Historical

tantalising period romances

DID YOU PURCHASE THIS BOOK WITHOUT A COVER?
If you did, you should be aware it is **stolen property** as it was
reported 'unsold and destroyed' by a retailer.
Neither the author nor the publisher has received any payment
for this book.

First Published 2008
First Australian Paperback Edition 2010
ISBN 978 1 742 55393 1

MORE THAN A GOVERNESS © 2008 by Sarah Mallory
Philippine Copyright 2008
Australian Copyright 2008
New Zealand Copyright 2008
Except for use in any review, the reproduction or utilisation of this work in
whole or in part in any form by any electronic, mechanical or other means,
now known or hereafter invented, including xerography, photocopying and
recording, or in any information storage or retrieval system, is forbidden
without the permission of the publisher, Harlequin Mills & Boon®, Locked
Bag 7002, Chatswood D.C. N.S.W., Australia 2067.

This book is sold subject to the condition that it shall not, by way of trade or
otherwise, be lent, resold, hired out or otherwise circulated without the prior
consent of the publisher in any form of binding or cover other than that in
which it is published and without a similar condition including this condition
being imposed on the subsequent purchaser.

All rights reserved including the right of reproduction in whole or in part in
any form. This edition is published in arrangement with Harlequin Books
S.A..

This is a work of fiction. Names, characters, places, and incidents are either
the product of the author's imagination or are used fictitiously, and any
resemblance to actual persons, living or dead, business establishments,
events, or locales is entirely coincidental.

Published by
Harlequin Mills & Boon®
Level 5
15 Help Street
CHATSWOOD NSW 2067
AUSTRALIA

® and ™ are trademarks owned by Harlequin Enterprises Limited or its
corporate affiliates and used by others under licence. Trademarks marked
with an ® are registered in Australia and in other countries. Contact
admin_legal@Harlequin.ca for details.

Cover art used by arrangement with Harlequin Books S.A.. All rights
reserved.

Printed and bound in Australia by
McPherson's Printing Group

MORE THAN A GOVERNESS

Sarah Mallory

SARAH MALLORY

was born in Bristol, England, and now lives in an old farmhouse on the edge of the Pennines with her husband and family. She left grammar school at sixteen to work in companies as varied as stockbrokers, marine engineers, insurance brokers, biscuit manufacturers and even a quarrying company. Her first book was published shortly after the birth of her daughter. She has published more than a dozen books under the pen name of Melinda Hammond, winning the Reviewers' Choice Award in 2005 from Singletitles.com for *Dance for a Diamond* and the Historical Novel Society's Editors' Choice in November 2006 for *Gentlemen in Question.*

DEDICATION

To Terry,
my rock and inspiration

Chapter One

Juliana Wrenn thought she had rarely entered a more un-inviting chamber than cousin Pettigrew's drawing room in Bouverie Street. Unpolished panelling, dark hangings and dull green paint on the ceiling seemed to swallow up the sunlight that was valiantly fighting its way through the dirty windows. She felt a little hand gripping her fingers and looked down, summoning up a smile.

'Are you cold, Amy? I am sure Cousin Pettigrew will not keep us waiting much longer.'

Her little sister hugged her rag doll closer.

'I want to go home!' she whimpered.

Juliana sat down on a worn sofa and pulled the little girl on to her lap.

'You know we can't do that, love. We must see if Cousin Alfred can help us.' She smiled up at her younger brother, a stout twelve-year-old who was hovering beside them.

'Come and sit down, Tom.'

'I would rather go back to the kitchen,' said Thomas, thinking of the fruitcake he had left behind when they had been summoned upstairs.

At that moment the door opened, and the three of them

jumped to their feet, their eyes fixed on the florid-faced, bewhiskered gentleman who came in.

Juliana gave him her best curtsy.

'Good afternoon, Cousin. Thank you for seeing us.'

Alfred Pettigrew advanced into the room, stripping off his gloves and dropping them, together with his silver-topped malacca cane, on to a side table.

'Yes, well, I have just got in—had to carry out the reading of a will in Mount Street. I gather you have been here all morning?'

'Yes, sir. We asked if we might wait for you and your housekeeper, Mrs Churwell, kindly looked after us.'

'She gave us cake, and a glass of milk,' added Amy and was nudged by Thomas, who hissed at her to be quiet. Juliana ignored the interruption.

'I wrote to you, Cousin.'

'Aye, you did, and I responded, did I not? Even more, I paid for your father's funeral, and saw to the settlement of his affairs for you.'

'Yes, sir, and we are very grateful. But that was three weeks ago, and circumstances have changed.' She hesitated, for the first time losing some of her self-assurance. 'The bailiffs called yesterday and removed everything, and Mr Crewe, the landlord, said he had already let the rooms, so we had to leave this morning.'

Mr Pettigrew looked at her.

'And what am I supposed to do with you?'

'We were hoping—that is…' Juliana took a deep breath. 'We need somewhere to stay. It need only be for a short time, until I can find employment—'

He gave an impatient snort.

'And what sort of employment could you find, miss, that would allow you to support the three of you?'

She drew herself up, her hands clasped in front of her rather shabby pelisse.

'Well, Cousin, I was thinking that if you could advance me a small sum, I could find a house for us and earn a living as a tutor. I am very good at French and Italian, and could possibly do a little translation, too…'

'Out of the question!' He waved a hand impatiently. 'Why, I would not see my money again for many a year, if ever.'

Juliana closed her lips firmly, quelling her retort. It was common knowledge that Alfred Pettigrew was a rich man, but it was equally well known that he was not a generous one. She had seen enough of the house to convince her that he was indeed what her father would have called a nip-farthing. She sighed. It was not a charge that could be laid at Papa's door.

'Well, then, what are we to do, Cousin Alfred?' asked Thomas. 'You are the only relative we have.'

'You have no need to remind me of that.' Mr Pettigrew scowled and his heavy jowls shook with disapproval. 'That my cousin Wrenn should leave his affairs in such disorder, with no means of support for the three of you—unforgivable.'

He paced the room while three pairs of eyes watched anxiously. At length he stopped.

'Very well. I'll tell you what I will do. I will send you all to Hinton Slade, my house in Devon. My mother lives there; she is not in the best of health and would welcome a companion, I am sure. That way, Miss Juliana, you can earn your keep. Thomas can help out in the stables and young Amy there can train as a lady's maid.'

Juliana looked at him in horror.

'But what about their schooling?'

'Tush, a boy of twelve doesn't need schooling. He is better earning his living. And as for the young 'un, well, you can teach her all she needs in your spare time.'

Juliana looked down at her siblings, fighting the urge to take their hands and walk out of Cousin Alfred's house. Instead she said calmly, 'That is very kind of you, Cousin. Perhaps you would allow me a few days to consider the matter?'

'Don't see there's anything to consider.' His lip curled. 'Unless you have had any better offers?'

'No, but I would like to make a few enquiries.' She tried a winning smile. 'Please, Cousin, may we impose upon your generosity for a few days? I promise you we will be in no one's way.'

'Of course you will be in the way! This is a bachelor establishment—it would be most improper for you to be here.'

'Not if we kept to the servants' rooms, sir. Mrs Churwell told me that she was obliged to dismiss one of the kitchenmaids, so the three of us could sleep in her room for a few nights. We would be most discreet.' Remembering the housekeeper's advice on dealing with the master, she added, 'I'm sure Mrs Churwell would be grateful for a little help now she's one girl short in the kitchen.'

She held her breath. Mr Pettigrew frowned at the carpet, puffing out his cheeks. Amy moved restlessly from one foot to the other and Juliana put a reassuring hand on her shoulder.

'Very well, you can stay, but only for a few days. I can't have the three of you eating me out of house and home. If you've found nothing in a se'ennight, then it's off to Devon with you.'

'Oh, thank you, sir!' Juliana beamed at him. 'We will be no trouble, I promise you. You will not even know we are in the house.'

Juliana hurried Amy and Thomas back to the kitchens where the housekeeper was waiting for them.

'Well, miss?' she asked. 'It must be good news or you would be out the door by now.'

Juliana smiled. 'We can stay, and I can help you with the maid's work until you find a replacement.'

'Aye, I guessed that would sway him,' Mrs Churwell

tutted. 'Miserable old skinflint, and him with more money than he knows what to do with.'

'He did say we could go and live with Aunt Pettigrew,' said Thomas, brightening when he found his half-eaten cake was still on the table.

The footman, sitting in one corner blacking his shoes, gave a derisive snort.

'Ha! She's worse than the master. You'd work your fingers to the bone for that one and not a penny would you get for it. I had a cousin as was groom there for a while, until he joined the army to fight the French. Said he preferred to face Boney himself than old Mrs P.'

'Aye, Lawrence is right,' agreed Mrs Churwell, shaking her head. 'The Pettigrews is a miserly family and no mistake.'

'And that makes it all the more imperative that I find employment,' said Juliana, sinking down into a chair by the table.

'Well, that's a problem for the morrow,' replied Mrs Churwell comfortably. 'Poor dear, I dare swear you have had no end of worry these past few weeks. Now you sit and rest, dearie, and these two youngsters can make themselves useful by shelling peas for dinner.'

Juliana rose early the next morning to find that Mrs Churwell had brought a pile of the master's newspapers to the kitchen, smiling as she put them down on the table.

'I thought you might find a suitable post advertised in here, miss. Sit yourself down and study these news-sheets while I take up the master's breakfast. And don't you worry about Thomas and little Amy, I've set them to folding sheets upstairs, so you can have a bit o' peace.'

When the housekeeper returned to the kitchen some time later, Juliana was still sitting at the table with the news-papers spread out before her.

'Well, dearie?'

Juliana sighed.

'It seems there are far more advertisements for those seeking employment than requiring someone. Listen— "Governess seeks position, no salary required." What straits must that poor creature be in?'

'The same as you, Miss Juliana,' responded Mrs Churwell. 'You are not to be letting that kind heart o' yours worry about everyone else's problems. You have your family to consider, and if you let the master send you all off to Hinton Slade you'll be stuck in the middle of nowhere, and don't think old Mrs Pettigrew will help you to better yourself, because she won't, not when she sees she can have the three of you doing her bidding for a pittance!'

'I suppose you are right. Oh, Mrs Churwell, it seems a hopeless case.'

'Not a bit of it,' came the robust reply. 'Now, miss, what you must do is to place your own advertisement in the newspaper. And you must write down all the things you can do, just like you told them to me, so that everyone will know what an accomplished young lady you are and they will come begging you to teach their children.'

'That would certainly be very welcome!' laughed Juliana. 'I suppose I *could* advertise.'

'Of course you could! Mr P. will be in his office by now, so there will be no one in the morning room, and you'll find paper, pens and ink there. You go and write it now, my dear. Strike while the iron's hot, as they say.'

'I will, Mrs Churwell.' Juliana rose. 'I will go and write the best advertisement you have ever read!'

She ran up the stairs, but checked as she reached the top. She could hear voices in the hallway and guessed that Mr Pettigrew was meeting a client. Peeping around the door, Juliana saw her cousin making a deep bow to a tall gentleman. The visitor had his back to her, so that all she could see of the man himself was his black hair and his many-caped driving coat which added even more width to his already large frame.

'Major Collingham—' Cousin Alfred's nose was almost touching his knee '—I am most honoured by this visit, sir, following on from our conversation yesterday. But you should not have come out in this rain, sir—I should have been quite happy to bring the papers to you.'

'No need, Pettigrew. I had to come this way this morning. I needed to place an advertisement and thought I could do it myself and call upon you on my way. I want to get everything signed and sorted before I leave town next week; thought I was doing well, too, until the children arrived yesterday evening, with the news that their governess had given notice!'

'How unfortunate for you, sir. Come into my office and I will find those papers for you.'

Juliana drew back behind the door as her cousin led the gentleman on, but before the door closed on them she heard the stranger say bitterly,

'Unfortunate? It's damned annoying, man! Particularly now, when I need to take the children into Lancashire with me. That's the third damned woman I've hired in as many months! What can be so difficult about looking after a couple of brats? I tell you, Pettigrew, I'd give a king's ransom to find a governess who could stay the course…'

The door closed upon the two men and Juliana stepped slowly into the hall, nibbling the tip of her finger. She looked at the footman, who was shaking out the man's greatcoat.

'Lawrence, that man—do you know him?'

'Major Collingham, miss?'

'Yes. Is he…is he one of Mr Pettigrew's clients?'

The footman shook his head as he laid the greatcoat gently over a large chest.

'No, miss. But he is trustee for one of 'em.' He added knowledgeably, 'He is the sort of well-set-up gentlemen that people like to appoint as executor to manage their affairs when they turn up their toes.'

Juliana smoothed her hands over her gown and said as casually as she could, 'And, do you perhaps know where he lives?'

'Oh, aye, miss. I've taken papers to his house in Burlington Street many a time.'

Juliana nodded, then turned and made her way back to the kitchen, where Mrs Churwell was busy making pastry.

'Well, now, that was quick!' exclaimed the housekeeper, up to her elbows in flour. 'Have you written your notice already?'

Juliana shook her head, and sat down at the table.

'No, but I think I have found a solution to my problems!'

Chapter Two

Later that afternoon Juliana put on her best walking dress of holly green with its matching bonnet and set off for Burlington Street. She was fortunate that the rain had stopped, but it remained overcast, and a chill wind stung her cheeks. Following Lawrence's directions, she found herself staring up at an imposing double-fronted façade. For a moment her courage failed her. Then, squaring her shoulders, she marched up to the front door and knocked loudly.

'Oh, come along, Juliana Wrenn,' she muttered to herself. 'He can't eat you, after all.'

A liveried footman admitted her to the house and showed her into a small study on the ground floor while he went off to carry her message to his master.

Too nervous to sit down, she stood in the middle of the room and looked about her. The walls were lined with oak panels from floor to ceiling in the same manner as her cousin's drawing room, but there all similarity between the two houses ended. The panelling in Major Collingham's study gleamed and several lively hunting scenes hung on the walls. She was just wondering if any of the figures depicted could be the master of the house when a deep voice sounded behind her, making her jump.

'You wished to see me, madam?'

'Oh—I did not hear you come in!'

'I am sorry if I startled you,' responded the Major, sounding not a whit remorseful.

Juliana looked at him. In her cousin's hallway she had only seen the back of his head. Now, staring up into the harsh, unsmiling face, her spirits began to fade. He was very tall, and dressed with military precision—there was nothing of the dandy about him, she noted with approval; the long limbs encased in buff-coloured pantaloons and black boots hinted rather at the athlete. His blue coat fitted perfectly about his broad shoulders and the crisp whiteness of his shirt and cravat enhanced his dark complexion, tanned by years in the sun—she knew he had been a soldier, and guessed he had seen action in the Peninsula. His bearing was upright and looked as solid and unyielding as his countenance. His voice, when he spoke again, was tinged with impatience.

'Well, madam, what can I do for you?'

'I—I came because—because you require a governess.'

Her words came out in a rush.

'Then it is my secretary, Brasher, you should see. I made it quite clear in the advertisement.'

He turned to go.

'Oh, I have not seen the advertisement—and it is *you* I wish to see, Major Collingham.'

He stopped and turned to face her.

'Not seen the—then how the devil…?'

His frown was not encouraging, but she screwed up her courage—she must do this for Thomas and Amy's sake.

'I am a cousin of Mr Pettigrew, the lawyer. I overheard your conversation with him this morning, about requiring a governess urgently. It—it is a fortunate circumstance for you, sir, that I am looking for just such a post.'

'I see. Well, if that is the case, I am of course delighted that you have come, but my secretary can handle the details—'

'But I do not wish to talk to your secretary, Major.' She swallowed. 'I—I want to talk to you about my terms.'

The Major raised his black brows.

'Terms?'

'Yes.' She drew a breath and put up her chin. 'I believe you require a governess to take up the post immediately, sir. Well, I am free to do that, upon condition.'

The Major stared at her. Juliana returned his gaze steadily, praying that he could not hear the rapid thudding of her heart. His countenance relaxed a little.

'I see this is not going to be the work of a moment.' He moved to his desk. 'Pray will you not be seated, miss...?'

'Miss Wrenn, Major.' She sat down on the edge of the chair, facing him.

'Well, Miss Wrenn, it is true that I am in need of a governess, but, as the employer, I was of the opinion that it was my place to set the conditions.'

She did not flinch from his hard gaze. Mrs Churwell had told her to have faith in herself, and she must do just that.

'In the normal course of events, yes, but you do not appear to be having much success; you told my cousin you would pay a king's ransom for a governess who could—ah—*stay the course* was your term, I think?'

He laughed suddenly, and the rather harsh lines of his face softened into something much more attractive.

'Quite right, Miss Wrenn, I did. Very well, why do you think you would suit my requirements?'

'Because I have had an excellent education, I am used to dealing with children and can teach them all the usual accomplishments of reading, writing, a little arithmetic and geography, the use of globes; my French and Italian are very good, I play the pianoforte and the harp, I paint and draw, I am a skilled needlewoman and—'

'And you are desperate for employment.'

She blinked.

'You do not deny it, Miss Wrenn.'

'No, sir.' She looked him in the eye and said with more confidence that she was feeling, 'But I have imp—impeccable credentials.'

He sat back, folding his arms across his chest and fixing her with a hard stare.

'You are very young for such a post.'

'I am one-and-twenty, sir.'

'What is your experience?'

She clasped her hands in her lap.

'I was educated in a select seminary in Clapham until I was seventeen years old, and had some teaching of the younger girls while I was there. I learned all the usual accomplishments, and was especially good at languages—a gift from my father, I think. My mother's demise made it necessary for me to come home and for the past four years I have had the care of my brother and sister.'

'And what has changed, that you must now seek employment?'

She looked down at her hands. It was not easy to admit her straitened circumstances to a stranger, but it must be done. 'My father died a month since and all his effects were seized to pay his debts. That is why we are staying with my cousin, until I can find a way to support us all.'

'And how old are your brother and sister?'

'My brother is twelve years old, sir. My sister just nine.' She looked up at the Major, but his face was impassive. She said, with a touch of defiance, 'I am not looking for sympathy, sir.'

'I have offered you none. You have been very frank, Miss Wrenn, so let me be equally open with you. I am a widower and have been so for the past eight years. My three children have been in the care of my mother—their grandmother—in Hampshire. Unfortunately, my mother died twelve months ago. Bonaparte had just escaped from Elba and it was impossible for me to leave my regiment at that time, so my sister took the children in; she lives nearby with her own young family. After Waterloo I was eager to settle my affairs and return to England, but it took me until a few months ago to complete my duties and get away.' He paused and sat forward, resting his arms on the desk. 'While in the care of my sister, my daughters were taught in the schoolroom with their young cousins, but I was naturally desirous to have the children with me, so I moved them back into Kewhurst, their old home, with a governess to look after them while I completed my business prior to taking them all to Lancashire. To date, as you pointed out to me, Miss Wrenn, I have been singularly unsuccessful in my choice of staff. The first governess lasted less than a week and left the house claiming that the place was haunted. The second I turned off when I discovered her addiction to strong liquor. The third, well, I thought she was settled, so I came on to London to put my affairs in order. I sent for the children to join me, and instead of the governess, they came with their aunt and their old nurse, and the information that the governess had discharged herself.'

'Oh…dear.'

'As you say, Miss Wrenn, oh dear.'

'How old are your daughters, Major?'

'Gwendoline is twelve years old, and Wilhelmina is eight. They are quite normal, Miss Wrenn—high spirited, perhaps, but not demons.'

'I do not doubt it. But you said you have three children, sir?'

'Yes. My son, Giles, is fifteen years old and for the past

few years has been under the tutelage of a learned reverend. When I arrived in Hampshire I discovered that this gentleman has accepted a much more attractive position as bearleader to a young gentleman embarking upon the Grand Tour. However, Giles need not concern you; once we are settled in the north, I will engage another tutor for him.'

'You said you are leaving town at the end of next week?'

'Yes, on Friday. I have property in Lancashire that requires my attention. I want the governess to travel with us, and to take charge of the children on the journey.' Again Juliana found that harsh stare fixed upon her. 'After what you have heard, are you still eager for this position, Miss Wrenn?'

She sat up and adopted her most businesslike tone.

'I think it would suit very well, sir, if we can agree terms.'

'Miss Wrenn, I hardly think you are in a position to make demands....'

'Then we need discuss this no further.' She rose. 'Let me see, today is Saturday, your advertisement should be published on Monday, at the earliest. No doubt your secretary is very efficient; if he interviews the candidates quickly, I *suppose* it might be possible to engage a suitable person in time to travel on Friday, assuming he has received suitable references, of course...'

He held up his hand.

'Very well, Miss Wrenn, you have made your point. Can *you* supply me with suitable references?'

'I am sure Mr Pettigrew will vouch for my character, and you may apply to Miss Shaftesbury at the Academy in Clapham. As to my education, you can test me, if you so wish.'

'No, I do not so wish!' he growled at her. 'Pray sit down again, madam, and tell me these terms of yours.'

Resuming her seat, she gave him a beaming smile.

'They are not really so outrageous. I will engage to look after the children, Major Collingham, and educate them for the next four months, that is, to the end of September. I would like you to pay me a lump sum at the end of that time.'

'How much?'

Juliana took a deep breath and named her price.

'What?'

She winced, but held her ground.

'You said you were willing to pay a king's ransom for this service, sir; I think you will agree that it is hardly that, but it would be sufficient for me to rent a little house in, say, Harrogate or Bath, and support my family by teaching. That is all I ask, Major.'

There was no more she could say. Juliana forced herself to sit still while the Major stared at her, his fingers drumming on the desk top. The remuneration she was asking was high, but discreet enquiries of her cousin had convinced her that the Major could afford twice that sum. Now she only needed to hold her nerve. She smiled to herself; perhaps she had something of her father's gambling spirit after all. At last he spoke.

'Very well. I will have Brasher draw up an agreement today.'

She found she had been holding her breath, for it now came out in a long sigh.

'Thank you, sir. I will not disappoint you.'

'I trust you will not. I shall make sure you do not get a penny if you do not keep your side of this bargain. One more thing. What do you propose to do with your siblings for the next four months?'

She hesitated.

'I am hoping to persuade my cousin—'

He shook his head.

'Pettigrew is a lawyer and a bachelor. I'd wager he knows less than I do about children. You had best bring them with you. They will be companions for Gwen and

Minna on the journey, and there will be plenty of room for them at Blackthorpe.'

'Th-thank you.'

He stood up and came round the desk towards her.

'Then let us shake hands upon it, and I will send for the children.'

Juliana rose and put out her hand. As he took her fingers in his strong grip she looked up into his face and wondered how she had ever managed to bargain with such a man. At close range he was even more intimidating. His eyes were as hard as granite; his countenance bleak and unforgiving. Dangerous. But even as she began to wonder if perhaps she had made a mistake, she saw a gleam of amusement in his grey eyes.

He said, 'Now what are you thinking, Miss Wrenn?'

She did not even consider prevaricating.

'That you would make an implacable enemy, sir.'

His grip on her hand tightened.

'True. But I am also a very good friend. Which would you have, Miss Wrenn?'

Juliana could not break away from his gaze. A small voice in her head was warning that he should not be asking her such a question. She swallowed and tried to answer calmly.

'Neither. I look only for a fair employer.'

He stared at her, a faint crease in his brows. Juliana looked down at his hand, still holding her own. Abruptly he released her and walked towards the window saying,

'I—um—I plan to marry—when we arrive in Lancashire: a neighbour's daughter, widow. There is an arrangement between the families. It has long been agreed. My wife will, of course, take over arrangements for the girls' education.'

'Then why not wait until you get to Lancashire to employ a governess?'

Even as the words tumbled out, Juliana wished them unsaid; she had signed no contract yet, and she did not want him to change his mind. The Major did not hesitate over his reply.

'I had considered that, but their nurse is far too old to have sole control of the children on such a long journey.'

Juliana's evil genius prompted her to play devil's advocate once more.

'But—forgive me—did you not say you will be travelling together, as a party?'

He turned to look at her, his brows raised in surprise, and just for a moment she thought there was a shade of unease upon those harsh features.

'I know nothing of the needs of young girls,' he said shortly. 'If it was only Giles, I should not hesitate. As it is—' He broke off. 'I shall summon the girls to meet you.'

He strode over to the door, barking his orders to a lackey.

Moments later, two little figures trooped into the room.

'Goodness, that was very prompt!' exclaimed Juliana, smiling at the Misses Collingham.

They were dressed in identical redingotes of claret-coloured wool with matching bonnets. The eldest girl raised her eyes, so like her father's, and looked directly at Juliana.

'We were waiting in the hall for Aunt Louisa, Papa.' She addressed the Major, although she kept her eyes upon Juliana. 'She is taking us for a drive in the park.'

'Well, I shall not keep you long.' Major Collingham beckoned them to come forward. 'I want to make you known to your new governess. Gwendoline…' He paused as the older of the two children bobbed a curtsy.

Juliana curtsied back.

'How do you do, Miss Collingham?'

'Gwendoline was twelve years old last month,' said the Major. 'And this is Wilhelmina.' He nodded at the smaller child, who stepped forward and bobbed, saying as she did so,

'And I'm eight.'

'Indeed?' marvelled Juliana. 'You are very grown up for eight, I think. I am very pleased to meet you both.'

'Miss Wrenn will be joining us next week,' said the Major. 'You will have your first lesson with her at two o'clock on Monday—yes, Miss Wrenn, did you say something?'

'So—so soon,' stammered Juliana. 'I thought we should get to know one another first.'

'If that is what you wish to do, Miss Wrenn, I have no objection, as long as you do it in the schoolroom.'

'And out of the way, Major?' she murmured, bringing that frowning stare upon her again.

Whatever retort the Major was about to make was interrupted as the door opened and a tall woman in a rose-pink pelisse erupted into the room.

'Damon, do you have the girls here? I was about to take them out.'

'The children are here, Louisa, dressed and ready for you. I was introducing them to their new governess. This is Miss Wrenn—my sister, Lady Varley.'

Juliana found herself subjected to a head-to-toe scrutiny and forced herself not to fidget. Her walking dress might not be as stylish as Lady Varley's fine wool pelisse, and one small ostrich feather could not compete with the three nodding plumes that adorned Lady Varley's high-crowned bonnet, but she knew her simple attire was perfectly suited to a young lady of modest means, and more than adequate for a governess. Lady Varley seemed to agree, for she gave a nod of approval.

'So, Damon, you have found someone already. How clever of you.'

The Major's lips curved up slightly.

'It would be more accurate to say that Miss Wrenn found *me.*'

Lady Varley waved one pink-gloved hand.

'Whatever the case, it would seem that I need not take

the children out with me after all.' She paused, glancing down at the two little faces looking up at her. 'But they are dressed now, so I suppose I must. Come along, then. The carriage is at the door and you know your father does not like to keep his horses standing!'

She hurried the children out of the room, turning at the door to say, 'We shall not be too long, Damon. I have to stop off at Madame Fleurie's to look at the new muslin she had brought in for me and then I shall take the girls for a quick turn around the park, to give them an airing before dinner.'

'You must not mind my sister, Miss Wrenn,' remarked the Major as the door closed upon the little party. 'She felt obliged to come to London with the children when their governess walked out. She has not yet forgiven me.'

'That was very good of her; some aunts might have considered it sufficient to send the children with a servant.'

'Ah, but then I would not have felt obliged to pay for the gowns she has ordered from Madame Fleurie.'

Juliana was surprised into a laugh, which she quickly stifled—levity was not becoming in a governess. She should take her leave. As if reading her mind, Major Collingham walked to the door.

'Very well, Miss Wrenn. I will send my carriage to Bouverie Street on Monday morning at, say, eleven o'clock. You will bring your brother and sister with you. I shall have rooms prepared for your arrival.'

'Thank you, sir. You are very good.'

'No, it is a business arrangement. My man will have the contract ready for you to sign when you arrive.' He bent that hard gaze upon her again. 'I shall expect you to earn your money, Miss Wrenn.'

She met his gaze squarely.

'I expect nothing less of you, Major Collingham.'

★ ★ ★

She hurried back to Bouverie Street and made her way directly to the kitchens, where Mrs Churwell was waiting to hear her news. Juliana could not suppress her elation.

'He's hired me,' she cried. 'Major Collingham is sending the carriage here for me on Monday, and he says Thomas and Amy can come too. I was most surprised at that, I can tell you, but it is ideal for us all.'

'Oh, well done, dearie! I'm that pleased for you, I really am.' The housekeeper turned to the footman, who was relaxing in a chair with his feet up on the fender. 'You hear that, Lawrence? Miss Wrenn is to be a governess to the Major, and him a hero of Waterloo, no less!'

'Is he? I never knew that.' Juliana smiled, taking off her bonnet and placing it on a side table.

'Aye.' Lawrence poured himself another mug of ale. 'My brother was in his regiment, the 30th Foot. They fought off the French at Quatre Bras. Praised by Lord Wellington hisself, they was. But that's not all.' He grinned. 'Devil Collingham, they call him. Heard it from the man's groom hisself, I did, last time I delivered some papers to the house and stopped off for a glass of daffy on the way back. Devil Collingham—devil on the battlefield, and devil in the bedroom. They say in Brussels it was nothing for him to pleasure three women in one night.'

With a shriek Mrs Churwell cuffed him round the ear.

'I'll have none of that talk in my kitchen, my lad! You had best get back upstairs, now, before the master starts shouting for you. Go on, now! Don't you be taking any notice of what Lawrence says,' she added, when the footman had lounged away. 'I don't hold with servants' tittle-tattle.'

'No more do I,' agreed Juliana. She looked up at the housekeeper, a mischievous twinkle in her green eyes. 'However, it seems I have just made a pact with the devil!'

Chapter Three

'Well, what do you think of her?' Wilhelmina whispered to her sister as Lady Varley gave her instructions to the driver. Gwendoline wrinkled her nose.

'Miss Sevenoaks was much prettier, except when she had been drinking too much, then her face became very red.'

'Well, I think she's pretty,' replied Wilhelmina. 'And she had kind eyes.'

Gwendoline gave her a nudge as their aunt climbed into the carriage.

'Whispering again?' Lady Varley shook her head. 'I hope this new woman Damon has hired will teach you both some manners.'

They travelled in silence to New Bond Street; when they reached the fashionable dressmaker's establishment, Lady Varley took the children into the shop, declaring she would prefer to keep them under her eye. The girls gazed around them in wide-eyed wonder. At first glance the walls seemed to be decorated in rainbow colours, but closer inspection revealed shelves from floor to ceiling, packed with rolls of fabric, shiny silks and satin, soft muslins and cottons of every shade. There seemed to be half a dozen ladies in the room, but the girls soon realised that these were life-size dummies displaying the very latest fashions. Madame Fleurie herself appeared from the back of the shop flanked by two simpering assistants, each carrying rolls of creamy-coloured muslin for Lady Varley's inspection. The modiste curtsied, bowed, flattered and fawned over her patroness, uttering so many compliments in her lilting French accent that Gwendoline turned away, her lip curling. She led her sister to a satin-covered couch, half-hidden between rolls of fabric and piles of hatboxes.

'What are we going to do about the new governess, Gwen?' Wilhelmina climbed on to the couch.

'Well, I think we should try to send her away. We certainly don't want to have her with us all the way to Lancashire. It will be much more fun with just Nurse, because she always lets us have our own way.'

'We could play ghosts again,' suggested Wilhelmina. 'It worked very well with Miss Gillimore.'

'But she was very stupid.' Gwendoline's tone was dismissive. 'This one does not look stupid.'

Wilhelmina regarded her silently. It was clear that Gwendoline was thinking hard. Wilhelmina bore it patiently for a few moments, but soon wriggled off the couch and went in search of something more interesting to look at than Gwendoline's pensive face. Aunt Louisa was engrossed in discussing fabrics and patterns with the modiste, while the assistants hurried back and forth with bolts of cloth and pieces of lace for her inspection. Wilhelmina walked around the shop; it seemed a nonsense for Aunt Louisa to be taking so long to choose a gown—the dummies were all so elegant she could surely want nothing better. The one nearest the door was dressed in a beautiful gown of apricot silk with a demi-train of shiny beads. Rows of beads also decorated the sleeves and hem, glistening in the light. Wilhelmina went closer, then closer still. It was all a cheat! It was not a dress at all—the silk had been cunningly draped around the dummy with lengths of beaded ribbon pinned into place. In fact, Wilhelmina could see where one of the pins on the sleeve had worked itself loose—perhaps if she just pushed it back in....

'Wilhelmina, what are you doing?'

Aunt Louisa's voice cut across the room and Wilhelmina jumped back. Unfortunately, as she did so, a loose thread on one finger of her glove caught around some of the beads, dragging them off the dummy and pulling the apricot silk with them. With a little cry Wilhelmina shook her hand, the beads fell away, but it was too late; before her horrified gaze the beautiful creation was falling apart, the silk dropping into a blushing cloud around the base of the cloth dummy.

'You tiresome child, how many times have I told you not to touch?' Lady Varley's chilling accents brought a hot flush of guilt and embarrassment to Wilhelmina's cheeks. She ran back to the couch and scrambled up beside Gwendoline.

'Really, I do not know why I brought you. Just look at what you have done!'

'No, no, *madame*, it ees nothing, nothing,' cried Madame Fleurie, hands fluttering as she sought to placate her wealthy client. 'It ees the work of a moment to put it right.' She signalled to her assistants to attend to the disorder while she gently escorted Lady Varley back to the counter to finish making her selection.

Wilhelmina looked up at Gwendoline, who frowned and turned away, hunching a shoulder as if to disown her troublesome little sister. Wilhelmina felt the tears gathering in her eyes. Her bottom lip began to tremble.

'There, there, missy, don't cry.' The younger of the two assistants came past, winding up the beaded ribbon into her arms. 'There's no 'arm done, my pet. We was about to re-dress that model anyway.'

Wilhelmina gave a shuddering sigh.

The assistant dropped the bundled ribbon on to the counter and came back to kneel in front of Wilhelmina, her round face creased into a kindly smile.

'Ah, now, dearie, there's no need for tears.' She drew out her own handkerchief and mopped Wilhelmina's cheeks. 'All this fuss over a bit o' cloth, well, I never.' She sat back on her heels, then suddenly dived down beside the couch.

'Here.' She held up a small wooden doll, beautifully dressed in a brocaded gown with a silk apron and a mass of grey curls. 'Take it, my pet, and you dry your eyes. *Madame* gets them sent to her from France all the time, dressed in the latest fashions, to show to her lady clients, but heaven knows where this one came from—why, look at those panniers! We haven't made gowns like this for the past ten years at least!'

Wilhelmina gulped and stared at the doll.

'Oh, but—I shouldn't take her.'

'Oh, yes, you should, my lovely. She will only be thrown away, so you might as well have her, if you like.'

'Like? Oh, I should love her.' Wilhelmina's small hands closed round the doll. 'If you really think…'

Madame Fleurie called, and after a final nod at Wilhelmina, the assistant rose quickly and trotted off.

'Gwen,' breathed Wilhelmina, 'Gwen, what do you think?'

'Keep her, if you wish,' muttered Gwendoline. 'Although it does seem odd to be rewarded when you have caused so much trouble.' Seeing her little sister's lip begin to tremble again, she gave her a quick hug. 'Goose. I know you didn't mean to do it. Come on, Aunt Louisa has finished; we must go.'

With regal grace, Lady Varley shepherded her two charges back to the coach, while Madame Fleurie bowed and scraped at her heels.

The children scrambled into the carriage and Lady Varley climbed in after them, dropping back with a sigh on to the well-padded seat.

'Well, thank heaven that is done. I shall not need to come back now. Madame Fleurie can call at Burlington Street next week for a fitting. Now…' she smiled brightly at her nieces '…let us take that turn around the park. It is a pity the weather is too inclement to put down the hood, but you will get an airing, none the less.' Her glance fell to the doll Wilhelmina was holding and she tutted. 'Oh, Minna, surely you are too old to be bringing dolls for a ride with you?'

'No, Aunt, you see—'

'Next time you must leave her at home.' Lady Varley carried on as if Wilhelmina had not spoken. 'Dolls should be kept in the nursery. Dear me, your new governess will have some work to do with you!'

Chapter Four

Juliana had wondered how Cousin Pettigrew would take the news that she had obtained a post and was relieved that he appeared quite sanguine. Once she had explained that she had overheard the Major's comments in the hallway of Bouverie Street, Mr Pettigrew seemed to believe that he had somehow engineered the whole thing himself, and had solved the problem of providing for his cousins at very little expense. He was therefore able to wave them off with perfect good humour. Mrs Churwell shed a tear at the thought of them all going so far away, and even pressed one last slice of fruitcake upon Thomas. He devoured it on the short journey to Burlington Street, explaining to his sisters that he would not wish to carry it with him into the Major's house, in case his staff thought it a slight upon their hospitality.

There was no sign of the Major when they arrived and they were greeted by the housekeeper who led them upstairs. She introduced herself as Mrs Hartley.

'The master sends his apologies that business takes him out this morning, but he has asked me to ensure you have everything you need, miss.' She opened the door of a large apartment on the second floor. 'The master thought this might suit you, Miss Wrenn—there's a bed made up in the corner for your sister, and another in the adjoining dressing room for the young gentleman. It is for less than a week, but the Major thought you might prefer to be together, being in a strange house.'

'Yes, thank you.' Juliana looked around her in surprise. She had expected to be tucked away in an attic room, yet this apartment bore all the trappings of a guest chamber. 'The Major is most kind.'

'That he is, miss. Now, your trunks are on their way up, so I shall leave you to unpack.' She gestured towards the round table by the window. 'I shall send up a light luncheon for you shortly, and Nurse will bring the Misses Collingham to the schoolroom for you at two o'clock.'

When the housekeeper had gone, Thomas let out a low whistle.

'Lord, sis, this is much grander than I thought it would be.' He opened the door to the dressing room and peered in. 'My own room, too!'

'Yes, well, enjoy it while it lasts,' said Juliana, taking off her bonnet. 'I expect there was no room for us with the servants and he was obliged to put us in this guest room. But do not expect such luxury when we are travelling, or when we reach the Major's Lancashire estate—remember I am a paid employee.'

'And what are we?' piped up Amy, bouncing on the edge of her bed.

'You are to be travelling companions for his nieces.' She sat down beside Amy and pulled the little girl on to her lap. 'He has two little girls: one is twelve years old, the other eight, just a little younger than you, Amy.'

'Huh, I hope you don't expect me to play with girls!' declared Thomas, pulling a face.

'I expect you to behave like a gentleman, sir. The Major

also has a son, some years older than the girls. I haven't met him yet, and he is not one of the schoolroom party, so perhaps we will not see much of him.'

Thomas shrugged. 'I don't see how we can avoid it, if we are all travelling together—'

He broke off as a large corded travelling trunk was brought in by two liveried footmen and, under Juliana's instruction, the two children spent the remaining time until luncheon unpacking their clothes and putting them into the chests of drawers and the big linen press that Mrs Hartley had told them they could use.

At two o'clock Juliana made her way to the schoolroom, Thomas and Amy hard on her heels. As she reached the door, Gwendoline's voice could be heard quite clearly coming from the other side.

'But we do not want her, Nurse! Why should we have a governess now, what can she teach us while we are travelling? Why, if she tries to make me read in the carriage, I shall be *sick*! It would be much better to wait until we get to Lancashire—Papa can hire a proper governess for us there.'

Juliana grasped the door handle and rattled it before opening the door. She moved into the room, smiling as if she had heard nothing of Gwendoline's tirade.

The young Misses Collingham were standing on each side of their nurse, an elderly, rosy-cheeked woman with curly wisps of snow-white hair peeping out around the edges of her cap. Juliana thought she looked a good-humoured creature, but just now her face displayed a mixture of mortification and embarrassment as she realised her charge's outburst must have been overheard.

Juliana gave her a brief smile and turned her attention to the children. They, meanwhile, had realised that Juliana had not come alone, and were staring open-mouthed at Thomas and Amy.

'I dare say your papa forgot to tell you that I would be bringing two travelling companions for our journey.' She led her siblings forward and performed the introductions. Gwendoline and Thomas greeted each other with frosty politeness, while the two younger children merely stared solemnly at one another. An awkward silence ensued and Juliana was about to break it when Amy spoke up.

'I have a doll, too,' she said, staring at the handsomely dressed little lady that Wilhelmina was clutching before her. 'She's sitting on my bed at the moment. She is called Sarah. What do you call yours?'

Wilhelmina hugged her doll even closer. 'Her name is Lady Arabella,' she said.

Amy stared at the wooden figure in its brocade gown. 'She's very beautiful.'

Wilhelmina held it out. 'Would you like to hold her?'

Amy glanced at Juliana, who nodded, then stepped forward to take the doll and the two girls moved off together, talking in low tones.

'Well now,' murmured Nurse with a smile.

'A good start,' agreed Juliana. 'Thomas, perhaps you would help me by making a list of the books on the shelf over there. I am sure Nurse will help you to find a pen and paper. Miss Gwendoline, shall we sit down, and you can tell me just what you have learned with your last governess.'

Shortly before the dinner hour, Juliana was summoned to Major Collingham's study. At the door she paused to shake out the skirts of her grey silk gown, the only mourning gown she owned, then she knocked and went in. Major Collingham was seated at his desk, but he rose as she entered. He did not smile as she approached, confirming her belief that his request had not been one of courtesy, more a command. He was dressed for dinner in a plain dark coat and biscuit-coloured knee-breeches, the snowy whiteness of his shirt and necktie contrasting sharply with the black cloth of his coat and his equally black hair. He motioned her to a chair.

'I am sorry I was not here to receive you. I trust you have everything you need?'

'Yes, Major, thank you. Our rooms are very comfortable, and more luxurious than I had expected.'

'It was more convenient to put you and your family together. After all, it is only for a few days.'

'Have no fear, Major, I shall not forget my position here.'

'Is that comment designed to put me in my place?'

Her eyes flew to his face.

'Not at all, sir, I—'

'If I sounded impolite, I apologise,' he said bluntly. 'I am not in the habit of making pretty speeches. I understand that you have made your brother and sister known to my girls.'

'Yes. The older ones are still painfully polite, but Miss Wilhelmina and Amy are already firm friends.'

'Good. You may, of course, include your brother and sister in your lessons, if you wish.'

'Thank you, Major. I would rather they were occupied and under my eye.'

He nodded. 'Brasher tells me you signed the contract. Did you read it first?'

'Of course.'

'And?'

'The terms are very generous. It is good of you to allow either party to terminate the agreement upon two weeks notice, should it prove necessary.'

'That was Brasher's doing. I never contemplate failure, Miss Wrenn.'

Her chin went up.

'No more do I, sir.' She hesitated, recalling Gwendoline's hostility towards her. 'However, if it should prove impossible for me to win the children's regard, I should not wish to inflict myself upon them for the full four months.'

'Then you may be sure that you would not be paid for the full four months.'

A scorching glance accompanied these words, and Juliana had no doubt the Major had used such a look to make young soldiers quail. She had to remind herself that she was no raw recruit to be intimidated.

'I would expect to be paid for work carried out, Major. Mr Brasher assures me that you treat your employees fairly, and I am told you are an honest man.'

'Oh, so you have been making enquiries about me?'

'Of course, since I am entrusting the care of myself and my family to you.'

A faint gleam of approval lit his eyes.

'Then welcome to my household, Miss Wrenn.' He got up and went to a side-table where a selection of decanters and glasses rested on a silver tray. 'Will you take a little wine with me, madam, to seal our bargain?'

'Yes sir, thank you, for there is something that I wish to discuss with you.'

He threw her a frowning glance, but said nothing until he had given her a full glass.

She sipped her wine. It was smooth and fruity, nothing like the weak potions served in Mr Pettigrew's house. It confirmed her opinion that Cousin Alfred watered down his wines to make them go further.

'What is it you wanted to discuss with me, Miss Wrenn?'

He had returned to the side-table to fill a glass for himself.

'Oh, I beg your pardon. Yes, I know I said I wanted to be paid with a lump sum at the end of our agreement, but my visit to the schoolroom today has revealed a sad lack of books and games for the children. Oh, there are plenty of religious and educational tracts, but I need to make a few purchases if I am to keep the children amused, especially on a long journey.'

'Very well, madam. See Brasher tomorrow morning and tell him how much you need. You may also have my carriage for your shopping expedition. Brasher will arrange it, if you tell him what time you wish to go out.'

'Thank you.' Her eyes were straying around the room, and they alighted upon a small painting on the wall: three children at play in a garden. 'Oh, is that your family, sir?'

'Yes. My mother had it done for me, when I was in the army. I think it was to remind me that I had a family.'

She rose and went over to the picture. It hung on the wall above a console table, upon which rested a glass case of miniatures. She leaned forward to study the figures more closely.

'They were much younger, then, of course,' said the Major, 'but I think it is a good likeness.'

'Yes, indeed. They are all handsome children, sir.'

He came to stand behind her.

'Giles takes after his mother. As does Wilhelmina.'

'They are fairer, certainly, while Gwendoline has your own dark colouring—oh!' She turned back, but he was so close that she found herself trapped between his body and the table. She stared at his neckcloth, at the cleft in his strong chin, then raised her eyes to his mouth and found herself wondering what it would be like to be kissed by him. Her heart leapt to her throat as the Major reached out and took her arms. What was it Lawrence had said about him, a devil in the bedroom? She felt scandalised, elated and frightened all in a moment.

He said quietly, 'You are almost sitting on the glass case, Miss Wrenn.'

He gently moved her aside, then let her go and returned to the desk. She could feel her cheeks burning. How had she been so foolish. Had he noticed? Did he think she was trying to…it was too embarrassing even to think of it!

'Now,' he said. 'Is there anything else?'

'No, sir, I believe—'

She broke off as the door opened and she heard a deep, cheerful voice saying,

'No need to announce me, Fraser, I'll find him—and lay another cover for dinner, there's a good fellow!'

Unable to curb her curiosity, Juliana turned to see who dared to walk in upon Major Collingham with such insouciance. She saw a gentleman dressed in the first style of elegance, his short fair hair brushed forward to frame a handsome, good-humoured countenance supported—or more properly confined—by a collar whose points came up to his cheeks. A tight-fitting blue coat and white embroidered waistcoat encased his body, while inexpressibles of the palest cream and gleaming Hessians completed the picture of a top-of-the-trees man-about-town. If the gentleman heard the Major's curt demand to know what the devil was going on he gave no sign, but stopped just inside the door and made an elegant bow.

'Well, now, Fraser did not tell me you had company, Damon. How very remiss of him.'

The Major was regarding the newcomer with a mixture of amusement and exasperation. 'Would it have stopped you charging in, had you known?'

The gentleman gave a grin. 'I dare say I'd have allowed him to announce me.'

Major Collingham sighed. 'Your manners really are appalling, Richard. Miss Wrenn, may I present to you Sir Richard Mondwyck?'

Juliana stepped forward, her cheeks still warm from her recent embarrassment.

'Yes. That is, we—we have met.'

'By Jove, yes, I thought you looked familiar! I knew her father,' he explained to the Major. 'Clever fellow, Jonas Wrenn. Could always rely on him to decipher the more difficult codes I put to him.' Sir Richard took her hand. 'I was very sorry to hear of his death, Miss Wrenn. I was in France at the time or I should have attended his funeral. He was a very good man.'

'Thank you, sir.' She gently withdrew her fingers from his grip and Sir Richard moved across to the side-table to pour himself a glass of wine.

'Well, now, Miss Wrenn—what are you doing here with this reprobate?'

'Miss Wrenn is in my employ,' the Major responded curtly. 'She has agreed to act as governess for a few months, until I have settled the girls into Blackthorpe.'

'My father was not a rich man, sir,' she answered the question in Sir Richard's look. 'So now I must earn my living.'

She ended brightly, smiling, and Sir Richard merely nodded, understanding in his eyes.

'As must I, Miss Wrenn,' he replied in the same light vein. 'Fortunately, there are wealthy men such as Damon here who have need of our services occasionally.'

Major Collingham's lip curled. 'Thank you, Richard. Now, before my patience is quite worn out, perhaps you will tell me what you are doing here?'

'I wanted a little company, so I invited myself to dinner, Damon.'

'Really? Louisa will be overjoyed.'

Sir Richard almost choked on his wine. 'No! Is your sister in town? Well, I didn't know, but no matter. I shall be delighted to see her again. This really is a superb burgundy,

Damon—shall I refill your glass? And we are all standing around like perfect strangers! Miss Wrenn, will you not be seated, ma'am?'

'Thank you, but I think Major Collingham and I have finished our business, and I must get back to my charges. If that is all, Major?'

'It is for now. You will oblige me by bringing the girls to the drawing room after dinner, Miss Wrenn.'

'As you wish, sir.'

Sir Richard opened the door for her and Juliana gave him a fleeting smile as she went out. She was feeling a little light-headed as she made her way back to the schoolroom. She attributed this to the wine, but could not deny her pleasure at seeing Sir Richard again. He had been an infrequent visitor to her father's house, always on business, but on the rare occasions they had met he had treated her with respect and she felt now that his acknowledgement of her had added to her standing with her new employer. All at once she found herself looking forward to going downstairs after dinner.

Chapter Five

'So you are taking the children back to Lancashire,' said Sir Richard.

'Blackthorpe Hall is their home, and mine, too.' Major Collingham tossed off his wine and walked to the side-table. 'I have hardly been there since their mother died. There is much to be done.' He held up the decanter and Sir Richard came over with his empty glass.

'And you plan to marry that neighbour of yours—the widow?'

'Lady Frances. Yes. She was in town with her father a few weeks ago. Nothing was said, of course, but much was hinted at.'

Sir Richard grimaced.

'Too cold for my taste, old friend. I cannot ever recall seeing a spark of warmth in her.'

Damon shrugged. 'She will make the girls a good mother. That is all I want.'

Sir Richard sipped his wine, saying nothing. The Major eyed him for a moment, then set down his glass with a snap.

'Damnation, man, say what is on your mind.'

'If I did that, my friend, you would call me out.'

'You think I am making a mistake?'

Sir Richard looked down at the toe of one gleaming Hessian as he traced the pattern on the carpet. 'I do not think Lady Frances will make you happy.'

'I am five-and-thirty, Richard, past the age of romantic notions. So, too, is Frances. I want a mother for my children, nothing more.' He paused, then said with some difficulty, 'I loved Harriet. To lose her was—agony. I have no wish to go through such pain again. Frances and I understand each other—we have been neighbours for many years. She will bring up the girls and look after my house, leaving me free to get on with the business of running the estate. We shall be very comfortable.'

'Then I wish you happy. And you have found a governess to look after the children. How did you manage that so quickly?'

'Miss Wrenn is related to Pettigrew, the lawyer dealing with my cousin Willoughby's affairs—you will remember he made me trustee before he died. Miss Wrenn and I struck a bargain—she is contracted to me until September, which will give me time to arrange matters in Lancashire.'

'There were other children in the Wrenn family, as I recall.'

'Aye. Two. They are travelling with us.'

'The devil they are!' Sir Richard laughed. 'What has come over you, Damon? I thought you didn't like children above half!'

'Nor do I.' He scowled. 'You may take that look out of your eye, Rick, I'm not going soft in the head, if that's what you are thinking. They would have to follow their sister at some stage, so it seemed expedient to take them with us. They will be company for my own girls.'

'True, and Miss Wrenn will be looking after them, will she not? I doubt they will bother you.'

'That is my hope. You knew her father, you said?'

'Aye. He spent some years in France as a young man and

his knowledge of the country and language was quite exceptional. In my work for the government, I often have need for someone to decipher the notes we intercept from French spies. Wrenn was one of the best.'

The Major studied his wine glass. 'And how well do you know his daughter?'

'We met once or twice, when I called on her father. That is all.' Sir Richard laughed. 'You need not worry, Damon. She was never one of my intrigues. Her reputation was—and is, I am sure—spotless.' He bent his shrewd gaze upon his host. 'Perhaps you have an interest there yourself?'

Damon thought of the little governess in her dull clothes with her soft brown hair braided so modestly around her head. 'Not my line at all, my friend. She might be quite pretty, if she were dressed up.' He sipped his wine, imagining the girl in an evening gown. Silk, he thought. It would cling to her slender body. And emerald green, to match her eyes, eyes that could suddenly gleam with mischief. He gave himself a little mental shake. 'No, I've no interest there, Rick. It has never been my way to tamper with innocents, or raise false hopes.'

'No, your taste has always been for more dashing beauties, eh, *Devil* Collingham?'

Damon laughed. 'Will I never live down that damned Brussels party?'

'It would appear not, my friend. The stories grow more outrageous every time they are retold.'

Damon shook his head. 'We were at war and a little reckless. Who wants such stories now? The war ended over a year ago.'

'But it pleases the ladies to remember. And it seems you *did* please 'em, Damon, the married ones, at least.'

'Safer that way.' The Major raised his glass. 'They know I don't offer 'em marriage. A flirtation, a little pleasure on both sides, then we go our separate ways.'

'Like Lady Ormiston? You were very close when you came home for the Peace Celebrations in 'fourteen.'

'That affair lasted only as long as the peace,' said Damon, his lip curling. 'Veronique is indeed a beauty, but she has a heart of stone.'

'You make a fine pair, then,' retorted Sir Richard, smiling faintly. 'Ormiston is still playing least in sight. It seems he prefers his Scottish acres to living with his wife. I believe she has young Leeson paying court to her now; they say he's besotted.'

'Silly young fool.' The Major lifted the decanter again. 'We might as well finish this off before we go into dinner. For God's sake, sit down, man, and you can tell me the real reason you are here.'

Sir Richard lowered himself into an armchair on one side of the empty fireplace. 'I am chasing diamonds, dear boy.'

'The devil you are! Is that what brings you back to England?'

'Yes. Bonaparte's followers have been trying to raise a force to free him from St Helena. From the letters we have intercepted we know that the Princess Borghese donated a pair of diamond earrings to the cause.'

The Major raised his black brows. 'Bonaparte's sister? How was she persuaded to part with them?'

'No idea, my friend. Her passion for jewels is legendary—the Emperor himself acquired these stones in Egypt and had them made up into ear-drops for the princess. Perhaps she wanted to make a gesture of sisterly devotion.'

'Then it would be her first! More likely one of her other—ah—admirers persuaded her to be generous.'

'One of her lovers, you mean? Possibly. In any event, the diamonds were sent from Italy to Paris. We arrested a number of conspirators, but the gems had already been moved on.'

'Did you identify the courier?'

'No. We caught one or two suspects at the coast, but it seems the diamonds were hidden in rolls of cloth bound for London. We have traced the consignment and are going through all the delivery papers and bills of exchange, but that is slow work. I am investigating other possibilities.' He crossed one elegantly shod foot over the other. 'One thing is certain: the diamonds have not been sold. I have my contacts in the markets and there is not a whisper of such fine stones being available.'

'What is their value?'

'Enough to buy and fit out a ship to take Bonaparte off St Helena.' He studied his wine glass. 'I was going to ask you to help me track them down.'

'Alas, Rick, I am leaving town on Friday. Besides, I am no longer in the army.'

'True, but you do have an uncanny ability to ferret out information. Oh, never fear, I have some very clever fellows looking for these gems, so I shall find 'em.' He finished his wine. 'Now, you had best take me to meet the lovely Louisa, since I am joining you for my dinner.'

Nurse and the children were gathered in the schoolroom when Juliana went in, and she found herself facing a row of expectant faces.

'Tomorrow,' she announced, 'we are going shopping. We shall make a list of everything we need for the schoolroom; we seem to be especially deficient of books.' She saw their horrified looks and burst out laughing. 'Do not look so shocked, it will not be so bad, I promise you.' She swept Amy up into her arms. 'There will be plenty of time for playing games, too.'

'Miss Sevenoaks said games were for babies,' scoffed Gwendoline.

'Then I pity her pupils,' chuckled Juliana. She looked around as the door opened.

A young man walked in. Despite his light brown hair he was so much a younger version of her employer that Juliana guessed immediately his identity. His first words confirmed it.

'My father said I should come up and make myself known to you. I am Giles Collingham.'

Juliana immediately brought her brother and sister forward to be introduced.

'You have been with your friends today, I understand?'

'Yes, which is why Papa has said I should join you for dinner, and get to know you, since we will be travelling together.'

'Oh, poor you.' Juliana gave him a sympathetic smile. 'How dull for you to be consigned to the schoolroom.'

Giles coloured a little. 'Yes, well, it is not so bad, you know.'

'I am sure you would prefer to be dining with Papa when you know who is with him,' put in Gwendoline as they took their places for dinner. She cast a quick, triumphant look around the table. 'Sir Richard Mondwyck! Nelly told me he walked in, bold as brass, and directed Fraser to set another place for him.'

Nurse tutted. 'Now, Miss Gwendoline, you should not be listening to servants' gossip, nor repeating it, neither.'

'I'll wager Aunt Louisa will be in high dudgeon,' grinned Giles, ignoring Nurse's mild strictures.

'Oh, he will turn her up sweet,' returned his sister, giggling. 'She thinks he is a charmer.'

'Enough, if you please,' said Juliana firmly. 'Such talk shows little respect for your aunt or your father's guest.'

Giles flushed and Gwendoline scowled across the table at her governess.

Wilhelmina looked up. 'Sir Richard was in the Peninsula with Papa, was he not, Giles? But he was only a mister then.'

'He was knighted last year, for services to the country,' said Giles. 'Father says he is an intelligence officer, collecting information against our enemies.'

'A spy!' Gwendoline's eyes grew round.

'If he is, then it is perhaps best we do not talk of it,' responded Juliana. 'Wilhelmina, shall I help you with your napkin?'

Juliana thought back to Sir Richard's visits to her father, the bound notebooks and closeted meetings. Suddenly, it all seemed to make sense.

While the soup was being served there was a sudden clatter to Juliana's right, where Wilhelmina was sitting.

'Oh, dear, Minna,' said Nurse. 'You have dropped your spoon.'

'I'll get it!' Gwendoline was out of her seat and racing around the table.

'Gwendoline, there is no need,' Nurse expostulated mildly. 'Really, dear, do stop waving your arms, your napkin is almost in Miss Wrenn's face.'

With mumbled apologies Gwendoline returned to her place. Juliana picked up her spoon, but as she was about to dip it into her soup she stopped. There, in the middle of her bowl, was a small, black beetle.

She heard Wilhelmina stifle a giggle. Across the table, Gwendoline was addressing herself to her food, a picture of innocence. Juliana put down her spoon and began to talk to Nurse on some unexceptional topic until the soup bowls were removed and she could help herself to one of the other dishes on the table.

As soon as the meal was over, Giles excused himself and went downstairs, but Juliana waited until she received word that the gentlemen had joined Lady Varley in the drawing room. Nurse promised to take care of Thomas and Amy, and Juliana glanced at her two charges to make sure they were looking neat and tidy.

'Very well, shall we go?'

As they went down the stairs, Juliana let Wilhelmina run on ahead while she moved a little closer to Gwendoline.

'That was a very neat trick you played at dinner—no, please do not deny it. Where did you find the beetle, in the schoolroom?'

Gwendoline tossed her head. 'Yes, if you must know.'

'Well, let me warn you, Gwendoline, that I will not be put off by your tricks or stratagems. Your papa has engaged me until the end of September and I do not intend to give up this position, however unpleasant you try to make it.' She glanced down at the mutinous little face beside her. 'Please try to make the best of it, Gwendoline—the time will pass much quicker if we work together. And remember that I have a younger brother and sister, so I have a few tricks of my own.' She lowered her voice, 'Beware how you get into bed tonight!' She laughed at Gwendoline's quick, alarmed glance and patted the girl's arm. 'Come, Gwendoline, cry friends with me; I am not an ogre, I promise you.'

They had reached the drawing room and Juliana took Wilhelmina's hand. The footman threw open the door and, with a bright smile pinned in place, Juliana escorted her charges into the room.

Lady Varley greeted the schoolroom party with regal graciousness and called the children to her. Juliana would have taken a seat in one corner of the room, but Major Collingham beckoned her forward.

'So you have spent your first day with my girls, Miss Wrenn.' He led her to a chair next to Sir Richard. 'I hope they have been no trouble?'

She saw Gwendoline look up quickly, and gave her a reassuring smile. 'I think we are in a great way to understanding each other, Major.'

Even if she had not made peace with Gwendoline, it was, she hoped, a truce.

'And you are to accompany the family to Blackthorpe Hall, Miss Wrenn,' said Sir Richard. 'I hope you have a strong constitution. Collingham here likes to travel at a fearsome pace.'

'The children's needs will dictate our progress,' returned Juliana calmly.

'I have already allowed for it,' nodded the Major. 'Brasher has written to the hotels where we shall stay. He will go on ahead with Benns to check the accommodation personally, and they will then travel on to Blackthorpe.'

Lady Varley looked up. 'You are sending your valet on ahead, Damon? Is that wise?'

'My dear Louisa, I am quite capable of dressing and shaving myself, you know,' retorted the Major. 'Besides, we shall only be on the road for three nights.'

Sir Richard grinned. 'Everything organised with the efficiency of a military operation,' he said. 'I hope you are impressed, Miss Wrenn?'

'I shall be impressed if we carry it off.'

Juliana found herself subjected to the Major's steely gaze.

'Do you doubt my planning, then?'

'No, sir. I am sure your planning is impeccable, but it is not wise to rely too heavily upon plans and timetables where children are involved.'

'Very true,' put in Lady Varley. 'I know from my own little ones that they are the most delightfully unpredictable creatures.'

'Good Gad, Miss Wrenn, do you follow Rousseau's philosophy for the education of children?' cried Sir Richard gaily.

'Certainly, I believe they should be allowed to express

themselves, and have room to play.' She felt a flush stealing into her cheeks and she added quickly, 'Not that I expect such considerations to affect our journey.'

'I am very glad to hear it,' growled her employer.

'However,' she continued, 'the children are very young, and if they need to stop a little more frequently I shall not hesitate to bring it to your attention, Major. But it is by no means certain; they may prove themselves to be excellent travellers.'

Major Collingham stepped closer, frowning down at her. 'Let me make myself plain, Miss Wrenn. The journey is set. It is up to you to ensure my girls are looked after at each stage. Keep them amused, by all means, but you will not bother me with trifling concerns.'

She gave him back look for look, refusing to be intimidated by his menacing tone. 'Of course not, sir. I should not dream of troubling you with trifles.'

His eyes narrowed. 'But?' he said. 'I feel sure you are about to add a rider to that last remark.'

Juliana regarded him with an innocent stare. 'We are both concerned with the children's welfare, Major. If that is in question, then of course I will bring it to your attention.'

'By Gad, Damon, she's got you there,' murmured Sir Richard. 'But you have the right of it, Miss Wrenn. Damon will like nothing better than to know his children are being cared for.'

One glance at the Major's tight-lipped face convinced Juliana that at that moment he would like nothing better than to strangle her. With a curt nod he moved away and began to converse with his sister.

Juliana turned to Sir Richard. 'Oh dear,' she said ruefully. 'Do you think I shall be turned off before we even leave London?'

'Not a bit of it!' he reassured her. 'Damon would be the

first to tell you he knows nothing about children. He will welcome your advice, despite his frowns. He is not nearly so harsh as he would have us believe.'

As there was no one to overhear them, she murmured, 'Not really the devil he is named, perhaps?'

'Oh, so you've heard that tale, have you? Well, you may rest easy, Miss Wrenn. Collingham is a true gentleman. As a member of his household you fall under his protection, and he'll take dashed good care of you, take my word for it.'

Chapter Six

The following morning Juliana sallied forth upon her shopping expedition, accompanied by the four children. No sooner had the Collingham carriage departed than another, much less elegant equipage pulled up and the occupants were shown to Lady Varley's sitting room.

'Madame Fleurie!' Lady Varley came out of her bed-chamber, her eyebrows raised in surprise. 'I had not expected to see you so soon. You have made up the gowns already?'

'We 'ave been working through ze night, *madame*, but ze primrose muslin is of such a complexity that I need *madame* to try it on, if *madame* would be so kind?'

'Oh, very well, but you must be quick, for I am very busy today.'

Lady Varley called for her maid and allowed herself to be draped in the soft fabric, which had been cut and par-tially sewn. Madame Fleurie set her minion to pin up the hem of the gown.

'It ees a very becoming colour for you, *madame*,' she said. 'If I may mention it, my lady, when you did me the honour to visit me earlier this week, one of my assistants made a mistake: she gave one of your leetle girls a fashion doll. It was an error, *madame*, and I have reprimanded her, *naturellement*, for you see this was a special doll, dressed expressly for another of my clients. *Madame*, I am *desolée*, but I must have thees doll. Do you think—would it be possible for me to take it with me today?'

Lady Varley looked blank for a moment, then she nodded and instructed her maid to go to the schoolroom. 'You are to find a doll.'

'A leetle wooden lady, dressed in cherry brocade, *à la Pompadour*,' added Madame Fleurie.

'Yes, well, go and find it, and bring it here directly.'

'*Madame*, you find me very grateful. If eet was for myself I would give your little children all my dolls, but this one is for a very special client, a very exacting lady…' She let the words trail away, giving the impression that not all her clients were as accommodating as Lady Varley.

'If you please, ma'am,' said the maid, coming back into the room, 'there is no doll in the schoolroom, nor in the children's bedrooms either. And Miss Wilhelmina and Miss Gwendoline have gone out with the new governess.'

Lady Varley shrugged. 'No matter, I will ask the children about it when they come back. Now, can we get on?'

The fitting had just finished and the gown was being packed away when a footman entered with a letter for Lady Varley. She snatched it from the tray, her brow clearing as she recognised her husband's distinctive scrawl.

'It is from Sir James. At last. I have been waiting to hear how the family goes on without me.' She looked at Madame Fleurie. 'I take it we have done, now?'

'Indeed, *madame*, thank you for your time.' She ushered her assistant out of the room, stopping at the door to turn back. 'And if I may remind my lady, you will not forget the doll?'

'Yes, yes, I will see to it,' responded Lady Varley, impatiently waving her away.

She barely waited for the door to close before she tore open the letter and immersed herself in news from her home.

Juliana returned from her shopping trip feeling that she had achieved a great deal. She had made her purchases and placed orders for several books at Hatchards in Piccadilly, but, more than that, she thought that her charges had begun to accept her. Wilhelmina was no trouble at all; she and Amy had become firm friends. By the time they returned to Burlington Street, Wilhelmina was chattering away to Juliana as though she had known her all her life. Gwendoline was more reserved, but she had been perfectly well mannered during their excursion and Juliana was encouraged to think that the child was unbending a little towards her.

With the move to the north so imminent, Juliana did not attempt to establish a routine to the afternoon lesson, but chose instead to show the children maps and pictures of the north country, well aware that such a long journey to a place they had not seen for many years must be exciting and somewhat unnerving for her charges. She asked Mr Brasher for details of their route, and used the guidebook she had bought to describe the various towns they would pass through.

Juliana dined in the schoolroom again with the children, although Giles did not join them. He dined instead with his father and aunt, and Juliana found him in boisterous good spirits when she brought the girls to the drawing room later. He teased Wilhelmina about her freckles and then drew Gwendoline to one side, whispering to her to make her giggle. Juliana was aware of Lady Varley's frowning looks and knew she would be expected to act. She waited until she was sure the Major was engrossed in conversation with his sister, then walked over to the youngsters. Giles rose as she approached.

'Gwendoline, you know how impolite it is to be whispering thus. If it is such a good joke, then let us all share it.' She spoke quietly, but her words made the girl scowl.

'It is no crime to talk to my brother!'

'No, indeed.' Juliana's smile embraced them both. 'But when you are in company, you are insulting those around you by such secretive behaviour. Master Giles must know that, even if you are not quite old enough to appreciate it.'

Her mild rebuke hit its target. Gwendoline flushed and her brother muttered an apology.

The entrance of the tea tray caused a distraction. Lady Varley called Gwendoline over to help her prepare the tea. Juliana watched her go and turned back to Giles.

'If your sister resents me, I am sorry for it,' she said gently. 'However, your father hired me as her governess and I am obliged to correct her when it is necessary. It will help me greatly if you do not encourage her to flout my authority.'

'I—I don't, I wouldn't!'

She smiled at him. 'Then I am relieved, and very grateful to you.'

Flushing, Giles bowed, muttered his excuses, and lounged away. With a sigh, she went back to sit beside Wilhelmina.

'So, Gwendoline, what have you been doing today?' Lady Varley posed the question while she prepared the tea. 'What have you learned with Miss Wrenn?'

'In truth, Aunt, nothing.' Gwendoline put her chin in the air and cast a defiant look at Juliana.

The room was suddenly very still. Wilhelmina wriggled uncomfortably on her chair. The Major had been talking to Giles on the far side of the room, but now he looked up.

'What do you mean by that, Gwen?'

'That Miss Wrenn is a fraud, Papa,' declared Gwendoline with awful clarity. 'This morning we did nothing but shop—a frivolous exercise—and this afternoon…'

'This afternoon we studied England,' said Juliana calmly. 'With the use of maps Mr Brasher looked out for us, we plotted our journey, once we had calculated how far we might travel in one day. That, of course, meant we had to decide how fast the carriage could go. What did we decide was our likely speed, Wilhelmina?'

'Eight miles in an hour.'

'Yes, very good. Then we had to work out the distance between towns.'

'And stops for changing horses,' put in Wilhelmina, glad to be able to contribute again. 'Thomas thought of that!'

'Yes, he did.' Juliana nodded at her. 'So you see how we practised our powers of calculation and arithmetic. Then, of course, we looked up in the guidebook the towns we are likely to pass through. Barnet, of course, where we shall look out for the Barnet Pillar, put up to mark the famous battle.'

'That was where Edward IV beat Henry VI to become king,' said Wilhelmina.

'Yes, in 1471. And St Albans—what can you remember of St Albans, Wilhelmina?'

The little girl wrinkled her nose. 'There was a battle when Queen Margaret brought her army and rescued King Henry, but he could not have been a very good king, because Edward beat him at the Battle of Barnet.'

'Yes, and where else might we be travelling?'

'Derby,' said Wilhelmina, swinging her legs. 'Where the rebels turned back in the 'Forty-five and they were followed back into Scotland, where the King's brother followed them and killed them all!'

The Major raised his brows. 'A very bloodthirsty summary.'

Juliana chuckled. 'More interesting than mere dates and places, Major.'

'Undoubtedly. And from there, Minna?'

'Macclesfield,' cried the little girl. 'Where there are mills that weave fine silks for Aunt Louisa's shawls!'

Major Collingham laughed and patted her head. 'Very good.' He looked hard at Juliana. 'Perhaps Gwendoline was not paying attention today.'

'No, Major, I cannot blame her—for she was sewing a fine lawn handkerchief for Lady Varley as I talked. After all, it was never intended to be a serious lesson.'

Wilhelmina tugged at her father's sleeve. 'When we were out this morning, Miss Wrenn gave us a whole sixpence each to spend, as long as we could reckon up the pennies we had in change. And I did, Papa.'

He lifted her into his arms. 'How clever of you. Now, ten more minutes while we drink a dish of tea, then bed for you, children.' He set her on her feet and smiled over her head at Juliana. 'Congratulations, Miss Wrenn. You make the journey sound exciting, even to me. I have no doubt Gwendoline will take more interest in future.'

'I have always maintained that girls should be taught to know their way about,' declared Lady Varley, pouring tea into the delicate porcelain cups. 'Gwendoline, my dear, please take this cup to your father. Thank you. Yes, girls need to be able to read and write, and to reckon a column of figures, but beyond that there is little value in book learning for them.'

'But, ma'am, how are they to stand their ground with their brothers, or their husbands, without a matching education?' objected Juliana.

Lady Varley shook her head. 'A man doesn't want a clever wife, Miss Wrenn. He wants a dutiful one. Gwendoline, this cup to Miss Wrenn, if you please.'

'An educated woman may still be dutiful,' put in the Major.

'Unless her husband is particularly dull-witted,' murmured Juliana.

Major Collingham laughed.

'A clever woman will learn to have her own way,' replied Lady Varley, 'but she does not need an education for that.'

Juliana looked up. The Major was watching her, and she found herself responding to the smile in his eyes. Gwendoline approached with a cup of tea, but as she reached out for it, the girl stumbled and the contents of the cup were thrown over Juliana's best grey gown.

There was an immediate commotion. The Major berated Gwendoline on her clumsiness and she burst into tears. Giles came forward to defend his sister, while Lady Varley bewailed the broken cup.

Juliana stooped to collect up the pieces.

'Pray, Major, do not scold her. I am sure it was an accident. Master Giles, ring the bell and fetch a servant to clear up this mess, if you please.' She rose, looking down at her wet gown and trying to hide her dismay. 'Let me take the children upstairs, sir. It is their bedtime.'

He was still looking thunderous.

'Very well. Leave them with Nurse and give your dress to Mrs Hartley. She will know what to do to clean it. You will then put on a fresh gown and come back here.'

Lady Varley stared at him. 'Damon!'

'Really, sir,' stammered Juliana, 'I should retire—'

'You will come back, Miss Wrenn.'

His tone was implacable and she knew it was useless to argue. Closing her lips firmly, she nodded, took Wilhelmina by the hand and led the two girls out of the room.

Her silence as they went up to the schoolroom seemed to unnerve Gwendoline. She said, 'It was an accident, you know.'

'If you say so.'

'Will the stain come out?'

What do you care? thought Juliana, and immediately scolded herself for being as childish as her charges. She said, 'I hope so. I do not have the luxury of another silk gown.'

'We could buy you one in Macclesfield,' suggested Wilhelmina.

Juliana squeezed her hand and forced a smile. 'Yes, we could. In the meantime, let us hope the housekeeper is as good as your papa says.'

She handed the children over to Nurse and went off to change into her only other evening gown, a cream robe with long sleeves caught up with lime-green ribbons. It was the last gown her father had bought for her, and she had been saving it for a special occasion. It occurred to her that there would not now be any special occasions, for a while at least. She threw a black silk shawl about her shoulders and looked at herself in the mirror.

'Far too bright for mourning.' She sighed. 'However, he insists I return, so it will have to do.'

Pausing only to say goodnight to Amy and Thomas, who were already in their beds, she ran lightly down the stairs and back to the drawing room. There was a martial light in her eyes as she walked in, but the Major merely nodded at her and Lady Varley addressed her with unusual graciousness. 'I have made more tea so that you may join us, Miss Wrenn. I was mortified at my niece's clumsiness.'

'No matter, ma'am. Mrs Hartley has taken the gown to clean it.'

'You shall have a new one, I will buy it for you,' announced the Major abruptly.

Lady Varley cast a sympathetic look at Juliana as she handed her a cup.

'It is so simple for my brother, Miss Wrenn. He says he will buy you a new gown, as if there were any number made up, just waiting for you to choose one. You forget, Damon, that you leave town on Friday. Why, even Madame Fleurie could not turn out a decent gown in such a short time. Although I have been most surprised at her endeavours on my behalf this week—she called here today for a fitting and I had only chosen the muslin yesterday! And that reminds me, dear brother. I must crave your indulgence and ask you to let me stay on here for a few more days after you leave for the north, because my gowns are not complete, and although I have had word from Sir James, begging me to return as soon as ever I can, I really must stay in town until all my gowns are ready.'

'Yes, yes, Louisa, but you are straying from the point. Surely you know where to buy a new gown for Miss Wrenn that she can take with her?'

'Sir, I pray you, it is no matter,' put in Juliana, distressed by so much attention. 'I am sure there will be no lasting damage; besides, I will not be requiring such a gown again for some months.'

'Well, you may leave one of your old dresses with me, Miss Wrenn,' pronounced Lady Varley. 'I will have my modiste make up another to fit and it shall be sent on after you. Not another word, Miss Wrenn, my mind is made up. Now, let us talk of something else—Damon, did you go to White's today? I hear Meyler was there, telling everyone that Mr Brummell is quite done up.'

The Major frowned. 'Aye, I saw him.'

'I have never liked Meyler. Bad *ton*, I always thought.' She refilled her brother's teacup. 'How has Mr Brummell taken it?'

'I have no idea. He was not there.'

'But this is not good enough, brother. I made sure you would know.'

The Major shook his head. 'I admire Brummell's style of dress, Louisa, not his way of living.'

Giles had been sitting quietly in the corner all this time, but now he came forward. 'I thought you were one of his friends, Papa.'

'Sufficiently so that I would not listen to Meyler's accusations. However, it is for the Beau to refute them.'

'And will he do so, do you think?' asked Lady Varley.

'With Brummell one never knows. He has come about in the past: we shall see what he does over the next few days.'

However, Thursday morning brought even more exciting news for Lady Varley. Juliana had already joined the Major and his daughters in the breakfast room when she came in, saying as she took her place at the table, 'Damon, you will never guess! I have had word that Lady Maltby is in town. I must call upon her this morning.'

'Must you, Louisa?' asked the Major, helping himself to a cup of coffee.

Lady Varley gave a little sigh. 'Of course I must. She is James's cousin, you know, and I would not want to be thought backward in paying her any attention.'

'Especially since she is a viscountess,' he murmured.

'And what if she is?' retorted Lady Varley. 'Family connections are important. I shall take Gwendoline and Wilhelmina with me, if Miss Wrenn will give them leave—Lady Maltby was very taken with the girls when she came to stay with us last year.'

'Ooh, yes, please. May we go, Miss Wrenn?' asked Wilhelmina.

Gwendoline said nothing, but Juliana saw her hopeful glance.

'Of course,' she said, 'if Major Collingham agrees.'

He shrugged. 'If that is what you wish, Louisa…'

'Damon, how can you be so tiresome! A connection

with the viscountess could be very useful for the girls when it comes to finding them husbands.'

Major Collingham gave a bark of laughter. 'Good God, I trust I have several years before I need to address that issue!'

'One should always be prepared,' replied his sister. 'Now, come along, girls, finish your breakfast, for we must make you ready. Miss Wrenn, I do hope I am not interfering with your plans?'

'Not at all. I have to collect some last-minute purchases, which I can do this morning while you are out.'

'I will send one of the maids with you—'

'Oh, there will be no need for that, Major,' Juliana interrupted him quickly. 'I shall have Thomas and Amy with me—there is no need for any other companion.'

The Major would not countenance Miss Wrenn and her family taking a hackney carriage and, as Lady Varley would be using the landau, he ordered his own travelling carriage to be made ready. This was a large, impressive vehicle complete with liveried servants hanging on the back, and Juliana was not surprised to see a group of ragged boys standing on the opposite side of the road, watching with interest as the carriage rolled away.

'This is the carriage we shall be using for our journey,' she told Amy and Thomas. 'Miss Gwendoline and Wilhelmina will be travelling with us, while Nurse and the Major's man will follow in the baggage coach.'

'And Major Collingham will be leading the way in his curricle, with Mr Giles beside him,' added Thomas. 'We shall create quite a stir when we drive through the town.'

'And there will be plenty of room for the five of us in here,' Juliana observed, leaning back with an appreciative sigh against the padded seat.

'Then we will be able to bring Sarah and Lady Arabella?' asked Amy, holding her doll on her lap.

Juliana smiled at her. 'Yes. They shall have a seat to themselves.'

Due to the press of traffic in New Bond Street, Juliana had decided it would be quicker to walk between the shops and she ordered the coachman to pull up and wait for her. The errands were soon accomplished, ending with a visit to Hatchards the booksellers, and with the children beside her she began to retrace her steps. They had not gone far when she saw Major Collingham walking towards them. He stopped, looking a little surprised.

'Miss Wrenn. I had thought you would be in New Bond Street, buying bonnets and gloves.'

'I would not bring Tom and Amy along for *that*, they would find it very tedious work. No, you will see that our parcels are quite small—paper and pens for drawing, and I have purchased more reading books. I ordered them Tuesday and they promised to have them ready for me today. We are on our way back to the carriage now.'

'I, too, have concluded my business, so I will walk with you, if I may?'

He turned to accompany her. Juliana took his proffered arm, glancing back to make sure the two children were close behind.

'And have you ordered another gown, Miss Wrenn, as I instructed?'

'No. Mrs Hartley has worked miracles with my grey silk and it will be ready to take with me tomorrow.' She saw he was looking severe and added, 'Lady Varley has already wrested an old gown from me, and will use it as a pattern for the new one that is being made up for me. She has promised to send it on as soon as it is ready.'

'Quite right. I am very sorry for what happened last night.'

'It was an accident.'

'We both know it was nothing of the kind,' he retorted. 'Gwendoline does not want you to come with us. I shall talk to her today, and make sure she understands I will not tolerate her disobedience.'

She stopped. 'Oh, pray do not be harsh on her, sir. It—it might make her resent me even more.'

Major Collingham turned to look at her. 'Then what would you have me say, Miss Wrenn?'

Juliana hesitated. She said slowly, 'I think we should agree that if Gwendoline is of the same mind when we reach Lancashire, we will terminate the contract. She will learn little from me if we are constantly at loggerheads.'

'Rousseau's teachings, Miss Wrenn?'

'Common sense, Major. I will do my best to make her like me, but you know that we cannot always order our affections.'

'And you would have me tell her that she may decide once we get to Blackthorpe?'

'Why, yes. I would like Gwendoline to know that I have no wish to inflict myself upon her against her will.'

'But to leave then—you would be miles from your home, Miss Wrenn.'

'I have no home now, sir,' she said quietly. 'There are no relatives to make it desirable for me to remain here. I can as easily find employment in the big towns of the north, and—'

A scream and commotion behind them made her break off. Turning, Juliana saw that Tom and Amy had fallen some way behind, and Thomas was fighting with two larger boys while Amy stood behind him, screaming for help. Passers-by hesitated, but the Major was there before any of them could act. Grabbing Thomas's assailants by their ragged collars he pulled them away and banged their heads together. The two boys staggered back and, as the Major turned his attention to Thomas, they tore themselves free and took to their heels.

Juliana had snatched Amy into her arms, but now she turned to her little brother. He was panting heavily and holding a handkerchief to his bloody nose.

'In heaven's name, what happened?' she asked as Amy sobbed against her shoulder.

'They—they pounced on Amy,' Thomas said thickly.

'Aye, I saw it.' An old gentleman stopped beside them. 'Dashed footpads, to attack a child, and in daylight too. Scoundrels!'

Juliana nodded, unable to speak. Silently she hugged Amy and watched while the Major took out his own hand-kerchief and began to wipe the blood from a cut over Thomas's eye.

'Don't worry, this looks worse than it is. There, that's better. Well done, my boy. You gave a good account of yourself there. But you are sadly lacking in science.' He straightened and patted Thomas on the shoulder. 'Remind me to give you a few lessons.'

'I will not have you teaching Thomas such a rough sport,' objected Juliana.

'I would teach him to defend himself better, Miss Wrenn,' retorted the Major.

'Coo, sis, this is nothing,' said Thomas. He looked up at Major Collingham and added shyly, 'I should very much like to learn to box, sir. To learn properly, that is.'

'Well, we can discuss that later,' said Juliana. 'For now we should take you both back to the carriage. If I stand you down, Amy, do you think you could walk a little? There's a good girl.'

She gathered up her packages and the parcel of books that Thomas had dropped when he had rushed to defend his sister, then, with the children walking safely between herself and Major Collingham, they set off towards New Bond Street.

It was not to be expected that such exciting news could be kept secret. As soon as they were back at the house, Juliana took the children upstairs, where it was necessary to explain their dishevelled appearance to Nurse. Thomas and Amy lost no time in giving the kindly old retainer the full story, while she and Nelly, the chambermaid, did their best to repair the damage to clothes and persons.

Nurse confided only in Mrs Hartley, the housekeeper, but Nelly thought it a fine tale with which to regale her colleagues in the servants' hall, and although Lady Varley's superior dresser did not consort with the lower servants, she overheard enough to pass on the story to her mistress.

Thus it was that when Juliana brought Gwendoline and Wilhelmina to the drawing room that evening, the subject under discussion was not the visit to viscountess Maltby, but the attack upon Miss Amy Wrenn.

'My dear, I have made Damon tell me the whole.' Lady Varley addressed Juliana as soon as she entered the room. 'How is little Amy, and Thomas, the brave boy?'

'They are fully recovered, ma'am, thank you. Thomas has an interesting black eye and a few cuts, but that is all, and he has enjoyed himself thoroughly over dinner, telling the Misses Collingham how he acquired his wounds.'

Lady Varley shook her head. 'You see, brother, why I insist on taking a footman about with me when I am in town? The streets are no longer safe.'

'You refine too much upon it, Louisa. Such attacks are not common.'

'I should not have let the children fall behind,' admitted Juliana. 'I can only think they believed Amy to be alone and unprotected.' She shuddered, then said in an attempt to throw off the gloom, 'At least the ruffians did not get away without some punishment; they will have very sore heads now, I think.'

She smiled gratefully at the Major.

'I hope so, Miss Wrenn, although I wish I had held on to them, and handed them over to the magistrate.'

'Well, 'tis too late for that now,' said Lady Varley. 'Tomorrow you leave for the north. What are your plans, Damon?'

'I have arranged three nights on the road, at Northampton, Derby and Macclesfield. We leave early tomorrow morning.'

'I am to ride in the curricle,' said Giles with a grin. 'I hope you will let me handle the ribbons, Papa.'

'Aye, for part of the journey.'

'But what of Fewell?' asked Lady Varley. 'You told me Benns is to go on ahead, but surely you will not travel without your groom as well as your valet.'

'By no means. He can sit up behind us or on one of the coaches, if he would prefer it. Giles will act as my groom, when necessary.'

'Oh, by Jove, yes!' cried Giles. 'I can handle the yard of tin, and make sure we are not delayed at the turnpikes—'

'We will not be racing, Giles. I intend to keep in sight of the carriages.' The Major saw the disappointment in his son's face and his lips twitched. 'Well, most of the time.'

Lady Varley shuddered. 'Well, I wish you luck, brother. I brought the children with me from Kewhurst. Less than half a day's travel and that was enough for me.'

The Major's good humour was not diminished. He turned his sardonic glance upon Juliana. 'I think it is Miss Wrenn who needs your good wishes, Louisa. She will have charge of the children, not I!'

Chapter Seven

Inside the Major's elegant travelling carriage an air of excitement prevailed, even though the rain beat steadily against the roof and the windows were already misted.

Juliana smiled at her companions.

'I have bought a scrapbook,' she said. 'It is to be a record of our journey. We will all add notes and drawings of everything we see and do on our travels.'

Gwendoline looked at the rain-streaked window and pulled a face. 'There will be precious little to put in it.'

Juliana laughed. 'But we have not yet been travelling an hour. There will be plenty to add during our journey, never fear. But I agree that for the present there is very little to see, so we shall entertain ourselves instead with making up a story.'

Thomas looked up. 'Juliana is very good at make-believe.'

'Thank you, Thomas, but I want everyone to join in. We shall make up a story of great adventures and when we stop in the evenings you can write it down, if you wish, and draw pictures to illustrate it.'

'Well, I cannot think of anything.' Gwendoline pouted and turned to the window.

'No matter,' said Juliana. 'I am sure that Minna and Amy will start us off. First of all we need our characters.'

Amy held up her doll. 'One can be called Sarah.'

Wilhelmina leaned forward. 'And can we have Lady Arabella, too?'

'Of course.' Juliana smiled. 'But we must also have some male characters. Thomas?'

'Leo,' said Wilhelmina. 'And he can be a farmer.'

'That's too dull,' said Amy. 'He should be a...a doctor!'

'No, a sailor,' cried Thomas. 'And he can have a wooden leg, and just one eye!'

Gwendoline looked round. 'That's silly,' she said. 'He would not be a hero.'

'Oh, yes, he would,' retorted Thomas. 'Lord Nelson had only one eye, and one arm.' He saw Juliana frowning at him and added pacifically, 'We could have another hero, if you want.'

'Very well.' Gwendoline thought for a moment. 'He will be called Roland, and he will be a soldier.'

Juliana sat back while the children continued to create their make-believe world. Even Gwendoline was drawn in, and the morning was spent discussing the lives of their favourite characters, until they made their first stop at a wayside inn and the children tumbled out of the carriage and into the inn, still chattering.

The Major raised his brows as he helped Juliana to alight.

'Congratulations, Miss Wrenn. I thought you would have been at cap-pulling by now.'

He took her arm and hurried her through the rain to the inn.

'Not yet, Major. They have decided to write a novel, where the hero and heroine will undergo the most appalling hardships.' She laughed as she preceded him indoors. 'You would be amazed to know the gruesome fate they have in store for the poor villain.' She stopped and put a hand to her mouth. 'Oh—that is, pray do not think that I allow them to run too wild in their imaginings, sir. I—'

'You do not need to explain to me,' he said, stripping off his gloves. 'I trust you.'

He reached out and brushed a curl of wet hair off her face. She flushed, partly at his words, and partly at his touch. She had to steel herself not to rub her cheek against his hand.

'You t-trust me? Oh, but…'

He looked amused.

'Come, Miss Wrenn. You told me yourself that you have impeccable credentials.' He took pity on her confusion and explained. 'I drove to Clapham on the day you moved into Burlington Street, to follow up your references with your old schoolmistress. She gave a glowing account of you. You look surprised—do you really think I would entrust my children to the care of a stranger?'

'Many fathers do so.'

'I am not one of them.' He guided her through the passage, where the landlord was holding open the door to a private parlour. 'So, Miss Wrenn, I have every confidence in you.'

It was not to be expected that the good mood of the party would last for ever. As soon as they had eaten, Juliana shepherded her charges back to their coach, but the novelty of travelling had worn off and the two younger girls were tired and fractious. The older children took two of the corner seats, where Thomas proceeded to fall asleep and Gwendoline stared out of the window at the rain, yawning openly and declaring that she was bored. Sitting between Wilhelmina and Amy on the other bench seat, Juliana settled the children against her and began to tell fairy stories.

Another hour passed. There was no easing of the rain, and as they travelled farther from London the state of the roads became worse until they were little more than rutted tracks that slowed their progress at times to walking pace. Juliana soon realised that the Major's first easy stage would not be accomplished until well into the evening.

Chapter Eight

The Northampton hotel that the Major's secretary had arranged for them could not be faulted, but by the time the travelling carriage drew up at its welcoming portal, the children were too tired to do more than pick at the choice dinner set out for them in the private parlour that had been reserved for the sole use of the schoolroom party. As soon as the children were settled in their beds, Juliana went in search of Major Collingham, who had been allocated private rooms on the first floor away from the bustling main street. She found the Major and his son sitting over the remains of their dinner.

'Oh, I am sorry. I will come back....'

They rose.

'No, come in, Miss Wrenn. We have finished now, and Giles was about to go out and check the horses for me.'

Giles laughed.

'As any good groom should,' he said, and with a bow to Juliana he went off.

Juliana waited until the door had closed behind the young man, then looked at the Major, clasping her hands before her. 'I wanted to speak to you, sir.'

'I realise that. Have you eaten?'

'Yes. I dined with the children.'

He took her elbow and led her to the table. 'With four tired children to look after, I doubt you had time for more than a mouthful. Sit down. There is plenty of food here.'

'Oh, but I had Nurse to help me. I—I couldn't—'

He ignored her protests and she found herself sitting at the dining table, a clean plate set before her and instructions to help herself from the assortment of cold meat on the platter. The Major poured her a glass of wine, topped up his own glass, then pulled up a chair and sat down, watching her.

'I was right, you are hungry. Did you eat *anything* of your own dinner?'

'At the time it seemed more important to feed the children,' she admitted. 'That is why I wanted to talk to you….'

'Later, Miss Wrenn. Let me recommend you to take a peach—they are excellent.'

'Peaches, so early?'

'I had them sent up to town from my own succession houses and brought some with me.'

She watched him select a ripe fruit from the dish and carefully cut it into pieces for her.

'You are very kind.'

'Nonsense. I am merely looking after my investment. If you do not eat, you will not be fit to take care of the girls.' He pushed the plate of prepared fruit towards her, his eyes narrowing as he saw her hesitate. 'Eat it, Miss Wrenn. Or would you like me to feed you?'

He had turned to face her, one arm resting along the back of her chair. He was too close, too intimate, the gleam in his eye definitely dangerous. Suddenly it was easy to imagine him as Devil Collingham, choosing a slice of peach to offer her, those strong fingers picking up the delicate fruit in a gentle clasp that did not bruise it and holding it to her lips…

Juliana felt herself blushing. Heavens, what had come

over her? She sought to cover her confusion by saying crossly, 'Do you always impose your will on people, sir?'

'Only when it is necessary. You eat barely enough to sustain a bird. A wren, perhaps.'

She ignored him and popped a slice of peach into her mouth. It was sweet and succulent, made all the sweeter because he had prepared it for her. As she raised her napkin to her lips, her hand trembled. Sweet heaven, such idle thoughts must be suppressed. She had heard of many poor women who had developed a slavish adoration for men with power over them. Indeed, in her own home some of the female servants had become infatuated with her father and she knew of more than one family where the governess was blatantly besotted with the master of the house. She had thought them all poor creatures, objects of ridicule. It would not happen to her, she would not allow it.

'Miss Wrenn?'

'I—oh—my apologies, Major. Wh-what did you say?'

'I merely asked if you would like more wine.'

'No. No, thank you.' She pushed her chair back and rose. 'Your kindness has almost made me forget my reason for being here.'

He sat back in his chair and watched her. 'And what was that?'

She began to pace the room, frowning over her words. 'To ask if you could send a message to Mr Brasher, to make new arrangements for the morrow. This wet weather has turned the roads to a quagmire and I fear it will disrupt your—our plans. It was full eight o'clock before we reached Northampton, sir. Far too late for the children.'

'Impossible.'

She stopped before him. 'For myself, sir, I do not object to the long hours in the coach, but the children—'

'Madam, I have no wish to make the children suffer, but

Brasher is even now at Derby. How do you expect me to contact him?'

'You could send a messenger.'

He got up and strode to the window. 'No, Miss Wrenn. I am sorry, but the arrangements must stand. We travelled greater distances in the Peninsula, you know, and over rougher ground.'

'But you are not eight years old,' she persisted. 'And then there is Nurse. She says nothing, but I know her hip is paining her from sitting for such long periods.'

She waited anxiously for his reply. He did not speak, but looked out at the leaden sky and the steady rain puddling in the lane below.

'Tomorrow may be better. If that is the case, we shall reach Derby and the hotel Brasher has secured for us with time to spare.'

'But—'

'No more, Miss Wrenn.' He turned to face her. 'It has been an exceptionally wet spring, but the rain cannot go on for ever, you know.'

Juliana knew it would be useless to argue further. She returned to her rooms, where she found Nurse waiting for her, sitting in a chair with one foot upon a gout stool, her hands busy with her knitting.

'Well, miss, what did he say?' She lowered her knitting to her lap.

'The Major thinks we shall do better tomorrow, if the rain stops.'

'There you are, then,' said Nurse, picking up her needles again. 'If the master sees no difficulties, then we shall do. He is a seasoned traveller, after all.'

'But even he cannot control the weather,' Juliana pointed out.

Nurse gave a comfortable smile.

'When you've known the master a little longer, miss, you will learn to trust him, as I do.'

Closing her lips against an unwise retort, Juliana retired to her bed, aware that Nurse was exhibiting the trait she most despised in a female, slavish devotion to the master.

Chapter Nine

Juliana made sure her charges were ready to travel at the appointed time the following morning and greeted the Major with determined cheerfulness. It was a dry morning, but from the lowering clouds Juliana thought the respite would be brief, and by the time they had reached Market Harborough a steady rain was falling. The muddy road was stony and uneven and the coachman was obliged to slow down to walking pace, for the large puddles gave no sign of how deep the ruts might be. At last they pulled into the stable yard to change horses at Oadby, and even before they had come to a halt Giles was at the door.

'It was not planned, but Father says we will stop here for a short while, so that the children may have luncheon,' he announced, preparing to hand Juliana out of the carriage. She threw up her hood over her bonnet and descended to the yard, where she was glad to hang on to Giles's arm as they crossed the slippery cobbles. Giles left her at the door, saying he would go back and help Nurse. Juliana gathered the children together and they followed the landlord to a large parlour, where they found the Major standing before a cheerful fire.

'Now that is a welcome sight,' she exclaimed, untying

the strings of her cloak. 'There is nothing like a good blaze to make one feel more the thing on a wet day.'

The Major took her cloak from her. 'We have not made the progress I intended. No doubt you would like to say I told you so?'

She twinkled up at him. 'No, sir. That would be very ignoble of me.'

His lips twitched. 'It would indeed, Miss Wrenn, and you are too magnanimous for that, are you not?'

'Of course. Now, if you have bespoken a bedroom from our host, I will take the children upstairs to tidy themselves.' She glanced at the large table set with eight chairs. 'Are we to eat together?'

'You will hardly expect an inn of this size to have more than one private parlour.'

The Major's retort made her smile. She shepherded the children towards the door, saying over her shoulder, 'Then we shall be delighted to have you join us, Major Collingham.'

Juliana had to admit that the party gathered for luncheon was a large one. She had suggested that she and Nurse could dine with Thomas and Amy in an upstairs chamber, but the Major would have none of it.

'Good heavens,' said Nurse as she came in, 'this is a real family party and no mistake.'

Following Nurse into the room, Juliana bit her lip hard to prevent herself from laughing aloud at the look of unease on the Major's face.

'You need not fear, sir. The children's table manners are excellent.' She smiled at him. 'They will not disturb you with their chatter.'

'No, but we have not started our meal yet, so I can ask Papa how he likes my hair,' said Wilhelmina. 'Miss Wrenn braided it specially, so that I would look well for you.'

'Very smart,' he replied gravely. 'And did Miss Wrenn help you with your hair, Gwen?'

'Miss Gwendoline did not need assistance,' said Juliana. 'She is very able.'

'But you showed me how to make the ends curl,' admitted Gwendoline, determined to be fair.

'Does this betoken a truce?' murmured the Major to Juliana as he held her chair for her.

'I hope so,' she replied quietly.

'Well, well, so like old times!' Nurse beamed around the table. 'It quite takes me back to when I had Master Damon and your aunt Louisa in my nursery.'

'And were they troublesome?' asked Giles, grinning at his father.

'Not a bit of it. Good as gold, they were, although it did help that I could get about better in those days, and did not need a stick. Such a lot of travelling as we did then. The family would spend the spring and summer at Kewhurst or London, then off to Blackthorpe Hall for the autumn and winter, when the old master wasn't away visiting his friends.'

'Did the children go too?' asked Gwendoline.

'Of course, my dear. The mistress, your grandmother, God rest her soul, liked to have Master Damon and his sister with her whenever she could, so we travelled with them to each one of their houses. Of course, I was younger then, and the journeys didn't affect my bones so much.'

'You have only to travel a little farther today,' said the Major, helping himself to a slice of the huge pie in the centre of the table. 'I have spoken to the landlord, and there is a very decent inn, the Queen's Head, at Loughborough. Less than twenty miles from here.'

Giles looked up.

'I thought we were stopping at Derby tonight, Papa.'

'It would take too long to reach Derby.' His glance flickered to Juliana. 'I have sent Fewell ahead to reserve rooms at the Queen's Head.'

'Will Lady Frances be waiting for us at Blackthorpe, Papa?' asked Wilhelmina.

'No, silly, she has her own house,' said Gwendoline. She turned her dark eyes towards her father. 'Is she already in Lancashire, sir?'

'I have no idea,' returned the Major. 'I expect so; she knows I am coming north.'

'Then we will meet her before the wedding.' Wilhelmina nodded. 'I am glad of that.'

Major Collingham looked amused. 'Of course you will meet her. I would not foist a new mother on you without giving you time to get to know her.'

'You foisted Miss Wrenn upon us,' said Gwendoline.

A nervous silence fell over the table. Outside the rain pattered against the window, the sky as dark as the scowl on Major Collingham's face. Juliana caught his eye and gave a tiny shake of her head, silently begging him not to reprimand his daughter. He seemed to understand her. Instead he growled, 'It would not have been necessary, had you not driven away your old governess.'

'Well, I am *glad* Miss Wrenn is with us,' declared Wilhelmina, 'because now I have Amy to play with.'

'Perhaps, sir, you would tell the children a little something about Lady Frances,' said Nurse, anxious to turn the conversation.

'Yes, Papa, please do,' Giles urged him.

The Major shrugged. 'What would you have me say? I have known Frances since she was a girl. She married Ridlington, my neighbour, but since his death she has spent much of the time with her parents.'

Gwendoline looked up. 'She is the daughter of an earl, is she not, Papa?' she asked.

'Yes, Lord and Lady Mattishall.'

'And is she very beautiful?'

'I believe she is considered so.'

'And accomplished?' persisted Gwendoline. 'Can she sing, and play the piano, and speak many languages?'

'Of course. She has had the benefit of an excellent education.'

A veritable paragon, thought Juliana, her spirits sinking.

The road into Loughborough was in a particularly poor state of repair and the constant rain had turned much of it into a running stream. The carriages bumped and jolted along at a snail's pace. Juliana amused the children with songs and stories until they reached the edge of the town, when they all gave their attention to looking out for their destination. The Queen's Head turned out to be a good-size coaching inn with an impressive frontage, two bay windows flanking a wide doorway. Juliana climbed down thankfully from the carriage and took the children inside, where Major Collingham was already in discussion with the landlord, who was explaining regretfully that he did not have sufficient rooms to meet the Major's requirements. Juliana listened for a moment, then she went over, put a hand on the Major's arm and drew him aside.

'I believe we could manage, sir. From what I overheard, the landlord has four bedrooms free for tonight: Nurse and the two younger girls could share one room, Gwendoline and I another. That would leave a room for Giles and Thomas, and one for yourself. I am sure he could find somewhere for your groom.'

The children had gathered round, and Amy now tugged at her sister's sleeve.

'Yes, please, I want to share with Minna.'

Juliana smiled down at her. 'I know, my love,' she said

gently, 'but it is for Miss Gwendoline and Wilhelmina to decide. Well, girls?' She looked at Gwendoline, well aware that she was torn between choosing to sleep with her little sister or sharing with a governess she was determined to dislike.

'Let Minna and Amy sleep together. I will share with Miss Wrenn.'

Juliana tried not to allow too much of her relief to show. She looked an enquiry at the Major.

'That still leaves the problem of one parlour.'

'I am sure you endured much worse hardships in the army, Major.'

'Of course, but that was with…'

'That was with your comrades?' she finished for him. 'Then surely to share a parlour with your family will be a pleasure.'

His eyes narrowed. 'I can hardly contradict you, madam, when they are listening to every word.'

She laughed. 'No, so pray tell the good man that we will take it, and we can order dinner.'

Juliana approached the dinner table that evening with some trepidation. In Burlington Street it had been the custom for the Major to see the children at breakfast and for only an hour after dinner. Now, not only had they all taken luncheon together, but would be confined to one room for the whole of the evening. Nurse had elected to take her dinner in her room and Juliana had at first suggested that Thomas and Amy should join her, but Major Collingham had overruled her, saying that if he was obliged to dine with his own youngsters he did not see that another two would make much difference. His tone was not encouraging, but Juliana was becoming used to his brusque manner and she hoped he would not find himself out of patience with such childish company. In the event she found the Major perfectly affable, the children were all on their best behaviour and since the dinner was good, if plain, fare, the meal passed off much better than she had expected. However, the long day's travel had taken its toll, and by the time the covers were removed both Amy and Wilhelmina were almost asleep at the table. Juliana rose to take the girls to their rooms, but the Major waved to her to sit down again.

'You have not finished your wine. Giles will take them all upstairs and deliver them to Nurse.'

'Of course, Father.' Giles rose. 'With your permission, sir, I was going to check the horses. Fewell thought one of the carriage horses was blowing too much, and feared a touch of colic.' He hesitated. 'Perhaps Tom would like to come out with me?'

'Ooh, yes, please!'

Juliana nodded.

'What a kind young man he is,' she said, as the young people left the room. 'Thomas is very impressed with your horses, Major, and will welcome the chance to see more of them.'

He refilled her glass from the decanter on the table. 'I will ask Dawlish to let him sit up on the box for a spell tomorrow.'

'Tomorrow? Surely you will not travel on a Sunday, sir.'

'We are already behind on our journey, Miss Wrenn.' She did not reply, and after a brooding glance at her face he set down his glass with a snap. 'Hell and damnation, we will never get to Lancashire if we do not press on.'

'It is only one more day, Major.'

He scowled, but she was not to be intimidated.

'Naturally if you were travelling alone the case might be different, but you would not wish to subject your children to censorious gossip.'

'And who the devil is there to see them?' he demanded.

Juliana did not reply, and feigned deafness as he cursed quietly beneath his breath.

'Oh, very well,' he said at last. 'We will remain here for another night. I shall send a man ahead to Blackthorpe to advise Brasher that we will be delayed.' He bent a frowning look at her. 'I hope you don't object to a *servant* riding on a Sunday?'

'I believe that will be unavoidable, Major.'

The scowl disappeared and he laughed suddenly.

'By God, you are a cool one.'

'You employed me to do a job, sir, and I take my responsibilities very seriously.'

'I'm glad to hear it. So what do you plan to do with yourself tomorrow?'

'Perhaps you would like the children to go to church. Then, if it is dry, I shall take them for a walk.'

He glanced out of the window. 'The sky is certainly clearing, but even if it does not rain again tonight, the road will be muddy.'

'The girls all have pattens to put over their shoes. I am a great believer in exercise.'

The rain held off that night, and the following morning, after a visit to the local church, Juliana took the girls out for the promised walk. Thomas had made good use of his introduction to the stables and there was more than a touch of pride in his voice when he told his sisters that he would not be able to walk with them because he was going to help Fewell in the stables. The walk was a pleasant one, keeping to the main streets of the town. Amy and Wilhelmina skipped ahead and Juliana used the time to talk to Gwendoline, asking questions and gradually drawing the girl out. They returned to the inn to find a fashionable cabriolet stopped at the front door. The driver of this handsome black equipage was leaning down to converse with the landlord, who was scratching his head. Seeing

Miss Wrenn approach with the children, the landlord nodded towards her.

'Perhaps you should address yourself to the lady, sir. She is with Major Collingham's party.'

The gentleman looked up and seemed a little discomposed.

'Oh—oh, yes. Well, my good man, if you will have one of your boys drive this rig to the stables, you can take my bag up to my room.'

'Well, if you'd said in the first place that you was wishing to stay…' the landlord grumbled as he took the gentleman's bag; calling to one of his lads to take the gentleman's carriage round to the back, he disappeared inside.

Juliana was at the door by this time. The gentleman jumped down and swept off his curly-brimmed beaver hat as he made her an elegant bow. He was a pleasant looking young man, with sandy hair brushed back from a pale brow and light brown eyes that held a hint of diffidence as he smiled at her.

'Your pardon, madam, you must be wondering who I am.' His smile encompassed them all, and the three girls looked up at him with undisguised curiosity. 'My name is Leeson, Charles Leeson. I believe Major Collingham is putting up here?'

Juliana nodded. 'I am merely governess to the children, sir. If you have business with the Major—'

He disclaimed quickly, 'No, no, I am travelling north to visit relatives and have to break my journey, and if this is good enough for Collingham…'

'But is it just gone noon, you could travel for hours yet,' observed Gwendoline.

Mr Leeson looked a little taken aback, but after a slight hesitation he laughed. 'I could, indeed, Miss Collingham, but my horse has been on the go since dawn and I need to keep him fresh for the long haul tomorrow.'

'Papa would not let us travel on a Sunday,' remarked Wilhelmina.

Mr Leeson nodded. 'Yes, well, there you have it. I should not carry on today, should I? But you will not want to be standing out here with me, you will have a private sitting room, I suppose? Allow me to escort you to it.'

Juliana was surprised at this excess of gallantry, but gathered the girls together and ushered them into the wide passage. They had just finished removing their muddy pattens when the door of their parlour opened and Major Collingham came out, only to pull up short in the doorway when he saw them.

'Ah, Collingham, well met!' Mr Leeson stepped forward, nodding genially. 'Taking the family to Black-thorpe, I suppose?'

'Yes.'

Juliana was stooping to help Wilhelmina remove her gloves, but she looked up at the Major, surprised how discouraging he made the one word sound. However, Mr Leeson pressed on.

'Strange that we should both choose this inn to stop. Of course, the landlord was telling me that you have the only parlour, but I have a very pleasant room, he assures me, so I shall manage.'

Juliana wondered if he was expecting the Major to invite him to join them but if so, he was to be disappointed. Major Collingham merely looked at him until the gentleman gave another bow and moved off into the taproom in search of refreshment.

'What a strange man,' said Gwendoline, leading the way into the parlour. 'Is he a friend of yours, Papa?'

'An acquaintance, merely,' said the Major, shutting the door behind them.

'I think he wanted to share our parlour,' observed Wilhelmina.

The Major grunted. 'Enough that I must have the whole family plus their attendants in here!'

Juliana looked up. 'You have had the room to yourself all morning, sir, have you not?'

'Well, yes. Nurse has kept to her chamber and Giles and your brother have not yet come in from the stables.'

Juliana removed her bonnet. 'Then you will not object to a little company this afternoon,' she told him serenely. 'The children will be making a start on our journal, and then we shall be reading *Gulliver's Travels*. You are very welcome to join us.'

'Thank you, but I have letters to write.'

The entrance of Giles and Thomas at that moment caused a diversion, and as the talk turned towards horses, Juliana took the girls upstairs to change out of their muddy dresses.

The day passed quietly enough and when they sat down to a family dinner, Juliana was relieved to find that the Major was in a particularly mellow mood. He was persuaded to tell them a little of his life as a soldier. His stories were told with humour, and tailored to his young audience, but Juliana guessed from the tightening of his jaw when he spoke of the heavy casualties suffered in the Peninsula, and then at Waterloo, that he had suffered deeply from the loss of his comrades. She was pleased to think he was not one to glory in the violence of war.

She did not linger after the meal, but took the four younger ones upstairs to their rooms, leaving the Major to discuss with Giles the revised plans for their journey north. The rain had kept off all day, and the Major had ordered an early start the following morning, so Juliana and Nurse were agreed that they should all go to bed at a reasonable hour. Juliana had never travelled so far before and she found the long hours in the coach exhausting, even though the

Major's travelling carriage was very luxurious. She was glad to climb into her own bed as soon as she had settled her charges. She bade Gwendoline goodnight, snuffed out the candle and was soon fast asleep.

Chapter Ten

The Queen's Head was a busy posting inn with coaches arriving and departing throughout the night. The rooms allocated to Major Collingham's party stretched across the front of the inn and although there was some inevitable traffic driving past their windows, the noisy business of changing horses was carried out at the back. Thus when Juliana was awoken in the early hours of the morning she lay for a moment, wondering what had disturbed her. Then she heard it: the scraping of the door handle being turned. She lay in her bed, her heart thumping wildly. The door was bolted, and she thought that if the person outside should attempt to force an entry her screams would soon bring help. She opened her eyes, wondering what time it could be; it was very dark, a low cloud blotting out any light from the moon and stars. The handle turned again and Juliana sat up, fumbling for the tinder box. It was the work of a moment to light her candle and scramble out of bed. At the door she paused, straining her ears, but she could hear nothing. Finally she unbolted the door and stepped out in to the passage, holding her candle aloft.

'Where the devil do you think you are going?'

Juliana jumped and almost dropped her candlestick. She

looked round to see Major Collingham standing outside his room. From the dim glow of her light she could see he was dressed only in his shirt and breeches.

'Someone tried the door of my room,' she said in a low voice. 'Was it you?'

He came towards her, his bare feet making no noise on the boards.

'At this ungodly hour? Of course not. Someone tried my door, too.'

A sudden shriek interrupted them. The Major pushed past her and dashed to the next room along, where Nurse was screaming and shouting while another, deeper voice struggled to make itself heard.

'Madam, my apologies—ouch! Madam, please—aah!'

As the Major reached the door a man appeared, followed closely by Nurse, who was setting about him with her stick. The Major grabbed his arm.

'Got you! Bring that candle closer, Miss Wrenn. Now then, let's have a look at you. Leeson! What in hell's name—?'

'Thief!' cried Nurse, still brandishing her stick. 'Breaking in, creeping about the room…'

'No, no, you mistake me!' cried Mr Leeson, cowering away from her. 'Damme, Collingham, tell her I ain't a thief! Merely mistook the room, that's all.' He was slurring his words, and even in the gleam of the single candle Juliana could see he was looking sheepish.

Major Collingham nodded to Nurse. 'The children are stirring, go and reassure them, if you please.'

'All a misunderstandin',' muttered Leeson as Nurse went back into the room. 'B-been imbibing a little too freely with our host, so I went out for a walk to clear my head— damned bad brandy he serves here, Collingham. Be advised by me, don't touch it.'

'The landlord shut up some hours ago,' said the Major, still holding his arm.

Mr Leeson swayed slightly.

'I know, but there was that p-pretty little chambermaid out in the yard, just waiting to—ah—entertain me.' He dug the Major in the ribs. 'You understand me, eh, Collingham? I know your reputation, devil in battle, devil in—'

'Yes, yes, enough.' Major Collingham pushed him away, his mouth twisting. Leeson did not appear to notice his disgust.

'Anyway,' he slurred on, 'came back in, couldn't remember my room. Simple mistake.'

'Then why did you not withdraw immediately, when you saw the room was occupied?' demanded Nurse, coming back out of her room.

'Too dark to see anything at first. I had just turned to leave again when the lady woke up.' He gave a shaky bow. 'My profound apologies for frightening you, madam.'

They heard footsteps on the stairs, and the landlord appeared, carrying a lantern in his hand, his nightcap askew on his head.

'What is it? What's amiss?' he hissed.

'Ah, our host.' Mr Leeson staggered towards him and clasped his shoulder. 'Can't for the life o' me remember where I'm sleepin'. Can you help, my good fellow?'

The landlord raised his brows as he looked at the little group.

'He went into one of our rooms,' explained the Major. 'Disturbed us all.'

'Then I am very sorry for it, sir.' The landlord took Leeson's arm. 'Your chamber is this way, sir, on the next floor. Come along, I'll show you the way.'

'Well, what a to-do!' exclaimed Nurse as the landlord led his guest to the stairs.

'I will check on Giles and Thomas,' muttered the Major,

disappearing into the darkness. Finding that Gwendoline had not stirred, Juliana slipped next door and went over to where Amy and Wilhelmina were tucked up in their beds.

'They are not harmed, miss,' Nurse whispered, standing beside her. 'They went back to sleep as soon as I told them all was well. In fact, I doubt if they will remember any of this in the morning. But it fair shook me up, it did, to wake up and find a man in the room, standing over the children's cots, he was! I feared for their lives, I did, so I set up such a scream and he turned and would have run out the door, but I got to him, and laid about him with my stick.'

'Well, no harm done,' said Juliana. 'Go back to bed, now, and let us hope the rest of the night passes more peacefully for you. There is a bolt on your door, Nurse—be sure you use it.'

'Yes, and so I will, miss. Goodness knows why I didn't do it first thing, then we would not have had all this commotion.'

'No, well, goodnight now.' Juliana left the room and was surprised to find the Major waiting for her outside. She said, 'The little ones are both asleep, and no sign of the room being disturbed. Gwendoline slept through the whole.'

'So did the boys.' Major Collingham nodded.

'They will be sorry to have missed so much excitement.' He did not smile, and she continued, 'It would appear the gentleman really did lose his way. He certainly smelled strongly of spirits.'

'Yes.' He frowned at her. 'But what were you thinking of, to come out here dressed like that?'

For the first time Juliana realised that she was wearing only her nightgown. She flushed.

'I might ask you the same question!' she retorted.

'I was prepared to apprehend a villain—what did you plan to do, swoon at his feet?'

'I never faint. Of course I was not going to accost him, but—'

'Well, thank God for that!' he interrupted her. 'He would have ravished you as soon as he saw you.'

Juliana gasped. She glanced down at herself: the ribbons at the neck of her nightgown had come loose and one white shoulder was exposed. The Major reached out and gently pulled the thin muslin back up over her arm. Juliana froze. She found she was unable to move as he calmly re-tied the ribbons at her neck. She noted how his white shirt seemed to glow in the candlelight. His fingers brushed her skin, setting up a tingle that raced through her veins and down into her very core.

'Th-thank you.'

Embarrassment seared through her; what a silly thing to say. She wished she could think of something witty, but her mind was as stodgy as the porridge slowly cooking in the kitchens for their breakfast. Suddenly he laughed.

'Jenny.'

'My name is Juliana, sir.'

'Jenny Wrenn,' he said firmly. 'You look up at me like a fragile little bird, entrusted to my care.'

She swallowed hard. It was very tempting to think that there was someone to care for her. She dare not raise her eyes, and found herself staring instead at the opening of his shirt, where a few crisp dark hairs were visible on his chest. Juliana felt a strong desire to step forward into his arms, to feel them close around her, protecting her from the world. Her heart began to race, as if she had suddenly become aware of some danger. Her hand holding the candlestick trembled so much that the hot wax dripped on to her fingers, recalling her to her senses. She moved back, putting more space between herself and the powerful figure who threatened her peace.

'I am a governess, Major Collingham.'

She could see the flame of the solitary candle reflected

in his eyes as he looked at her. In the sudden silence the shadows danced eerily around them.

'Then you had best go to bed, Miss Wrenn, lest we forget that.' He turned and strode back to his own room, saying over his shoulder, 'And bolt your door!'

Despite the excitement of the night, Nurse brought the children to the breakfast table in good time the next morning. There was no sign of Mr Leeson, and upon enquiry the landlord shrugged and said the gentleman had not yet left his room. None of the girls had any recollection of the night's events, and after a warning glance from Juliana, Nurse merely said that a gentleman had been a little the worse for drink and caused a disturbance. As they settled down for another long day's journey, Juliana was left with an uneasy conviction that the greatest disturbance of the previous night had been to her own composure.

Chapter Eleven

Monday had dawned cloudy but dry, and the party set out in high spirits, to arrive in good time at Derby, where they stopped to take luncheon. The inn was large and commodious and when Juliana remarked upon it, Major Collingham informed her that he had originally planned to stop there overnight.

He was escorting her back to the carriage to resume their journey and she glanced around her. The inn was built up on three sides, with several floors of rooms reached by open galleries that overlooked the bustling courtyard.

'It is an excellent hostelry, I am sure, Major, but I have no doubt that the children's rest would have been disturbed by the constant noise of the coaches coming and going through the night.'

'If I know my man, Brasher would have booked rooms for us on the quiet side of the inn, with the two parlours as I ordered.'

Juliana paused at the coach steps. 'Then the children would not have had the pleasure of your company at dinner for the past two nights, sir.'

'A pleasure for them, perhaps, but I did not expect to spend my evenings with a schoolroom party.'

'No, of course not,' she said soothingly. 'And I admire the way you moderated your behaviour to suit the company.'

His black brows drew together. 'Just what are you implying, madam?'

She met his darkling look with her own innocent gaze. 'I know very little of the ways of gentlemen when they are on their own, Major, but is it not the fashion to drink to excess and to—er—swear like a trooper?'

'Not amongst my particular friends!'

'Oh. I thought that was why you needed a separate parlour for yourself, sir.'

He gave a crack of laughter. 'Baggage! Up into the carriage with you, Miss Wrenn, and after another full day with your charges, you tell me whether you, too, would not like a separate parlour!'

Their next overnight stop was to be at Leek; without the constant rain, Major Collingham was able to make much better progress in his curricle. Juliana soon lost sight of it and when at last the travelling carriage pulled up at the Greyhound Hotel, Giles was waiting to hand them down.

'Did you have any trouble at the turnpike?' he asked, assisting Nurse to alight. 'I am getting quite handy with the yard of tin now, and blew up in good time, but the old fellow moved at a snail's pace. We have been here for an age, and I have had time to see Father's cattle safely stabled and the curricle too, is under cover, which is a good thing, for it is threatening to rain again and it does it no good to be stood in the wet overnight, as it was at Loughborough. Here at least Fewell will be able to get the hood waxed to make it watertight again.'

Juliana looked up at their accommodation. The Greyhound was a large new building, erected to meet the needs of a prosperous, growing mill town.

'This looks big enough to afford the Major his separate room,' she murmured as Giles turned to help her down.

'Very likely, but Papa has reserved only the one parlour. I hope you do not dislike it, Miss Wrenn, but I told him that by some chance I had never read *Gulliver's Travels*, which you have been reading to the children, and I thought I might sit in again this evening, if you was to read some more, so Papa said that if we were all intent on being together, he would not sit in majestic isolation.'

Thus it was that once dinner was over and the dishes cleared away, Juliana found herself in a particularly domestic scene. The large room set aside for them faced full east and therefore did not benefit from the evening sun, but it glowed with the light of a dozen candles. Thomas and Gwendoline were playing backgammon on a small table while Minna and Amy worked on their samplers. Giles had taken a chair close to the empty fireplace where he was whittling a piece of wood into shape to replace a missing knight from his chess set. Juliana sat at the table with a pair of branched candles at her elbow as she read from Mr Swift's entertaining book. Nurse was dozing in her chair, her knitting lying abandoned in her lap, and only the Major had no secondary occupation. He had taken a chair in the far corner of the room, where he sat at his ease, his long legs stretched out before him and crossed at the ankles. Juliana was aware that he was watching her as she read aloud, but she did not allow it to affect her. Major Collingham had been driving all day, and it was quite reasonable to suppose that he was tired, and wanted only to relax.

At the end of a chapter she put down the book. Immediately Gwendoline looked up.

'Oh, can you not read a little more?'

'I am sorry, it is time for you to go to bed.'

Roused from her slumbers, Nurse tutted. 'I should think so, indeed. Why it is quite dark now.'

Gwendoline looked ready to argue and Juliana said cheerfully, 'An early start in the morning and we shall be at Blackthorpe Hall by tomorrow night, is that not so, Major?'

'Aye. It is little more than fifty miles from here.' He rose. 'Come, Gwen. Kiss me goodnight and go to bed— tomorrow you shall be in your own room.'

'I will, Papa!' Wilhelmina ran forward to be swung up into the Major's arms.

'Goodnight, sweeting.' He kissed her and set her back on her feet. 'Off you go now, and be a good girl. Gwen…' He bent to kiss her cheek, '…goodnight, my dear.'

'What a tiring thing it is to travel,' sighed Nurse when they had finished putting the children to bed. 'I declare I am ready to drop, and it is not yet ten o'clock. And I have the children's samplers to pack away, yet.'

'I will go down and take care of that,' said Juliana.

'Would you, dearie? I would take it as a kindness, for my old knees object to going up and down these stairs more than once, I can tell you.'

Juliana patted her arm. 'Then stay here and rest. I will make sure the children's sewing and games are all packed away in readiness for the morning.'

She went back to the parlour, where only the candles on the table were still burning. She jumped as a figure detached itself from a shadowed corner.

'Oh, Major Collingham. I thought everyone had retired…'

'Not yet. I did not expect you to come back.'

'The girls' sewing things.' She waved towards the litter of silks and fabric on the table. 'It will be in the way when the maid comes to set the table for breakfast in the morning.'

'Well, then, when you have packed that away, if you are not too tired, perhaps you would indulge me in a game of backgammon?'

'Oh. Well, yes, of course, if you wish. But—could not Master Giles…?'

'My son has gone to bed, taking with him your book. I hope you do not mind that he has borrowed it?'

'Not at all. I am pleased that he has taken an interest.'

'It is an entertaining tale, and a good choice for a journey, Miss Wrenn.'

She gathered up the silks and put them into the work-basket, but as she did so she watched him setting out the backgammon counters.

'The table is cleared now—perhaps you would like to move the board here?'

'Why? This little table was sufficient for Gwen and Thomas.' He came to pick up the branched candlestick. 'This should be sufficient light for us. When you are ready, Miss Wrenn.'

She quickly finished packing away the children's samplers and threads and placed the basket in the windowsill. Then she took her seat at one side of the low table. The Major had placed the candlestick on the mantelshelf, from where it cast a flickering yellow light over the board.

'I should tell you that I am considered something of an expert at this game,' she warned him.

'Then at least you should be good enough to give me some sport.'

She put up her chin. 'I do not think you will find me deficient, Major.'

He glanced up at her, a smile glinting in his eyes. 'That's put you on your mettle.'

She scowled. 'Oh, be quiet and play, sir!'

★ ★ ★

The first two games went to Juliana, and earned her a word of praise from her opponent. The Major narrowly won the third game, and Juliana did not object when he suggested they should play again. She was enjoying herself, and in concentrating on the game she forgot that they were master and employee.

'Our landlord has left a bottle of burgundy—would you care for a glass, ma'am, or would you prefer brandy?'

'Is it usual for ladies to drink brandy, Major?'

'No, but you are an unusual lady, Miss Wrenn.'

She laughed at the unexpected compliment. 'A glass of wine would be very welcome, sir.'

She set out the counters again while he poured the wine and brought it back to the table, with a glass of brandy for himself. The fourth game was closely fought, but an error by Juliana gave her opponent an advantage, and she shook her head as she watched him bearing off his counters to win.

'I allowed you too many hits,' she remarked. 'Should I plead fatigue, Major, or accuse you of trying to befuddle my brain with the wine?'

'Neither. Merely admit I am the better player.'

'Such arrogance! We have won two games each, sir. The honours so far are even.'

He sat back, sipping at his brandy. 'So they are. Shall we play a deciding game?'

She nodded eagerly.

'Do you wish to change colours, ma'am?'

'I am happy to let you have the black.'

He gave her one of his rare smiles. 'The devil's colour, is that it?'

She chuckled. 'Precisely.'

★ ★ ★

From the first throw of the dice Juliana was determined to win. The wine had warmed her, but she did not believe it had lessened her ability to think clearly. The Major grunted as she moved her pieces into blocks, leaving no counter exposed.

'Defensive play, Miss Wrenn.'

'Necessary play, Major, when I know you are ready to pounce upon my slightest error.'

They were sitting forward, leaning over the board, intent on the play. A false move by her opponent allowed Juliana to make some gains, but the Major countered immediately and the advantage was lost. Vexed, Juliana rattled the dice-box and cast a little wildly. One die bounced over the edge of the board and on to the floor.

'Oh, how careless of me!' She slipped off her chair, searching the shadows under the table. 'Ah, there it is. A six! Will you allow that, Major, or will I have to throw again? It would be very ungentlemanly of you to deny me!'

She was on her knees beside him, laughing up into his face, quite forgetting any restraint. The Major sat motionless. The light from the candles was behind him and she could not see him clearly, but she caught his sudden stillness. Silence settled over the room. Juliana's laughter died away, but she remained at his feet, transfixed. He reached out and cupped her face in his hands. He was going to kiss her, she knew it, and with a sudden, blazing certainty she realised there was nothing she wanted more. He leaned forward, his black shadow enveloping her as his lips touched her own. It was a gentle kiss that sent icy threads of fear and excitement through her body. It was everything she had expected, but nothing as she had imagined it. Instinctively she reached up her hand to touch his face, and the whole world exploded.

He dropped down beside her, his chair scraping back and catching the edge of the little table, sending the backgammon board and pieces flying. The table toppled over, counters skittered in all directions across the floor, adding a brighter tapping to the drumming of blood that already filled Juliana's head. His mouth was hard on hers now, demanding. His hands moved down to grip her shoulders. She was aware of no pain, only an urgent desire. She clung to him as he lowered her unresisting to the floor. He pulled the muslin fichu from her neck and his lips left her mouth to trail lightly down across her throat. Pushing her gown from her shoulders, he pressed his kisses on the exposed skin while his fingers moved on, slipping inside her bodice to cup one breast. Juliana gasped, feeling the nipple grow hard and erect under his circling thumb. She threw her arms about his neck, excited by the feel of his taut body pressing against her. There was a tingling ache between her thighs, an urgency that she did not understand. When his lips returned to her mouth, she kissed him ardently, her body pressing against his, inviting his caresses. He raised his head and the next moment his mouth closed over the breast where his hand had been so effective in rousing her. Juliana closed her eyes, giddy with new sensations. Her fingers slid up from his neck to bury themselves in his sleek black hair; the pleasure was exquisite, almost unbearable. Juliana arched against him, her body aching for more, and she gave a little whimper, murmuring his name. The Major grew still. He lifted his head to stare at her, his breath ragged and warm upon her face. He stared at her for a long moment, as if trying to bring her into focus. With a groan he turned away.

'I—am—sorry,' he said curtly, his back to her. Juliana's hand crept to her cheek. She was stunned, unable to think clearly. She became aware of the hard wooden floor beneath her and slowly she sat up, readjusting her gown with trembling fingers. She did not understand the tumult of emotion he had aroused. Her reaction to his touch had overwhelmed her, and she was frightened at her loss of control. She wanted to cry, and in defence tried to be flippant.

'Is—is that why they call you a devil in the bedroom?'

He jerked to his feet and crossed to the window. 'So you have heard that. A stupid jest, born of the, ah, the wild parties we held before Waterloo.' He turned and came back to her. 'One thing you will *not* hear is that I tamper with innocent young women. What has just happened—I apologise for my lack of control, Miss Wrenn.' She was on her feet now, and he bent to scoop up the fichu and hand it to her, a strange smile twisting his mouth. 'I must blame it on being cooped up in this damned inn. It will not happen again.'

'It was indeed foolish beyond permission,' she muttered, shaking out her gown. The excitement had drained away, leaving her exhausted and depressed.

He raked one hand through his hair.

'What can I say? Miss Wrenn, I am more sorry than I can tell you. Please forgive me.'

Juliana moved towards the window, away from the candlelight. She had been about to say that she was equally to blame. True, he had kissed her first, but she had made no attempt to repulse him. Indeed, she was well aware that she had encouraged him. The thought of what might have occurred had he not broken away made her shudder. She had the instincts of a harlot. It was a lowering thought. Juliana drew a steadying breath. She was at an inn, miles from anyone that she knew, without money, without power. She must tread carefully.

'I am contracted to you as a governess, Major.'

He sighed. 'Of course. No doubt you wish to have nothing further to do with me or my family.'

His tone was harsh, but Juliana knew his anger was directed at himself. She wanted to run to him, to take at least some of the blame for what had happened, but then what would he think of her? Why, to admit her desire would show herself to be no better than a strumpet.

But she did not want to leave him.

'I have grown very fond of your children, Major Collingham, and my financial position has not changed in any way. I am contracted to you until September and I would like to fulfil my obligations.'

He was watching her closely. 'And this?' he said. 'Would you have us pretend this did not happen?'

She swallowed. 'I believe you are right, sir. It was the consequence of being too much thrown together. And the wine, Major. I shall be at pains to ensure that there is no opportunity for such a thing to happen again.'

She walked towards the door, but his voice stayed her.

'But you will stay? For the children?'

She looked back. 'Yes,' she said quietly. 'I will stay for the children.'

Chapter Twelve

Juliana dreaded meeting the Major at breakfast the following day and her cheeks grew warm when he greeted her, but his manner was curt, and his subsequent behaviour so politely indifferent that she began to wonder if she had dreamed the previous night's encounter. He did not escort her to their carriage, but stood talking to his groom while Giles performed the service. That he was trying to spare her embarrassment Juliana was sure, but still she found his coldness depressing.

With the prospect of reaching Blackthorpe that evening the children were happy to be on their way. Gwendoline and Thomas had discovered a travel chess set Juliana had purchased for them and were soon engaged in a deep combat while the younger girls were busy making up stories. With no need to entertain the children, and Nurse settling down to sleep in her corner, Juliana had nothing to do but look out at the undulating hills and pleasant scenery. Unfortunately, this gave her far too much time to think, and her mind kept returning to the Major's caresses and the way she had abandoned herself to him.

The Major's kiss had surprised, but not outraged her. Men, she knew, were prone to such lusts. A lady would have pushed him away, not encouraged him to continue with his gallantry. Juliana reflected sadly that her reactions had been most unladylike. She cast a quick look around the carriage, half-expecting to see the children regarding her with disapproval. If they knew the wanton way she had behaved, they would look upon her with horror. The fact that the Major had not turned her off instantly was a relief. With no money, if he had abandoned her then she, Thomas and Amy would have become beggars. They had seen many such pathetic figures during their journey from London. Some were ex-soldiers, discharged from the army now the war was over and left to fend for themselves. At one farm they passed, she had seen a ragged woman taking food from the pig trough to feed her child. It was a frightening prospect, and one Juliana would do anything to avoid.

She closed her eyes, but the memory of the Major's kiss would not go away. She had wanted him to kiss her! Juliana remembered reading of monks who flayed themselves with birch sticks to rid themselves of lustful thoughts. If such good men had problems, why should not she? A small, treacherous voice whispered that she should be making efforts to attach the Major, not keep him at a distance. As an impecunious teacher with two children to support, she was unlikely to attract a husband—would it really be so bad to enjoy the Major's attentions for a while? Marriage was out of the question, she was well aware of that, for he was promised to his paragon of a neighbour with all her fortune, and Juliana was not fool enough to think her charms sufficient to make him give up his plans. Indeed, the idea of Damon falling at her feet in blind adoration was laughable— so why did it make her want to cry?

Her little demon whispered that it was not too late, that with a few smiles and compliments he would again take her in his arms, but she resolutely crushed such thoughts.

Damon had hired her as a governess for his children and that is what she would be. Last night's encounter was a salutary lesson to her: she would be on her guard in future. She would earn her money, then walk away from Major Collingham and his family with her pride and her virtue intact.

Such a resolution should have brought contentment, but it did not, and Juliana was settling down to enjoy a prolonged spell of self-pity when the carriage lurched to one side and she was thrown off her seat and on top of Nurse, who awoke with a shriek.

For a few moments all was confusion. The carriage body was resting at a drunken angle and there were shouts and cries from inside the coach and out. Juliana pushed herself away from Nurse and tried to comfort the children, who were tangled in a heap in the far corner.

'I think we have broken a wheel,' said Thomas, clambering towards one door, which now hung down over the bank. He managed to open it, and jumped down, calling cheerfully, 'Come on, it is quite easy to get out.'

Within a few minutes the children had all climbed down and Juliana helped Nurse to alight before nimbly jumping out and scrambling up the bank on to the road. It was easy to see the cause of their accident. The road at this point was built around the contours of the hill, with dense woodland rising up to the east and on the west the ground falling steeply away to the valley bottom. A sudden dip in the road surface had been filled with loose rubble, which had given way under the weight of the coach and the subsequent jolt had shattered the front wheel.

The coachman was calming his frightened team, and as soon as Juliana assured him they were all safely out of the coach he coaxed the horses forward, dragging the carriage back on to the road, until it was in no immediate danger of slipping farther down the hillside.

'I was right, Mr Dawlish,' declared Thomas, surveying the damage. 'It is the wheel.'

The driver climbed down and walked round the carriage, shaking his head.

'Aye,' he muttered. 'Smashed beyond repair, she is.' He kicked at the road with his boot. 'Just look how this crumbles away. It's all the rain we've had this spring, it's breaking up the surface, and doubtless it has washed away the foundations, too. We was lucky the whole carriage didn't go a-tumbling down the bank.'

As they all surveyed the wreckage, Major Collingham came bowling back along the road in his curricle.

'Fortunately we were not too far ahead and Giles saw you stop.' He jumped down. 'Is anyone hurt?'

'No, sir, everyone is well,' replied John Dawlish, tugging his forelock. 'It's just a broken wheel, but she's smashed, and we'll need to find a wheelwright to repair her.'

Juliana looked up and down the road; the fields and woods stretched away in every direction.

'Where are we, do you think?'

'We have gone no more than five miles from Leek,' said the Major.

'Heavens, don't say we have to walk all that way back,' cried Nurse in alarm.

'No, no, Rushton Spencer is no more than a mile farther on, and it's downhill into the village,' responded the Major. 'There might be a wheelwright there, I think. What say you, John?'

The coachman rubbed his nose.

'I disremember, sir. There will be a forge, of course, but we might have to go back to Leek to fetch a new wheel. However, if I remember rightly, there's a respectable inn at Rushton Spencer where the ladies can rest.'

'Then that is the way we shall go.'

By this time the baggage coach had lumbered up and the situation had to be explained to the driver and to Fewell, the Major's groom, who was sitting up on the box. A quick discussion, a few instructions and Major Collingham had everything arranged.

'Giles will drive Nurse in my curricle to Rushton Spencer, and find the inn John mentioned. Is it on this road, John?'

'Aye, Major. On the crossroads, you can't miss it.'

'Good, then you go there, Giles. We shall follow on foot. Fewell and the coachmen will send on the baggage wagon and arrange for a new wheel.'

Gwendoline pouted. 'I do not want to walk.'

The Major shrugged. 'Then you had best see if Fewell will let you sit up on the roof with the trunks—there is no room inside.'

Juliana looked at the two coachmen who were moving the small trunks from the broken vehicle into the already laden carriage. It was clear that there would be very little room for a passenger. She smiled and held out her hand.

'Come, Gwendoline. I need you to help me show the little ones the way. Perhaps the Major will tell us how he used to march when he was in the Peninsula.'

Major Collingham had been giving final instructions to Giles in the curricle; as that vehicle set off, he turned back, his harsh features softening as he regarded the little party looking up at him so expectantly.

'Well, let me see. First we need a drummer. Thomas, you shall lead the way, and the others shall follow two by two.'

'And you, Papa, shall be the Duke of Wellington,' declared Wilhelmina. 'Keeping us all in order.'

They set off, the two younger girls marching along quite happily beside the Major, swinging their arms in time to the beat of Thomas's imaginary drum. The day was dry and warm, and the Major was persuaded to recall from his army days some of the more acceptable marching songs to help them on their way.

Juliana walked behind them with Gwendoline at her side. Major Collingham turned occasionally to speak to Gwendoline, but not once during their walk to the village did he address Juliana, and in the face of his seeming indifference it cost her an effort to remain cheerful.

Fortunately the section of road leading down to Rushton Spencer was smooth and well drained and they soon covered the mile down the hill, where Juliana was heartened by sight of the freshly painted inn at the crossroads.

'That looks pleasant enough,' she said. 'I have no doubt we shall comfortable here.'

Thomas looked up at the inn sign. 'The George. And look, sir, there is your curricle standing in the yard.'

At that moment Giles appeared in the doorway and hailed them. 'I have been looking out for you,' he said, grinning. 'They have a parlour, sir, and sufficient bedrooms for us all, so I have told them we will take them, because I cannot see the wheel being mended for us to travel on today.' He led them into the inn, throwing open the door to a large comfortable room where Nurse was sitting in a chair in the deep bay window.

'No, don't get up,' said the Major as she went to rise. 'We shall stand on no ceremony here. Have you ordered food? Good. Perhaps by the time we have eaten, Fewell will be here to tell us how long a delay we may expect.'

Juliana untied the strings of her bonnet. 'I am sure Nurse and I can look after the children, sir, if you wish to go on: you could still reach Blackthorpe Hall before dark.'

'Thank you, ma'am, but we have travelled thus far together. I can wait a little longer to reach Lancashire. I have no intention of abandoning my family.'

He looked towards her as he spoke, but his gaze was somewhere over her head and a bolt of remorse shot through Juliana. It could not be more clear that he was keeping his distance. She turned away, tears starting to her eyes at his brusque tone. Biting her lip, she walked to a far corner to divest herself of her bonnet and cloak, keeping her back to the room while she tried to regain her composure. She jumped when the Major spoke again, close to her shoulder.

'I have upset you,' he murmured. 'I am sorry, I did not mean to imply I do not trust you.'

She muttered a quiet thank you, blinking away her tears. Two strong hands caught her shoulders, obliging her to turn and face him. She could hear the children chattering away to Nurse, describing their march down the hill, and she was thankful that she was shielded from view by the Major's body, made even broader by his many-caped driving coat.

'Come, what is this?' He placed two fingers under her chin and forced her to look at him. 'You have never minded my rough tongue until now.'

She turned her head away. 'I am tired, that is all.'

'I would that it were all. Ju, I—'

'Papa, did you see the bills posted on the wall when you came in?' Giles came up, excitement bubbling in his voice. 'There is a mill hereabouts tomorrow—well, at Congleton, which is very close! If we are to stay here, sir, can we go?'

The Major's hands dropped to his sides. Juliana turned away quickly and busied herself with her cloak, taking some comfort in his use of her name. She heard him speaking to his son.

'A mill, you say?'

'Aye, sir. I do not know who is fighting, but the landlord tells me there should be some good sport. I know Thomas would like to go too, wouldn't you, Tom?'

Juliana moved around the Major and saw that her brother was standing hopefully beside Giles.

'I would,' he said shyly. 'And you did say you would teach me to box, sir, so would it not be a good idea for me to see a real sparring match?'

Major Collingham reached out to ruffle his hair. 'I did promise, you are right, and I have been sadly behindhand with you, have I not?'

'So can we go, sir, please?' said Giles.

'Well, let us wait for Fewell to tell us the state of the carriage. Then, if we are to remain here, and Miss Wrenn has no objections, we shall go.'

Juliana found two pairs of eyes fixed upon her.

'I do not like the sport, I admit, but if the Major sees no harm…'

His unfathomable gaze rested on her again. 'You may be sure I will take good care of your brother, Miss Wrenn.'

'Ah, refreshments,' exclaimed Giles as the landlady came in with a tray. 'I ordered wine, cakes and lemonade to be brought in…oh, and ale for ourselves, sir—I hope you do not object?'

'Not at all, my son. I admire your foresight.'

'Well, I only thought of the wine and the ale,' Giles admitted. 'It was Nurse who said that the young 'uns would like lemonade.' Giles beamed at them all. 'So we have something for everyone to enjoy. All we have to do now is wait for Fewell to turn up.'

It was mid-afternoon before Fewell arrived at the George. Juliana had collected the children at the table with pencils and paper from her sketching block and they were engaged in drawing pictures for their journal. Major Collingham and Giles had gone out to the stables and Juliana looked up as she heard their voices outside the door. The Major entered with Giles and the groom behind him.

'And he cannot be persuaded to have the carriage ready for the morning?' demanded the Major as he came in.

Fewell touched his forelock towards Juliana before answering.

'No, sir. The wheelwright says he cannot have the wheel ready before noon at the earliest, then there's the fitting.'

'And by the time the carriage is ready to travel it will be too late to set out,' growled the Major. 'We shall be here until Thursday.'

Juliana glanced from his dark frown to Giles's cheerful countenance and smiled inwardly. She had no doubt the young man was thinking of the boxing match at Congleton. Major Collingham exhaled.

'Well, if there's no help for it. Miss Wrenn, are you happy to stay here for two nights or would you like me to see if there is another, larger hotel in the vicinity? We could go back to Leek, if you wish…'

'This inn seems clean and comfortable enough, sir. I think we shall do very well here, thank you.'

He nodded. 'Then it is settled. Fewell, you had best find accommodation for yourself and the others, and see if you can arrange for the carriages to be under cover for our stay, in case it comes on to rain again.'

The groom went out and Giles looked hopefully at his father.

'So we are to stay, Papa. And shall we go to the mill?'

'Would you have me leave your sisters here for the whole day?'

Juliana looked up. 'Pray do not worry about the children, Major Collingham. Nurse and I will take care of them. It is, after all, what we are employed to do.'

His gazed scorched her. 'Thank you for reminding me of the fact, Miss Wrenn.' Looking at Thomas, he continued in a milder tone, 'Well, my boy, do you want to come with us tomorrow?'

'Would I? Oh, sir, yes, please!'

For the rest of the day the Major treated Juliana with a punctilious politeness that she found more daunting than his abrasive manner, so it was with relief that she saw the curricle drive away towards Congleton the following morning. The children were persuaded to spend the morning at their reading, but after so many days of rain, the blue skies and sunshine were too good to be wasted and when Gwendoline suggested they should play out of doors after luncheon, Juliana was happy to agree.

'The maid says the landlord owns the orchard at the back and would not object to our playing there, as long as we do not climb the trees or damage the fruit,' added Gwendoline.

'Bless your hearts,' Nurse beamed at them. 'A little fresh air will do us all good, for we shall be cooped up in that carriage again tomorrow. If we could have a chair moved outside for me, I would happily sit with the children, Miss Juliana. I could take my knitting and watch them play.'

'We shall all go outside,' declared Juliana. 'I will talk to our host about it now.'

Half an hour later they were established under the trees in the small orchard behind the inn, with two chairs for the ladies and a stool for Nurse's feet, plus a rug for the children. The orchard was bounded by trees on two sides and the inn buildings to the west, so they were sheltered from any breeze. A lane ran back behind the inn, but was separated from the orchard by a low wall that prevented the children from running out into the path of any farm wagons or animals that might be on the move. Juliana leaned back in her chair and closed her eyes, turning her face to the sun, enjoying its warmth on her skin. The children were playing tag around the trees, their happy laughter filling the air.

'Ah, 'tis wonderful to see the little ones so happy,' remarked Nurse, her fingers busy with her knitting. 'I am so glad the master let you bring young Amy and Thomas along with us. Amy and Minna play together so well, and even Gwendoline is settling down.' She chuckled. 'Lord, how she disliked the idea of having a governess with us, but now it is Miss Wrenn says this, and Miss Wrenn does that—you are a firm favourite with her.'

'I am glad. I had said I would leave you when we reached Blackthorpe Hall, if she was still set against me.'

'The child was against anyone, Miss Wrenn. Such a stubborn, headstrong girl she is, just like her father, but they are both of them good at heart.'

'Did they miss Major Collingham, while he was away with the army?'

'Dear me, miss, he was in the Peninsula for several years, so they hardly knew him. Indeed, I think they have seen more of him during this journey than ever before.'

Juliana gave a little laugh. 'Then perhaps it was a good thing Mr Brasher's plans were overturned.'

A sudden anguished cry made her open her eyes. Amy was running towards her.

'Gwen has fallen and cut her knee!'

Juliana hurried towards Gwendoline, who was sitting on the grass holding her leg. Her stocking was torn at the knee and a little blood was already oozing from a jagged gash.

'There was a stone in the ground,' she said, clenching her teeth.

Juliana took out her handkerchief and wiped carefully around the wound. 'It is nothing serious, but it will be sore for a few days. Oh, you have torn your hem, too. Come indoors with me and we shall bind you up and repair your skirts. Then you will be as good as new.'

She helped the girl to her feet and they made their way to the inn. As she held open the door for Gwendoline to go in, Juliana looked back towards the orchard. The younger girls had given up their game of tag and were playing with their dolls on the rug with Nurse sitting close by in her chair, her feet resting on the footstool. Her hands were no longer moving the knitting needles and Juliana thought it would not be long before the old lady was asleep.

'Look after each other,' she called to the girls. 'We will be back very soon.'

Juliana took Gwendoline up to her bedroom where the cut on the knee was soon washed and dressed, but the stitching up of her hem took a little longer.

'You are unlike any governess we have had before,' remarked Gwendoline, watching Juliana as she plied her needle.

'Because I mend your skirts? Surely anyone would do as much.'

'No, that's not it.' She stopped, then said slowly, 'I have been very unfair to you—I tried to make Papa think you were not a good teacher, and you have not said anything about it.'

'Well, there has been no need.'

'And I *did* spill the tea on you deliberately,' Gwendoline confessed.

Juliana's eyes twinkled. 'I know, and you may think yourself fortunate I could not find a toad to put in your bed that night!'

'I am very sorry.'

'If that is so, then we can forget all about the matter.'

'Yes, but—I don't want Papa to dismiss you now, and I am afraid that he will do so, because you have given us no lessons, no *real* lessons. You have given us nothing to learn by heart.'

'There will be plenty of time for that when you are settled in your new home. Until then we shall do what we can to improve your reading and writing while we are travelling, and perhaps do a little sketching.'

'I like drawing.'

'Yes, I thought as much—your drawings for our journal are very good.'

Gwendoline shook her head. 'Faces,' she said. 'I can never draw faces as I would wish.'

'Then we shall work on it. There, your hem is mended. Let me put away my scissors and needle and we will go back and join the others.'

'Papa says our new mama will want to choose a governess for us.'

'Well, that will suit me very well. I am only contracted to your father until September.'

'Do you not *want* to stay with us?'

'I thought you did not want a governess.'

'Well, if we must have someone, I would as soon it was you as anyone.'

'Thank you,' said Juliana, smiling. 'However, we agreed you should not make any decision until we reach Lancashire.'

'But if I decided I wanted you to remain, would you not stay longer?'

'I am afraid not, my dear. I have my own family to think of.'

'So what will you do?'

'I shall rent a little house where Thomas and Amy and I can live together.'

'But you could all live with us.'

'I do not think your new mama would want that, Gwendoline.'

'Well, I cannot see that she should object,' the girl replied, shaking out her skirts. 'Papa says Lady Frances is a great lady, and used to large households. And in all likelihood we shall see little of her—Papa will take her off on a long honeymoon and we shall be left at Blackthorpe, all alone, and when they come back they will have new babies that they will both love, and we shall be forgotten.'

'That is nonsense, Gwendoline. I am sure that your new mama will love you all very much indeed.'

'How can she do that when she does not know us?'

'She will come to know you, my dear, and to love you, just as I—' Juliana bit her lip and continued after a pause, 'Come along, let us go back outside and enjoy the sunshine while it lasts.'

Juliana ushered her charge before her, suddenly feeling very tired and dispirited. She should be glad that at last Gwendoline had given her approval, for she could now look forward to continuing her contract and earning enough to secure her independence. She told herself she should be happy, that there was no reason for these megrims; she could only think that the journey was proving more tiring than she had anticipated.

As they made their way to the back of the inn, Juliana noticed that the door to their private parlour stood open. She looked in to see her little sister sitting at the table, drawing on her slate.

'Amy? I thought you were playing with Wilhelmina.'

'She wanted to play tag again, but I was tired and wanted to sit down,' said Amy, not looking up. 'Minna called me a *baby*.'

'Well, we are going outside now,' said Juliana. 'Bring your slate and we will play some word games—would you like that?'

She waited for Amy to climb down from the chair and the three of them made their way through the narrow corridor and out of the door at the back of the inn. As they passed a window Juliana noticed that the clouds were growing thicker, and she was wondering if she should go back for her shawl when there was a cry from outside.

'That's Minna,' said Gwendoline, pushing open the door. 'I expect she's fallen out of a tree or some such thing.'

Juliana followed her outside and looked towards the orchard. The rug was empty and Nurse was sitting up in her chair, rubbing at her eyes as if she had just woken up. A feeling of foreboding crept over Juliana. She ran forward until she was clear of the inn buildings. A black cabriolet was drawn up in the lane, close to the orchard wall.

'Minna!' Even as she called, there was a crack of a whip and the carriage moved off. Juliana raced for the wall, and saw with chilling horror that the driver was holding on to a small, struggling figure on the seat beside him.

'Oh, heavens!'

Juliana scrambled over the wall, and followed the cabriolet towards the crossroads beside the inn, but even as she reached the corner, the vehicle picked up speed and drew away from her, heading up the hill and into the trees. Juliana watched, aghast, but just as she turned to head back to the inn and call for help, another vehicle swept into sight from the Congleton Road. She recognised Major Collingham's curricle and she ran towards it, waving frantically. The Major had already slowed to turn into the inn yard but now he pulled up beside her on the road.

'Good God, what is the matter?' he called.

'Minna—kidnapped!' she gasped, gripping the edge of the carriage for support. 'He—he has driven off with her, up that road. You must go after them, now!'

The Major turned to the two boys sitting beside him.

'Get down. You must look after the ladies.'

Giles hesitated. 'Should I not go with you?'

'No, Fewell can stay on the back. You will be needed here.'

'I am coming with you.' Juliana ran round and prepared to climb into the curricle.

'No. Stay with the others.'

She ignored him and climbed into the curricle. 'Minna may need me when we catch up with them.'

His mouth tightened. 'Very well.'

She hardly had time to sit down before he had turned the horses and set off up the hill at a canter.

'It was the man from the Queen's Head,' she said. 'The one who stole into the girls' bedroom.'

'Leeson?'

'Yes.'

'Tell me what happened.'

Briefly she told him all she knew.

'I am sorry,' she ended. 'I should not have left her alone.'

'She was not alone, Nurse was with her. You cannot blame yourself.'

'But why? What can he want with her?'

'That we shall find out when we catch up with him,' muttered the Major, whipping up his team.

Juliana clung to the side of the curricle as they bounced over the uneven surface.

'If my memory serves me, this is the old road back to Leek,' said the Major. 'They built the new section about ten years ago, to avoid the hill. I know this area quite well; we shall catch him, never fear.'

Charles Leeson set his horse to a gallop along the straight road that stretched ahead of him and glanced down at the sobbing child beside him. What a fix he was in now! He would not blame Lady Ormiston for this. How could he? He had sworn to help her, vowed that he would give his life for her if necessary. Veronique had explained it to him so carefully. It had all sounded so simple, but Charles had younger sisters of his own, and in his experience they were the very devil to deal with. He had nearly succeeded at the Queen's Head, when the children were asleep, but just as he had been about to lay his hands on the prize, the old biddy had set up such a screech! He flicked his whip across the horse's rump. He had carried it off rather well, he thought, convincing them all that he was in his cups. Since then he had kept his distance, waiting for another opportunity, and it was a stroke of luck that he had come upon them here and seen the girl playing with her doll, with no one near her save the old dame sleeping in her chair. The brat had remembered him from the Queen's Head, and she did not run away when he climbed over the wall to talk to her. But then she would do nothing more than sit on the rug, hugging her doll so there was nothing for it but to clap a hand over her mouth and bundle her into the carriage. He thought of Veronique. How grateful she would be; she would smile upon him again; he would be in favour once more. Not only that, she had promised to pay him handsomely if he succeeded, more than enough to settle his gambling debts. He did not know how he had managed to lose so much, but it would have to be paid: it was a matter of honour.

The road levelled out and he allowed the horse to slacken its pace and glanced idly over his shoulder.

'Damnation!'

Just coming into view behind him was a curricle, thundering along at breakneck speed.

Chapter Thirteen

'There they are!'

Juliana's cry was unnecessary; she knew Major Collingham had seen the cabriolet as soon as they crested the rise on to a long straight. It was about half a mile ahead of them.

'He's stopping.'

'No,' said the Major, his eyes fixed on his quarry, 'he's picking up speed again. He has seen us.'

Juliana looked at her companion. His face was impassive, the hands on the reins were quite steady, his eyes fixed on the carriage ahead of them. It soothed her frayed nerves to see him so calm.

'How far will he go?' she asked.

'I have no idea, but he won't escape me now. I've a pair to his one horse, we shall soon catch him.'

The harsh note in his voice made her shiver.

The cabriolet turned off the road and was lost to sight. Juliana said nothing, but she held her breath as the Major raced to the turning, barely checking his horses as he swung into the lane. She saw the cabriolet briefly before it was hidden by a bend in the road. They were racing along through an avenue of trees, with hedges and fields on both sides, permitting them only occasional glimpses of their quarry. The distance was closing, but slowly. Juliana glanced at the Major.

'You have just driven back from Congleton,' she murmured. 'Your team must be tired.'

'They'll do,' he said shortly.

'Don't you worry, miss,' said Fewell from his perch on the back of the curricle, 'This team would run all day if you'd let 'em.'

The clouds that had been gathering during the afternoon had blotted out the sun, and beneath the canopy of the trees the lane was damp and rutted. The Major held his team together, setting a cracking pace. Juliana kept her eyes fixed on the vehicle in front, wanting only to reach Wilhelmina and find her safe. Occasionally she saw the child's head appear over the back of the chaise. Juliana closed her eyes and prayed that she would not panic and jump out.

'Now we've got him!'

Juliana opened her eyes. Ahead of them, a herd of milch cows were making their leisurely way in the same direction, and effectively blocking the lane. The carriage slowed and she saw the driver standing up, gesticulating towards the farmer's boy who was following the cows. She almost laughed to see the boy staring up at Leeson, and even from a distance his stance showed that he was not intimidated by the raging figure demanding that he move his animals to one side.

'He'll never get by!' she muttered, her voice breaking.

'No, he's going to try to cross the field,' muttered the Major. 'The fool, he's likely to be overturned, if he doesn't break the axle first.'

Juliana watched in horror as the carriage lurched on across the field, coming to a halt by the wall on the far side. Leeson jumped down, pulled Wilhelmina from the chaise and set off across the fields.

'Now what is he doing?' she said, her throat tight with fear. 'Why is he taking Minna?'

The Major pulled a deadly-looking pistol from its holster.

'Because he knows I cannot shoot him while he has her so close. He must be heading for the moors. I'll follow him on foot, it will be as quick as trying to drive.'

The curricle came to a stand by the gap in the hedge. Juliana climbed down even as the horses were plunging in their harness.

'I'm coming with you. Fewell can stay with the horses.'

'Then you must keep up with me. I will not wait for you.'

Leeson was running up the hill towards the ridge, dragging Wilhelmina with him. Juliana followed Major Collingham into the field. The ground was wet and the mud clung to Juliana's soft kid boots. The crop, whatever it should have been, was stunted and sodden and she lifted her skirts to prevent them from getting too wet as she struggled to keep pace with the Major. He was striding across the ground, his eyes fixed upon his quarry. Juliana was out of breath by the time they reached the stile into the next field. Major Collingham helped her across and took her hand.

'Come on, we must hurry.'

He moved off and Juliana was forced to run to keep up with him, but she did not complain, her whole attention fixed on the fleeing man in front of them. Grey clouds moved across the sky, and a breeze had sprung up, cooling Juliana's hot cheeks. When Major Collingham slowed, she looked at him anxiously.

'I have no idea what's on the far side of the ridge,' he said, pulling the pistol from his pocket. 'I will not lose him.'

Juliana shivered.

'But what of Minna?'

His lips drew into a thin line.

'I will not hit her.'

He took careful aim. The shot rang out across the fields, sending the rooks flying from the trees behind them.

'He's hit!' cried Juliana. 'He stumbled. You have winged him.'

'Aye—if Minna had not been so close, I would have aimed to kill him.'

The Major dropped the pistol back into his pocket and began to run, leaving Juliana to follow. She caught up with him again on top of the ridge. A low wall separated the field from rough land that stretched away for miles in every direction.

'He's heading across the moors,' said Damon. 'There's no cover for him amongst the bracken—he will not get away. Come on.'

He helped her over the wall and they set off again. Leeson was following a sheep track through the bracken. He had thrown Wilhelmina over his shoulder and was running and stumbling along in the distance.

'I should have gone back for a horse,' muttered the Major. 'I could run him down.'

'But we are gaining on him,' panted Juliana.

They continued at a steady pace across the bleak landscape. The sun made an occasional appearance between the heavy clouds, each time a little lower in the western sky. The moors stretched out around them, not a sign of a building and only the mournful cry of birds to be heard on the wind. Juliana's world had become one vast, desolate expanse of heather and bracken, her only goal the figure of Charles Leeson trudging tirelessly onwards before them.

'There's a small copse down there,' said Damon at last. 'He is heading for cover, but we can catch him before he reaches it.'

He quickened his pace, dragging Juliana with him and

gaining on Leeson with every step. They were heading towards the trees, which filled a small, sheltered hollow in the land. They were only yards from the edge of the woodland when the Major shouted out. 'You will not reach the trees, Leeson. Stop now, and let the child go.'

Leeson turned, lowering Wilhelmina from his shoulder and pinning her in front of him. He drew out a small silver-mounted pistol and held it to her head.

'If you come any closer, I'll shoot her!' he cried, his voice quivering with a mixture of fear, exhaustion and panic.

The Major stopped. 'Put that down, lad. You know you do not want to harm the child.'

'I—I will if you come nearer.'

Juliana put her fist to her mouth to prevent herself from crying out. She marvelled at the Major's control and his calm, reasonable tone.

'Then I will stay here,' he said. 'Will you tell me what this is about, Charles?'

'I c-can't.' Leeson's voice quivered.

'Let the child go, lad, and we can talk this out. Your arm is bleeding. Let me bind it up for you.'

'Too late!' Leeson shifted uneasily from one foot to the other, the pistol shaking dangerously. 'It's all up with me now.'

'If that's true, then what good would it do to harm Minna?' Damon took another step forward, holding out his hand. 'Give me the pistol. Let me help you.'

Leeson shook his head, looking down at Wilhelmina.

'No one can help me now. I'm ruined. I'm… Damn you all to hell!'

With an anguished cry he pushed Wilhelmina away from him, turned on his heel and dashed for the trees. Juliana rushed forward to Minna, who was shaking uncontrollably. She saw the Major running past her and reached out for him.

'Where are you going?'

He stopped. 'To kill him.'

'No! Damon—no, please. He is armed, he might kill *you*.'

'Let him try.'

Her fingers clawed at his sleeve. 'No, you must not—we need you here, Damon, *please*.' Her voice sank to a desperate whisper. 'Please don't leave us.'

She saw the tightening of his jaw. His eyes narrowed as he watched Leeson disappear into the woods.

'You are right, of course,' he muttered, 'But he won't get far, I promise you I'll find him one day.' He looked at Wilhelmina, who was clinging tightly to Juliana. 'How is she?'

'Very frightened, but unhurt, I think. As is Lady Arabella,' added Juliana, glancing at the doll that Minna was hugging to her. She knelt down and said quietly, 'Can you tell us what happened, dear?'

Wilhelmina laid her head on Juliana's shoulder.

'Lady Arabella and I were playing on the rug when the man stopped and said hello.'

'And Nurse was asleep?' put in the Major.

'Yes.' She hiccupped. 'He—he climbed over the wall and picked me up and threw me into his carriage.' She looked up. 'I banged my head.'

'Did you, my dear? Let me see.' Juliana gently kissed her forehead. 'You will have a bruise there, I think. Poor Minna.'

'What happened then?' asked Damon.

'He drove off and held me so that I couldn't get out. Lady Arabella was very frightened.'

'It was fortunate she had you to comfort her,' responded Juliana. Wilhelmina's head dropped back on her shoulder. Juliana looked up. 'We must get back, Major. She is very tired.'

'We will have the doctor look at her as soon as we get back to the inn.' He reached out. 'Here, let me take her, she is too heavy for you.'

She looked anxiously over her shoulder.

'And Leeson? What—what if he should come back?'

'I don't think he will. Leeson is no killer, he panicked. But you must walk ahead of me, just in case. My body will shield you both.'

The walk away from the woods was an ordeal. Juliana looked repeatedly over her shoulder and wanted to run, afraid at any minute that a figure would break from the cover of the trees and take aim at them. The thought that any bullet was most likely to hit the Major did not comfort her at all.

'We are safe now, Ju,' Damon said at last. 'He could not hit us from this distance even if he wished to do so.'

She gave a long, ragged sigh.

'I hope you are not going to faint on me,' he remarked, striding on.

'Of course not,' she flashed.

'I'm glad to hear it. I should be obliged to leave you here if you did.'

She managed a shaky laugh and looked up to find him smiling at her.

'I'm glad you are here, Ju.'

She felt herself blushing, inordinately pleased.

'Yes, well,' she said gruffly, 'I shall be glad to get back to the inn and out of these muddy clothes.'

Major Collingham stopped. 'Unfortunately I am not sure when that will be.'

He nodded towards the west and Juliana's heart sank. On the far hills was a wall of low cloud and it was rolling towards them, enveloping the moors in a thick, grey blanket.

'How far can we go before it reaches us?' she asked, trying to stay calm.

'Not far enough. Our route back is not a well-defined one, we could be stranded on the moors all night if it does not lift. You and Minna have no surcoats, and your gowns are too thin to offer much protection from the damp and cold.'

She looked around her desperately.

'Look,' she pointed. 'There is a cart track; hopefully it leads to a farm of some sort. If we can reach the track before we are caught in the mist, we should be able to follow it, don't you think?'

'It is certainly a possibility,' he said, shifting Minna more comfortably into his arms. 'Come along, and stay close to me.'

They set off down the hill and were only yards from the cart track when the grey mist rolled around them. The air was cold and damp; Damon pulled his coat around Minna to protect her, but the mist clung to them, leaving droplets like tiny diamonds on their hair and clothes. Juliana shivered in the unearthly light, and moved closer to the Major.

'Hold on to my coat,' he said to her. 'I do not want to lose you in this fog. And watch your footing, the stones are very uneven.'

'But at least the track looks well used, sir. Let us pray it leads to a house.'

They walked on, and Juliana uttered up a silent prayer of thanks when they reached a gate. The stony lane was replaced by a cobbled yard. The sounds and smells of a farm greeted them, and Damon walked forward, shouting for the farmer.

A tall, shambling figure in a ragged coat emerged from the mist, a pitchfork clutched in one large, bony hand.

'Good day to you,' said Damon. 'Is this your farm?'

'Aye.'

'Is there somewhere we can shelter until the mist clears?' Damon persisted. 'We have come from Rushton Spencer.'

The farmer turned his shaggy head and spat. 'No ways you're gettin' back there, then.'

'No, so we require somewhere to stay for the night. We would, of course, pay you for the inconvenience.'

A sly look came over the man's features. 'You'd pay?'

'Of course,' said Damon. 'Handsomely.'

'You'd best come in, then.'

They followed the figure across the yard until a large, stone farmhouse loomed out of the mist before them. He pushed open the door and led the way into a long, low room. A sullen fire smouldered in the hearth and beneath their feet the floor was little more than hard-packed earth. He picked up a lamp that was burning on a side table and held it aloft. Juliana took the opportunity to observe the man. She was not encouraged. He was as tall as the Major, but thin and stooping, with an unkempt appearance. His sandy hair hung in a shaggy bush about his head, while an equally unkempt beard covered most of his face. A pair of curiously light eyes peered at them from beneath thick brows. She thought he had a sly, calculating look about him.

'You'll pay, you say?'

Damon patted his pocket, and a faint jingle of coins could be heard. 'Aye, for a room, and a little food.'

The farmer nodded. 'Then I can let you have a room, and one for the woman—'

'My wife and I will share with the child, thank you,' cut in Damon. 'One room will suffice. We would not put you and your wife to too much trouble.'

The old man spat again. 'Ain't got no wife, see, but I can find you a bite to eat and a bed, like,' he added quickly. 'If you've the money to pay for it. Foller me.'

He led them through a maze of small rooms, up a creaky staircase and along a dark passage to a large chamber. Juliana guessed it was directly above the room she had seen below. It was of similar proportions, with a wide stone hearth at the far end. In the dim light of the lamp it could be seen that the room was sparsely furnished with an ancient tester bed, a wooden settle beside the fire and a small table under the window. The bed hangings were missing, and there were no curtains at the window, but a once-handsome rug was stretched out before the hearth.

'Ye can have this room, then, and welcome to it. There's the bench that will do for the bairn, and you and your missus can get cosy on the bed.' He leered at them. 'Payment in advance.'

Damon handed Minna to Juliana and reached into his pocket.

'Ten shillings on account,' he said, fixing the man with his hard stare. 'We will settle up the rest in the morning.'

The farmer squinted at the coins for a long moment, then nodded. 'Very well.' He pulled a taper from his pocket and lit it from the lamp, then he went around the room, lighting the tallow candles in their holders. 'I'll have to fetch you up sheets and blankets. You'll be wanting a fire as well, I suppose.'

'And a hot brick for Minna, if it is possible,' added Juliana.

The man dragged his sleeve across his nose. 'I'll see what I can do.'

'I'll come with you and help you,' said the Major. He shrugged off his jacket and placed it around Wilhelmina, murmuring to Juliana as he did so, 'Stay here; I will have a fire for you as soon as may be.'

The two men went out, and Juliana shivered in the gloomy chamber. The room smelled of old soot and dust and the dim light cast menacing shadows. Wilhelmina stirred and began to cry. Juliana sank down upon the settle and cuddled her, rocking her gently until she grew quiet again. She began to sing softly, as much to cheer herself as Wilhelmina. By the time she heard footsteps outside the door she had exhausted her store of nursery songs and her arms were aching from holding the child.

The farmer came in with an armful of wood, followed by Damon carrying a pile of sheets and blankets. Juliana noted idly that they looked as grey as everything else in the house. While their host proceeded to build a fire, the Major began to make up the bed. In a very short time there was a cheerful blaze in the hearth and the farmer withdrew, promising to bring up the hot brick as soon as it was ready. Juliana carried Wilhelmina to the rug in front of the fire.

'Come along, my dear, we had best get you out of your damp clothes.'

Wilhelmina blinked and said querulously, 'Where's my nightgown?'

'At the inn, Minna. Tonight you must sleep in your chemise.'

'Why must I?' Wilhelmina rubbed her eyes sleepily.

'Because we are on an adventure,' said Juliana as she stripped off Minna's gown. 'Good, the wet does not seem to have soaked through to your undergarments. Come along, Minna, up into the bed with you. You are very honoured,' she continued as she tucked the girl up between the sheets. 'I'd wager very few people have had your father make up a bed for them.'

'True,' agreed Damon, coming forward to lay a hand on his daughter's head.

Minna gave a sleepy chuckle. 'What a lot I shall have to tell Gwen and Amy tomorrow.'

'Indeed you will.'

'You will not leave me?' Wilhelmina reached out to cling to Juliana's hand.

'No, Minna.' Juliana squeezed her fingers. 'I promise I shall not leave you, my dear.'

Damon stooped to plant a kiss on the child's brow. 'I am with you too, Minna. You will be quite safe.'

Wilhelmina smiled. 'Yes,' she said sleepily. 'I shall be safe enough if you are both with me.'

Juliana sat on the edge of the bed, holding Minna's hand.

She looked up to find the Major watching her. She gave a faint smile.

'She seems unharmed by her ordeal.'

'I pray you are right,' he murmured, walking over to stand before the hearth. 'Our host's name is Stopes, by the way. He has a farm lad who seems bright enough. I have sent him off to find Fewell and bring him back here in the morning. He seems to think he can find his way across to Rushton Spencer in any weather.'

'I hope so; I would like to get Minna back to Nurse's care as soon as possible.'

'As would I. In the meantime, let us think about your health, Miss Wrenn. Your clothes must be as damp as Minna's.'

She began to unbutton her short jacket. 'My spencer is a little damp.'

'But your muslin skirts are wet and muddy. Take off your gown and we will dry it before the fire.' He observed her hesitation and added roughly, 'Come now, Miss Wrenn, this is no time to be prudish. As you said to Minna, we are on an adventure.' He picked up one of the spare blankets and shook it out. 'You may wrap yourself in this, if you wish, but do not worry on my account—you will not shock me.'

'No,' she muttered, slipping out of her gown, 'I have no doubt you have seen many women in a state of undress.'

'Dozens,' came the cheerful reply. He lifted two corners of the blanket so that it formed a triangle and placed it about her shoulders. 'And you need not fear that I have any designs upon your virtue—tonight at least.'

They heard a shuffling step in the passage and the next moment the farmer came in. Juliana pulled her makeshift shawl about her.

'Here, for the bairn,' said Stopes, holding a hot brick wrapped in flannel cloth.

She thanked him and quickly pushed the brick into the

bed, close to Wilhelmina's feet. Stopes watched her for a moment, then nodded and shuffled out of the room. Juliana tucked the covers around Wilhelmina again and held her hand until she was sleeping soundly. Major Collingham collected up the damp dresses and spread them out over the back of the settle together with his jacket.

'At least we have plenty of firewood; we shall keep the fire burning well tonight to dry out our clothes.'

Juliana smiled. 'I am impressed, Major. Tending fires, making beds—I had not thought you so accomplished.'

'Did you think me a gentleman of leisure, capable only of making pretty speeches?'

She laughed at that. 'I have never yet heard you making *pretty speeches*, Major.'

'No...' He gave her a wry smile. '...I am more likely to snap your head off, am I not?' She watched him piling more logs on the fire.

'Why did you say we were married?'

'At first glance I had little opinion of our host. If there was any other choice I would not stay here, but if we must do so I would rather we remain together overnight.'

She nodded. 'I admit I shall feel happier if you are close by, but where will you sleep? I had considered the settle, but it is far too narrow even for me.'

'You will share the bed with Wilhelmina,' he replied. 'I shall use the remaining blankets to make up a bed on the floor in front of the fire.'

'Will that not be uncomfortable?'

'Not half so uncomfortable as sleeping out on the moors.'

'No, of course not.'

There was a knock at the door and Stopes entered with a supper tray.

After he had left them, Damon inspected the contents by the light of two of the tallow candles. 'Hmm, rye bread,

butter, cheese and meat—although I would not like to guess
what sort—and small beer. A pity our host has no woman
to keep house for him—there is no tea for you.'

'No matter,' said Juliana. 'I shall share the beer, if you do
not object. Mr Stopes has sent up a pan of gruel to heat up
for Minna when she wakes. That was kind of him. Perhaps
he is not as bad as we first thought.'

'No? Did you not see the way he looked at you?'

'Thankfully, no. I avoided looking at *him*.' She shuddered.
'How fortunate that you are with me.' He looked at her, a
faint smile lifting the corners of his mouth. She put her head
on one side. 'What is it, Major?'

'You are a remarkable woman, Juliana Wrenn. You
should be railing at me for embroiling you in this damned
uncomfortable fix. Instead you make light of it.'

She shrugged.

'A fit of the vapours would help no one at the moment.
Now, perhaps you will help me bring the table closer to the
fire, then we can enjoy our supper in comfort, although I
vow I am so tired I have little appetite.'

'That will never do.' He smiled at her. 'You cannot be a
heroine on an empty stomach.'

'Is that what you think me?' she said, feeling her cheeks
grow warm again. 'How very foolish of you, Major Collingham. Pray now, stop your teasing and pour me a little
of that small beer.'

Once they had finished their supper, Major Collingham
collected up the dishes and carried the tray downstairs,
saying he did not wish their host to have to come to their
room again. He returned a few moments later to find Juliana
trying to peer out of the window.

'You will see nothing,' he said to her. 'The mist has not
lifted, it is completely black outside.'

She came away from the window. 'I hope the farm boy managed to reach Fewell.'

'We shall not know that until the morning.'

'Then I suppose we should try to get some sleep.'

A rueful smile lit his eyes. 'I don't think I shall have any difficulty there. I shall put the table across the door, in case our host should try to come in during the night.'

'Do you think that is likely?' asked Juliana, looking anxious.

'No, but I would rather not be taken unawares. Come now, get you to bed.'

She watched him place the remaining bedding on the floor before the fire.

'Here.' She took the blanket from her shoulders and held it out to him. 'I shall not need this now.'

'Thank you.' He caught her hand and held it. 'Thank you for coming with me.'

Juliana awoke to find sunlight streaming in through the dusty windows. For a moment she lay still while she remembered the events of the previous day. Minna was sleeping peacefully beside her and Juliana raised her head to look about her. The logs had burned away to a pile of grey ash, leaving the air sweet with woodsmoke. Damon was still asleep on the floor, his breathing deep and regular. Juliana slipped out of bed and padded across to the settle. Her dress was clean, but sadly muddied. Shaking it out, she slipped it on and was tying the sash when the Major's deep voice made her jump.

'So you would deny me the pleasure of watching you dress.'

She did not look at him. 'I want to be ready when Fewell arrives.'

'How practical you are, Miss Wrenn. How eminently sensible.'

'Do not mock me, sir.'

'I do not mock you, Ju, I mock myself, for wanting to prolong this interlude. We are about to go back to our real world, where you are the governess and I am your employer. We must behave the way our world demands, and I will no longer be able to talk with you, to eat with you and to…sleep with you in the same easy manner that we have enjoyed here. And, apart from the danger to Minna, I *have* enjoyed it, Juliana. Although I have not laid a finger on you I have revelled in your company.'

Juliana blinked rapidly. Her fingers trembled as she finished tying the ribbons on her gown. 'You have said yourself sir, this is not real. We have to go back to our duties and responsibilities.'

'Juliana—'

A whimper from Wilhelmina made him break off and they both hurried to the bed.

'So you are awake now, Minna,' said the Major. 'How do you feel?'

'Hungry,' said Wilhelmina after a slight pause.

'And the bruise on your head, does it hurt?' he asked.

'Only if I touch it.'

Juliana put a gentle hand on her brow and nodded at Damon. 'She is quite cool. There is no fever.'

'Good. I shall go and see what Mr Stopes has to offer.'

'And while your papa is away we shall get you dressed,' said Juliana, pulling aside the bedclothes. 'Fewell should be here soon with the carriage to take us back to the George. What an adventure we shall have to tell the others!'

Damon looked at her, the ghost of a smile on his lips. 'Are you never out of spirits, Miss Wrenn?'

Her lips curved involuntarily. 'Never in front of the children, Major.'

* * *

Their arrival at the George brought the whole party out to meet them. Wilhelmina was handed down to Giles to be borne gently up to her room while the Major barked out his orders. A doctor and magistrate must be summoned, pens, paper and ink to be brought to his room immediately. Juliana climbed wearily down from the carriage and went indoors with Thomas and Amy, reassuring them that all was well. As she went upstairs to change out of her muddy gown, Gwendoline followed her.

'Miss Wrenn, is Minna injured? What can I do?'

'She was very frightened yesterday, Gwen, and was a little wet from the mist, but I think she has suffered no other hurt. Perhaps you should go and ask Nurse if you can help her, I am sure she would be glad of your assistance.'

'Yes, yes, I will.' Gwendoline brightened perceptibly and ran off to find Nurse.

The rest of the day passed in a bustle of activity. Once she had changed into a dry gown Juliana went to help Nurse. She was on hand to see the doctor and ordered lunch for the children, a meal which seemed to have been forgotten in all the excitement. The doctor was optimistic that, although distressed by her ordeal, Wilhelmina was suffering from nothing more than exhaustion, but upon hearing that she had banged her head he recommended that she should not be moved for a few days and that someone should sit with her throughout the night. Since Nurse was the obvious person to look after the invalid, it fell to Juliana to look after the other children until they went to bed.

At ten o'clock she relieved Nurse in the sickroom. Wilhelmina was sleeping soundly, and Juliana settled down in her chair to watch her. Half an hour into her vigil there was a light scratching on the door and the Major came in.

'Oh, Miss Wrenn. I thought Nurse would be here.'

'She has gone to lie down for a few hours. We are sharing the night watch.'

'Of course. How is Minna?'

'Peaceful, thank goodness. The doctor left a sleeping draught in case she grew restless, but I am hopeful that it will be a very tedious night, with little to do but watch her.'

'May I join you?'

He pulled up a chair and sat down on the other side of the empty fireplace. A lamp on a table in the corner cast a warm glow over them, but left the bed and its occupant in semi-darkness. In Farmer Stopes's dusty chamber Juliana had been comforted by the Major's presence—now it unsettled her. She sought for a topic of conversation.

'Thomas has told me something of the prize fight you attended—not everything, of course, for he is old enough to know that some things are best not shared with a sister. However, I am grateful that you allowed him to go with you.'

'It was no hardship. Thomas is a fine boy, and he and Giles get on very well, despite the difference in their ages. Giles has even started to give him sparring lessons, since I have not yet had the time to do so. I hope you do not object?'

'No, not at all. I am pleased that he has some male company and I do not believe you or Giles will lead him into bad ways.'

'Thank you, Miss Wrenn. Your confidence almost un-mans me.'

'Nonsense,' she retorted, flushing. This was dangerous territory, she moved away from it. 'You—you have seen the magistrate, Major?'

'Yes. I have given him my statement, but do not expect much to come of it. I hope that my letter to Mondwyck will be more effective. If Leeson turns up in town, Richard will apprehend him.'

She shuddered. 'I dread to think what would have happened if you had not come back when you did.'

'Well, it is over and you need have no fear now. Fewell and my coachmen are on watch in case Leeson should come back, although I think that is unlikely.'

'So, too, do I. But I cannot understand why he should abduct Minna. You know Leeson, sir—could it be some sort of revenge against you?'

He shrugged. 'I wish I knew. I have seen Leeson in town, of course, but I know little of him, except that...' He paused. Juliana waited expectantly. He looked up at her, then continued gruffly, 'We have...we *had*, a mistress in common. There, I have said it. Are you shocked, Miss Wrenn?'

'I am too anxious to understand Mr Leeson's actions to worry about social niceties, Major Collingham,' she responded coldly.

'I had a brief, ah, flirtation with a lady I believe is now Leeson's mistress. Or perhaps it would be more truthful to say that he is *one* of the lady's lovers.'

Juliana studied her hands.

'And your...connection with the lady?'

'Ended within weeks of its beginning. Satisfied, Miss Wrenn?'

'It is really of no interest to me, except where it concerns the children, of course.'

A chilly silence descended. The Major spoke again. 'Do you propose to sit here all night with nothing to do?'

'I have my book to read, and there is some mending...' She waved vaguely towards her workbox.

'Excuse me.'

Major Collingham rose and left the room. Juliana sighed; disturbing as she found his presence, it was preferable to sitting alone in the darkness. She went over to the bed to

Wilhelmina, who was still sleeping soundly. The lack of light had robbed that part of the room of its colour, even the scarlet gown on Wilhelmina's precious doll was almost black. As Juliana straightened she heard the door click again and looked around to see that the Major had returned, carrying a bottle and two glasses.

He smiled, his teeth gleaming white in the low light. 'You are confined to this room, but there is no reason why you should not enjoy some pleasures.'

'I—I am not sure,' she stammered. 'Perhaps a little water for me—'

He put down the glasses and proceeded to fill them, ignoring her protests.

'Here.' He held one out and she looked at it doubtfully. 'Do you think I am trying to make you drunk?' he growled at her. 'To seduce you in my daughter's sickroom?'

'No, no—of course not! I—'

'You look with suspicion upon everything I do for you.'

'No!' She looked anxiously towards the bed, knowing her voice had risen, but Minna did not stir. 'No,' she said more quietly, hanging her head. 'It is my own weakness that frightens me.'

He put his fingers under her chin and forced her to look at him.

'I am an ogre to distress you so. If I give you my word to behave with the strictest propriety, to treat you with unimpeachable politeness, will you cry quits with me?' He dropped his hand. 'Now, what have I said to make you smile?'

'Propriety and politeness are not words I associate with you, Major Collingham.'

He laughed. 'That's better. Lord, how I like your frankness, Miss Wrenn. Are we friends again?'

'Yes, sir.'

'Good.' He raised his glass to her. 'I want to thank you for your help in rescuing Minna.'

'I did very little.'

'I was glad to have you with me.'

'Th-thank you.' She was unaccountably cheered by this, and managed to give him a small smile. It was reflected in his eyes.

'That's better. Now, we shall sit down and drink a glass of wine together while we keep watch over the patient.'

When a clock somewhere in the house chimed one, Juliana suggested he should retire.

'There is no need for you to give up all your sleep, sir. Besides, Nurse will be returning shortly to relieve me.'

'And you would not want her to find us together?'

'She might not understand the nature of our…friendship, sir.'

'I'd wager Nurse knows me as well as anyone, but I can see from your expression that you are adamant, so I will take my leave of you. Until the morning, Miss Wrenn.'

When Major Collingham had gone, Juliana sat for a long time, staring at the chair he had vacated. In the day there had been anxiety for Wilhelmina, but the doctor had put her worst fears to rest and she had been able to enjoy her glass of wine. The Major had been with her for more than two hours, yet she could not recall what they had talked about—everything and nothing. She thought she had never felt so content as in that quiet, dark room with the occasional hooting of an owl outside the window, and Minna as their chaperon. Juliana felt a sudden constriction in her throat. She took out her handkerchief and blew her nose defiantly. There was a saying that half a loaf was better than none. Well, she had only a few crumbs, and she feared that they were proving to be infinitely worse than no loaf at all.

Chapter Fourteen

The next morning Nurse came downstairs to report that Wilhelmina was recovering well. The rest of the party were gathered at the breakfast table, and the old lady beamed at them all.

'She is sitting up, and Gwen helped her to take a little gruel for her breakfast.'

'When may I see her?' asked Amy.

'The doctor is to call again at noon,' said Juliana. 'We had best wait for his opinion. To pass the morning we will take a walk across the fields to the tiny church on the far side of the valley. Look, you can see it from the window here.'

Gwendoline pouted. 'Will that not be muddy?'

'Perhaps a little, but there will be a path leading from the village, so we shall go and see. We can always come back if it is too bad.'

'You will not go unattended,' put in the Major. 'The landlord must send one of his servants with you.'

'It is already agreed,' she replied, meeting his harsh gaze with a bland smile. 'It will mean taking his man away from his duties, but I said you would not begrudge the extra charge.'

His frown deepened, but she observed the twinkle in his eyes and turned away to hide her smile.

'Do you mind if I do not go with you?' put in Thomas. 'Giles and I wanted to see the carriage.'

'Oh, is it mended?' said Juliana.

'The new wheel was fitted yesterday and the carriage is now safely under cover,' replied the Major. 'I would like the boys to look it over and make sure my driver is happy with it. And Giles, ask Fewell to make sure the leather hood of the curricle has been waxed again; it was leaking yesterday.'

'So may I go with Giles, Juliana?' Thomas turned his hopeful gaze upon his sister.

'Very well. I will take Gwendoline and Amy for a walk, and we will look for more wild flowers to press for our journal.'

The Major held the door as she ushered her young charges off to collect cloaks and bonnets.

'You are never at a loss for amusement, Miss Wrenn,' he muttered as she passed him.

'Activity prevents boredom, Major Collingham,' she told him. 'And boredom, as we know, leads to mischief, for adults as well as children.'

The doctor called again promptly at noon and declared himself satisfied with Wilhelmina's progress. He recommended another night of rest, but agreed that Major Collingham could resume his journey the following day, if Wilhelmina continued to improve. The children went to bed in good time that evening in readiness for their early start and, after wishing them all goodnight, Juliana returned to the private parlour where she found the Major and his son engaged in a game of chess.

'Are the children asleep already, Miss Wrenn?' asked the Major, not looking up.

'No, sir, but they have been persuaded to lie down on their beds—Gwendoline is reading to Amy and Nurse will look in upon them later to make sure they do not leave a candle burning all night. She tells me she will sleep on a truckle bed in Minna's room tonight, so I am relieved of my sickroom duties.'

'Careless, Giles.' Major Collingham's hand hovered over the chessboard. 'You allow me to take your bishop. So, you are at leisure to please yourself, Miss Wrenn. What do you propose to do? You never seem to be idle.'

'Well, tonight I shall be,' she declared, going to the window seat. 'Our host tells me there will be a fine moon rising tonight, and I intend to sit here and watch it. Pray do not let me disturb your game.'

Juliana made herself comfortable in the window, but instead of looking out for the moon she watched the game of chess and studied the two opponents. They were very alike, both tall, but Giles was fairer and still had the ranginess and exuberance of youth; by contrast, his father exuded an air of calm strength. Juliana watched the Major as he gave his attention to the chess pieces. The flickering candles highlighted the strong lines of his face, giving him a harsh, intractable look. Many called him a hard man, but she had seen the tender way he had carried Wilhelmina back across the fields, and she remembered the way they had talked, late into the night. There was kindness beneath his harsh exterior. She was glad he had not gone on to Blackthorpe and left the school party to follow. With an effort she tore her eyes way from the two men and looked out at the butter-yellow moon climbing over the valley. Really, she was becoming quite weak-willed, quite mawkish. It would not do. The sooner she set up her own establishment the better.

'Papa, you have me in checkmate! I made sure you could not do that.' Giles's laughing protests cut through her reverie.

'I told you that you were too careless with your smaller

pieces,' said the Major. 'Next time take more care over your moves. Will you pack the set away, please?' He rose and came over to the window, bending a little to look out at the sky. 'If you wish to see the moon, Miss Wrenn, perhaps you would care to step outside. You will have a clearer view from the road.'

She hesitated, and he turned to his son.

'Giles, would you like a little fresh air before you retire?'

'Thank you, no. That replacement knight I made does not sit quite steady, so I am going to work on it again.'

Major Collingham looked back at Juliana. 'So it is just you and I, Miss Wrenn. It is a fine night; you will come to no harm.'

The temptation was too great to resist. She uncurled herself from the window seat. 'I will get my shawl.'

The heavy rain clouds of the day had broken up and a full moon was climbing high and bathing the village in a silver-blue light. The road outside the inn was in good repair and the few puddles were easy to negotiate. She walked beside the Major, making sure she kept a distance between them.

'So,' she said at last, ' tomorrow you will be at home.'

'Aye, if all goes well.'

'I have never been so far north—will you tell me about Blackthorpe?'

For a moment she thought he had not heard her but at length he began to speak.

'It lies amid the hills and high moors to the north of Manchester. At one time Blackthorpe was a hunting lodge, but the forests and woods have for the most part been cleared for farming, although there is still a fine park surrounding the house.'

'Has it been in your family for long?'

'Aye, generations. The Collinghams made their money

as wool merchants, then my grandfather wanted to be done with trade and to live as a gentleman.'

'You do not sound as if you approve of his decision,' she observed.

'He sold off the best of the farming land on the northern estates. What was left was not sufficient to support the life-style my father adopted and the estate was reduced even further. I am not a pauper, far from it, but the income is dwindling and will continue to do so, unless I can turn around our fortunes.'

Juliana pulled her shawl more tightly about her. 'With an advantageous marriage, perhaps?'

'Yes,' he said curtly. 'Marriage to Lady Frances will combine our estates—indeed, a fair portion of her inheritance is land her husband's family bought from mine. The alliance will more than double the income and allow me to pass on a healthy inheritance to Giles as well as providing good dowries for the girls.'

A dull ache had settled inside Juliana. She raised her eyes to the moon, idly noting how it had turned from a large yellow ball to the cold silver disk now shining down upon them.

'My first marriage was a love match,' he continued. 'Harriet and I were both very young. My father tried to advise me against it but I would not listen. I did not then understand how matters stood, and even if I had done, it would not have made a difference: the estate would support us as it had always done. It was not until the children were born that I realised how little there would be to pass on to them.'

'Then your duty is clear.'

He stopped. She risked a look at his face, grey in the moonlight, with a muscle working in his jaw as if he were trying to control some inner turmoil. Suddenly he turned and dragged her into his arms, his fingers biting into her flesh.

'Duty be damned!' he muttered.

Even as she opened her mouth to protest he kissed her, so hard that her senses reeled under the assault. His arms came round her like steel bands, almost crushing the breath from her.

'No, Damon. Pray don't—stop!' Juliana tried to push him away.

He did not release her, but he raised his head, and with a sob she buried her face in his coat.

'You promised me!' she cried, her voice muffled against the cloth.

'I know, but talking of marriage to Frances, I—' his hold tightened. 'Juliana, I love you.'

She whimpered softly. 'Oh, Damon, no. You cannot love me.'

He gave a shaky laugh that Juliana, her cheek resting against his chest, heard as a deep rumble.

'But I do. God knows why, for you use no arts to attract me, and take delight in crossing me at every turn! But after these past few days, I cannot contemplate a life without you.'

She blinked away her tears and raised her head. His eyes burned down into her soul; it would do no good for her to deny she loved him, he would read the lie in her face. As he went to kiss her again, she reached up and put her fingers against his lips.

'No, Damon, we must not. You have told me now why you must marry. There is no other way. You must provide for your children, as I must look after Thomas and Amy.' The thought of her family gave Juliana the strength to push herself out of his arms. 'When we get to Blackthorpe, I will look for another appointment. I—I do not think I could bear to stay now until September.'

He gripped her hand. 'You will—you must,' he said savagely. 'We have a contract.'

'You cannot hold me to it.'

'I can and I will. Leave me now and you will get not one penny.'

She looked up at him, anger sparking in her own eyes. 'I will serve my two weeks' notice.'

'And leave the children to wonder why you are deserting them?'

'That is too cruel, sir!'

'Perhaps, but it is the truth.'

She felt her resolve weakening. 'I will not stay in the house once you are married. Surely you would not ask that of me.'

He let her go. 'No. No, I would not ask that.' He looked up at the sky. 'But there are ways other than marriage—you do not have to leave the area…'

She gave an exasperated sigh. 'Would you make me your mistress? Would you take away the little dignity I have left?' She hunted for her handkerchief. 'I—I joked when I first embarked upon this venture that I had made a contract with the devil. How true that has turned out to be!'

'Ah, love, don't cry.' He pulled her into his arms again, his anger gone. 'We will find a way out of this coil.'

She allowed herself to lean against him, to breathe in the heady mixture of wool and skin and spices that she associated with him. She sighed. 'If I were to discover I was an heiress, perhaps there could be a solution. Until such a miracle, we must both do our duty.'

He buried his face in her hair. 'Even though it tears at my very soul?'

'To do otherwise would destroy us. You know it is so, Damon.'

With a growl of frustration he pulled her closer. 'I want you as I have never wanted anyone, Juliana. *Why* should I not have you?' he muttered savagely, driving the fingers of one hand into her hair and forcing her head back until she could not avoid his searing gaze. 'What is to stop me dragging you into that barn yonder and taking what I want? After all, it is not as if you are unwilling; I know you want me as much as I want you. And once I have taken you, I will set you up as my mistress—you will have nothing more to lose then.' His arms tightened. 'Why should I not do that?'

He held her so close she found it hard to breathe, and her blood ran cold at his words and the wild look in his face. Struggling to free one hand, she reached up and touched her fingers to his cheek.

'You will not do such a thing because you are an honourable man, Damon Collingham, and you know that such an action would kill my love for you.'

Juliana held her breath, watching his face. It was grey and hard as stone in the moonlight. His fingers curled in her hair, straining painfully against her scalp, but she did not regard it.

'I could break you,' he muttered. 'You are so small, so frail here in my arms. With one swift movement I could extinguish you. And yet you have such power over me.' With a long sigh he let her go and half-turned from her, staring up at the moon with his hands clenched at his sides. 'I would lie down and die for you, Juliana Wrenn, yet you want me to live—without you. You condemn me to purgatory.'

'I ask the same of myself.' She waited a moment, and when he did not reply she slipped her hand through his arm. 'We must go back, sir. To the inn.'

He looked down at the fingers lying against his sleeve, then covered them with his free hand.

'Yes, of course. You will not go without telling me?' he asked her as they turned their steps back towards the George. 'You will not take Thomas and Amy and disappear? When you leave me, I want to know that you are safe. Promise me.'

'I give you my word I shall not leave in such a way. Unless you give me cause.'

'Hah! I should have known you would put the responsibility on my shoulders.' They had reached the door of the inn and he stopped. 'I will bid you goodnight, Miss Wrenn. I will not wish you pleasant dreams. I am selfish enough to want you to suffer, as I do.'

She gave a sad little smile. 'Oh, you may be sure of that, sir. Are you not coming in?'

'No.' He kissed her fingers, gave them a squeeze and let them go. 'I shall walk on for a while. I have a sudden desire for some vigorous exercise.'

Juliana watched him stride away, then turned and slowly made her way up to her room. She felt desperately tired, but guessed that no amount of sleep would relieve the black depression that filled her heart. She did not believe Major Collingham would refuse to pay her something if she chose to leave, despite his harsh words. She would look for another post, but how long would that take? Weeks, at least, which would give her time to see Gwendoline and Wilhelmina settled into their new home. She realised that she was almost as fond of them as she was of her own family. She thought dismally that, if it were not for the children, she could end her own misery by drowning herself in the local horse pond. As it was, she would continue the journey to Blackthorpe and hide her despair as best she could.

Chapter Fifteen

'Here we are, dearies.' Nurse leaned forward to peer out of the coach window. 'You'll soon have your first view of Blackthorpe Hall.'

They had been climbing for some time, travelling across wild desolate moorland with only the occasional farmhouse and its stone-walled enclosures to relieve the emptiness. Now the road was curling about the side of a hill and as they swept around for their descent a wide, green valley came into view below them covered with a mix of woodland and pasture. Winding through the lowlands was the new canal, the ground around it brown and scarred by the recent construction. To the west and east the land rose up gently, but in the far north smoky grey peaks indicated a wilder landscape.

'Look!' cried Gwendoline, 'There's the Hall. You can just see the gables.'

'Bless you, dear, and you nought but a tot when you was last here,' exclaimed Nurse, admiring.

'There is a painting of the house in the drawing room at Kewhurst,' put in Wilhelmina, 'so I remember it too!'

Juliana followed Gwendoline's pointing finger. To the eastern side of the valley was a small park with a ribbon of white drive curving through it to a long, low house of creamy stone. There was an occasional glimpse of stone-mullioned windows but the gables and twisting chimney-stacks were plainly visible above the trees.

'I love this part of the journey,' said Nurse, settling back into her seat. 'I am always reminded of the devil taking our Lord up on to a high mountain and showing him all the kingdoms of the world to tempt him.'

'Yes,' nodded Wilhelmina, remembering her lessons. 'And the Lord said, *"Get thee behind me, Satan."*'

Nurse chuckled. 'So he did, well done, Minna.'

'Yes, well done,' Juliana echoed, watching the tiny figures in the curricle ahead of them—Wilhelmina's words were a timely reminder of the task she had set herself. She said aloud, 'Blackthorpe is beautifully situated.'

'Aye, miss, 'twas always the master's favourite. In his grandfather's time, of course, the family owned nearly the whole valley, but it is all gone now.' Nurse shook her head, and mouthed the word 'gambling' over the children's heads to Juliana. 'But the Major still owns the land to the east of the house, as far as the eye can see.'

Juliana looked up at the hills, stark and bare against the rich farmland to the west. Her spirits sank; if this was the remains of the Major's estates, it was no wonder he needed to marry well.

'Of course,' Nurse continued, 'some days the cloud is so low there's nothing to see but a grey mist until you reach the valley bottom, but today we are fortunate—we can see clear up to the mountains of Westmorland, where the poet Mr Wordsworth lives, but Miss Wrenn can tell you all about that in your lessons.'

For the first few days at Blackthorpe Hall, Juliana was busy organising the schoolroom and settling the children into their new home. In such a large, rambling building it was not difficult for her to avoid seeing Major Collingham. The great hall was the oldest part of the house, containing the main entrance and an open gallery that linked the two main wings with the grand staircase that rose majestically from the centre of the hall. The nursery, schoolroom and the rooms set aside for herself, Thomas and Amy were all in the east wing above the library, while the family rooms and the estate offices occupied the ground floor of the west wing with the main bedchambers and guestrooms above. She wondered if some previous owner had planned it for just such an occasion, in order that the schoolroom party would cause as little inconvenience as possible to the lives of the parents. The two main corridors leading from the gallery were almost identical, each lined with carved oak panelling, the long stretches of polished wood broken by plinths bearing a series of marble and alabaster busts. The housekeeper, Mrs Plumstead, told Juliana that there were thirty-two of the busts around the house.

'The master's grandfather was a great collector, miss,' she said, when she was giving Juliana her first tour of the house. 'He had been to foreign parts, you see, and took a fancy to the old statues he saw there. There's everything from Greek gods and goddesses to the likeness of Milton outside the blue guestroom. You will find them all over the house, miss, but the finest examples are displayed in the main passage, which leads to the master's rooms and the guest rooms. Mostly marble they are.'

'But did I not see some examples outside the school-room?' enquired Juliana.

'Oh, yes, miss, although most of them are chipped or marked.' She lowered her voice. 'If it was up to me, I would throw out the damaged ones, but the master won't hear of it. Ancient, he says they are, to be preserved for the family. But

I says Miss Gwen and Miss Minna would much prefer some nice new statues to look at, if they was given the choice.'

Juliana smiled to herself as she accompanied Mrs Plumstead on the rest of the tour. It was plain that despite her disapproval of the old relics with which Blackthorpe was filled, the housekeeper was proud of her domain and kept everything in gleaming good order. She was also proud of her master, and was willing to tell more anecdotes of the Major than Juliana could bear to hear.

Juliana took her dinner with the children in the schoolroom and sent them with Nurse to visit their father for an hour after dinner each evening. Thomas had been given permission to visit the stables, and on the second evening he came back with the news that the Major had instructed Fewell to find ponies to suit him and Amy, and that they were to be given riding lessons with his own girls. Juliana could not but be pleased at their inclusion and to feel gratitude for the Major's kindness, but there was no mention of her joining in this treat and she was obliged take herself to task for feeling disappointed; after all, the Major spent a great deal of time with his horses, so it would be much better if she avoided the stables altogether. No, she told herself, if she was careful, it was very possible that she could go for weeks without seeing Major Collingham.

The dry weather of their arrival was replaced by a lowering cloud and a fine, chilling rain that blew across the land in hazy drifts, as though Nature was regretting her earlier kindness. The schoolroom windows faced east and looked out across the high moors to the back of the house. The tops of the hills were shrouded in cloud, but there were plenty of tracks through the heather and gorse, and Juliana was eager to explore. A few days after her arrival she sought the secretary in his office to inform him of a crack in one of the schoolroom windows and was emboldened by his friendly attitude to ask him about the moors.

'Mr Brasher, I wonder, can you tell me—are the hills accessible from here? I would dearly love to walk out that way, once the weather improves.'

'Why, yes, miss, there's a track leads directly from the Hall up on to the moor, but you would be wise to keep to the wide tracks and within sight of the Hall. The land is very wild, and the weather can turn in the wink of an eye, and you would not want to be caught out overnight in these bitter winds. It is a dangerous place, Miss Wrenn.'

'You are not native to these parts, I think,' she ventured.

Mr Brasher gave her a rueful smile. 'No, miss, I'm a Hampshire man, born and bred, and more used to Kewhurst, where the soil favours crops and cattle. Farming at Blackthorpe is a perpetual struggle, given the house's situation. Still, with investment, the returns can be improved.'

'And that will happen when the Major marries Lady Frances?' she asked.

'Aye, miss,' beamed the secretary. 'A good day that will be, I am sure.'

On her fourth day at Blackthorpe Juliana was able to escape from the house and set out alone to explore. A stony track led away from the grounds and wound its way upwards. Green pastures soon gave way to gorse and heather and large tracts of rough grassland dotted with sheep. It was a bright, blustery day, with thick white clouds sailing high in a blue sky. Although it was the end of May, a chill wind was blowing and Juliana was glad of her thick pelisse, although the exertion of the ascent soon had her cheeks glowing. She stopped and turned to look back over the valley. The westerly wind whipped at her bonnet and she ripped it off, laughing as the breeze tugged at her hair, pulling strands free from the clips she had so carefully placed earlier in the day. She was breathing hard from her climb, but the exercise had refreshed her, and she felt happier than she had done for months. The sad death of her father and the worry over how she would support the children seemed to have lessened, and even her longing for the Major could be contained as a dull but constant ache. She could be happy here, she thought. If she could find a small house in one of the towns, she could survive in this rough land. Immediately below her she could see Blackthorpe Hall, its stone walls almost glowing in the sunlight. It resembled a large creamy letter E against the green of the lawns and gardens, with the gravel drive winding away through the small park. She would bring the children up here, she decided. On the next dry day they would bring their drawing materials and sketch the house.

'Beggin' yer pardon, miss, but ye should be headin' down now.'

Juliana jumped when the guttural voice spoke behind her. She looked round to find a small, weatherbeaten face peering up at her from under the brim of a battered hat. An old man in brown homespuns touched his forelock, then nodded towards the southern sky.

'Clouds rollin' in. You had best be getting 'ome.'

Juliana looked around and saw the heavy grey cloud massing on the horizon. 'Yes, I will, thank you.' She gave the old man her friendly smile. 'Do you work at Blackthorpe?'

He shrugged. 'Not at the Hall, no, but I does work for the family. Aye, man and boy, I bin tendin' sheep on the moors. Without me most of the families in yon valley would starve.'

'Oh, you provide their meat, then? Do the sheep not belong to the estate?'

The man gave a cackling laugh. 'You bain't from these parts, I can tell! Staples, miss.' Juliana looked blank. He said patiently, 'Wool. The womenfolk spins it, and the men sits up at their looms and weaves their pieces to take to the market.'

'Oh. And does that provide a good living?' she asked him.

The old man spat. 'It suits some. Me, I'd rather be out 'ere under the clouds than cooped up with a clacking loom all day.'

'You must love these moors.'

'Aye, miss, I do. And there's riches 'ere, for them as knows where to look. Gold,' he whispered.

She could not prevent her smile. 'I think not,' she said, putting on her bonnet. 'Because I am new here does not mean I am a simpleton.'

'No more than the rest,' he called after her. 'They can't see it, but it's here, right enough. Black gold.'

With a laugh and a wave of her hand Juliana set off down the hill. The clouds to the south were billowing over the sky, and by the time she reached the park the sun had disappeared and the fresh breeze had grown chilly. Juliana headed for the stable yard and the quickest way into the house. As she turned in through the gateway, she saw a diminutive groom leading a beautiful long-tailed grey to the mounting block. Almost immediately Major Collingham came out of the house, escorting a tall woman in a deep-blue riding habit.

Juliana hesitated, but only for a moment. They had seen her, and to turn back and scuttle away would only draw attention to herself. Squaring her shoulders, she walked quickly across the yard towards the side door, pausing only when the Major called her name.

'Lady Frances, let me present Miss Wrenn to you before you leave.'

'Ah, yes, the governess,' murmured Lady Frances, giving Juliana a faint, cold smile. 'I had expected her to be in the schoolroom.'

In that few moments Juliana learned everything she wanted to know of Lady Frances Ridlington. The lady was built on queenly lines, and the velvet riding suit had been tailored to accentuate her generous figure. An abundance of flaxen hair was swept up beneath a wide-brimmed beaver hat trimmed with ostrich feathers that curled around her face. Her features were regular, there was nothing to displease. Juliana had heard her described as serene, but thought she looked smug, and immediately castigated herself for this uncharitable opinion.

'Yes,' remarked Major Collingham, 'Why are you not in the schoolroom with your charges, Miss Wrenn?'

'We have finished our lessons for the day, sir, and I left them in the care of Nurse, sewing their samplers.' The wind tugged at the curls that were escaping from her bonnet and she became aware of her windswept appearance. 'I took the opportunity to walk up on to the moor.'

The Major's eyes narrowed. 'So I see.'

Lady Frances laughed gently. 'Do not be too angry with her, Damon; the wind here is enough to make any female look positively frightful. No doubt you will allow Miss Wrenn to bring the children to the drawing room after dinner tomorrow night, and she will be a little more prepared for a meeting with me.'

Juliana's cheeks flamed. She bobbed a curtsy and walked to the house, using all her will-power to prevent herself from breaking into a run—she would not scurry away like a frightened minion.

She spent some moments at the door, vigorously scuffing the mud from her boots while her anger cooled. Behind her she could hear the muted voices as Lady Frances took her leave, and the clatter of hooves on the cobbles, but Juliana went inside without a backward look. She had reached the main staircase when she heard the Major calling her. She stopped and looked back.

'What were you doing on the moors?'

'I told you, I went for a walk.'

'Alone? I gave orders to the contrary.'

She raised her brows. 'I thought that applied only to the children.'

As she put her foot on the first stair he reached out and caught her wrist.

'No, you foolish girl, you are as vulnerable as they…and as dear.' His thumb rubbed gently into the palm of her hand and a sudden sting like lightning shot down through her body. She tried to pull away, but he held her firm. 'Did you see anyone while you were out?'

'Only an old man—wizened and brown as a nut. He told me he looked after the sheep.'

'Old Caleb. He's harmless enough.'

'If a little confused; he said there was gold on the moors.'

He smiled faintly.

'If only that were true! Very well. Go and look to your charges.'

'I had best tidy myself first.'

'Aye.' He scowled at her. 'How dare you walk through my yard looking like a regular blowsabella and frightening my guest?' The scowl disappeared. He chuckled. 'Oho, that's made you show hackle, eh?'

'I have no idea what it means, but I infer that you are trying to insult me,' said Juliana furiously. 'Let me go!'

'It means a country wench,' he said, smiling.

With a little cry of frustration and anger Juliana swung her hand up to slap his face, but he was too quick for her, and in an instant she found herself pinned to his chest, both wrists held firmly behind her back. She glared up at him.

'How dare you!'

'I would dare a great deal more,' he growled, his hard eyes glinting down at her.

She felt the tears pricking her eyelids and suddenly the fight left her. She hung her head, whispering into his coat, 'Damon, you promised.'

He sighed. 'Aye, so I did.'

He released her and stepped away so quickly that she was obliged to reach for the baluster to steady herself.

'I have tried to keep out of your way,' she said. 'It would be best if I did not come down to the drawing room tomorrow night....'

'No, you must be there. Frances wants to talk to you about the children.' He raked his fingers through his hair. 'Promise me one thing: you will not leave the house again unaccompanied. Until I know why Minna was abducted, I would not put any of you at risk. My people will not take it amiss; I have told them something of the danger, and asked them to be on the watch for strangers.'

'Very well, sir. But may I take the children on to the moors? I would like them to sketch the house from the hills.'

He turned, saying over his shoulder, 'Yes, yes, as long as you take Fewell or one of the footmen with you.'

Juliana watched him walk away and felt her heart sinking. This was intolerable: she must find another post. How were they ever to bear this torture until September?

Chapter Sixteen

High winds and frequent heavy showers put an end to any hopes of going out of doors the following day and Juliana kept the children in the schoolroom for most of the morning. Thomas sulked at first, because Giles had asked him if he wanted to go out rabbiting, but Juliana was firm— Thomas was behind on his lessons and must stay indoors. A diversion was caused shortly after luncheon when a large parcel was brought up to the schoolroom.

'It is addressed to you, Juliana,' cried Gwendoline, taking the package from the footman and carrying it to the table. 'And there's one of Papa's visiting cards tucked under the string, look.' She lifted it out and turned it over to read the message scrawled on the back. *'Louisa has sent this for you,'* she read. *'You will oblige me by wearing it this evening.'*

'It is the new dress Aunt Louisa has had made up for you,' said Wilhelmina. 'To replace the one Gwen spoiled.'

'Yes, well, never mind that,' said Gwendoline hastily. 'Will you open it now?'

Juliana smiled. 'Why don't you open it for me?'

'I'll fetch a knife,' said Thomas, running to the desk.

With Amy and Minna looking on, Thomas cut through the string and Gwendoline carefully peeled away the paper to reveal a large printed box. She threw back the lid and pulled out a long, creamy dress packed in layers of tissue paper.

'Oh, it is lovely!' breathed Amy as Gwendoline shook out the material and held it up for inspection.

Juliana caught her breath. The gown was made of the finest muslin and seemed to float on the air. The frilled hem was decorated with pink ribbon and appliquéd acanthus leaves, with a matching decoration around the deep neckline and tiny puff sleeves.

'Oh, I cannot wear it!' she whispered, pressing her hands to her cheeks.

'Of course you can,' said Gwendoline, holding the gown against herself and taking a few skipping steps across the room. 'It is perfectly exquisite.'

'That is just it,' sighed Juliana. 'It is far too fine for me.'

'No, it isn't,' declared Amy, 'you will look beautiful.'

'But I am still in mourning for Papa.'

Wilhelmina spread her hands. 'Aunt Louisa did not know that,' she said.

'The Major insists that you wear it,' said Thomas, waving the visiting card. 'Besides, when Papa died and we had no money for mourning clothes, you said people in straitened circumstances should not worry about their dress, as long as their grief was sincere.'

Juliana frowned. 'Your memory is far too good, Thomas,' she said severely. She took the gown from Gwendoline and carefully folded it back into the box. 'No,' she said, trying not to sigh, 'my grey silk will be much more suitable for this evening.'

'Oh no, please, Juliana!' Gwendoline caught her hand and gazed up at her imploringly. 'If you are taking us down to meet Lady Frances, please wear your new dress. Lady Frances is always so…so *bang-up prime* that you will want to look your best!'

'Gwendoline, where in heaven's name did you pick up that phrase?' demanded Juliana, trying to sound severe. 'If Thomas taught you that—'

'No, no, it was Giles,' said Gwendoline quickly. 'But that's not the point—Nurse is always telling us that Lady Frances is terribly modish.'

'And she is an earl's daughter,' put in Wilhelmina.

'Yes,' nodded Gwendoline. 'So *surely* you would not wish to look like a dowd tonight?'

Remembering her encounter with Lady Frances, Juliana was aware that she desperately wanted to look her best that evening. She tried one last argument. 'But I have no gloves or slippers to match.'

'Yes, you have!' cried Amy, diving into the box. 'Lady Varley has sent you some.' She held up a pair of shell-pink slippers and matching long gloves.

'And a fan, too,' added Wilhelmina, who had been rummaging through the packaging.

'How—how kind of Lady Varley,' uttered Juliana in failing accents.

'So you see, you have no excuse not to wear it,' concluded Gwendoline.

Juliana looked at the happy, expectant faces around her and capitulated.

Juliana stared at her reflection.

'I suppose it will do,' she sighed.

'Do?' cried Nurse, bustling around the room behind her. 'You look as fine as fivepence, and no denying it!'

'The children are behaving as if this is some sort of special treat for me.'

'And so it is: you have the perfect opportunity to wear your new gown. They are very much looking forward to going downstairs; they have heard so much about Lady

Frances and at last they are going to meet her.' She sighed. 'It was said she would have married the Major first time round, if he had not set his heart on Harriet Blakeney. Now, well…he's a widower and she's a handsome widow; 'tis only natural they should think of marriage.'

'Yes.' Juliana felt as if a lump of lead was lodged in her chest. She squared her shoulders. 'Are the children ready, Nurse? It is time to take them downstairs.'

'Aye, Miss Juliana, they have been ready and waiting these ten minutes past.'

Juliana cast another look in the mirror. 'The neck is so low; if only I had a shawl to put about me…'

'Nonsense, you look positively lovely.' Nurse came over and kissed her cheek. 'Now off you go, dearie. Keep your head up, and smile; you look as fine as any lady, I promise you.'

With these words of support ringing in her ears, Juliana called to Gwendoline and Wilhelmina to join her, adjured Thomas and Amy to be good and set off for the drawing room. Plumstead, the Major's butler, was waiting to open the door for them.

After the gloom of the main staircase and hall, the drawing room was glaringly bright. The rain clouds had given way at last to a blue sky and the evening sun blazed in through the long windows, filling the room with a dazzling, golden light. Juliana stopped in the doorway, blinking. When her vision cleared, she observed that the dinner party had been a small one. There were only two ladies present: Lady Frances Ridlington and an older lady whom she guessed was Countess Mattishall, Lady Frances's mother. Besides the Major and his son, the only other gen-tleman was a cheerful-looking man in a green frock-coat. Earl Mattishall, she concluded.

Major Collingham came forward to greet her. 'So you

came.' He added in a low voice, 'I wondered if you would heed my request.'

'Request, sir?' Juliana murmured, bringing the children into the room. 'I thought it more in the nature of an order.'

'And you are wearing your new gown.' The Major continued as if he had not heard her. 'I knew it would suit you; Louisa has such excellent taste.'

She blushed, and could not think of a reply, but none was necessary for he was already taking his daughters forward to introduce them to Lady Frances. She immediately embraced them and presented each of the girls with a small, elegantly wrapped package. She smiled down at them.

'Now you must open them immediately, and tell me if you like your gifts.'

The bows were untied and the wrapping speedily torn away.

'Ooh, a stocking purse!' cried Wilhelmina, holding up a long knitted tube ornamented at each end with coloured beads. 'Thank you, ma'am.'

'My cousin-companion Beatrice made it,' explained Lady Frances. 'She is for ever knitting, so I thought she might produce something useful for me.'

'And I have a brooch,' said Gwendoline, holding the ornament on her hand. 'Look, Papa, emeralds, fashioned like a bow of ribbon. How pretty, thank you.'

'They are only paste, so you may be easy, Damon,' said Lady Frances. 'I know how careless children can be. If it is broken or lost, it is of no great moment.'

Gwendoline opened her mouth to protest, but Juliana caught her eye and urged her to silence with the tiniest shake of her head.

Major Collingham took Lady Frances by the hand. 'You are very kind to think of them,' he said, raising her fingers to his lips.

Lady Frances inclined her head, and gave a little smile. 'I am glad they like them. I trust Giles is as happy with his sketch block and pastels.' She raised her voice as she spoke, and directed a look of enquiry towards the young man, who was sitting in one corner.

'Oh, yes,' he said, flushing slightly. 'Thank you, ma'am, very useful. Although it is Gwen who is the artist.'

But Lady Frances was not listening. She was giving the Major an arch smile.

'Having no brothers of my own, I have no knowledge of just what a young boy would like.'

'It was very good of you to think of the children at all,' he replied.

'Yes, thank you,' Giles said again. He rose. 'Papa, if you will excuse me, one of the pointers picked up a thorn while we were out this afternoon, and, although I pulled it out, I want to make sure there is no infection.'

With a bow to the company Giles strode to the door, but the glance he gave Juliana as he passed was eloquent of the relief he felt to be escaping from the drawing room. Juliana was moving away to a quiet corner when she was called back by Lady Frances.

'Miss Wrenn, I shall not allow you to hide yourself away. You must come and sit over here, where I can talk to you without having to shout across the room. Mama, this is Miss Wrenn, the children's governess. You will recall I mentioned her.'

Juliana made her curtsy towards the large, iron-haired lady sitting in majestic state in a winged chair and the man in the green frock-coat, standing behind her.

'My parents are paying me a short visit before they go off to the Continent,' continued Lady Frances. 'It was so fortunate that they arrived in time to accompany me here, Damon, for it means that I could give Beatrice the night off.' She gave a tinkling little laugh. 'So tiresome she must find it to follow me everywhere.'

'Nonsense, my love, I am sure she is very glad to repay you for taking her in.' Lady Mattishall returned her attention to Juliana, looking her up and down in a considering way. 'So, Major, Frances tells me you had three governesses before Miss Wrenn.'

The children had come to sit beside Juliana on a sofa, and she was aware of Gwendoline's anxious glance at her father.

'Yes,' he said shortly. 'They did not suit.'

'I have always considered it most important that children are taught correctly,' declared Lady Mattishall. 'A really good governess is a very rare thing. Miss Wrenn, you do not look to be long out of the schoolroom yourself—I suppose you must have sufficient experience for your position?'

'I like to think so, ma'am,' Juliana replied coolly.

'The children like her, at all events,' added the Major.

'The children's wishes in this matter are of little importance,' stated Lady Mattishall with majestic finality.

Juliana closed her lips firmly to suppress her retort, reminding herself that it was not her place to express an opinion.

'Oh, fie on you, Mama,' cried Lady Frances playfully, 'I vow you would have us think you an ogre, but I know you would not wish any child to be miserable. I remember I was very happy when I was at school.' She turned to Juliana. 'Major Collingham tells me that your younger brother and sister participate in the lessons, Miss Wrenn. Do you not find that difficult? I mean…' she gave another little laugh '…do you insist they call you *Miss Wrenn* when you are teaching them?'

'They call her Juliana, as do we,' put in Wilhelmina, who was playing with the shells on her new purse.

Lady Frances raised her finely arched brows. 'Indeed? Is that not a little…irregular? Does not the lack of respect engender a lack of discipline?'

'Not at all,' returned Juliana. 'I find they all mind me very well.'

'Perhaps they do, for now, but you have been with them for, what, a couple of weeks.' She raised her eyes to Major Collingham. 'I am surprised at you, sir, allowing such laxity. I cannot think that you, as an army man, approve.'

The Major shrugged. 'I leave the running of the schoolroom to Miss Wrenn. It is, after all, why I employ her. Lord Mattishall, I have ordered coffee to be brought in, but there is a very fine cognac here that I think you will like…'

Lady Frances accepted the Major's rebuff without demur and began to talk with her parents about their plans to tour the continent.

'Think of it, Damon,' she said. 'Paris, then Switzerland in the summer months, and for the winter, Naples and Rome! How I would love to see Rome.'

Lord Mattishall chuckled as he accepted his glass of brandy from Major Collingham. 'Aye, my little puss likes to be on the move—London, Brighton, wherever society is at its liveliest.'

'And what of the country?' asked the Major.

'Oh, one tires of the country quicker than anything,' said Lady Frances, rising. 'Unless, of course, one is kept well entertained.'

She smiled at the Major, who raised his glass to her.

'Then we must do our best to amuse you.'

Lady Mattishall questioned Juliana about her family, and although she thought some of the lady's questions impertinent, she answered truthfully, glad that she need not give her attention to the little group in the corner, where Lady Frances was conducting a lively conversation with the two gentlemen. Once the coffee was finished Juliana sought leave to take the children away. The Major gave his permission and she prompted the children to bid the guests goodnight.

* * *

'Lady Frances really is beautiful,' said Wilhelmina as they trooped up the stairs.

'Yes,' agreed Gwendoline. 'Just as Papa told us she would be. Did you notice her gown? The bodice studded with pearls and little embroidered roses all round the hem and sleeves.'

'Just like a fairy princess,' breathed Wilhelmina. 'And she gave me a purse, even if I have no pennies to put in it at the moment.'

'That was very kind of her,' said Juliana.

Wilhelmina turned to her sister. 'Do you like your brooch, Gwen? It looks very well against your gown.'

Gwendoline looked down at the bow-shaped ornament pinned to her bodice. 'Yes, it is very pretty.'

'Tomorrow you shall both write a thank-you note to Lady Frances; then she will see how neat is your handwriting.' *And she will know that I am teaching them something*, she added silently.

Chapter Seventeen

The following week dragged by. The rigours of the journey north paled for Juliana as she struggled to maintain a cheerful demeanour while an aching unhappiness grew within her. She took her meals in the schoolroom, sending the children down to the drawing room each evening with Nurse. Her only glimpse of Major Collingham was from the schoolroom windows. In fair weather or foul the Major rode out every day, and every day Juliana stood by the cracked window pane and watched him trotting out of the yard and cantering through the park on his powerful black hunter. She tried to tell herself that he was merely riding over his own lands, but it was difficult to continue with this comforting thought when Nurse made constant allusions to the changes soon to come to Blackthorpe.

'It is a match, you mark my words,' she said to Juliana. 'He will soon propose to Lady Frances, I am sure.'

The children had gone to bed and they were alone in the schoolroom. Juliana did not reply, but continued to tidy the room, putting away the books and returning the globe to its place on the top of a large cupboard. Nurse lowered herself into the rocking chair by the hearth and gave a contented sigh.

'I have always said it's time the master married again. It's not natural for a man to live alone, and the children need a mother. I don't deny that he was head over heels in love with Miss Harriet, but it is eight years now since the poor lamb died.'

'Lady Frances is a very suitable match,' remarked Juliana, feeling that some response was required.

'Aye, that she is, and it's not as if the master will be marrying her for her wealth alone, for Lady Frances is an accredited beauty, and that's enough to gladden any man's heart—oh, Miss Wrenn, now you've dropped the chalks on the floor. Dear me, let me help you…'

'No, no, it will not take me a moment.' Juliana dropped to her knees and began to gather up handfuls of chalks. 'So careless, I do not know what came over me.'

'Why, my dear, you are tired, and no wonder, when you have been obliged to keep those children occupied indoors these past few days. Take yourself off to bed now, Miss Wrenn; there's nothing here that won't wait for the morning.'

Juliana took Nurse's advice, but it was long before she slept that night. It was not enough to hide herself away from Major Collingham; she was living in his house, there were reminders of him everywhere, his whip and gloves discarded in the hall, his portrait in the gallery—she could even sense his personality in the fabric of the house, with its dark panelled corridors and the rooms full of vibrant colour, as bold and energetic as the man himself. And then there were the girls. She had been told that both girls had inherited their mother's beauty, but Juliana could see the Major in the tilt of a head, a sudden, fleeting expression, or in Gwendoline's granite-grey eyes, so like her father's that Juliana's heart would clench in despair and longing for what she could never have. Then there was Thomas; her little brother slipped away from the schoolroom as often as he could to help out in the stables or to join Giles for his sparring lessons with the Major. He returned from these forays in high spirits and eager to talk. Thomas declared that Major Collingham was true as a gun, never talking down to one and a good teacher. His conversation became littered with things the Major had said. Juliana endured it all with a calm smile, but each mention of the Major stung her like salt on an open cut. She would not for the world dissuade Thomas from confiding in her, and she was wise enough to realise that if he was looking to Major Collingham for his model, she could not wish for a better example for him to follow. Juliana therefore struggled to overcome her own unhappiness, comforting herself with the thought that she need only endure life at Blackthorpe until September, or the Major's marriage, whichever came the sooner.

The next day brought a welcome break in the weather with a dry, bright morning that gave Juliana her chance to take her pupils to the moors with their paints and sketchbooks. Thomas excused himself, saying that Giles had invited him to ride out with him and visit a new mill that was being built, so it was only Juliana and the three girls who toiled up the hill, accompanied by one of the under-footmen, Juliana having requested Plumstead to provide her with an escort, in accordance with the Major's wishes. She had also asked Mrs Plumstead to pack up a picnic for them; with such a treat, it was no wonder that they all enjoyed the break from routine, and came back down the hill late in the afternoon in the highest of spirits.

The sunshine and fresh air had acted as a tonic for Juliana and she returned to the house much refreshed. She brought the children into the great hall just as the Major was coming down the stairs with a gentleman at his side. Juliana smiled in delight as she recognised Sir Richard Mondwyck.

'Miss Wrenn, I was just asking Collingham about you. How are you?'

'Very well, sir, thank you. How good it is to see you again.'

He took her hand and raised her fingers to his lips. 'Damon was telling me that you have been sketching from the hills—did you not see my coach arrive?'

'I did indeed see a carriage, but I thought it was Lady—' She broke off, smiling. 'Do you mean to make a long stay?'

'Oh, well now, that depends upon how long Damon can put up with me.'

Major Collingham had been talking to the children, but now he came up to stand beside his friend. 'As long as you like, Rick, you know that.' His eyes, dark and hard as the rocky outcrops on the moors, rested on Juliana. 'Perhaps your presence will persuade Miss Wrenn to come down to the drawing room after dinner.'

'Yes, pray do, Miss Wrenn.'

Juliana found herself responding to Sir Richard's friendly smile. 'I will,' she said, preparing to follow the children up the stairs. 'I will come down this evening, with pleasure!'

Chapter Eighteen

'You appear to be much more at ease with your children here,' remarked Sir Richard.

Damon watched the little party disappear from the upper landing.

'During our journey north I was in much closer proximity with them than I had ever before—enjoyed.'

'Good for you!' Sir Richard laughed as he followed his host to the library. 'And they like their new governess?'

'I think so. Yes. Very much.'

'And yet it is not usual for Miss Wrenn to accompany them downstairs of an evening?'

'No. She has the care of them all day. Their nurse is quite happy to be with them for that short time.' Damon saw the knowing look in his friend's eyes and felt the colour mounting to his cheeks. 'God damn you, Richard, let it be! I am as good as married.'

'You have offered for Lady Frances, then.'

'No. It is implied, but not yet agreed.' He gave an exasperated sigh. 'You did not come all this way to discuss such matters. Out with it, Rick.'

'Very well. It was your letter that brought me here.' Sir

Richard accepted a glass of wine and settled himself into one of the armchairs.

The Major filled his own glass. 'Any word of Leeson?'

'Not yet. My men are looking out for him, but we fear he may have escaped abroad.'

'Damnation, I was afraid of that. I wish I could have caught him, I would have found out what his game is.' He thought back to that day, the hectic chase across the fields, Juliana clutching his arm, fearing for his safety. He remembered it so clearly: her green eyes dark with alarm, her voice begging with him not to leave them. His instinct had been to go after Leeson, to beat him senseless, but Juliana's pleas had cut through his white-hot anger. Dear heaven, how she had got under his skin! Sir Richard's voice brought him back to the present.

'Your letter said this was not the first incident.'

'No. Just before we left town, Miss Wrenn's little sister was attacked.'

'She is of an age with Wilhelmina, I think,' mused Sir Richard. 'Child abductors?'

The Major frowned. 'I wondered about that, but Amy was attacked on a busy street by two young ruffians. God knows what they thought they were about, for I was only a few paces away. And Leeson, well, he made off with Minna, but...Rick, he did not seem like a man acting for himself. I would swear he never meant to harm her; why, he was shaking so much he could not even hold the pistol. Yet I cannot believe these were random attacks.'

'Do you have any enemies?'

'No more than any other man, I dare say. But until I know the reason for these attacks I am taking no risks. I have warned my people to be on their guard, and Ju—Miss Wrenn has instructions that none of the children are to go out of the house without a manservant to attend them.'

'And I am here now, so I will help you to watch over them,' said Sir Richard.

'Thank you, Rick, but can you be spared? I thought you were busy searching for the Borghese diamonds.'

'Alas, that trail has grown cold. My men will keep looking, of course. They know what they are about, and if they need me they will send word. I can be in London in a couple of days.' He grinned. '*I* am travelling light, old friend.'

Damon gave a crack of laughter. 'You are fortunate. You do not have to transport a parcel of brats with you.'

'You could have gone on ahead.'

'Aye, but heaven knows what might have happened to Minna if I had not been there.' He paused. 'The children are all I have now, Rick. What I do is for them, to provide for their future.'

'And the little governess, Juliana Wrenn?'

Damon rose abruptly. He went to the sideboard and refilled his glass. 'We have a contract. She stays until September, or until the wedding.'

Sir Richard tossed back his wine. 'If that's the case, you'll marry as soon as possible and let the girl leave here. It will not do to let the children grow too fond of her.' He stood up. 'Now, we had best change for dinner. Did you tell me that Lady Frances will be joining us tonight?'

'Yes, with her parents. They are visiting the north before going off to the Continent.'

'No doubt they want to see the banns posted before they leave the country.' The Major's growled reply was inaudible, but Sir Richard merely laughed and clapped his host on the shoulder. 'Come on, you old bear, if we delay much longer you will not be ready to greet your future bride.'

Dinner in the schoolroom was a noisy affair. Thomas had returned from his visit to the new mill with Giles and was full of the wonders of water, steam and power looms.

'They are building such big mills, now,' he told them, in between mouthfuls of food. 'Whole families work there, day and night, and they use the power of the local water supply to spin the cotton and work the looms, too.'

'How did you learn so much?' asked Juliana. 'I hope you did not get in the way.'

'Not a bit of it,' returned Thomas, helping himself to more potatoes. 'Fewell's brother is the engineer there, and we had a letter of introduction to him. Of course he would have received Giles in any event, as Major Collingham's son, but when he found we were *truly* interested in the machinery, he showed us all over, including the new steam engine.'

'Lady Frances is coming to dinner tonight,' said Wilhelmina, bored with the subject. 'We have not seen her since the night she gave us our presents. Nurse says you are to take us down, Miss Wrenn.'

'That is so.' Juliana nodded.

'Is that why you are wearing your new gown?' asked Gwendoline

'That's to impress Sir Richard,' giggled Amy.

Juliana frowned at her. 'It is not to impress anyone. I merely want to look my best for the Major's guests.'

'I wish I could come down,' sighed Thomas. 'I would dearly love to meet Sir Richard. Giles says he is a real topper.'

'Does that mean he is interested in machinery?' asked Juliana, her eyes twinkling.

'Yes, but not merely for the mills. Giles says he invests in foundries—iron and steel—and he knows a great deal about the new steam engines.'

'I have no doubt you will meet him tomorrow, Master Thomas,' said Nurse, giving him her kindly smile. 'But you know it wouldn't be right for you to go to the drawing room.'

'But Juliana is going,' argued Amy, waving her knife.

Juliana gently pushed her arm down. 'That is because

someone must be there to look after Gwen and Minna,' she said.

'Well, I wish Amy could come down as well,' said Wilhelmina. 'It would be much nicer if I had someone to play with.'

'Heavens, you mustn't play in the drawing room!' exclaimed Nurse, half-shocked, half-laughing. 'You are there for your father to show you off to his guests.'

Juliana shook her head. 'You make them sound like trophies, Nurse, not children.' She rose. 'Now, if you have finished your meal, girls, I think we should make you as neat as pins before we join your father.'

Gwendoline and her sister ran ahead of Juliana to the drawing room, eager to meet Lady Frances once more. Juliana was forced to hurry to catch up with them, afraid they might burst into the drawing room without her. As the footman opened the door she entered, flushed and a little out of breath, not at all as composed as she would have liked. She was relieved to see the gentlemen had already come in from the dining room. Sir Richard was talking to Giles, who was looking very smart, if a little uncomfortable, in his dark coat and knee breeches; Lord Mattishall was standing beside his wife's chair, smiling benignly at no one in particular; and Lady Frances had taken up her position on a sofa in the centre of the room and appeared to be holding court. Juliana could not deny that she looked magnificent in a high-waisted gown of bronze lustring with diamonds adorning the slender column of her neck and winking from her ears. The thought that she was a trifle overdressed for a country dinner Juliana quickly dismissed as springing from jealousy. She sighed, and began to wish she had not come. Gwendoline and her sister immediately went forward to make their curtsies.

'Ah, look, Mama, the little Misses Collingham,' cooed

Lady Frances. She patted the sofa beside her. 'Come and sit by me, my dears.'

'You see, I have my purse with me,' said Wilhelmina, climbing up on the sofa. 'And Gwen is wearing her brooch.'

'Lovely, but you must hush now, my dear, because young ladies must learn to sit quietly until they are addressed. Now, Sir Richard, what were we saying? Ah, yes, poor Mr Brummell. It is true, then—he has fled the country?'

'Yes, ma'am. It would appear he quit London a few hours earlier than Damon.'

'Then I hope he enjoyed a better journey,' returned the Major, smiling at his friend. 'I heard nothing of it on Thursday.'

'No, it was very quietly done,' explained Sir Richard. 'He was seen at the opera on the Thursday night, but it seems he had a chaise waiting for him, for he did not go to his rooms again.'

'No doubt the creditors were waiting there,' remarked Lord Mattishall, shaking his head. 'Dashed wolves, waiting to pounce as soon as they hear a man's pockets are to let.'

'They have their own families to feed,' remarked Major Collingham. 'Brummell has existed for years on credit.'

'As do many in town,' put in Sir Richard.

'Aye, and pass their debts on to their children,' growled the Major, a frown in his dark eyes.

'Well, I for one will miss Brummell's wit,' announced Lady Frances. 'But such dismal news is all of a piece with this dreadful weather. We have had such a wet spring here. My steward was telling me this cold wet weather has rotted the seed in the ground. And it is the same everywhere, is it not, Papa?'

Lord Mattishall nodded. 'Aye, my love. I fear we are in for a poor summer.'

Juliana had chosen a seat in one corner of the room, well away from the main party, but where she could watch the girls and be ready to step in should they forget their manners or grow too noisy. She was grateful for the opportunity to regain her composure after her hasty entrance, but scarcely had the flush died from her cheeks than Sir Richard approached.

'I will not ask how you go on, Miss Wrenn, for I can see that you are in high bloom.'

'Thank you, sir. To be out of doors today has been of benefit to us all.'

He sat down beside her. 'You know Damon wrote to me about your journey and what happened at Rushton Spencer?'

'Minna's abduction? Yes. It was truly terrifying.'

'He has had nothing but praise for your cool actions.'

'Me?' Her cheeks grew warm again. 'I did very little, Sir Richard.'

'But you saw as much as anyone, and you went with Collingham to chase Leeson. If it would not upset you, I would like you to tell me everything—and also I would like to hear about the attack on your sister.'

She looked up. 'You think there is a connection?'

'I hardly know. Damon has already told me about it, but I am hoping that there may be some clue to help us unravel this mystery. Until we know why these attacks occurred, we cannot be sure that the danger is over.'

'Of course I will help, if I can.' She frowned a little and after a slight hesitation began to recount everything she could remember until the moment they had Wilhelmina safe. The night spent in the farmhouse she skipped over, and was thankful that Sir Richard did not question her too closely.

'Thank you, Miss Wrenn,' said Sir Richard, when she had finished. 'I know it must be painful for you to relive these events.'

Juliana nodded, aware that the pain of recollection was not wholly connected with Wilhelmina's adventure. There was a general bustle as Plumstead entered with the tea tray and Sir Richard rose and held out his hand to her.

'I think it is time we were a little more sociable. We should join the others.'

'Oh—no, sir. Pray, go and take your place, but I am merely the governess, I should remain here.'

He took her hand and pulled her to her feet. 'I insist, Miss Wrenn. Damon does not wish you to be so excluded, I am sure.'

'Goodness, Sir Richard, you and the little governess have had your heads together for a full half-hour,' exclaimed Lady Mattishall as he escorted Juliana to a sofa nearer the centre of the room. Gwendoline and Wilhelmina immediately ran across to join her.

'Hush, Mama.' Lady Frances gave a soft laugh. 'Can you not see that you are putting Miss Wrenn to the blush?'

Juliana felt a spurt of anger at the insinuation. Her indignation grew when she saw the Major frowning at her, for surely he must know why Sir Richard wanted to talk to her. She allowed Sir Richard to bring her a cup of tea, his easy manner doing much to calm her agitation as he gently teased the children and included them in his conversation. At first Juliana struggled to respond, but soon she relaxed and even laughed aloud at some of his more amusing anecdotes. Giles, she noticed, was talking in an animated fashion to his father, and she realised that he was holding forth very much as Thomas had done earlier, although with slightly more clarity, on the wonders of the new mill being constructed at Burnley. Even while she listened to Sir Richard, she was aware of the mention of spinning mules, water frames and jennies. It was impossible to ignore his enthusiasm, and even Sir Richard cast an amused glance at him.

'Young Mr Collingham has a great interest in machinery,' he murmured to Juliana. 'I took him to see the new mint building at Tower Hill when he was in London. He was enthralled by the coining presses, worked by steam power, of course. I begin to think he has the makings of an engineer—what do you say, Miss Wrenn?'

Before she could respond she heard Lady Frances say in a bored, carrying voice, 'Really, Giles, your papa cannot be interested in all this talk of mills.'

Giles flushed a little. 'I think we should consider building some ourselves. We have the land and sufficient water, and there is the new canal almost running past our door—'

She threw up her hands in mock dismay. 'Really, Giles, that smacks of trade.'

Giles ignored her and turned back to his father, enthusiasm shining in his face. 'But we should consider it, sir.'

'I did consider it some years ago,' replied the Major. 'There is barely sufficient head of water in Blackthorpe Clough for one small engine.'

'But we have coal in the hills,' said Giles. 'Steam is the new way of powering the machines.'

Greatly daring, Juliana raised her voice to join in. 'When I was on the moors, the old man—Caleb—said something to me about black gold. Do you think he meant coal?'

The Major considered her words. 'Possibly. They used to collect it from the tops, but it was close to the surface and easily dug out. However, that seam was worked out in my father's day.'

'There are new ways of mining now, sir,' put in Giles. 'When we were in Leek, the wheelwright there was talking to a man, an engineer—'

'My dear Giles, you must accept that your father knows best in these matters.' Lady Frances's voice cut across the room, carrying clearly to everyone present. 'Damon, Mama tells me they plan to be in Rome by the autumn. You have been there, have you not? Do come and tell us all about it...'

Giles, flushed with embarrassment at the snub, looked as if he wanted to stride out of the room, but Sir Richard beckoned to him.

'That new mill has fired your imagination,' he said, smiling.

'If there is coal in the moors, then we should mine it,' muttered Giles in a furious undervoice.

'It should certainly be investigated,' put in Juliana. 'I read that there is a way of finding out these things, of looking at the landscape.'

The boy nodded enthusiastically. 'It is in the layers of rock, the way they are laid down. The—the strata.'

'I, too, have heard that,' said Sir Richard, nodding. 'A man named Smith has produced a geological map of the country.' He looked up at Giles. 'You should find out a little more— I will help you if you like, then you can put the case to your father. But not,' he added with a twinkle, 'when you have company. Choose a time when he is not occupied with social niceties!'

Chapter Nineteen

For the first time since arriving at Blackthorpe, Juliana awoke from her night's sleep refreshed and eager for the day. Looking back at the evening, she thought it the most pleasant she had spent at the house. The conversation had been lively, and Sir Richard's kindness had ensured that she had not been excluded. She acknowledged that there was nothing of the lover in Damon's attentions to Lady Frances, and although it did not lessen the dull ache of longing inside her, she felt her emotions were under good regulation.

Juliana set the children to work on their lessons and ran down to the library in search of an atlas. The morning was well advanced, and she knew enough of the household's routine to be confident that Damon and his guest would be engaged in some outdoor pursuit. She skipped downstairs, humming and went into the library without knocking.

'Oh!' She stopped in the doorway. 'Oh, I am sorry—I thought you had gone out…'

Major Collingham was sitting at his desk, engaged in mending his pen. He looked up as she entered. 'As you see, I am still here. Richard has gone out riding with Giles and left me to attend to my business—no, don't run away. Come in and close the door. I want to talk to you.' He said as she came towards him, 'You were singing when you came in, and you were in spirits last night.'

'Sir Richard is charming company. He went out of his way to entertain me.'

'As I do not.'

His voice was taut with anger. She forced herself to speak calmly.

'I do not expect it, sir.'

'You enjoy Mondwyck's company?'

'Why, yes.'

'No doubt that is why you were so delighted to see him yesterday afternoon.'

'Yes, I was pleased to see him,' she retorted, nettled. 'As I would be pleased to see any old friend.'

He walked to the window and stared out. 'Perhaps you would like him to be more than a friend.'

'No!'

'Why not? *I* cannot marry you, so why should you not set your cap at him?'

Her cheeks flamed. She replied furiously, 'I would never *set my cap* at anyone. That is a crude term and I find it offensive.'

'Oh, do you?' He flung himself across the room and stood before her, frowning down at her with such a dreadful scowl that she stepped back, only to find the unyielding edge of the desk behind her. 'Well, *I* find it offensive that you are flirting with him in my house!'

She gasped. 'How dare you accuse me of flirting. How dare you!' she railed at him, seething with anger. 'I see what it is— you are jealous. You think because you cannot have me—'

'Can I not?'

With something that sounded like a snarl he grabbed her. She looked up to protest and his mouth swooped on her.

The force of his attack made her senses reel, and all the emotions she had held so rigidly under control were released. She was overwhelmed by him, by the familiar hint of spice on his skin, the strength of his arms around her—it was intoxicating. For a moment she clung to him, then reason reasserted itself and she pushed against him, tearing her mouth free.

'No, Damon, this is wrong.' She glanced up into his face and suffered a shock; there was a wild look in his eyes, no sign that he understood her. He cupped her face with one hand and kissed her again, even more savagely. When she pushed her hands against his chest, it was not the Major who gave way. With the desk behind her she felt herself bending backwards. Damon was pushing her down, using his arm to sweep everything out of the way as he lowered her on to the desktop. She heard the clatter as the inkwell and pens fell to the floor, followed by the heavy thud of the paper-weight. She found herself looking up at the strapwork on the ceiling, noticing the carved cornices on the top of the tall bookshelves; her world was quite literally turned on its head. Then every thought was obliterated as he kissed her again. Inwardly she fought against her own desire while struggling against him, but her feet no longer reached the floor, and she had no strength to fight him off. She had no *will* to fight him off; her resolve was slipping away. *This must not happen*, she told herself, turning her head aside to avoid his mouth, knowing that if he continued to kiss her she would be unable to prevent her body giving in to his demands. Her heart was thudding so hard it made the blood sing in her ears. Denied her lips, his mouth moved over her cheek, gently now, the tip of his tongue tracing the line of her jaw up to the tender lobe of her ear. She bit her lip hard to stop herself from responding. Her panic grew as he began to trail kisses down her neck—she was losing control. He tore aside the muslin fichu and began to kiss the swell of her breasts. A groan was wrenched from her.

'Damon, we should not be doing this.'

He raised his head and stared at her, his eyes blazing. 'You want me,' he muttered, breathing heavily, 'You know you do.'

'Yes, yes, I do, but not like this!' Even as she spoke he lowered his head again, his body crushing her on to the desk. She gasped, for his touch had turned her insides to molten fire. She arched towards him, giving the lie to her whispered pleas for him to stop. She was losing control. Her hands beat a futile tattoo on his shoulders. Another minute and it would be too late, the hot liquid in her belly was spreading to her limbs, making them wayward, responding to his touch rather than her will. It would be so easy to give in to him, to abandon herself to the heat of the moment, but there was a part of her that told her she would regret it; even more painful, she was sure that Damon would hate himself when he realised what he had done to her. Unable to push him off, her hand groped around the desk, knocking a sheaf of papers to the floor, brushing against the feathers of a pen. Then her fingers touched metal. She stretched out and grasped the handle of the pen knife. Summoning up the last shreds of her resolve, she brought her arm round and drove the knife with as much force as she could muster into his arm. Restricted as she was, the blow had little force, but it was enough.

With an oath the Major pulled away from her. Juliana rolled off the desk and scrambled away from him, holding the knife before her.

'That may be the way you take your whores, but you shall not treat me thus!' she hissed at him.

She had moved out of reach, watching him, ready to fly if he should come towards her, but he remained by the desk, feeling his arm.

'You stabbed me, you little vixen.'

He was breathing heavily, but she noticed with relief that the mad light had gone from his eyes.

'Have—have I hurt you very much?' She could not resist the question.

'Not as much as I deserve,' he said ruefully. 'Ju, I am sorry.'

'I asked you to stop.' She blinked away the tears that were welling up. Silently she straightened her bodice. He sat down on the edge of the desk, clutching at his arm with his good hand.

'You did. I am sorry.' He looked chastened. 'I never expected you to defend your honour so fiercely. I thought you cared for me.'

'I do!' She dashed her hand across her eyes. 'I *do*. But you are engaged to marry another woman and I cannot—will not—come between you. Do you not see? You are an honourable man; I would not have you demean yourself—or me.'

'But we love each other, Ju. There can be no shame in that.'

She shook her head at him, raising her hands in frustration.

'What would you have me do—become your mistress? If I did that, I could no longer teach your children. And what of Thomas and Amy? Are they to grow up knowing that their sister is—is a—' She turned away, her voice suspended in tears.

'No, you are right.' He sighed. 'You see everything so clearly, and you are so much stronger than I. You must be my example, Juliana. I will try to match your fortitude in future.' He paused. 'Do you think you could help me out of my coat? You need not look so suspicious, I give you my word I will not touch you, but I would like to see how deep you have cut me.'

Juliana went to him and eased the coat away from his shoulder. The woollen sleeve had taken most of the force and there was no more than a tiny tear in the shirt, but it was surrounded by a bright red stain.

'Oh, heavens, what have I done?' gasped Juliana, tears coming to her eyes again.

'Well, let us see.'

He shrugged himself out of his flowered waistcoat, un-buttoned his shirt and pushed it off the shoulder to expose the wound on the top of his arm. Juliana blinked and swallowed hard. Not at the sight of his injury, which was nothing more than a small cut, but at the shadow of dark hair on his chest, and the hard bare muscle of his shoulder.

'There is a clean handkerchief in the pocket of my coat,' he said. 'Perhaps you can find it; we must bind up the arm until it stops bleeding. I could call for Plumstead, of course, but I would rather the servants did not know of this.'

Juliana found the handkerchief, shook it out and pro-ceeded to fold it into a bandage. The Major watched her as she bound up his arm, but she kept her eyes resolutely on her task, aware that the emotion sizzling between them a few moments ago was in abeyance, but it had not disappeared.

'There.' She stepped back. 'I think that will hold. I am relieved it is nothing more serious. Truly.'

He grunted. 'It is merely a scratch, but you have ruined a perfectly good coat.'

She did not smile. 'It will not work, sir. I cannot stay here.'

There was a silence, broken only by the steady tick, tick of the clock.

'So you will leave me.'

'I think I must. I *know* I must.'

Silently he put on his waistcoat and walked over to the window. He sighed. 'Yes, you must. I cannot be trusted when you are near me. I shall buy you a house. Do not argue with me, Ju. I will not let you leave here unless I know that you are safe. If not for yourself, accept it for Thomas and

Amy. It shall be wherever you please. Harrogate, or perhaps Manchester—that is a growing town, there will be many rich merchants who want a good education for their daughters. You may be sure that I shall give you a glowing reference.'

Juliana nodded. Her heart felt like lead and she did not care where she went since it meant she would not see him again.

'I will set Brasher on to it. You can tell him what it is you require; I shall not interfere.'

He began to collect up the pens that were scattered across the floor.

'I must be gone within the week, sir.'

He looked up at that. 'So soon? You would have me pay dearly for my loss of control.' He suddenly saw the tears rolling down her cheeks and jumped to his feet. He would have taken her in his arms, but Juliana put out her hand, mutely shaking her head at him.

'If you will not let me comfort you, then dry your tears,' he said roughly. 'To see you cry is more than mortal flesh can stand.'

'I must go. The children will wonder where I am.' She wiped her eyes, then turned to the mirror and arranged the muslin around her shoulders. Her hair had escaped from its pins and she did her best to scrape it back into some sort of order. In the mirror she watched the Major go back to his desk and sit down. The tears welled up again when she saw how tired he looked. It would be better for them both once she was gone away. Damon would busy himself with his estates and soon forget her: she would retire to a genteel little house in Harrogate and wait to die.

Juliana squared her shoulders. That was silly talk. She had Amy and Tom to look after. She could not afford to indulge in such maudlin behaviour, and neither could Damon.

'I shall see Brasher in the morning, and when I have decided upon where to live I shall ask him to find me lodgings until such time as we can find a house. If you have no objection, I would like to continue teaching the children—I would prefer not to tell them I am leaving until I have some idea of my direction.'

'They will miss you.'

She raised her chin. 'I shall miss them, but they have much to occupy them, a wedding and a new mama.'

'Yes, there will be a great deal to do in the next few weeks. Which reminds me…' He began sorting through the papers he had retrieved from the floor. '…Brasher informs me that the glass has arrived to replace the cracked window in the schoolroom. They plan to do the work tomorrow—would you be able to teach the children in the morning room?' He looked up, his mouth twisting into a humourless smile. 'It should only be for the day, and you have my word I will not disturb you.'

'Thank you, sir. I am sure we will manage very well.'

'Then it is settled. You had best go now. Have no fear, Miss Wrenn: your colour has returned to normal, and with that muslin wrapped around you so demurely no one would guess how near you have come to being ravished.'

A thread of laughter fluttered inside her; how like Damon to show humour when they were in the midst of a nightmare.

Chapter Twenty

Heavy, lashing rain delayed the replacing of the window and three days later Juliana was still using the morning room as a makeshift schoolroom. When the day dawned dry and bright, Juliana took the children out of doors for an early morning walk to collect leaves and flowers for a drawing lesson. They were all quietly employed at this task when the door of the morning room burst open and Lady Frances swept in, the velvet skirts of her riding dress caught up over one arm. She stopped in surprise when she saw them.

'We have been ejected temporarily from the east wing by the workmen,' Juliana explained. 'Did Brasher not say?'

'I did not see Brasher,' came the curt reply. 'I came in through the garden door. I expected to find Collingham here.'

Juliana blinked. 'Major Collingham went out early this morning, with his son and Sir Richard,' she said quietly. 'If he is expecting you…'

'No, no.' Lady Frances strode about the room, tapping her riding crop against her gloved palm. 'We made no plans, but he should have known I would ride over on the first fine day.'

Something very like a pout marred her serene features.

She walked around the room, looking at the children's work. She stopped beside Wilhelmina and picked up the sheet of paper at her elbow. It bore sketches of several different leaves.

'Ju—Miss Wrenn drew that,' offered Minna, holding up her own attempt. 'This is mine.'

Lady Frances put the paper back down. 'I wonder the Major does not hire a drawing master for you.'

'Perhaps he will,' murmured Juliana, 'if they show an aptitude for the art.'

Lady Frances raised her fine brows. 'And are you qualified to tell if they have a talent, Miss Wrenn? Really, I think they would do a great deal better at school.'

Thomas looked up from his sketchpad, quick to take offence at this insult to his sister. Juliana gave him a little smile and the tiniest shake of her head. She thought it best not to reply. After all, in a few days' time she would be gone, and the Major would be free to consult his future bride about his children's education. She withdrew to a sofa at the side of the room.

'And these…' Lady Frances pointed her riding crop at the dolls propped up on a chair. 'What place have such toys in a schoolroom?'

The two younger girls looked up anxiously and Juliana smiled to reassure them.

'It is usual for Wilhelmina and Amy to leave their dolls in their bedrooms, but with the workmen making such a noise upstairs, we decided to keep them with us today.'

'I do not hold with such indulgence,' announced Lady Frances, continuing her perambulation. As she moved away, her crop caught the hair of Wilhelmina's doll and it toppled off the chair. Wilhelmina gave a gasp. Lady Frances did not notice, and continued to walk up and down the room with quick, angry strides. Wilhelmina waited until she had turned away again, then scrambled down from her chair to retrieve her doll.

Unfortunately, Lady Frances had allowed her skirts to slip from her arm, and as Wilhelmina jumped down, her feet caught the edge of her train. There was a ripping sound, and Lady Frances jerked to a halt.

'Oh, oh.'

Wilhelmina stepped back quickly, whimpering. Lady Frances swung round.

'You clumsy child!' she cried, her cheeks scarlet with anger. 'Why can you not be more careful? It is no wonder you were the death of your mother.'

A sudden stillness fell over the room. Gwendoline gasped, Amy and Thomas looked anxiously at each other and Wilhelmina, white-faced, turned and ran to Juliana, who pulled the little girl on to her lap. Lady Frances noticed none of this; she was examining her skirts, and muttering to herself.

'No great damage done, thank heaven. The stitching is pulled, but with a little pressing it might not show.'

Juliana gave Wilhelmina a quick hug and set her down on the sofa. She rose and went across to Lady Frances.

'Ma'am, it was an accident. Wilhelmina is distraught—will you not find a kind word for her?'

'I will not,' retorted Lady Frances, shaking out her skirts. 'The child is wild to a fault. And I lay the blame firmly at your door, Miss Wrenn.'

Juliana fought down her indignation. She said quietly, 'But to imply that Minna was responsible for the death of her mother—'

'It is no more or less than the truth,' came the terse reply. 'Everyone knows that Harriet died giving birth to that child.'

'You cannot blame Wilhelmina for that.'

Lady Frances drew herself up. 'And why not? Would you

tell me that Major Collingham would not rather have his wife than that…that brat?'

Juliana gasped. 'Madam,' she said, 'that is an unjust and heartless thing to say.'

'How dare you criticise me!' Lady Frances's face flushed with anger.

Juliana saw that Gwen had gone across to sit beside Wilhelmina, who was sobbing uncontrollably. She tried again.

'Pray consider, ma'am. Will you not tell Wilhelmina that you did not mean those words? Will you not retract?'

'I will not. Let me remind you that you are nothing more than a servant here.'

'I am governess to these children,' retorted Juliana. 'Their welfare is my first concern and I cannot allow you to upset them so.'

'You cannot allow—' Lady Frances stared at her. 'Why, you impertinent hussy. How dare you speak to me in that way!'

'I do dare, madam,' flashed Juliana, thoroughly roused, 'And I also dare to warn you that your callous words will not endear you to these children.'

Lady Frances went pale with fury. She lifted her riding crop. Juliana raised her chin, daring her to strike. After a long, tense silence, Lady Frances lowered her arm.

'Such behaviour is not to be tolerated,' she snapped. 'You and your family will leave Blackthorpe immediately. I—'

'What is going on here?'

They had not heard the Major come in. He strode into the room, still dressed for riding in his brown coat, buckskins and muddy top boots.

'What the devil is the meaning of this?' he demanded. 'I heard your voices from across the hall.'

'Damon, thank heaven! This—this *creature*—' Lady Frances pointed to Juliana '—has had the effrontery to criticise me—*me*! You cannot allow such behaviour in a servant.'

'Certainly not, if it is true.'

Juliana had walked across to the table, but she turned her head now, her anger barely concealed.

'Oh, yes, it is true,' she said. She took Amy's hand. 'Come, you too, Thomas. We must pack.'

She did not look at the Major, but swept out of the room with her head held high.

'Are we really leaving?' asked Amy, running to keep up with her. 'Where will we go?'

'I neither know nor care.' Juliana strode up the stairs and into the bedroom where she dragged her trunk into the middle of the room.

'But we have no money,' said Thomas.

'Then we shall walk into Burnley and I will take a post as a chambermaid if I must!' She sighed, her shoulders sagging. 'No, no, that is anger speaking. I shall seek out Mr Brasher and ask him for the wages I am due.' She looked down at the two anxious faces. 'You must not worry, my loves. We are no worse off than when we applied to Cousin Pettigrew.'

'But we are hundreds of miles away from London.'

'So we are, Tom. We must make a new life for ourselves. Is that not exciting?'

The words sounded hollow, even to Juliana. She shrugged, and set her mind to packing. There was a knock at the door. The Major came in without ceremony.

'Miss Wrenn, I would like to speak to you. Privately.'

She continued to throw the children's clothes into the trunk. 'You can have nothing to say that the children should not hear.'

From the corner of her eye she observed the tightening of his jaw. He addressed Thomas.

'Will you take Amy outside for a while, if you please? You will find the girls having luncheon in the breakfast room.'

Juliana looked up. 'You will stay where you are, Thomas! We will take nothing further from this house.'

'Now you are being foolish in the extreme,' retorted the Major. 'Go along, Thomas; Giles is out with Sir Richard, so you will find only Gwen and Minna there, no one else,' he added with a meaningful glance.

He waited until Thomas had taken Amy out of the room and closed the door behind him. Even then he did not speak, but stood watching Juliana as she continued to pack.

'Gwen told me what happened.' He waited. 'Will you not talk to me?'

'There is nothing to say.'

'There is much to say! I understand Frances said Minna was to blame for her mother's death.'

'Yes.'

'It is not true and I said as much to Minna before I came upstairs.' He walked over to the window. 'I have also done my best to reassure her—and Gwen, too—that much as I loved their mother, I would not give them up now. They are my world.'

'That was kind.'

'It is the truth.' He cleared his throat. 'Frances has gone. I—we decided we should not suit.'

Juliana found her hands were shaking as she dropped another pile of clothes into the trunk. She said nothing, mechanically folding Tom's shirts and putting them away. After a short pause he continued.

'The—sacrifices I have been prepared to make have all been for the sake of my children. It has been forcibly borne in upon me that to marry Lady Frances might provide for their future security, but it would scarcely make them happy.'

She closed her eyes.

'Well? Have you nothing to say to that?'

She shook her head, her throat too tight with unshed, angry tears for her to speak. He turned towards her.

'Damnation, woman, will you not answer me?'

She continued to bundle her clothes into the trunk. 'It is not my place to offer an opinion.'

'Then it will be the first time since we met that you have not done so!'

'I am merely a governess—'

He swore roundly, making her wince. 'You have never been merely a governess and you know it! You are a most outspoken and opinionated young woman!'

She threw back her head at that, incensed. 'And if I am, it was because I found it necessary to combat your arrogance!'

He continued as if she had not spoken. 'You are head-strong, hot at hand, damnably independent and you have become quite indispensable to my family.'

She froze.

'Juliana, please don't go.'

She swung round, unwilling to face him. Her anger had carried her thus far; now the contrition in his voice confused her.

'You—you cannot want me to stay,' she murmured, her voice barely above a whisper. 'I—I stabbed you.'

'A scratch, and nothing more than I deserved.' She felt his hands on her shoulders, the heat of his body close behind her. She resisted the impulse to lean back against him. 'Ju—I have been such a fool. Can you forgive me for putting you through all this? Can you…love me?'

'I will always love you,' she whispered.

Damon gave a deep sigh. His breath was on her neck. He turned her round and gathered her into his arms. She leaned against him, her cheek resting against the rough wool of his coat. For a long time they remained thus, standing in each other's arms, and Juliana thought she would ask for no greater happiness.

'So you will stay?' His words rumbled against her cheek and she smiled into his coat.

'Yes.'

He tilted up her face and kissed her. 'Unpack, then. This is your home now. For ever.' He threw up his head. 'Now what the devil is that racket?'

From the stairs came the sounds of running feet and loud voices. Damon opened the door and stepped out, almost colliding with a chambermaid.

'Beggin' your pardon, sir. There's a coach arrived.'

'A coach? What the devil is this now?' He strode away and Juliana followed, bemused.

The long passage to the gallery echoed faintly with the sounds of voices from the hall below. The sounds became louder as they approached the stairs.

'What the…?'

Coming to a halt behind Major Collingham, Juliana peeped around him. Below, the floor of the hall was littered with bandboxes and trunks, while a thin woman in a severe black redingote was directing the servants as they brought in even more bags. Standing quietly in the midst of this confusion was a lady in a pale-blue travelling gown. Hearing the Major's voice, she turned and looked up, and Juliana found herself looking at the most beautiful face she had ever seen.

Chapter Twenty-One

'Lady Ormiston, what a pleasant surprise.'

As Major Collingham descended the stairs to greet his visitor, Juliana drew back into the shadows of the gallery. The lady in the hall was a ravishing brunette with glossy ringlets peeping out from beneath her modish bonnet while the excellent cut of her travelling robe showed her figure to advantage. She had large black eyes fringed with long, curling lashes, smooth cheeks delicately flushed and a pair of red lips that had curved now into a dazzling smile.

'Damon, my dear! You are surprised, no? I am travelling to Scotland to join Ormiston, and when I realised how close we would be to you, I ordered my driver to divert.' The enchanting little face showed a moment's anxiety. 'You will not turn me away, *mon ami*? If it is inconvenient…'

'Not at all,' he said politely 'You are very welcome, Veronique, if unexpected.'

She gave a light, tinkling laugh and cast a roguish glance at her host.

'I was ever that, *non*?' A harsh, hacking cough made her look around at the woman in the black redingote. 'Ah, poor Sophie. Major Collingham shall tell us which rooms we are to have and then, while you unpack, we shall have a tisane prepared for you, is that not so?' She directed a look of enquiry at Plumstead, who gave a stately bow.

'Of course, madam.'

'Bon.' She looked up at the gallery. 'But who is that little thing, hiding up there? Is it one of your children, Damon?'

He laughed.

'Hardly. Come down, Miss Wrenn, and let me present you to Lady Ormiston. This, Veronique, is my children's governess.'

'Ah, and do they make your life very difficult, *mademoiselle*?' asked Lady Ormiston as Juliana came down the stairs. 'My sister and I, we were very naughty for our tutors, but perhaps Damon has little angels?'

Juliana allowed herself a faint smile. 'They are children, *madam*, nothing more.' Now she was closer she could see that Lady Ormiston was older than she first appeared, with tiny lines around her mouth and at the corners of her eyes, but these merely added character to her beauty, as did the lilting French accent.

The Major turned to Juliana. 'It is time you went back to your charges, Miss Wrenn. They should have finished their luncheon by now.' He held her eyes for a moment. 'We will talk later.'

Juliana nodded and began to walk away. She did not look back, but as she heard Lady Ormiston's playful tone she imagined her taking the Major's arm and fluttering her absurdly long lashes at him.

'Now, Damon my dear, tell me truly if I am in the way. But this is such a big house, and you must have a *little* room somewhere that I can use for a night or two? I require very little luxury, after all; during the Terror in Paris, I slept in a hovel on straw, you know.'

'I am sure we can do better than that for you…'

Juliana heard the laugh in the Major's voice. She

slipped into the morning room and closed the door firmly behind her. Instead of making her way to the breakfast room in search of the children, she sank down on to one of the cushioned window seats. Her head was spinning with the events of the past few hours. It could not be much past noon, yet already she felt she had not slept for several days. She had never known such anger as she had felt for Lady Frances that morning. Even now her hands clenched tightly at the memory of her callous words to little Minna. She had been prepared to take Thomas and Amy out of the house that very hour rather than make an apology. Then, when her temper was cooling and the first threads of anxiety had started to wrap themselves about her heart, Damon had come to her and told her what she had dreamed of hearing for weeks past; that he was not going to marry Lady Frances.

The sudden transition from despair to elation had shaken her, but Lady Ormiston's arrival had robbed her of the opportunity to talk to Damon about her situation, and her feelings were still in turmoil. She remembered Damon telling her that Lady Ormiston had been his mistress. It had been a brief affair, he had said, but he had not told her who had ended it. Now her own particular demons whispered that the lady was far too bewitching to be cast aside, that it must have been the lady who had ended the affair. Juliana had no illusions about Damon. He was too masculine not to be attracted by the lady's luscious beauty. Juliana sighed. There was nothing she could do to mend matters, she told herself; she had best put aside these melancholy thoughts. She rose and went briskly to the breakfast room, where the children were coming to the end of their luncheon.

'Ah, Miss Wrenn, such goings on as the children have been describing to me!' Nurse greeted her with a shake of her head as she came in. 'I was mortified when Gwen told me what that woman had said to Minna, and not a word of it true, as the master told her first and as I have been telling her since, for I was there when Mrs Collingham gave birth to my little poppet, and I know how happy she was about it. "Another girl," she says to me. "A beautiful healthy little sister for Gwendoline."' Nurse wiped her eyes. 'It was a few days later that my poor mistress caught the fever and died, and even then she bade me to take Minna away to the wet nurse rather than risk her becoming ill. "Nurse, you look after my little angels," she says, and so I have, all these years, bless her memory.'

The children looked at one another and fidgeted uncomfortably at this display of emotion.

'The Major is not going to marry Lady Frances,' announced Amy.

Juliana sat down at the table. 'So I understand,' she said cautiously.

'It is true.' Wilhelmina nodded. 'He sent us away, but Gwen and I listened at the door. He told her he was sorry, but it would not work, and it was fortunate there had been no announcement.'

'You should not be eavesdropping, and you certainly should not be repeating anything you overheard,' said Juliana, trying to look severe.

'Well, under normal circumstances we would not do so,' said Gwendoline. 'But this was too important to miss. And we shall only tell *you*. Well, then there was a pretty kick-up—'

'Gwendoline!' gasped Nurse.

'Thomas says it.'

'Then he should reserve it for when he is in the stables,' retorted Juliana, frowning at her little brother.

'Very well, then,' continued Gwen. 'Lady Frances railed at Papa, saying he should send us to school to learn some manners, and how everyone knew they were to be married, and they would all say he had lost his senses—'

'And Papa says, "No, madam, I have just found them,"' growled Wilhelmina, and went off into a fit of giggles.

'And then Lady Frances stormed out of the house.'

'And Papa saw us in the hall, and he must have known we heard everything, but he never said a word about it.' Wilhelmina's cheeks grew flushed. 'Instead he—he told us about Mama…'

'I am very glad he did so.' Juliana kissed her.

'Now,' said Nurse, rising from the table, 'Plumstead came in earlier to tell us that the workmen have finished in the east wing, and we can go back to the schoolroom. Miss Wrenn, would you like something to eat before we leave the table?'

'No, thank you. I am not hungry.'

'You are a little pale.' Nurse looked at her closely. 'Are you sure you're not sickening, miss?'

Juliana tried to smile. 'No, I am just—I feel a little faint. Perhaps I should take some air.'

'Bless you, dearie, why didn't you say so?' declared Nurse. 'You take a turn around the garden, miss; the children will come upstairs with me. Unless you would like me to come with you?'

'No, I shall be quite well again in a moment.'

Juliana slipped out through one of the long windows on to the terrace. It was but a step from there to the shrubbery, where the gravel path was sufficiently well drained for her to walk without ruining her thin slippers. A few deep breaths calmed her and she could appreciate the warm sun on her skin, the soft breeze rustling through the bushes. She was not given long to enjoy her solitude. She heard the scrunch of footsteps on the gravel and turned to find Major Collingham striding towards her.

'I saw you come out here. Are you unwell?'

'No, not now.'

He held out his arm and with only the tiniest hesitation she took it.

'An eventful day,' he said.

She smiled at his understatement.

'You are silent, Ju—do you not agree with me?'

'I am still trying to organise my thoughts on all that has happened. But—if you are not to marry Lady Frances, what of your plans to improve Blackthorpe and provide for the children?'

'Oh we shall come about.' He squeezed her arm. 'I am not exactly a pauper, you know.'

'Of course not, but…'

'But?'

'You wanted to rebuild your fortune.'

He stopped and pulled her into his arms.

'I already have my fortune here.'

He kissed her, and Juliana relaxed against him, admitting to herself for the first time how she had longed for this, to feel his arms about her, his mouth on hers, and to know that he was as free to give his love as she was to accept it. Her lips parted beneath his, and as his kiss became more urgent the liquid heat surged through her, pooling somewhere between her hips, which pressed against Damon of their own accord. All too soon the kiss ended. Damon threw up his head, listening.

'Someone is coming.' Disappointment washed through her as she heard the approaching footsteps. He kissed her again, quickly. 'I am thwarted at every turn.' He stepped away from her just as Sir Richard appeared from a side path. 'Rick, are you looking for me?'

'Aye. Plumstead tells me Lady Ormiston has arrived.'

'Yes, alone, too,' said the Major. 'It is too much of a coincidence. Do you think Leeson has contacted her?' He observed Sir Richard's hesitation and continued bluntly, 'You need not mind Miss Wrenn, she knows as much of this affair as anyone, including the fact that Leeson and Lady Ormiston were lovers.'

'Very well, then. I believe she plans to succeed where Leeson failed.'

Juliana gasped. 'The children!'

'They have Nurse and Matthew, one of my footmen, looking after them at the moment,' said Damon. 'I made sure of it before I came out here.'

'Good, but I do not believe they are in any immediate danger,' mused Sir Richard. 'It is more likely that Leeson snatched the child as a way to manipulate Damon.' He looked at the Major. 'What could he hope to gain from that?'

Damon frowned. 'Do you think I haven't considered that, Rick? I have no influence at Court, no state secrets to hand over. Good God, I do not even have a fortune to tempt him.'

They began to stroll along the path, Sir Richard swinging his quizzing glass gently to and fro on its black ribbon.

'Then if you will let her remain here as your guest, Damon, we must watch and wait for Veronique to make her play. You look troubled, Miss Wrenn. What is on your mind?'

Juliana felt the colour rising to her cheeks.

'Come, Ju,' said the Major roughly. 'What is it?'

'You—you say you will wait for Lady Ormiston to make her play, but what if it is for…for—' She broke off, blushing furiously.

'You think she might try to seduce me?' The Major laughed. 'I am not a man to be caught twice by that trick. However, you are very right to remind us of the proprieties, Miss Wrenn. You had best go off and change your dress, Giles has sent word that he is dining with Fewell's brother in Burnley—and will be talking of engines all night, I have no doubt! We need you to make a fourth at dinner.'

Chapter Twenty-Two

Juliana dressed with care, not with the intention of pleasing the gentlemen, but more in the spirit of going into battle. She rejected her new cream gown in favour of the grey silk, which showed no signs of the tea Gwendoline had spilled over it, and the rustle of the skirts gave her confidence as she made her way to the drawing room. She found Major Collingham there alone, and stood, hesitating, at the door.

'Come in, Miss Wrenn. Our guests have not yet left their rooms.' He came forward and said, as the butler closed the door and left them alone together, 'You look nervous. There is no need, I am sure you have not forgotten the social graces required at the dinner table.'

'No, sir, but—'

He continued as if she had not spoken.

'As my hostess, I expect you to take your place opposite me, at the foot of the table.'

'Oh no, surely—'

'It is essential.' He stood before her and ran one finger down her cheek. Even that light touch made the blood sizzle in her veins. 'If I have you any closer to me, I shall not be able to keep my hands off you.'

That treacherous finger moved past her chin and began to trail down her neck. She reached up to clasp his hand in both her own.

'Oh, please don't say such things to me. How can I remain calm when you treat me thus?'

His blazing look turned her insides to water and she closed her eyes, fighting to maintain her composure. How could she doubt that he loved her? She heard him laugh softly.

'You are quite right, Miss Wrenn. We must observe the proprieties this evening, must we not?' He gently withdrew his hand from her grasp and stepped away from her. It was not a moment too soon, for the door opened and Plumstead ushered Lady Ormiston into the room.

Juliana sank down on to one of the straw-coloured sofas and began to fan herself gently, as much to disguise her shaking fingers as to cool her cheeks.

Lady Ormiston immediately crossed the room to Major Collingham. 'Forgive me for keeping you waiting, Damon.'

He kissed her fingers. 'You did not, ma'am. We still await Sir Richard.'

She did not look too pleased with this answer, but her smile widened and she turned to look about the room.

'Well, this is to be a cosy little dinner, is it not?' She appeared to notice Juliana for the first time. 'Oh, is it the custom for the governess to dine with you, Damon?'

The Major replied easily, 'Miss Wrenn has agreed to act as my hostess while you are here, Veronique.'

Lady Ormiston's silvery laugh rang out. 'But, Damon, you and I do not need a chaperon, I am a married woman!'

'All the more reason not to give Ormiston cause for suspicion. And while I think of it, Veronique, how long are you planning to stay? Thursday is the day of the Burnley fair, you see. It is a tradition at Blackthorpe that the staff are given a half-day's holiday. That is the day after tomorrow.

There will be nothing but a cold luncheon for us and we take pot luck with our dinner when Cook returns. For the afternoon we will be left to our own devices.'

She gave him a roguish look. 'Oh, I am sure we shall contrive to amuse ourselves, Damon.'

'I am sure we will.' Damon looked up as Sir Richard entered. 'Ah, in good time, Rick.' He held out his arm to Lady Ormiston. 'Madam, shall we go in to dinner?'

'Miss Wrenn?'

Juliana looked up at Sir Richard and relaxed a little when he winked at her.

'My knees are shaking,' she confessed in a whisper as he escorted her to the dining room. 'I depend upon you, Sir Richard, to help me through this.'

When Juliana had left the garden, she had taken a circuitous route through the back rooms to avoid a chance meeting with Lady Ormiston. She had seen the footmen storing the mahogany leaves from the table in their green baize-lined slots in the corridor behind the dining room, so she knew the table had been reduced for what Mrs Plumstead described as a snug little party, yet when she was seated at one end of the table with the Major facing her and their two guests on either side, Juliana was aware of a strong sense of isolation. A dazzling array of silver covered the space between her and the other diners, and the distances seemed vast. Her spirits drooped as she watched Veronique flirting with the gentlemen. She was recounting an amusing anecdote and flashing those huge black eyes towards each man in turn. As the meal progressed, Sir Richard left the Major to entertain the vivacious Frenchwoman and turned instead to talk to Juliana, who responded gratefully, while part of her attention remained fixed on Lady Ormiston. She wondered if she was being too sensitive, but the lady seemed intent on fixing her interest with her host. She was leaning forward, turned slightly towards Damon as he replied to a question, as if she was telling him he was the only man in the room.

Juliana glanced at Sir Richard, who was calmly eating the lamb fricassee. The occasional glances he cast at his guest were merely amused. Juliana wished she could be so complacent, or that she was close enough to deliver a well-aimed kick at Damon's shin, since he had designated her as a chaperon for the evening. As it was, she could only curb her frustration and wait for the Major's sign that the ladies should retire. When it came, she rose solemn-faced from the dining table and led Lady Ormiston from the room.

'Well,' said Sir Richard, once the ladies had gone, 'what do you think she wants?'

Damon watched as Plumstead filled their glasses with brandy, then dismissed him with a gesture.

'Veronique is too clever to let me know that yet,' he said when they were alone. 'I believe she is trying to set me at my ease.'

'Have a care, my friend,' said Sir Richard. 'She is a fascinating woman.'

Damon gave a crack of laughter. 'A lovely piece of work, ain't she?' He frowned at his glass, then tossed back the brandy, saying in a quite different tone, 'Miss Wrenn was very quiet at dinner—I depended upon you to look after her, Richard.'

'We talked a little, but in the main we were enjoying the performance you and Lady Ormiston were putting on for us.'

Damon frowned. Even while Veronique had been flirting so outrageously, a blatant invitation in her eyes, he had been aware of the grave little figure sitting opposite him, picking at her food.

'You may have enjoyed it, my friend, but I am damned sure Miss Wrenn did not.'

. 'No, you are right.' Sir Richard reached for the decanter. He gave his host a speculative glance. 'Taking little thing,' he said. 'Of course, in looks she cannot hold a candle to the lovely Veronique.'

'But she has a heart, and I would not see it bruised,' retorted Damon. 'I must talk to her. I would to God I had refused to let Veronique stay. I should have sent her away and foiled her little scheme.'

'But then we would never learn what that scheme is, and I am very anxious to find it out.' He sat back, holding up his glass to study the contents through half-closed eyes. 'It will do no harm to let her think she is succeeding in charming you—she may let slip just what she wants.'

Damon frowned. 'But you think she is involved in something that could have national importance.'

'Yes, I do.'

'Out with it, Rick.' Damon refilled their glasses. 'What is in your mind? Come, my friend, we have known each other too long for secrets, even state ones.'

'Very well. I suspect the lady to be involved with the plot to rescue Bonaparte. You will recall I mentioned it to you in London. Somehow, you and your family have become embroiled in her scheme.'

'Then we must try to find out what it is.'

'Exactly, but I would not ask it if I thought there was any real risk of harm to your family. The fact that Veronique has come here so openly suggests that she means to take what she wants by stealth.'

'Don't worry, Rick, I will protect my own.'

Juliana glanced at the clock. The gentlemen had been sitting over their brandy for nearly an hour. She knew such rituals could go on for much longer, but surely if they suspected Veronique of planning mischief they would come in soon. The ladies had made themselves comfortable on the satin sofas that flanked the empty fireplace and engaged in desultory small talk that Juliana found extremely trying. Now a difficult silence had settled over the room.

'Will we see the Major's delightful children this evening, Miss Wrenn?' asked Lady Ormiston at last, when other subjects like the weather and the state of the roads had been exhausted.

'Yes, I believe Major Collingham has requested that they should come down.'

'And what are they like, these little girls—are they in awe of their papa?' She gave a soft laugh. 'No doubt he is very strict with them, is he not? He is an army man, after all, and used to order.'

'Naturally he likes the children to behave well.'

'But children like to play and run wild, do they not, Miss Wrenn? No doubt they have much more freedom here, to use up their energies. The moors must be an exciting place for them to roam free.'

'The children are never allowed out of doors unaccompanied,' said Juliana, choosing her words carefully. 'Major Collingham is very conscious of the children's safety.'

She looked round hopefully when the door opened, but it was not the gentlemen as she had hoped. Nurse stood on the threshold, asking diffidently if the children should come in.

'But of course!' cried Lady Ormiston, spreading her arms wide to welcome them. 'Bring them in—ah, little darlings, come here, that I may look at you.'

Gwendoline and Wilhelmina approached and made their curtsies to their father's new guest, who gave them her dazzling smile, complimented them on their pretty gowns and asked them how they liked Blackthorpe. Gwendoline made some polite reply, but Minna merely stood beside her sister, staring wide-eyed at their beautiful visitor. Lady Ormiston put her head on one side and smiled at her.

'Little Wilhelmina, you have said nothing—you are not afraid of me, are you? Of course not. And you have your little doll with you—how charming. What is her name?'

Wilhelmina drew back a little, hugging the doll even closer.

'That's Sarah,' offered Gwendoline, adding with the superiority of her twelve years, 'It is Amy's doll. Minna couldn't bring her own doll downstairs because her arm came off and Thomas is mending her. She wouldn't come downstairs without a doll. She takes one everywhere.'

'Everywhere?' Lady Ormiston's amused glance turned to Juliana. 'Even into the schoolroom?'

The two children looked towards Juliana. She realised from their anxious faces that they were thinking of Lady Frances's visit that morning.

'Not generally, ma'am. We leave the dolls to Nurse's care while we take our lessons.'

'Papa!' Wilhelmina ran across the room as Major Collingham and Sir Richard came in. With a laugh, he swung her up into his arms.

'Well, Minna, have you been entertaining our guest?'

'She has not said a word,' scoffed Gwendoline.

'She is a little shy, but I think we will all be great friends.' Lady Ormiston waved her fan gently as she watched the Major set his daughter gently on her feet. 'This is a side of you I have not seen before, Damon.'

'I believe Collingham is becoming quite a family man,' observed Sir Richard, following his host into the room.

'I think you are right, Rick, and you may believe I will go to any lengths to protect them.'

The Major's implacable tone sent a shiver through Juliana—was he trying to warn Veronique off? If so, the lady did not appear to notice. She continued to talk to the children, but, despite her best efforts, Wilhelmina could not be induced to give her more than monosyllabic answers to her questions. The little girl stood beside Juliana, clutching her doll and watching Lady Ormiston with a direct, solemn gaze.

'Oh, dear me.' Veronique gave an uncertain little laugh. 'I fear I have frightened poor little Wilhelmina, she looks at me so sternly.'

Juliana put her hand on the child's shoulder. 'I think she is a little tired. We have had an eventful day.'

'Then what are you doing, allowing the children to stay up so late?' growled Major Collingham. Impatiently he waved her back into her seat as she made to rise. 'No, no, there is no need for you to go—Nurse will take them upstairs.'

He beckoned to the old woman, who left her chair in one shadowy corner and came forward.

'Goodnight, my dears.' Lady Ormiston smiled at them fondly as they left the room. 'What little dolls, I vow I am quite smitten. Perhaps I should find myself a pageboy.'

'Pageboys grow up,' replied Sir Richard. 'Perhaps you should buy a pug instead.'

'Yes, perhaps. Damon, do you remember that frightful Lady Corston and her three pugs? She insisted on taking them everywhere with her, even the Duchess of Almonham's rout.'

'Where they disgraced themselves on the Aubusson carpet.' The Major grinned.

Juliana sat back and listened as the conversation ranged around London society with anecdotes and gossip about people she did not know. She did not object, for she felt battered by the day's events and was glad to sit quietly and allow her thoughts to wander. However, by the time the party broke up it was nearly midnight and Juliana was fighting to stay awake. Lady Ormiston declared she must retire or fall asleep where she stood.

'Perhaps, Damon, you will escort me to my room? The corridors in this house are so very dark.'

'No need,' he replied easily. 'Miss Wrenn can do that.' Lady Ormiston pouted prettily, but he carried on inexorably. 'You will find Plumstead has put the bedroom candles ready at the bottom of the stairs. Our guest is in the blue room, Miss Wrenn, in the west wing, beyond the bust of Milton.'

'I know it, sir.'

Juliana watched from the door as Lady Ormiston said goodnight to the gentlemen. They both kissed her hand, but it seemed that Damon held on to those slim fingers a fraction longer, that his eyes followed her as she glided out of the room. Juliana led the way up the stairs and along the landing to the west wing.

'No doubt all the bedrooms are here,' remarked Veronique as they turned to walk along the main corridor, where their candles reflected dimly in the polished oak panelling. The tall plinths with their marble busts threw out long shadows as they approached them; the cold, impassive faces with their sightless eyes appeared ghoulish in the candlelight. Juliana thought of the less-than-perfect head of Prometheus on display outside the schoolroom. She had passed it many times in the dark and never found it as disturbing as these less familiar sculptures. They seemed to look upon her with disapproval.

'Which room does Major Collingham occupy?' asked Lady Ormiston.

Juliana blinked at the blunt question. 'I—I am not sure.'

It was a lie. Mrs Plumstead had pointed out the master's room to her during their tour of the house. It was the door nearest the gallery, but Juliana was not sharing that information with Lady Ormiston.

'No, this is not your side of the house, is it, Miss Wrenn?'

The contempt in the lady's voice was unmistakable. Juliana closed her lips firmly and walked on, offering no reply. The only sounds to break the silence were their slippered feet pattering on the boards and the whisper of silken skirts. As they reached the bust of Milton, Juliana stopped.

'Your room is here, ma'am. I am sure you will have all you need, but I understand this part of the house has a new bell system. You only have to ring if you require anything more.'

'So there are no lackeys on duty during the night?' she murmured. 'No footmen standing outside my door?'

'No, madam.'

With a nod of dismissal, Lady Ormiston disappeared into her chamber and Juliana made her way back through the corridor and across the gallery to the east wing. Upon her arrival at Blackthorpe Hall she had been allotted a suite of rooms for herself, Thomas and Amy, but Nurse had suggested it would be much more sensible for the children to sleep in the spare bedrooms in the nursery, where she and the Major's daughters had their own chambers. Thomas and Amy had not objected to this, but now as Juliana entered her apartment, she was aware of the emptiness, and for the first time wished that she had the children with her. The clock in the schoolroom began to chime: midnight. She decided it was too late to look in on the children. The nursery was situated under the eaves, reached from another flight of creaky stairs at the far end of the passage, and Juliana did not wish to disturb their slumbers. She must go to bed.

It took her some time to undress and slip into her thin cotton bedgown. With her father's diminishing income she had not had the luxury of a maid for many years and generally did not regret it, but tonight all she wanted to do was to lie down and sleep and she did not relish the thought of tidying away all her clothes. However, she knew that if she did not smooth her gloves flat and shake out her gown before folding it away carefully in the linen press, then they would be sadly creased when next required. Even when all her clothes were put away, Juliana had to unpin her hair and brush out the tangles. She snuffed the candles around the room and sat on her bed with only the bedroom candle still alight as she pulled the brush through her hair with long, even strokes, allowing her mind to wander. In the space of one day, she had known raging anger at Lady Frances, despair at the thought of leaving Blackthorpe, then elation when Damon had come to ask her to stay. But even her happiness had been short-lived. Now, with Lady Ormiston's appearance, there was a new fear gnawing at her. If Sir Richard's suspicions were correct, then Lady Ormiston was a dangerous enemy to be carefully watched. But even if she was not the enemy the gentlemen considered, she was very beautiful, and she had been Damon's lover once before. To Juliana's inexperienced eye, Lady Ormiston seemed intent upon reviving that relationship.

The brush snagged on a tangle of hair and Juliana gently teased the bristles through until the brush ran freely again, but the little doubt nagging in her head was not so easily smoothed away. Damon was a strong-willed, passionate man, and she had no doubt that he could withstand Veronique's blandishments, should he wish to do so.

'Aye, there's the problem,' she muttered to herself. 'What if he does not wish to resist her? Oh this is ridiculous!' Juliana tossed her hairbrush on to the dressing table and scrambled into bed. She blew out the candle and tried to make herself comfortable, but although she had entered the room feeling almost too tired to undress, now sleep eluded her. She longed for Damon, wanted to feel his arms around her, wanted him to kiss away all her doubts. If he had knocked on her door at that moment, she would have welcomed him into her arms and into her bed without a thought for the consequences. But he did not come, and she tossed and turned in the darkness. After an hour she gave up the struggle and felt around in the dark for her tinderbox.

Not only did the occupants of the east wing have to do without ladies' maids, she thought resentfully, they also had to manage without a personal closet. On her tour of the house, Mrs Plumstead had proudly shown Juliana the guest chambers, each with their own servant's room and a separate closet, but the schoolroom wing did not have such luxuries. The nursery rooms up under the eaves were equipped with a closet of their own, but Juliana's suite of rooms had not been similarly improved and her nearest privy was in a recess on the far side of the schoolroom. Preferable to a chamber pot under the bed, perhaps, but not ideal. With a sigh she slipped out of bed and picked up her lighted candle. At least it was warm enough for her to make the trip without her wrap.

Juliana opened her door and padded along the silent corridor to the little closet. A wind had sprung up, rattling the windows and whistling through the old house, but Juliana paid no heed. Old buildings were noisy places; she had even made it a game with the children to find all the creaking floorboards in the long corridors. Juliana reached the closet, taking care not to let the door bang and rouse the children sleeping above. She was just as careful when she left a few minutes later, quietly closing the door and re-tracing her steps. As she turned into the main corridor she gave a gasp and nearly dropped her candle when she saw a ghostly white figure hovering before her.

Chapter Twenty-Three

'L-Lady Ormiston!'

Holding up her candle and stepping closer, Juliana realised that the floating effect was caused by the diaphanous folds of the lady's fine muslin wrap swaying around her feet. Veronique's candle wavered.

'I could not sleep, and lost my way.' She stepped aside into the schoolroom and held her candle aloft. 'Is this where you hold your lessons for the little ones? How charming.'

'Yes, madam.' Juliana followed her into the room.

'Oh—so many toys.' Veronique moved closer to the shelves, casting the candle's feeble glow over each in turn. 'But some of the shelves are empty—why is this?'

'The carpenter has been fitting new windows to this room,' explained Juliana, watching her. 'Not everything has yet been put back.'

'It must be difficult, Miss Wrenn, to make sure all the children's playthings are suitable for them. I suppose you must know every toy that they own?'

'I had not considered it.'

Lady Ormiston's free hand crept inside her wrap.

'Well, consider it now, Miss Wrenn. I would like—' She stopped.

Above the keening wind was the sound of footsteps on the boards, a heavy-booted tread. Light flickered in the corridor and the next moment Major Collingham stood in the doorway, dressed only in his shirt, buckskins and top boots.

'Is anything wrong, ladies?' The light from the branched candlestick in his hand threw the angular planes of his face into strong relief, giving him a hawkish appearance. 'I was in the stables checking on my horse and saw the light up here.'

The white shirt billowed over his broad shoulders, unconfined by even a waistcoat, and his body seemed to fill the doorway.

'Lady Ormiston lost her way,' murmured Juliana. She had not realised how tense she was until she tried to speak, and the effort rasped her dry throat.

'So silly of me,' confessed Veronique with a little laugh. 'I could not sleep, and when I found myself up here, I was enchanted by all these reminders of childhood.' She moved towards Major Collingham. 'You will remember I told you, Damon, when I was a child in Paris during the Terror, we lost everything, my home, my nursemaid and my little friends.' She delicately wiped a tear from her cheek. '*Mon Dieu*, those were dark days.'

'Indeed they were, madam.' He held out his handkerchief to her.

'*Merci*. You are too kind.'

'Dry your eyes now,' said Damon. 'Miss Wrenn will take you back to your room.'

Juliana opened her mouth to protest, met his fierce stare and closed it again. She did not understand this game, she certainly did not like it, but if Damon did not wish to challenge the lady, she could hardly do so. She moved towards the door.

'Ma'am, if you are ready?'

As the Major stepped aside to let them pass, he caught Juliana's arm.

'Do not be alarmed if you meet one of the footmen on the stairs, I have asked Matthew to sleep at the foot of the nursery stairs tonight. Minna was looking a trifle feverish and I want someone on hand, should Nurse call for assistance.'

His tone was light, but there was no mistaking the message. Juliana nodded and went on her way, guiding Lady Ormiston back through the darkened house. They did not speak, and although Veronique dabbed at her eyes, she did not seem overwrought. At the door of the blue bedroom Juliana bade her goodnight, and when the door had closed again she began to make her way back along the empty corridor. She was about to step out onto the gallery when a door opened behind her and she heard her name called in a fierce whisper.

She turned to see Damon, his figure black against the glow of candlelight from the room behind him.

'We cannot talk here. Step inside.'

Juliana hesitated.

'This is my dressing room, Ju. You need go no farther.'

He stepped back and, gripping the candlestick a little tighter, she crossed the threshold into his apartment. As she passed him she realised Damon was wearing a brightly coloured dressing gown, the belt pulled tight and knotted at the waist. It enveloped him from neck to toe, covering those long limbs she found so unnerving.

The room was dark, the shutters had been closed across the window and the only light came from the two candles in a branched holder on a small side table. Outside their warm glow everything was in shadow, the curtains, the panelling all robbed of their rich colours. Instinctively she moved towards the table, her own candle adding to the pool of light. The room smelled of brandy and spices. And man. It was a very masculine room. Damon's room.

'Veronique is safely back in her chamber?' he asked, closing the door.

'Yes. I saw her go inside. I doubt she will stir again tonight, knowing Matthew is on the stair.'

He grinned. 'Yes. Not at all subtle, but I hope she has taken the hint.'

'What does she want, Damon?'

'I don't know.'

'But you know something,' she persisted. 'I can see it in your face. Please tell me.'

'Very well.' He walked to a daybed and sat down. 'Come over here.'

The daybed was in a shadowy corner of the room, and Juliana took her candle with her, placing it on a nearby console table.

'Afraid of the dark, Ju?'

He sounded amused.

'No, sir,' she replied calmly as she sat down beside him. 'But I would like to see you.'

'So you like to look at me.'

She took her bottom lip between her teeth to prevent a smile escaping her. 'That is not what I meant.'

Damon put one arm around her shoulders and turned her towards him, tilting up her chin with his free hand. She put her hands against his chest, feeling the heavily embroidered silk beneath her fingers.

'Damon, let me go or I shall have to move away.'

'Don't you like being in my arms?'

His voice had deepened suddenly and she felt the now-familiar fever coming over her. A shiver tingled through her spine.

'No,' she lied, trying to sound severe. 'You were going to tell me what you suspect.'

With a sigh he let her go and threw himself back against

the padded scroll of the daybed. One arm was lying along the backrest and Juliana sat up very straight, knowing that his fingers were only inches away from her.

'Tell me,' she repeated.

'Very well. Richard was investigating a plot to free Bonaparte from St Helena. He had discovered that supporters in France were sending diamonds here to pay for a ship and enough men to storm the island. He was hoping to intercept the diamonds and catch the plotters, but he did not succeed, and those involved went to ground.'

'But who would do such a thing? Surely no true Englishman—'

'Of course not, but there are many in London who owe no allegiance to our country. Richard has his suspicions, but without proof he can do nothing.'

Juliana was thinking, a tiny frown creasing her brow.

'Lady Ormiston,' she breathed. She looked up, her eyes wide and dark. 'Sir Richard suspects that she is involved, and that Leeson, as her lover, was drawn into her schemes.'

'Well done, my love. You have your wits about you tonight.'

She brushed aside his approval. 'From what you have told me, it was the obvious conclusion.'

'And you are happy to think Veronique a villain?'

She felt her cheeks growing warm.

'Well, yes,' she said, unable to meet his eyes. 'But you cannot let her stay here, Damon, it is not safe!'

He caught her hands.

'Richard thinks she intends no harm, and I agree with him.'

'No harm—but what of Mr Leeson—he ran off with Minna!'

'I think that was a mistake. He panicked.'

'But—'

'Hush.' He laid a finger on her lips. 'If we send Veronique away now, we will never know what she was

(

planning, and Richard is very keen to find out. And, I admit it, so am I. Now, will you help me?'

Juliana looked up into his eyes. 'Of course,' she said simply.

'Good girl.'

She knew she should object to his calling her a girl, but his tone turned the words into a caress that tingled through her body. She could feel his fingers at her back, playing with her hair. She looked away quickly.

'I must go.'

'Must you?'

'Yes.' Her mind was telling her to get up, but her body refused to move. She sat very still, feeling as if she was a glass that might shatter at any minute. Damon leaned towards her. She could feel the heat of him through the silk. He was smiling at her. His fingers curled under her chin, forcing her head round until he could brush her lips with his own. The touch was featherlight, but the effect was to send the familiar liquid heat surging through her.

'You are cold,' he murmured, drawing back.

'No,' she followed his gaze and saw that her nipples were pushing against the thin cotton of her nightgown. 'Oh, heavens,' she gasped, horrified, 'I should have put on my wrap!'

'Indeed you should, but it is too late now.' He pulled her towards him and kissed her again, fiercely this time. Juliana did not resist him. Instead her body seemed to melt into his arms of its own accord. His mouth teased hers and she found her lips parting voluntarily. She began to kiss him back, the pleasurable excitement growing within her so that when he broke away she found herself almost moaning with disappointment. Suddenly she found herself being pushed backwards while with one hand he swung her legs up until she was lying fully on the daybed. Damon was kneeling beside her and even in the light of the single candle the glow in his eyes was unmistakable. Juliana felt her breath catch in her throat.

He lifted a hand to smooth a strand of hair from her cheek. Her eyes widened.

'You are trembling,' she whispered.

'I know.' He drew an audible, ragged breath. 'You had best tell me to stop now, Ju, or by God I swear it will be too late for you.'

'Oh, Damon, my love, it is already too late.'

With a groan she reached up her hands to cup his face and pull him down so that she could kiss him again. Her lips parted beneath his mouth, and his flickering tongue tantalised her senses. Without warning Damon broke away and she found herself being lifted into his arms.

'Not here,' he muttered, burying his face in her hair. 'I want to be able to enjoy you without fear of falling off that damned couch.'

Her hands crept around his neck and she rested her cheek against him, listening to the thud of his heart. He carried her into the bedroom, walking with an unerring step through the darkness to lay her tenderly on the bed. For a moment she panicked as he moved away from her, but it was only for a moment as he shed his dressing gown. She stretched out her hand and touched not cloth, but skin. Damon climbed up beside her, and she felt a jolt of excitement to know that only her thin nightgown lay between them. And then even that was gone. Damon gathered it up and began to pull it gently over her head. She lifted her arms to free herself of the garment and gasped as Damon used the opportunity to swoop down upon her breasts, catching one taut nipple between his teeth while his fingers circled its twin and her body writhed beneath his touch. Freeing her arms from the nightgown, Juliana drove her fingers into his thick hair as her body arched towards him. She was aching for him to do more, although she had no idea what it was her body wanted. She could feel his lean, hard limbs pressing against her own. She breathed deeply, inhaling the heady mix of soap and spices and skin. Her excitement grew. An unfamiliar sensation was building deep within her.

He trailed kisses up over her neck and captured her mouth again while one hand moved gently over her body. Tentatively she moved her own hands, exploring the unfamiliar curves of his shoulder. The firm skin beneath her fingers excited her. She drew her hand across his chest, threading her fingers through the fine covering of hair and all the time his hand was caressing her, tracing the curve of her waist and massaging the flat surface of her stomach. As her hand moved up to his face, his moved gradually downwards and she found her body moving instinctively beneath his fingers. She felt relaxed, fluid, all tension gone.

Juliana gave a little gasp as his fingers crept between her thighs and moved into her most private space. She felt herself opening for him, lifting her hips to offer herself up to him completely. With a groan he shifted on top of her, measuring the length of his body over hers while he kissed her cheeks and her eyelids, his lips gentle as a breeze on her skin. She became aware that Damon was tense above her, holding himself off as though afraid that his weight would crush her. Juliana shuddered and sighed, desperate for his embrace. She twined her arms around his neck and pulled him closer. He lowered himself on to her, gently easing himself into the space his fingers had prepared so well. She was surprised into a little cry and immediately Damon froze.

'Do I hurt you—do you want me to stop?' he muttered.

'No, no.' Her fingers dug into his shoulders. 'Go on, go on!'

She took her bottom lip firmly between her teeth as he moved within her, feeling pain, but even more aware of a savage satisfaction. She tried moving her hips and heard Damon groan. She moved again and he gasped, his body tensing over her. His rigidity frightened her, but the next moment he was relaxing, falling on to the bed beside her, breathing heavily as if he had been running hard.

'Darling Ju,' he murmured. 'Did I hurt you?'

'Not much,' she answered truthfully.

'I wanted to take longer, to please you, but you—moved.'

She frowned in the darkness. 'I don't understand.'

'No.' He pulled her into his arms, wrapping his body around her. 'No, but you will soon.'

Juliana lay very still, cocooned in the warmth of the very male body pressed against her own. She could tell by his steady, regular breathing that Damon was asleep. It was very pleasant, to be sure, but she was nagged by a vague sense of disappointment. On several occasions her feelings had threatened to overwhelm her, and when Damon had kissed her she had been obliged to fight to prevent herself from yielding to him, but now she had done so, and there had been a brief moment of pleasure, but surely it was a very small reward that hardly satisfied the terrible, aching love she felt for Damon. His breath tickled her cheek and she snuggled closer against him. She was very innocent, she knew that, and Damon had told her she would understand soon. She would have to trust him, she thought drowsily.

It was still dark when she woke again. She was still wrapped in Damon's arms, but something was different about the body that lay entwined with hers: he was aroused. Gently she shifted her position, turning on her side until she was face to face with him. She could not see his eyes, but she guessed that he was awake. Her hand snaked up around his neck and she moved her head to kiss him gently. Immediately his arms tightened about her. The gentle kiss became a long, languorous one. She felt his tongue flicker against her own and the sensation sent ripples of excitement down through her body. Damon's hands began to caress her, gently moving over her ribs and into the deep curve of her waist, then down over the swell of her hip and once again those long, sensitive fingers moved between her thighs, sliding into her and moving with tantalising slowness while an aching wave of desire was slowly building within her. She began to move restlessly on the bed, her breath coming in short gasps and still the desire was growing. She groaned, unwilling and unable to escape those teasing fingers that were rousing such exquisite feelings. Suddenly she knew the wave of desire was about to break, and at that moment Damon shifted his weight to lie above her. She lifted her hips to receive him and felt him moving within her, rousing her to a fever of excitement so that she matched him move for move and she cried out, arching her back and digging her fingers into his skin as he held her at the crest of the wave before she subsided on a sobbing, shuddering sigh.

Damon collapsed beside her and she clung to him, saying impulsively, 'Oh, thank you!'

'I take it that was better?'

'Oh, yes, I never knew—'

He laughed softly and kissed the tip of her nose. 'No, how could you?'

'Did—did you enjoy it too?' she asked shyly.

'Very much.'

'You are sure?' She frowned in the darkness. 'You spent so much time giving me pleasure, there must be more for you—'

He kissed her.

'There will be many other nights, my darling, when we will spend hours pleasuring each other. Now, though, you must go back to your own room before the servants are abroad. You must be respectable Miss Wrenn for a little longer.'

He helped her into her nightdress, then put his own garish dressing gown about her shoulders.

'You will take my banyan. I will not risk you catching a chill,' he told her.

'But if I am seen wearing this—'

'You will not be, if you go now.'

He pulled on his nightshirt and guided her back through the dressing room. She was surprised to see that the candles had not quite burned out.

'Here.' Damon found her a fresh candle and lit it from one guttering flame. He crossed to the door, opened it and looked out. 'Go now, quickly,' he whispered. As she passed him in the doorway, he stopped her and took another swift kiss. 'Goodnight, dearest Ju. You had best stay away from me in the morning, for I fear Richard will guess our secret if he only sees me look at you.'

After the warmth of Damon's arms, Juliana's bed looked cold and uninviting. She pulled the banyan around her and lay down upon the covers, taking comfort from the feel of the garish fabric, the faint muskiness that reminded her of Damon. The first grey fingers of dawn were already creeping into the room, and Juliana slept only fitfully, her mind too full to rest. It was still early when she eventually decided to get dressed and go to the schoolroom to prepare for the day's lessons. She pulled out a white muslin dress embroidered with white spring flowers about the hem and sleeves. Although the lack of colour made it suitable for a mourning dress, she had considered it too ornate for general use, but today her mood was buoyant and she wanted to wear something to reflect it. She picked up Damon's dressing gown and hugged it to her, knowing it must be returned. With no fires to light in the bedrooms, the servants would not come upstairs for some time yet. She smiled to herself—the temptation to see Damon was too great. She would take the banyan back to him. She would scratch quietly on the door, and if he was asleep she would leave it outside his room. If he was awake, however... She shivered deliciously at the thought.

It was barely light enough to see her way, but as she came out onto the gallery she could hear footsteps in the hall below as the servants made their preparations for the coming day. Juliana hung back, waiting until the hall was empty and there was no possibility of being seen, then she slipped across to the entrance to the west wing. She padded silently into the corridor and stopped as she heard the creak of a hinge. At the end of the passage a bar of early morning sunlight cut through the gloom as a door was thrown wide. It illuminated the bust of Milton, making the marble glow. Juliana watched, unable to move, as Damon stepped out of the room. He was wearing only his nightshirt, and one arm was stretched behind him, as if holding on to someone within the chamber. He looked back and said softly,

'Go back to bed, Veronique.'

Juliana whisked herself out of sight and leaned against the wall, shaking. Part of her wanted to confront Damon, but her legs would not carry her, and even as she realised this she heard the soft click of his door. For several moments she remained, motionless, her brain refusing to function. Then, in a daze she pushed herself away from the wall and forced her wayward limbs to take her along the now empty corridor. *Another moment and this was all I would have known. I should have seen nothing. I would have been happy.* The thought came to her in a detached way, rousing no emotions. At Damon's door she laid the dressing gown on the floor and walked away.

There were no tears. Juliana shut herself in her room,

but would not allow herself to cry; the children would be up soon and swollen, red eyes would only invite comment and questions. She curled up on the bed and tried to think calmly, to persuade herself there was some reasonable explanation for what she had seen, but she knew there could be none. She recalled sitting in Cousin Pettigrew's kitchen with Lawrence the footman. 'Devil Collingham, pleasuring three women in one night...'

Is that how it was? Had Damon taken her to his bed last night merely because he could? Surely not, surely he loved her—but if that was so, then why had he gone to Veronique? Her hand crept to her cheek. She had no experience of this. Perhaps her innocence had left him unsatisfied—a lowering thought. She blinked away a tear—she would not cry. Desperately she sought another explanation. Sir Richard was convinced that Lady Ormiston was involved in some intrigue. If that was so, was it not possible that Damon had gone to her room to discover the truth? Juliana found that explanation no more acceptable. Having admitted that she loved Damon, she realised that she would not share him with any other woman. She *could* not share him. She pressed her clenched fist against her mouth.

'Oh, Damon, what have you done?'

The morning lesson dragged by, and if the children noticed their governess was unusually quiet they did not say so. Juliana felt as if she had split in two, and that she was some disembodied spirit, watching herself going through the routine of teaching the children their letters, correcting their mistakes. She excused herself from luncheon and afterwards set the children to drawing in their sketchbooks, when her bruised and tired mind could think of no other occupation for them. The clatter of hooves in the stable yard took her to the window and she looked out to see Damon and Lady Ormiston riding out through the gates. It was too much; the pain was too great to be borne in silence. Leaving the children to Nurse's watchful eye, Juliana made her way downstairs.

Sir Richard was strolling through the shrubbery. He stopped and turned when he heard Juliana behind him.

'Miss Wrenn, have you come to enjoy the air? I confess I thought the rain would continue all day. Damon and Lady Ormiston are taking advantage of this dry spell to go riding.'

'I know.' Juliana came up to him. 'I saw them leave. I— I wanted to talk to you, Sir Richard.'

His brows rose fractionally, but he smiled and held out his arm for her. 'Then shall we walk?'

Juliana strolled beside him, trying to find words that would not expose her inner turmoil. 'You said you thought Lady Ormiston to be in league with Mr Leeson.'

'That is correct, Miss Wrenn. I have no proof, of course, but I have my suspicions.'

'And…is Dam—is Major Collingwood helping you to discover the truth?'

'Well, yes, he said he wanted to help. That is why he is gone out with the lady now. He thinks if we set her at her ease, she will make some slip.'

Juliana closed her eyes. 'And, M-Major Collingham can be quite…ruthless, I think.' She forced herself to speak normally.

Sir Richard considered the matter. 'He is a soldier, Miss Wrenn. He was trained to be ruthless to achieve his goals. Yet to those fortunate enough to win his friendship, he can be very kind.' He looked down at her, a slight frown in his eyes. 'These are odd questions, Miss Wrenn—what is on your mind?'

Juliana looked down at the ground. If her face showed only a fraction of the anguish she felt, it would not do to let him see it.

'I—I merely wonder how far the Major will go to—to put Lady Ormiston at her ease.'

'Ah, now I understand your concerns.' He squeezed her arm. 'You need not fear that Damon is in danger of losing his heart to the lovely Veronique, Miss Wrenn. He may flatter her and flirt with her, but only until he can discover her purpose in being here.'

Greatly daring, she said, 'But they were l-lovers once, were they not?' Sir Richard hesitated. She continued, 'You may be frank with me, sir. Damon has already told me of it.'

'Well, then, yes, but it was a couple of years ago and there was never any serious intention. Good lord, Miss Wrenn, I hope you will not hold it against Damon, that he has had a mistress?'

'Heavens, no.' She forced a laugh. 'I am merely trying to understand the situation.'

Sir Richard nodded, and patted her arm. 'You need have no fear, Miss Wrenn. Trust Damon to look after everything.'

By dinner time Juliana had developed a sick headache and she sent the children down to the drawing room with Nurse to say goodnight. In the silence of the nursery wing Juliana lay on her bed, watching the summer light slowly fading from the sky outside her window. The carving on the tester above her head had disappeared into a black shadow by the time she heard the children come back upstairs.

'Can we not go in and wish Miss Wrenn goodnight?' Wilhelmina's piping voice was directly outside her door.

'Not tonight, dearie. In all likelihood Miss Wrenn is asleep by now, and we should let her rest.' Nurse's kindly tones made her smile in spite of her unhappiness. 'Come along now, and you can tell me what story you would like me to read to you tonight…'

She should get up and go to them, to make sure they

were settled securely in their beds, but she felt too dull, too tired to move. She closed her eyes and tried to sleep.

'Juliana.'

There was a soft knock on the door. Juliana opened her eyes to find the room washed in blue-grey moonlight. She was curled up in a ball on the bed and did not want to get up.

'Juliana.'

Damon's voice called again from the other side of the door, more urgent this time. She remembered that her door was not locked, and she could not be sure that the Major would go away if she did not answer him. She eased herself off the bed and padded to the door to open it a little. Damon was standing outside, still dressed for dinner, but his loosened cravat suggested that it was late. The light from the candle he was holding flickered over his face, illuminating the upward curve of his lips, but not his eyes.

'So you are awake,' he murmured. 'Will you let me come in?'

'No. No, it—it is unseemly.' His frown made her add quickly, 'Go to the schoolroom, and I will join you there.'

Juliana closed the door and stood for a moment in the moonlight. She must do this. It could not be delayed. She must talk to him. She shook out her dress and made her way to the schoolroom, where the Major was lighting candles. He turned and smiled at her as she came in.

'Poor Ju, is your headache so very bad? Let me kiss it better.' Damon started towards her, but she stepped back, putting up her hands to ward him off. He stopped. 'What's this? Ju, you are shaking. Did I frighten you last night?'

'No.' She twisted her hands together. 'I returned your banyan this morning.'

He grinned. 'I know. Benns fell over it when he brought my hot water.'

She did not feel inclined to smile. 'I saw you. I s-saw you coming from Lady Ormiston's room.'

'Did you.'

'You do not deny it?'

'Deny it?' He laughed. 'No, of course not. I—'

She did not wait for him to finish. His laugh had seared through the brittle control she had placed on herself all day. A wave of anger swept over her.

'How dare you!' Her voice shook with rage. 'How dare you sneer at me—or at her! What a fine day's work you made of it, Major Collingham. Within four-and-twenty hours you have rid yourself of a fiancée, compromised me beyond redemption and made up the rift with your ex-lover.'

His black brows snapped together. 'For God's sake, Ju, you know it is important we learn Veronique's motives for being here.'

'And did your seduction do the trick?' She threw the words at him as she paced feverishly up and down the room. She was beyond reason, wanting only to hurt him, to make him suffer as she was doing.

'I did not seduce her—I did not touch her. Listen to me.' He caught her arm. 'Listen to me, damn you!'

'Let go of me!' she cried, struggling to free her arm. 'I saw you, Damon—you were coming out of her room *dressed only in your nightshirt!*'

'I had no choice since you had my damned dressing gown!'

He released her and stepped away. 'For Heaven's sake, Ju, let me explain why—'

'There is nothing to explain!' she interrupted him. 'It is perfectly clear—she had been making eyes at you all evening, and you could not resist, could you, *Devil* Collingham.'

He gave a crack of mirthless laughter. *'My reputation, Iago, my reputation!'*

'Yes, you may joke about it,' she threw at him, shaking

with fury. 'Did you laugh at me, too? Why did you take me to your bed, Damon? Because you *could*, I suppose.'

She noted with savage satisfaction how his face paled at that. His mouth tightened.

'You have a poor opinion of me, madam.'

She threw up her head. 'I have *no* opinion of you!' She saw the anger flare in his eyes and raised her chin defiantly. 'No, that's not true,' she said slowly, deliberately. 'I hate you.'

The words hung in the air, echoing through the stillness as they faced each other across the room, each now in a towering rage. She saw the muscle working in his cheek and knew his anger was barely contained.

'If I am so disgusting to you, then you will not wish to stay here.'

'I shall have Thomas and Amy ready to leave by noon. If you will order your carriage to take us to Blackburn, we will trouble you no further.'

'Where will you go?'

'That is none of your concern.'

'Damnation, woman, of course it is my concern. You have no money—or do you plan to make a living lying on your back?'

She threw him a look of scorn. 'Alas, I do not have your expertise in that area.'

'You would soon pick it up.'

She wanted to fly at him, to claw out those eyes that looked at her with such fury, but she was close to tears, only her anger kept her going. She turned on her heel and walked away. She hurried to her room as fast as she could without running, her spine tingling with anticipation—any moment she expected to hear his step behind her, to feel his hand on her shoulder, but he did not follow her.

Chapter Twenty-Four

When Juliana announced to her pupils that she would be leaving, her words were met with a stunned silence. They were in the schoolroom, with only Gwendoline, Wilhelmina and Nurse present. Juliana had already given the news to Thomas and Amy and set them to work packing their few belongings. She had forestalled their questions by saying she would explain everything later, but Gwendoline and her sister were not to be fobbed off so easily.

'By why?' cried Wilhelmina. 'I do not want you to leave.'

'My contract here was only ever a temporary one, Minna.'

'But it was until September,' said Gwendoline, 'Papa can insist you stay until then.'

Juliana hesitated, then said carefully, 'I have been offered a position I cannot afford to ignore, and—and your father has agreed to let me go.'

'Well, he had no right to do so!' declared Gwendoline, two spots of colour staining her cheeks. 'You said I could decide if you should leave us!'

'No, Gwendoline,' she replied gently. 'We agreed that if you found me intolerable I would remove as soon as we arrived here.'

Wilhelmina ran to Juliana and clambered on to her lap

while Gwendoline came more slowly. She put an arm about Juliana's neck and laid her cheek on her shoulder, saying, 'I shall miss you.'

Juliana blinked away her tears.

'And I shall miss you both, very much. And you, Nurse.'

'Oh, dearie, we have all grown so fond of you.' The old woman shook her head and wiped away a tear. 'It will seem strange without you, and what are the children going to do for their lessons?'

'Yes,' said Wilhelmina, sitting up. 'You cannot go until Papa has found somebody else to teach us.'

'I'm afraid I must, my love.' She looked round as Thomas came into the room.

'Well, I suppose you have told them,' he said, observing their miserable faces.

Amy came running in behind him and went immediately to put her arms about Wilhelmina. 'It is perfectly horrid, and I don't want to go away from here,' she said.

'I d-don't want you to go either,' muttered Minna, her lip trembling. 'You are my *bestest* friend.'

'Perhaps you can write to one another,' suggested Nurse.

Juliana said nothing. She had no intention of giving Damon her direction, wherever it might turn out to be. She could not be sure he would not come after her.

'Well, we shall see,' was all that she would say when Gwendoline pressed her.

'And it means we won't be going to the fair this afternoon,' grumbled Thomas.

Gwen looked up.

'No, and neither shall we, for Papa said we could only go if Juliana would escort us.'

Thomas turned to his sister. 'Could we not stay for one more day, Ju, please?'

She had to steel herself to withstand the four pairs of eyes fixed beseechingly upon her.

'I am afraid not, my dears. Never mind, there will be other fairs. Now, our coach is not due until twelve. We still have a little time—what would you like to do?'

'We could finish the pictures for our journal,' suggested Gwendoline.

'Oh, yes,' said Wilhelmina. 'Then we shall have something with which to remember you.'

Juliana settled the children at the big table, but they were none of them inclined to work, and had achieved very little when Giles came in, frowning.

'Juliana, I have just come from Papa. He says I am to take Gwen and Minna to the fair today because you are leaving us.'

'Oh, that is famous,' declared Juliana. 'They were disappointed to think they would have to miss it.'

'Yes, well, never mind that! I want to know why you are leaving, and why so suddenly?'

Juliana was studying Wilhelmina's drawing and did not look up. 'Goodness, such blunt questions,' she said lightly. 'I—I have received a very good offer and agreed with your papa that I will leave immediately.'

Amy looked up, about to speak, but a kick under the table from Thomas made her close her mouth again.

'Well, if it is so, I suppose you must go as soon as possible,' admitted Giles grudgingly. 'But it is very sudden.'

Juliana straightened and summoned a tiny smile. 'Sometimes that is best—I do not like long goodbyes.'

'No, of course not.' Giles looked down at his boots, then blurted out, 'I shall be sorry to see you go.'

'Thank you, Giles, but you will do very well without me, I am sure.'

He nodded, looked solemn for a few moments, then the twinkle returned to his eyes.

'There is *some* good news today. Lady Ormiston is leaving, too.'

'No!' exclaimed Gwendoline.

'Yes. She came to the study while I was with Papa and I heard her telling him that she was off to join Lord Ormiston in Scotland. She's ordered her carriage and is even now preparing to set off. Good thing, too.'

'Don't you like her?' asked Thomas.

Giles pulled a face.

'Lord, no. Silly creature. Set fire to her curtains the other night: went into her dressing room to see to her maid, who had disturbed her with her coughing, and left her candle unattended. When she saw the flames she went screaming fit to burst to m'father, when anyone but a nodcock would have made at least some attempt to put out the flames. As it was, that dour-faced maid of hers pulled down the curtains and stamped on them, so that by the time Papa got to the room there was nothing for him to do.'

Juliana froze. Was that the reason Damon had gone to her room? Why had he not told her? Why had she not listened to him?

'Where did you learn all this?' asked Gwendoline, round-eyed.

'From Papa. He was telling Sir Richard when I came upon them in the library yesterday. At first he didn't see me, until Sir Richard indicated that I had come in, and Papa stopped, then he decided to continue, saying he thought it was as well if I knew what "that damn fool woman" had been doing—his words, Nurse, not mine,' Giles added hastily as Nurse uttered a faint protest.

Juliana leaned on the back of Minna's chair, hoping her knees would not buckle beneath her. She had been mistaken, but it was too late to go back—she had said she hated him. He could never forgive that. A leaden despondency was added to her misery.

'So, I had best go and make sure the gig will be ready for us this afternoon,' Giles continued. 'Oh, and before I forget—Juliana, Papa says you are to see Brasher before you leave.'

'So you will be able to buy those ribbons after all, Gwendoline,' said Juliana with a smile, when Giles had left them.

'Yes, but there will be no one to put them in my hair for me.'

Juliana thought it wise to ignore her grumbles, and did her best to turn their interest again to their drawing.

At twelve precisely the carriage rolled up at the door. Juliana tied the strings of her bonnet under her chin and hurried the children into the hall. She stepped outside to direct the footmen, who were putting her small trunk and portmanteau into the boot, and as she came back indoors she saw Major Collingham coming down the stairs, his children beside him.

'Did you think to leave without saying goodbye?' he barked.

'I knew you would be at luncheon, and I said my goodbyes to Giles and the girls in the schoolroom.'

'But you would not eat with us. True, it is only a cold collation, since all the servants are off to the fair, but it would have set you up for your journey.'

There was accusation in his tone, and because it was not without foundation Juliana could not meet his eyes.

'Mrs Plumstead has packed up a hamper for us.'

She watched the children taking a polite leave of each other, their solemn little faces mirroring the grave looks of the adults. Wilhelmina was asking Amy if she had seen Lady Arabella, and Juliana was only just in time to stop the two girls running off in search of the doll.

'There is no time for that, Amy, I am sorry. Enough now, we must go to the coach.' She gave Amy a little push, then turned towards the Major. 'Pray give my regards to Sir Richard for me—he is out riding, I believe.'

She went to follow Giles and the children out of the door, but Damon caught her arm.

'You told the girls you have obtained another post,' he said in a low voice. 'Why did you not tell them the truth?'

She pulled herself free. 'They worship you,' she said. 'I would do nothing to change that.' She waited, her eyes fixed on the marbled floor.

Ask me to stay. Silently she begged him to speak. One word, one sign, and she would fall into his arms and admit that she had been wrong. If he loved her, surely he would not let her go. She remembered the night in Rushton Spencer when he had said he loved her—he had even threatened to take her by force rather than let her leave him. *Then* he had been desperate to keep her; now his very silence told her that his passion had died. Her resistance had been the attraction; once she had given in to him, he had lost interest in her. Stifling a sigh, Juliana turned and hurried outside, stooping to hug Gwendoline and Wilhelmina and to take Giles's hand for a moment before she stepped quickly up into the carriage. Then the door was shut and they were moving away down the drive. Amy and Thomas hung out of the window, waving furiously, but Juliana dared not look back. Tears were very close, and in an effort to drive them away she lay back against the squabs and closed her eyes.

From the doorway Damon watched the carriage bowling along the winding drive. He scarcely noticed Giles hurrying his sisters back inside to collect their cloaks, telling them that if they tarried he would be off to the fair without them. When they had gone, the silence settled about him as he watched the carriage disappear amongst the trees.

'Damnation, have I missed her?' Sir Richard was hurrying across the hall. 'Plumstead told me when I came in that Miss Wrenn was leaving, but I thought I should have time to change out of my muddy clothes.'

Damon turned back to fix his eyes again on the wooded horizon.

'You are too late, my friend. She is gone. I have lost her.' His hands balled into fists. 'I have lost her, Rick. She saw me coming out of Veronique's room after the fire and thought—'

Sir Richard put a hand on his shoulder.

'Nonsense. Miss Wrenn is a sensible young woman. Surely when you explained it all...'

'I didn't. I didn't even try to explain it. I lost my temper.' He rubbed his hand wearily across his eyes. 'I was angry that she should doubt me. I don't know what I said, something damnable...I have driven her away.'

'Well, then, go after her, man. I have never known you at a loss with a woman before.'

'This one is different.'

Sir Richard smiled. 'You say that because you care for her. Go after her, Damon.'

'If I thought there was a chance—' He broke off and shook his head. 'It is too late, my friend. I disgust her. When we said goodbye just now, she could not even look at me. She....she hates me, and with good reason.' He turned suddenly and drove the side of his fist against the doorpost. 'She thinks I tricked her. Well, perhaps it is better this way—I am over a dozen years her senior. Let her find another, younger man, one more deserving of her than I could ever be.' That thought could not be borne. He shook it off and drew himself up. 'Enough. Come, Richard, there is something to celebrate at least. Did Plumstead tell you that Veronique has also quit the house? She went off to Scotland this morning.'

'Has she, by God!' Sir Richard cocked an eyebrow. 'So soon after you refused to fall for her little seduction? Perhaps I have misjudged her—mayhap you were her only reason for coming here.'

Damon's lip curled. 'You think me that attractive, that she would follow me the length of the country to win me back?'

Sir Richard grinned. 'Actually, no, my friend! My suspicion still stands, but there is little I can do about it at this moment.'

'True.' Damon pushed himself away from the wall and linked his arm through his friend's. 'Come on into the library. Giles is taking the girls to the fair, most of the servants have already set out, so we are left to our own devices. I suggest we get damnably drunk!'

'Where are we going?'

Juliana roused herself. Amy was tugging at her sleeve. Blackthorpe and its park had long since disappeared and they were travelling through countryside she did not recognise. She took off her bonnet and tossed it aside, hoping it might ease her headache.

'To Blackburn. I shall look for work there.'

Amy looked puzzled. 'But I thought you already had a post.'

'Silly, that was only what she told everyone,' said Thomas. 'So they would not worry about us. That's correct, is it not, Ju?'

'There is no need for anyone to concern themselves over us,' she replied firmly. 'We shall do very well.'

'But you did not see Mr Brasher before you left, did you?' persisted Thomas. 'So we have no money.'

Juliana looked at their anxious faces and was determined to be cheerful. 'I have my pearls to sell, and Papa's watch. That will give us a little money until I can find work.'

'Well, if you are going to sell your pearls, you might like

to take these too.' Thomas dug his hand into the pocket of his coat. 'They are only glass, but quite pretty, so you might get something for them.'

Juliana stared. There on his open palm lay a pair of exquisite diamond earrings.

Chapter Twenty-Five

'Thomas! Wh-where did you get them?'

'I ought to have given them back to Minna, I know,' he confessed, looking a little shamefaced, 'but to be honest I had forgotten all about them until now.'

'What pretty beads,' said Amy, craning her neck to see them.

'I don't think they are beads,' murmured Juliana. She looked closely at her brother. 'Tell me where you found them, Tom. The truth, now.'

He flushed. 'I didn't steal them, if that's what you think.'

Juliana managed a little smile. 'No, of course not, but I must know where they came from.'

'No, well, it was when I mended Minna's doll. Giles had gone out, so I said I would look at it. The arm had come off, you may remember, and before I could mend it I had to take off the dress. That was when I found these earrings. They must have been caught up in the material in some way.'

Juliana was thinking quickly.

'Could they—could they have been hidden *inside* the doll?' she asked.

Thomas shrugged.

'I suppose so, the body is hollow, but I did not notice where they came from, only that as I removed the dress they fell on to the workbench. I was in the workroom next to the stables at the time, and I didn't want to leave them around, so I put them into my pocket, meaning to give them to Minna when I gave her the doll, but it was getting late, and I had to hurry to repair it and get her back before Minna went to bed and—well, I forgot all about the earrings.' He looked up. 'If you like, I will put them in a letter and post them back to Blackthorpe.'

Juliana picked up the earrings and looked at them. 'I think they are rather too valuable to be sent in the post, Thomas. I think they are diamonds.'

'Diamonds!' He laughed. 'That's silly—who would give Minna such a thing? She is just a baby.'

'Perhaps they belonged to her grandmama and she hid them in the doll at Kewhurst.'

'Oh, Lady Arabella was never at Kewhurst,' piped up Amy. 'She was given to Minna in London.'

'Oh?' said Juliana. 'How do you know that, Amy?'

'She told me all about it. She and Gwendoline went with their aunt to visit the dressmaker, and one of the assistants gave Minna the doll to stop her crying.'

'A dressmaker?'

Amy nodded.

'Minna and Gwen didn't like her because she took no notice of them, and spoke to their aunt in her funny French voice.'

Juliana sat back, her face pale. 'She was French?' she said at last.

'Yes, Aunt Louisa says she is the best dressmaker in London.'

A succession of thoughts and ideas were running riot through Juliana's head. If the dressmaker was so very fashionable, it was very likely that Lady Ormiston would know her. Her thoughts raced on—Lady Ormiston had left this morning, and Wilhelmina's doll was missing…

'We must turn back!' She sat up and pulled the check string.

'Back!' the children cried out in unison and she held up a hand to stem their questions while she issued her instructions to the driver. When the carriage was moving again, she dropped the earrings into her reticule and sat back to find Thomas looking at her with anxious eyes.

'I am sorry, Ju, I did not know they were diamonds, I never thought…'

'And why should you?' She patted his knee. 'I shall give them to Sir Richard. He will know what to do with them.'

Amy clapped her hands. 'I will be able to see Minna again!'

'No, my love. You forget, Giles is taking the girls to the fair this afternoon. I shall stop only long enough to give the diamonds to Sir Richard, then we must be on our way again. But pray do not look so gloomy, my loves. Who knows, there may well be a reward for finding these jewels.'

'A reward!' said Thomas, brightening. 'Then it should be mine, since I discovered them.'

'Indeed it should,' admitted Juliana, a glimmer of humour lightening her depression. 'But perhaps you would be very good and let me borrow a little of it, just until I can establish myself, of course.'

Thomas drew himself up. 'Don't worry, I shall look after us all, since I am head of the household now.'

By the time the coachman had found a place to turn around and they were at the palings of Blackthorpe Hall, an hour had passed. Juliana called to the coachman to drive in through the woods.

'We shall save a good twenty minutes if we take the back lane rather than drive all the way round to the front gates,' she told the children. 'I am not too proud to walk in through the housekeeper's door.'

However, when the carriage had made its way up the muddy drive that led to the servants' quarters, the house was strangely quiet.

'It's the fair, miss,' said the footman as he opened the carriage door for her. 'The master always lets the servants go off at mid day to attend the fair.'

The tone of his voice indicated that he too should have been at the fair rather than escorting a governess and her family around the countryside. Juliana suppressed her inclination to apologise.

'Pray stay here with the children,' she said. 'I shall only be a few moments and we can be on our way again.'

The outer doors at the back of the house were all locked, and she wondered if she would be obliged to go to the front door after all, but the coachman suggested she should try the side door leading in from the stable yard.

'There's a wicket gate into the yard in the wall over there, miss, and you should find a key to the side door underneath the bucket beside the doorway.' The coachman touched his hat and gave her a fatherly smile. 'It's the way here at Blackthorpe, so we don't have to wake up the porter every time we comes in late.'

Juliana found the key just as the driver had said. She had just unlocked the door when she heard the faint jangle of harness and the scraping of hooves upon gravel. She walked towards the arch and saw the back wheels of a travelling coach pulled up on the front drive. Moving cautiously forward, she could see the driver hunched in his seat, then came the sound of a loud, hacking cough from inside the coach. Juliana froze. Lady Ormiston's maid was in the carriage. That could only mean that Veronique had returned.

Juliana hurried back to the side door and quietly entered the house. There was no sound from the lower rooms. Without its servants the house seemed eerily quiet. Juliana had just reached the great hall when she heard a noise from upstairs, as if some piece of furniture had been knocked over. Her heart beating wildly, she ran swiftly up to the landing. Which way? The corridor to the main bedrooms was silent, deserted. She went back to the gallery, straining her ears to catch the slightest noise. There was the faint rumble of voices ahead of her. Following the sound, she realised it was coming from the nursery wing. Some instinct told her that she must not be heard. She crept along, moving her feet cautiously over the old boards, thankful that she remembered which ones creaked. She was halfway along the corridor when she heard a groan quickly followed by a laugh, brittle and tinkling as glass. Common sense told her to turn and run, to get help, but her feet continued to carry her forward and she could hear the voices more clearly now. They were in the school-room. The door stood half-open, allowing a band of strong, white light into the passage. Damon's deep tones were un-mistakable and Juliana's heart clenched when she heard the lilting tones of Lady Ormiston.

'So tell me where they are, Damon.'

'I have no idea.'

'Come now, Damon. I have my pistols, you see, and I know how to use them. Would you have me kill your friend?'

'Of course not, but I tell you I haven't seen the damned stones.'

'Be sensible, *mon ami*. They were in the doll when it left London—Charles swore to me the doll was intact when he caught up with you.'

'So it was you who set him to follow us.'

Veronique's heartless laugh echoed through the quiet rooms.

'Such a simple task, to recover the doll. Those two imbeciles should have managed it in Bond Street, before you left town, but they bungled the attempt. So I sent Charles to bring it back to me. I thought he would accomplish it easily, but no, he panicked and snatched the child as well. What a pity your bullet did not kill him, Damon. He was such a fool.'

'Was?'

'You do not think I could let him live, knowing so much? He was weak, Damon. One should never deal with weak men. Now you, *mon cher*, you are not weak.'

'Neither am I a fool, madam. I can see only one way this can end.'

Juliana marvelled that Damon could sound so cool. She edged closer to the doorway, desperate to know what was going on. She peered through the crack between the door and the frame and what she saw made her feel suddenly faint. On the far side of the room Sir Richard was slumped against one wall, blood trickling from a gash on his head. Damon stood a little in front of him, as if to shield him from further attack. She could not see Veronique, but guessed from Damon's watchful look that she was standing just inside the room. Juliana moved forward a little more towards the shaft of light, then drew back quickly. Veronique was standing in the doorway, holding a slim silver pistol at her side. In that brief glance Juliana had not seen her other hand, but she had spoken of pistols, and from her stance she guessed she was levelling another one directly at Damon. His next words confirmed her fears and a cold chill ran through her.

'Perhaps before you kill me, you will tell me how those diamonds came to be in my daughter's doll?'

'It is a fashion doll, of no interest to anyone but the *modiste*. We arranged for the doll to come from Paris; it should have been foolproof, but her assistant gave the doll to one of your infants before the diamonds had been removed.'

'And without them you cannot pay for the ship that is to snatch Bonaparte from St Helena.'

'So you know of that, too,' purred Veronique. 'You are too clever, Damon. I was going to spare you, for the sake of our former friendship—'

'Even though I would not make love to you the other night?'

'I am generous, *mon cher*, I can forgive you for that. I thought I would lock you in here while I go in search of your children. Now I will have to shoot you after all.'

Juliana knew an impulse to hurl herself into the room, to shield the Major as he was shielding his friend, but it was not possible. Veronique stood between them. She looked around helplessly. She must do *something*.

'You will not touch the children, madam.' Damon spoke quickly, his tone cold as ice.

Lady Ormiston laughed harshly.

'No? And what can you do to stop me? In a few moments you will be dead, and then I shall wait on the road until the children come back from the fair. I shall make them tell me what they have done with the diamonds.'

'I tell you, they know nothing.'

'My dear sir, if you cannot tell me, what else am I to do but ask the children? You tell me the doll has not been out of their possession, so one of them must know about the stones.'

Damon's voice cut through the air like steel, quiet and deadly. 'If you touch them, I swear I will kill you!'

Juliana flinched, tensing herself for the inevitable shot, and when it did not come she knew she dare not wait any longer. She began to inch forward until she was directly behind Lady Ormiston. She was in the light now and clearly visible. She prayed that Veronique's attention would remain fixed on Damon, and that he would not give her away by so much as a glance. The lilting, taunting voice continued.

'No, no, Damon. It is *I* holding the pistol, not you. But I have tarried long enough, let us end this.'

Veronique raised her arm to take careful aim. At the same time Juliana grasped the only object within her reach. She swept the bust of Prometheus from its pedestal and raised it above her head as she stepped forward.

'You will—not—touch—my man!' she gasped as she brought the bust crashing down. Veronique had become aware of someone behind her, but even as she looked round the bust shattered against her head before she could squeeze the trigger. The weapon fell from her fingers as Veronique crumpled to the floor.

'Oh, well done, Ju.'

There was the faintest tremor in Damon's voice. He strode forward and dropped to his knees beside Veronique. Juliana leaned against the doorpost, staring in horror at the lifeless form.

'Don't worry, you haven't killed her, although you might have done so if that bust had been marble instead of ala-baster, and Veronique had a less flamboyant taste in hats.'

Juliana looked at the shattered bust and the crumpled wreck of Lady Ormiston's fashionable bonnet, the ostrich feathers fluttering gently amongst the fragments of alabaster.

'I am glad I am not a murderess,' she said unsteadily. A movement across the room caught her attention and she hurried to Sir Richard, who was beginning to stir.

'Be still, sir.' She knelt beside him. 'Do not try to rise until I have looked at that cut on your head.'

'I have a damnable headache,' he muttered.

She took out her clean handkerchief and pressed it to the wound. 'You have had a nasty blow to the head.' She looked at the red rag on the floor beside him.

'Oh—it is Minna's doll.'

'Aye,' said Sir Richard. 'I heard a noise and looked in here to see the thing lying on the floor. I bent to pick it up and as I turned something hit me.'

'She used the poker on you,' added the Major.

'Damned foolish of me to be taken unawares.' Sir Richard winced as he put his fingers to his bruised head.

'Even more foolish of me to come running in,' growled Damon. 'Veronique had hidden herself behind the door and caught us both.' He helped Sir Richard up on to a chair. 'That was just before you arrived, Ju.'

Leaving Sir Richard to hold the handkerchief to his brow, she dug her hand into her reticule. 'I wish I had been a little earlier, then you might have been prepared for her. She was looking for these, I think.' The two men stared at the diamonds winking on her palm. 'Thomas discovered them when he mended Minna's doll for her, but he thought they were glass and forgot about them.'

Damon gave a low whistle. 'The Borghese earrings, I presume, Rick?'

'Yes, by God. Well done, Miss Wrenn. With these and what the lady has let slip today we have a case, without doubt. I shall take her back to London and interrogate her further, of course, and hope we can flush out the rest of the group.'

'Amy told me Minna was given the doll when she went with Lady Varley to visit her dressmaker.'

'Madam Fleurie,' said Damon. 'That would explain Louisa's postscript on her letter that she wanted a doll returned. I didn't know what she meant and gave it no more thought.'

'Better and better.' Sir Richard grinned. He stood up, a little unsteadily, and pointed to Lady Ormiston. 'She's coming round. Damon, have you somewhere secure we can keep her until I can take her to London?'

'Aye, there's a cellar with a stout door, and nothing in it save a few boxes. She will not be able to harm herself or others from there.'

Juliana held out the diamonds to Sir Richard. 'I have done now, and had best be on my way—'

Sir Richard gripped her hand. 'Not yet, if you please, Miss Wrenn. I would be glad of your help in cleaning up this cut on my head. Foolishly I have let my man go off with the others. He has his eye on that pretty little chambermaid who comes to make up the bed and I thought it would be cruel to keep him here. Had I known this would happen, of course, I would never have consented to his going…'

She felt the corners of her mouth lifting almost reluctantly.

'There is a pump in the kitchen,' said Damon, stooping to gather Lady Ormiston into his arms. 'Perhaps Miss Wrenn would be good enough to escort you there, Rick, and clean you up a little while I see to our prisoner.'

Juliana hung back, unhappiness welling within her. Damon would not look at her, could not even bring himself to talk to her, it seemed. He would not give her an opportunity to admit she had been mistaken. She wanted to be away, to leave the house and enjoy her misery to the full. Sir Richard's grip on her hand tightened.

'Please, Miss Wrenn.'

His gentle tone worked: she could not ignore his plea for help. She nodded.

'Of course, sir. Lean on me.'

The kitchen was unnaturally tidy, the big table scrubbed and empty and all the copper and pewter dishes put away. Juliana helped Sir Richard to a chair, then went over to the sink where she began to pump water into a small bowl. Whipping a cloth from the drying rack as she came back to the table, she proceeded to clean the blood from Sir Richard's brow with gentle strokes.

'Let us hope I shall look a little less frightening when you have finished,' he remarked as she worked away.

'You look almost respectable already, sir, although there is a little blood on your cravat.' She put down her cloth. 'There, I have finished. The wound is not too deep and has stopped bleeding, so I think we need not subject you to the indignity of a bandage. Now, if you will excuse me, Sir Richard, Thomas and Amy will be wondering what has happened to me.'

'Must you go?' he asked her. 'It is very late to be setting off.'

'I know; that is why I must make haste.'

'Is your new employer expecting you? Let a servant ride over with a note, to explain.'

'No. I will not stay in this house.'

Her voice broke on the words. He gripped her hands.

'At least give me your direction. There could be a substantial reward…nay, I am sure of it—for the capture of Lady Ormiston, and for the diamonds—you must have your share. Tell me where you are going.'

Juliana closed her eyes and sank down on to a chair. Exhaustion weighed her down. She said dully, 'I will not lie to you, Sir Richard. I have nowhere to go when I leave here, which is why I must go now if I am to find decent lodging for us tonight.'

'Oh, my poor girl—' He broke off.

A hasty step sounded outside the door and the next moment Damon came in.

'Well, she is safe enough, although not too happy with her quarters.' His lip curled. 'She's not so much to be pitied. I found her maid outside in the carriage and locked her in the cellar with her mistress, along with the coachman. I promised to feed them all presently, if they behave themselves.'

Sir Richard nodded. 'Good. You should warn the servants not to go near the cellar, Damon. I wouldn't want to lose her now.' He paused, looking down at his chest. 'Dear me, I believe there is a bloodstain on my cravat, so if you will excuse me I shall go and find a fresh one.'

Juliana rose. 'And I must go, too.' She made to follow him out of the door, but Damon blocked her way.

'One moment, Miss Wrenn. You have not yet let me thank you for your services today.'

She kept her eyes lowered. 'I need no thanks, sir.'

'For saving our lives? I think you do.'

He spoke evenly, but she knew him too well to miss the hint of amusement in his voice. How dare he laugh at her, when she had been through so much? She gathered the remains of her strength.

'I would do the same for any man,' she retorted coldly. 'Please, let me go. Thomas and Amy are waiting for me outside.'

'No, they are not. I have sent them upstairs.'

She raised her head at that and gave him a scorching look. 'You had no right to do so.'

'It is far too late for you to travel today.'

'Surely, sir, that is for me to decide.'

'Not when you are using my servants.'

She eyed him resentfully, but it only seemed to increase his amusement. He put up his hands. 'You have my word that if you are still of the same mind tomorrow, my carriage shall take you wherever you wish to go.'

She considered this, and nodded. 'Very well. Then if you will excuse me, I am very tired and wish to rest.'

Still he barred her way. She clenched her jaw, determined not to lose control.

'Major Collingham,' she said carefully, 'please let me pass.'

'Not until you have explained yourself.'

'I have told you, I came back here to bring the diamonds to Sir Richard—any true Englishwoman would do as much.'

'That does not explain your behaviour in the schoolroom.'

She sighed in exasperation. 'She would have shot you both. I am very sorry if you were attached to that particular sculpture—'

'No, I had always considered that representation of Prometheus a very poor example.' He laughed. 'Quite apt, though, don't you think? The Greek myths,' he explained, observing her puzzled look. 'There's one version that says Prometheus smashed a rock against Zeus's head and Athene came out, fully formed.'

The suspicion that Damon was not quite sober entered her head. She stepped back a little.

'I fear we are straying from the point, Major.'

'Indeed we are,' he agreed cordially. 'I have no objection to you smashing the bust—it was what you said that intrigues me.'

'I don't understand.' She found herself fixed with his unrelenting gaze.

'It was your words as you came in, as glorious as any avenging goddess, and felled Veronique. Say it again for me.'

'I—I don't remember,' she said, blushing.

'Oh, I think you do.' Damon came towards her.

'I was frightened. S-surely you take no notice of what people say when they are in *extremis*?' She stepped back and found herself pressed against the panelled wall.

'Say it again.' He took another step forward.

'No!'

He placed his hands on the panelling on either side of her head, and fixed her with those dark, hawk-like eyes.

'Say it again.'

She swallowed. 'Y-you cannot bully me, Damon. I am not a r-raw recruit to be ordered about by you.'

He smiled. It was so unexpected that it caught her by surprise and her heart turned over.

'You are right. *Please* say it again.'

'I—um—'

He leaned closer. 'Go on.'

'I think I said…you shall not…Damon.'

His lips brushed her cheek. 'Say it all,' he murmured.

'I said…you shall not…'

His mouth had moved to her brow, where he dusted a featherlight kiss on the edge of her hair. 'Say it. All of it.'

He was standing so close she could feel the heat of his body. She pressed back against the wall to prevent herself leaning into him. She raised her face, inviting him to kiss her, but his mouth was just out of reach. It was difficult to breathe.

'Go on, Ju.'

'You shall not…touch…'

'Yes?'

Her eyes were level with his lips. She could not look away.

'You shall not touch…' she whispered the words, then swallowed again. He was so close, around her and above her. There was no escape. She thought wildly that she wanted none. 'You shall not touch…my man.'

There. She had said it. Now he would kiss her, surely he would kiss her! Instead he brought his hands forward to cup her face and scowled at her.

'You said just now that you would do the same for any man. Would you have said that about any man?' he demanded.

'Not—perhaps anyone,' she conceded.

His eyes narrowed. 'Richard, then—were you talking about Rick perhaps?'

With a small squeal of frustration, she reached up and pulled his dear, frowning face down to hers, giving him her answer with her lips. Only for a second did he resist her, then his hands slid over her shoulders and the next minute she was crushed against him and answering his passionate kiss with her own. Her arms slid around his neck and she clung to him. She revelled in his savage embrace, rejoiced in the feel of his hard body against hers; clearly his passion had not died. When at last he lifted his head she buried her face in his coat.

'I doubted you, Damon, I should not have done so. I am so sorry.'

He hugged her. 'You must never be sorry,' he muttered fiercely into her hair. 'I should have explained, made you believe me. We must be married, as soon as possible. I won't risk losing you again.'

She pushed away from him and looked up. 'Is—is that a proposal?'

He kissed her again. 'No, it is a command.'

'Because the children need a mother?'

He scowled at her. 'No, because I need a wife. A friend. A lover.'

A bolt of liquid fire ran through her body and she trembled. She would have looked away, but he caught her chin and forced her to meet his eyes. The glow in their granite-grey depths made her breathless.

'You know I have a damnable temper, God knows you have felt the lash of my tongue already. I will try to mend it; but I make no promises: in any event you are more than a match for me and will give me my own again if I grow too tyrannical.' He gave her a wry smile. 'Do I not have the wound on my arm to prove it?'

'Pray do not remind me of that, Damon. I never wanted to hurt you.'

'It was only a scratch, Ju, but enough to bring me to my senses.'

She smiled up at him mistily. 'For days afterwards I was afraid it would become infected and give you a fever,' she told him, her voice breaking.

He hugged her tightly. '*You* gave me a fever, Ju. I could think of nothing but you.' He looked up at the ceiling and gave a deep sigh. She waited patiently and at last he looked at her again, a touch of uncertainty in his eyes.

'I love you, Juliana. I have no great fortune to offer you, but Giles's engineer is confident the coal mine is viable and I plan to build the cotton mill—in a few years they could both be giving a good return.'

'Do not forget the reward Sir Richard spoke of,' she added shyly.

He shook his head. 'That shall be settled on Thomas and Amy. Well, Ju, will you agree to marry me, and to share my life and my fortune, such as it is?'

She lifted her hand to his cheek.

'*You* are my fortune, Damon. And my life.'

Chapter Twenty-Six

Juliana woke up to the sound of birdsong. She stretched languorously and felt Damon's sleeping form beside her. She reached out a hand and ran her fingers over the silky hairs on his naked thigh. He stirred.

'Good morning, Mrs Collingham.'

Mrs Collingham! She had been married for a whole month and still smiled when she heard that name. Damon turned and pulled her back against him, kissing her neck. He cupped her breast in his hand and she sighed with contentment.

'What shall we do today, sir?'

'Fewell's brother is bringing his plans for the new mill.'

'Have you told Giles he is coming?'

'Yes, he will be there. He is interested in machinery and has a natural gift for such things—I think he will be very useful. I am sending him to Birmingham; Sir Richard has contacts there amongst the engineers and Giles is to work with them, learn what he can.' His arms tightened slightly. 'You will come to the meeting with me, will you not? You won't find it dull work?'

'By no means.'

His fingers moved down over her body, caressing her

stomach, then down to thread themselves among the soft curls at the hinge of her thigh. She caught her breath.

'It is still early.' Damon nibbled at her ear.

He was curled around her and she smiled as she felt the hardness of him pressing against her skin.

'Then I think you should be looking to maintain your reputation in the bedroom,' she murmured provocatively. '*Devil* Collingham.'

With something like a growl, he pulled her round to face him. 'You will be gaining something of a reputation yourself, madam, insatiable as you are.' He captured her mouth, her lips parted invitingly and her body moved sensuously beneath his caressing hands until the ache deep within her was too great to be denied and she rolled on top of him, taking him within her as he had taught her and revelling in the exquisite, joyful pleasure of their mutual love.

★ ★ ★ ★ ★

Historical™

tantalising period romances

DID YOU PURCHASE THIS BOOK WITHOUT A COVER?
If you did, you should be aware it is **stolen property** as it was
reported 'unsold and destroyed' by a retailer.
Neither the author nor the publisher has received any payment
for this book.

First Published 2010
First Australian Paperback Edition 2010
ISBN 978 1 742 55393 1

WICKED CAPTAIN, WAYWARD WIFE © 2010 by Sarah Mallory
Philippine Copyright 2010
Australian Copyright 2010
New Zealand Copyright 2010
Except for use in any review, the reproduction or utilisation of this work in
whole or in part in any form by any electronic, mechanical or other means,
now known or hereafter invented, including xerography, photocopying and
recording, or in any information storage or retrieval system, is forbidden
without the permission of the publisher, Harlequin Mills & Boon®, Locked
Bag 7002, Chatswood D.C. N.S.W., Australia 2067.

This book is sold subject to the condition that it shall not, by way of trade or
otherwise, be lent, resold, hired out or otherwise circulated without the prior
consent of the publisher in any form of binding or cover other than that in
which it is published and without a similar condition including this condition
being imposed on the subsequent purchaser.

All rights reserved including the right of reproduction in whole or in part in
any form. This edition is published in arrangement with Harlequin Books
S.A..

This is a work of fiction. Names, characters, places, and incidents are either
the product of the author's imagination or are used fictitiously, and any
resemblance to actual persons, living or dead, business establishments,
events, or locales is entirely coincidental.

Published by
Harlequin Mills & Boon®
Level 5
15 Help Street
CHATSWOOD NSW 2067
AUSTRALIA

® and ™ are trademarks owned by Harlequin Enterprises Limited or its
corporate affiliates and used by others under licence. Trademarks marked
with an ® are registered in Australia and in other countries. Contact
admin_legal@Harlequin.ca for details.

Cover art used by arrangement with Harlequin Books S.A.. All rights
reserved.

Printed and bound in Australia by
McPherson's Printing Group

WICKED CAPTAIN, WAYWARD WIFE

Sarah Mallory

Mills & Boon™

DEDICATION

To the Romantic Novelists' Association,
for the unstinting friendship and support
I have found there.

Chapter One

Makerham Court, Surrey—July 1783

'Ouch!'

Evelina jumped as the rose thorn pricked her finger.
How timely, she thought, staring at the tiny bead of blood.
She had just been thinking that this was the most dangerous activity she undertook; cutting flowers. She sighed.
These sheltered ornamental gardens at Makerham summed
up her life; ordered, secure, protected. She wiped the blood
from her finger and firmly suppressed the vague feeling of
dissatisfaction. She had become more aware of it recently,
this impression of being stifled. But she was happy, wasn't
she, keeping house for her grandfather? He had promised
to take care of her, to provide for her. She need not worry
about anything.

Evelina picked up her basket of summer flowers and was
walking back to the house when she heard the sound of hoof-
beats on the drive. She looked up to see a rider approaching
on a rangy black horse. At the stone bridge that gave access to
the ancient, moated house she stopped, her head tilted enquir-
ingly as he rode up. The man drew rein and jumped down.

He was very tall, she noted. Strong, too, judging by the width of shoulder beneath his dark riding jacket and the powerful legs encased in buckskins and gleaming top boots. His black hair was caught back with a ribbon and there was a rakish look in his laughing blue eyes. He looked like an adventurer, she thought. Tall and dark and…

'You must be Evelina.' His voice was rich and warm as honey. 'How do you do?'

Without waiting for her reply he reached out, pulled her into his arms and kissed her. Eve was so shocked she dropped her basket. She made no effort to pull away; with his arms holding her so firmly it would have been impossible to do so, even if she had wanted to. She had never been kissed by a man before and the sensation was surprisingly pleasant, jolting her senses alive so that she was aware of the scent of his skin, the mingled smell of soap and spices and horses and…she did not know what. Man, she supposed.

He raised his head and gave her a rueful smile, although Eve thought the glint in his deep blue eyes positively wicked.

'Oh Lord,' he said, stepping back from her. 'That was not meant to happen.'

Eve stared up at him, shaken, and wondered what a well-bred young lady should do in this situation. With some deliberation she brought her hand up and dealt him a ringing slap across the face.

He flinched a little, but continued to smile down at her, mischief glinting in his blue eyes. 'I suppose I deserved that.'

It took an effort for Eve to look away from that hypnotic gaze. Her basket was lying on the floor, roses, irises and common daisies tossed on to the drive. With shaking hands she began to gather them up. The man dropped onto one knee beside her, unsettling her with his nearness.

'You do not seem very pleased to see me,' he remarked.

She concentrated on collecting up the flowers and putting them back into the basket. She said stiffly. 'I do not know you sir.'

'Oh, did your grandfather not tell you?' Laughter trembled in his voice. 'I am Nick Wylder.' He picked up a rose and held it out to her. 'I am the man you are going to marry.'

Eve jumped to her feet. The man rose in one agile movement and looked down at her with pure amusement in his eyes. A devil-may-care man, she thought. His lean, handsome face was too attractive. Dangerous. Instinctively she drew away from him.

'Your jest lacks humour, sir.'

Those mobile black brows drew together slightly. 'Has your grandfather not told you? Then my apologies, Miss Shawcross.'

She regarded his flashing smile with suspicion. 'I see no remorse in you sir. I do not believe you know how to apologise.'

He stepped back, his smile softening into something gentler as he said contritely, 'I have truly offended you. Pray, ma'am, forgive me. I did not mean to do that.'

She was not proof against his beguiling look and found herself weakening. She made an effort to maintain her scornful attitude. 'It seems to me, sir, that there is much you do not mean to do!'

He treated her again to his devastating smile and this time she noticed the dimple in his cheek. It was so very distracting.

'Aha, you are not so angry after all. I see the twinkle in your eye, Miss Shawcross. You would laugh, if you were not determined to put me in my place! Am I forgiven, ma'am?'

She turned away that he would not see her smile. 'That depends upon your future conduct Mr…Wylder. Am I to understand that you have come to see my grandfather?'

'I have indeed, ma'am, if he is well enough to receive me. I sent my man over this morning to advise you of my arrival.'

She inclined her head. 'I have not seen Grandpapa since we broke our fast together, so I know nothing of your message. However, that does not mean you are unwelcome. Pray come in, sir, and I will ascertain if he can see you.'

She left the visitor in the great hall with its walls lined with armour. Shields, swords and halberds battled for place between the long windows, a reminder of the turbulent period when the hall was built. As she ran up the stairs she glanced back at him. He was standing before the huge fireplace, studying the crest carved into the overmantel. His head was thrown back and she was treated to an excellent view of his profile with its straight nose and strong jaw-line. Powerful. Confident. She thought how well he would fit into those unsettled times.

As soon as she was out of sight at the top of the stairs she stopped and leaned against the wall. Her heart was thudding uncomfortably in her chest. So it had happened; her grandfather had always promised her that one day he would bring home a husband for her. He had told her to trust him to find a suitable gentleman, one who would look after her as he had always done. One who would make her happy. She pressed her hands to her cheeks. She had expected Grandfather to bring home someone like Squire Amos from Makerham village, someone solid and respectable. There was no doubt that the gentleman now standing in the great hall was solid—when he had crushed her to him he had felt very solid indeed—but she doubted very much that he was respectable. Eve was aware that she had led a very sheltered life, but she knew that respectable gentlemen did not kiss young ladies before they had even been introduced! And respectable young ladies did not stay to exchange banter with such scoundrels. Eve wondered why she had not run away when the man released her. Somewhat to her surprise she realised that he had not frightened her. She had been shocked, yes, and outraged, but never afraid. She took a deep breath and smoothed her hands down over her gown. If only it was as easy to smooth her disordered nerves. If Grandpapa discovered the cause of her agitation he would be alarmed; he might even send his visitor away. With a little jolt of surprise she realised that she really did not want that to happen.

Eve found her grandfather in the morning room. His winged chair had been moved to the window and he was sitting now with a blanket across his knees, gazing out over the park.

'Grandpapa?'

Sir Benjamin Shawcross had been a good-looking man in his youth, but ill health had aged him prematurely and although he was not much more than sixty, his skin had grown sallow and the flesh hung loosely on his large frame.

However, despite the great effort it cost him every morning, he insisted that his valet, Rooney, should help him out of bed and dress him in his velvet coat and fresh linen. His sparse grey hair was hidden by a curly wig in the old style and there was always a twinkle in his faded blue eyes. It was in evidence now as he looked at his granddaughter.

'Eve, my dear, come in. Rooney has made me comfortable here, you see, where I can look out of the window. I have a visitor, you know.'

'Yes, sir, I do know.' Eve put down her basket and slipped across the room to his side.

As she bent to drop a kiss on his forehead she glanced out of the window. The room looked out over the front drive, but thankfully any view of the little stone bridge was

blocked by the bulk of the Gate House tower. Her grandfather would not have seen her first encounter with his
guest. She dropped down to sit on the footstool beside his
chair and gathered his gnarled old hands between her own.
'Mr Wylder is even now in the hall, Grandpapa.'

'Captain, my love; he is Captain Wylder. He sailed with
Admiral Howe against the French and acquitted himself
well, by all accounts.'

'That may be so, sir, but before he is brought up I want
you to tell me just why he is here.'

'A pretty thing, child, if I must answer to you for inviting
a guest to my own house!'

Eve was not deceived by his blustering tone. She saw the
consternation in his faded eyes, but she was not to be swayed
from her course. 'Please, Grandfather, tell me.'

'I have known the family for years. Nick Wylder is the
younger brother of the Earl of Darrington. Of course we
are not well acquainted, for he is so much younger than I
am and he has spent most of his time at sea. He resigned
with Howe in '78, you know. Neither of them thought
very much of the government's handling of the American
War but before they could return to England they were
caught up in the defence of Rhode Island. Clever bit o'
work, that.' Sir Benjamin chuckled. 'Outwitted the French
all right and tight, and young Nicholas in the thick of it.
Commended for his bravery, mentioned in the newspapers.
You may remember it—'

'That was five years ago, Grandpapa,' Eve interrupted
him quietly but firmly. 'And I do not remember you ever
drawing my attention to a Captain Wylder.'

'No, well, perhaps not. In fact I did not recall much
about it myself, until young Nicholas sought me out at Tunbridge Wells last month. It was Percy Anderton told me his

history. Percy lost his son in the action, you see, and Captain Wylder came to see him as soon as he returned to England, to pay his respects. Percy was very impressed. Captain Wylder has friends in the government, too it appears— young Pitt and Lord North—'

'But you said Captain Wylder sought you out, Grandpapa,' Eve persisted, frowning. 'Why should he do that?'

'Why should he not? Old family friend, after all.'

'Yes, but why should he wait until now to look you up?'

'I have no idea, but I am very glad he did. A fine young man, Eve, and very attentive to me. I invited him to call upon us…'

'But you have not said a word about him to me, Grandpapa.'

Sir Benjamin stirred uncomfortably in his chair. 'No, well, the time did not seem propitious, and after all, I did not know if he would really come.'

'Have you brought him here as a husband for me?' she asked in her direct way.

'He did mention to me that he was looking for a wife, and…'

'And you want me to take a husband.'

'Only if you are inclined to do so, Evelina.'

'I have told you, Grandfather, I have no wish for a husband yet.'

'But you will need someone to look after you when I am gone.'

'Grandpapa!'

'Do not frown at me, Eve. We both know that I am failing. Doctor Scott has warned us that my heart is very weak now; the end cannot be far away—'

'You must not say such things,' she said fiercely.

'Ignoring the inevitable will not prevent it, my love. If

Nick Wylder wants to wed you I recommend you to accept him. I shall not insist, of course, but I would ask that you consider the matter very carefully.' He squeezed her fingers and released them. 'Now, we must not keep our guest waiting any longer. Have Captain Wylder fetched up, Evelina.'

'But, sir—'

He waved his hand impatiently. 'Would you have me thought uncivil, gel? Tell Green to show him up.'

The order was given, and Eve went back to stand beside her grandfather. He reached for her hand.

'Trust me on this, love; I am thinking only of you. Ah…' He turned towards the door as the butler announced his visitor. 'My dear sir, you are very welcome! Forgive me for not getting up to meet you, but my legs are very weak today. The baths at Tunbridge did not help me overmuch on this occasion.'

'I am sorry to hear it, Sir Benjamin.'

Evelina watched Captain Nick Wylder stride into the room, his healthy vigour even more in evidence when contrasted with her grandfather's feebleness. He came forwards and bowed to his host, exuding energy. Sir Benjamin smiled and nodded.

'You have met my granddaughter, Evelina?'

Eve found those blue eyes fixed upon her. She had the strange impression that he could read her innermost thoughts. She put up her chin and returned his look defiantly.

'Yes indeed.' Nick Wylder turned and made a fine leg to her. 'That is, we introduced ourselves, but I am glad of this opportunity to be more formally presented, sir.' His eyes laughed at her. 'I fear Miss Shawcross disapproves of me.'

She sank into a curtsy, her cheeks burning. How was it possible to want to laugh and be cross at the same time? She had no experience of gentlemen like Captain Wylder, but instinct told her to beware of him.

Eve determined she would not talk to the captain but her resolve was unnecessary. By the time she had risen out of her curtsy, he had engaged Sir Benjamin in conversation, discussing with ease such diverse subjects as the efficacy of hot baths, the pleasures of hunting and the grand tour. There was nothing for her to do but to arrange her flowers in the vase Green had provided for her. She was out of reason cross that she could not deliver a snub to the laughing gentleman.

'I saw you ride in, Captain,' said Sir Benjamin. 'I take it your baggage follows you?'

'Yes, sir. Richard Granby, my valet, accompanies it in my travelling carriage.'

'You are staying?' Eve blurted out.

Once more those disturbingly blue eyes rested upon her.

'I am afraid so. Will that inconvenience you?'

'N-no…' she faltered. 'That is, you are staying no more than the one night, I hope.'

Sir Benjamin chuckled. 'Take no notice of my grand-daughter, Captain Wylder. She is a great one for jesting.'

'So I have noticed, Sir Benjamin.' He smiled across at her in a way that made Eve want to hit him.

'Captain Wylder is making a prolonged visit with us,' explained Sir Benjamin.

'Really?' Eve pinned on a brittle, sugar-sweet smile.

'I am greatly indebted to your grandfather for allowing me to stay with you,' Nick bowed to her. 'I shall have plenty of time to grow used to your funning.'

Eve turned back to her flower arrangement. Her angry, jerky movements broke one of the stems and she was obliged to breathe deeply and calm herself before she continued. The butler came in with a decanter and two glasses and after that the gentlemen paid her no attention, engrossed in their discussions of hunters and bloodlines, so, as soon as she had finished, Eve muttered her excuses and made her escape.

Nick watched her leave the room, her little heels kicking up her skirts as she crossed the floor. A slight cough from Sir Benjamin made him turn and he found his host was holding out his empty glass, indicating with the lift of an eyebrow that it should be refilled. Nick hesitated and the older man winked at him. 'Come along, my boy. My butler and my granddaughter might argue that brandy is not good for me, but *you* have not heard my doctor say so. Life is for living, sir, and I mean to enjoy what little time I have left.'

'I cannot fault that philosophy, Sir Benjamin.' Nick grinned and carried both glasses over to the decanter. 'Miss Shawcross seems a little agitated,' he remarked. 'I do hope my visit is not inopportune…'

Sir Benjamin chuckled. 'Her feathers are ruffled because I omitted to tell her you were coming.'

'I gathered that much.' Nick smiled to himself as he recalled his first meeting with Evelina Shawcross. 'I am afraid I might have ruffled her feathers even more.'

'No matter, she'll come round.' Sir Benjamin sipped his brandy. 'She's a good gel, my granddaughter. Level-headed and with as sweet a nature as any man could wish. She's not the flighty sort, never shown any desire to go off exploring.' The old man sighed a little. 'Her mother was quite the opposite. Never happier than when she was travelling the world. Took my son off all over the place when they was married. But Eve's different, a quiet gel. She needs a husband who can give her all the comforts she has enjoyed here at Makerham. A man who will look after her properly. Can you do that, Captain?'

Nick suddenly found himself fixed with a fierce stare from those faded eyes. He returned the look steadily.

'You know my circumstances, Sir Benjamin. I believe I can keep a wife in tolerable comfort.'

'Yes, yes, but will you make her happy?'

Nick fought down a smile.

'I have never had any complaints yet, sir.'

'That's what worries me, a good-looking dog like you. I saw the women at Tunbridge making eyes at you, throwing out lures—and some of 'em old enough to know better!'

'But what you didn't see was my responding to any of their—er—lures,' replied Nick evenly. 'Let us be clear, Sir Benjamin. I am not a monk; there have been plenty of women in my life, but none of 'em more than a flirtation. If I take a wife, she will have nothing to fear on that score.'

'I'm glad to hear it. Well, sir, if you are wishful to marry my granddaughter, then go to it. But mind you; it must be her decision. I'll not have her coerced into anything.'

Nick raised his glass.

'From the little I have seen of the lady, sir, I think she will make up her own mind.'

When Eve went to her room to change for dinner, her maid Martha was laying out her new gown.

'My blue silk?' she exclaimed. 'Is that not a little grand for a family dinner?'

'We must make you look your best for your visitor, miss.'

'I am not sure the occasion warrants such a display,' Eve objected mildly, but Martha was not to be deterred.

'Captain Wylder is a fine gentleman, miss. Son of an earl, his man says.'

'I know that, Martha.'

'Ah, but did you also know that he is a hero? In the Americas he was, fighting the rebels. Captain *Wyldfire* they called him.' She spread out the petticoats for Eve to step into them.

'Martha, what have I told you about repeating servants' gossip?'

'This is not gossip, miss,' Martha corrected her; 'It is *information*. He was a bold and fearless captain, Mr Granby told me, always to be found where the fighting was thickest. That's where he got the name Wyldfire, they say, because he blazed his way through the enemy lines.'

'And who says so? His own servants, I don't doubt.'

'Aye, well, Mr Granby told me some of it, but William the coachman also had it from his groom, who has been with the family for ever.'

Eve gave a little huff of disbelief. 'I believe they are all besotted with their master. I shall write to my old school-friend Maria Scott—Lady Gryfford as she is now. Her letters are always full of society gossip so I am sure she will be able to furnish me with a true account of our guest.'

'I am sure she will, miss,' replied Martha comfortably. 'And I am sure it will bear out all that has been said. Well, you only have to look at him, so tall and handsome as he is. A real hero, is Captain Wyldfire.'

'Well there will be no need for him to be a hero in this house,' retorted Eve crossly. She glanced at the red leather box on the dressing table. 'What is that?'

'Your sainted mother's sapphires.' replied Martha. 'Sir Benjamin ordered them to be sent up to you. He wants you to wear them tonight.'

Eve put a hand up to her bare neck. 'G-Grandpapa sent them?'

'Why, yes, miss. Most insistent he was.'

She stared at the box. At last she said quietly, 'Then, of course, I must wear them.'

Nick stood by the fireplace in the little parlour and looked down at the flames leaping merrily in the hearth. One of the logs had fallen forward; he resisted the temptation to push it back into place with his toe. Richard had worked hard to coax him into his dark blue frock-coat and the knee breeches that were the required mode of evening dress for a formal dinner and he knew his trusty servant would think his efforts wasted if he was to end up with wood ash on his soft leather shoes or, even worse, spattered on his white silk stockings. Instead he picked up the tongs and rearranged the logs until the flames were licking hungrily around them. He straightened as the door opened and Miss Shawcross entered. After their encounter on the drive he thought he had himself well under control, but it was an effort to prevent his jaw from dropping as he looked at her. She was a vision in cobalt blue and silver lace, her glorious hair piled on her head and one glossy black curl falling on to her shoulder. Nick smiled to himself; he had come to Makerham determined to court Evelina Shawcross, even if she had been hunchbacked and with a squint. This glorious creature was like a gift from the gods. She aroused in him all that was good—and bad! There was a troubled look on her face as she came into the room and he said hurriedly,

'I understood this is where you meet before dinner…'

'You are perfectly correct, sir. I am only sorry that there was no one here to greet you.'

He smiled.

'You are here now, that is all that matters.' He walked forwards to give her his arm. The sapphires around her neck twinkled, enhancing the beauty of that slender column. He longed to put up a hand and touch the creamy skin, but she was like a wild animal, tense and ready for flight. He must go carefully.

'Miss Shawcross, you are not happy with me here.'

'Oh—no, I—'

Her hand fluttered on his arm and he covered her fingers with his own. She was trembling.

'Please,' he murmured, 'while we are alone let me say this. If you would prefer me to leave, I will make my excuses to Sir Benjamin—'

She stopped, her eyes downcast, the long lashes black against her pale cheeks. Nick watched the play of emotion on her countenance; saw the resolute set of her mouth.

'You are my grandfather's guest, sir. It is his will that you should stay, and to me his will is paramount.'

'But I shall be guided by your wishes, lady. Tell me what you want me to do.' He continued softly, 'We made a wretched beginning. Forgive me for that, Miss Shawcross, and allow me to show you that I can be a gentleman.'

He saw the delicate blush tinge her cheeks, read the uncertainty in her eyes when she looked at him, then his gentleness was rewarded with a shy smile.

'Very well, Captain Wylder, I am ready to be persuaded.'

There was a twinkle in those soft brown eyes, a hint of mischief. The temptation to steal another kiss was very strong, but he resisted. That would *not* be the action of a gentleman! Instead he escorted her to a sofa. He intended to sit down beside her, but as she sank down she spread out her blue skirts, completely covering the seat. With a wry grin he moved to a chair on the opposite side of the fireplace. It would be slow work to win her round, but he found himself warming to the challenge.

★ ★ ★

Evelina was aware of an irrational disappointment. She had been convinced that he was going to kiss her again, and her heart leapt into her throat at the thought of it. The man had about him an air of danger, a delicious sense of the unknown that set her pulse racing. But now he was determined to be the gentleman. She was glad of it, of course. She flounced down upon the sofa, her silken petticoats billowing around her.

'Your grandfather explained to me that you and he live here alone,' remarked the captain, lowering his long frame into a chair. 'He told me your parents died when you were a child. I am very sorry.'

'Thank you, but you do not need to pity me; it was more than ten years ago. My parents liked to travel a great deal and I was left at home with Grandpapa, so I never knew them that well; I think they were a very restless couple.' His sympathetic silence encouraged her to say more. 'It was a fever; they were on the Continent when they were struck down.' She paused briefly then forced a smile. 'But I am very happy living here with Grandpapa, I want for nothing.'

'But you are very secluded here; do you not find it a little…lonely?'

'Grandpapa is companion enough for me,' she responded quickly. 'I have no wish for female company—and I am beyond the age of needing a chaperon.'

The corners of his mouth lifted fractionally. 'Remembering our first encounter, I beg to disagree with you on that last point, Miss Shawcross.'

Eve blushed hotly. She was relieved that her grandfather's entrance created a timely diversion.

Sir Benjamin came in, leaning heavily on his stick and declaring that they should go directly into the dining room.

'If I sit down here I shan't be able to get up again,' he explained with a chuckle. 'No, no, my dear, I do not need your arm; let Wylder escort you.'

They processed slowly to the dining room, where Eve found herself sitting opposite Nick Wylder.

'I told Green to rearrange the table,' said Sir Benjamin, correctly interpreting her look of surprise. 'Silly for you to be sitting at the far end and Wylder here, halfway between the two of us. Much better to have you near me, where I can see you both. Just a snug little dinner, Wylder,' he continued. 'We do not stand upon any ceremony here. It's plain cooked fare, but you won't find better in the county, and you have Evelina to thank for it.'

'Grandpapa!' She shook her head at him.

'No need for this modesty, miss! It is only right that our guest knows what a treasure you are. She has been mistress here since she finished her schooling.' Sir Benjamin laughed. 'Just seventeen years old, she was then, Wylder. I wanted her to go off and stay with her young friends, to enjoy herself, but she would have none of it. She insisted upon coming home to live with me. Not that she needed to, for we have a very capable housekeeper in Mrs Harding, but Evelina was determined that she would look after me. And she has done so, magnificently.'

'I do not doubt it,' returned Captain Wylder. 'And how many years has that been, sir?'

'Seven,' responded Sir Benjamin instantly.

While her grandfather turned his attention to his plate, Eve glared across the table at Nick Wylder. He met her look with a glinting smile.

'Four-and-twenty,' he murmured. 'Far too old for a chaperon.'

'Positively on the shelf!' she retorted. Eve signalled to

the footman to refill the glasses. 'So, Captain, you were at Tunbridge Wells. Were you taking the waters?' She added sweetly, 'A touch of gout, perhaps?'

His eyes acknowledged the hit, but he said merely, 'No, I was there on business.'

'Oh? And is your business now concluded, that you have time for a *prolonged* stay here at Makerham?'

Again that wicked glint flashed in his deep blue eyes. 'I hope to conclude my business while I am here.'

'And just what is your business, sir?' Eve picked up her wine glass.

'Marriage.'

She choked.

'Oh dear, dear,' muttered Sir Benjamin. He bent a reproving look upon his guest. 'I had not planned to broach this delicate subject for a day or so, sir.'

'Then I apologise, Sir Benjamin, but given your granddaughter's advanced years I did not wish to waste time.'

Evelina, still recovering from her choking fit, could only gasp. Sir Benjamin's mouth fell open, then his face creased into a smile.

'Ah, you are funning, sir! Giving my girl her own again, what? Eve, my dear, I think you have met your match, here. Captain Wylder is as big a jokesmith as yourself!'

Evelina forced her lips into a smile, but the look she threw at Nick Wylder promised dire retribution.

Nick turned his attention to his dinner. Damme, but he was enjoying himself, and far more than he had anticipated. Sir Benjamin was a considerate host and although he was confined to the house by his poor health he was remarkably knowledgeable and the conversation did not flag. Then there was Miss Shawcross. She was a mixture of spirit and adorable innocence; an unforeseen bonus to his plans. Nick realised with a little jolt of surprise that he wanted to know more about her.

Eve excused herself after dinner and went to her room to dash off a letter to her old school friend.

I understand Captain Wylder to be something of a hero, she wrote at the end her letter. *But however highly he is regarded as a sailor, I hope you can furnish me with some information as to his character as a man.* 'There,' she said to herself as she applied her seal. 'If I know anything of Maria, she will be only too delighted to find out everything there is to know about Captain Nick Wylder.'

Sir Benjamin did not keep late hours at Makerham, so it was not until the following morning that she saw their guest again. It was her custom, upon summer mornings such as these to take a stroll through the ornamental gardens that surrounded Makerham. Sheltered and secluded at the bottom of a wooded dell, the moated manor house was always inviting, but looked at its best in summer. She loved the way the old stone seemed to glow and the golden sunlight twinkled in the leaded windows; it gave the old house a fairy-tale quality. She was wandering through the lavender-lined paths when she heard footsteps on the gravel behind her. She turned to find Captain Wylder approaching.

'Good morning, Miss Shawcross. You are an early riser.'

'Yes. I often take a walk at this time; the gardens are at their best with the dew still on the flowers.'

'Then I will join you, if I may?'

After a brief hesitation Eve nodded. She would not take his arm, but walked along beside him, keeping a safe distance between them. At Nick's request she pointed out the more unusual flowers and described to him the history of the building. When they reached the end of the ornamental gardens they stopped and turned, looking back at the old house.

'It's beautiful,' said Nick. 'It is clear that you love Makerham.'

'It is my home.'

'But it is entailed.' At his words she glanced up at him and he spread his hands. 'Your grandfather told me.'

'Yes. When Grandfather dies the estate will pass to my cousin, Bernard Shawcross.'

'And you will have to leave.'

Evelina thought of her cousin with his clammy hands and air of ownership. He seemed to assume that she was included in his inheritance. Eve knew she would do everything in her power to avoid that fate.

'Yes,' she said quietly. 'I will have to leave.' The chiming of the bell in the clock tower brought her head up. 'It is time I went indoors. Grandfather will be coming downstairs shortly.'

Nick accompanied her back to the house, but any plans for furthering his suit were dashed when she announced that they would meet again at dinner.

'But you will be breaking your fast now, Miss Shawcross?'

She shook her head. 'Breakfast will be served to you and Grandpapa very shortly, Captain. I have arranged to walk into Makerham.'

'Will you not wait for me? I should like to escort you.'

Again a little shake of the head. Nick was convinced there was a mischievous twinkle in her eyes.

'I go to take a little food to the poor in the village. They would not thank me for bringing a stranger into their homes. Grandpapa will be very pleased to have your company for the day,' she added with a sunny smile. 'And I shall be happy to know that he is entertained.'

Nick watched her walk away, a little smile playing around his own mouth. Out-manoeuvred, by Gad. Miss Evelina Shawcross might be an innocent, but she was not unintelligent. To win her over would be a challenge. Nick's smile grew.

He could never resist a challenge.

Chapter Two

'Evelina, my love, you are being quite tiresome!'

Sir Benjamin's mild reproof brought his granddaughter's wide-eyed gaze to his face. They were sitting together in the morning room where Rooney had helped Sir Benjamin to his favourite chair and was tenderly placing a rug over his legs. Eve waited until the valet had finished and was making his way out of the room before she answered.

'Grandpapa, I have no idea what you mean.'

'What game is this you are playing, Eve? I bring Captain Wylder here as a suitor and you seem bent on avoiding him.'

'No, no, Grandpapa, I have been most attentive!'

'You have presided over my dinner table and served him tea in the drawing room after,' retorted Sir Benjamin. 'Hardly effusive behaviour, my love. I understand from Rooney that you are gone from the house before breakfast every day and do not return until late in the afternoon. Are there suddenly so many distressed families in Makerham that require your attendance?'

'The summer has brought on a deal of sickness and ague, sir.'

'Then you must send Martha with a basket of food, child. I will not have you neglect our guest.'

Eve cast down her eyes. 'Yes Grandpapa.' She stole a glance at Sir Benjamin and saw he was frowning at her. She put out her hands. 'Oh, sir, pray do not be angry with me. It is such a novelty to have any man save yourself in the house and it is taking me a little time to grow accustomed.'

She might have added that she found her grandfather's guest far too attractive for her comfort, but decided against it.

'Well I consider four days is long enough for you to *grow accustomed*, as you put it. I don't say that the captain isn't excellent company, but it's not me that he has come here to see. If you continue to absent yourself, he will think you do not like him.'

'It is not that, Grandpapa—'

'My dear child, I know this is very sudden for you. When I took you to Tunbridge Wells a few years ago I had hoped that you might form an alliance, but none of the gentlemen took your fancy, and you could not be persuaded to stay with your friends in London—'

'I could not leave you, Grandpapa,' she said quickly. 'You were ill and I wanted to look after you.'

He patted her hands. 'Your heart is too kind, Eve my love, but I should have made you go; imprisoned here with me, you have no opportunity to meet eligible gentlemen.'

'But I have not been unhappy, sir.'

'That is not the point, Evelina,' Sir Benjamin leaned forwards, saying urgently, 'I am growing weaker, my love. When I am gone there will be no one to protect you. Your cousin inherits Makerham, there is nothing to be done about that, but I do not like him. I have seen the way he looks at you when he is here. I would not have you left to his care.'

She shivered at the thought. 'You are right, Grandpapa, I do not think I should like that.'

'So you will consider Captain Wylder's suit?'

'Yes, Grandpapa. If he should offer for me, I will consider his suit.' Eve smiled. She had made up her mind that she would not relax her guard until she had received word from London about Captain Wylder. Now, with her friend Maria's letter nestling in her pocket, she had decided upon a course of action. 'I am sorry if I have not been as attentive to our guest as you would like, Grandpapa. I promise you I am now quite ready to entertain Captain Wylder. In fact,' she added with a twinkle, 'I will start this very day!'

Nick looked up from the letter he was reading as Richard Granby came into the room.

'Bad news, Captain?'

Nick shook his head.

'No news at all,' he said. 'Our quarry has gone to ground.'

'I'm sorry to hear that.' Granby hesitated and then said delicately, 'And, if I might enquire, how are your plans progressing with the young lady?'

Nick tossed the letter aside. 'They are not,' he said shortly. 'I am wondering if we should weigh anchor and try another tack. The admiralty wants answers and there are other leads to follow…' his lips twitched '…though none so attractive.'

A knock at the door interrupted them. Nick hurriedly took up his letter and put it away while Granby answered the door. He heard a murmur of voices and turned to see his valet approaching, a folded paper in his hand.

'A note for you, Captain.'

'Well.' A slow grin appeared as he read the missive.

'Perhaps all is not lost. Miss Shawcross wants to see me. In the garden.'

Nick strode along the gravelled paths until he reached the yew walk. At the far end was a small clearing where a statue of Pan nestled against the surrounding hedge. On either side white-painted benches had been placed for those who wished to rest for a while in this sheltered retreat. Evelina was sitting on one of the benches, reading a letter. As Nick approached she looked up and gave a slight smile. He bowed.

'You wished to talk to me, Miss Shawcross?'

She gestured towards the opposite bench and Nick sat down.

'I did indeed, sir.' Her soft brown eyes rested upon him. 'You said at our very first meeting that you came here to marry me. Is that truly your intention?'

'A direct attack,' he said approvingly. 'I like that.'

'You have not answered my question, Captain.'

'Then, yes. It is indeed my intention, Misss Shawcross.'

Her gaze did not falter. 'Why?'

Nick's brows rose. This was blunt indeed. 'It is time I settled down. My family has been nagging me to do so ever since I came home from sea.'

'But you know nothing about me.'

He smiled at her. 'You are beautiful, witty, accomplished—and Sir Benjamin assures me you are an excellent housekeeper. Is that not enough?'

She dropped her gaze, a delicate flush mantling her cheek. 'But you knew nothing about me when you sought out my grandfather at Tunbridge Wells.'

She raised her eyes again and Nick hesitated. How much should he tell her?

'I did go to Tunbridge in search of Sir Benjamin,' he admitted. 'I planned merely to renew my family's acquaintance with him. It soon became clear to me that Sir Benjamin was looking for a husband for you.' A smile tugged at his lips. 'He seemed to think I might be a suitable candidate.'

'Do you mean that *he* suggested it?' She looked shocked. 'And you agreed to…to…'

He spread his hands, saying apologetically, 'This seemed an opportunity not to be missed. I am glad now that I came.'

For a moment she looked delightfully flustered, but she soon recovered. 'Very well, sir.' She settled herself more comfortably on the bench and glanced at the papers in her hand. 'Grandpapa may consider you suitable, but you have yet to convince *me*! I would like to ask you a few questions.'

Nick leaned back and crossed one booted leg over the other. 'I am at your disposal, ma'am.'

'We have already established that you are a sailor, and, one cannot deny it, a brave one.'

'Thank you,' he said meekly.

'But you have something of a reputation in town, Captain.' She stared down at the letter. 'Last year your name was linked with a Mrs Stringham.'

He blinked. The chit had been checking up on him!

'We were…friends for a few months, yes.'

'I understand she is a lady with a somewhat tarnished reputation.' She shrugged. 'No doubt much more interesting for you than an ingénue.'

He choked, but she did not seem to notice and was again peering at her list.

'Then there was Lady Alton.'

'What of her?' he asked warily.

'She was your mistress, was she not? You look shocked, Captain Wylder. I thought you liked the direct attack.'

Nick sat up. By heaven, the wench was teasing him! 'May I ask how you came by this information, Miss Shawcross?'

She held the letter to her breast. 'You may ask, but I shall not divulge my sources.'

He leaned forward. 'And what else do your…sources… say of me?'

She studied the sheets of paper again. 'Well, there was Miss Brierley from Rochester, many people thought you might offer for her.'

'What, because I took her driving in the park?'

'Apparently so,' she murmured, not raising her eyes from her letter. 'And Dorothy Chate, the actress, not to mention the opera dancers—'

'I would much rather we did *not* mention the opera dancers!'

She regarded him sternly. 'Since quitting the navy, your life seems to have been one of dissipation, sir.'

He tried to look remorseful. 'Alas, I am very much in need of a wife to keep me in order.'

'I am not at all sure that anyone could keep you in order, Captain Wylder. Are you saying that if we were to marry you would give up your dissolute ways?'

'I would try.'

He gave her a soulful look and noted with satisfaction the smile tugging at the corners of her mouth. She was having difficulty keeping her countenance.

'I am not at all sure that I believe you.'

'I fear I am in need of an occupation.'

She turned the page. 'My correspondent tells me that you *have* an occupation.'

Nick froze. Now how the devil did she know that?

'Or you *should* have one; you should be managing your

properties in the north, Captain Wylder, not wasting your time in idle pursuits.'

He breathed again. 'I would not call looking for a wife an idle pursuit.'

'Captain Wylder,' she said seriously, 'I am not at all sure I am the wife for you.'

'Miss Shawcross, the more I know of you the more I am convinced that you are the *perfect* wife for me!'

'But I am not at all worldly. What I mean is...' She blushed again, looking so adorable that he wanted to cross the space between them and take her in his arms. 'What would happen when you grew tired of me?' When he did not respond she said quietly, 'I am not quite as naïve as you might think, Captain. I know my parents' marriage was unusual; they were so much in love they did everything together, as equals.' She gave a sad little smile. 'They even died together. I do not expect that, but...'

Nick half-rose from his seat, then sank back down again. He knew that any attempt to comfort her was more likely to frighten her away. 'But what, Miss Shawcross?'

The colour flared in her cheeks, but she was determined on her course. Her words were almost inaudible. 'I w-would not want to share you with a mistress.'

Nick took a deep breath. By heaven, he admired her bravery. Now he must honour it with an honest reply. 'Miss Shawcross, whatever else you may have heard about me, pray believe that I am a gentleman. If we were to marry, I give you my word you would always be treated with respect, and I would do my best to make you happy. I can promise you that I have no mistress hidden away.' He laughed suddenly. 'Now what is that look, do you not believe me?'

She glared at him. 'I do not think you understand, sir.'

'Then perhaps you can explain.'

He sat back, as she threw him another scorching look. He felt more sure of his ground when she was angry with him.

'I have always expected Grandpapa to arrange my marriage for me, but I thought it would be a local gentleman. Someone…'

'Someone safe and staid and boring,' he put in helpfully.

'Well…yes.'

He spread his hands. 'Even the most upright country gentlemen take mistresses, you know.'

'But they are less likely to have women falling at their feet,' she retorted. She brandished her letter. 'My correspondent tells me the ladies in town find you fatally attractive.'

'Does she indeed?'

'How do you know it is a woman?'

'I have an instinct for these things. Does your correspondent find me fatally attractive, too?'

'Captain Wylder I do not think you are taking this seriously.'

'But I am! And your grandfather has already spoken to me of this.'

'He—he has?'

'Yes.' Her consternation made him smile. 'It is a question that would occur to any loving guardian. I have already assured him that, if I take a wife, she will have nothing to fear on that score.' He paused. 'Sir Benjamin approves of me, you know. Will you not at least consider my suit?'

She held his eyes for a moment, then folded her papers and put them into her reticule. 'Yes, Captain Wylder, I will consider it,' she said quietly. 'But it is not a decision to be taken lightly.'

'No, of course not.'

'Thank you for being so frank with me, Captain.'

As she rose he jumped up and reached for her hand, carrying her fingers to his lips.

'I hope we understand one another now, Miss Shawcross.'

'I am not sure.' She regarded him with a tiny crease between her brows. 'I still do not understand why you should want to marry me, but we will let that pass, for now.' She withdrew her fingers and, with a slight, regal nod of her head, she turned and walked away from him.

Eve returned to her room, her mind going over and over her interview with Captain Wylder. He had not denied any of the liaisons Maria Gryfford had detailed in her letter, but he had looked wary. Were there even more lovers that she did not know of? Eve realised she did not care how many lovers he might have had in the past; only the present and the future concerned her. A line from Lady Gryfford's letter flitted through her mind; *If the dashing Captain Wyldfire has made you an offer, then snap him up immediately, my dearest Eve. We are all mad for him!* But why should he want to marry her? He did not look like the sort of man who would marry merely to please his family. But then, she had been brought up to believe she would marry to please her grandfather. Were they so very different? She put her arms around herself. It was a big decision, to leave the safety of the only home she had ever known and put herself under the protection of Nick Wylder. After all, what did she know of him? Did she trust him?

'Yes,' she said aloud. 'Yes, I do. Perhaps I should not, but I do.'

'Your pardon, Miss Eve, did you say something?'

Martha came bustling into the room.

'What? Oh, no, no. I was merely talking to myself. Is it time to dress for dinner already? I think I will wear my blue gown again tonight, Martha.'

'Ah, you want to look your best for the captain, is that it?'

'Do not be so impertinent!'

Eve frowned at her handmaiden, but Martha had been part of her household since Eve had been a baby and was not so easily snubbed.

'Well, what else is one to think, when you and he have been in the garden together this afternoon?'

'Who told you that?'

Martha shrugged. 'Mr Granby mentioned it…'

'How dare you gossip about me!'

'Lord love you, Miss Eve, we wasn't gossiping. Mr Granby just happened to mention it in passing. Heavens, miss, how you do take one up. And what does it matter anyway, since you are going to wed him—'

'Martha! Who says so?'

The maid stared at her. 'Well, is it not so?'

'No. Yes—that is…' She dropped down on the bed, crying, 'Oh, Martha I do not know what to do!'

'Don't you *want* to marry the captain?'

Eve spread her hands. 'I must marry someone.'

'And the captain *is* very handsome, miss.'

Eve felt herself blushing. 'Yes he is. Very handsome.'

And exciting, and witty: Eve had never felt so attracted to any man before. Not that she had much experience, one short visit to Tunbridge Wells being the nearest she had ever been to entering society, but she had read lots of books. She knew exactly what a hero should be like, and although the gentlemen she had met at Tunbridge had all fallen well short of her expectations, she was forced to admit that Nick Wylder was the embodiment of her secret dreams. The thought was a little frightening.

'Well, if you'll be guided by me, you will listen to Sir

Benjamin and do as he bids you, miss,' Martha advised her. 'He has never let you down yet.'

'I know, Martha, but this is…marriage.' She whispered the word, suddenly nervous of it and the thoughts it conjured.

'Lord love you, that is just the time to be advised by your grandpapa,' said Martha cheerfully. 'If Sir Benjamin thinks the captain is the right man for you, then so it is, and a sight better catch than your cousin Bernard,' she added, suddenly serious. 'And that's who you'll end up with if the master dies and leaves you alone. I've seen 'im sniffing round you when he's been here on a visit.'

'Stop it, Martha.' Eve shuddered. 'Besides, I have heard that my cousin is hanging out for a rich wife.'

'Aye, well, maybe he is,' opined Martha darkly. 'But that won't stop him trying to get you between the sheets, with or without a wedding ring!'

With this dire warning she went off to fetch Eve's gown, leaving her mistress to stare after her.

By the time she went down to dinner Eve was no closer to making a decision, but she was too well-bred to let her inner turmoil show and she greeted Sir Benjamin and the captain with her usual calm smile. Despite her assured performance in the garden that afternoon she was a little nervous of meeting Nick again, but his polite, gentle friendliness soon put her at her ease. However, Sir Benjamin's suggestion after dinner that the young people should take a stroll in the garden while it was still light threw her into a panic.

'An excellent idea,' murmured Nick, his eyes glinting, but not unkindly. 'Come, Miss Shawcross, indulge me in a little walk.' He leaned closer and murmured. 'It need be nothing more, I promise you.'

Feeling the hot blood in her cheeks, she hurried away

to fetch her wrap and returned to find only Nick waiting for her in the hall.

'Sir Benjamin has retired,' he informed her as she came down the stairs towards him. 'He asked that you go up to see him when we come back in.' He held out his arm to her. 'Shall we walk? You need not worry,' he added, seeing her hesitation. 'We shall talk of the most unexceptional subjects, if you like.'

His understanding calmed her jangled nerves. She put her hand on his arm and allowed him to lead her out of the house.

At first they discussed the weather, then books and music, but when they had strolled past the parterre and into the shrubbery, Nick said suddenly, 'I think, Miss Shawcross, that I owe you an apology.' She glanced up at him and he continued, 'It seems Sir Benjamin truly did not prepare you for my visit.'

She flushed. 'This is not the unexceptional topic you promised me, Captain.'

'I know, but you are very reserved with me tonight. You are trying to make up your mind whether or not to marry me, is that not so?'

'Of course not!' she exclaimed, startled. 'It is…' She trailed off. 'To be truthful with you, yes,' she admitted.

He stopped and turned to her, catching at her hands. 'And what is so difficult about that decision, Miss Shawcross?'

He lifted her hand to his lips and began to kiss her fingers, one by one. She watched, transfixed.

'I, um…'

He lifted her other hand and, when he had finished with her fingers, his lips moved on to her wrist, sending a fiery shock the length of her arm.

'I cannot think,' she confessed.

He raised his head and smiled at her. Eve's fingers were

still tingling and she found herself staring at his mouth, wondering at the havoc his lips could cause. The smile in his eyes deepened. He cupped her chin.

'Sometimes it is best not to think,' he murmured and gently brought his mouth down upon hers.

It was the lightest of kisses, a mere brushing of lips, but it sent Eve's senses reeling and as Nick pulled away her face remained upturned, inviting him to kiss her again. He gazed down at her.

'A young lady should not allow a gentleman to kiss her unless she means to marry him,' he murmured.

'Then perhaps you have made my decision for me,' she replied.

He laughed, pulled her hand back on to his arm and they resumed their stroll.

'I shall not coerce you into this, Miss Shawcross; it must be your decision.'

'It is in truth my grandfather's decision,' she told him. 'Or at least, his wish. But your assumption was correct, Captain. He did not mention you were coming. I should not be surprised by it, however. He always said that one day he would bring home a husband for me.' She sighed. 'I never really believed him.'

'Surely he has not kept you locked away here all these years?' He sounded slightly shocked and she gave a little gurgle of laughter.

'Like a princess in a fairy-tale? No, of course not. I have attended assemblies in Makerham village upon occasion. And I went to Tunbridge a few years ago.'

'Then of course you know all you need to know about the world!'

'I know enough to realise that I am very happy to remain here at Makerham. Everything I want is here.'

'Is it? Do you never long to know what is going on outside these walls?'

'There are the news sheets—'

'That is not the same! There are towns and cities—whole countries waiting to be explored. Does that thought not fill you with excitement?'

The thought filled Evelina with dread. She stepped away from him to cup a particularly lovely rose between her fingers, breathing in its fragrance while she formulated her answer. Apart from one or two early memories of life with her parents and a few brief years at school, Makerham was the only world she had ever known. Outside was alien and full of danger, like the infection that had carried off her parents. Her life here at Makerham was safe, secure; the thought of her cousin taking possession was something she did not want to consider.

'I am very happy here,' she said again.

Nick strolled along beside Evelina, his hands clasped firmly behind his back to prevent them reaching out and pulling her into his arms. He had never known such a glorious summer's evening; bees hummed around the plants and the scent of lavender filled the air. Then there was Evelina herself; she was beautiful, but there was an air of calm about her, serenity. It was like finding a safe harbour after stormy weeks at sea. When he had sought out Sir Benjamin at Tunbridge Wells he had already formulated his plans; if he needed to marry to obtain his ends, then he was prepared to do his duty, but never had he expected *duty* to be quite so pleasurable.

He stopped and gently turned her to face him. 'I understand how much you love Makerham, but could you consider living elsewhere?'

'I think I must, sir, since the house will pass to my cousin when Grandpapa dies.'

'That is not quite what I meant. Sir Benjamin brought me here as a prospective husband for you. I am not sure what he has told you about me...'

'Only that your father was an earl: that is looking pretty high for a baronet's daughter.' Her lilting smile jolted his senses. It took all his will-power not to drag her into his arms and cover her face with kisses, but he needed to talk to her.

'Evelina—Eve, from our discussions this afternoon you know I have not led a blameless life, but I told you that will change when I take a wife. I have a comfortable income and two estates in the north. I can afford to give you a Season in town every year, should you wish it. You will have your own carriage and we could buy a property nearer Makerham, closer to your grandfather, if that is what you want.'

'Captain Wylder, this is too soon!'

He put a finger against her lips. 'Perhaps, but I do everything in a hurry, my dear; as soon as I saw you I knew that I wanted to wed you.' He saw the confusion in her face and stopped. He drew away a little, took a breath and said gently, 'You need not answer immediately. I merely want you to understand what I am offering you.'

There was a slight shadow in her eyes as she looked up at him. 'That is all very well, Captain, but I do not understand what *I* can offer *you*.'

He hesitated, then said lightly, 'I believe that you bring with you your mother's property at Monkhurst.'

She laughed. 'A rundown house on the edge of Romney Marsh! I love it, and spent some happy times there as a child, but no one has lived there since Mama and Papa died. It is a poor dowry, Captain Wylder. I fear I will get the best of this bargain, sir!'

His spirit soared. She was almost his, he could read it in her eyes. A dizzying happiness shook him. He ran his hands down her arms and caught her fingers.

'No, Eve, I think I will have a great deal more than I bargained for!'

Eve stared at the dark head bent over her hands. This could not be happening to her; when she was at school she had read novels of handsome knights carrying off damsels in distress, but that was fantasy. Besides, she was not in distress. Or was she? She was twenty-four years old and she had never found anyone she would like to marry, nor was she likely to meet anyone while she lived in such seclusion. Her grandfather was much weaker than he had been even a few months ago. If he should die while she was still unmarried, then what would become of her? The vision of her cousin filled her mind. She had never liked Bernard, sensing in his nature a cruel streak that made her a little afraid of him. And now here was this handsome, dashing sea captain offering her his hand and he came with her grandfather's blessing. There really was no choice.

Eve realised Nick was looking at her with a steady, unsettling gaze. She needed to say something. 'How soon do you wish to be married, Captain Wylder?'

Goodness, how matter of fact she sounded.

'By the end of the month.'

'The end of the——!'

'Why, yes, I see no reason to rush into this with a special licence. We have time for the banns to be read in church. We shall be married here, of course. I have no doubt that is what you would like——'

'But I haven't agreed to it yet!'

With a laugh he pulled her into his arms. 'No, but you will.' He was grinning down at her. Eve found it difficult to concentrate, her thoughts seemed to centre on the dimple in his left cheek.

'Wh-what will Grandpapa say to such a hasty marriage?'

'Oh I think he will agree.' He kissed her, a sizzling, burning kiss that sent shockwaves tingling right down to her toes. 'What say you, Eve, will you be my wife?'

'But—' She tried to collect her wayward thoughts. 'We have only just met!'

'And we have more than three weeks until the wedding to get to know one another.' He kissed her again. 'Well?'

She struggled out of his arms. 'No, no. It is out of the question,' she said crossly. 'You appear out of nowhere, big and brash and—and totally overwhelming, and you expect me to agree to be your wife! No, sir, I will not do it!'

He dropped to his knees before her, throwing his arms wide. 'Evelina, don't you *want* to marry me?'

She clapped her hands over her mouth to stifle a giggle. 'Get up, sir, before someone sees you!'

'Not until you answer my question.'

Evelina stared at him. His blue eyes twinkled and that irrepressible dimple cut into his cheek. Heavens, was the man never serious?

'Well, Evelina; will you give me your answer?'

A stillness settled over the garden. The birds were silent, not a breath of wind stirred the bushes; the whole world was hushed, waiting for her reply. Suddenly she knew that there was nothing she wanted more than to be married to Nick Wylder.

'Very well,' she said quietly. 'I will marry you.'

Chapter Three

'Oh heavens, what have I done?'

Evelina paced about her bedroom, her clasped hands pressed to her mouth. The arrival at Makerham of a prospective husband should not have come as a surprise, her grandfather had told her often that he would find her a suitor and she had told him that she would abide by his judgement. But she had not expected that gentleman to be so dazzlingly attractive as Captain Wylder, nor had she foreseen that he would propose to her upon such short acquaintance. Even more extraordinary was the fact that she had accepted him!

Eve paused by the window. The last remnants of daylight had disappeared and the glass reflected her image like a dark mirror. She had always considered herself a sensible, level-headed young woman, so what madness had possessed her, standing in the garden with the heady scent of summer roses in the air, to accept his proposal?

'No, no, it will not do,' she said aloud, resuming her perambulations. 'Tomorrow I must tell him I have changed my mind—*not* changed my mind,' she amended. 'Merely that I want a little more time to think over his proposal.'

She climbed into bed and snuffed out her candle, satisfied that she had resolved upon a very sensible course of action.

'Hell and damnation we're in the suds now.' Nick shrugged himself out of his coat and tossed it to his valet. 'I had not planned this, Richard!'

'I thought the whole point of coming here was to propose to the young lady,' murmured Granby, folding the coat and laying it tenderly over a chair.

'Yes, of course, but I behaved like a veritable mooncalf!'

'But I understand Miss Shawcross has accepted your offer, Captain.'

'Aye, she has.' Nick slumped down into a chair and gave a heavy sigh.

'Then I wish you happy, sir.'

'Damn your impudence! This wasn't meant to happen— or only as a last resort.' A wry smile tugged at one side of his mouth. 'The truth of it is she's bowled me over, Dick. She floored me with the very first glance from those great brown eyes and I haven't recovered since.'

'Her maid tells me Miss Shawcross is a very accomplished young lady.'

'Aye, so she is. The wonder is that she wasn't snapped up years ago.'

'Martha—that's her maid, Captain—Martha says that she's lived here very quietly since she finished her schooling. Sir Benjamin's health being so poor they have never been in the habit of entertaining.'

Nick gave a short laugh. 'So she's been waiting here all these years, like a Sleeping Beauty! But the devil of it is I'm no Prince Charming.'

A ghost of a smile flitted across Richard Granby's impassive features. 'If you'll pardon me, sir, I think there's plenty of ladies would disagree with you there.'

Nick waved his hand impatiently. 'What if she finds out why I am really here?'

'Perhaps you should tell her.'

'Damn it all, Richard, what would she think of me, marrying her to get control of her property? No, I'll keep my own counsel. After all, another few weeks and this business will be finished, so there's no reason for Miss Evelina Shawcross to know anything about it.' Nick ran a hand through his hair. 'But I do not like the idea of rushing her into this marriage. Mayhap we will merely go through the ceremony. After all, I shall need to get back to the coast almost as soon as the wedding is over. That way, if she finds she really cannot stomach me—'

'If you'll forgive me saying so, Captain, whenever your *liaisons* have finished it's rarely been the lady's choice to end it.'

'Aye, but Miss Shawcross is different.' He pushed himself out of the chair and stretched. 'Look out my nightgown, if you please, Richard. It must be well after midnight by now and time I—' He broke off, frowning. 'Now what the devil is the matter?'

From the corridor outside his room came the sound of urgent whispers and hurrying footsteps. Nick strode over to the door and flung it open. Sir Benjamin's valet was making his way along the passage and by the glow of the lamp he was holding aloft Nick observed that his coat was unbuttoned and his hair tousled, as if he had been roused untimely from his bed. Nick stepped out into his path.

'Well, Rooney, what's amiss?' he demanded.

'It's the master sir. He's had one of his turns.'

'Can I be of help—can Granby ride for a doctor?'

'Thank you, Captain, but no. I've already despatched a groom to fetch Dr Scott. If you will excuse me, sir, I must get back to Sir Benjamin. Miss Eve is with him, but I do not like to be away for too long.'

'Of course.' Nick stepped aside and, after watching the valet hurry out of sight, went back into his room.

'Is it the old gentleman sir?' asked Granby. 'I heard he was very down pin.'

'Yes, he is. Go along and see if there is anything we can do, Richard. Sir Benjamin's man is reluctant to trouble *me*, but he may be more forthcoming to you.'

Having despatched his man, Nick found himself alone. Silence settled around him but it did nothing to relieve his anxiety. He was a guest in the house, but it was unthinkable that he would sleep while Eve was sitting up with her grandfather. He snatched up his coat. There must be something he could do.

When Eve left Sir Benjamin's room her eyes were gritty with lack of sleep. She held aloft a bedroom candlestick to light her way through the dark passages and down the stairs. The arch leading to the great hall glowed with a welcoming light and as she moved forwards she could see that the fire had been built up and several candles burned brightly in the wall sconces. Nick Wylder was bending over the fire, stirring a large black pan that seemed to be balanced precariously amongst the flames. He straightened and turned as he heard her approaching footsteps.

'I was told that you were here, Captain.' She nodded towards the fireplace. 'I doubt anyone has cooked upon that fire for generations.'

'Punch,' he said, smiling. 'Nothing like it for restoring the spirits in the middle of the night.'

'I am sorry if we woke you.'

'No need, I was not asleep.' He reached out for her hand and led her to the settle on one side of the hearth. 'How is Sir Benjamin?'

'Quieter now. Grandfather panics when an attack comes on and he cannot get his breath, but Dr Scott always calms him.'

She sat for a moment, staring into the flames.

'I hope you do not mind, I built up the fire. It is summer, I know, but somehow a good blaze always seems more comforting at times like these.'

'It does, thank you, but you should not have had to do that.'

He waved his hand dismissively.

'Your servants are busy with their master. I would not add to their load.' He turned back to the cooking pot and ladled some of its contents into a cup. 'Here, try this.'

She curled her fingers around the warm cup. She had not realised how cold she had become. A sweet, pungent aroma rose from the liquid and her eyes widened.

'Rum.' Nick grinned. 'Try it.'

Cautiously she took a sip. It was warm and sweet with a fiery bite that made her cough, but it was strangely comforting. Nick was watching her and she managed a small smile.

'Thank you. That is just what I need. Perhaps we should offer some to Dr Scott before he leaves.'

'Of course. Are these attacks a regular occurrence?'

'They have been more frequent in recent months.'

'I did not realise Sir Benjamin was so ill.'

'He hides it well. He does not like people to fuss over him.' She read the question in his eyes and her gaze dropped to the cup clutched between her hands. 'The attacks weaken his heart. The doctor says we must be prepared…' She did not trust her voice to continue so she sipped at the punch.

When she looked up again Nick was watching her, such kind concern in his face that she found herself smiling at him. 'Perhaps now you understand why Grandpapa is so eager to see me settled,' she said, handing him back the empty cup. 'He worries so about what is to become of me when he is gone.'

He sat down beside her on the settle. 'Then at least I can relieve his mind on that account, and perhaps on another.' He reached for her hands. 'When we are married we need not remove to Yorkshire immediately. I think you would prefer to remain near your grandfather.'

His words allayed her barely acknowledged anxiety. She fixed her eyes on his face.

'Truly, you would not mind if we lived here for a little while?'

'Truly. I have an excellent steward who has managed my affairs for a good many years; he will cope for a little while longer.'

'Thank you.' Her relief and gratitude were palpable. Without thinking she leaned towards him and he enfolded her in his arms. It is, she thought, nestling her head contentedly against his shoul-der, like coming home after a long and tiring journey.

Nick rested his cheek against her hair, breathing in the sweet, flowery fragrance. She felt so fragile, so delicate within his arms that he was afraid to hold her too tightly lest she should fracture. His heart ached. He wanted not only to possess this dainty creature but to protect her. It was an unfamiliar feeling, and not altogether comfortable.

They remained locked together in companionable silence for several minutes while the long case clock ticked steadily and logs crackled in the fireplace. He wondered if now was the time to talk to her, to take her into his confidence. He held his peace. It was government business, not his to share. She was so fragile that he did not want to add more worries to her slender shoulders. Besides, in a few more weeks it would all be settled.

Chapter Four

'Dearly beloved, we are gathered here…'

The little church at Makerham was packed. Evelina stood, eyes modestly lowered, and wondered how she had come to this. A month ago there had been no thought of marriage in her head, then Nick Wylder had ridden into her life and changed it for ever. A month ago she had not known of his existence; now she could not imagine life without him.

With the exception of a few days when he had been obliged to go to town on business, Nick had been her constant companion at Makerham Court. They rode through sun-dappled lanes, walked in the gardens and in the evenings they played cards with Sir Benjamin, or Eve would sit in the corner with her embroidery while the two men talked or played backgammon together. Nick's energetic presence filled the house. Eve woke every morning with a little thrill of anticipation, knowing he would be waiting for her. They talked for hours, although she had little rec-ollection of what they talked *about*. Occasionally they would argue, and it would end with Nick pulling her into his arms and kissing her. She had never known such happiness. It was especially gratifying to see her grandfather's approval of her future husband and not even the business of the marriage contract upset this happy state of affairs; Sir Benjamin talked to Eve with smug satisfaction about jointures and settlements and Eve did not press him for details: it was enough for her that he was happy.

And now they were in Makerham church, standing side by side, exchanging marriage vows. A fairy-tale. Some might say it was too good to be true. Eve had to keep pinching herself to believe in her good fortune. Nick's brother, the Earl of Darrington, came to act as his groomsman. Eve thought he looked rather disapproving, but his greeting was kindly enough and he even kissed her hand when she came out of the church on her husband's arm. Her husband. A *frisson* of excitement trembled through her.

'So, you are my sister now.' The earl smiled, lightening his rather sombre expression and all at once looking much more like Nick. 'Welcome to the family, my dear Evelina. I look forward to the day when I can welcome you to Wylderbeck Hall. It is a long way north, but Nick will tell you it is well worth the journey. I wish it was not necessary for me to leave immediately after the wedding breakfast, but so it is; if Nick had given us more notice of your nuptials we would have had time to become acquainted—'

'And have you cut me out, brother?' put in Nick. 'I wanted to make sure of my lady first!'

The earl's smile was a little strained.

'Take care of her, Nick. And bring her north very soon, that she may meet the rest of the clan.'

'I should like that, my lord.' Eve cast a questioning look at Nick.

'I will bring her to you as soon as I can, brother. Our plans are a little uncertain for the moment; we will be staying at Makerham for a few weeks yet.'

'My grandfather's health is not good,' explained Eve. 'The wedding has been a great effort for him, although he was determined it should be held here.'

Nick put his hand over hers. 'I said I would not take you away from Makerham until he is better. You have my word on that.'

She nodded and leaned against him, drawing comfort from his presence at her side. They both knew there was little chance of her grandfather growing stronger. She did not wish to consider the more likely outcome, but it was there, unspoken, and Nick understood. The message was in his eyes now as he looked at her. They would not leave Makerham while Sir Benjamin had need of her.

'I am only sorry that more of your family could not be present,' she said later, when they were standing at the entrance to Makerham Court, ready to receive their guests at the wedding breakfast.

'Do not be,' laughed Nick. 'They would have turned our little celebration into a riotous occasion! Darrington is the serious one, the rest of them are rakes and rabble-rousers, as you will see when I take you to Yorkshire to meet them!'

'I am sure they are not as bad as you make out. Indeed, there are some from my own family that I would as lief not see here,' she murmured, directing his attention to a tall, heavy-browed gentleman who was approaching them. She raised her head, saying more loudly, 'Captain, may I introduce to you my cousin, Mr Bernard Shawcross?'

Mr Shawcross swept off his hat and made such a deep bow that his nose almost touched his knees.

'We have met in town, Cousin. Let me tell you, Captain Wylder, that you have stolen the march on me, it was always my desire to wed my lovely Cousin Evelina.'

She gave him a honey-sweet smile. 'A pity then that you did not apprise me of the fact, Cousin.'

'Ah, but I did not wish to deprive Sir Benjamin of his most devoted companion,' came the smooth reply.

'Oh?' she murmured, 'from the number of times I have read your name in the society columns of the London newspapers I thought you were far too busy chasing heiresses to think of *me*. A pity that you have been unsuccessful thus far, Bernard.' His mouth tightened in displeasure and her smile widened.

'Mere gossip, Evelina,' he replied shortly. 'I am surprised you should take note of such tittle tattle.'

'And have you come directly from town today, sir?' asked Nick.

Bernard Shawcross shook his head. 'I am currently staying with friends near the coast. I regret, Cousin, that I have engagements there I cannot break and will be returning to Sussex in the morning. I shall leave you my direction, in case you need me.'

'Thank you, Bernard, but I can't think that we shall ever *need* you,' she murmured wickedly. 'However, let us not quarrel; I bid you welcome, Cousin. We are delighted that you have graced our wedding with your presence.'

'It was the very least I could do, Evelina, even though the event has taken place with——er—indecent haste.'

Her smile widened at his obvious annoyance.

'We are merely following Grandpa's wishes,' she returned, coolly. 'Have you spoken to him yet? No? Then perhaps you should do so now, while he is free.' She added quietly, as he turned on his heel and stalked away, 'It would do you no harm to play the dutiful heir once in a while.'

Nick drew his breath in with a hiss. 'Remind me never to get on the wrong side of you, madam wife,' he murmured.

'At one time Bernard was forever calling at Makerham, asking Grandpapa to advance him loans against his inheritance. Thank-fully he has not called at all for the past year, so I can only suppose that he has learned to live within his means.'

'That, or he has found an additional source of income,' observed Nick. 'You will note that his coat is of the very finest cut: such tailoring only comes at a price.'

'I do not care how he comes by his money as long as he stays away from Makerham.' Eve shuddered. 'I cannot like him, his manner towards me has always been…possessive, and I dislike the way he fawns over Grandpapa, as though his well-being is his only concern, yet when he leaves he never writes to enquire after Grandpapa's health—but perhaps I refine too much upon it.'

'You need not concern yourself with your cousin any longer, sweetheart. I will not let him trouble you.' Nick squeezed her fingers. 'Come, my dear, our guests have all arrived now, I think we may take our places at table.'

They feasted in the great hall, which had been decorated for the occasion with garlands of summer flowers. Even though she was the bride, Eve was also the hostess and it was her duty to announce the wines for the diners and to direct their attention to the cold meat dishes and salads available on the sideboard. She also had to watch the servants to make sure no guest was neglected. With so much to do it there was little time for reflection. It was not until the meal was ending that she allowed herself to think about the coming night.

Her wedding night.

'That went off very well, I think,' declared Sir Benjamin as the last of the carriages drove away. 'I do wish, however, that we had invited at least some of our people to stay here.'

Eve came to stand beside his chair.

'You know we would not have been able to accommodate more than a few of our guests—and we should have been obliged to offer Bernard a room; you know how much you would dislike that.'

'You are very right, my love. They will be a deal more comfortable at the White Hart. Ah, and here is Rooney come to take me to my room. Goodnight, my dear, Captain Wylder. Such a tiring day, I shall sleep well, I think.'

As she watched her grandfather leave the room, leaning heavily upon his valet's arm, Eve knew a moment of panic. For the first time that day she was alone with her husband. There had been no awkwardness on previous evenings; she had merely bade him goodnight and they had gone their separate ways, but tonight she knew that the oriel bedroom had been prepared for them. It was the principal bedchamber in the house and legend had it that Henry VIII had slept there. On Sir Benjamin's instructions it had been cleaned and the huge tester bed furnished with new bed linen. Eve had a sudden, wild fancy to ask Nick if he would like to play a game of backgammon.

'We should retire,' he said gently. 'Your maid will be waiting to put you to bed and Richard will be looking out for me also; we must not disappoint them.' He took her hands and lifted them one after the other to his lips. Even that small gesture made her knees grow weak. 'Off you go, my dear. Send word when you are ready for me.'

She found Martha bustling around the oriel bedroom. Her new linen nightgown was laid out on the bed. It looked pale and insignificant against the blood-red velvet of the bedhangings. Eve shivered.

'Martha, I don't know what to do,' she whispered, desperately.

Her maid chuckled. 'With the two of you smelling of April and May ever since Captain Wylder arrived? You will have no prob-lems, Mistress. Leave it all to the captain. Now then, Miss Eve, let me help you out of your gown.'

Send word when you are ready, Nick had said. Perhaps she need not send for him at all. She thought wildly that she would lock the doors and spend the night alone, but she knew that would not do. In the event it was not her decision. Once Martha had put her into her nightgown and arranged her hair becomingly around her shoulders, she gathered up her clothes.

'There. You look as pretty as a picture, mistress. I will send word to the captain that you await him. Shall I light the candles before I leave you?'

'No.' The summer night was drawing in, but it was not yet dark. 'Leave them.'

Outside the open window Eve could hear a night bird singing. Her nerves were on edge and every sound seemed louder, sharper.

I'm not ready for this, she thought suddenly. *Nick Wylder is a stranger.* She wrapped her arms about her, closing her eyes to conjure his face in her mind. She pictured him smiling at her with that warm, understanding look in his eyes and her panic subsided. Nick was no stranger. In her heart she had always known him.

Nick stood in the doorway and regarded the little figure by the window. She had her back to him, and her head was bowed as if in prayer.

'Eve?' He spoke her name quietly.

She jumped and turned. The light from the window provided a gleaming halo for her hair as it flowed down over her shoulders. He could see every curve of her body through the gossamer-thin nightgown. The sight inflamed him, rousing the desire he had kept under control for the past four weeks. His breath caught in his throat. By heaven, how he wanted her! As he crossed the room he saw how nervous she was. He felt a desperate desire to tell her everything, but he dare not. Not yet. He must control himself, play for time. As long as they did not consummate the marriage then he could set her free, when it was all over and the danger was past. He would explain why it had been necessary to marry her in such haste and then, if she still wanted to be his wife, so be it, but it must be her choice. He owed her that much. He reached out and placed his hands gently on her shoulders. Her eyes, dark and luminous in her pale face, looked towards him for reassurance. His mouth was dry; suddenly *he* was anxious. What if he broke her heart?

'Eve, we do not have to do this tonight…'

She put her fingers against his mouth. 'I want to, Nick. I want to, very much,' she murmured, then with her hands on his shoulders she reached up and kissed him.

Nick felt the touch of her lips and he was lost.

Evelina marvelled at her temerity, yet when she had seen the concern in Nick's eyes her own doubts had fled and she had desperately wanted to comfort him. She felt his arms around her and her own crept about his neck. As Nick kissed her back with increasing urgency her lips parted and his tongue explored her mouth, flickering and teasing and stirring up the hot fire that burned deep in her belly. He was wearing a brightly patterned dressing robe, but through the heavy silk she could feel his body, hard against hers and she experienced a heady, exhilarating sensation of power even as he swept her up and carried her to the bed. She kept her eyes on his face, marking every line and shadow, the purposeful curve of his lips and the deepening colour of his eyes—they were almost black as they looked at her now and she trembled at the passion in their depths. He laid her on the covers and she reached up for him, wanting to kiss him again, but he resisted while he untied the belt of his robe. Eve's eyes widened as he shed the heavy satin. She had expected him to be wearing a nightshirt and the sight of his naked body surprised her. Nervously she ran her tongue over her lips. Nick lowered himself gently on to the bed beside her, measuring his length against hers, propping himself upon one arm while he ran his free hand gently across her cheek.

'You are so beautiful,' he murmured. 'More than I ever imagined.'

Eve swallowed hard. 'So, too, are you,' she managed to say with a shy, tremulous smile.

He bent his head, capturing her lips again while his hands moved over her, caressing her body through the thin nightdress. Eve's own hands were exploring too, running over Nick's arms, stroking his shoulders, tracing his spine. His body was smooth and firm beneath her fingers, the muscles rippling beneath the skin. His kisses deepened and her own desire mounted. She wanted to be closer to him; even the thin muslin of her nightgown between them was too much. She broke away and sat up, scrabbling to drag off the last scrap of fabric that separated her from Nick. After a heartbeat's hesitation he helped her, his breathing as ragged as her own. As she raised her arms to drag the gown over her head she felt his hands capturing her nakedness. Collecting up her breasts, he buried his face in their softness. Gasping, she freed herself from the flimsy material and they fell together on to the covers in a tangle of limbs.

Nick's lips moved back up her body, slid over her mouth, his kiss urgent and demanding while his hands on her skin caused her body to writhe out of her control. She threw back her head, shuddering with surprise and delight as his hand moved between her thighs, gently easing them apart. She arched beneath his questing fingers, moving against them, not knowing why, only aware of the ache in her groin and the pleasurable sensations he was arousing deep, deep within her. He kissed her neck; she felt his lips briefly on her collar-bone, then they fastened over one erect nipple and she gasped. The pleasure was so heady and intense that she thought she might faint. She was soaring, flying and falling all at the same time. Her hands gripped him, fingers digging into his shoulders as the first spasm shook her, then a second. She knew a moment's panic as those pleasuring fingers eased away and Nick rolled over and entered her. She gave a little cry and he froze. Desperately Eve pushed against him.

'No, no, do not stop,' she gasped.

She heard him give a shaky laugh. 'I don't think I could, even if I wanted to.'

The blood was pounding in her ears, singing through her body as they moved together. The wave of pleasure had receded, but it was building within her again. She matched her movements to Nick's, running her hands over his muscled back, keeping pace with him as the tempo increased, the heady wave building and building until at last, when she thought she might die of pleasure, it crested and broke. She heard a cry, but did not know if it came from her or Nick. He tensed and tensed again before they subsided together, shuddering and gasping for breath.

They lay side by side on the silken bedcovers, fingers entwined. The daylight had gone now, replaced by a fine silvery moonlight that cast a magical gleam over their naked bodies.

'Nick?' Eve raised herself upon one elbow and looked at him. Her heart lurched. Could this handsome man really be her husband? Was it possible that he could love her, that she could satisfy him? She gently brushed her hand across the scattering of crisp black hairs that grew on his chest. 'Was— was that how it is meant to be? Was it, I mean, was I—?'

His hand came up to trap hers against his chest. He grinned at her. 'You were magnificent, Eve. I am a very lucky man.'

She flushed with delight. He reached up, hooked his fingers around her neck and began to pull her down to him. 'In fact,' he whispered, 'I think we should try that again, just to be sure…'

Chapter Five

Eve awoke the next morning to the sound of birdsong outside her window. As her sleepiness disappeared and memories of the previous night returned, a delicious feeling of well-being spread through her body. She reached out, expecting to feel Nick next to her, but she was alone in the bed. Eve opened her eyes.

Nick was standing by the window. With the early-morning sun behind him she could not see his face but she knew that he was watching her.

'Nick?'

As he came towards the bed she noted that he was dressed for riding, already booted and spurred.

'I did not want to wake you. You looked so peaceful.'

'You are going out? Will you not wait for me and I will go with you—'

'That is not possible,' he murmured, sitting on the edge of the bed and taking her hand. 'I have to go away for a few days. The messenger came this very morning from Hastings. Business, I am afraid, my love, that requires my urgent attention.'

Eve sat up. 'Hastings! What business can be so important it takes you away so soon after the wedding?' she demanded.

'That I cannot tell you.'

'Oh, but—' He put a finger on her lips and shook his head at her.

'Hush, my dear. You must trust me on this.'

He was still smiling at her, but there was something in his blue eyes that gave her pause, made her bite back the host of questions she wanted to ask him. He leaned forwards and kissed her, very gently. 'Only the most urgent business could tear me away from you at this time,' he said. 'Can you believe that?'

She nodded, suddenly feeling sick with misery. This was nothing unusual, she told herself. Gentlemen did not discuss business affairs with their wives. She shivered, suddenly aware of her nakedness. Nick walked across the room to fetch her wrap of apricot silk. She slipped out of bed and scrambled into it, giving her attention to fastening the ties so that she did not have to look up. He reached out for her.

'I am sorry, sweetheart.'

As he hugged her to him, Eve leaned her head against his chest, willing herself not to cry.

'How soon will you be back?'

His arms tightened around her. 'I do not know. A week, if all goes well. Longer, if not.'

'And—you cannot tell me what is this business that takes you away from me?' Eve knew he would not tell her, even as she asked the question. He put his fingers under her chin and tilted her head up. She looked up into his eyes, blinking to clear her own of the tears that threatened to spill over.

'I must ask you to trust me, my love.'

'I do,' she said passionately.

He kissed her. 'Then stay here, keep yourself safe for when I return.'

She shuddered suddenly and had a vague premonition of danger. 'Promise me you *will* return!'

He laughed down at her, the light glinting in his blue eyes. 'You adorable little goose, of course I shall return!' He kissed her soundly and she leaned into him, returning his kisses and hoping he would sweep her up and carry her back to the bed for one final act of lovemaking before he left. Her disappointment as he gently put her aside was so strong it almost made her weep. 'I must get on, my sweet.'

'Can you not give me ten minutes to dress? I would like to come downstairs and take my leave of you.' She noted his hesitation and added quietly, 'Please, Nick.'

He relented. 'Very well. Ten minutes.'

Nick watched her walk out of the room, her head held high. A wave of tenderness welled up in him. She did not understand why he must go yet there were no tears, no tantrums. He had asked her to trust him and she did. He put out his hand, opened his mouth to call out to her, but something held him back. The moment was lost; the door had closed behind her.

'Just as well,' he told himself. 'The less she knows of this affair, the better.'

A little over ten minutes later, Eve accompanied Nick out of the house, trying not to cling too tightly to his arm.

'Will you be able to write to me, sir?' She tried to keep her voice light.

'I shall try, but it may not be possible if I am very busy.' He lifted her hand to his lips. 'Be strong for me, my love, until I return.'

Looking up into his laughing face, she remembered her

first impression of him; an adventurer, a man who courted danger. Her fingers suddenly clenched on his hand. 'You will be careful?'

He gave a merry laugh. 'Sweetheart I am always careful!' With a squeeze of her fingers he turned away and mounted nimbly upon his black horse.

'Granby will be following me with the carriage in an hour or so.' He grinned down at her, his eyes glinting. 'I do not want to hear that you have gone into a decline, madam.'

She dragged up a smile. 'I am not such a poor creature, sir. I shall keep myself busy until your return.' His warm look turned her heart over.

'Good girl. Come up, Admiral!' He raised his whip in a salute as he turned and galloped away down the drive.

Eve watched from the little bridge until Nick was out of sight, then with a sigh she went back into the house. There was an aching void in her chest and she had a desperate desire to burst into tears. She glanced at the clock in the great hall; it was still very early. She had been married for less than twenty-four hours and already her husband had given her both more pleasure, and more pain, than she had ever known before.

When Eve joined Sir Benjamin in the morning room some time later, he held out his hand to her. 'Rooney told me Nick has been called away, my love. That is a great pity. But it means I have you to myself again.'

She smiled as she grasped his outstretched fingers. 'Indeed you do, Grandpapa.'

'And are you happy with the husband I have found for you, my love?'

She smiled down at him. 'Can you doubt it, sir?'

'No, love. You have been glowing with happiness these past few weeks.' Sir Benjamin sighed. 'But we shall miss him.

He is a very lively fellow, Nick Wylder—Wyldfire, they called him, when he was at sea.' He chuckled. 'He certainly sets the house alight with his energy! And he has entertained us royally, has he not, my dear?'

'Yes, sir, and while he is gone we must entertain each other,' said Eve bracingly. 'It is a beautiful day, Grandpapa, will you not take a stroll with me through the garden? I should like you to see the flowerbeds; the roses are particularly fragrant just now. Rooney will give you his arm...'

'I think not, my love. My legs do not feel so very strong today.'

'Then let me bring the backgammon board into the morning room. I know Nick's skill is superior to mine, but I can acquit myself creditably, I think.'

Sir Benjamin patted her hand. 'Not just now, Evelina. I am very tired. I think I should like to rest here quietly in the sunshine for a little while.'

'Of course, Grandpapa.' She bent to kiss his cheek. 'There is plenty for me to do. I fear I have neglected my household duties recently.'

Poor Grandpapa, she thought as she went out. *He will miss Nick almost as much as I do.*

Evelina kept herself busy. She threw herself back into the life of Makerham, for she was still its mistress, and would remain so until Nick came back and carried her away to run his own houses in the north. During the long, lonely nights in the big tester bed she stifled her longings with thoughts of her new life so far from the only home she had ever known. She would be sad to leave Grandpapa, of course, but the thought of moving away did not frighten her: with Nick at her side she knew she need not fear anything.

A week had gone by and there was no letter from Nick,

only a hastily scribbled note, telling her that if she had need of him she could leave word at the Ship in Hastings. Eve was philosophical about this; her grandfather had been a very poor correspondent when she had been at school, sometimes a month would pass without a letter and then when it came it would be little more than a few lines dashed off in haste. She folded Nick's note and placed it under her pillow; she would not worry. Besides, she had a much more pressing concern. Sir Benjamin's health was failing rapidly. She sent for the doctor, and came hurrying downstairs to meet him as soon as he arrived.

'Thank you for coming so promptly, Dr Scott.'

'It is no trouble at all, Miss Eve—I mean, Mrs Wylder,' responded the doctor, a twinkle in his kind eyes. 'Now tell me, what is the matter with my patient? Is it his legs again?'

Eve nodded. 'He is complaining of pains in his chest, too. Since the wedding he has not been out of the house,' she said as she escorted him up to her grandfather's room. 'I thought at first he was a little tired from all the celebrations, but this past week he has kept to his bed. And he is eating so little.'

'Well, take me to him, Mrs Wylder, and I'll see what I can do.'

Eve was busy arranging a bowl of roses in the great hall when the doctor came in search of her.

'I thought I would take these up to Grandpapa,' she said, as he descended the stairs. 'He is so fond of flowers and the perfume from these is delightful.' Her smile faltered as she looked at him. 'It is not good news, I fear, Dr Scott.'

'You must remember he is an old man,' said the doctor gently. 'And a very sick one.'

'I do,' she murmured. 'I am very grateful that he has been with me for so long…'

'I have often thought that he was determined to keep going for your sake. Now that you are married—'

'Oh, pray do not say that!' cried Eve, distressed.

'No, well, perhaps not.' Dr Scott patted her shoulder. 'Go to him, my dear. Take him your flowers. I will call again tomorrow.'

'Grandpapa, I have brought you some roses. Since you cannot go to the garden, the garden must come to you. I shall put them here, near the window where you can see them. There, are they not beautiful?'

Sir Benjamin smiled a little. He was propped up on a bank of plump pillows, but his eyes were shut. He looked gaunt and grey and very frail in his nightcap and gown.

Eve went over to the bed and took his hand. 'Will you not look at the roses, Grandfather?'

His eyes opened a fraction. 'Very pretty,' he murmured. 'You must excuse me, my love. I cannot seem to get my breath.'

'Then do not waste it on words,' she whispered. 'I shall sit here beside you: we need not talk.'

By the time Dr Scott returned the next morning it was all over. Evelina met him with a black shawl wrapped around her shoulders. Her eyes, she knew, were red and swollen from crying, but she made no excuses.

'Oh, my dear.' He took her hands.

Evelina lifted her head a little higher. 'It was very peaceful,' she said. 'Rooney and I were with him.'

'I'm glad, the two people who loved him most in the world. He would like that. But what will you do now? You should not be here alone.'

'Why not? I am accustomed to that.'

'But not in these circumstances. There are arrangements to be made,' said Dr Scott. 'The funeral, for instance…'

'I shall instruct Grandpapa's lawyers today; they will know what is to be done. And I shall write to my husband.' A new burst of sadness clogged her throat making it difficult to speak. She missed Nick so badly. 'He is away for the moment.'

'Then I wish him God speed to return to you, Mrs Wylder.'

Evelina wished it, too, but she could not allow Nick's continued absence to fill her thoughts, there was too much to do. Letters had to be written, lawyers consulted and funeral arrangements to be put in place. Evelina left the running of Makerham to Mrs Harding while she busied herself with the rituals of bereavement. She sent off her note express to Hastings and wondered how soon she could expect a reply.

Two days later she was in one of the attic rooms, searching through trunks of her mother's clothes for anything that might be altered and used as a mourning gown when from the open window she heard the sounds of a carriage on the drive. Her heart began to thud painfully at the thought that Nick had returned. She hurtled down the stairs, arriving in the great hall just as the door opened.

'Oh I knew you would come! I—'

She broke off, fighting back a wave of anger and disappointment when she saw Bernard Shawcross stepping through the doorway.

'I am delighted to think I have not disappointed you, Cousin,' he said smoothly. As he straightened from his bow he put his hand to his neck. 'You see, I have adopted a black cravat. Thought it fitting.'

'Y-yes, thank you,' she stammered. 'You received my letter.'

He inclined his head. 'I came immediately. I thought you

would need me. This is a very distressing time for you. You have my deepest sympathy, dear Cousin. Such a shock for you.'

'Shock? No...no. Grandpapa's health has been of concern for some time. That is why we did not remove to my husband's home in the north country. But you must think me very rag-mannered. Pray sit down, Bernard; you must be wondering why Captain Wylder is not here to greet you. He is away, you see. On business.'

'Ah.' His close-set eyes under their heavy brows were fixed upon her. 'So you have not heard from him?'

'N-no, not yet. It is my hope that he is even now on his way to Makerham.'

Bernard's mouth stretched into a smile. 'Let us hope so, indeed. But in the meantime I am here to support you. If you would ask Mrs Harding to prepare a room for me...' He waved one hand. 'I know, by rights it should be the master's room, but perhaps it is a little soon.'

She knew a little spurt of anger at his presumption. 'Far too soon,' she retorted. 'Grandfather's bedchamber is still as he left it—' She broke off, gathered herself and said more calmly, 'One of the guest rooms shall be prepared for you.'

Eve was glad of the excuse to leave her cousin and she hurried away to consult the housekeeper. Mrs Harding's reaction to his arrival was typically forthright.

'So he's turned up, has he? Like a bad penny, that one.'

'He is the master here now, Mrs Harding,' Eve reminded her gently. She ignored the housekeeper's scornful look. 'I must clear Grandpapa's room for him, but not yet.'

'No of course not yet, Miss Eve! Why, the master ain't even in his grave. We'll strip the room out completely after the funeral, miss, and we'll do it together. It's not a job for a young lady to take on alone.'

'And...' Eve bit her lip '...and will you join us for dinner,

Mrs Harding?' She could not explain her uneasiness, but the older woman nodded immediately.

'Of course, miss, and I'll be in the drawing room of an evening, too. You shouldn't be left alone with that man.'

'Oh, I am sure there is nothing…'

'You cannot be sure of anything with that one,' retorted Mrs Harding grimly. 'He's trouble, you mark my words. I just wish the captain was here, he would know how to look after you.'

Eve forced a smile. How easily the staff had taken to Nick.

'Perhaps we shall have news of him tomorrow.'

Chapter Six

It was not until the day of Sir Benjamin's funeral that they received word of Nick and when it came, the news was shattering. Evelina was in the morning room with her cousin, waiting for the carriage to take them to Makerham church when Green announced that Captain Wylder's valet had arrived and wished to speak to her.

'At last!' She gave a brief look of apology to her cousin as she hurried away to the great hall where Richard Granby was waiting for her.

'Well,' she greeted him, 'what news have you from your master?' She heard footsteps on the stairs behind her and knew a moment's irritation that her cousin should follow her, but it was forgotten as she observed the grave look upon Granby's face. 'What is it?' she said sharply. 'Tell me.'

'There has been an…accident, ma'am.'

Evelina stared at him. Bernard put his arm about her and guided her to a chair.

'You had best sit down, Cousin,' he murmured.

She kept her eyes fixed upon the valet. 'An accident? Is he badly hurt?'

Granby shifted uncomfortably and Eve put her hands

to her cheeks as a shocking idea forced its way into her head.

'Not—?'

Bernard's hand clenched on her shoulder. 'Is he dead?' he said harshly. 'Out with it, man.'

'Yes, sir.'

Eve could only stare at him. The world was shifting, unbalanced. She was having difficulty thinking. She heard Bernard asking what had happened and tried to concentrate upon Granby's answer.

'Drowned. Fell overboard from the yacht. On Saturday last.'

'Perhaps he survived,' suggested Bernard. 'Might there not be some hope?'

Granby shook his head. 'No sir. They were somewhere beyond the Rocks of Nore, too far out for an injured man to swim. But we did check the beaches...'

'Yacht?' Eve frowned. 'But he went to Hastings on business. What was he doing on a *yacht*?'

Granby looked even more uncomfortable.

Bernard patted Eve's shoulder. 'There will be time for such questions later, my dear. For now I think you should lie down.' His calm assumption of authority put new spirit into Eve.

Impatiently she shook off his hand. 'I have no intention of lying down. I am not ill, Cousin, and I shall not fall into hysterics because my husband is—' She could not bring herself to say the word. She knew her composure could shatter at any moment and she would not let that happen. She must stay strong. Eve took a deep, steadying breath. 'You must have ridden half the night to reach here so early, Mr Granby. Thank you for that, I suggest you rest now.'

'Yes, ma'am. I am very sorry, Mrs Wylder.'

'Mrs Wylder,' she murmured. 'No one calls me that

here.' She looked up. 'One more thing, Mr Granby. My husband's body…?'

The valet hesitated. He avoided her eyes as he murmured, 'Lost, ma'am.'

'It might still be recovered,' put in Bernard.

'The news was spread along the coast.' Granby nodded. 'They have promised to send word if he is…found.'

'They?' said Bernard. 'Who would that be?'

'The master's business acquaintances.'

In spite of the numbness that had settled over her, Eve almost smiled. The valet's haughty tone and the look that accompanied his words said very clearly that Nick Wylder's business was his own affair, certainly not to be shared with Bernard Shawcross. She rose.

'We will talk later, Mr Granby.' She turned to her cousin, 'Perhaps you would escort me to the carriage, Bernard.'

'My dear cousin, it is not necessary—indeed, it is not usual—for females to attend a funeral.' Eve stared at him and he continued gently, 'I have no doubt you would prefer to go to your room. Shall I send your maid to you?'

'No, Cousin. I will go to the church. I need to be active.'

'But surely—'

She put up a hand. Her voice, when she spoke, was barely under control. 'I wish, Cousin, you would stop trying to order my life. I shall go on much better if I am allowed to keep busy. Please let me have my way in this.'

'My dear Evelina, I am head of the family now—'

Granby coughed. 'Beggin' your pardon, sir, but Mrs Wylder is part of Lord Darrington's family now.'

Eve felt a flicker of gratitude for Richard Granby. Bernard scowled, but as he opened his mouth to retort she forestalled him.

'Yes, thank you, Mr Granby. That is all for now. You may

go.' She reached up to her bonnet and pulled the veil down over her face. 'Cousin, our carriage is at the door.'

Sir Benjamin had been an important figure in Makerham and the little village church was packed with those wishing to pay their last respects. The sight of Evelina in her flowing black robes and leaning heavily on her cousin's arm caused more than one stolid parishioner to blink away a tear. When the coffin was carried out of the church and Miss Shaw-cross fainted clean away, there were many that said it was a blessing she should be spared the sight of her beloved grand-father's body being consigned to the earth.

Martha accompanied her mistress back to the house and half-carried her up to her room, but it was not until her maid had tucked her up in her bed and departed that Eve allowed her pent-up grief to spill over. Tears burned her eyes and huge, gasping sobs racked her body as she mourned for the loss of her grandfather and her husband. She curled herself into a ball and sank her teeth into her fist to prevent herself screaming with rage and grief and pain. Sir Benjamin's death had long been anticipated, but Nick's loss was unbearable; she was not prepared for the agony and in some strange way she felt betrayed. He had ridden into her life and she had tumbled headlong into love with him. She had trusted him with her heart and now he was gone, as quickly as he had come. She dragged the covers over her head and allowed the tears to fall, crying for her grandfather, for Nick, for herself. Finally, as exhaustion set in, she buried her face in her damp pillow, praying that the expensive feather-and-down filling would deprive her lungs of air and suffocate her.

When Eve awoke to the grey dawn, her first conscious thought was disappointment. Disappointment that she was still alive. The silence in the house told her it was very early. She threw back the covers and crawled out of bed; there was a heaviness to her limbs that made every movement a struggle. She dragged herself over to the window and looked out. The garden was grey and colourless in the half-light. Very fitting, she thought. A house in mourning. She crossed her arms over her chest and tried to make sense of her grief. She had been prepared to lose her grandfather; they had said their goodbyes and she was comforted by the thought that he was no longer suffering from pain or ill-health. She was saddened by his death, but not bereft. But Nick—Nick with his dazzling smile and laughing blue eyes. He had ridden into her sheltered world and given her a glimpse of a much more exciting one. She had known him for such a short time, but now she missed him so much it was a physical pain inside her.

She gazed out at the horizon, where a watery sun was climbing through the clouds. Soon the house would be awake and Martha would come in with her hot chocolate. Life would go on and she was expected to do her duty. With a sigh she turned away from the window. The day stretched interminably before her. She had no idea how she would bear this misery.

Her fairy-tale had turned to a nightmare.

'Ah, Cousin, here you are.'

Evelina schooled her features as Bernard Shawcross came into the morning room. To smile at him was impossible, but she must not glower.

'So I have found you alone at last.' He laughed gently. 'I was beginning to think you were avoiding me.'

And with good reason, thought Eve. Aloud, she said, 'I have been very busy. Since the funeral there have been so many visitors wishing to offer their condolences, then there are all the legal matters to attend to as well as the household duties to be done…'

'At least with that I may assist you,' he said, sitting down near her. 'After all, Makerham is my home now, so I can remove that worry from your pretty shoulders.'

She repressed a shudder. 'Makerham was never a worry, Cousin,' she replied coolly.

'Green tells me that you have been closeted with your lawyer this morning. Is there any news of your husband?'

She shook her head. 'Mr Didcot urges caution. Without a—' she swallowed hard '—without a b-body he is loathe to pronounce me a widow. Both he and Granby advise me to go to Yorkshire and place myself under the protection of my husband's family.'

'Yorkshire is a wild, uncivilised country, Cousin. You would not like it.'

She raised her brows. 'You cannot call York and Harrogate uncivilised. Really, Bernard, you are quite Gothic at times.'

'Perhaps, but you have always lived in the south, always at Makerham. We are the last of the Shawcross family, Cousin. It is only right that I should want to take care of you.'

He reached out as he spoke and put his hand on her knee. Eve froze.

'Please, Cousin. I am a married woman.'

'You are a *widow*, my dear.'

'You are very certain of that.'

'I would not have you keep false hopes alive.' The hand on her knee tightened. 'And now that you have experienced a man's touch—'

She jumped up. 'Pray stop. It is far too soon for such a conversation, Bernard! Please, excuse me!'

She turned away but his hand shot out and caught her arm.

'Think, Evelina. What do you know of Wylder's family? You must not go north. You would be far from everything you have ever known, ever loved. Consider what I can offer you.' He was standing behind her now, his breath hot on her neck. 'He was a hellraiser, that husband of yours. Did you know that? Did you think you could reform him? Impossible, madam: you cannot tame a tiger, only cage him. If he was truly changed, how could he leave you so soon after your marriage?'

She shook her head. 'No,' she protested. 'I shall not listen to you!'

'But you must! He tricked you, Eve. He never really loved you. Had he done so, he could not have left you. How could any man leave you?' He pulled her back against him and murmured in her ear, 'You love Makerham, and you need never leave it. You can stay here, run it as you have always done. We will marry, of course, as soon as that is possible, but until then, we can be… discreet.'

Eve fought down her growing panic. His grip on her arms was like iron, biting into her flesh. She knew she could not free herself by force. She must stay calm if she was to escape. She said in a low voice, 'Please, Cousin. This is all so, so unexpected. My thoughts are in turmoil.'

'Of course. I should not have spoken yet.' She felt his lips on the back of her neck. 'Off you go, my dear. We will talk more of this later.'

Eve forced herself to walk slowly out of the room, her back rigid with fear, as though there were some wild animal behind her, ready to pounce. As soon as she reached the hall she picked up her skirts and fled to her room, trying to blot out the memory of Bernard's mouth upon her skin.

Eve changed her gown and at the dinner hour she made her way down to the drawing room with some trepidation.

She was relieved to find only the housekeeper awaiting her. 'Mrs Harding, I must get away from Makerham.'

'Away from the new master, you mean.'

The blunt statement made Eve smile.

'His intentions are—ultimately—honourable.'

Mrs Harding gave a scornful laugh. 'Aye. He'll have to marry you if he is to get Monkhurst.'

'I beg your pardon?'

'I heard him talking to Lawyer Didcot when he came to read the will.' The housekeeper flushed slightly. 'I needed to pick some rosemary from the bush outside the study window, so I couldn't help but overhear, mistress. He questioned Mr Didcot very closely, he did, about who would get Monkhurst now you was married. Mr Didcot said of course he wasn't at liberty to discuss the marriage settlement, but he *could* tell him that Monkhurst was secured on you and your heirs. Unless you died without issue,' she continued, her brow furrowed in concentration. 'Then of course it would go directly to your husband. It seems Bernard was hoping it might revert to the family, but as Lawyer Didcot explained to him, it belonged to your mama's family, the Winghams, and was never part of the entail.'

'But why should he want Monkhurst? The house has been shut up for years, since Mama died, in fact.'

Mrs Harding spread her hands. 'Mayhap 'tis greed, Miss Eve. He wants everything.'

'Well he shall not have it,' declared Eve. 'Any more than he shall have me!'

Mrs Harding put up her hand. 'Hush now, dearie, I hear his step in the hall. And you need not look so anxious, I am not about to leave you alone with that man.'

The housekeeper was as good as her word, and after an uncomfortable dinner Eve made her excuses to retire to her room. There she was careful to make sure her door was locked securely. She crept into her bed and lay rigidly beneath the covers.

It was little more than a week since she had tried to cheat sleep and stay awake each night to think about Nick Wylder, to go over their conversations, relive their moments together. Since the news of Nick's death, when her whole being ached for the oblivion of sleep, it would not come. But at least now, following Bernard's sudden declaration, she could spend the long, sleepless night making her plans.

Early the next day she summoned Granby to the morning room, and when he came in she began without preamble. 'Granby, I am leaving Makerham.'

'Ah. We go to Yorkshire, ma'am?'

'No. I plan to go to Monkhurst.'

'Monkhurst! But, that's impossible!'

'It is very possible,' she replied crisply. 'The marriage settlement is quite clear; Monkhurst remains my own.'

'But surely it would be better for you to be under the protection of the master's family.'

'No, why should it? My grandfather provided for me very well in his will, and Mr Didcot assures me that it will not be affected by my—my widowhood. I am dependent upon no one, Mr Granby.'

'Of course, ma'am. But—'

'My mind is made up.'

The valet stared at her, his usually impassive countenance betraying his consternation. 'I pray you, mistress, reconsider. You said yourself Monkhurst has not been lived in for the past ten years! It—it could be derelict. Allow me to escort you to Yorkshire. You will be made very welcome, and—'

'Now why should you be so horrified at the thought of

Monkhurst?' she asked him. 'It is my own property, after all. I lived there with Mama and Papa for the first few years of my life. And as for being derelict, no such thing! I was used to help Grandpapa with the accounts and I know he is still paying the housekeeper and her husband to look after the house. I shall feel more comfortable amongst my own people, under the present circumstances.'

'Of course, ma'am, but surely—'

'Yes?' There was a touch of impatience in her voice now.

The valet bowed his head. 'I am sorry, madam, if you think I speak out of turn, but the master would want you to go to his family.'

'But the master is not here.' She was not able to keep the tremor from her voice.

'No, ma'am, but—'

'Enough, Mr Granby. My mind is made up. Since you returned from Hastings in the travelling carriage I should like to use it to go to Monkhurst. You may use the baggage wagon to take Captain Wylder's trunks on to Yorkshire. I shall ensure you have sufficient funds for the journey.'

'No, ma'am.'

'I beg your pardon?'

Granby tilted up his head, his chin jutting obstinately. 'I cannot leave you, Mrs Wylder. The master would never forgive me. I mean,' he added hastily, 'if you are going to Monkhurst, then I should like to come with you, mistress. I could be useful to you. As a courier, perhaps, or a steward at Monkhurst.'

'A steward! Do you know anything about such matters?'

'I sailed with the captain for years, madam, and only became his valet when he left the sea. I know a great deal more than how to dress a gentleman, and I cannot like the idea of you and Martha travelling so far without a man.'

Eve regarded his solid figure. 'I confess it would be a comfort to have a manservant with me.'

A look of relief flashed in his eyes. He bowed. 'Then it is settled. Mrs Wylder. I shall go and pack.'

'Hurry, then, for I wish to be away from here by noon.'

It was not to be expected that Bernard would take Eve's decision calmly, but in the presence of Mrs Harding and the servants he could not argue too strongly and Eve was careful not to give him the opportunity to speak to her alone. By noon the carriage was packed and ready to depart.

'I fear you will find the house in a dreadful state,' Bernard warned her as he helped her into the carriage.

'Perhaps, but I sent a messenger off at dawn to advise the staff there of my arrival.'

'The devil you did! You planned this and never a word to me!'

'Come, Bernard, do not scowl so. Let us part as friends.'

After a slight hesitation he took her hand and bowed over it. 'Very well. But I cannot like it.' He kissed her fingers. 'Remember, Evelina, you will always be welcome here at Makerham.'

It was shortly after noon when Eve left Makerham. She dare not look back at the house that had been her home for so many years, nor at the churchyard where Sir Benjamin's remains now rested. Instead she kept her gaze fixed upon Granby, who was riding alongside the carriage. It reminded her of her first sight of Nick Wylder, when he came cantering towards her on his magnificent black horse. The memory brought a lump to her throat. She could not yet believe that she would never see Nick again. Eve wondered what had become of Admiral. She must ask Mr Granby. If the animal was still at Hastings then he must be fetched, even if he had to be sold. Yes, he most definitely would have to be sold, she thought, trying to be practical. But not yet. Not until she was settled in her new life.

The day dragged on. Even the thought of seeing Monkhurst again, a house Eve had not visited for a decade, did not have the power to excite her. Her grandfather's loss had not been unexpected and although she grieved for him she was not overcome. It was Nick who filled her thoughts. Nick with his devastating smile and that twinkle in his blue eyes, his energy and enthusiasm for life. She remembered the night they had shared, a single night that had transformed her from a girl into a woman. Nick had made her feel alive, he had aroused emotions in her such as she had never known—and now would never know again. Eve closed her eyes and turned her head towards the window so that Martha should not see her tears.

Their progress had been slow through the lanes around Makerham, but once they reached Guildford the roads improved and they made good time. Eve had given instructions that they were to press on as quickly as possible, but even though their stops to change horses were brief, and Eve had alighted only once at Tenterden to partake a hurried dinner, it was nearly ten o'clock when they arrived at their destination. As the carriage pulled up at the closed gates Eve let down the window.

'I can smell the sea on the breeze,' she murmured. 'I had forgotten how the winds carry the salt air inland.'

'There's no lights in the house,' muttered Martha, peering out of the window towards the shadowy building, outlined against the darkening sky. 'We're locked out.'

'Nonsense,' Eve replied. 'There is a light in the

window of the Gate House. Mr Granby is even now knocking on the door.'

A few minutes later the valet approached the carriage followed by a large, ambling figure. 'This is Silas Brattee, Mrs Wylder, the gatekeeper. He says your message never arrived.'

'But I sent it express!'

Granby shrugged. 'I will follow that up tomorrow, madam.'

Eve waved him aside and peered at the figure behind him. 'You are Aggie's husband, are you not?' she said. 'You will not know me, for you were at sea when I lived here as a child.'

'Aye, I was, mistress. Went off to sea about the time that you was born, I'm thinking. The mistress was dead by the time I came home for good, but Sir Benjamin kept me an' Aggie on here to look after the place.' Silas was shifting from foot to foot as he spoke to her. 'If we'd known you was comin' ma'am, we'd've spruced up the house. As it is, the place ain't fit...'

'Well, it will have to do,' replied Eve. 'Unlock the gates, please.'

'Mebbe the Bell would suit, or the Woolpack,' suggested Silas hopefully.

'That is only a mile or so back,' added Granby. 'They will have rooms for the night.'

'Nonsense. I took the precaution of bringing my own linen. It will not take a moment to prepare beds for us.'

'Nay, mistress,' said Silas. 'You'd be much more comfortable in the village, miss, believe me.'

Eve peered through the darkness at him. 'I am beginning to wonder if you received my message, but decided to ignore it,' she declared. 'Let me in now, Mr Brattee.'

'The house has not been lived in,' Granby warned her. 'It may well be damp.'

'I do not care if the roof is falling in,' retorted Eve. 'I will stay in my own house tonight.'

Her fierce glare had its effect. Granby nodded and muttered to Silas to unlock the gates.

'Well,' sighed Eve as they clattered onto the grass-covered drive and drove up to the front door. 'This is a poor beginning.'

'Mrs Brattee is going to bring coffee and some food up to the house later,' said Granby as he helped Eve to alight. 'However, I fear you will not be very comfortable.'

'I am so exhausted now I think that as long as I can lie down I shall be happy,' she said, following him into the dark entrance hall. She stood for a few moments, pulling off her gloves while the valet moved around the walls, lighting candles. As the feeble glow strengthened, the outline of the large panelled hall could be seen. It was furnished with a large table that filled the centre of the room and a number of solid chairs and heavy dark chests pushed against the walls.

Martha gave a gusty sigh. 'Ooh, miss, this reminds me of the last time we was here, when your sainted mother was alive. I was nobbut a girl then, o' course, like yourself. My first post away from home, but I remember your mama saying how glad she always was to come back here after her travels.'

'I am sure she never had to come to an unprepared house!' retorted Eve with asperity.

'No, miss, but she wouldn't have worried about it. A very spirited lady was your mother and one who loved adventure, God rest her soul.'

'Well, *I* want nothing more than a quiet life!' Eve sighed. 'Let us see what we can do, Martha. Fetch a candlestick and we will go upstairs. I had best take the main bedroom; if my memory serves, there is a maid's room adjoining. Ask

Dan Coachman to bring up the trunks and we will search
out the sheets.'

'You are never going to be making up beds, miss!'
Martha was shocked. 'Rich—I mean, Mr Granby can help
me with that.'

'Well, if you think I am going to sit alone down here like
a great lady while you are labouring away you are very much
mistaken,' replied Eve, amused. 'I am just as capable as you
of putting sheets on a bed—well, almost—and we shall have
it done in a trice. Mr Granby would be better employed in
the kitchen, helping Mrs Brattee to prepare our supper!'

Eve was thankful that the main bedchamber was still furnished and once they had removed the dust sheets she declared
herself very well satisfied. She gave a cry of delight when she
found her mother's portrait propped against the elegant little
writing desk and immediately charged Martha to assist her in
hanging it on the empty hook above the fireplace.

'There,' she said, bringing the candles closer. 'Now I feel
much more at home.'

'She was a beauty, Miss Eve, and no mistake,' remarked
Martha. 'And you have the look of her, too.'

'Do I?' Eve gazed up at the painting. She saw an elegant
woman in a gold sack-backed gown standing very erect
with one hand resting on a large atlas. Eve recognised some
similarities, the thick, luxuriant dark hair, straight little nose
and smiling mouth, but there was a confidence about her
mother that she had never felt in herself: those dark eyes
seemed to look out upon the world with such self-assurance.

'This was painted just before her marriage,' she
murmured. 'Even then she yearned to travel the world,
whereas I—I have always been content to live quietly at
home. What a disappointment I would be to her.' She

stared at the portrait for a few moments longer, then gave her head a little shake, as if to throw off some unwelcome thought. 'Well, such musings will do no good! Open those trunks and find our sheets, Martha, we must prepare for bed.'

There were no hangings on the tester bed, but the mattress was in place beneath its protective cover and it did not feel damp. Martha grumbled as she pulled the sheets from the trunk, but Eve was glad to be active, it helped her forget her unhappiness for a while.

That night Eve dreamed Nick was still alive. In those darkest hours just before dawn, when dreams are at their most vivid, she saw him clearly, heard his ringing laugh and knew in her very core that he was near her. The disappointment, when she opened her eyes and memory returned, made her feel physically sick. Eve looked around at the unfamiliar furnishings and knew a moment's panic. This was not Makerham, neither was it the warm sunny place of her dream, the place where Nick was. She closed her eyes again, trying to bring the dream back, but it was impossible. All that was left was a vague, half-remembered happiness and she clung to it, holding on to it like a talisman, to be touched and rekindled when the demands of the day grew too great.

As Eve made her way downstairs she thought that Monkhurst looked much more welcoming with the morning sunshine flooding in. She found Mrs Brattee waiting to escort her to the small parlour where breakfast was laid out for her.

'Aggie!' Eve smiled fondly upon the housekeeper. 'I am so sorry I missed you last night. Martha insisted that I take supper in my room, and to tell you the truth, by the time we had finished making the beds I was ready to fall asleep!

You have not changed a bit, yet it must be all of ten years since I was last here!'

'Aye, ma'am, that it is,' replied Aggie, her harsh features softening a little. 'And you a grown lady now. I'm that sorry for last night, Mrs Wylder. If only we'd known…'

'It cannot be helped. We shall soon make everything comfortable.'

'You are planning to stay here?'

Eve observed the look of horror upon the housekeeper's face and knew a strong desire to laugh. 'Why, yes,' she said, taking her seat at the breakfast table. 'Granby is very keen for me to go to Yorkshire, to his master's house, but I would rather stay here, for now.'

'But it's not fit for you, mistress. It's been empty for years.'

Eve sipped at her coffee. 'I made a quick inspection before coming downstairs, the house is in much better order than I dared expect. One would never believe it has been ten years since it was occupied. In fact…' Eve fixed her eyes upon the housekeeper '…one of the rooms—the one I used to know as the blue room—has every appearance of having been used recently.'

'Well, mistress, how that can be I cannot say, I'm sure,' replied Mrs Brattee, bustling about the parlour.

'Can you not? Grandpapa always said Mama's family had links with the free traders. I thought perhaps they might have been here.'

There was a loud crash as the dish the housekeeper had been holding dropped to the floor and shattered. Eve raised her brows.

'Oh? Am I correct, then?'

'No, mistress. I swear there was no smugglers sleeping in the house!' declared Aggie, looking thoroughly alarmed.

'Well, who?' Eve said gently, 'I do think I have a right to

know who has been sleeping in my house.' She waited, fixing her eyes upon the housekeeper, who shifted uncomfortably. 'Tell me,' she commanded.

'I can't, mistress. I promised I wouldn't say.'

'I think you must.'

The old woman eyed her doubtfully and Evelina tried again.

'Come,' she coaxed her gently. 'Tell me who it was. Well?'

The housekeeper twisted her apron between her hands. 'It was the master,' she blurted out.

'Grandpapa? But he has not been near the place for years.'

'No, no, the *young* master,' replied Mrs Brattee. 'Captain Wylder.'

Chapter Seven

Evelina stared at her housekeeper. She began to tremble and clasped her hands together, digging the nails into her palms to fight down her panic.

'When was this?'

'About a week since.'

'Then you saw him just before he, before—'

'Aye, miss.' Aggie nodded. 'He—he came down to talk to Silas, said that now he was wed to you it would be quite proper for him to stay at Monkhurst. Showed Silas the marriage papers, he did. Everything looked to be in order so Silas let him in. Didn't think there'd be any harm in it…'

Eve jumped to her feet. 'No harm! Richard Granby knew of this, and he did not tell me! Where *is* Granby?'

'He's taken the old gig to the village, ma'am. Said he would fetch me some provisions, to tide us over until Silas can take me to Appledore in the cart.'

'Then he will be gone for hours.' Eve sank down again, her brow furrowed with thought. 'Nick, stayed here?' she mused. 'But why?'

'That I can't say, mistress, but Silas was never one to refuse the captain—'

'Wait.' Evelina put her hand to her head, trying to make sense of what she was hearing. 'Did—did my husband *know* Silas?'

'He did, ma'am. They sailed together, years ago. Silas was always talking about Captain Wyldfire and he was that pleased when the captain came looking for him, but he wouldn't let him into the house, ma'am, not until it was all legal, like.'

'Do you mean that…that C-Captain Wylder came here *before* we were married?'

'Oh, yes, ma'am.' It seemed that now Mrs Brattee had made her confession she was happy to talk. 'Back in the spring he fetched up here. Silas was so surprised—'

'But what did he want?' The closed look returned and Eve said impatiently, 'You have told me this much, Aggie I do not think you can stop now.'

'He…he was asking about the free trading.'

'Is Silas—I mean—does he know about such things?'

The housekeeper gave her a pitying look. 'There's not a family hereabouts that doesn't, miss.'

'But I don't understand. Why should Nick come *here*?'

'That I couldn't say, mistress. He stayed in the village for a week or more, went out with Silas and the boys—do you remember my sons, ma'am, Sam and Nathanial? You wouldn't recognise 'em, they're strapping men now. Both married; my Nathanial has twins and Sam has a babe on the way.'

Eve smiled reminiscently. 'We used to play together on the Marsh, did we not? I know you did not always approve of my running wild with the boys, but Mama did not mind, and we were very young. It all changed when I was sent away to school.'

'You had to learn to be a lady, Miss Eve.'

'I suppose I did.' Eve sighed. 'But we digress. You were telling me about Captain Wylder's visit.'

'Ah, yes. As I was saying, Silas keeps a galley on the Marsh, you see, and Captain Nick went out with them—'

'Wait, wait, wait!' Eve interrupted her again. 'Are you saying Captain Wylder helped them to *smuggle* goods into the country?'

'Silas prefers to call it free trading,' said Mrs Brattee, affronted. 'They brings in a few barrels of brandy, sometimes a bit of Brussels lace—it's not as though anyone hereabouts could afford to buy it, if they had to pay the duty, so it ain't doing any harm.'

Evelina realised it would be useless to argue and turned her mind to her main anxiety. 'But why Nick? What interest did he have in such things?'

'There's many a seafaring man turns to free trading to repair his fortunes, mistress.'

Eve shook her head. 'Nick Wylder was not in need of money. I know that because Grandpapa discussed the marriage settlements with me. Not only did my husband have property, there is also a great deal of prize money invested in the Funds. So why should he come to Monkhurst?'

'The captain was very interested in the house, but Silas was adamant. Apart from the odd visit from your grandpapa, Monkhurst has been shut up since your parents died.' Aggie gave a noisy sigh. 'Very attached to your mama, was Silas. Apple of his eye, she was, so he wasn't about to let anyone into her house. Even when your cousin, Mr Bernard Shawcross, came down here a couple o' years ago. Silas turned him away, sayin' he'd had his orders from your grandpapa to shut the house up and shut it would remain.' She snorted. 'And your cousin didn't take it anything like as well as Cap'n Wyldfire. Raged at Silas, he did; said he was family and entitled to be let in, but Silas said if that was the case he should go and get permission from your grandfather.'

'Yes, but what of Captain Wylder?' Eve prompted her gently.

'The cap'n went off. Back to London, we thought. Then, next thing we knows, he comes back to tell us he's wed—and to our own Miss Shawcross!'

'But why did he not tell *me* he had been to Monkhurst, or that he was coming back here?'

The housekeeper's blank look was genuine, and Eve forbore to press her further. However, the question continued to plague Eve. She played with the gold band on her finger, turning it round and round as an answer lodged itself in her brain. Nick had not trusted her.

Only because he did not know me, she told herself fiercely. *He would have learned to trust me, in time.* If only… A little scream of frustration forced its way up through her. She banged her fist into her palm. 'Ooooh, I hate that man!' she hissed. 'How could he do this to me? I hate him, I *hate* him!'

Tears welled up again but she fought them down. She would be strong. And she would get to the bottom of this mystery.

However, an interview with Silas proved even less rewarding, for the old man merely shook his head, saying he had no idea why Captain Nick had come looking for him.

'But you took him out in your boat with you when he was here in the spring.' She added quickly, 'Come now, Silas, I know all about your…activities.'

'The captain ain't concerned with the piddlin' little bits we bring in,' he said. 'He's after bigger fish, that much I do know. But he was impressed with the galley that we uses to go in and out to the sea. Deal-made, she is, and fast in the water. Me brother Ephraim 'as another just such a one over at Dimchurch and I told the cap'n how in the old days we used her to row across to Boulogne. Can't beat Kentish oarsman, mistress, although these days when there's a drop we just meets the lugger off shore and brings in what we need through Jury's Cut.'

'I am sure you do, but it is still illegal, Silas, and I cannot have it.' She regarded him steadily. 'You must promise me to give up the trade, Silas. I will find work for you, and for Nat and Samuel, but you must not take part in any further smuggling.'

It was not to be expected that Silas would capitulate immediately, but Eve was adamant and eventually she wrested from him a grudging promise that he would cease his illegal activities. Satisfied on this point, Eve could once more give her attention to finding out why Nick had come to Monkhurst.

'What did Captain Wylder want here, Silas? How long did he stay in the house?'

'No more'n a couple o' nights. We took a dinghy out on the Monkhurst Drain, Miss Eve, that leads down to Jury's Cut and the sea, and I showed 'im the boathouse, but that ain't been used for years.' Silas twisted his cap in his hands and looked at Eve anxiously. 'I didn't think there was any harm in it, mistress, knowing the cap'n, and him now being family…'

'And you trusted him, Silas?' she said, a little wistfully.

'With my life, mistress. The cap'n knew I'd follow him anywhere,' he ended proudly. 'When we was fighting the rebels in the American War he was never happier than when he was kicking up a dust. Unpredictable, see, like his nickname, Wyldfire. He was here one minute, then the next, he's up and gone to Hastings.' Silas frowned, shaking his head. 'Not but what that was a mistake, God rest his soul.'

There was nothing more to be learned from the old man. Evelina dismissed him, but the problem nagged at her throughout the morning while she worked her way through the house, trying to decide what was required to make it a comfortable home. The early morning sun had given way to heavy storm-clouds and a blustery wind whistled through the passages, signalling a change from the dry, sunny weather of the past few weeks.

It was noon before Eve heard the sounds of the gig returning. A glance out of the window showed her that it was raining heavily and she felt a certain grim satisfaction when she saw that Granby had omitted to take a greatcoat with him, and was soaked through. She hurried to the kitchens and found the valet drying himself off before the kitchen fire. Paying no heed to Mrs Brattee, who was busy unpacking the baskets Granby had brought in for her, Eve went straight into the attack.

'Why did you not tell me my husband stayed here?'

Granby swung round and she saw the flash of surprise before he schooled his countenance to its usual inscrutable mask. 'I thought it might distress you, ma'am.'

'I am more distressed to think you lied to me. What else have you omitted to tell me?' she demanded. 'What was Captain Wylder doing here?'

'I believe he wished to renew his acquaintance with Mr Brattee and his family,' said Granby, smoothly.

'But he had already done that, he had visited Silas before he made Grandpapa's acquaintance at Tunbridge Wells.'

The valet bowed. 'As you say, madam.'

Eve watched him closely, 'Captain Wylder told me he had business in Sussex.'

The valet inclined his head. 'That is true ma'am. The

master stayed here only a few nights before going on to Hastings.'

'And this…business: did it involve smuggling?'

Granby looked shocked. 'Captain Wylder's acquaintances in Hastings are most respectable people, ma'am.'

'I do hope so, Mr Granby.'

He smiled a little and spread his hands. 'You have my word upon it, Mrs Wylder.'

'I shall have more than that.'

'Ma'am?'

Eve put her hands on her hips and looked at him. 'Go and change into dry clothes, Mr Granby. And order my carriage. We are going to Hastings.'

Granby's smile vanished. 'Hastings! Now?'

'Yes, now. As soon as we are packed.'

'But, madam, there is not the least need—'

'There is every need,' she flung at him. 'I am anxious to know that I am not the widow of a common villain!'

'Mrs Wylder, I beg of you, at least postpone your journey until this storm has eased.'

Richard Granby stood beside Eve in the doorway, looking out with dismay at the rain that lashed the house while the coachman packed the trunks securely, water running from the brim of his hat and his oiled coat.

'I am determined to reach Hastings today,' she retorted. 'You may ride in the carriage with Martha and me, if you do not wish to get another soaking.'

The valet declined the offer, and clambered miserably up beside Dan Coachman.

'He is afraid I shall interrogate him further,' remarked Eve cheerfully as she climbed into the carriage.

Her maid sniffed as she settled herself beside her

mistress. 'Mr Granby was only trying to save you unnecessary worry, Miss Eve.'

'Is that what he has told you, Martha?'

'No, madam, but I know he's a good man.'

'Is he?' Eve looked closely at her maid. 'You seem to be uncommon friendly with Richard Granby.'

Martha flushed, but she said stiffly, 'Given his position and mine, it is only natural that we should talk.'

Eve forbore to tease her. 'Of course it is,' she said, turning her mind back to her own worries. 'And if Mr Granby has passed on anything concerning my husband's death, I would like you to tell me, Martha. I shall not be easy until I know what sort of business it was that took my husband away from Makerham in such haste. I hope we may find some answers at Hastings.' She leaned back against the thickly padded seat. 'And I confess I want to see where Nick spent his last days,' she murmured to herself.

The wind howled around them, rocking the carriage while the heavy rain drummed on the roof and pattered against the windows. The pace was necessarily slow. The storm grew worse as they neared the coast and it was a relief to drive through Rye, for although the cobbles shook the coach until Eve's teeth rattled in her head, at least the houses gave them some shelter from the buffeting winds. The carriage slowed to a stop and Eve leaned forwards to peer out of the window. A horseman had stopped beside them and was shouting something at the coachman.

Eve let down the window. 'What is it, is there a problem?'

The rider turned to look at her, touching his hand to his sodden hat.

'Aye, ma'am. The Winchelsea road is closed. They wanted to take advantage of the dry weather to repair the

road, but the dam—dashed fools didn't start it until yesterday. Now the grass verge is too wet to take the weight of a
carriage and there's only room for a horse to squeeze by.'

'Is there another route?' asked Eve.

The rider nodded. 'Aye, you can go via Broad Oak Cross
and then south through Battle.'

Granby leaned down from the box, shaking his head at
her. 'That's a long journey, Mrs Wylder. Dan says he must
proceed slowly if we are not to be overturned by the high
winds on the open road.'

'Then that is what we shall do,' said Eve decisively. 'Tell
him to drive on!'

'Very well, madam.'

Martha sniffed. 'The poor man will very likely catch his
death sitting up on the box in this weather.'

'Very likely,' replied Eve, unmoved.

'We should turn back,' said her forthright handmaiden. 'No
good can come of this, Miss Eve, you mark my words. What
do you want to go traipsing all the way to Hasting for? What
if you hears things you didn't want to know about the master?'

Eve did not answer. Martha had voiced the fear that had
been nagging at her, that Nick was involved in some vil-
lainous activity, but it was no good. She had to know the
truth, however bad. Besides, illogical as it was, she wanted
to visit the place where he had died.

To say goodbye.

Tears filled her eyes again and she blinked them away,
angry at herself. Why should she feel such sorrow for a man
she had known for less than a month? Yet the tug of attraction had been so strong, she could not resist it. He still
haunted her dreams. Nick had wound his way so effectively
into her heart that now his loss threatened to break it.

'You are a fool, Evelina,' she told herself angrily. 'You let yourself believe that Grandpapa had brought you a knight in shining armour!'

The sudden stopping of the carriage dragged her away from her depressing thoughts.

'Oh, Heavens, what is it now?' cried Martha.

The cab rocked as someone climbed down from the box and Eve pressed her nose to the window, trying to see out. It was impossible; inside, the glass misted with her breath and outside the raindrops distorted her view. She let down the window and immediately the driving rain slapped at her face. There was another carriage stopped in front of them, and Granby was talking in earnest conversation with the driver, one hand clamped over his hat to prevent the wind from whipping it away.

'There is some sort of hold up,' she said to her maid as she put up the window once more. 'Granby is looking into it now.'

Moments later the valet yanked open the door. Even though he was standing on the most sheltered side of the carriage the wind swirled around and threatened to drag the coach door out of his hands.

'The road is under water, ma'am. A culvert has collapsed. One wagon has already tried to drive through and has broken an axle. No one is hurt,' he hastened to assure them, 'but we must turn back.'

Reluctantly Eve agreed. She glanced past him at the rain, still sheeting down. The thought of spending another couple of hours returning to Monkhurst was not a pleasant one.

'Very well, Granby. Tell Dan to drive back to the nearest village. We will put up for the night.'

But when they drove into Udimore, Eve took one look at the rundown hostelry and quickly changed her mind. She ordered Dan to drive back to Rye.

'What I saw of the slatternly maids and greasy landlord convinced me we should not be comfortable there,' she said to her maid as the carriage set off once more. 'Granby tells me we passed several well-appointed inns at Rye. We shall do better there.'

'I do hope so, madam,' replied Martha in a failing voice. 'I fear if I don't get out o' this jarring, jolting cab soon I shall have to ask you for your smelling salts!'

Eve laughed. 'Then I would have to disappoint you, Martha, for I do not carry such a thing!'

'Well then, it's a good job I put a bottle of Glass's Magnesia in your dressing case! With your permission, Miss Eve, I shall take some as soon as I can lay my hands on it.'

'You would be better advised to take a little walk and get some fresh air,' replied Eve, 'but as you wish.'

She looked out of the window. The rain had eased a little and looking up she saw the squat tower of Rye church, secure on its hill, a black outline against the lowering sky. The clatter of hooves on the cobbles told Eve that they had reached the town and she knew a few moments' anxiety when they pulled up at the George, only to be told that every available room had been taken, but minutes later the carriage turned into the yard of the Mermaid, another busy coaching inn, and Granby was holding open the door for her to alight. Evelina had the impression of overhanging eves and a half-timbered building surrounding the yard as she hurried across to the entrance. She was immediately shown into a small private parlour filled with gleaming brassware and polished panelling.

'This is very much more the thing!' she exclaimed. 'A warm, clean room and the most appetising smell from the kitchens. I vow I am quite famished. Granby must bespeak dinner for us as soon as maybe.'

Her maid groaned. 'I feel as sick as a cat, miss.'

'Poor Martha. Sit you down then and rest until the landlord brings us coffee. Or should I ask him for some tea?'

'Just as you like, miss. I wants nothing more than to sit quiet for a bit.'

'Then you shall do just that. Granby is organising our rooms for us and will see that our bags are taken upstairs. I never realised before how useful it is to have a man to do these things for one. Perhaps I shall keep him on, after all, as my major-domo.' A glance at the pale figure sitting beside the fire showed her that Martha was not listening, so she busied herself instead with making them both comfortable. She helped her maid to remove her bonnet and cloak and put them with her own over a chair. A rosy-cheeked maid brought in her coffee, apologising for the delay.

'We've been that busy, what with the storm and everything. Every table's took.' She looked around, smiled and bobbed a curtsy. 'You'm lucky to have this parlour, madam. You'll be comfy enough in here.'

As the maid went out, Martha opened one eye. 'Will you not sit down, miss? You must be exhausted, all that travelling—'

'Not a bit of it! I did not like being bounced all over the road, but I am more excited than tired. You know how little I have travelled. My last real journey was to go to Tunbridge with Grandpapa two years ago and the pace was so slow and decorous I think we would have moved quicker had we walked!' She went over to the window and looked out. 'If it would only stop raining, we could take a walk now and see the town.'

Her handmaiden groaned again and Eve turned back to her.

'Poor Martha, here am I, chattering on when you are feeling so poorly. You do look very pale, you poor thing.

Perhaps a little Magnesia would settle your stomach. I wonder where Granby can be. He will have taken the dressing case to my bedchamber. Well, perhaps the landlord can show me the way.'

She went to the door and looked out. The corridor was very busy and through the doorway opposite she could see that the taproom was packed with men enjoying a mug of ale and pipe of tobacco while they sheltered from the rain. To her right was a much more ordered scene, for the corridor opened on to the coffee room where travellers were seated at small tables and were served refreshments by a number of harassed-looking waiters. Of the landlord or the cheerful maid there was no sign. Undeterred, Eve stepped out of the room to go in search of her host. The ancient building was large and irregular, and for a moment Eve could not decide on the best way to go. She had seen a number of people using a door on the far side of the coffee room and surmised that it would lead to an inner hall where she might find an obliging chambermaid who would take her upstairs. Eve made her way quickly through the coffee room, trying to ignore the inquisitive stares of its patrons. She kept her eyes fixed upon the door, putting out her hand as she approached. It opened easily, swinging away from her and she spotted Granby in the corridor beyond, talking with a group of ragged-looking men. In her haste she did not see the slight step down and she found herself hurtling through the doorway, off balance. She cannoned off the man nearest the door.

'Oh, I beg your pardon,' she gasped as strong arms shot out to steady her. 'I—'

Her words died away as she looked up and found herself staring up into the all-too-familiar face of Nick Wylder.

Chapter Eight

Evelina's breath caught in her throat and for an instant she thought she might faint. The look of surprise on Nick's face gave way to one of wry humour. The corners of his mouth lifted.

'Oh, lord,' he murmured. 'This was not meant to happen.'

Eve regained her balance and pushed away from him. Something was wrong. It was her husband, but it was not the fashionable beau she had married. The superbly tailored frock-coat and snow-white linen were replaced with a worn frieze jacket and a coloured shirt, while his raven-black hair was no longer neatly confined by a ribbon and one black lock hung rakishly over his eyes. The blood was drumming in her ears as she sought to make sense of the situation.

'You are alive.' She could not take her eyes from his face. 'But how, why—?'

One of the other men shook his head and said warningly, 'Cap'n…'

Nick put up his hand. 'I cannot explain now, sweetheart, but you must not been seen with me. Richard shall take you back to your room.'

'No—I—'

Nick reached out and caught her arms. 'I will explain it all later.' He gave her a little shake. 'Go back inside, Eve. You must act as if you have not seen me, do you understand?'

Eve swallowed hard. She understood nothing and wanted to argue.

'Eve.' He held her eyes. 'I need you to do this for me.'

'Y-you'll come to me?' she whispered, her hands still clutching at his coat.

'You have my word.' He looked down at her, then in one sudden movement he pulled her to him and kissed her once, hard, on the mouth. 'I'll join you in your room, very soon. Now go.' He turned her away from him and gave her a little push.

Richard Granby took her arm and walked her back to the private parlour. There was so much conjecture in her head that this time she did not notice the diners in the coffee room or the raucous laughter as they passed the taproom.

Granby ushered her into the private parlour. Martha, who had been dozing in her chair, uttered a shriek and jumped to her feet.

'In Heaven's name, Richard, what have you done to her?'

Granby guided Eve to a chair and gently pressed her down. 'She has had a shock. Can you fetch a glass of wine?'

Eve raised one hand. 'No,' she said, her voice unsteady. 'I want nothing, only to know what is happening.'

'It will all be explained later, ma'am. For the moment you must stay here and say nothing.'

'May I not tell Martha?'

'Tell me what?' demanded her maid, looking bewildered.

Granby gave her a reassuring smile. 'Oh, I think there would be no harm in that, as long as it goes no further. I shall return in a little while and escort you to your room.'

He bowed and retired in his usual unhurried style, leaving Martha almost hopping with impatience.

'What is it, Miss Eve, what are you to tell me?'

Eve stared at her anxious face. 'I have just seen Captain Wylder. He is alive.'

Martha's reaction was as noisy as Eve's had been controlled. She screamed and fell back on her chair, drumming her heels on the floor. It was unfortunate that the tavern-maid chose that moment to come in with a fresh pot of coffee. Remembering Nick's words, Eve knew it was imperative that Martha did not blurt out her secret, so she immediately took her by the shoulders and shook her.

'Stop it, stop it this instant!' Her sharp treatment had its effect; Martha stopped shrieking and subsided into noisy sobs. Eve dismissed the round-eyed tavern-maid and waited patiently until Martha had stopped crying and mopped her eyes. With no more than the occasional hiccup she apologised for her outburst and quietly requested her mistress to tell her everything. Eve obliged, but she found that relating her meeting with Nick only added to her frustration, for Martha kept asking her questions she could not answer.

Eve wanted nothing more than to sit quietly and consider her own feelings. The first shock of finding herself face to face with her husband had been followed by a surge of elation, but that had been replaced almost immediately with consternation. Why had he wanted her to believe he was dead? Answers crowded in upon her, none of them satisfactory, most too painful to contemplate, so she resolutely pushed them aside, determined to remain calm and to await Nick's explanation. Martha's reaction to the news was much more straightforward. The master was alive, and she was glad of it. Eve wished she could be so easily satisfied. She was relieved when at last Granby came in the room and announced that the landlord was waiting to escort her to her room.

'It is our finest apartment, madam,' their host told her as he led the way through a winding corridor and up the stairs. 'It has been said that good Queen Bess herself slept there. I am sure you will find it very comfortable.' At the end of a dim corridor he threw open the door and stood back for her to enter. 'There, is it not a handsome apartment?'

Eve had to agree with him. It was a large, square room with an ornate plaster ceiling and richly carved panelling on every wall. Candles glowed from the wall sconces, illuminating the rich scarlet-and-gold hangings that decorated the huge tester-bed and the matching curtains pulled across the window to blot out the gloomy rain-sodden sky. A large chest of drawers and a sofa covered in wine-red damask occupied the far corner of the room and the only other items of furniture were two chairs and a small gate-legged table set before the stone fireplace, where a merry blaze crackled. The table was already laden with dishes and it was set with two places. Eve's eyes flew to the landlord. He beamed at her and tapped his nose.

'Mr Granby suggested a collation, so you need have no servants interrupting you. There's meats, bread, pastries, fruit—everything you could wish.' He pointed to a little door in the corner of the room. 'That is a private stair, madam. Leads up to your maid's room and down to the back hall, so even she can come and go to the kitchen for her dinner without disturbing you.' He gave her a knowing wink and Eve felt her cheeks grow hot.

'Thank you.'

With another beaming smile the landlord bowed himself out and shut the door carefully behind him. Martha was already bustling around, inspecting the room.

'Very comfortable, Miss Eve. Everything just as it should be. And very clean, not a speck of dust. Shall I unpack your trunk, ma'am? Seems such a lot of work for just one night.'

'Yes. No. That is, no.' Eve tried to think of practical matters, but her brain did not want to work.

'Then I'll lay out your nightgown—'

'No! No, leave it where it is, Martha. Go now. I shall call you if I need you again. Oh, Martha—' she pulled a small bottle from her dressing case and handed it to the maid. 'You never did dose your self with Glass's Magnesia.'

'No, ma'am, I'll take it now, if you don't mind. Thank you. That is, if you don't want it yourself?'

Eve looked towards the table, where a decanter and two glasses stood in readiness for the coming meal. She felt in need of something more than medicine. 'No, but you may pour me a glass of wine before you go.'

Eve watched the maid fill up one glass with blood-red wine before making her way to her own room. The little door closed behind her with a click and Eve was alone. But it was not the peace of the old room that enveloped Eve: it was a brittle, ice-cold fury.

'I will not see him!' she said aloud. 'He has treated me abominably. I shall not see him.'

She walked over to the main door and bolted it. There was a wooden peg on the door to the servants' stairs and she used it to secure the latch. She gave a long, deep sigh. There, it was done. Slowly she removed her pelisse, folded it neatly and placed it upon her trunk before returning to the table and picking up her glass of wine. The storm had passed and there was a stillness about the room. No noise filtered through to her from below and the air seemed to settle around her, calm and tranquil, in complete contrast to her own nerves, which were stretched tight as a bowstring. Let him knock. Let him hammer on the door, she would not admit him.

She stood in the middle of the room, facing the door, straining to hear the slightest sound. Clutching at her wineglass, she silently berated herself for her anxiety. No one could surprise her, the room was secure. Or was it? The scrape of wood on wood made her spin around in time to see one of the panels beside the fireplace swing open and Nick Wylder step into the room. He still wore the frieze coat, but instead of the tattered coloured shirt he now wore a fresh white one, fastened with a froth of white lace at his throat, and a black ribbon at the nape of his neck confined his black hair, glossy as a raven's wing. The baggy sailor's trousers and worn shoes had been replaced by buckskins and topboots. With the skirts of his coat swinging around him the inconsequential thought came to her that he looked every inch a pirate. Nick gestured towards the panel.

'The stair leads up directly from the alley. You need not be alarmed; I have bolted the door at the foot of the stairs; no one else can come in that way.'

He stood, feet slightly apart, hands at his sides, watching her. Like a cat, she thought. Alert, wary. Eve's heart had misssed a beat but now it was thudding painfully against her ribs. She did not know whether she was going to laugh or cry, to be thankful or furious.

'You did not drown,' she said at last.

'No. Sweetheart, I am so sorry I was not there to help you when Sir Benjamin died.'

'You lied to me.'

'Evelina, I—'

A red mist descended over Eve, blotting out reason. The wineglass flew from her hand, its contents leaving a dark trail across the floor. Nick side-stepped neatly and the glass sailed past him to smash against the wall.

'How dare you!'

'Sweetheart, listen to me—' He ducked as she snatched up the second glass and hurled it towards him. 'Eve, I am sorry. Let me explain—'

His words were lost as the glass shattered on the panelling and fell in tinkling shards to the floor. With a shriek of rage Eve picked up the carving knife and advanced upon him.

'I hate you, Nick Wylder!'

As she hurled herself at him he caught her arm, holding the lethal blade away.

'Eve, I had no choice.'

Unable to plunge the knife into his heart, Eve brought up her other hand, her fingers curled ready to scratch his eyes out. With an oath Nick caught at her arm, easily over-powering her.

'I know you are angry, my love, but I am not going to let you kill me.' His fingers tightened on her wrist; her grip loosened and the knife clattered harmlessly to the floor. 'That's better.' He grinned and released her. 'No wonder my father said never trust the carving to a woman!'

'Are you *never* serious?' She gave a sob of frustration and began to beat at his chest with her fists.

Nick reached out and put his arms about her, pulling her closer. 'I know,' he said quietly as she continued to pound him. 'I know I was a monster for doing this to you.'

She hammered her fists against his hard, unyielding body until there was no strength left in her arms. Then, as her anger evaporated, it was replaced by tears. She found herself crying; huge, gulping sobs that could not be controlled. She did not resist as Nick pulled her closer, stroking her head and murmuring softly. He continued to hold her while she cried herself out and at last she collapsed against him, taking deep, shuddering breaths. He reached into one of the capacious pockets of the old coat and pulled out a clean handkerchief.

'I thought this might be needed,' he murmured, pressing it into her hand. 'I had no idea my wife had such a temper.'

'Nor I,' mumbled Eve from beneath the handkerchief.

He touched his lips to her hair. 'Now will you listen to me? Will you let me try to explain?' He guided her across to the sofa and they sat down together, Nick keeping one arm firmly around her shoulders. 'I did not plan this, Eve. Believe me.'

'Why should I believe you?' Angrily she shrugged off his arm and sat up very straight while she wiped her eyes. 'You have lied to me from the beginning. You married me to gain control of Monkhurst, did you not?'

'Richard told me you had gone there. Yes, it is true that I wanted access to Monkhurst. Marrying you was one way to get that.'

Misery clutched at her heart. 'You are despicable!'

He sighed. 'Perhaps I am, but I never meant to hurt you. I admit I went to Tunbridge Wells in search of your grand-father, knowing he owned Monkhurst. I soon learned that the property was part of your marriage settlement and that Sir Benjamin was looking for a husband for you.' The irre-pressible smile tugged at his mouth. 'It all fitted neatly with my plan—and my family have been nagging me for years to settle down so I knew I would be pleasing them, too. So I accepted Sir Benjamin's invitation to visit you at Makerham. What I had *not* anticipated was finding such an adorable young lady waiting to meet me.'

Evelina stifled the traitorous surge of pleasure she felt at his words. She dare not consider them or her brittle self-control might shatter. She injected a touch of impatience into her voice. 'And just what were your plans? *Why* did you need Monkhurst?'

'I suspected Monkhurst was being used by smugglers.'

'Very likely.' She shrugged. 'Nearly every house in the area would be the same.'

'Yes, I know that, but—I think I should go back to the beginning.' He paused and Eve waited, pulling his handkerchief through her restless fingers. 'My—ah—adventurous career in the navy brought me to the attention of the Admiralty, and since returning to England I have been working for them, investigating certain…activities.'

'Smuggling. You have said that.'

'Yes, but not the innocuous practice carried out by Silas and his friends, a few barrels of French brandy and bundles of Brussels lace. The villains I seek are involved in a much bigger enterprise. Not only are they depriving the government of duty—and before you interrupt me let me say that I have heard all the arguments that the duty is too high! The people I seek are flooding the country with a tea that is, at best, illegal and at worst, poisonous.

'They call it smouch. It is made from leaves gathered from the English hedgerows and mixed with chamber-lye, green vitriol and other choice ingredients, including, very often, sheep's dung. Then it is baked and rubbed to a black dust. Quite,' he said, observing her look of horror. 'I traced the most recent consignments to this coast. It is being shipped to Boulogne, then sold to our—er—freetraders.'

'But they wouldn't,' she exclaimed. 'Silas would never carry such a cargo.'

'Not knowingly, but he has been duped into bringing it ashore. Did you not think it odd that Mrs Brattee had no tea in her store cupboard when you arrived at Monkhurst?

Now Silas knows the truth he will not trust any tea coming from the Continent.'

Eve's eyes darkened. 'It is some horrid French plot to poison us!'

Nick shook his head. 'I wish I could say that was it; the evidence points to it being made in this country, and in this area.'

'And you suspected Monkhurst? My house?'

'One of the cargoes we intercepted contained a fragment of a letter. Monkhurst was mentioned in it. Silas swore there was no connection, but I wanted to see for myself.'

'So you married me to gain access to my house.'

'Yes.'

She threw him another savage look. 'You do not apologise for it.'

He smiled. 'I am not sorry I married you, Evelina. I never could be.'

Her skin tingled when saw the glint in his blue eyes. It was difficult to remain angry when he smiled at her like that. She reminded herself that his smiles meant nothing. They were as worthless as his honeyed words. She looked away, scowling. 'Go on.'

'Once Silas was persuaded to let me into the house we searched it thoroughly. There are extensive cellars, and a very interesting underground passage leading to the boathouse on Monkhurst Drain, but no sign that it has been used in recent years.'

'Well there is nothing secret about that! Mama showed me the tunnel when I was a child. She told me her grandfather had built it so that the family need not get wet walking to the boathouse on rainy days, but if that was the case why does it come up into the kitchen? And why is the entrance hidden behind the panelling at the back of the boathouse?

From the outside the tunnel is well hidden; it appears that the boathouse is built into the bank.' Eve shook her head. 'I always believed it was built for smuggling goods into the house, but Mama would never admit it.' She forgot her anger as a half-forgotten memory surfaced. 'I remember having nightmares about people stealing into the house through the tunnel, so Papa took me down there. He showed me the iron grating at the far end. It had a big lock and the key was kept on a hook in the tunnel, so that anyone from the house could get *out*, but no one could get in.'

'That is still the case, Eve, so you may still rest easy. But the boathouse is in a sad state of repair.'

'When Mama and Papa died the boats were sold. Grandpapa kept the house in order, but we only visited Monkhurst once or twice after that.'

Nick had stretched his arm along the back of the sofa. His fingers were playing with one of the curls at her neck. It was a great temptation to turn her head and rest her cheek against his hand, but she resisted it.

'And what about you, Eve?' he said softly. 'Do you dislike the house?'

'Oh, no, it holds only good memories for me. We lived there until I was about nine, you see, then I went to stay with Grandpapa while my parents went abroad and…they never came back. They died in Italy.'

His fingers left the curl and squeezed her shoulder. 'I know, you told me they caught a fever. I am sorry.'

'So, too, am I, but it was a long time ago.'

'I am sorry, too, about your grandfather, and even sorrier that I could not be with you.'

She drew herself up, not prepared to accept his sympathy. She hunched her shoulder to shake off his hand, yet was disappointed when he removed it. She said gruffly, 'We are straying from the point, sir. Why did you leave Makerham so suddenly?'

'My enquiries had led me to suspect that Lord Chelston was involved in this business. He owns a sizeable property near Northiam and keeps a yacht at Hastings. I have had people watching him for some time now, but he is very elusive. On the morning after our wedding I received word that a rendezvous had been arranged. After so many months of work I could not leave my men to deal with it alone, so I had to come here to the coast.'

'But you have not arrested Lord Chelston?

'He is a powerful man. We need hard evidence before we make our suspicions known. Besides, I want to catch *all* the main players and close down the whole operation. If we move too soon they will merely go underground, move production to a new location.

'These people are clever; they have a warehouse in Boulogne. The French are not averse to helping anyone who is working against England. You said yourself, smuggling is a way of life in these parts; the local gangs are trusted by their regular customers who believe they are purchasing good Black Bohea.' He leaned forwards, resting his elbows on his knees. 'There were reports that a consignment of smouch was ready to be shipped out of Hastings on a brigantine and transferred to a French lugger cruising off this coast. We thought it would be possible to catch Chelston's men red-handed with the goods; with their evidence we could convict him. Captain George has a cutter at his disposal, the *Argos*, but on the night of the rendezvous some of us were in disguise on a small fishing smack, hoping to get close enough to the brigantine to board and overpower the crew, but they discovered the plot.'

'What happened?' asked Eve, enthralled in spite of herself.

'In the fighting I was shot and toppled into the water.'

'Shot!'

'A flesh wound, just below the ribs. Nothing serious, but it carried me over the side. Thankfully I managed to swim to the *Argos*, but having been lost overboard it was decided it would be to our advantage to let everyone else think I had perished.'

Eve kept her eyes on his profile, noting the fine laughter lines etched at the corner of his eye and at the side of his fine, curving lips. It would be so easy to lose her heart to him all over again. She squared her shoulders, determined to resist the temptation.

'I understand that you would not want these villains to know you were alive, but what of me?' she said quietly. 'Why did you send Granby to tell me you were dead?'

He turned his head to look at her and for once there was no smile in his blue eyes. 'I never intended to tell you. I thought we could wrap up this matter quickly and there would be no need for you to know. Then I received your note, saying your grandfather had died, and I knew I would have to send Granby to you.'

'But why? I do not understand.'

'Because the man who shot me was your cousin, Bernard Shawcross.'

Chapter Nine

'Either the world has gone mad or I have lost my wits!' Eve put her hands to her cheeks. 'Confess you are joking me.'

'It is no joke, Eve,' Nick said quietly. 'When you wrote to tell me of Sir Benjamin's death, I knew Shawcross would go to Makerham. When your note reached me I was too weak to leave my bed or I promise you I would have found some way to get to you. Instead I had to send Richard to protect you.' With a sudden, impulsive move he slid from the sofa to kneel on the floor before her, taking her hands and looking up earnestly into her face. 'I never meant to cause you such pain, Evelina; we had known each other less than a month, only one night married—I did not think you could care for me so very much.'

'Well, you were wrong,' she muttered, pulling her hands away. She rose and walked about the room, trying to make sense of all he had told her.

Nick sat back down on the sofa, watching her. At last he said, 'You are looking very pale, love. Are you hungry? When did you last eat?'

She stopped her pacing, frowning as if she did not understand his words. 'At breakfast.'

'Then we must dine.' He jumped up. 'But first, my little termagant, we need to call your maid.'

Martha was quickly summoned and came into the room, dipping a slight curtsey towards Nick as she did so.

'I am very pleased to see you looking so well, Captain Wylder.'

'Thank you, Martha,' he responded cheerfully. 'Would you be good enough to bring up some fresh glasses? We had a—er—little accident with the others. But mind, not a word to anyone that I am here.'

She nodded solemnly. 'No sir, I'll keep mum, my word on it.'

Nick smiled at her and Eve noted with a stab of irritation how her usually stern-faced maidservant softened under the force of his charm.

'And I'll fetch a brush to clear up the glass in the corner, too, Cap'n.'

When she had gone Nick shrugged off his coat and tossed it aside. 'I hope you do not object to me dining in my shirtsleeves, sweetheart, but this is a very rough, workaday garment, not at all suitable for sitting down to dinner with a lady.'

He was not wearing a waistcoat, and the linen shirt fell softly over his powerful shoulders. Eve observed the contrast between the billowing white shirt and tight-fitting buckskins that hugged his narrow hips and powerful thighs. Memories of that strong, athletic body pressed against hers made her tremble and she resolutely pushed them aside. As Nick came to the table she realised that he was not walking with his usual grace.

'Your wound,' she said. 'Is it very painful?'

'Only if I move too quickly.' The corners of his mouth lifted. 'Or if I have to fight off an angry lady.'

She ignored that. 'May I see it?'

'There is little to see,' he said, pulling his shirt away from the waistband of his buckskins. 'It is almost healed.'

'Then why is it still bandaged?'

'Protection,' he told her. 'The wound still bleeds occasionally.' He lifted his shirt away and Eve gazed down at the white linen strips that were bound around his body. 'Well,' he said, 'do you want me to remove the bandages, so that you may see I am telling the truth?'

Eve flushed. 'I believe you.' She waved her hand at him. 'Pray, tuck in your shirt.'

He unbuttoned the waistband of his buckskins and she could not resist the temptation to look at the exposed skin on his stomach and abdomen, smooth and taut with a shadow of crisp black hairs, a shadow that continued on down towards—

Eve dragged her eyes away. She must not think of such things because it made the excitement stir deep inside and her knees grew weak. She sat down abruptly at the table, her hands clasped tightly in her lap while he finished tidying his clothes. Nick Wylder was a scoundrel. She must not think of him as anything else.

Martha bustled back into the room and while she busied herself sweeping up the broken glass, Eve tried to concentrate upon Nick's story, and not upon his body. The mere thought of dining together made her mouth dry; the little table was so small their knees would almost be touching beneath it. She watched Nick follow the maid to the door and lock it after her. She was not sure if that made her feel more or less safe; might as well be locked in with a tiger, she thought as he prowled back towards her.

'I cannot believe Bernard is involved in smuggling.' Nerves made her voice sharper than she intended. 'He is an odious little toad, but I cannot think so ill of him.'

Nick poured wine into her glass. 'Can you not? It is a very lucrative trade.'

Eve was silent. After a moment she said slowly, 'I think I told you that at one time he was always calling upon Grandpapa, asking him for money, coming to Makerham to hide from his creditors.'

'But not recently?'

'No. You saw him at the wedding; a modish new coat and his own carriage.' She paused while he carved a slice of ham and put it on her plate. 'He asked Mr Didcot about Monkhurst. He thought it was part of Grandpapa's estate.' She clasped her hands together, her fingers tightening until the knuckles showed white. 'He began to—to hint that I should marry him, now that you were—that I was...'

'Now that you were a widow.'

'Yes.' She did not look at him. 'That was why I left Makerham. I feared he might...compromise me.'

'For that alone I would thrash him,' he muttered savagely.

She smiled slightly. 'Thank you. But you cannot blame him; he believes you are dead. Is that not what you wanted, to catch the villains unawares?'

'Yes, but it wasn't only that; I thought it would protect you. Once Chelston knew I was on to him, I feared that he might try to get to me through you. Making Chelston think I was out of the way removed that threat. However, when Sir Benjamin died I knew your cousin would be swift to claim his inheritance and if he suspected news of my death was a ruse then you would be in even greater danger. That is why I asked Richard to take you to my family in the north. I could be sure you would be safe there.' His eyes softened. 'I did not know then what a stubborn little minx I had married.'

'If Mr Granby had told me the truth—'

'Poor Richard was merely following my orders.' Nick hesitated. 'I did not know—I did not know if I could trust you.'

She shrugged, the core of misery hardening in her heart. She had thought as much. 'And now?' She looked up. His eyes were midnight blue in the candle-glow. Inscrutable.

'Now I have no choice.' He reached across the table for her hand. 'I cannot be sorry that you know the truth, Eve, but this is a dangerous game; you would be advised to let Granby escort you to Yorkshire, to the protection of my family. I will join you there when I have finished my work here.'

'But you could still be killed.'

He laughed. 'Faith, sweetheart. I have faced greater dangers than Chelston and his cronies!'

Nick was holding her hand, his grasp warm and comforting and he was smiling at her in that reckless, devil-may-care fashion that invited her to enjoy the adventure. She swallowed.

'Let me stay.' She heard the words come out of her own mouth. 'Let me stay and play my part in this.' Suddenly *she* felt reckless, no longer afraid of the world. She put up her chin. 'If you are going to get yourself killed, I want to be on hand to know of it!'

He was staring at her intently. 'Are you sure, Evelina?'

She met his gaze steadily. The weeks since he had left Makerham had been the most miserable of her life; Grandpapa was at peace, there was nothing more to be done for him, but the idea of being more than two hundred miles away from Nick was not to be borne. Not, of course, that she cared a fig for him now, but he was her husband and she knew her duty.

'Yes, I am sure,' she said at last. 'I will live at Monkhurst and be your eyes and ears there.'

His chair scraped back. He stepped around the table and pulled her up into his arms. She put her hands against his chest, holding him off, but all the while her heart was beating a rapid, heavy tattoo against her ribs, leaving her breathless. He looked down at her, his mouth tantalizingly close.

'It could be dangerous,' he murmured.

'Being your *wife* is dangerous, Nick Wylder!'

With a laugh he bent to kiss her and it took all her willpower to turn her head away.

'No,' she gasped, closing her eyes as his lips feathered kisses down the line of her neck, causing her traitorous body to shiver with delight.

'You cannot deny you want me,' he murmured. His warm breath on her skin made her tremble, weakening her resolve.

'No, but I—do not—trust—you.'

The butterfly kisses stopped. He raised his head. 'Ah.'

'I'm sorry,' she whispered.

'You have nothing to be sorry for, sweetheart, it is my fault.' He cupped her chin and tilted her face up towards him. 'And I am to blame, too, for these dark circles under your eyes.' He ran his thumb gently across her cheekbone. 'What a villain I am to embroil you in this.'

Angrily she knocked his hand away. 'Yes, you are, and I shall *never* forgive you.'

'Never is a long time, sweetheart.' He grinned at her. 'I must try to make you change your mind.'

She hunched one shoulder and turned away from him. 'It will not work. I am wise to your charming ways now, Captain Wylder.'

He laughed softly. 'We shall see. But for now, we must feed you.'

'I do not think I could eat anything.'

He pushed her gently back on to her chair. 'Oh, I think you can.' He pulled a little piece of flesh from the chicken carcase with his fingers and held it out to her. 'Try this. The most succulent pieces are near the bone.'

Patiently he coaxed and cajoled her, offering her tasty slivers of cheese and the most succulent pieces of meat until she put up her hands, protesting that she was full. Only then did he look to his own needs. While he dined, Eve leaned back in her chair and sipped her wine.

'Nick? Why did you come to the Mermaid?'

'I was meeting a sea-captain, one with more information on the black-sailed lugger.'

'Did you see him? And did he help you?'

'Yes, and yes. He knows the lugger; she's called the *Merle* and sails out of Boulogne.'

'Is that not where you said Chelston has his warehouse?'

'It is. All I need now is evidence of where the smouch is being made and we can make our move.' He looked up at her. 'A few weeks more, my love, and all this will be over.'

Eve did not reply, but she watched him while he finished his meal. Light from the candles and the fire cast a warm golden glow over his face, enhancing the lean cheeks and strong jaw line, glinting off his raven-dark hair when he moved his head. A stab of longing shot through her and she clamped her teeth into her bottom lip to prevent a sigh. She must be careful or her wayward body would betray her. At last he pushed his plate away and gave a sigh of satisfaction.

'Our host knows how to please his guests, excellent food washed down by the finest French wines.' He refilled their glasses.

'And has the duty been paid on the wine?'

He grinned at her. 'I doubt it, but I am not going to ask. Now, one more thing to finish our meal.' He picked up an orange.

'No, really, I have had sufficient—'

'We will share it, then, but you will have some; it will do you good.' His lean fingers deftly removed the peel and broke the orange into segments. He leaned forwards, holding a piece out for her. 'Eat it,' he said. 'No, don't touch it; you will get juice on your hands.'

Obediently she leaned forwards and allowed him to put the segment in her mouth. She nodded, smiling slightly. 'It is good.'

He held out another piece and this time his fingers touched her lips; she yearned to take them in her mouth, to lick the sharp-sweet juice from his skin. It took all her willpower to pull away. Nick's eyes were on her face, reading her thoughts, piercing her very soul. In turmoil, Eve tried desperately to think of something to say. Anything, to break the dangerous mood that had settled around them.

'We should build a hot-house at Monkhurst. Fruit would do very well there. The gardens are sadly neglected but I have set Nathaniel and Sam to clearing the ground—'

'Eve.'

'We will need to employ a gardener, but Silas may know someone…'

Nick's chair scraped back. 'My love, you may employ as many gardeners as you wish, but we will not talk of it now.' He pulled her to her feet and wrapped his arms around her. She kept her head down and braced herself. Her instinct was to give in, to lean against him and yield to his embrace, but she would not. She could not, for she knew only too well the heartbreak he would cause her. He cupped her chin with his hand and forced her to look up at him. When she saw his eyes darken with desire, felt his aroused body pressing hard against hers, she panicked.

'Of course as my husband you are entitled to take your

pleasure of me, but I pray you will take it speedily. I am quite worn out with travelling.'

His brows snapped together. 'What is this? Do you think I am a monster, that I would force myself upon you?'

His hold slackened and she stepped back, turning away from him while she gathered her defences, dredged up every feeling of anger and resentment to protect herself from the attraction she felt for him.

'You are no monster, sir, but you must understand that I have suffered a severe shock. I set out this morning thinking myself a widow, only to discover that I have been deceived.'

'And I have explained to you why it was necessary!'

Eve spun around. 'Oh, so that is sufficient to make everything well again! You think that you only have to smile and say you are sorry and you will be forgiven.'

'No, of course not—'

She began to catalogue his offences, counting them off on her fingers. 'First, you married me because you suspected my family of being involved in smuggling. The day after our wedding you disappear, then you send your man to tell me you are d-drowned. I have told you, I shall *never* forgive you!' She put her hands over her face, fighting back the tears that were choking her. She longed to feel Nick's arms around her, to hear him utter some words of comfort, but there was only silence and it seemed to stretch on forever.

'You are quite right,' he said at last. 'I have behaved abominably towards you.'

She looked up. He was putting on his coat.

'Where are you going?'

'I must leave. I have no wish to force my attentions upon you, nor my company, if you find me so repulsive. Forgive me, Evelina.'

'Go, then!'

No, don't leave me! The words echoed in her head but Eve could not voice them. Nick buttoned up the old frock-coat.

'Richard will escort you back to Monkhurst tomorrow. If you are happy to remain there it will be a comfort to me to have you so close, but it could be dangerous. You need only say the word at any time and Richard shall take you to my brother.'

'Monkhurst is my home now. I shall stay there. What do you want me to do?'

'Watch and wait. But you must be careful, and tell Martha she must watch her tongue, because no one else at Monkhurst knows I am alive. Send a message with Richard if you want to contact me.'

'I will.'

Eve's heart leapt as he took a step towards her, but he stopped just out of arm's reach and gave her a wry, apologetic smile.

'Do not turn me into a monster while I am away from you, sweetheart. I shall give you no cause to distrust me ever again, I swear, but I need time to prove it to you.'

'Wait!' She gazed at him. Phrases such as 'do not go' and 'stay with me' rattled in her head, but instead she heard herself say, 'Should I not go on to Hastings? Granby will have told you it was my intention to visit the spot where you…died. It might look suspicious if I do not continue.'

'As you wish.' He smiled at her and the sight of that wickedly attractive dimple made the breath catch in her throat. 'Aye, go to Hastings. Let the world know that someone mourns my passing!'

Nick kissed his fingers to her, turned on his heel and disappeared through the door in the panelling. Eve watched the door close behind him, felt the stillness of the room envelope her again. Then, as if released from a trap, she dashed across the room and ran her fingers over the wood, trying to find a handle or lever to open the door. There was nothing. She pressed her ear to the panel. Straining, she thought she heard his boots on the wooden stairs and the dull thud of the outer door closing behind him.

He was gone.

There was a scratching on the servants' door and she went across to unlock it. Martha peeped in.

'Shall I clear away now, mistress? It's growing late and I don't want to be traipsing through these passages once they have snuffed out the candles.' She looked over Eve's shoulder. 'Where's the master?'

'He's gone.' Eve took a long breath, but she could not stop the tears spilling over. Martha put her arms about her and guided her to the bed.

'There, there, Miss Eve. You come and sit here and tell Martha all about it.'

'Th–there's nothing to tell,' sobbed Eve. 'I—we…had a disagreement and…he l–left.'

Eve subsided into tears and Martha clucked over her like a mother hen.

'Good heavens, Miss Eve, never say he forced himself upon you!'

'No,' cried Eve in a fresh flood of tears. 'No, of course he did not, I told him to g–go and…and he d–did! Stupid, stupid man!'

Chapter Ten

The journey to Hastings was accomplished with ease, the Winchelsea road having been repaired and opened again for coaches to pass through. There was no reception party waiting for her when she reached the town and the road leading down the hill to the little harbour was rutted and ill-used. As Richard Granby opened the carriage door for her to alight she glanced at him.

'There is nothing here except fishing smacks. Tell me, Mr Granby, where are these business acquaintances that my husband was visiting?'

The valet's impassive countenance did not alter. 'I cannot say, madam.'

She pulled her veil down over her face. 'Well, help me out, Granby. We must continue with this charade, although there is no one here to witness it.'

'Oh I think you are wrong there, madam,' muttered Granby, giving her his hand. He nodded towards a group of fishermen who were mending their nets in the shelter of an upturned boat. Eve had noticed them looking at the carriage and as she stepped down one of the men came across to her, tugging at his forelock with his gnarled fingers.

'Beggin' yer pardon, mistress, we sees yer coming down the road and thinks—well, seein' yer widder's weeds—we wonders if you be the cap'n's widder? Cap'n Wyldfire?'

Eve looked towards Granby and, as if aware of her eyes through the thick veil, he nodded slightly. She turned back to the fisherman. 'Yes, I am,' she said softly. 'Did you—did you know my husband?'

A wide, black-toothed grin split his weather-beaten face.

'Aye, mistress, we all knew Cap'n Wyldfire. Proper sailor, he was, from the King's navy, no less, and very generous 'e was, too, allus ready to stand buff in the Stag of an evenin'. He told us he'd come down 'ere to take out the villains what is givin' us a bad name, sellin' us their smouch that was no more real tea than that there seaweed.' The grin disappeared and he shook his head. 'It were a sad day when he drowned, mistress, an' no mistake. We was all of us sorry to see the end o' such a brave one.'

Eve's heart skipped a beat. 'Were you with him, then? You saw my husband the night he—he—'

'Lor' bless you mistress, 'twas my boat, the *Sally-Ann*, he used that night. Wanted to get close to a brig that was sailing out o' Hastings, see?'

'And what happened?'

'Oh, we got close, right enough, the cap'n and some of us had already boarded the brig, being friendly-like, and pretending we was interested in taking some o' their cargo, but the Revenue cutter came up too soon. There was only a donkey's breath o' mist and as soon as they spotted her they set up the cry, knowin' as how they'd been tricked. Set upon us, they did. The cap'n was quick to sound the retreat, got us all safely back on board the *Sally-Ann*, but one o' they villains, he levels his pops at the cap'n and shoots him afore he can escape. Killed-dead he was. Went over the side without a murmur.'

'And did you not try to find him, to recover the body?'

'O'course we did, but there was no sign of him and we had to make sail, for the sea was carryin' us towards Nore rocks. It were dulling-up by that time and with the brig bristling with guns we decided to make for the shore. The Revenue cutter did give chase, but not long enough.' The fisherman showed his contempt for their efforts by turning his head to spit. 'They may've scared 'em off for now, but they'll be back, especially now they knows the cap'n ain't here to gainsay 'em.' The fisherman shook his head, and said in a reminiscent tone, 'Aye, a great one, was Cap'n Wyldfire; allus on the gammock he was, looking for excitement or any sort o' bobbery. We've been watching the beaches every day since then, missus, hopin' his body would be washed up so we could give 'im a proper Christian burial up at All Saints. And there's still time. We'll keep a look-out, don't 'ee worry.'

'Thank you.' Eve opened her purse and took out a handful of coins. 'Here,' she said, pressing them into the man's hand. 'When you and your crew go to the Stag tonight, I pray you drink a toast to my husband's memory.'

Again she was treated to the black grin.

'Well now, missus, that's very generous of 'ee, very generous. The sort o' thing the cap'n would approve, if you don't mind me sayin' so.' He tugged his forelock once again and turned to the little group behind him. 'Stan' up, lads, stan' up and pay yer respects to Wyldfire's widow!'

He tugged his forelock yet again as Eve turned back to the carriage.

'Back to Monkhurst, madam?' asked Granby, holding open the door.

'Yes, if you please. But we will stop at the church before we leave Hastings, I think.'

* * *

All Saints Church stood on the eastern edge of the town, high above the harbour and surrounded by its graveyard. As Eve climbed down from the carriage a shiver ran through her to think that this was where Nick might have been buried. The wind blew in from the coast, tugging at her bonnet and pressing the black veil to her face. She folded it back and breathed in the fresh sea air.

'What is beyond those houses?' she asked Granby, pointing to the cluster of buildings and the little lane beyond the church.

'Fields, madam, and the cliff.'

'Does it overlook the rocks the sailor mentioned?'

'The Rocks of Nore? Yes, madam.'

'Then let us go there.'

She strode off across the graveyard and through the little gate at the far side. She found herself in a lane that ran between rows of small, rundown houses. Raggedly dressed women and barefoot children stared at her with dull, unfriendly eyes as she hurried by and Eve was relieved that Granby was following close behind her. When they emerged from the lane on to the open grassland, there was no shelter from the elements and Eve was suddenly brought to a halt by the strong onshore wind. It buffeted her remorselessly, whipping at her pelisse and skirts and she put up one hand to hold her bonnet. Granby stepped up beside her.

'Allow me, madam.'

She took his arm and together they battled towards the cliff edge, until they could see the restless, grey-brown water breaking into creamy foam against the rocks beneath them.

'If last night had not happened,' Eve remarked, 'if we had not stopped at the Mermaid, I suppose you would have spun me a yarn about my husband's friends having left Hastings by this time.'

'I would have been obliged to think of something, Mrs Wylder.'

'Then you are an unmitigated scoundrel,' she told him. 'Now move away and allow me a moment alone to contemplate my fate.'

'Pray do not go to close to the edge, madam!'

Eve waved him away. She stood for a moment looking out at the choppy grey waters while the wind tugged at her skirts. She thought how much her life had changed. No longer was she Grandpapa's darling, living sheltered and secure at Makerham. She was a married woman now and there was no going back. Nick had married her for Monkhurst, but what else did he want from her? Was hers to be a marriage of convenience, was she to be installed in one of his houses and left there to run the estate while he was off adventuring? She squared her shoulders, narrowing her eyes a little against the wind. She had no idea what the future might hold, but as for the present…well, she had a part to play. She was a widow. Eve conjured up a picture of Nick as she had last seen him, wearing his old frock-coat with all the swagger and panache of a buccaneer. She was Captain Wyldfire's widow.

'What on earth am I to do now?' Evelina stood in the panelled drawing room and looked about her. She had returned to Monkhurst excited at the thought of playing her part in Nick's adventure, but now, as the comfortable stillness of her old home settled around her, she found it hard to believe that anything exciting could happen here. She turned to look at Granby, who had followed her into the room.

'I have no doubt your master thinks me safely out of the way here, while he pursues his dangerous games.'

'He is concerned for your welfare, madam. It was his

wish that you should go north, to his own family, where he could be sure you were protected.'

'And do you blame me, Granby, do you think I am wrong not to take his advice?'

'I would not presume to criticise your actions, mistress.'

'Damn your eyes, you criticise me with every look!' she exclaimed, shocking herself with her unladylike language. With a sigh she sank down into a chair and dropped her head in her hands.

'Madam, I—' Granby broke off. She heard him take a few paces about the room before he began again, his voice devoid of all emotion. 'Captain Wylder ordered me to remain with you and I know he thought you would be safer at Wylderbeck Hall. Naturally, I do my best at all times to carry out his orders, but I admit that in this instance I was not—unhappy—to remain in Kent.'

She lifted her head. 'Thank you Mr Granby,' she said softly. 'We neither of us want to be too far away from him, do we?'

'No, madam.'

Nick's words came back to her. *It will be a comfort to me to have you so close.* It was a tiny crumb of consolation and it put new heart in her. Eve jumped to her feet.

'Well, there is no reason why we should not make ourselves useful here while we are waiting for this business to come to an end! We can at least make Monkhurst a home again.' She untied her bonnet and cast it aside. 'I may have to play the grieving widow, but there is no reason why I cannot be active in my own house!'

Over the following week Evelina found some outlet for her pent-up energies in making the old house comfortable. She accepted Richard Granby's offer to act as her general factotum until Nick returned and agreed that Aggie should bring in more girls from the village to help her with the cleaning. In an effort to prevent Silas and his sons from returning to smuggling she set them to work repairing windows and clearing even more of the garden. Eve herself donned an old dimity gown and joined Martha in the attics. They were packed with broken furniture, most of it only fit for firewood, but some of the better pieces she sent downstairs to be used in the house. It was hard work, but it helped to fill her days and at night she was so tired she would fall asleep as soon as she climbed into bed.

Once the attics had been cleaned, Eve turned her attention to the trunks that were stacked there. They were full of linen and fine fabrics, carefully packed away by some previous owner and Eve made a note of their contents for future use. There was one trunk, however, that caused her to cry out in delight when Martha dragged it forwards for inspection.

'I remember this one!' she exclaimed, running her hands over the battered top. 'It was kept in Mama's bedroom.'

'Nay Miss Eve,' exclaimed Martha. 'You can't recall so long ago, surelye.'

'Well, she is right,' agreed Aggie, who had come upstairs to help them sort through the trunks. 'This case was kept beneath the window in the mistress's bedroom.'

'Yes!' cried Eve excitedly. 'It had cushions on the top, like a window-seat. Look, it has Mama's initials on the lid: H. W.—Helena Wingham.'

Aggie reached out one gnarled hand and traced the letters. She gave a loud sigh.

'I remember Miss Helena's father giving her this trunk when she was a girl and she always had it in her bedroom here, even after she was married and she couldn't come here quite so often. When your parents died Sir Benjamin moved all their personal effects to Makerham and closed up the house. If he left this behind, it cannot hold anything of value.'

'We must open it and see,' said Eve. 'It is locked. Try your keys, Aggie; one of them may fit.'

But after a fruitless quarter of an hour they were forced to admit that none of the housekeeper's keys would open the trunk.

'We could break the lock,' offered Martha.

'No-o, there were a few old keys in Mama's writing desk,' said Eve. 'I saw them when I was hunting for a seal to put on my letter to my Cousin. I did not tell you Martha, I received a note from him yesterday, such a wheedling letter, apologising for frightening me away from Makerham and asking if he could visit me here at Monkhurst.'

Martha snorted. 'I hope you told him it was not to be thought of.'

'I did indeed. I made it very clear that I will not have him in my sight.'

'You did very right, Miss Eve. Mr Granby will give him short shrift if he comes anywhere near this house, you may be sure o' that, miss. I told 'im how Bernard was makin' up to you, and you having just learned that the master was drowned.'

Eve shot her handmaid a warning glance.

'Yes, well, if my cousin should decide to visit Monkhurst I shall rely upon Granby and Silas to turn him away. And talking of those two, do you think you could run and find them now, Martha, and ask them to bring this trunk down to my room? Then we can try the keys I have found.'

The trunk was duly carried downstairs. Martha and the housekeeper accompanied it, Aggie declaring that the mistress should not be wasting her time with such trifles.

'It will be filled with old rubbish, you mark my words,' she said, shaking her head while Eve hunted through the drawers of the little writing cabinet.

'Perhaps, but I should like to be sure. I know I saw them here somewhere…ah, here they are.' She pulled a small bunch of keys from the back of a drawer and held them aloft, smiling triumphantly. 'Now we shall see!' She selected the likeliest key and fitted it into the lock while Aggie clucked her disapproval. At first the key did not move, but Eve gripped it tightly and tried again. This time it turned with a soft grating noise.

'You've done it Miss Eve!' Martha stared open-mouthed as Evelina lifted the lid.

'There,' said Aggie, peering into the trunk. 'What did I tell you? 'Tis full of old clothes. Let it be, madam.'

Eve ignored her and rummaged through the contents. 'I do not understand.' She frowned. 'I know this to be my mother's trunk.' She pulled out an old brown jacket. 'But this is a boy's coat. It is far too small to belong to my father.'

'Now, Miss Eve, leave off, do,' exclaimed Aggie as Eve pulled out more clothes.

'Shirts, stockings, buckskins…and a pair of boots.'

'The stable-lad's cast offs, mayhap,' offered Martha.

Eve picked up one of the boots and held it against her own dainty foot. Excitement bubbled within her. 'Do you know what I think?' she said softly. 'I think these clothes belonged to Mama.'

Martha laughed. 'Now where are your wits gone a-begging, mistress? They's lad's togs.'

'I do not think so.' Eve fixed her eyes on the old house-keeper, who shifted uneasily. 'Well, Aggie?'

'Now, mistress, how should I know aught about these things?'

'Because you have lived at Monkhurst all your life. You were here when Mama visited the house as a child and you would have seen her grow up here. I can tell from your face that you know something.' She jumped up and caught at the old woman's hands. 'Do tell us, Aggie.'

'No, miss, 'tis nothing. It's all in the past. Let it be,' she implored, an anguished look upon her face.

'No, I insist.' Eve gave her hands a little shake. 'Tell me, Aggie. When did Mama wear these clothes?'

'They could be dressing up clothes,' suggested Martha, her eyes wide.

Eve shook her head and kept her own gaze fixed upon the housekeeper. 'No, I do not believe that. Well, Aggie?'

The old woman looked at her, read the determination in her face and capitulated. 'The mistress would sometimes go out in these clothes.' She paused, looking uncomfortable, but Eve's gaze did not waver and she added, in a whisper. 'At night. She would go out with the boys, the free traders.'

Eve clapped her hands. 'I knew it,' she breathed. 'She was a smuggler.'

'No!' declared Aggie, shocked. 'Your mama would be mighty offended to hear you speak so. There has always been trade twixt here and the Continent. Silas and the other lads from the village would bring in a few ankers of brandy every now and then. Only small, mind you— we had no truck with the big cutters bringin' in tea and brandy for the towns, we've only ever brought in enough for local use. Everyone knew about it and turned to the wall if the pack-ponies were coming through the village. Miss Helena discovered it on one of her visits here with the family. She could twist Silas round her little finger. Apple of 'is eye, she was, so when she wanted to go out with 'em, he couldn't stop her, short o' telling old Mr

Wingham, and that 'e would never do. After all, it was only the local lads plying their trade, not one o' them nasty, vicious gangs that would cut yer throat as soon as look at you.'

'And did she stop going out with them once she was married?'

'Of course. She gave it all up when she became Mrs Shawcross.'

Eve gazed up at the portrait of her mother. Looking into the demure smiling face, she thought now she could detect a gleam in those dark eyes that she had not noticed before. She laughed suddenly. 'Perhaps I am not such a poor match for Captain Wyldfire after all!'

'I beg your pardon miss?' said Martha.

Eve shook her head, smiling mischievously. She began to pack the clothes back into the trunk. 'It is nearly dinner time and this is such dusty work, I think I will have a bath, Aggie. We will continue sorting through the trunks tomorrow.'

However, the following morning, Evelina had barely risen from the breakfast table when Granby came in to tell her that she had a visitor.

'Lady Chelston has called, madam. I have shown her into the morning room.'

Eve stared at him. 'Lady Chelston! What in heaven's name can she want with me?'

'To offer her condolences, perhaps?' he suggested quietly.

She swallowed. 'And you think I must see her?' His steady look gave Eve her answer. 'Oh, heavens!' She bit her lip. 'I suppose I must do so, but I will not see her wearing this old gown! Do you go back to her, Mr Granby, and tell her I shall be with her presently—and if she objects and will not wait while I change, then so much the better.'

★ ★ ★

But when Eve entered the morning room some twenty minutes later she found her guest sitting at her ease, flicking through one of the periodicals that Eve had left on a small side table. Eve came in quietly, smoothing her hands over the heavy black bombazine skirts of her mourning gown. She wore no ornament save the plain gold wedding band upon her finger, and her hair was covered by a black lace cap. She looked, she hoped, very much the grieving widow.

'Lady Chelston. I am so sorry to keep you waiting.' She gave a little curtsy before raising her eyes to observe her guest.

Catherine Chelston was a tall, spare woman. Her once handsome face was heavily lined and at odds with the improbably black curls that peeped from under her large hat. Her Pomona-green travelling dress rustled as she hurried towards Eve, holding out her hands and saying impetuously, 'Oh my poor child, so beautiful, so like your dear mama.'

Eve blinked. 'You—you knew my mother?'

'Yes, yes. That was many years ago now, of course, we lost touch once we were married. When I heard you had taken up residence at Monkhurst, I was determined to pay a morning visit and make myself known to you. And to offer you my condolences. So tragic, my dear, to lose your grandfather *and* your husband in so short a time. I thought to find you prostrate.'

'We bear it as best we can, ma'am.' Eve gently withdrew her hands and gestured to her guest to sit down. 'News travels fast here, I see.'

Lady Chelston laughed softly. 'It is the way in these country areas, and neighbours must offer each other such solace as they are able.'

'Oh, ma'am? Are we, then, neighbours?'

Again that soft, assured laugh. 'Chelston Hall is not much

more than a dozen miles from here, and in an area where there are so very few *good* families, I do not like to be backward in my attentions.'

Eve inclined her head. She did not know how to respond, but was spared the necessity of a reply for Lady Chelston continued with barely a pause for breath.

'By the bye, my dear; who is that delightful young man who showed me in here? Not your butler, I vow.'

'No, that is Mr Granby. He was my husband's valet and has agreed to stay on with me,' explained Eve, deciding that it would be best to stick as closely to the truth as she could. 'I have not yet set up my household here, and Granby is very useful. He fulfils the role of a major-domo very well.'

'He is certainly very personable,' murmured Lady Chelston, her eyes half-closed. 'When you have finished with him, my dear, you must send him to me and I shall find him a place in my household. I like to be surrounded by attractive young men. Oh, have I shocked you? I am sorry, Mrs Wylder, I allowed my tongue to run away with me, but you are so like your sainted mama that I quite forgot myself.'

'Did—did you know my mother well, ma'am?'

'Oh, yes, we were the greatest friends. Helena and I went off to school together, you know. We were both sadly wild, always falling into scrapes. It is difficult to know who was the leader! I was quite surprised when Helena married Shawcross—he was such a very quiet gentleman, not at all what I thought she would—' She broke off suddenly and smiled. 'But I am running on to no purpose and you will be wishing me at Jericho.'

'Not at all, ma'am,' murmured Eve politely.

'Now, my poor Mrs Wylder, you are here, all on your own, no family, no friends—'

'I have many loyal people around me.' Eve was quick to correct her, but Lady Chelston merely waved her hand dismissively.

'Servants. That is not at all the same thing. Life can be very lonely here on the Marsh. I know you will wish to live quietly, but it will do you no good to become a hermit. I know what you must do, you must come to Chelston Hall and stay with me! There is room and to spare, and you will very welcome.'

'That is very kind, Lady Chelston, but—'

'Better still,' cried my lady, ignoring her interruption, 'you must join my house party! I have friends coming to stay in a se'ennight and it would be just the thing for you to have some company. I am holding a masquerade, too, which is very exciting. I have already ordered a costume for myself and for Chelston. He is to be Hades and I am Persephone. It will be such fun…oh, do say you will come!'

'Really, madam, I cannot. My mourning is too recent—'

'Nonsense. Mourning in the country is a very different matter from the public show you would be obliged to put on in town, where everyone would know you and your circumstances. Here you are not known, and no one will be offended if you go about a little. I have never held with widows shutting themselves away, that only leads to deep melancholy. And you are not to think that I would be wishing for you to be merry all day long; Chelston Hall is a large house and you will be able to take yourself off and be quiet now and then, if you wish, but I shall be there to look out for you, to make sure you do not succumb to your dismal thoughts. Of course, you will not *dance* at the ball, but think how well you will look at the masquerade, dressed all in black and with a black satin mask to hide your identity! You will look so elegantly mysterious that all the ladies will be jealous and the gentlemen will be wild to discover who you are!'

Eve recoiled, shocked. 'Madam, I could not! It would be most improper.'

'La, but who is to know?' replied Lady Chelston, smiling. 'It is just such a spree as your mama would have liked.'

'Not if she was newly widowed!'

Lady Chelston's smile slipped a little, as if she realised she had gone too far. She sighed. 'Perhaps you are right,' she said, rising. 'I can see that you are not convinced, my dear, but believe me, a little lively company, a little stimulating conversation—it can work wonders in assuaging your grief. But your countenance tells me you are determined to refuse me today. Well, I shall send you an invitation nevertheless; perhaps when you have thought it over you may change your mind.' She reached out for Eve's hands and took them, smiling down at her. 'You are far too young and pretty to bury yourself away, my dear. Send me word at Chelston Hall if there is anything I can do for you.'

'Thank you, my lady, but I am at a loss to know why you should be so eager to befriend me.'

Lady Chelston's blue-grey eyes widened. 'So frank—how refreshing,' she murmured. 'Let us say it is for your mother's sake. Now, I must go.' She squeezed Eve's fingers. 'To stay longer would be beyond the bounds of the propriety you set such story by. Goodbye to you, Mrs Wylder, and think upon my invitation!'

Eve could think of nothing else and when her disturbing visitor had left the premises she walked slowly to the kitchen, where she found Aggie shelling peas for their dinner. Richard Granby was piling logs into a large square basket beside the great fireplace.

'It is not for you to do that,' she told him, frowning.

'You have only one manservant in the house besides

myself and he has been on duty in the hall, waiting for your visitor to leave.' He grinned. 'I thought it best to play least in sight and let Matthew show her out; the lady seemed disposed to question me.'

'Lady Chelston did indeed ask about you. I told her you were my husband's valet and that you had stayed on to manage my house for me.' She chuckled. 'She was very taken with you and told me to send you to her when I have no further need of you.'

'I hope you will do no such thing, madam!'

'No, of course not, but I could not make her out. Aggie, Lady Chelston says she knew my mother. They were neighbours, and they went to school together. Do you remember her?'

Aggie shook her head, a crease furrowing her brow. 'I disremember any close schoolfriends of your mama's, madam, except—yes, there *was* one: Catherine Reade, merchant's daughter, about a year younger than Miss Helena she was. Spoiled little thing, nothing would do for her but she should follow Miss Helena to school in Tenterden. Yes, we thought it a good joke at the time, for Mr Reade was no more than your grandfather Wingham's tenant at the time, though 'e did buy the house at Abbotsfield from your grandfather later. But what little Cathy wanted she must have. Made a good marriage, though; caught a lord with property across the border. We never saw her after that.'

'In Sussex? That could be Chelston Hall.' Eve sat down at the table and cupped her chin in her hands. 'If Catherine really had been such good friends with Mama, I would have thought you would know of it, Aggie, even if I couldn't remember her.'

'I am certain sure she never called upon your sainted mama after her marriage, at least not here at Monkhurst. I wonder why she should be calling upon you now?' mused the housekeeper.

Eve saw the warning look in Granby's eyes and shrugged. 'I think she was curious to see Helena Wingham's daughter.' She hesitated. 'She invited me to stay with her.' Aggie dropped the pea pod she was shelling and stared. Eve nodded. 'She thinks I will be lonely here on my own.'

'Well there is no denying, Miss Eve, that there's precious little company here for you. You should perhaps consider hiring a companion to live with you.'

Eve dared not look at Granby. 'I shall consider it, Aggie, but not yet. I am quite content here on my own for the present time. And there is plenty to do. Mr Granby, if you will meet me in the attics in quarter of an hour, I will go and change and then you can help Martha and me to empty the last few trunks.'

The busy afternoon passed quickly enough, but Catherine Chelston's visit still played on Eve's mind. It was not until dinnertime that she found the opportunity to talk it over with Granby. It had become the habit for the valet to wait upon her at dinner, overriding her objections by saying that he had done the same for his master on numerous occasions. She was glad of his company; it was a link with Nick and it was a comfort to be able to talk to him about his master. The September sun was shining in through the dining-room windows, making candles unnecessary as he cleared away the remains of her meal and placed a small bowl of sweetmeats upon the table before her.

'Aggie has surpassed herself,' said Eve, reaching for her wineglass. 'The lamb was delicious. Have you tried it, Mr Granby?'

'No, madam. I shall take my meal later. Mrs Brattee will

leave a plate on the hob for me before she goes back to the Gate House.'

'Tell me what you make of Lady Chelston's visit.'

'I am not sure. I think she was sent here by her husband, but for what purpose I do not know.'

'We must tell Captain Wylder of this,' she decided.

'That is what I was thinking, madam.'

'Can you get a note to him, Mr Granby? He said you would know how to contact him.'

'Yes madam, I—'

'Good.' She rose. 'I shall write to him directly.'

'That will not be necessary, Mrs Wylder.'

'No, you are right, it would be best if we did not commit anything to paper.'

'That is not what I meant, madam.' Something in the valet's tone made her look at him intently. A glimmer of a smile was just discernible on his usually impassive face. 'You will be able to tell him so yourself, Mrs Wylder. The master is coming here tonight.'

Since their last meeting at the Mermaid Inn, Eve had spent many hours wondering just how she was going to deal with Nick Wylder. He was her husband, it was impossible for her to cut him out of her life, no matter how badly he had treated her. He had vowed to win her trust and she wanted to give him that chance, but that did not mean she was going to fall into his arms as soon as he smiled at her. No, she would be polite, she would help him catch his smugglers, but he should not have her love until he had earned it!

As the clock in the hall chimed eleven, Eve picked up her candle and left the drawing room to make her way through the dark, silent passages to the kitchen. Granby was sitting at the big table in the centre of the room, playing patience by the golden light from a single oil lamp. He glanced up as she entered.

'It is all right, madam, we are alone. Aggie has returned to the Gate House.'

'And I have told Matthew he may go on to bed,' she replied. 'He is not here yet?'

'No,' said Granby, rising. 'Have patience, madam, the captain will come. Pray, return to the drawing room; I will bring you word as soon as he arrives.'

Eve shook her head slightly and set her candlestick down upon the table.

'I will wait for him here. I cannot settle to anything. There is a chill in this house tonight, at least here the fire has been burning all day—'

She broke off as the valet threw up his head, listening. Soon Eve could hear it, too, the soft thud of a footfall followed by a quiet knocking on wood. Granby crossed the room and dragged aside the log basket. Seconds later the floorboards beside the fireplace began to rise.

'Welcome, sir!' Granby pulled back the trapdoor and Nick Wylder's head and shoulders rose from the black aperture. He grinned at Eve.

'Permission to come aboard, madam!'

She was so surprised by his unorthodox entry that her plans to remain cool and aloof were forgotten. 'You have used the riverside passage,' she exclaimed. 'But it is locked!'

Nick stepped up into the room. 'I know.' He patted his pocket. 'Dick left the key within reach for me.'

'You had no difficulty navigating the channel?' asked Granby.

'No, the waterway is clear from Jury's Cut as far as the boathouse.'

Nick drew up a stool and sat down, wincing slightly.

Eve said quickly, 'Your wound is still paining you.'

'It has not healed yet.' He gave her a wry smile. 'I do not rest enough.'

'When was the bandage last changed?' His shrug told Eve all she needed to know. She went to the door. 'Stay there while I fetch some clean linen. I will re-dress it for you.'

'But I came here to talk to you!'

'You can do that while I bind you up.'

Chapter Eleven

When Eve returned to the kitchen, Granby had built up the fire and lighted more candles so that the room glowed with a rich golden light. A pitcher of ale stood on the table and three tankards had been filled to the brim.

'Richard has poured one for you,' said Nick, waving to the mugs. 'It is small-beer, but he will fetch you a glass of wine if you prefer.'

'No, I will drink ale with you.' She began to tear the old sheet she had brought with her into strips. 'You must take off your jacket and shirt, if you please.'

She did not look up as Granby helped Nick to take off his coat, but as he stripped off his shirt she found her eyes straying to Nick's broad shoulders. She watched the way the muscles rippled under the skin as he pulled the shirt over his head, the sinuous contours accentuated by the candlelight.

Swallowing hard, she forced herself to concentrate and shifted her gaze to the tight bandaging around his ribs. There was a dark stain low on his left side.

'Good God, sir,' exclaimed Granby, frowning. 'Has it been changed at all since I last saw you?'

Nick perched himself on the table and held up his arms as Eve began to remove the bandage.

'Of course,' he said. 'Rebecca did it for me about a week ago. She is landlady at the Ship, ma'am, in case you were wondering.'

'Is that where you are staying, at an inn?'

'Yes, outside Hastings. The risk of being recognised is too great to stay in the town, but I am well hidden at the Ship. It was Rebecca who looked after me when I was first brought ashore.'

Something of Eve's thoughts must have shown in her face for Nick laughed. 'You need not be jealous, sweetheart; she is married, and old enough to be my mother.'

'I am not at all jealous,' she retorted.

He reached out for her. 'No?' he murmured, pulling her closer.

She put her hands against his chest and pushed hard. 'Of course not!' she said crossly. She went over to the pump in the corner and worked the handle vigorously. The water slopped into the bowl. She drew more than she needed, but she wanted the heated flush in her cheeks to die down before she went back to Nick. She heard Granby's angry mutter.

'I should have stayed with you, Captain.'

'It would have made no difference. Besides, Dick, I needed you here to look after my wife.'

Eve refused to allow herself any comfort in Nick's words; he was merely looking after his interests, scoundrel that he was! However, when she turned her attention to the wound in his side, all other thoughts were driven out by the sight of the red, angry gash.

'You told me it was a little flesh wound.' Her hands trembled slightly as she washed away the dried blood and gently cleaned around the injury. 'This is very deep. You are fortunate it did not touch any vital organs.'

'I've had worse than this,' he reassured her cheerfully.

'But I have always been there to look after you!' put in the valet quickly.

'Oh.' Eve paused. 'Then perhaps, Mr Granby, you would like to carry on here—'

'No he would not!' exclaimed Nick. 'Richard's ministrations have always been of the rough-and-ready sort. I much prefer your gentle touch.'

Eve scowled, revolted by her pleasure at his words. She picked up a small ointment jar.

'What's that?' asked Nick suspiciously.

'Comfrey paste, to help the skin to heal.'

'It is healing well enough alone,' he muttered, looking sceptically at her.

She held the jar in front of her. 'I made it myself,' she coaxed.

At length he sighed and raised his arm. 'Very well, apply your witch's potion!'

She dipped her fingers into the jar and began to smooth the ointment over the wound. Standing so close to Nick was playing havoc with her insides, making it difficult to concentrate. She was aware of his chest rising and falling just inches from her face, the faded scars on his skin reminding her of the adventurous life he had led.

She did not realise she had stopped applying the comfrey paste and was staring at a neat round scar on his shoulder until she heard him say, 'I told you it was not the first hole I've had in me.'

'I think you court danger,' she said in a low voice.

'No, but it seems to find me.'

She looked up to see that devil-may-care smile curving his

lips. He held her eyes, inviting her to share in his excitement and, oh, she wanted to! She wanted to throw her lot in with him and declare the world well lost, but it frightened her.

Eve dragged her eyes back to the red, ugly wound in his side. Just looking at it made her shudder for what might have happened. She was about to suggest that Mr Granby should apply the final bandage when she heard the valet cough and excuse himself. When the door closed behind him, the silence that settled over the kitchen was heavy with tension.

She took up a strip of clean linen and turned to face Nick. Obligingly he raised his arms for her but he was still sitting on the table, and Eve had to move forwards, to step in between his legs and put her arms about him to pass the bandage around his back. Her face came very close to his chest, so close she only needed to lean a little more and her cheek would press against him. His skin smelled of the outdoors, of salt and sea air, overlaid with hints of spice and soap. She breathed deeply; he was so strong, so reassuringly solid. Safe. Nick jumped.

'Oh—did I hurt you?' She looked up quickly.

'No, sweetheart. I had forgotten how good it was to have you near to me.'

The dark glow in his eyes sent her heart skidding round in her chest. She knew an overwhelming desire to stretch up and kiss the dimple that appeared at the side of his mouth when he smiled down at her. With an effort she wrenched her eyes away, reminding herself what a troublesome individual he was.

'I am only doing this because I do not want your death laid at my door!'

'Yes, of course.'

She bit back a smile at his meek tone and continued to pass the bandage around him. When she had finished, her hands lingered on his skin, reluctant to move away. Nick reached up and covered her fingers, trapping them. He slid off the table and stood before her, his body tense and aroused. A thrill of anticipation trembled through her, quickly followed by a terrible, aching pain as she remembered his betrayal. She had mourned him, grieved for him and he was not dead.

'You need your shirt.'

'Eve.'

With a tiny shake of her head she pulled her hand away from him and stepped back, blinking rapidly. 'I have no time for dalliance, sir.'

'Dalliance! I merely desire a moment's tenderness from my wife.'

Eve stared down at her hands, clasped tightly before her. The room was silent save for the merry crackle of the fire that seemed to mock her unhappiness. She said in a low tone, 'I do not trust you. Not yet. It is still too painful for me—'

'Then I will wait,' he replied quietly. 'Until you are ready.'

The constriction in Eve's throat threatened to choke her as the tears welled up. There was a heavy tread from the passage, a rattling of the door handle and Granby entered the kitchen. Nick quickly turned, putting himself between Eve and the door. Retreating to the shadows, she pulled out her handkerchief and wiped her eyes.

'I have brought in more ale,' said Granby. 'I thought you might care for another cup?'

'Thank you, yes, but I cannot stay too long, the tide will be turning soon.'

He guided Eve to a chair, then sat down beside her. Granby refilled his tankard.

'So, Captain, what news have you?'

'Very little, I am afraid. I have been to Boulogne and can

find no sign that they are making this false tea there. It brings me back to my original suspicions that the stuff is made here, in this country, but where? My searches around Chelston Hall have drawn a blank. I cannot find out that Chelston is carrying out any large-scale production of the smouch on his estates.'

'Surely it would be very dangerous for him to do so,' murmured Eve.

'It would, of course, but the production needs to be somewhere secluded, and he has acres of woodland. Unfortunately, after the fiasco at the Rocks of Nore there has been very little activity; the Revenue men's sources have no new leads for us to follow. It is like the Marsh, the villages are isolated and people do not talk readily to strangers.'

'So what happens now?' asked Granby.

'We continue to watch and wait. Chelston cannot hold off indefinitely, he will need to move the goods soon.'

Despite Nick's cheerful words Eve felt the chill of despondency curling around them

'Well, we have had some excitement,' she said, trying to be cheerful. 'I had a morning visit today, from Lady Chelston.'

'The devil you did!' exclaimed Nick.

'Yes. She knew my mother. She said they had lost touch when they both married. I cannot imagine that Mama liked her—I did not take to her at all.'

'And what did she want?' asked Nick eagerly. 'Did she ask to look around the house, or was she looking for you to invite her to stay?'

'Quite the contrary, she wanted me to join her house party next week. At Chelston Hall. Of course I declined. It would be most improper, especially as she is holding a masquerade.'

'Is she, by Gad?'

'Yes. Although she tells me I need not attend.' A reluctant smile dragged at the corners of her mouth. 'She sees herself as Persephone, with Chelston as Hades.'

Nick laughed. 'How appropriate, Hades being known as both the unseen one and the rich one! That fits very well with my idea of the man.'

'But not so appropriate for his lady.' chuckled Eve, 'Persephone was an innocent, and I cannot think that term applies to Lady Chelston!'

'True, but I like the idea of a masquerade, it could be very useful to us.'

'Now what are you planning?' she asked, suspicious of Nick's wicked grin.

'Well it would be an advantage to have someone inside Chelston Hall. We might learn something.'

Eve backed away, shaking her head. 'Oh, no!'

Nick gave her a pained look. 'I would not expect you to search the house, sweetheart, merely to open a door or a window to let me in.'

'Certainly not! It is impossible for me to go. I am a widow.' Nick raised an eyebrow at her. 'Well,' she temporised, 'I am still mourning my grandfather.'

'Of course you are,' he agreed, reaching out to clasp her hand. 'You could not be expected to attend the ball, or even to join the company after dinner. Your widow's status would make it perfectly acceptable for you to keep your room a good deal, but think how useful you could be, inside Chelston Hall.'

'I thought you wanted me to live retired,' she argued. 'It would be most improper for me to go out in public.'

'This is a private party at a country house where no one knows you. Your situation would allow you to keep your distance from the other guests.' He squeezed her hand and gave her the full force of his charming smile. 'I promise you will come to no harm.'

She felt herself weakening and rallied a final, desperate argument. 'You cannot know that. Lord Chelston may be planning to coerce me into giving up Monkhurst, or even to have me murdered in my bed.'

'Chelston is outwardly very respectable. I would not send you if I thought you would be in any real danger. I do not believe he would show his hand quite so plainly. You will take Martha with you, of course.'

'And where will you be?' asked Eve suspiciously. She was not reassured by the wicked gleam in his eyes.

'Oh I shall be close at hand, never fear.' He squeezed her fingers. 'Say you will do this for me, sweetheart. Write to the lady and tell her you have changed your mind.'

'I shall do no such thing! I can think of nothing more likely to rouse her suspicions.'

'I thought you *wanted* to help me.' His reproachful gaze made her falter.

'Lady Chelston did say she would send me an invitation, even though I told her I should not come. If she does so, then I will accept.'

He lifted her hand and pressed it to his lips. 'Thank you. I knew I could rely upon you.'

'Should I go too, sir?' asked Granby. 'If there is any danger—'

'No, I do not think Mrs Wylder will be in any serious danger while she is at Chelston Hall, Richard. I would rather you stayed here, in case they try to break into the house.'

'You still think there is something here that they want?' exclaimed Eve, snatching her hand away. 'And you are happy that I should continue to live here, when I may be in mortal danger? Oooh…' She almost stamped her foot in vexation. 'You are despicable!'

Chapter Twelve

Eve wanted to believe that Lady Chelston's visit had been no more than a neighbourly gesture and that, having done her Christian duty, the lady would forget all about it. She was therefore disappointed and somewhat surprised when an invitation to visit Chelston Hall arrived a few days later. Having given her word to Nick, Eve sent back a civil acceptance, but it was not to be expected that her decision to visit Chelston Hall would be welcomed by her household. Aggie tut-tutted at the idea of her mistress going away so soon after her arrival at Monkhurst.

'There is so much yet to do here, mistress,' she complained. 'We have but emptied the attics!'

'I shall not be gone more than a se'ennight,' said Eve. 'And you do not need me in residence to have the house swept out from top to bottom. In fact,' she added, 'I would as lief *not* be here.'

They were sitting in the kitchen, where Eve had been going through the week's menus with her housekeeper. She looked up from her lists as the outer door opened and Sam strode in with an armful of logs.

'Morning, mistress,' he greeted Eve cheerfully as he

dropped the logs into the basket. 'There now, Mother, dry logs from the store. Nat and I should finish clearing the shrubbery today and then I'll chop some more firewood for 'ee.'

As he straightened and turned to go, Eve noticed his left eye was blackened and there was a livid bruise spreading over his cheek.

'Heavens,' she exclaimed. 'What has happened to you?'

Sam grinned and put his fingers to his face. 'Oh, we had a set to a few nights ago with some lads down at Jury's Cut. There was a bit of argle-bargle going on: they wanted to stop us using the inlet. Jumped us, they did, when we was lying up there.'

Aggie shook her head as she stirred the contents of the black kettle hanging over the fire. 'There's been a fair few fights recently,' she said. 'I do hope we aren't going back to the bad days. Some says it's the Hawkhurst gang come back.'

Eve frowned at Sam. 'Silas promised me that if I could find you work you would all give up the smug…free-trading.'

'And so we will, mistress, surelye, but there's some obligations that has to be dealt with first.'

'It is a matter of honour,' put in Aggie, anxious that Eve should understand. 'Some o' the villagers has already paid you see, but once the final orders are settled then the boys will not be going out again. And glad of it I shall be; I shan't rest easy in my bed until they've completed their final run.'

Sam looked pained. 'Now then, Mother how can you say that when Father has been free-trading all his life?'

'Ah, but it weren't so dangerous in the past, it's been a gentlemanly business since the worst o' the gangs was taken out…'

Eve went out, leaving them to argue, and ran upstairs to inform her maid of the forthcoming visit. Martha was even more disapproving than the housekeeper, and much more vocal.

'Well I don't like it, Miss Eve and so I tell you! To be putting yourself in the hands of that villain, not to mention the disrespect to your sainted grandfather.'

'There will be no disrespect,' returned Eve with quiet dignity. 'I shall wear full mourning, and I have made it clear in my letter to Lady Chelston that I will not participate in any of her entertainments.'

Martha sniffed 'Nevertheless, to be staying in the house of the captain's enemy is a risk, miss, you cannot deny it.'

'You seem to know a great deal about this, Martha; I suppose you have been talking with Richard Granby.'

Her maid blushed rosily. 'Mr Granby and I do have an understanding, madam.'

'Ahh. So that's it; you do not wish to leave him and come with me to Chelston Hall.'

'Miss Eve! How could you think that I would ever see you go off without me to look after you! And you to be thinking that Rich—Mr Granby would countenance such a thing! Now cease your teasing, do, and leave me to get on with the packing, since you are determined to go!'

Chelston Hall was a sturdily-built Palladian villa which had been extended at some recent date with two new wings and an imposing pediment over its entrance. It stood atop a slight hill, affording its occupants unrivalled views over the surrounding countryside and even, on a good day, a glimpse of the sea. The wind whipped around Eve as she stepped from her carriage. Through her black veil she observed the tall, wooden-faced lackey who welcomed her to the house and took her into the huge marble hall. A grand staircase led up to a gallery that ran around the upper floor, supported on gleaming marbled pillars. A second footman escorted her to her room. Sounds of laughter drifted down to her from the main reception rooms leading off the gallery, but she was in no hurry to see her fellow guests and requested that Lady Chelston be informed that she would rest until the dinner hour.

Her allotted bedchamber was in the east wing, overlooking a wide terrace and formal flower gardens. Ivy leaves surrounded the window and spilled over the stone windowsill, the growth so abundant it threatened to invade the room. A quick glance assured Eve that the stout door to her room had a serviceable lock and key and there was a small adjoining dressing room that also contained a narrow bed for her maid. She set Martha to the task of unpacking her trunk, deciding that her gowns would be better hung on pegs in the dressing room rather than folded in the large linen press, which already contained a colourful assortment of folded satins and velvets. Eve then lay down upon her bed until it was time to join the other guests for dinner. Despite her outward calm she was excited at the thought of what was to come: she had a part to play, but although she was a little nervous, she did not think that any harm could come to her in a house full of guests. Eve wondered how soon Nick would contact her. She had sent Richard Granby to him with the news that she was going to Chelston Hall, but Nick's reply had been disappointingly brief; he would seek her out.

'What?' she had exclaimed upon hearing this. 'Did he give no indication of when I might expect to see him?'

'The captain prefers to leave matters to take their course, Mrs Wylder,' Granby replied woodenly. 'He finds that the most satisfactory way to work.'

'Well, I find it most unsatisfactory,' retorted Eve. 'I am to put myself into danger with no idea what I am expected to do.'

She thought she saw a faint curving of the valet's lips,

but it was gone in an instant. He said quietly, 'Captain Wyldfire runs with the wind, ma'am. That is his way. But you need not be anxious. He will always come about.'

'Well, let us hope that this time is no exception!'

'Mrs Wylder, how glad I am that you could join us!'

Catherine Chelston hurried forward in a rustle of satin skirts to greet Eve as she came into the drawing room. Lady Chelston gestured to the lavishly dressed gentleman following more slowly in her wake. 'Madam, may I present to you my husband?'

Eve observed the man bowing before her. Lord Chelston was of slight build, not above average height, but there was a sense of ruthless strength beneath the satin and lace, and when he fixed his eyes upon her they held such a cold, calculating look that Eve had to suppress a shiver. His thin face was very pale with a high forehead and she guessed that beneath his powdered wig his own hair would be thin and receding. He took her hand in a limp, almost damp clasp.

'My dear Mrs Wylder, it is very good of you to honour us with your presence, especially when you have suffered not one, but two losses so recently—'

'I told my lord that you were reluctant to take up my invitation,' broke in Lady Chelston.

'I am still not sure if I should be here,' murmured Eve, withdrawing her hand and resisting the impulse to wipe her fingers on her gown.

'Your scruples do you credit,' returned Lord Chelston. 'And be assured, no one will intrude upon your grief, but on these occasions it is sometimes better to be amongst friends.'

Eve inclined her head. 'Did you know my husband, sir?'

'I regret I did not have that pleasure, but you are not to be thinking that you are totally alone here in your grief, for your cousin is also staying with us.' He stepped aside and Eve saw Bernard smiling at her from across the room. She looked away without acknowledging his bow. Catherine laughed gently.

'Poor man, he told us he had allowed his passions to run away with him and declared himself far too early. But you need not worry, my dear Mrs Wylder; I have his word that he will be on his best behaviour here.'

'You will forgive me, madam, if I reserve judgement on that,' returned Eve.

'Of course.' Lady Chelston reached out and touched her arm briefly. 'But I beg you will allow him to take you into dinner tonight. We would not wish to give the gossipmongers cause to think there was any dissention in your family, now would we?'

'Very well, ma'am, to oblige you. However, please let me say, as I made plain in my letter, I cannot join in all your entertainments, and I certainly cannot attend your masquerade.'

'No, no that is quite understood,' agreed her hostess. 'I hope you will be able to join us for the dinner beforehand, but after that you may keep to your room and you can send down for such refreshments as you require.' Lady Chelston patted her hands. 'We want you to feel at home here, my dear; I hope we can be of some comfort to you at this time. Mayhap your visit here will help you to forget your grief, at least for a short time.'

Eve inclined her head. 'I think we can be sure it will do that, Lady Chelston.'

'We have been here for three days, and still no word from him!'

Eve stared into the mirror as Martha brushed out her hair.

'Hush madam. The captain will come to you when he is ready.'

'And in the meantime I feel such a fraud,' sighed Eve, keeping her voice low. 'Everyone is so very considerate to me as the poor, grieving widow. My host and hostess have not said or done anything out of place and even Bernard is keeping his distance!'

'As well he might,' growled Martha. 'Now sit still Miss Eve, do, while I put up your hair again. You cannot go down to my lady's grand dinner looking a fright.'

Eve slumped a little. 'I wish I did not have to go. Lady Chelston knows I will not attend the ball, but she has planned her dinner table to include me. I shall feel so out of place in my widow's weeds.'

'The black show off your fine complexion,' returned Martha in a bracing tone. 'Every lady will envy you and the gentlemen will all admire you excessively.'

Eve pulled a face in the mirror. The thought shot through her mind that there was only man she wanted to admire her, and he would not be present. She watched as Martha fixed the black lace cap over her curls, then she stood up and shook out her gown. She had chosen to wear a black overdress of cobweb-fine lace over her silk skirts, the deep mourning relieved only by a single string of pearls around her neck. 'I thought it an unnecessary extravagance when I bought this gown, but now I am glad I have it. The feel of the silk gives me more confidence. Well…' she gave her skirts a final twitch '…wish me luck.' An irrepressible gleam of humour tugged at her mouth. 'I may well find that my grief is too great and I shall be obliged to rush away from the dinner table.'

She set off along the maze of corridors, keeping her gaze modestly lowered and taking no notice of the statue-like footman who were on duty at regular intervals along her route. Within hours of their arrival at Chelston Hall, Martha had passed on to her the servants' gossip that the mistress of the house had a predilection for handsome young footmen and Eve noted that every one of the liveried menservants in the house was over six feet tall. Observing Lady Chelston's lingering glances at these lackeys, Eve suspected that some of them at least provided her with more intimate services than was usually required of a footman. She was approaching the main gallery when one of these liveried statues spoke to her.

'Good evening, sweetheart.' The sound of the familiar voice was so unexpected that Eve's knees threatened to buckle and she put out a hand to the wall to support her. Raising her eyes, she gazed in astonishment at the tall figure in the white-powdered wig and blue coat with its gold facings. The deep blue eyes and wicked grin were unmistakable.

'Nick! What in heaven's name are you doing?' she hissed.

With a quick glance to make sure the corridor was deserted, he gripped her wrist and pulled her through the nearest door into a small, empty bedroom. 'I told you I should come.'

'But not like this! You look…strange.'

He grinned. 'And you look breathtaking. I have missed you.' His eyes darkened with desire and she looked away quickly, finding it difficult to catch her own breath.

'This is madness! You will be recognised.'

'*You* did not know me,' he pointed out.

'That is different.'

'No, it is not. People only see what they expect to see. Besides, who is there here that knows me?'

'My cousin Bernard, for one!'

Nick shrugged. 'He will not notice me. I had thought to look through Chelston's papers while I am here.'

'As far as I can tell, there are two places where he might keep important documents. There is a desk in the library, but that room has been opened up for his guests tonight. However, his office is below here, on the opposite side of the hall to the kitchens and servants' rooms. The passage leads only to the office and the back stairs for the east wing, so it should be very quiet this evening.'

'Well done, Eve. You have been busy.'

'I have had little to do but acquaint myself with the house.'

'I commend your foresight.' He cast an appraising glance over her. 'Are you going down to dinner in that? The gentlemen will have eyes for no one else.'

She flushed. 'That was not my intention.'

'No, but you do not appreciate just how beautiful you are.'

She tried to ignore this, but was aware of the flush creeping into her cheeks and the fluttering excitement in her stomach. 'How did you get in?'

'It is common knowledge in this area that the Chelstons take on more staff when they are entertaining. Once I learned that Lady Chelston likes to pick the servants herself, it was not difficult to be chosen.' The wicked laughter was in his eyes again. 'After all, I have all the attributes she looks for in her footmen.'

'You would be well served if she was to select you for her favours tonight!'

'It is the lady who would be well-served,' he murmured.

Eve gasped at his audacity. Nick merely laughed and swept her into his arms.

'No, no, I am jesting, sweetheart. There is only room for one woman in my life now, and you know it.'

His words and the feel of his arms about her sent Eve's senses spiralling out of control. She had no time to gather her scattered wits and turn her head before he was kissing her, his mouth rough and demanding against her own. Her fingers clutched at his coat as she responded, urgent desire heating her blood.

'Must you go in to dinner now?' he muttered, covering her face and throat with warm, tender kisses.

'We will be discovered,' she whispered as reason threatened to leave her.

He groaned. 'You are right. You will be missed.' He gripped her shoulders and possessed her mouth for one last, lingering kiss. 'There. Go now before I forget that I am a servant and ravish you.'

She did not smile as she stepped away from him. 'Will we speak again?'

'I shall find you later, trust me.' He opened the door and cautiously looked out. 'It is clear. Off you go now.'

Still bemused with the shock of the encounter, Eve made her way to the drawing room. She was one of the last to arrive and her entrance went almost unnoticed in the noisy confusion. The room was packed with guests who laughed and chattered and exclaimed over each other's masquerade costumes. Lady Chelston came up, looking magnificent in green and gold.

'Persephone in Spring, my dear,' she said, when Eve uttered a compliment. 'Chelston had these yellow diamonds made up into the shape of a primrose cluster for my corsage—are they not exquisite?'

She hurried away and Eve watched her flit around the room, too distracted to spare more than a few words to anyone. A small group of houseguests welcomed Eve in a kindly manner, then continued their discussion with no more than an occasional glance or word in her direction. This suited her perfectly, unlike the protracted dinner, which proved to be a sore trial.

She was seated next to her cousin and she nearly fainted when Nick filed in with the other footmen to serve the first course. She kept her eyes resolutely lowered, praying that she would do nothing to give him away. Conversation ebbed and flowed; Eve had no idea what she said or what was said to her. The elegant and colourful dishes prepared for the delectation of Lord Chelston's guests tasted of nothing in her mouth. Eve filled her plate and ate mechanically and all the time she was aware of the footmen gliding silently around the room, refilling glasses, clearing dishes and setting down fresh ones.

'Cousin, let me help you to a little of the baked pike,' said Bernard presently. 'It is quite delicious.'

'No, I thank you.'

'You are still angry with me,' he said in a low voice. 'I should not have declared myself so soon. It was the violence of my regard for you that made me so precipitate.'

Eve froze. Nick was directly before them, serving the gentleman seated on the opposite side of the table. Anxious that Bernard should not look up, she gave him a much warmer smile that she had intended, desperate to keep his attention. 'So you told me in your letter, Cousin.'

'Your reply did not lead me to hope you had forgiven me.'

'*Your* letter implied you thought your suit might still succeed,' she countered.

'And will it not?'

Nick had moved out of sight and Eve relaxed slightly. 'No,' she said. 'Never.'

'Never is a long time, Cousin.'

The complacent smile on Bernard's face made her long to slap him. She restrained herself, regretting her earlier friendliness. She said with false sweetness, 'Then you will have plenty of time to recover from your disappointment.'

Very deliberately she turned her shoulder and began to converse with the gentleman on her right. *There*, she thought. *I have told him; I will not speak to him again, and Nick must look out for himself!*

The meal progressed with no oaths, no clatter of dropped dishes to draw attention to a clumsy servant. A glance at each end of the table showed Eve that Lord Chelston and his wife were both at ease and too engrossed in their guests to look at the footmen. When at last her hostess gave the signal for the ladies to withdraw, Eve knew a moment's panic. What if something happened to Nick later, when she was not there? Reason told her there was nothing she could do to help, but she would have preferred to remain near him. As the ladies slowly processed out of the room she risked one swift glance along the line of liveried servants. She saw Nick almost immediately, but although he met her eyes for a brief moment, he gave no sign of recognition. A wild bubble of laughter welled up within her; he might be daring, but he was not so reckless that he would risk a look being intercepted. It gave her some comfort, but it was still a struggle to maintain her composure, knowing he was courting danger.

After a brief word to her hostess Eve slipped away to her room. As she passed along the gallery she could hear the orchestra tuning up below. The notes reverberated around the empty hall, but Eve knew that once the vast space was filled with people the hollow echo would be replaced by a much more melodious sound. It would be very busy, she thought, all the footmen would be required to attend to the guests and Nick would not be able to slip away unnoticed.

She paced around her bedchamber, her body buzzing with nervous energy. It was absurd for her to sit idly doing nothing. The idea nagged at her so much that after an hour she could bear the uncertainty no longer and she went back to the gallery. There were no servants now in the dimly lit upper corridors and she guessed that they had all been pressed into service downstairs. Eve peeped over the balustrade. The hall was packed with a noisy, colourful throng. Many of the guests were in elaborate costumes with silk masks over their eyes, but dotted between them were mysterious figures enveloped in swirling silk dominos. The liveried footmen moved through the crowd offering fresh glasses of wine. She walked round the gallery until she could see the entrance to the saloon that opened off the hall. The double doors had been thrown wide and more servants were busy setting out supper on long tables.

'Mrs Wylder, does the noise disturb you?'

She jumped and turned to find Lord Chelston beside her. 'N-no, sir.' She tried a wan smile. 'I merely wished to see how the ball was progressing.'

He held out his arm. 'Let me take you down—'

'No, no, my lord, I thank you.' She shrank away. 'My black gown does not lend itself to such gaiety, and it might make some of your guests uncomfortable. Forgive me, I have seen enough and will retire now.'

'Then allow me to escort you back to your chamber.' He pulled her hand on to his arm and walked beside her through the dimly lit corridor. 'To find you watching the dancers makes me wonder if you are perhaps lonely, ma'am.'

'L-lonely, my lord? No, I assure you—'

'Shawcross informs me that Makerham was your home for many years. It must surely be a wrench for you to leave it, to leave all your friends and move to Monkhurst, which I am well aware is very isolated. You are young, would you not prefer to be living in Tunbridge, or Bath, where you would find a little more society?'

'I am very content at Monkhurst, my lord.'

He stopped, his sharp eyes searching her face. 'Are you sure?' he said gently. 'Are you not putting a brave face upon your plight? If it is money, madam, then perhaps I can help you. I could buy Monkhurst. I know this country, Mrs Wylder; Monkhurst is not like to suit everyone. I would be happy to take it off your hands for a generous sum—and we need not wait for the legalities to be complete. I could make you an advance to allow you to move immediately to somewhere more suited to your nature.'

She put up a hand. 'Please, my lord, say no more. I assure you Monkhurst suits me very well. Perhaps, perhaps in a year or so, when my grief has lessened...' She allowed the sentence to remain unfinished and lowered her eyes before his cold, piercing gaze. After a moment he bowed.

'As you wish, madam. I shall take you to your room now. But do not be afraid to send your maid to me, if there is anything you require. Anything at all.'

'You are very good, sir.'

He escorted her to her door and when she entered she found Martha anxiously waiting for her.

'Oh, Miss Eve, thank heaven you are back safe! I was that worried.'

'And rightly so.' Eve pressed her ear to the door, listening. 'Lord Chelston discovered me on the landing. It is plainly not safe for me to wander the house like this.' Excitement fluttered in her chest. She crossed to the linen press and opened the doors.

'Whatever are you about, madam?' Martha demanded. 'We never put any of your things in there.'

'I know it,' Eve said, hunting through the cupboards. 'But I saw something when we arrived...ah, here it is.' She emerged from the cupboard, a triumphant smile upon her lips, and held up a cherry-red domino.

'Lawks, miss, you are never going to join the dancing?'

'No, but I saw several red dominos amongst the revellers, so no one will recognise me if I wear this tonight!'

Creeping out of the room again a short time later and enveloped in cherry-red silk, Eve made her way along the empty corridor and slipped down the backstairs. As she reached the ground floor there was shrieking and loud laughter, and she flattened herself against one of the panelled walls as a lady dressed as Gloriana rushed past, dragging a puffing and be-whiskered Falstaff behind her. They paid no heed to Eve, shrouded in her domino, and once they had disappeared she moved on. Reaching the study, she tried the handle. The door opened easily, but the room was in darkness. Calmly she picked up a candlestick, stepped along the corridor and held the candle to the lighted ones burning in the wall sconces. With some small, detached part of her brain she marvelled that her hand was so steady, but she was aware that a show of nerves now could be her undoing. She slipped into the study and closed the door carefully behind her. Lifting her candlestick higher, she looked around the room.

Eve was suddenly at a loss. She had no idea what she was looking for. Glass-fronted cupboards lined two walls, while shelves flanked the chimney piece and the window, where a large map-chest stood, its top level with the sill. A heavy mahogany desk occupied most of the floor space with a selection of stamps, inkwells and pens arranged neatly on the top, but it was clear of papers, as was every other surface in the room. She moved to the fireplace and inspected the mantelshelf, but there were no invitations propped against the snuff-jars nor opened letters tucked behind the ormolu clock. Eve scolded herself for naïvety in thinking Lord Chelston would leave evidence of his wrongdoing lying around for anyone to find. The sudden scrape of the door handle made her jump and she almost dropped the candle-stick. She swung around, her heart leaping into her mouth, but it settled into a rapid tattoo against her ribs as Nick stepped into the room.

'I saw the light under the door,' he said quietly. 'Chelston is dancing, so I knew that it must be you here. What have you discovered?'

'Nothing yet.' Eve put the candlestick down upon the desk. 'I was about to try the drawers.'

'A very good notion.' He crossed the room in a few quick strides and slid open the top drawer. Eve watched him lift out a pile of papers and carefully flick through them.

'But is it likely that he would keep anything here that could incriminate him?' she asked.

'No, but there may well be some clue for us.'

'What sort of clue?'

'I have no idea, but I shall know when I find it.'

Eve stepped back. The glow from the single candle was barely enough to light the area where Nick was searching so she did not attempt to help. Instead she wandered over to the window. A half-moon was rising, bathing the gardens in a silver-blue light and casting a soft gleam on the top of the map-chest. Idly she pulled open the first drawer. The moonlight illuminated a large and detailed map, but there was insufficient light to read the names. She lifted the document out of the case and held it closer to the window, but it was no use. She thought it might be a map of the Chelston estate, but the writing was too faint to read in the poor light. Eve was about to put it back when the next map in the drawer caught her eye. The outline of the coast was picked out with a bold, dark line and even in the pale moonlight she recognised it immediately.

'Nick,' she whispered, 'here is a plan of Monkhurst.'

She pulled out the map and laid it on the top of the chest as Nick crossed the room. He held up the candle and its feeble glow was just enough to show the bright colours of the map and the carefully marked place names.

'Look.' She pointed to the map. 'The River Rother, Jury's Cut and the inlet leading up to the boathouse. It is all picked out in a darker ink.'

Nick peered closer. 'Yes, but it is not primarily a map of Monkhurst. It is the neighbouring estate that is at the centre of this map.' He moved the candle slightly and peered closely at the writing. 'Abbotsfield.'

'Nick,' breathed Eve, her voice trembling with excitement. 'Aggie told me that Lady Chelston's father bought Abbotsfield from my grandfather Wingham. It might have been part of her marriage settlement.'

'In which case Chelston might be using it. This shows Abbotsfield to have a substantial portion of woodland. Perhaps we have been looking in the wrong place for Chelston's manufactory,' said Nick slowly. 'Perhaps it is not in Sussex, but in Kent!'

Eve gripped his arm. 'Earlier this evening Lord Chelston offered to buy Monkhurst from me. He offered to fund me to leave the house immediately.'

'So there might well be a connection,' said Nick. The little clock on the mantelshelf chimed repeatedly. 'Midnight,' he muttered. Carefully he placed the maps back in the drawer. 'I must get back. And you should return to your room, now. The unmasking will take place soon and it would not do for you to be found out.' He moved to the desk, checking that nothing was out of place, then he put down the candlestick and turned to take Eve by the shoulders. 'I am sorry I must let you go again so soon. I—' He froze, listening.

Eve heard footsteps and a stifled giggle outside the door. As the handle rattled she hurled herself at Nick, throwing her arms around his neck.

'Oh, we are too late—someone is here before us. A thousand apologies, madam, for intruding upon your...assignation.' Eve recognised the voice as that of the man sitting on her right during dinner. She kept her face buried against Nick's chest, thanking Providence that she was still covered from head to toe by her domino. The door clicked shut and Nick exhaled with a long, low whistle. He hugged her, giving a low laugh that rumbled against her cheek.

'Quick thinking, sweetheart.'

She leaned against him, suddenly weak. 'This is too much excitement for me,' she murmured. 'I fear I shall faint.'

His arms tightened. 'Not you, my love. You are made of sterner stuff.' He put his hand under her chin and tilted her face up. 'Admit it,' he said, his eyes glinting, 'you are enjoying this adventure.'

The familiar tug of attraction liquefied her insides. She was exhilarated, reckless. 'When I am with you...' she began.

'Yes?'

Eve closed her lips tightly. It would be madness to confide in him. 'You bewilder me,' she ended lamely.

Nick held her eyes for a moment longer, then kissed her brow. 'I wish I had time to ask what you mean by that, love, but you must go back to your room now.' He snuffed the candle and took her hand as he led the way out of the study.

The sounds of revelry coming from the hall were even louder than before. Shrieks and wild laughter echoed between the panelled walls of the dark corridor and several empty glasses had been abandoned on a narrow shelf. They approached the back stairs; grunts and sighs were coming from the darkness beyond and Eve tried not to think what might be going on there.

Nick's hand pressed in the small of her back. 'Go,' he whispered. 'Quickly.'

She turned for one last, fleeting look at him then picked up her skirts and fled.

Nick watched her run up the stairs and disappear into the darkness without one backward glance. He had seen the spark of desire in her eyes when he held her, but he had also noticed her withdrawal, her lack of trust. She was not ready to give herself to him, not yet. But she would, for he had glimpsed in her a passionate spirit to match his own and he was determined to capture it.

As he turned away from the stairs he heard heavy foot-steps and voices and the butler appeared around the corner, talking to one of the regular footmen. They stopped at the sight of him.

'Now, my lad,' barked the butler, 'what do you think you are doing here?'

Nick scooped up some of the empty glasses. 'Collectin' these.'

As another dance ended and the music in the hall died away, the heavy grunts and gasps from behind the staircase could be clearly heard. Nick grinned and jerked his head in the direction of the noise. It drew an answering grin from the footman, but the butler merely scowled.

'Your place is in the saloon attending the guests, not skulking here in the passage! Get back there now. You can collect up the glasses when everyone has gone.'

Nick dipped his head. 'Aye, sir.' He slouched away,

grinning to himself as he heard the butler complaining to his companion.

'Heaven help us, the mistress takes on these extra hands for what they have in their breeches rather than in their heads…'

Nick made his way downstairs to the kitchen where he found Lord Chelston's bad-tempered French cook shouting at his minions. He slipped past them and into the servants' hall where a tired-looking scullery maid was clearing the remains of the servants' dinner from the table.

'Here, let me help with that.' He began to stack up the plates. 'Do you always eat so well?'

She giggled. 'No, silly, 'tis only when there's guests that there's so much left over for us.'

'So have you worked here long?'

'Aye, since I was a nipper.'

'Then you've seen lots of balls like this one.'

The maid paused and rubbed her nose. 'None so many. But I do believe they is always having balls and parties at the house in Lunnon.'

'Oh? Is that their only other house, then?'

'Lawks, no! The master has his huntin' lodge somewhere up north, and there's another house in Devon.'

'What about Kent?' asked Nick. 'I thought I heard one of the stable lads mention property in Kent. Abbots-something.'

'You means Abbotsfield. 'Tidn't a house, though. That burned down years ago.'

Nick carried the plates through to the scullery and the maid gave him a quick, appraising glance.

'But you isn't supposed to be 'elping me, you should be upstairs, serving supper.'

'I should, I know, but I reckons there's enough of 'em up there for now. I'll go up in a minute, when we've finished clearin' the tables.'

'Well, mind you don't get the mess from the plates on yer coat,' she warned him. 'They'll knock a charge off your money for cleaning if you do.'

He grinned. 'Well then, they'll have to pay me first!'

Eve hurried up the stairs and through the empty corridors to her bedchamber. She launched herself through the door and quickly locked it after her, leaning against the heavy wooden panels, breathing heavily. A single candle burned on the mantelshelf and Martha was sitting on a stool, gazing dejectedly into the empty fireplace. When she saw her mistress she jumped up.

'Ooh, Miss Eve, thank heavens! Where have you been, and why on earth are you smiling in that way?'

'I am smiling, Martha, because I think I am having an adventure!'

Eve quickly scrabbled out of her clothes and into her nightgown. The cherry-red domino was neatly folded and returned to the linen press and Martha took away her gown to hang it with the others in the dressing room. By the time she returned, Eve was sitting at the dressing table, unpinning her hair. She resisted her maid's attempts to take the brush from her. 'Get you to bed, Martha. You must be very tired.'

'Not so tired that I cannot see you safely tucked up, Miss Eve.'

'I am quite capable of blowing out my own candle, I assure you! Off you go now; as soon as I have finished brushing my hair I shall retire, I promise you.'

However, it was long before Eve slept that night. She could not say that she was disturbed by the masquerade because very little noise reached her bedchamber, save Martha's gentle snores coming from the dressing room, but the events of the evening had left her brain racing with conjecture and there was the underlying fear that Nick had been discovered. She tossed and turned in her lonely bed, wondering where he was, what he planned to do next. It did not matter that she told herself this was a fruitless exercise, it kept her awake until the grey light of dawn crept into her room.

It was with some trepidation that she went down to breakfast the next morning but the few guests who were not sleeping off the excesses of the night before greeted her quite normally, and there was no sign that she was about to be denounced as a fraud or a spy. She asked about the ball and was told it had been an outstanding success with the last carriages rolling away soon after dawn. No one mentioned intruders posing as footmen, and the servants in attendance in the breakfast room looked as sleepy and indifferent as ever, so she could only hope that Nick's disguise had gone undetected.

It was not to be expected that the party would be very animated after such an exhausting entertainment and the day passed quietly, with Eve making sure she remained in the company of the ladies at all times. She was relieved that neither Bernard nor Lord Chelston made any attempt to single her out, but her cousin's very civil attentions during dinner tried her patience and, pleading fatigue, she fled to her room before the gentlemen joined the ladies in the drawing room.

Eve was indeed very tired after her sleepless night and she lost no time in donning her nightgown and dismissing Martha. Within minutes she was asleep, only to wake with a start some time later. The room was very dark, for her maid had closed the curtains to shut out the bright moonlight which might disturb her mistress. Eve lay still, straining every nerve to listen. She had locked the door herself, but wondered if it had been the sound of someone trying the handle that had woken her. Then she heard it again, a gentle but insistent tap-tapping on glass. For a moment she hesitated, wondering if she should call Martha, but she decided against it. Eve slipped out of bed and padded across to the window. With her heart hammering hard against her ribs she threw back the heavy curtains.

There was no one there.

The nearly full moon sailed in a cloudless sky, bathing the gardens in its serene light. Eve threw up the sash and cool night air flooded into the room. She rested her hands upon the sill, puzzled. There was no wind, nothing to cause a loose tendril from the ivy to tap at her window.

She gasped as a hand shot out and grabbed her wrist.

'Stand back, sweetheart, and let me come in.'

Chapter Thirteen

The ivy rustled and creaked as Nick hoisted himself across and in through the open window. He was wearing soft boots, black breeches and a dark linen shirt, clothes chosen deliberately so that nothing would stand out against the ivy-covered walls. He grinned at Eve, who was staring at him, open-mouthed. His heart contracted as he looked at her. She was so appealing, standing there with her hair in a dark cloud about her shoulders. 'Well, will you not welcome me?'

She ignored his open arms. 'How did you know this was my room?'

'I saw Martha at this window when I was here yesterday. By the bye, where is Martha?'

Eve indicated the dressing room. 'She sleeps very heavily, but pray keep your voice down. Have you been here all day?'

'No, we were paid off this morning. Which reminds me, how much do we pay our servants, Evelina?'

She blinked at him. 'I—um—I do not know…'

'Well, whatever it is we must increase it. I was given a paltry sum for working here last night, and I've never worked so hard in my life. I'd rather be a raw recruit on board a man o' war than to do that again.'

Eve tried to stifle a giggle and failed. She pressed her teeth into her full bottom lip, but could not suppress an unruly dimple. Nick was enchanted. He resolved to make her laugh a great deal more in future.

'You have led too pampered a life, sir!' she told him severely.

'I am beginning to think so, too.'

'Well, never mind that. Why are you here? What have you learned?'

'In one day? Not much. Catherine inherited Abbotsfield when her father died. It would appear all the old retainers were turned off when the house burned down about five years ago and no one knows much about the place since then. I have sent someone to search the woods and report back to me.' He moved away from the window, taking care that his feet made no noise on the bare boards. 'I wanted to tell you that I have sent a couple of men to Monkhurst. They will act as your servants, but they are Revenue men and are there to protect you. I still think Chelston's schemes involve Monkhurst in some way, and I want to be sure you are safe.'

'Thank you, but you could have sent me word of that. There was no need for you to put yourself at risk by coming here.'

'But I wanted to see you. No—' he held up his hand. 'Don't move.'

'Why not? What is wrong?'

'Your nightgown.'

'What about it? It is a very fine nightgown.'

'I know, sweetheart. With the moonlight behind you I can see every line of your body.' And a very shapely body it was, long legs tapering down from the swell of her hips and above that the narrow waist that seemed to beg for his hands to span it. He remembered how she had stood before the window on their wedding night. It had been his undoing. With a gasp she stepped quickly out of the moonlight and Nick laughed softly.

'You are no gentleman!' she hissed.

He reached out and pulled her to him. The feel of her body against his brought an instant reaction. 'If I were not a gentleman I would carry you to that bed and ravish you!'

He must not rush her, but he could not resist pressing just one kiss on her neck, where the lacy edge of her nightgown had slipped off her shoulder.

'That would be the action of a true scoundrel!'

Reluctantly he raised his head. 'I know,' he agreed mournfully. 'And I have vowed I shall not impose myself upon you.'

She put her hands against his chest and his heart thudded, as if trying to reach her. She tilted her face up, her lips parting to form a very inviting O of surprise. His arms tightened and the next moment he was kissing her, slowly, sensuously. For a brief, exultant moment she responded, then he felt her struggle and push against him.

'No,' she hissed, turning her head away. 'I will *not* give in to you, Nick Wylder!'

She tried to pull away from him but he caught her wrist, saying impatiently, 'By God, woman you are *my wife*!'

Her head went up. Even in the moonlight he could see the haughty flash of her eyes. 'You forfeited any rights you had when you deceived me,' she said, her voice vibrating with fury.

His head snapped back as if she had struck him. Nick looked at the tightly-coiled bundle of pride and passion standing before him and for the first time in his adult life he was afraid of doing the wrong thing. Pure, animal instinct told him to take her, to kiss her into submission. He knew he could do it, he had sensed the passion within her, had tasted it in her kiss moments before. But something held him back, warned him that passion might win her body, but it would not win her trust.

Eve trembled. In her head she was determined to fight him, but every nerve of her body strained with desire. If he ignored her protests and dragged her into his arms, she knew her defences would crumble almost immediately for her heart was crying out for him to hold her, to make love to her. She kept her head up and met his gaze defiantly. 'I think you should go now.' She marvelled at how steady her voice was when inside she was burning up.

'Yes,' he said, releasing her wrist. 'I think I should.' Nick saw the flicker of surprise in her eyes and smiled, knowing he had made the right choice. 'I do not consider that I have any—*rights*—over you, sweetheart. Neither do I want you to give in to me. You are my wife, my partner. We will meet as equals, you and I. Or not at all.' He flicked a careless finger across her cheek and slipped back out of the window.

Eve stood looking at the space where he had been. She told herself she was relieved, but there was also a vague sense of disappointment that he had given way so easily. Perversely she was not at all sure it was what she wanted. She ran to the window and leaned out. Nick was little more than a dark shadow amongst the bushes. His words echoed in her head: *my wife, my partner. We will meet as equals, you and I.* Equals. Could he really mean that?

As she peered down he stepped out into the moonlight and raised his hand to blow her a kiss.

Two days later Eve was back at Monkhurst. Lord and Lady Chelston had been reluctant to let her go, but she had stood firm, declaring that she must attend to her estate.

Richard Granby was clearly relieved to see her safely returned and lost no time in presenting to her Davies and Warren, the two men Nick had sent to protect her. They bowed to her and declared themselves happy enough to help Granby around the house.

'We thought it best to keep it quiet that we are with the Revenue,' grinned Davies. 'The people hereabouts are none too fond of us.'

Eve nodded. 'Then we shall just say that I asked Mr Granby to bring in extra staff. There should be no surprise at that; there is a deal to be done.'

However, Eve was surprised at Silas's reaction to the news.

'If you thinks I'm too old, missus, then just say so,' he told her when they met in the gardens later that day. Eve tried to be patient.

'You are not too old at all, Silas. But we can use the extra help, and it is always useful to have a few more men around the house.'

'What's wrong with Sam and Nat? They'll protect you, if that's your worry.'

'They are very useful, and have made a big difference already to the gardens, but they have families of their own to look after in the village, and cannot be at Monkhurst day and night. Pray do not be offended, Silas.'

'Well I don't see how you needs anyone else,' he grumbled. 'Especially when they're not Kentish men.'

'Perhaps you are right, but Granby did what he thought best. And they will be very useful in turning out the last few rooms for me.'

Eve was determined to continue with her plans for making Monkhurst into a comfortable home, but after the excitement of her visit to Chelston Hall, life at the old house seemed sadly flat. There was no news from Nick, but that did not surprise her; he was born for adventure, not the day-to-day domesticity that comprised her own life. Her depression deepened; she was far too ordinary to satisfy the dashing Captain Wyldfire for very long. She blinked back a tear. True, she was his wife and he would come to her occasionally, when he needed to rest, or perhaps—the thought turned her insides to water—when he wanted her body, but then he would be off again, seeking excitement. Well, thought Eve, if that was how it must be then she would not complain. To have such a man, even for a short time, was as much as she could hope for. She would not pine.

To keep herself from moping, Eve threw herself into the role of housewife, but this served only to highlight how humdrum her life was compared with the unimaginable dangers Nick was facing. The only drama at Monkhurst was provided by Silas, who fell off a ladder in the barn and cracked open his head.

'He should never have been on that ladder in the first place,' declared Aggie, bustling around the kitchen. 'Sam told 'im he would do it, only he was that determined to prove that he was every bit as good as these new lads you brought in, that he would go up.'

'Oh dear, poor Silas. Is it very bad?'

'Well, he can't see straight for the present, besides bein' sick as a dog, so he won't be able to—' Aggie closed her lips and shook her head before saying with a sigh, 'But don't you be worrying, Miss Eve, we shall manage.'

'Perhaps you would like to go back to Silas now,' suggested Eve. 'Martha and I will do very well with a cold dinner.'

'You will do no such thing, mistress. Why I never heard of such a thing! Silas has young Nat to look in on him during the day and I shall cook your dinner as I always do, so let's not hear any more about it!'

Eve hurriedly begged pardon and left her affronted housekeeper to her work.

She thought no more about it until Martha came in tutting because Aggie had left her basket by the back door. It was after dinner and Eve was in the drawing room, sitting by the window and making the most of the remaining daylight to work on her embroidery.

'Full of pies it is, too, Miss Eve,' said the maid, carrying a lighted taper to each of the candles. 'I hope Silas wasn't expectin' them for his supper.'

'Poor Aggie was looking very harassed today,' remarked Eve. 'She was in a hurry to get away, too.' She put aside her embroidery and looked out of the window at the golden sunset. 'Do you know, it is such a lovely evening that I would like to take a walk, so I will carry Aggie's basket to the Gate House. It will save her walking back for it.'

'Well, you can't go out alone in the dark. I'll fetch Davies to go with you.'

'There really is no need...' Eve began, but Martha's look silenced her. Meekly, she collected her shawl and set off towards the Gate House with Davies for company. It irked her to have someone dogging her every footstep, but she realised the necessity of it and smiled at the man. After all, it was not his fault that he had been ordered to protect her. Most likely he would prefer to be off chasing smugglers rather than walking behind her.

There was a lamp burning in the window, but when she knocked on the door it was a long time before there was any response, and then it was only Aggie's rather nervous 'Who's there?' from within.

'It is only me,' Eve called cheerfully. 'I have brought your basket. You left it in the kitchen.' The door opened a crack. 'Well, Aggie, will you not invite me in?'

Aggie peered out into the gloom.

'Aye, mistress, but your man must wait outside.'

'What is the matter, Aggie? Are you in your nightgown with your hair in rags?' Eve chuckled as she slipped in through the door but her smile was replaced by a look of surprise when she saw Aggie wearing one of Silas's smocks and a pair of baggy trousers. 'What on earth—?'

'There's a run tonight, and as Silas can't go I shall have to,' explained Aggie, looking anxious. She ran a hand over one leg of the trousers. 'These sailor's slops fits me better nor most of Silas's clothes.'

'Surely this cannot be necessary.'

Aggie's mouth pursed. 'Do you think I'd be going if it wasn't? There's not enough boys to go out tonight as it is, and without Silas they'll be short of hands. I'm waiting now for Nat to call for me.'

'You must not go,' said Eve, setting down her basket.

'That's just what I bin tellin' her,' said Silas, appearing at the door. 'I'll be fine as soon as I gets me sea-legs.'

He swayed as he spoke. Aggie and Eve both rushed to take his arms and help him to his chair.

'You ain't goin' nowhere,' Aggie told him crossly. 'You'd be a danger to yourself and to the boys.'

'She's right, I'm afraid, Silas,' said Eve.

Silas hunched in his chair, scowling. Eve took the older woman's shoulders and looked into her face. 'Why is it so important to go out tonight, Aggie?'

'It's the last run. You will remember, miss, that Silas promised they would do no more once the orders was filled, but John the waggoner and his son are gone off to Ashurst and we daren't wait for their return, because the moon's on the wane. It has to be tonight.'

'But there must be other men in the village.'

Aggie shook her head. 'Since Sam and Nat had the run-in with that other gang, the village lads is afeard to go out. So with Silas laid up they're too short-handed.'

'Well, you cannot go,' said Eve decidedly. She stood for a moment, tapping her foot. 'What time do you expect Nathaniel here?'

'Soon as it's properly dark.'

'Then I have half an hour. I can be back by then.'

Silas looked up. 'What d'you mean, mistress?'

'Miss Eve, what are you going to do?' demanded Aggie suspiciously.

Eve turned, her eyes shining with mischief. 'Why, go in your place, of course!'

Eve hurried back to the house, dismissed her escort and ran lightly up the stairs to her bedchamber, calling for Martha as she went. By the time the maid arrived Eve had pulled a selection of clothes from the trunk at the bottom of the bed. 'Quickly, Martha; help me out of this gown.'

'Whatever are you about now, mistress?'

'You must not ask me,' replied Eve. She was unable to keep the excitement from her voice, nor could she resist confiding in her maid, 'I am going out.'

'You never are, madam!'

'Yes, I am.' Eve stepped out of her skirts and reached for the soft leather breeches. 'But you are not to tell anyone.'

'Heavens to mercy! You cannot be going out in those!'

'I am. I only hope Mama's clothes fit me...they do, thank goodness!'

'Miss Eve—' Martha put her hands to her mouth. 'You're

never goin' out with the traders?' She collapsed on to the bed. 'Oh, gracious heart-alive!'

'Hush, Martha. Now where is the shirt—? Oh, and my hair, I cannot possibly wear it like this. Quick, now, remove the pins and I'll tie it back…there, what do you think?'

'I think it is a dreadful idea, Miss Eve, and I cannot let you go!'

'If you try to stop me, I shall turn you off,' retorted Eve, giving Martha such a fierce look that the maid went pale.

'You wouldn't,' she whispered.

'Of course not, as long as you do as I bid you.'

'But what would the master say!'

'The master is not here,' replied Eve. 'And if he was, it is just the sort of thing he would do.'

Eve clapped the battered tricorn hat upon her head and stared at herself in the mirror. In the flickering candlelight a stranger stared back at her. The tricorn shaded her eyes, leaving only the mouth and chin visible, and if Eve considered these far too dainty for a man, she thought that at least she could not be recognised. The breeches were close-fitting, but thankfully she could still move in them, and the shirt billowed out from her shoulders, adequately disguising her form. 'It will have to do,' she said, dragging on the dark woollen jacket.

'You need a muffler around your neck,' said Martha. 'You must make sure every bit of that shirt is covered and your face, too; your pale skin will show up bright as day under this moon.'

'Martha, how do you know about such things?'

'You can't live in these parts without knowing something of the trade,' retorted the maid. 'But oh, Miss Eve, I wish you would not go.'

'I have to, Martha. They are my people out there and

they need me.' She drew herself up as she said these words, a *frisson* of pride threading through her excitement. She kissed her maid. 'Now, you had best come down and lock the door after me. And remember, tell no one I am gone!'

Eve slipped out of the kitchen door and stopped for a moment, listening until she heard Martha slide the bolts back into position, then she ran silently through the garden and across the park to the Gate House. The moon that had been so full during her visit to Chelston Hall was no more than a sliver, giving barely enough light for her to find her way and she guessed that anyone watching would see little more than a shadow flitting between the trees. She arrived, breathless, at the Gate House and scratched at the door.

'Miss Eve, I cannot like this,' muttered Aggie as she let her into the house. She led the way through to the little kitchen, where Nathanial was waiting, twisting his cap in his hands. His mouth gaped when the saw her in her coat and breeches. Eve merely nodded at him.

'Good evening, Nat, I see you are wearing a smock, too—must I wear one?'

'The boys all do, mistress,' said Aggie. 'It's common garb here on the Marsh. That way the ridin' officers can't tell one from t'other.'

'Then I should put it on, I suppose. Help me, Aggie. There.' She grinned at them. 'Well, will I do?'

'Nay, mistress.' Nathanial cast an anguished look towards his mother.

Eve's grin disappeared. 'For heavens' sake, Nathanial! Would you rather it was your mother out on the marshes with you? I can handle the ponies as well as Silas—' she paused, then added with a touch of irrepressible humour, 'and run a great deal faster, if necessary.'

'I'd rather it was neither of you,' mumbled Nat.

'Now that is very uncharitable.'

'Well you mun promise to do just as I say,' he retorted, gaining a little courage.

'Of course I will.' He did not look very reassured by her assertion and she put her hand on his arm, saying gently, 'I have no wish to ruin your last run, Nathanial, but Aggie says you need an extra pair of hands, and I am offering you mine.'

Nathanial frowned at her for a long moment, then he seemed to make up his mind. He straightened. 'Well then,' he said, 'Let us be off.'

They walked for a mile or so along the shadowy lane until they reached a crossroads, where Nathanial gave a low whistle. At first, Eve could hear no sound on the still air, but after a few moments there was the faint clop of hoof-beats. Black shapes appeared, a line of ponies led by a stocky figure, his face a pale disc in the moonlight.

'Gabriel.' Nathanial's murmured greeting received only a grunt in reply, but there must have been some whispered question about her presence for she heard Nathanial say, 'Oh, he's my cousin's boy, from Tenterden-way.'

The man called Gabriel peered in her direction, Eve lowered her head so that the brim of her hat shadowed her face.

He grunted again.

'And Robert and Adam?' muttered Nathaniel.

Gabriel jerked his head. 'Bob's 'ere. Adam's comin' in on the galley with Sam. That's all the help we could muster this night.' Gabriel beckoned to them to follow him.

For the next few hours Eve found herself in a dark, alien world where familiar objects such as houses or trees loomed black and menacing around them. All her senses were heightened, every nerve alert to pick up the merest hint of danger. She strained her eyes to see through the near-darkness, and once she grabbed at Nathanial's arm. 'Look!' she hissed, pointing. 'A light over there!'

The pack stopped and for a moment there was a tense silence. Then she heard Nat's low rumbling laugh. 'It's nought but a shiney bug. You've seen they before, surelye.'

Eve was aware of the grins of the other men and she hastily begged pardon, hunched her shoulders and walked on, berating herself for allowing her nerves to get the better of her.

'Come up, Admiral.'

Nick touched his heels to the horse's glossy sides and the animal responded immediately. Soon they were moving through the lanes at a steady canter. There was no time to lose, but to press Admiral to go too fast across the dark, un-familiar territory was to risk a fall at best, and a broken neck at worst, neither of which would help his cause. He had learned only an hour ago that Captain George had received word of a run tonight at Jury's Cut. Privately, Nick had no doubt that it would be Silas and the boys, but although he argued strongly that these could not be Chelston's men, the Revenue officer knew his duty. He could not ignore the report and had despatched a party of riding officers to ap-prehend the smugglers. Nick was powerless to stop them. His only hope was to reach Silas in time and warn him.

The pale moonlight illuminated a stretch of flat, clear ground and he pushed Admiral on to a gallop. He could have found someone to carry the message for him, someone who knew the area better than he, but at the back of his mind was the thought that once he had discharged his errand he might call at Monkhurst. He laughed out loud, causing Admiral to throw up his head, nervously breaking his stride.

'Fool, it will be gone midnight by the time you get there,' he muttered to himself. No matter. He would wait until dawn, creep into her room and be there when she awoke.

He thought of Eve as he had last seen her at Chelston Hall, warm and drowsy with sleep, her hair tumbled over her shoulders. Damnation, just the thought of it made him hot for her! He eased himself in the saddle. Better not even to think of Eve until he had delivered his message.

He pushed on, cantering past Monkhurst village and through the leafy lanes until the Gate House was in view. He judged it was gone midnight and Silas might already have set off. Suddenly he was aware of a movement to his left. He pulled Admiral to a halt in the shadow of the trees and peered into the darkness.

'Richard!' His call brought the figure to a stop. Nick walked his horse forward. 'Richard? What are you doing here?'

'It's Mrs Wylder, sir.' Granby ran towards him. For once he had lost his imperturbable calm. Fear chilled Nick's bones. He said tersely,

'Well, man?'

'She's gone off with Nat and Sam to Jury's Cut!'

Chapter Fourteen

Eve had no idea how long they walked in the near-darkness. Their progress was silent save for the gentle clip-clop of the ponies and the creak of leather harness. Eve wanted to ask Nathanial where they were going, but she was afraid to speak and break the hush that lay over them like a palpable blanket, so she merely walked, striding out in her mother's old leather boots. It was a still night and only the lightest of breezes stirred the leaves. The steady walking gave her far too much time to think of Nick, and the darkness in her mind was even thicker and more engrossing that the night. She knew now that she loved him, but although she knew he wanted her she thought that his passion for her was cooling. What else could explain the way he had accepted her rebuttal at Chelston Hall? Twice now she had refused him and twice he had walked away. She was very much afraid that he no longer found her attractive. In fact, she thought miserably, he must be regretting ever having married her.

And did she regret Nick coming into her life and dragging her out of her cosy little world? *If I had not met him, I would not have disguised myself and searched Lord*

Chelston's office. Nor would I now be walking through the near-darkness to collect a cargo of contraband. Even as the words formed in her head, Eve realised with a little jolt of surprise that she would have been very sorry to miss the visit to Chelston Hall and, in a strange way, she was even enjoying being out on the Marsh in the middle of the night.

Eventually they left the houses and farms behind and the lane was no longer shadowed by high hedges. Instead deep ditches lined the causeway and the land stretched away on either side, a vast, flat expanse of marshland where the faint, salty breeze whispered through the rushes.

Eve could smell the sea and make out the line of sand dunes that rose up to meet the midnight-blue sky in the distance. A few yards away a narrow channel of water wound like a pewter ribbon through the Marsh towards the inlet known as Jury's Cut. Eve could feel the tension in her companions now: this was where Nathanial and Sam had been attacked and she looked about her nervously, her body tense and ready for flight.

Suddenly Nathanial stopped. The ponies came to a stand, blowing gently. Eve heard a short, low whistle and a quiet splash of oars. A long, low boat nosed its way between the rushes. Several figures leaped out and pulled the hull up on to more solid ground.

The men worked quickly and silently to unload the boat. Nathanial pulled Eve into line and she found herself part of a human chain, passing goods hand to hand from ship to shore. Her arms began to ache and soon she was uncomfortably warm in her smock and heavy coat, but she dare not remove them, nor unwind the concealing muffler from the lower part of her face. She realised now why they needed more men. There was some distance between the boat and the causeway where the ponies waited patiently to be loaded. When goods were passed she had to reach out to take each packet and stretch to pass it on to her neighbour. The bundles wrapped in oilcloth were weighty enough, but the half-ankers, the small barrels holding the brandy, were so heavy she had to take a step each time to complete the operation.

At last the final barrel had been strapped to a pony and the last packet of lace tucked away in a pannier. Eve eased her aching back and watched as half the men pushed the galley off the mud and began to row away, the oars dipping almost silently into the grey waters. A touch on her arm told her that they were ready to move off and she clambered back to the causeway where the ponies were already beginning the trek back inland. She tugged at Nathanial's sleeve. 'The last pony carries no pack,' she whispered.

Nat grinned, his teeth gleaming briefly in the pale light. 'We always keep one saddled and ready. In case.'

'In case of what?'

'Just in case.'

He put his hand to his lips and strode ahead. Eve followed on, puzzled and determined to demand an explanation as soon as they were safe.

The crescent moon hung low in the sky by the time the first farm came into sight, a black outline in the distance. Eve realised how tense she had become and made a conscious effort to relax her shoulders. Soon they would reach the comparative shelter of the tree-lined lanes again. She was about to say as much to Nathanial when there was a warning growl from the head of the line.

'Riding officers. Run!'

The ponies began to trot, their packs creaking ominously. 'Where are they?' muttered Eve, peering into the darkness.

Nathanial raised his hand and pointed. 'Between the barns over there.'

Eve only had time for one swift look. The blackness between the tall square outlines of buildings was shifting and moving. Riders, and they were coming swiftly towards them. When they realised their quarry had spotted them, the riders abandoned their stealthy progress and shouted, their cries carrying on the night air.

'Stop, in the name of the King!'

Nathaniel pushed Eve before him. 'Run.'

The little ponies moved with surprising speed and Eve followed, her heart pounding. The road snaked between deep drains and on one corner stood a small copse of stunted trees, which screened their flight from the pursuing riders. A sudden slackening of the ponies' pace made Eve look up. At the head of the line, Sam was leading the ponies off the road and into the ditch. She gasped, expecting the animals to plunge into deep water, but they merely dipped a few inches before disappearing into the shadows on the far side of the drain.

'Where are they going?' she asked Nathanial as one by one the ponies were swallowed up in the darkness.

'Sunken causeway,' he replied. 'Once the fence and reeds are in place no one can see us.' She heard him chuckle. 'We've been doing this, man and boy, for so long that we're experts at fooling the Revenue.'

As they trotted to the edge of the drain, Nathaniel untied the final pony and held him back while the others splashed across the ditch and into the darkness.

'Come along, Miss Eve,' called Sam with no attempt to hide her identity. 'The water's only ankle-deep.'

She hesitated. 'What about Nathaniel?'

'I'm going to draw them off.'

'But isn't that dangerous in the dark?' she asked.

'No, these ponies know their way,' said Nat. 'Better'n the Revenue men anyway.'

'Miss Eve, come *on*!' Sam was already pulling the reed-covered panels into place.

'Then let me go.'

'No, by heaven!' exclaimed Nat, revolted.

Eve put her hand out and took the reins. 'You must,' she insisted. 'I'm lighter than you and can make better time. And do not worry, I will find my way home.'

Nathanial gasped as she pushed past him and scrambled into the saddle. He reached up as if to pull her from the pony, then stopped, unable to bring himself to lay hands upon a lady.

'No, Miss Eve, 'tain't proper! What would the master say?'

'What would Aggie say if you were caught?' she countered. 'You and Sam have your families to think of. They need you.' *There is no one to miss me.* She pushed aside the unspoken thought and said briskly, 'Quick, now, they will be here any minute.'

'Mistress, please!'

'Go. We shall all be caught if you do not go now!'

Nathanial hesitated for another moment, until Sam's urgent hiss reminded him of the danger. He splashed through the water and helped Sam to put the final panels into place. Then there was silence.

The water in the drain grew calm again, mirroring the starry sky. Eve looked at the high wall of reeds; there was no sign of an opening. She stood up in the stirrups, but could see nothing more than the reed tops, rippling and whispering in the breeze. The pony stamped impatiently, but she held him still, curbing her own impatience to be moving as she looked back for her first sight of the Revenue men. She did not have long to wait. A rumble like distant thunder grew steadily louder, and as the first rider appeared round the bend she dug her heels into the pony's flanks and set off at a gallop. Shouts from her pursuers told her she had been seen. The race was on.

The track was a grey ribbon in front of her, occasionally disappearing into darkness where trees threw their black shadows across the path. Her capacious smock billowed around her as the little pony flew over the ground. Eve marvelled at his sure-footed flight, but drew on the reins, steadying the headlong pace; she must not lose her pursuers too soon. Ahead lay the outline of a jumble of buildings; a village or farm, Eve could not tell, but she knew that as they moved inland there would be more buildings and more roads where she might slip out of sight and escape. Through the gloom she could see that the road turned sharply to the left beside a large wall. Eve risked a glance over her shoulder. She still had a good lead, but it could not last; the pursuing horses were covering the ground much quicker than her little pony.

She leaned into the corner, pulling her mount round, but as she straightened up and settled into the saddle again she was aware of a black shape breaking away from the shadows behind her. Alarmed, she dropped her hands and leaned forwards over the pony's neck, allowing him his head. The lane was flanked by tall trees and they were galloping in and out of the shadows. The wind was in her face, tugging at the wide brim of her hat. She dare not lift a hand from the reins and moments later it flew off behind her. Eve pressed on at a gallop, praying there were no obstacles or deep holes in the path. They were flying through the darkness, but she could hear the drumming of other hoofbeats. Someone was close on her tail. Eve dug in her heels, her heart ham-

mering against her ribs. The little pony pressed on coura-
geously, but the thunder behind her was growing louder.
The next moment a wild-eyed horse was alongside her,
foam flecking its mouth. Panic jolted through her and for
one heart-stopping moment she imagined the devil was at
her side. A black shape loomed, Eve screamed as the rider
leaned over, grabbed her around the waist and lifted her
bodily from the saddle.

'Release the reins, sweetheart.'

The shock of hearing Nick's voice almost sent her into
a swoon. The reins fell from her nerveless fingers as he
pulled her up in front of him. The riderless pony galloped
away and Nick slowed his horse, swerving off the road into
the deep shadow of a high wall.

'Quiet now.'

His warning was unnecessary. Eve could not have spoken
even had she wished to. She watched the pony racing along
the road and minutes later a dozen riders thundered past in
hot and deadly pursuit.

They remained in the shadows, still and silent until the
riders had disappeared into the darkness. The thunder died
away and was replaced by the quiet whisper of the salt
winds through the trees.

'With any luck they'll be following that little fellow until
the morning.' Eve heard the words, felt Nick's breath warm
on her cheek. She wanted to pinch herself, to make sure this
was not a dream. He spoke again. 'Where are the others?'

'Safe, I hope. They took the hidden causeway.'

'Ah. Then they will be able to evade the Revenue men.
Time to get you back to Monkhurst, I think.'

Eve clutched at him as the horse began to move forwards.
His arms tightened around her, holding her fast.

'How did you know?' she murmured, breathing in the

familiar smell of his closeness, soap and spices and a male muskiness that made her close her eyes and inhale again.

'The officers received word that there was a drop tonight. I rode over to warn Silas, but I was too late. Thankfully so were the Revenue men. Hush now; let me see if I can find my way back to Monkhurst. I would be much more at home on the water than on these winding lanes.'

Eve settled herself more comfortably against him and wrapped her arms around his body, being careful to keep her grip well above the wound in his side. Admiral moved over the ground in a long, loping stride and she tried to relax, to sway with the movement of horse and rider. Her whole body was still buzzing with the excitement of the chase, the blood was singing in her veins. Was this how her mother had felt when she had gone out with the free-traders? Was this how Nick felt when he was engaged in some dangerous adventure? She hugged the question to her as they rode through the darkness, the rough wool of Nick's coat against her cheek, his arms enclosing her, holding her safe.

Nick settled Admiral into an easy canter and stared ahead into the near-darkness. The sliver of moon was low in the sky and the tall trees cast inky shadows on the road. He was very conscious of Eve's slim form leaning against him; wisps of her hair had escaped their ribbon and tickled his chin. He turned his head briefly to rest his cheek upon her tangled locks, relieved to have her safe within his arms. He had been surprised when Richard had told him that Eve had taken Silas's place with the boys. At first he had been far too intent upon racing after her to dwell on the danger, but gradually fear had crept into his mind, fear unlike anything he had experienced before. He knew the Revenue officers, they were good men, but ill disciplined and God knew they had no cause to love the free-traders. If they had captured Eve, there was no telling what they might have done to her when their blood was up. Now, with her soft body resting against his, he had nothing to do but to think of what might have happened if he had not seen her racing towards him, if he had not been in time to rescue her. The heady relief of finding her safe diminished and was replaced by an ice-cold chill as his imagination ran wild.

Admiral clattered into the stable block at Monkhurst. A sleepy groom fumbled with a lantern, but Nick did not wait. He lowered Eve to the ground, then jumped down and thrust the reins at the bewildered boy. 'Don't unsaddle him,' he barked. 'I will be leaving again shortly.' He took Eve's arm in a painfully tight grip and marched her towards the house. Granby opened a side door as they approached.

'I was looking out for you,' he said quietly. 'I'm glad to see you back safely, Miss Eve. If you would like to go to the morning room, Martha has built up a fire in there for you.'

Nick gave her no time to reply; he almost dragged her along the dark passageway and into the little room off the great hall, where they found the maid waiting for them, her hands twisting nervously in her apron.

'Oh Miss Eve, thank heaven—' Martha broke off, eyes widening in surprise. 'Captain Wylder! I didn't think you knew of this.'

'I didn't.'

'Yes, and why was Granby waiting for us?' asked Eve, shaking off Nick's hand. 'Did you tell him, Martha?'

The maid bowed her head. 'I did, miss. I'm sorry, I know you said not to tell anyone, but I was that worried!'

Nick stood by the door, holding it open. 'Leave us, please.'

The maid's face was alive with curiosity, but Nick merely

stared at her and without a word she bobbed a curtsy and scurried away.

'Poor Martha is agog,' remarked Eve, tugging off her gloves. 'She will not rest until I have told her everything.' She looked up at him, her face alight with laughter. The rage that had been growing inside Nick during their moonlight ride now boiled over.

'Of all the crack-brained starts! Whatever possessed you to be so foolish?'

She blinked. 'I beg your pardon?'

'Did you think it a good jest, to play at smuggling? Do you not realise how deadly serious it is?'

'Of course I realise it! That is why I wanted to help them. Silas had promised me this would be the last run they would do, but they could not let their people down.'

'Did you not stop to think about the risks you were taking? That you would be putting them all in jeopardy with your inexperience?'

She smiled. 'What experience does it need to follow a pack-pony, and to shift half-ankers from the boats?' She rubbed her arms. 'I think I did quite well.'

Her calm response only enraged him further.

'I credited you with more sense than to risk your reputation, your life even, going out with the Brattee boys.'

'They were short-handed. Silas must have told you—'

'Aye, he told me, but do you really think your presence made that much difference?'

'Yes, I do! The chain was stretched enough as it was, and you know that the risks are greatest during the unloading! It has to be done quickly.' She stared at him. 'You are really angry with me.'

'Of course I am angry!' He advanced upon her and before she knew what he was about he had wrenched the linen smock up over her head and dragged it off. 'The others might be able to put this on and pass for simple farm workers, but not you! Think what would have happened if you had been caught.' He bundled the offending cloth into a ball and hurled it into the corner of the room. 'How dare you do such a thing!'

Eve frowned. A shadow of uncertainty clouded her eyes. 'These are my people. I must help them where I can.'

His hands slammed on the table, making her jump. 'Do you think it would help them if you were to be clapped in gaol? Damned idiotic idea. And with Revenue officers in the house, too! How the hell do you think it would have looked if they had discovered what you were up to? Damnation, you are my wife!'

'I am your *widow*!' She drew herself up, her lip curling. 'You made me thus, and I have no wish to be anything else to you—ever!'

Eve dashed away a tear. This was no time to show weakness, especially to Nick. She had ridden back to Monkhurst in a mood of elation, relieved that the others had escaped, pleased with her own part in it. Nick's fury was like a bucket of ice-cold water, but her nerves were still tingling with excitement and anger swept through her; she would not be cowed by his irrational rage. He took a step towards her and she moved away, making sure the solid oak table was between them.

'And what makes it so different for you?' she flung at him. 'You have been engaged on far more dangerous enterprises.'

'That is different. I risk being injured, killed perhaps, but you, if they caught you—'

She slammed her own hands down on the table. 'Do you think my anxiety is any less, when I am left here to imagine what might be happening to you? Not that I care any more,' she added quickly. 'I have no wish to be deceived by you again. In fact, I shall be much happier without you.'

'Evelina—'

'I do not think you can have anything more to say to me.' She folded her arms and glared at him. 'Make sure Granby locks the door behind you.'

Nick was like a statue, looking at her from under his black brows. She forced herself to meet his eyes, hoping hers were showing nothing more than scorn and disdain. The silence was unnerving. Anger held her body rigid. She would not yield. Finally, after what seemed like an hour, but she knew could be only a few moments, Nick turned on his heel and strode out, slamming the door behind him.

All the anger and excitement in Eve drained away. Trembling, she sank down into a chair and dropped her head in her hands. She knew he did not love her, but she had been foolish enough to hope that he might like her better now she had shown him she had some spirit. He did not. It was not at all what he wanted and now she had lost him completely.

Nick had stormed out of the house, managing only a curt word for Richard as he strode past him. He had collected Admiral and was a mile away from Monkhurst before he even realised it.

I am your widow. I have no wish to be anything else to you.

Eve's words had hit Nick like a physical blow, winding him. She did not trust him, did not realise that his anger was born out of anxiety. He had never been afraid for himself, but the idea that the fragile little woman he had married might be in danger had almost driven him out of his wits.

You should have told her that. You should tell her you love her.

This blinding revelation jolted through him. He jerked on the reins and obediently Admiral halted. *Did* he love her?

He had always enjoyed his encounters with women, but he had never loved any of them. He had thought that love, when it came, would be a warm, comfortable feeling. What he felt for Eve was far from comfortable. It was a mixture of joy, desperate desire and anxiety. He was afraid for her, afraid she might be in danger, that she might be unhappy.

And for himself there was the dark, terrifying prospect of life without her.

He turned his horse. He would go back, explain it all, suggest that they should start afresh. A few yards on he stopped again. The first fingers of dawn were pushing into the sky. Eve would be asleep. She would not thank him for waking her when she had already been up for most of the night. Besides, he could offer her nothing until the business with Chelston was resolved. Better to wait. When all this was over he could woo her properly. He turned once more.

'Easy, Admiral,' he muttered as the horse snorted in disapproval. 'You think your master is an old fool, don't you?' He sighed. 'Well, mayhap you are right.'

Chapter Fifteen

Eve dragged herself through her morning duties. Her body ached from the unaccustomed activity of the night and there was a bleak heaviness within her as though some spark of hope had finally been quenched. It would pass, of course, but for the moment she felt desperately lonely. She knew a sudden, searing moment of agony as she thought of her grandfather. How she missed him and the quiet, peaceful life they had shared. How she wished he had never invited Nick Wylder to Makerham!

The thought of Nick brought her back to the events of the previous night. Nick's fury at her going out with Nat and Sam had hurt her deeply, all the more so because she had thought he would share her exhilaration. The heady excitement she had felt during the chase was intoxicating. She had wanted to explain that to Nick, to let him know that she understood now why he thrived on danger. But instead of catching her up in his arms and making love to her he had berated her, turning her adventure into a foolhardy scrape, causing nothing but trouble. The thought made her eyes sting and she blinked away her tears. She would not cry. It had all ended well; there had been word from Sam that everyone was safe and that was all that mattered.

'Pardon me, madam, there is a note for you.'

Granby approached, holding out a letter. Eve took it, but had to blink several times before the words stopped swimming before her eyes.

'It is from Catherine Chelston,' she said. 'She says that she is even now on her way here, determined to carry me off to Appledore to see the new muslins that have just arrived at Mrs Jameson's.' She refolded the note. 'I will not see her.'

'There will be some plan afoot,' murmured Granby. 'It would be interesting to know what it might be.'

'Interesting for you and your master, perhaps,' snapped Eve.

'I beg your pardon, madam.'

She rubbed her brow. 'No, it is I who must apologise, Richard. I am very tired, and have no heart for these games.'

'But, madam, the captain would—'

'No!' she exclaimed. 'After the rating I received last night I want nothing further to do with any of this. You may see Lady Chelston if you wish; after all someone must ride out to meet her, to tell her I will not go!'

She turned on her heel and swept away, leaving Granby to stare after her.

The day dragged by and after a solitary dinner Eve retired to her room, telling herself that everything would seem brighter after a good night's sleep. Eve guessed that Granby had told Martha of her outburst, for the maid was determinedly cheerful and bustled about the chamber lighting the candles and talking all the while, as though afraid of silence. Eve allowed herself to be undressed and coaxed into her silk wrap, then she sat quietly upon the stool in front of her mirror while Martha brushed out her hair with long steady strokes. The rhythm was soothing and some of the tension went out of her shoulders. Martha met her eyes in the mirror and smiled.

'There, Miss Eve, is that better? It's no wonder you are so tired, being out of doors until dawn! It's all Aggie can talk of, you goin' out on a run, just like your sainted mother. Well, that and the fact that the captain is alive. I must say I'm relieved that I don't have to watch my words with her any more. She and Silas are that pleased you'd think he was one of their own. Of course the captain told 'em not to spread it abroad, but he did say they could tell Nat and Sam, since they can all hold their tongues—'

'And I wish that you would do just that, Martha!' Eve dropped her head in her hands. Everyone wanted to talk of the captain, when all she wanted to do was to forget all about him. Before she could apologise for her incivility, Martha was patting her shoulder.

'Ah, my poor lamb! There I am, talking nineteen to the dozen, and I've no doubt at all that your head is aching. Well, my dearie, what you need is something to soothe you off to sleep. What say you to a cup of warm milk?'

'Thank you Martha, I would like that. If it's not too much trouble.'

'No, madam. The kitchen fire will still be warm enough to heat up a pan, I'm sure. You just slip into bed and I'll be back upstairs directly.'

She bustled away, but Eve remained on the stool, staring disconsolately at her reflection. She should plait her hair, she thought. It would prevent tangles in the morning, but it seemed too much effort. Perhaps she would ask Martha to do it when she returned.

She heard a light step on the landing, the click of the latch as the door opened and closed again. She expected to hear

Martha's breezy chatter, but there was nothing, only a continuing silence. Eve turned. Nick was standing just inside the room, his greatcoat hanging open and swinging slightly, as if he had been moving quickly only moments before. He regarded her intently, his eyes shadowed.

'I was frightened for you,' he said abruptly. 'Last night. Men can turn into animals in the heat of battle. That's why I was angry. I know what can happen if they find a woman. And riding officers are not all gentlemen.'

'But they did not catch me.'

'No. But it did not stop me thinking about it. My blood ran cold to think of what might have happened to you.'

She rose. A tiny spark of light glimmered. She knew him well enough to realise this was the nearest he would come to an apology.

'I did not think of the danger when I went out. I only wanted to help.'

'I know. You were very brave.'

The glimmer strengthened, but she damped it down, kept it under control. 'You said I was foolish.'

'Did I? Eve—' He took a step towards her and she put up her hand, savouring the feeling of power.

'*Damned idiotic* were your exact words.'

A smile lifted the corners of his mouth, 'That could equally apply to me. I should tell you now that I am very proud of you, Mrs Wylder.'

'Y-you are?'

'Oh, yes. Not many women would willingly put themselves in such danger.'

He was coming closer. Another few steps and he would be within arm's reach. The tug of attraction was very strong, but she fought it.

'M-Martha is coming back with a cup of milk for me.'

'No, she is not. I have sent her to bed.'

Eve gasped. Her hand fell to her side. 'Oh! Of all the arrogant, high-handed—'

He pulled her into his arms and stopped her mouth with a kiss. The shock of it sent a tremor right down to her toes. Eve gripped his coat as his tongue raided her mouth. She was so relieved to have him with her that she responded eagerly, kissing him back with a ferocity that left them both breathless. Eventually, when Nick raised his head, Eve rested her cheek against his chest, listening to the heavy thud of his heart, revelling in the feel of his arms around her.

'You were magnificent last night,' he murmured, pressing a kiss on the top of her head. 'You were riding like the very devil; I doubt they would have caught you.'

She pushed her arms around him under the greatcoat and hugged as hard as she could. 'I wanted to make you proud of me.'

'I *am* proud of you, my love.'

She almost purred with pleasure at that. 'Really?' she murmured into his chest and felt him growl in response. She raised her head to find him gazing down at her. She responded to the look of dark desire in his eyes by tilting her head up, inviting his kiss.

As his head swooped down he swung her up into his arms and walked across to the bed. Even before he put her down her fingers were reaching for the buttons of his shirt. She wanted to run her hands over his bare skin, to feel again the pleasure she knew he could give her.

When he lowered her on to the bed and released her, Eve scrabbled to her knees. She knew a moment's panic as she thought he might be leaving her, but instead he shrugged himself out of his coats and pulled off his neck-cloth. Impatiently she reached out for him, pulling him to her. As he climbed on to the bed she kissed him, throwing her arms around his neck, her lips parting beneath the on-slaught of his deep, urgent kisses. Desire raged through Eve, she found herself plucking at his shirt, desperate to touch his skin, to run her fingers over the smooth, hard curves of his body. There was more to discuss, many more questions to be answered, but for now she need to know he was really here, that it was not some sweet dream from which she would wake up, lost and unsatisfied. His fingers tangled with the ribbons at her neck and all the while he continued to kiss her mouth, his roving tongue wreaking havoc with her senses. He lifted his head and gently ran his hands over her shoulders, pushing away the nightgown. It slid down, unresisting, to pool around her on the bed. Eve reached out for his shirt and tugged at it.

'This is unfair,' she whispered. 'I must see you, too.' Eve grappled with the buttons of his breeches but her hands stilled as Nick pulled off his shirt in one sweeping movement and she saw the bandage just below his ribs.

'Merely a precaution now,' he said, following her gaze. As if to prove his words he unwrapped the dressing to reveal the thin, jagged line. 'There. It is almost healed.'

Gently she reached out and placed her fingers near the wound. The skin was pale and cool to the touch. No sign of inflammation. 'Does it hurt?'

'Not much.' He grinned at her and that wicked dimple peeped. 'It will not impair my performance, I promise you.'

While he slipped off the bed and quickly removed his boots, breeches and stockings, Eve pulled away her night-gown and tossed it aside, but all the time she kept her eyes on Nick, enjoying the way the candlelight played on the muscled contours of his back, enhancing the curving sweep of his spine. It was as if she was seeing him for the first time;

she marvelled at the broad width of his shoulders, the way his body tapered to the narrow waist and taut, finely carved buttocks. As he turned back to her the sight of his aroused body drew a faint gasp from Eve.

Nick tumbled her back onto the bed, laughing. 'I told you I had missed you.'

She pulled him down to her, driving her hands through his hair, cradling his head while he trailed kisses along her collar-bone. Her body arched as his hands cupped her breasts, thumbs gently caressing her. She breathed in the faint, spicy fragrance that clung to him. It was so familiar she had even dreamed of it. She threw back her head as his mouth trailed across her breast and closed over one hard peak. His tongue circled slowly, causing such sweet agony that a soft moan escaped her. She felt so alive, every inch of her skin was crying out for his touch and it positively burned beneath his fingers when they travelled over the flat plain of her stomach. The aching desire intensified as his hand moved downwards. Muscles deep within her pelvis seemed to be pulling her apart. Her thighs opened in anticipation, her body tilted, eager for his fingers to slide into her. Even so the shock of his touch jolted through her and she cried out as a surge of excitement flooded her body. Still his tongue continued to caress her breast, creating waves of almost unbearable pleasure while his fingers continued their rhythmic stroking. She writhed beneath him, crying his name, no longer able to control her body.

In one smooth movement he rolled on to her. His fingers slid away and she felt him inside her, hard and smooth. Gasping, she reached up to his face, pulling him close so that she could plunder his mouth, wanting to repay something of the pleasure he was giving her. He tasted of salt and wine. Her senses were reeling with the feel of his body upon hers, their limbs tangling together in the semi-darkness. She felt rather than heard his groan as his self-control slipped away. She matched her movements to his, revelling in the joyous release as they both approached the final, shuddering climax. Eve clung to him, crying out as a wave of passion crested and broke. Consciousness splintered and Nick's rigid body was above, around and within her, possessing her totally.

With a sigh Nick collapsed, panting, beside her on the bed. Gently he drew her into his arms. 'I think,' he murmured into her hair, 'that you have missed me, too.'

She snuggled closer and gave a sleepy sigh. 'I did not realise how much.'

He gave a soft laugh. 'Then we are equal in that.'

Eve awoke to find herself alone in the bed. The early morning sun peeped through the window and she raised her head to look around the room.

Not again! Memory stabbed at her.

Nick was already dressed, bending before her mirror to tie his neckcloth. She remembered their wedding night at Makerham, waking to find Nick dressed and about to leave her. An icy chill settled over her heart. Would it always be like this?

She sat up, pulling the sheet up in front of her. 'You are going?'

'I must.' In two strides he was at the bedside, cupping her face and kissing her. 'We had word yesterday that Chelston will be moving a large consignment soon—perhaps tonight. I have to get back. The Revenue cutter is patrolling the mouth of the Rother; nothing can slip by.' He kissed her again. 'Another couple of days should see this wrapped up. Then I promise you my roving days are done.'

'Do you really mean that?'

'I do.'

She released the sheet to put her arms around his neck for one final kiss. Her body arched upwards as his hands cupped her breasts.

'Damnation, Evelina, you make it hard for a man to leave you!'

She gave a low laugh, using all her new-found powers to detain him. 'Do I?'

He put his hands on her shoulders and held her away from him. 'Yes, but it must be done.' His eyes held a promise that made her tremble with anticipation. 'I shall return: be ready for me!'

One final, hard kiss and he left her.

Chapter Sixteen

As Eve made her way downstairs some hours later, Nick's words sang in her head. Her spirits soared when she recalled the way he had looked at her, his admission that his anger was not for what she had done, but for the danger she faced. It was true, it had been a reckless escapade and it was not something she should repeat, but she had known a wild pleasure in outwitting the riding officers. She chuckled to herself as she crossed the hall. Sam and his friends were very enterprising, the hidden causeway had been effective; no one would guess that there was any route other than the road.

Eve stopped. 'Of course!' she exclaimed. 'I wonder—' She looked up to find Granby had come into the hall and was watching her.

'Madam?'

She looked at him, hardly able to contain her excitement. 'Mr Granby, I want you to come with me, now, to the boathouse passage.'

'The passage? But why, mistress?'

'I cannot say,' she replied, her eyes twinkling with mischief. 'It may be nothing, but…come along. And bring a lantern!'

She was too excited to waste time changing her gown, but made Granby precede her down the stepladder and look away while she pulled her skirts about her and negotiated the narrow steps. Aggie, holding open the trapdoor, tutted her disapproval and uttered dire warnings about headstrong females.

'I have seen those novels you keep by your bedside, Miss Eve. They do you no good, filling your head with outlandish ideas and making you think you can act like the heroine in a romance!'

Eve paused long enough to laugh up at her. 'Tush, Aggie, if I really thought of myself as a heroine I should not tell anyone where I was going and put myself in great danger. As it is, I am being very sensible and taking Mr Granby with me. Now shut the door after us, if you please.'

By the time Eve had descended to the floor of the passage the trapdoor had closed above them and they were in darkness save for the pale gleam of the lantern. She shivered in the cold, damp air and was inclined to wish she had brought a shawl.

'So, madam, what are we looking for?' asked Granby.

'I am not quite sure. Let us go on to the boathouse— and keep the lantern shining forward. I can hear things scrabbling around in the dark, and I have no wish to see what it might be.'

Granby laughed. 'There might be the odd rat, Miss Eve, but they won't bother you. After all, we must look like monsters to them.'

'Your reasoning may be sound, Mr Granby,' said Eve with studied calm, 'but I really do not wish to think about it! Let us get on.'

She grabbed his arm as he strode along the passage, telling herself that the noises she heard were no more than the drip of water from the roof of the passage, or the soft moan of the wind blowing in from the grating at the end of the winding tunnel. She found herself breathing a little easier once they reached the final bend and the locked grating stood before them. Beyond it, the wooden panels that made up the back wall of the boathouse were sadly rotted and sunlight reflecting off the gently moving water of the drain glinted between the weathered boards. Instinctively Eve moved towards the light.

'Shall I unlock the grating, madam?'

'No.' Eve stopped, considering. 'The passage winds so I have lost my bearings. Tell me, Mr Granby, if we stand with our backs to the opening, on which side of this passage would be Abbotsfield?'

Granby did not hesitate. 'That side,' he said, pointing. 'To the north.'

Eve looked at the way the passage curved slightly northwards. 'Excellent,' she said. 'Then that is where we must look.'

'Look for what?'

'A concealed entrance. When I was out with Sam the other night he said that the families in these parts had been hiding their tracks from the Excise men for generations.'

'That is true, madam, but I don't see—'

She took the lantern from him and began to inspect the walls very carefully. 'We know Silas has always been involved in free-trading: the very presence of this tunnel suggests that Monkhurst was used for smuggling at one time, but my family also owned Abbotsfield, which is no more than half a mile north of here. What if there is a tunnel from Abbotsfield to here? Sam and his people use a sunken causeway; it is hidden from the road by fencing covered in reeds so that the riding officers went straight past it, following the road. If the King's men ever searched the boathouse they might well discover this tunnel and would follow it to

Monkhurst, but would they look for another opening? The bend in the passage makes this wall particularly dark...aha!' Eve held the lantern higher. 'There is a gap here!'

Granby stepped up, running his hands over the wall. 'This looks like part of the wall but—it's a door.'

'There's no lock,' said Eve, moving the lantern to and fro. 'No, but—there's a latch!'

The click echoed around the passage, Eve tensed, expecting the shriek of metal against metal as the door swung open, but it moved smoothly and in near silence.

'The hinges have been oiled very recently,' murmured Granby.

Eve's heart hammered painfully against her ribs. 'Careful!' she gasped. 'What if there is someone—?' Her words trailed away as the door swung wide and the lantern's glow illuminated the space beyond. The light did not reach very far, but it showed them a cavernous tunnel stretching back into the darkness. Piled high against its walls were dozens of wooden chests.

Granby gave a low whistle. 'You were right, Miss Eve.' He took the lantern from her and stepped through the doorway. He bent closer to one of the chests 'Tea,' he said. 'Or rather, not tea. Smouch.'

Eve swallowed. 'Nick said the Revenue men are watching the river,' she said slowly. 'They are watching the wrong place. These casks will be taken out through Jury's Cut.'

'Then they'll miss it, mistress.'

She turned and gripped his arm. 'Mr Granby, you must go immediately to tell Nick. There may still be time for him to act.'

They ran back along the passage.

'Quickly,' she said when they had once more reached the kitchen. 'Take the fastest horse and do not stop for anyone.'

'But what of you, madam? Captain Wylder ordered me to stay with you.'

'I shall be safe enough, I have Davies and Warren to look out for me. Now go!'

Eve went off to change her gown. She was sure she would not be able to settle to anything until she heard from Nick, but she could not be idle. After partaking of a very late breakfast she sorted out a pile of sheets for mending and was carrying them downstairs when she saw a figure crossing the hall.

'Bernard!' He stopped and looked up, raising his hat to her. 'How did you get in here?'

'I walked in from the kitchen garden, Cousin. Are you not pleased to see me?'

Eve hoped her face did not show her dismay. She was a little surprised to see him in topboots and breeches, and despite the warmth of the day he carried a travelling cloak over one arm. She said shortly, 'I am very busy, Bernard. Pray tell me what it is that you want.'

He followed her into the morning room, where she placed the sheets next to her sewing basket.

'I thought you might like to take a little walk with me. Let me put it differently,' he said as she opened her mouth to reply. 'You *will* take a little walk with me.' He lifted the travelling cloak slightly to reveal a small silver-mounted pistol in his hand. 'Do not think I will not use this,' he continued. 'From this distance I could not fail to kill you.'

Eve stood very still, her eyes upon the small black mouth of the pistol that was pointed at her stomach. 'What are you about, Bernard?'

'I will explain presently. For now you will precede me out on to the terrace, if you please, and from there to the park.'

'And if I refuse?'

'I will choke you or shoot you.'

Eve stared at his face. There was a grim determination in his eyes that made her think he would really do it. He gestured towards the door. 'Shall we go? And pray do not think to call to your servants,' he murmured as she went out before him. 'If I think you are giving them any signal at all, I shall shoot you.'

She stepped out of the house and upon Bernard's instruction walked ahead of him towards the archway that led into the park. It was a balmy day, yet Eve found herself shivering, aware of the pistol's muzzle only inches from her back. She could only hope for some distraction so that she could get away, but for the moment there was no one in sight, no one who knew of her plight.

'Where are we going?' she asked, trying to keep her voice calm.

'Walk straight on towards the row of beeches over there. My carriage is parked just beyond the wall.'

'You are kidnapping me.' It was a statement, and Eve was surprised that she could sound so matter of fact about it.

Bernard laughed. 'Yes, I suppose I am. It would have been simpler if you had agreed to accompany Lady Chelston yesterday, but there it is. She was most put out that you would not see her, but we thought it might arouse suspicions if she came bang up to the house and demanded you go out with her.'

'We? Who might that be, Bernard?'

'Why, Lord Chelston and myself, of course. I—'

A sudden shout behind them made him stop. He grabbed Eve's arm and pressed the pistol hard against her ribs.

'It—it is my maid,' she said, looking back. 'I will need to speak to her, to reassure her.'

'Then be very careful, Cousin. Remember the pistol at your back. I have its twin in my pocket and I can use it just as well with either hand. Do not give me cause to shoot your maid as well as you.'

Keeping close, he turned Eve to face Martha, who was running up to them.

'Madam, I saw you from the house—'

'Yes, Martha. I am going for a walk with my cousin.' The maid hesitated, frowning, and Eve found herself praying that she would say nothing out of place.

'You may return to the house,' said Eve quietly. 'I do not need you.'

Martha shifted uncomfortably from one foot to the other. 'Madam, it—it is going to rain; would you not be more comfortable indoors?'

'That is why we are taking our walk now,' said Eve smoothly. 'Although it means I shall not be able to ride out on Persephone this afternoon. When Mr Granby returns, Martha, pray tell him I shall not require Persephone.'

Eve smiled brightly while all the time she was in terror that her maid would look puzzled and ask her what she meant.

'Would you like me to come with you, mistress?'

The hard muzzle prodded warningly in Eve's back. She managed a laugh, although it sounded brittle to her strained nerves.

'Goodness me, no. You would be much better employed mending the sheets I have left in the morning room. You know I was going to tackle them myself, until my cousin here beguiled me with the idea of a walk. Of you go now. I shall not be long.'

'She is suspicious,' muttered Bernard, watching the maid make her way back to the house.

'Of course she is,' retorted Eve. 'She knows I dislike you.

However, it is not her place to question my behaviour. She will sit over her sewing until dinner.'

'By which time you will be far away.'

Another few minutes brought them to the edge of the trees. Bernard pushed her on to a narrow path and soon she saw a gap in the palings and a carriage beyond. Eve tensed. If she was going to run, it would be better to do it now. Once in the carriage she could be miles away before she had another chance to escape. Her hands had closed on her skirts, ready to lift them and take to her heels, when she felt a stunning blow to the back of her head. The force sent her down on to her knees, the daylight was replaced by blackness and she lost consciousness.

Chapter Seventeen

'Four o'clock.' Nick consulted his watch as he guided Admiral through the gates and into the park at Monkhurst. 'We have made good time, Richard, though not quite as speedy as your ride to me this morning!'

'I thought it necessary to get the information to you with all speed, sir.'

'And you were right. You arrived in time for me to discuss the new plans with Captain George, rather than send fresh instructions after him.'

'I only hope we've got it right, Captain,' murmured Granby.

'Well it all makes sense, Richard. And it explains Chelston's interest in Monkhurst.'

Nick urged his horse to the trot. His heart was singing, not only with anticipation of the forthcoming action, but with the thought of seeing Eve again.

As they clattered into the stable yard he was surprised to find it already bustling with people. Warren and Davies were leading horses out of the stables while Silas Brattee and his sons turned as Nick trotted up. Eve's maid pushed them aside to run forward. Richard was off his horse in a flash to meet her.

'Martha? What is it?'

'Oh, Dick, I'm so glad you've come.' Martha caught at his hands, then turned a tear-stained face towards Nick. His brows snapped together.

'What's happened?' he barked.

Silas strode forwards. 'It's the mistress, Cap'n. She's gone. We was just getting up a party to go and find her.'

'Gone? Where?' he demanded.

'We don't know, sir,' cried the maid. 'She went out walking with that cousin of hers and never came back.'

'Shawcross was here?' said Granby. He turned towards Nick, a frown in his eyes.

'Aye,' muttered Martha, wiping her eyes with her apron. 'Davies let him in.'

'That I did, Cap'n.' Davies stepped up, an anxious frown on his round face. 'I'm that sorry, sir, but when he came walking in by the side door and said he was Mrs Wylder's cousin—'

'You weren't to know,' said Nick. 'He's abducted her, that's certain.' He turned again to Martha. 'What time was this, when did you last see her?'

'It was about noon, Captain. When Davies told me Mr Shawcross was here I wasn't happy about it and went to find her, not wanting her to be alone with him. I saw them walking away from the house, so I ran after them, but Miss Eve sent me away, saying to tell Mr Granby that she wouldn't be needin' her horse this afternoon.'

Richard frowned. 'Horse? We had made no arrangement.'

Martha shrugged. 'I'd said it looked like rain—trying to get them to come back to the house, but she just laughed at me and said in that case she wouldn't be needing Pers—Persephone.'

Nick turned to stare at Granby, who shook his head. 'She doesn't own a horse by that name.'

'No,' said Nick slowly, 'but she used it for Lady Chelston recently.' He grinned. 'Clever girl, she's telling us where Shawcross is taking her!'

The unpleasant tang of smelling salts stung at Eve's nose and instinctively she twisted her head away. As consciousness returned she was aware that she was lying on a narrow couch. She did not open her eyes, but she could feel the slippery satin beneath her hand. A woman's voice sounded very close.

'She's coming round.'

There was something familiar in the low, husky tones, but her head ached and she could not quite remember where she had heard it before. Then she heard a voice that she knew only too well.

'She has been unconscious for hours; I did not think I had hit her quite so hard.'

Bernard's tone was querulous, defensive. Eve kept her eyes closed, as though by doing so she could avoid the truth of her situation. Her memory was returning. Bernard had carried her off. The soft, gravelly voice belonged to Catherine Chelston, and suggested they were at Chelston Hall. Eve knew she must find out for herself. Cautiously she opened her eyes a little. The room seemed very bright and she closed them again with a moan.

'It is very hot in here. Throw up the sash, then pour some wine for her!' Lady Chelston began to chafe one of her hands. 'Come along, madam, you have lain there long enough. We need you awake.'

With a shudder of distaste, Eve pulled her hand free and tried opening her eyes again. She found Catherine leaning over her, and beyond the painted face and powdered hair she could see a white rococo-patterned ceiling. She had seen that design before, it was Lady Chelston's drawing room.

Eve struggled to sit up. Bernard was standing before her, his eyes narrowed.

'What am I doing here?' she asked frostily.

'I apologise for the rough treatment, Cousin, but it was entirely necessary.'

'Was it necessary to hit me over the head?' she demanded, taking a glass of wine from him.

'Oh, yes,' he replied with a cold, self-satisfied look. 'I knew you were considering flight, and I had no wish to drive through the village with you struggling like a wildcat.'

'So what do you want with me?' She glared at them. Anxiety gnawed at her. Did they know Nick was alive? Did they know of his plans to intercept the consignment? Bernard's next words gave her some reassurance.

'It is very simple: Monkhurst.'

She took a sip of the wine, hoping it would revive her. 'And how do you propose to get it?'

Bernard's sly smile made her skin crawl with apprehension. 'You will marry me. I have to admit the idea holds some appeal for me. I have always had a fondness for you, Cousin.'

Eve turned away from him. She glanced at the clock on the mantelpiece; Five o'clock. Martha would know by now that something was wrong, but could she get word to Nick? And would she pass on her parting message? It was a very slim hope, but it was all Eve had. She must not lose her courage now. She must play for time.

'I feel very ill, is there somewhere I could wash my face, and perhaps brush my hair?'

Catherine Chelston regarded her for a moment. 'Very well, come with me.' She escorted Eve upstairs to one of the guest rooms, but any hopes Evelina might have had of overpowering her were dashed when Lady Chelston called to her dresser to accompany them.

* * *

Eve took as long as she dared tidying her hair and splashing her face with cold water. When she returned to the drawing room she felt considerably more alert, although no nearer finding a means of escape.

'Ah, my blushing bride. I trust you are feeling a little better, Cousin?'

Bernard stopped pacing the floor and tried to take her hand. She snatched her fingers away.

'You cannot force me into marriage. Everyone knows I detest you.'

'Do they?' Catherine pushed her down on to a chair. 'Your presence at my house party did not go unnoticed, Mrs Wylder, nor the fact that Bernard was so very attentive. What more natural than a lonely widow finding solace with her cousin and unable to wait to satisfy her passion? So you slip away quietly to be married by special licence—'

'Which I have obtained,' added Bernard, patting his pocket. 'I cannot wait to make you mine, Cousin.'

Eve tried not to think of it. 'But Mr Didcot advised caution; I might not yet be a widow.'

Bernard gave a snort of rude laughter. 'Didcot's an old fool. Wylder's dead. There's no one to contest our marriage. I'll have you wedded and bedded by dawn.'

A shudder ran through her. 'Why is Monkhurst so important to you?' she asked.

'There are certain—goods—at Abbotsfield that need to be shipped abroad,' said Lady Chelston. 'Revenue men are watching the Rother, so we want to move them out on the Monkhurst Drain. We have already taken steps to make sure that no one else uses the inlet at night.'

'So you have been attacking my people in Jury's Cut.'

'Your people—how feudal that sounds,' Bernard scoffed.

'Yes, we sent our men to frighten off the locals. And we made sure the Revenue was aware that there was going to be a drop the other night. Normally they would not concern themselves with such a small affair, but they are very active here at the moment; they think it will lead them to a large smuggling gang.'

'Led by Lord Chelston and yourself, perhaps?' retorted Eve.

Lord Chelston's cold voice came from the doorway. 'Very acute, madam, but it is dangerous for you to ask so many questions.'

Catherine turned to him. 'You are back, my dear! You have the parson?'

'He is in the chapel.' He nodded towards Eve. 'How much does she know?'

Bernard shifted uneasily. 'Very little, my lord. Mere conjecture—'

Lady Chelston lifted her fan. 'Still enough to make her a threat,' she said.

'She will be safe enough once we are married,' said Bernard. 'I promise you.'

'You promised me Monkhurst if I would make you a partner in this business,' snapped Lord Chelston. 'I want you and your new wife back at Monkhurst as soon as maybe. If her servants set up a hue and cry, there will be the devil to pay.'

'If he takes me back to Monkhurst, what is to stop me telling everyone the truth?' demanded Eve.

Lord Chelston's cold grey eyes settled on her. 'Do not underestimate your cousin, Mrs Wylder. If you give him too much trouble, he will have to kill you just as he killed your husband.'

Eve did not have to pretend to look shocked at these words. Although she knew the truth, she was horrified to hear Lord Chelston speak of murder so coolly.

'Wylder was working with the Revenue,' said Bernard. 'If I had not shot him, he would have ruined everything—'

'We have no time for this now,' Lord Chelston interrupted him. 'Bring her to the chapel.'

'Wait!' cried Eve as Bernard dragged her to her feet. 'What if I refuse? You cannot force me into this!'

Lord Chelston looked at his wife, who pulled a small bottle from her reticule. 'Laudanum,' she said. 'You will not be in a position to refuse.'

'No!' Eve protested as Lord Chelston stepped behind her and pinned her arms to her sides. Bernard took the bottle and removed the cork. Eve stared, horrified. If he forced her to swallow the laudanum she would be lost. She might even give away Nick's secret. She struggled desperately but Lord Chelston held her fast. Bernard stepped closer, a cruel curl to his lips.

'Now, now, my dear, why should you object so much to taking me for a husband?'

'Because she does not wish to commit bigamy.'

A stunned silence fell over the room. Eve's head snapped round towards the sound of Nick's voice. Relief flooded through her at the sight of him sitting in the open window, his legs astride the sill and a deadly-looking pistol in each hand. She knew a sudden and irrational desire to laugh; he looked completely at his ease and that familiar, gleaming smile made her heart leap.

Bernard dropped the laudanum bottle and its contents spilled out to make dark, spreading stain on the carpet.

'Wylder!' he spluttered. 'But it can't be. I sh-shot you. You are dead!'

'Obviously not,' drawled Lord Chelston. He gave Eve a little shake.

'Well, madam, did you know he was alive?'

'Not at first.'

Bernard turned to glare at Eve, his mouth working convulsively. 'No, I'll swear she did not. I was there when his man broke the news.'

She tried to shrug herself free, but Lord Chelston's grip only tightened painfully. He held her before him like a shield.

'Congratulations, Wylder,' he said coolly. 'You fooled us all.'

'Yes, I did, didn't I?' Nick grinned as he swung his leg over the sill and stepped into the room, Richard Granby and Sam following him. 'So much so that we know all about your plan to send out the next consignment of smouch through Jury's Cut. Captain George already has his orders to intercept the black-sailed lugger and haul in your people at Abbotsfield, to keep everything ship-shape. It is all up with you, Chelston.'

'Oh I think not. I still have one ace in my hand, Wylder.' He yanked Eve's arms behind her, holding them with one hand while his other reached into his pocket and pulled out a pistol. He pressed the cold muzzle against her head, just below the ear. Eve swallowed, trying not to tremble, and kept her eyes on Nick. His smile did not waver, but he was very still. Tension crackled around the room.

'Let her go, Chelston,' he ordered. 'There is no way you can escape now.'

'Perhaps not. But what have I got to lose if I shoot your wife first? I should like to think I made you suffer for your victory.'

Eve closed her eyes. It would not help Nick to see how terrified she was.

'Don't be a fool, man.'

Chelston laughed softly 'Oh I am no fool, Wylder. I have your measure. You will not risk the life of this pretty lady, now, will you? One wrong move by you or your friends and I shall pull the trigger.'

There was a brief, heart-stopping silence before Nick spoke again. 'We seem to have reached an impasse.'

'Whatever happens now, your wife will die,' said Chelston. 'Unless...'

The word hung in the air. Eve's nerves were at breaking point. She forced her tense muscles to relax, afraid that if she shuddered or trembled that deadly pistol might go off.

'Unless?' Nick prompted quietly.

'Call your men off, Wylder. Let the consignment go through.'

'That is out of my hands. Chelston. The Revenue is aware of your whole operation.'

'True, there is little I can do about Abbotsfield; if the government knows of its purpose then it is too late to save it. It matters not, since it would appear you have made it impossible for us to remain in England. However, this final consignment is valuable and I would rather not lose it. You can send word to your Captain George, Wylder; tell him you were mistaken and that the original orders stand: his ship should continue patrolling the Rother.'

Eve's eyes flew open. 'No,' she whispered, gazing at Nick. 'You cannot let him get away.'

'Would you rather he let you die?' sneered Chelston.

Eve ignored him. She kept her eyes upon Nick. *I'm sorry*. She mouthed the words, hoping he would understand her. Lady Chelston took a step forward.

'Everything depends upon how much our gallant Captain values his wife.'

Eve drew herself up. She said proudly, 'Not above duty to his country! I would not expect that.'

Nick stared at the little group in front of him and weighed up the odds. With Richard and Sam both armed he did not doubt that Shawcross, Chelston and his lady could all be overpowered, but neither did he doubt that the pistol pressed against Eve's head was loaded and that Chelston would use it if they made any attempt to rush him. His heart contracted painfully as he saw how bravely she stood her ground. He looked into her soft brown eyes. They were dark now, the dilated pupils the only sign that she was afraid. Bless her, did she really think he could put duty before her?

'Very well,' he said at last. 'I will call off the Revenue.'

Eve gave a little sob. 'No.' Her voice was little more than a whisper. 'You were sent here to prevent this,' she said. 'When they find out, you will be ruined.'

'Yes, that gives another pleasant twist to this episode,' Chelston jeered. 'The heroic Captain Wyldfire, a traitor to his country.'

Nick ignored this taunt. He signalled to Sam and Richard to lower their pistols. 'Release her, Chelston, and you have my word that you will not be intercepted tonight.'

'No, no, Captain, you have *my* word that once the *Merle* has loaded her cargo and set sail again I will let your woman go free,' Lord Chelston replied. 'I do not fear your ships once the *Merle* is moving. I would back her to outrun anything you may have in your fleet. You and your men will leave here now. You will send word to the Revenue officers that their cutter is to remain at the mouth of the Rother and make sure that nothing happens to prevent this last consignment from reaching the *Merle*, or to prevent my own little party boarding my yacht at Hastings. Is that agreed?'

'And my wife?'

'Mrs Wylder shall be my guest aboard the *Maestro* and we shall watch the proceedings from there. And now, Captain Wylder, I would ask you to make your decision quickly. My arm is beginning to ache and this trigger is so very sensitive.'

'What assurance do I have that you will keep your word?'

'Why, none, my good Captain; but then, what assurance have I that you will keep yours?' He laughed softly. 'Mrs Wylder is my guarantee of safe passage out of the country. But time is getting on. You must leave now if your instructions are to reach your gallant Revenue captain in time. And remember, Captain Wylder; your wife is safe only as long as matters go smoothly, so you had best make sure I see the Revenue cutter in Rye Bay this evening. I shall look out for her when we sail past in the *Maestro*. From this moment Mrs Wylder will be accompanied at all times by Shawcross, Catherine or myself; we are all like to hang if we are caught, so we are none of us afraid to pull the trigger, am I not right?' He looked at his companions, who nodded, and Chelston fixed his cold eyes on Nick again. 'If I suspect you are trying to trick me, then she will be the first to die. Well?'

'Your consignment will not be intercepted. You have my word upon it.'

It took all Nick's self-control not to react to the flash of triumph he saw in Chelston's face. He had schooled his own to a look of indifference and forced himself to watch without emotion as Chelston pulled Eve closer to him and stroked her cheek with the pistol.

'Well, my dear, do you trust him?' That purring voice grated on Nick's raw nerves. 'After all, he fooled you before, did he not? He allowed you to think he was dead. What sort of trick is that to play on a loving wife?'

Nick saw the anger in Eve's eyes and the scornful curl of her lip. He gave her a rueful smile and said quietly, 'Well, sweetheart?'

Her chin went up. 'Yes,' she said clearly. 'Yes, I trust him. Implicitly!'

Despite their desperate situation a blaze of happiness lifted Nick's spirits. He met and held Chelston's challenging look. 'You harm her and I will make sure you do not live to see the dawn.'

Lord Chelston's thin lips curled. 'I am no uncivilised savage; keep to our bargain and she goes free. Shawcross, ring the bell, if you please. Our guests will leave by the main door, I think.'

Chapter Eighteen

'Captain?'

Nick heard Richard call his name, but he did not answer as he strode out of the house. He made his way quickly to the walled garden where they found Silas and Nathanial waiting with the horses. A tight knot of anxiety twisted inside him, worse than any fear he had ever felt for himself. Walking away from Eve was the most difficult thing he had done in his life. Her brave smile had wrenched at his heart; although he had a plan forming, there was no guarantee that it would work. She had put her trust in him and he was not at all sure he would succeed.

'Captain?' Richard spoke again. 'What are you going to do?'

'There's enough of us, Cap'n,' said Sam, anxious eyes fixed on his face. 'What if we were to storm the house—?'

Nick shook his head. 'You heard Chelston, Sam. If we try anything of that nature he will shoot Eve. I cannot risk it. Let's get out of here.' He mounted and cantered down the drive, Richard and the others behind him. He did not stop until they were well clear of Chelston, then he pulled up in a wooded glade at the side of the road and waited for them to come up to him.

'Well, sir?' Richard's usually impassive countenance was grim.

'I do not think Chelston will harm her, at least until the smouch has been transferred to the lugger,' said Nick. 'The first thing to do is to get word to Captain George.'

'I'll go, Cap'n!' declared Sam eagerly.

Nick shook his head. 'I've other work for you, Sam. Silas, how many oarsmen does that galley of yours hold?'

'Why, twenty, sir, but we can manage with half that number—'

Nick interrupted him. 'For what I have in mind you'll need a full complement. You said your brother has a similar vessel, over at Dimchurch.'

'Aye, sir, 'e has.'

'You'd be better setting off from there. Could you find me enough oarsmen? Could you find them for tonight?'

'Aye, Cap'n, reckon we can, if it will help rescue Miss Eve.' Silas stuck out his chin. 'She helped us on our last run, now it's our turn to repay the debt.'

Nick grinned. 'Very well then, Silas. You are always telling me that the Kentish oarsmen are the best in the world, now you are going to prove it to me!'

Chapter Nineteen

It took all Eve's willpower not to cry out to Nick as he walked out of the room. As soon as the door had closed behind him Lady Chelston pulled one of cords from the window and bound Eve's wrists. After that she became the still centre of a whirlwind of activity. She was obliged to sit passively and watch while all around her bags were packed, orders shouted and servants despatched. Her forced inactivity was deeply frustrating. And at all times Lady Chelston, her husband or Bernard hovered near her, a constant reminder that if anything should go wrong she would be the first to suffer.

Eve half-expected an attack on Chelston Hall by the dragoons or a party of riding officers and she was a little disappointed when an hour dragged by with nothing more exciting than Lady Chelston's maid dropping a scent bottle on the marble floor of the hall and filling the air with the pungent, sickly smell of overblown roses. Eve told herself that Nick was protecting her, that he would do nothing to risk her life, but it irked her to be so helpless. She remembered Mr Granby's words: *Captain Wyldfire runs with the wind, ma'am*. Well, he was running with a very ill wind now and she did not see how he could turn it to his advantage.

★ ★ ★

The drive to Hastings was slightly more interesting, but less comfortable, for she was bundled into the carriage with Lady Chelston and her maid, who cried into her apron and declared that she did not want to leave her family.

'Why can't I stay behind, m'lady, like 'is lordship's man?'

'Griffin is not staying behind, you foolish wench,' retorted Lady Chelston, 'He is staying to pack the rest of the trunks and will follow us as best he can.'

'But I don't like the water, ma'am; you know I gets sick!'

In reply Lady Chelston boxed her ears and told her to control herself, but the maid's sobs only increased.

Eve looked away in disgust. Outside the windows she could see her cousin and Lord Chelston riding beside the carriage. She felt trapped and as the coach bounced and rocked over the uneven road she was obliged to reach up with her bound hands and cling on to the strap for the most uncomfortable journey of her life.

They boarded the *Maestro* at Hastings. With her hands tied Eve found it difficult to climb up on to the yacht, but she closed her lips stubbornly against any complaint. As Bernard helped her on to the deck she heard Lord Chelston addressing the first mate.

'Mr Briggs, where is your captain?'

The man snapped to attention. 'Sick, me lord,' he replied smartly. 'Flux. Running out of 'im somethin' dreadful…'

'Yes, yes, no need to give me all the details.' Lord Chelston waved him away. 'Well, get on with it, then man. You know what to do.'

Lady Chelston and her maid immediately retired to a cabin, complaining of sickness and Bernard bundled Eve to a quiet spot near the stern of the yacht while the bare-footed sailors moved quickly about their tasks as they prepared to put to sea. Everywhere she looked there was a profusion of ropes, wooden spars and huge canvas sails that to Eve's un-tutored eye made the *Maestro* look top-heavy. As the crew adjusted the sails to make the most of the light breeze, she heard the first-mate informing his master that with so little wind it would be fair nigh impossible to make good time. If that was true, then perhaps the *Merle*, too, would be late to the rendezvous; no one could blame Nick for that.

Eve waited until the first fevered activity of setting sail had died down, then she thrust her bound wrists towards Bernard.

'I would be obliged if you would untie me now. After all, I can hardly escape from here.' She looked out over the calm grey water that surrounded them. 'You know I cannot swim, Cousin. What harm can I do you here?' She directed a steady look across the deck at Lord Chelston, who nodded.

'Take off the rope, Shawcross, but watch her.' He turned to Eve. 'Any tricks, madam, and you will be trussed up and locked below. Do you understand?'

Eve met his eyes without flinching. 'Perfectly.'

Once her wrists were free, Eve made her way towards the bow of the ship where she hoped she would not be in the way of the crew. She rubbed her arms, hoping that the balmy night would stay warm since she had only the silk shawl Lady Chelston had given her to keep out any chill winds. The sun had set, the daylight a mere thin line of pale grey on the horizon. There was no moon and the only light came from the stars that were beginning to twinkle in the east, although above her head the mass of ropes, spars and huge sails blotted out the sky. She moved past the pin-rail, where a bewildering number of ropes were tied off, and dropped down by the railing so that she could peer out under the rigging at the empty sea before them. Despite the lack of wind the ship seemed to be travelling quickly through the water, the prow slicing effortlessly through the waves with a gentle rocking motion that she found quite soothing. The sea air was cool on her cheeks and she could taste the salt on her lips. It was invigorating; it reminded her of Nick. Bernard came up and sat down beside her. She hunched her shoulder and turned her back on him.

'Look, Cousin.' He pointed towards the dwindling coastline with the ancient town of Rye on its hill, standing guard like some medieval fortress. 'You see the sails over there? It is the *Argos*, cruising at the mouth of the Rother. Captain George will have a long wait.'

Eve did not answer. The Revenue ship looked so far away, she could expect no help from that quarter.

'The *Maestro* is a very fast cutter,' Bernard continued. 'She's clinker built with a lute stern so she's very light and fast. She's rigged fore-and-aft—'

'Bernard,' Eve interrupted him wearily. 'Do you have the slightest idea what any of that means?'

'It means, dear cousin, that we have the advantage of any government vessel. Chelston tells me the *Maestro* was built at the self-same shipyard as the lugger that is waiting for our longboats to row out to it with the casks full of smouch. It means,' he said with great deliberation, 'that even if your husband tries to give chase tonight he will not catch us.' Bernard gave a self-satisfied sigh. 'It is common practice, I believe, for the shipwrights to build boats for both the free-traders and the Revenue, but 'tis the free-traders who get the faster vessels.'

'With so little wind I do not see it makes any difference,' remarked Eve.

'Oh, it will pick up presently. For now we are in no hurry. The *Merle* is not expected at the rendezvous until midnight.'

He settled himself more comfortably. 'Seems damnably dark to me. Barely enough light to see your hand in front of your face, but I'm told the crews prefer it that way.'

'How will the *Merle* know this is not an enemy ship?' she asked. She added hopefully, 'It might turn around and sail away.'

'There are pre-arranged signals. Chelston informs me that we shall be able to watch the consignment being transferred to the *Merle* and when it is all done we shall follow her to Boulogne.' He reached out and put a hand on her shoulder. 'I am looking forward to getting you ashore, my dear.'

Angrily she shrugged him off. 'Lord Chelston gave his word that if the consignment went ahead I should be freed.'

She caught the quick gleam of his teeth in the near-darkness.

'Yes, Cousin; but Lord Chelston did not say where. If we set you down in Boulogne with no money, no maid and no baggage, I think you might soon find yourself in difficulties. What do you think, Cousin?' He leaned closer until she could feel his hot breath on her face. 'A young lady, unattended, in a busy seaport—you would not last five minutes. Much better to put yourself under my protection, my dear. Besides, I think your husband owes me something for obliging me to undertake this precipitous flight, with not even my valet to attend me. At least I shall have you to warm my bed—'

She brought her hand up and caught him a stinging slap on the face. With a snarl Bernard jumped up, his black shape looming over her.

'Why, you—'

'Quiet, damn you!' Lord Chelston's voice cut like a whiplash across the deck. 'We have reached the rendezvous.'

With a muttered curse Bernard lounged away. Eve watched

him go with some relief. She looked towards the shadowy figure of Lord Chelston, pacing to and fro across the deck.

'What happens now?' she asked him as he came near.

'Now we sit and wait to see if your husband is as good as his word.'

A heavy darkness fell, trapping them between the velvety sky with its myriad twinkling stars and the silky blackness of the sea. The only sound was the gentle lapping of the water against the hull or the occasional snap of a sail overhead. Eve hugged her shawl about her and wondered what she could do when they reached Boulogne. The idea of remaining under Bernard's protection was unthinkable. Nick would come for her, she was sure of that, but how soon? Perhaps she could find a priest to take her in while she sent word to him. She closed her eyes, summoning up that last glance he had given her before he had walked out of the drawing room at Chelston Hall. No words, but a look in his blue, blue eyes that had promised he would find her. It was a small hope, but it was all she had and she clung on to it desperately.

'There she is, m'lord.'

The first mate's quiet growl roused Eve. She strained her eyes until they watered. At first she could see nothing in the gloom, but at length she could just pick out a black shape in the distance. A light glimmered, the barest flash in the darkness. One of Lord Chelston's crew swung a lantern in response and a murmur of anticipation ran around the deck. Eve remained beside the rail, watching and waiting. Minutes passed. At last a faint movement caught her eye; she could see a line of small shapes on the water, inching towards the *Merle*. She knew they must be the long boats, laden with casks of bogus tea to be hauled aboard the lugger. Her pulse quickened; perhaps Nick and his officers had replaced the longboatmen and were even now aboard the *Merle*, overpowering the crew and capturing the ship for the crown. Perhaps...

A series of lights flickered from the black outline of the ship and Eve heard Lord Chelston give a grunt of satisfaction.

'Good. All is well; she's loaded. Any sign of enemy ships, Briggs?'

'No, sir.'

Eve's heart sank as she watched the tiny boats moving away from the *Merle*. At such a distance they looked like a string of jet beads on a bed of dark satin. Once the *Merle* set sail there was little chance that any Revenue cutter could prevent her from reaching Boulogne. Depression as black as the night settled over her. Once it was known that Nick had allowed the smugglers to escape, his good name would be lost. And she was to blame. Nick had sacrificed everything in a desperate bid to save her. Eve squared her shoulders. She must not be despondent; if the tales she had heard were to be believed, Captain Wyldfire had successfully recovered from worse situations than this. For now there was little she could do except to stay alert.

As Eve watched the black shapes of the longboats slip back towards the shore, a question occurred to her.

'What will happen to those men?'

Chelston shrugged. 'I have no idea.'

'But you could have warned them. If they return to Abbotsfield, they will be arrested.'

'That is not my concern; I have no further use for them.'

'How can you be so cold?' She shook her head, disbelieving. 'Have you no thought for the people you have abandoned?'

'No, none.' Lord Chelston put his telescope to his eye and slowly turned around, raking the seas. 'Well, well; the

Merle is underway and not another vessel in sight. Wylder was as good as his word. He must really love you, my dear.'

'Oh I do, Chelston. Never doubt it.'

'Nick!'

Eve hurtled across the deck towards the tall, familiar figure that had appeared by the main mast. Nick reached out and drew her to him with one hand, while the pistol in the other never wavered from its target, which was Lord Chelston's heart. She noted that Richard Granby was beside him, his pistol aimed at Bernard, who had raised his hands. Even in the darkness she could see that he was shaking.

Nick leaned down to plant a kiss upon her head. 'Have they hurt you, sweetheart?'

She clung to him, pressing her cheek against his rough wool jacket. 'No, not at all. But I am so glad to see you.'

'Curse you, Wylder, where did you come from?' snarled Lord Chelston.

'I was 'tween decks with Richard. We didn't want to ruin the surprise by your spotting us too early.'

'Much good it may do you, when you are outnumbered by my crew. Take them!'

Eve gasped as Chelston dived to the deck, but Nick did not move. No shots were fired, and no one attempted to lay a hand upon Nick, who merely laughed.

'Get up, Chelston, you look very foolish lying down there. I think you will find they are not your crew any longer. I've hired them.'

'You have *what*?' It was too dark to see Chelston's face, but Eve could hear the astonishment in his voice.

'I have hired them. You kept 'em too long ashore, Chelston, and on half-pay too. A mistake, but although they were anxious to get to sea again not one jack tar wanted to turn pirate, which I convinced them they would be if they followed you. I admit it was the reward for your capture that finally persuaded them to come over to me. I've a mind to have the *Maestro*, too; after all, you will have no use for her now. Of course, your captain could not be bought, so we had to leave him behind, but I think once he learns you have been arrested he will consider his contract with you void.' He raised his voice. 'Mr Briggs, take them aft and secure them, if you please.'

'Aye, aye, Cap'n.'

Eve gripped his coat 'Nick, Lady Chelston—'

'Safely locked in her cabin, sweetheart. I do not think she is yet aware of what is happening; she dosed herself with laudanum as soon as they set sail.'

'And the maid?'

'Locked in with her. She's cast up her accounts, but still looks decidedly green. But what of you, my love, no sea-sickness?'

Eve shook her head. 'I have been on deck all the time.'

'That's my girl.' His arm tightened around her, pulling her against his chest. He dropped his pistol into the pocket of his coat before cupping Eve's chin in his hand and turning her face up towards him. 'Are you sure you are not hurt?'

'Yes, I am sure.'

'Were you frightened?'

She smiled up at him lovingly. 'No. I knew you'd come for me.'

He threw back his head and laughed. 'What? No fits, no vapours? You are a woman after my own heart, Evelina! No.' He looked down at her, suddenly serious, and said softly, 'No, you *are* my heart.'

It was too dark to see his face clearly, so she reached up

her hand to touch his cheek. A muscle in his jaw quivered beneath her fingers, he pulled her even closer until she could feel his body hard against hers.

She drew his head down, turning her face up to him. The next instant his mouth was crushing hers, possessing her. She pressed herself against him, consumed by a fierce, urgent desire until Nick's hands moved to her shoulders and he held her off a little.

'Gently, sweetheart,' he said unsteadily. 'Much more of that and I'll have to take you here, on the deck. Think how that would shock poor Richard!'

She stared at him, dizzy, uncomprehending. All she knew was that she wanted him. She managed a shaky laugh. 'I said I was not frightened, but that's not true; I was afraid I would never see you again.'

He stroked her face gently. 'You'll never know how much it cost me to leave you at Chelston Hall.'

She covered his hand with her own and rubbed her cheek against his captive fingers. 'It is over now—'

She broke off at a sudden shout of alarm. Nick looked up and instantly pushed her away from him. As she hit the pin-rail Eve saw the dark figure of Lord Chelston crash into Nick, who fell to the deck with a grunt of pain. Chelston straightened. There was a flash as the starlight glinted on the blade in his hand. Eve seized a belaying pin from the rail and swung it as hard as she could. It caught Chelston's arm with a sickening, bone-breaking crack and the knife fell harmlessly to the deck.

There was an infinitesimal pause, a brief moment of stillness for Eve to catch her breath before she was surrounded by figures. One sailor gently prised the belaying pin from her fingers while two more laid hands on Lord Chelston, who yelped with pain. Richard Granby was helping Nick to his feet, Mr Briggs hovering beside him, anxious to make his apologies.

'I'm sorry about that, Cap'n. He was so quiet-like and I just took my eye off 'im for a moment—'

'Yes, well, don't take any more chances with this one,' replied Nick, putting a hand to his side.

'You're hurt,' said Eve, her voice not quite steady.

'No, no, merely winded,' he replied. 'He caught me on my wound, but no harm done, I hope. A capital hit, Evelina, well done, my love.' He reached out one hand for her and looked over her head to address the first mate. 'Briggs, take Lord Chelston away and bind him up securely this time— and be careful with his arm; I think 'tis broken. Now, Mr Granby, cram on all sail and let's see if Captain George has captured the *Merle*.'

'But how can he?' Eve frowned. 'The *Argos* is still in Rye Bay; I saw it myself, when we sailed from Hastings.'

'His ship may be at Rye, but Captain George and his men should be near Boulogne by now, as guests of Silas and his brother in the old galley!'

Chapter Twenty

There was no opportunity for Evelina to demand a full explanation. A freshening wind had sprung up and Nick was busy ordering his new crew to set course for Boulogne. The stars were already fading by the time they came upon the *Merle*, which was now flying a red customs ensign and pendant above its black sails. As the *Maestro* came alongside the lugger, Eve recognised several Monkhurst men on her deck and guessed they would be helping the customs officers to sail the lugger back to England. As the two ships prepared for the return journey Silas sprang nimbly over the rail on to the deck of the *Maestro*. When he saw Eve, he stopped and tugged his forelock.

'I'm glad to see thee well, mistress, and that's a fact. I tell thee straight I didn't think the cap'n's plan would work when he first suggested it—'

'Then damn your eyes for doubting me, Silas Brattee,' cried Nick, coming up. 'You'd best come below deck; we'll break out a bottle of rum and you can give me your report.'

Eve stepped forwards.

'I'm coming too.' She sensed the men's hesitation and added belligerently, 'I have been kidnapped, tied up and forced aboard this, this floating prison: I think I am entitled to know just what is going on!'

Silas looked stunned at this outburst, but Nick merely laughed.

'Very well,' he said holding out his hand to her, 'Come below, my dear, but you will find it very cramped!' He crossed to the companionway leading below deck. Eve hesitated at the dark, cavernous opening, wondering how she was going to negotiate the steep, ladder-like stairs and keep her dignity. 'Allow me,' said Nick, and before she could protest he threw her up over her shoulder and carried her to the lower deck where he set her down, grinning.

'Thank you,' she said through gritted teeth, 'You need not have done that. I managed the ladder in the boathouse tunnel and I could have managed this one.'

'I am sure you could,' he replied soothingly, 'but my way was much quicker—and far more enjoyable.'

Blushing furiously, she turned away as Silas climbed down the steps to join them. Nick lifted a lantern from its hook and led them to a small table. Moments later she was sitting beside him while he poured a red-brown liquid into three cups, saying as he did so, 'Well, Silas, tell me just how you enjoyed having a full complement of Revenue officers on board.'

The old sailor gave a slow smile. 'I think they considered our galley a bit beneath their dignity, Cap'n, but once we was underway they realised we could beat any sailing vessel on the sea last night, there being no wind, like.'

'So you rowed out in the galley to intercept the *Merle*?' asked Eve.

'Aye, mistress, that's right. The cap'n here daren't risk Lord Chelston spotting any ships *following* the lugger, so he sent a message to Captain George, asking him and his men to meet us at Monkhurst. From there we rode like the very devil across to Dimchurch, to me brother's place.' Silas tossed off his drink and gave a fat chuckle. 'You should've seen old Ephraim's face when we arrives with a parcel o' Revenue men! Thought we'd turned traitor, dang 'im, it took a fair few minutes to convince 'im to let us have the galley, but he come round in the end and we made good time after that. Sea was like a mill pond, she was.'

Silas paused and stared hard at his empty cup. His lips twitching, Nick finished his own drink and reached for the bottle. When he had filled Silas's mug and his own he looked at Eve, one eyebrow raised. She shook her head. She had taken a few small sips of rum and managed not to cough, although the thick, sweet liquor had made her eyes water. She realised she had eaten nothing since breakfast and wondered if it was wise to drink at all. She turned away from the mischievous glint in Nick's eyes and addressed Silas.

'But how did you find the *Merle*? After all, the sea is so…' she spread her hands and ended lamely '…big.'

'Lord love you, mistress, we just rowed for Boulogne like we always do—I mean…' he coughed, and looked a little sheepish. 'As we used to do in the old days. Then we just laid on the oars and waited for the *Merle* to come to us. Took some time, of course, with no wind for her sails. 'Twas dark and the galley so low in the water that the *Merle* didn't see us 'til it was too late. Cap'n George sends a volley o' shots across 'er decks and we boarded her with no trouble. French crew. No fight in 'em,' he ended almost sadly.

Eve took another cautious sip from her cup. The rum left a burning trail as she swallowed, but now there was a pleasant warmth spreading through her limbs. She leaned back and listened as Nick told Silas all that had happened aboard the *Maestro*. Their talk became steadily more animated, full of nautical terms as they passed from discussion of the night's activities to reminiscences of the adventures they had shared together in the King's navy. The little cabin rocked with their laughter.

'Aye, those were the days,' sighed Silas. 'I'll never forget '76, Cap'n—do you remember? Admiral Howe gave you command of your first ship.'

'How could I forget? We took Newport and Rhode Island, although we had to defend it from the French a couple of years later, before we could sail for home.'

'So we did—' nodded Silas as Nick refilled their mugs yet again. 'Rare times they was, so far from home and the enemy all around us. But we were all for 'ee, sir, every man jack of us wanted to sail with Cap'n Wyldfire. We'd all go to hell and back for you, Cap'n, 'cos we knowed you'd be there with us.'

Eve closed her eyes and let their talk wash over her. A tiny cloud was shadowing her heart. This was Nick's world, this life of adventure and danger. It was not hers. She heard the chink of glass against a cup. Nick was serving out more rum; most likely he had forgotten she was there. The cloud darkened as Bernard's words came back to her. *You cannot tame a tiger, only cage him.*

'Aye, they was good old days, surelye,' Silas was saying, his tone contemplative.

'And do you miss it?' asked Nick.

'That I do, sir. Pottering about near the shore ain't the same as sailing halfway round the world. No, the sea's a harsh mistress, Cap'n, but she don't ever let you go.'

Eve felt the depression settling more heavily inside her. She let out a sigh. Immediately Nick turned to her.

'Tired, my love?' The warmth in his voice was unmistakable; that was a comfort, but Eve realised just how weary she was, and when Nick called Richard Granby to escort her away she went quietly, content to rest in what Richard explained was once Lord Chelston's cabin. She lay down upon the narrow bunk, and even the muffled sounds of Lady Chelston's hysterical shrieks from her makeshift prison did not prevent her from falling into a deep, dreamless sleep.

Eve awoke some hours later to find that they were at Rye. Making her way to the deck, she found Richard Granby overseeing the crew. He turned and bowed when he saw her.

'Good morning, ma'am. The captain sends his apologies; he was obliged to meet with Captain George, and they are taking the prisoners to the gaol in the tower. He expects to return soon and begs that you will wait for him at the Mermaid. If you will give me but two minutes to instruct Mr Briggs, I will escort you.'

At the inn she found that Nick had already reserved a bedchamber and the genial landlord informed her that the small coffee room was also at her disposal. Eve declined any refreshment and allowed her host to escort her upstairs. The room set aside for her was the same one she had used on her previous visit, but she had no time for memories, because no sooner had she stepped through the door than Martha rushed across the room and enveloped her in a fierce, tearful embrace.

'Oh, Miss Eve, I'm that glad to see you! I was so frightened when I had the message from the captain, and he begged most politely that I should come to Rye to wait for you here. As if anything would stop me coming to you, mistress!'

'Yes, yes, thank you Martha.' Eve gently disentangled herself from her maid, resisting the urge to burst into tears. 'I am very glad you are here, and I shall be even more glad if you will fetch up some hot water for me to wash.'

'Of course, madam, immediately. And you will see that I have brought you some clean clothes. The master sent for his things, too, but without Rich—I mean Mr Granby to pack for him, we can only hope that we've brought the right clothes.'

'But where is his trunk? Oh…' Her spirits flagged a little. 'He bespoke a separate room, I suppose.'

'Why yes, Miss Eve, which the landlord tells me is just such a thing as the greatest lords and ladies do.' Martha chuckled. 'Nothing but the best for our Captain Wylder! But you are looking very pulled, mistress, and no wonder, being out on that nasty rough water all night. But don't you worry, we will soon have you feeling as fresh as a daisy. Um…' Martha stepped back, twisting her hands in her apron. 'I'm supposing you *all* came back safe? I mean, is Mr Granby…?' She trailed off, a rosy glow spreading over her round cheeks. Despite her low spirits a smile tugged at the corners of Eve's mouth.

'Richard Granby escorted me here,' she replied. 'It is very likely that he is still here at the inn.' She added innocently, 'Perhaps you could find him, and tell him I have no further need for him today.'

The blush on Martha's cheeks deepened. 'Ooh, yes, mistress, I will!' She dropped a series of hurried curtsies as she backed towards the door, then she was gone and Eve was alone.

She sat down on the edge of the bed and let the silence of the room settle around her. It was as if she was still for the first time in many, many weeks, for the first time since Nick Wylder had ridden into her life. She had lived a quiet and unexacting existence at Makerham; the most exciting thing in her life had been a short visit to Tunbridge Wells. But Nick's arrival in her sheltered world had changed all that. He was Captain Wyldfire indeed. She had been pitched headlong into the sort of adventure that should have left her swooning. Only she had not fainted away. Instead, she had relished the excitement. She regretted nothing. Except, perhaps, that she had fallen in love with an adventurer. And adventurers, like tigers, could not change their nature.

Eve wrapped her arms across her stomach. She could not tame her tiger, but neither would she confine him. To do so would surely kill any love he had for her. No, he must be free to go his own way, however much it hurt her.

Chapter Twenty-One

It was late morning before Eve received a message from Nick. She was sitting in the small coffee room when Martha came in with a note. Eve almost snatched it from her hands.

'Hmm,' she said, scanning it quickly. 'Typically high-handed. No apology, he merely says he will be here as soon as he can. *"I have ordered dinner to be served in your room."* Hah! I am tempted to countermand that.'

'Ooh, Miss Eve, I beg you won't! The captain don't want you eating with the common folk.'

'We could use this room. Well,' she said as Martha shifted uncomfortably from one foot to the other, 'why not?'

'Well, mistress, you see, Richard and me…' Martha almost squirmed before her.

'Ah, I understand,' said Eve, trying not to smile. 'You are planning a private dinner with Mr Granby. As your employer, I should perhaps ask him if his intentions towards you are honourable.'

'No, Miss Eve, pray don't do anything like that! 'Tis only a dinner, after all, and better for the both of us than listening to the coarse talk in the kitchens. I was so worried about him, you see…'

'Very well, Martha, but you must promise to behave yourself.' Eve looked out of the window. 'Now, the sun is shining and I would like some air. We will go out.'

'But what if the captain should come looking for you, Miss Eve?'

She put up her chin. 'Then he will not find me. Let him kick his heels and wait for *me*. Fetch my wrap, please Martha, and your own. We are going to explore the town, then we shall walk to the church and admire its fine architecture!'

Eve returned from her outing much refreshed and if she was disappointed to find that Nick was not waiting for her she would not admit it. It was still early and she sent Martha away to find out if it was possible for her to bathe before dinner. While the inn's servants built up the fire and toiled up the winding stairs with pails of water, Eve turned her attention to the clothes Martha was laying out for her.

'That is my cream polonaise, Martha. Have you nothing less…dashy?'

'No, ma'am, only the walking dress that you have been wearing all day.'

'But the cream gown is part of my trousseau.'

Martha gave her a sly look. 'Why so it is, mistress, and very romantical, too.'

Eve hunched a shoulder and turned away, knowing that any remonstrance would be wasted and would most likely lead to her own discomfiture. She allowed Martha to undress her and stepped into the hip bath to enjoy the hot scented water. It was very relaxing, but as the dinner hour approached her anxieties increased. When she had finished bathing she put on a clean chemise and allowed Martha to pin up her hair. Eve glanced at the creamy silk gown laid out on the bed. Its low neckline seemed to mock her.

As the maid picked up the linen stays she said, 'Lace me up tightly, Martha.'

'Very well, ma'am.'

The feel of the linen and whalebone enclosing her ribs brought to mind visions of knights in stiff, unyielding armour. Not unlike her own forthcoming meeting with her husband. 'Tighter,' she ordered, adding very quietly, 'I do not want to enjoy myself tonight.'

Martha helped her into the polonaise and arranged the folds of the skirt becomingly over the rose-coloured petticoat. It was not until the bodice was fastened that Eve realised the effect of the tight-lacing was not at all what she desired. She might feel restricted and unyielding, but the confining stays accentuated her tiny waist and pushed up her breasts so that they filled the gown's low neckline in a way that would draw any male eye. And Nick was most definitely male. Well, there was no time to ask Martha to undress her again now.

'Did you pack a kerchief for me, Martha?'

'Aye, ma'am, but—'

'Find it, if you please.'

Five minutes later Eve regarded with satisfaction the fine muslin kerchief that covered her bosom.

'There, that is much better.' Much safer. 'Now, Martha, if you will have dinner fetched up and make sure they remove the bath and all signs of my ablutions, you can take yourself off and join Richard Granby.'

Eve did not know whether she desired or dreaded Nick's appearance. She paced about the room as the hip bath, water and towels were carried away and the small table pulled out in readiness for dinner. Martha and the inn's servants moved quickly and efficiently, lighting the candles, drawing the curtains and building up the fire to ward off the slight chill of the evening. She watched them at work, reasoning that the longer they took over their tasks the more she could put off seeing Nick.

The hasty, booted footsteps outside the door told her she was mistaken.

Nick strode in, bringing with him a sense of urgency that had the servants hurrying through their tasks and scuttling away.

'Pray forgive the informality, madam.' He bowed to her. 'Will you allow me to dine with you in this attire?'

Eve's heart lurched as she looked at him. He was dressed as she had first seen him, in buckskins and topboots. His exquisitely-tailored riding jacket and the snow-white linen of his shirt and cravat signified the fashionable town beau, but his sun-browned face and the wicked twinkle in his blue eyes belonged to the adventurer. He spread his hands and said apologetically, 'I sent word to Monkhurst for my clothes to be brought here, but this is the best I can muster.'

She felt herself responding to his lazy smile. 'Then it shall suffice, sir.' She became aware that Martha was hovering by the door and waved her away. 'Yes, yes, you may go, Martha. I shall call for you if I need you.' She glanced at Nick, feeling awkward now they were alone. 'I believe she is dining with your man this evening, sir. I hope you do not object?'

'Not at all. He confided to me that he wants to make an honest woman of her, so I suggested he should wine and dine her in the coffee room tonight.'

'Oh. Is that why we must eat here?'

'No, sweetheart. We are eating here because it is more convenient.'

She observed his quick glance towards the bed and a little

spurt of excitement flamed within her. Quickly she damped it down. He came closer, a faint crease between his brows.

'What is that thing round your neck?'

'What? O-oh, this.' She touched the muslin kerchief. 'It—um—seemed a little cool in here.'

'Well the fire is blazing well enough now, so you won't need it any longer.' Before she realised what he was about he had grasped the kerchief and pulled it away. She felt the colour rush to her cheeks as his eyes fell on the full, rounded bosom. He put his hands on her shoulders, saying softly, 'Now why should you want to hide such beauty?'

He lowered his dark head and she felt his lips brush the soft skin just above the rim of her bodice. Immediately her breasts tightened. They seemed to want to push right out of their confinement, to offer themselves up to his waiting mouth. The breath caught in her throat. Dear Heaven, why did he affect her so?

'I...did not want to distract you,' she managed, her voice croaking pitifully. Another deep breath, another attempt to control her wayward senses. 'We have things to discuss, sir.'

He raised his head. 'Ah.'

A scratching at the door heralded the arrival of their dinner. As the two waiters set down their trays Nick escorted Eve to the table. His fingers burned through the silk sleeve of her dress. Heavens; a single touch and she was reduced to a quivering wreck! She looked at the food set out on the table; soup, a brace of pigeons, a dish of mushrooms, apple pie—her appetite had disappeared.

Nick took his seat at the table and watched Eve toying with her food. Something was amiss. She was upset; he could see it in her face, in the droop of her shoulders. She would tell him, before the night was out. Night. He wanted to pick her up now and carry her over to the bed and make love to her. Just the thought of it aroused him. She had been right to put that muslin about her shoulders; the sight of her soft round breasts pushing up from her gown was too damned distracting. He smiled, hoping he looked reassuring and not leering as he poured more wine into their glasses.

'I suggest we postpone our…talk, until we have eaten.'

He set to with a will, but he did not ignore her. He carved a few tasty slices of pigeon to tempt her appetite, spooned some of the mushrooms on to her plate and cut a sliver of the apple pie. She ate it dutifully, and he was relieved to see a little colour return to her cheeks.

The waiters brought in another set of dishes, including a ragout of mutton and a sweet pastry. Eve was once more in command of herself and they managed to talk of commonplace things until they were alone once again.

'So, is your investigation concluded now?' she asked him, nibbling on a pastry.

'Yes.' The tip of her tongue was running across her bottom lip in a most sensuous fashion. He dragged his eyes away. 'Yes,' he said again. 'I have made my reports. Captain George will escort the prisoners to London. I shall be obliged to go to town at some stage, but my work here is finished.'

She nodded. 'You will be anxious to return to your home, then. In Yorkshire.'

'There are matters there that require my attention, undoubtedly.' Now where was all this leading? 'Estate management can be tedious, I know, but it must be done.'

She was avoiding his eyes, looking into her wineglass as she murmured, 'You would much rather be at sea, I think.'

'Evelina—' He reached for her hand across the table, but she snatched it away. As the waiters returned at that moment he let the matter drop, but he waited with impatience for the table to be cleared.

'That will do,' he said at length. 'Leave the bottle and the glasses. You need not come back again.' He smiled again at Eve. 'Will you take a little more wine with me, madam? A toast to a job well done.'

'Very well, sir. But now I think we should—we must—talk.'

He rose from the table and held out his hand to her. 'Then shall we sit by the fire?'

He led her to one of the two armchairs placed on either side of the hearth. She sank down and spent a few moments rearranging her skirts. One dusky curl fell forwards and lay across the white skin of her shoulder. He resisted the temptation to reach out and touch it and instead sat down opposite her.

'Now, my love, what is it you want to say to me?'

She did not answer him, but kept her eyes lowered, her fingers smoothing the creases from her petticoats.

'Eve?'

She looked up then, her dark eyes fixed upon him. 'You said you must return to Yorkshire soon. I understand that. After all it is your home. I wondered if, perhaps, when you go north, you would allow me to remain at Monkhurst.'

Nick sat very still. He had the strangest sensation that his world was teetering, about to fall. Now, at last, when he knew what he wanted, was she about to snatch it all away from him? He said quietly, 'You regret our marriage.'

She looked up quickly. 'No! That is…' She sighed and waved one of her hands in a gesture of hopelessness. 'You married me to get Monkhurst. I know that, and I am not angry about it. I know that you did not intend to—to consummate the union. I believe you truly thought that if…if we did not suit, then the marriage could be annulled.' She gave a crooked little smile. 'It did not quite work out like that, did it? We are bound, now. Irrevocably.'

He shrugged. A cold hand was squeezing at his heart. 'We are man and wife, sweetheart. For better, for worse. Until death.'

Silently he cursed himself; he had not meant the words to sound so harsh. He saw the flicker of alarm cross her face. She jumped up from her chair and began to pace about the room.

'But that's so cruel, Nick. So unjust. We are too different. You crave adventure, excitement; catching smugglers, fighting for a cause, risking your life—it is what you do. I watched you, on board the yacht, dealing with the sailors. You are a natural leader, Nick. And—and when you were talking to Silas, about your life at sea, it all became clear to me. You miss it already.' She turned to him, her eyes dark and troubled. 'A life of quiet domesticity would not suit you, Nick. You would be miserable, and I do not want you to be miserable. You must be free to do as you wish. I know that, but I cannot bear the uncertainty of your life, knowing each time you ride off that you might not return. I would rather s-say goodbye now and live quietly at Monkhurst than have that recurring agony.'

Nick closed his eyes and breathed out slowly. The world was righting itself again. 'I thought we might go adventuring together.'

Eve put her hands over her face and shook her head. Why would he not listen? Why did he make it so difficult for her? She had to make him understand.

'No, no,' she said. 'Do you not see? I would be a hindrance to you.' Her hands dropped to her sides. 'This time you risked everything to rescue me. I know, I like to think, that you would do the same again.' She gave a sad little smile. 'But you will not always be able to save the world and to save me, too.'

He was out of his chair so quickly that she only had time

to blink. He stood before her and put his hands on her shoulders. 'Is that what you think?' he asked her. 'That I cannot be happy unless I am courting danger? My sweet life, that may have been the case in the past, but not any more. My life changed when I met you; suddenly I had someone to live for.' He gazed down at her, his eyes more serious than she had ever seen them. 'Eve, when Bernard Shawcross put that bullet in me, I thought it better to let everyone think I was no longer alive. I thought we would round up Chelston and his gang and I could get back to you without you knowing anything about it. Then you wrote to tell me that your grandfather had died. That was the worst time of my life, sweetheart; I couldn't be with you to comfort you in your loss and, even worse, I had put you in danger. I vowed then that when this was all over I would never put you at risk again. And I mean it, Eve. I intend to be a model husband from now on.'

Eve blinked, trying to clear the hot tears that crowded her eyes and prickled her throat, making it difficult to speak.

'I would like to believe you, Nick, but I cannot. I heard what Silas said, about the sea. It never lets go…'

He caught her agitated hands and held them firm, his thumbs circling on the soft pads of her wrists, calming her. 'Silas is a sailor to his core, but I—' a sudden smile lit his eyes. 'I am more of an adventurer. I enjoyed the navy, but I can leave it for a new challenge and there are plenty of those to be had. We are living in exciting times, Evelina; in my native Yorkshire there are manufactories springing up for spinning and weaving, with the new canals ready to carry as much as can be produced to London or to the coast. England is changing, Eve, and we should be part of that. I do not need to leave you, sweetheart; there are more than enough challenges for a man here at home, especially one with a wife at his side.' He squeezed her fingers. 'Well, what do you say? I am offering you everything, Eve, my heart as well as my hand. I love you, you know. Will you throw in your lot with me?'

She stared into his face. There was no sign of the devil-may-care look now, only an anxious, earnest expression of a man awaiting his fate. That vulnerability was her undoing, it demolished the last of her defences.

'Yes,' she whispered, 'Oh, yes, Nick!'

Slowly the earnest expression disappeared, replaced by a mixture of love and triumph and happiness. He gathered her in his arms and she melted into him. His mouth slid over hers and he kissed her in a thorough, unhurried manner that had her senses reeling. She leaned against him, dizzy and breathless. She felt his hands on her shoulders.

'Open your eyes,' he murmured. 'I need you to stand up.'

He was unlacing her bodice, his long fingers drawing out the strings with a smooth, steady rhythm.

'What are you doing?'

The wicked glance he gave made her racing pulse even more erratic. 'This is a beautiful gown, sweetheart, but it is in my way.'

Heat pooled low in her belly. It was an effort to keep still while the laces whipped out of the remaining eyelets and he pushed the bodice away from her shoulders. The silk fell to the floor with a whisper and she felt herself blush. The thought flashed through her mind that her cheeks probably matched her rose-coloured petticoats. She began to unbutton Nick's waistcoat. 'Sauce for the goose, Captain Wyldfire,' she murmured, provoking a shadow of desire in his blue eyes.

Once she had helped him out of his jacket and waist-coat his hands slipped around her waist and stopped. He threw up his head, an arrested look on his face. 'What's this?' He squeezed the large pad of wadding tied to her back.

'It is a false rump.' She choked on a laugh. 'It is all the fashion.'

'Well, we can do without it,' he said, undoing the tapes and casting it aside. 'You have a perfect rump without it.' As if to prove his words he cupped her buttocks with his hands and pulled her to him. She gasped, feeling him hard and aroused against her belly. He lowered his head and trailed a line of butterfly kisses down her neck, causing her to moan softly. His hands moved up again to her waist. 'I've a mind to take a knife to these stays,' he muttered as his fingers tugged as the ribbons. 'This is layer upon layer of armour.'

She laughed, feeling her power over him. 'That is exactly it, to protect me from your wicked ways.'

Nick tilted up her chin and gazed at her. 'Do you *want* to be protected from me?'

Her insides had turned to water. Eve ran her tongue across her lower lip and shook her head. She did not think she could speak. His smouldering glance held her eyes while his fingers eased the ribbons loose. The friction vibrated against her body, sending ripples of pleasure through her limbs. Once the confining stays had been cast off he pushed aside her chemise and gathered her to him, pressing her flesh against his. For a heartbeat she remained frozen in pleasure, arching towards him, then the world exploded around them. Nick was kissing her neck, her face, trailing hot kisses over her eyelids. They were both gasping, eyes wild as the remainder of their clothes were discarded. With a growl Nick swung Eve into his arms and carried her to the bed. She clung to him, pulling him down on top of her, wrapping her legs around his waist as if to bind him to her for ever.

She drove her fingers through his hair, guiding his lips back to her own where she gave him back kiss for kiss. This was no gentle embrace, it was fierce, furious possession and Eve revelled in it. She ran her fingers down his back, exploring the contours, delighting in the iron muscles rippling under the skin. Nick's hands roamed her body, exploring and caressing, gently arousing her until she groaned, arching her back and thrusting her hips forward, inviting him in. He shifted his body, covering her, their bodies moving together, faster, harder until Eve could no longer control her own responses. She dug her nails into Nick's broad back, crying out as a spasm of pure pleasure rippled through her. She heard Nick shout out. He gave one last, final thrust and she felt herself falling, tumbling as if from a great height.

Nick rolled over and collapsed beside her on the tangled bedsheets. He reached out and caught her hand, twining his fingers with hers.

'Well, madam, are you satisfied?'

She turned her head to look at him. His naked chest was rising and falling rapidly, his skin gleaming and golden in the candlelight. She smiled. 'For the moment.'

He raised himself on one elbow and gazed down at her. 'For the moment, hmm?' He drew one finger lightly across her breasts. They tightened immediately at his touch. 'You are going to be a challenge, Mrs Wylder.'

She rested her hands on her belly. 'I think we may have another challenge ahead of us, Nick. It is too early to be certain, but…'

He stared at her, a slight crease in his brows, then his eyes lit up and he gave a wide, unstoppable grin. 'Oh, lord, I never meant for *that* to happen.'

She sat up. 'Oh, you are not happy,' she said, dismayed.

'Happy?' He caught her to him. 'I think I must be the

happiest man alive! Oh, but should you not be resting? Should I not even be kissing you, or…you know?'

She blushed at the thought of 'you know', her toes curling up with pleasure. 'I do not believe we must give up our pleasures just yet, my love.'

He lowered her back down on to the bed and kissed her nose. 'Now that is a good thing. Because I have just realised that we have been apart for most of our married life. We have some time to make up.'

Eve allowed her glance to stray downwards. A tiny, mischievous smile curved her lips. 'Well, we have all night, my love…'

* * * * *

Historical™

tantalising period romances

DID YOU PURCHASE THIS BOOK WITHOUT A COVER?
If you did, you should be aware it is **stolen property** as it was
reported 'unsold and destroyed' by a retailer.
Neither the author nor the publisher has received any payment
for this book.

First Published 2010
First Australian Paperback Edition 2010
ISBN 978 1 742 55393 1

THE EARL'S RUNAWAY BRIDE © 2010 by Sarah Mallory
Philippine Copyright 2010
Australian Copyright 2010
New Zealand Copyright 2010
Except for use in any review, the reproduction or utilisation of this work in
whole or in part in any form by any electronic, mechanical or other means,
now known or hereafter invented, including xerography, photocopying and
recording, or in any information storage or retrieval system, is forbidden
without the permission of the publisher, Harlequin Mills & Boon®, Locked
Bag 7002, Chatswood D.C. N.S.W., Australia 2067.

This book is sold subject to the condition that it shall not, by way of trade or
otherwise, be lent, resold, hired out or otherwise circulated without the prior
consent of the publisher in any form of binding or cover other than that in
which it is published and without a similar condition including this condition
being imposed on the subsequent purchaser.

All rights reserved including the right of reproduction in whole or in part in
any form. This edition is published in arrangement with Harlequin Books
S.A..

This is a work of fiction. Names, characters, places, and incidents are either
the product of the author's imagination or are used fictitiously, and any
resemblance to actual persons, living or dead, business establishments,
events, or locales is entirely coincidental.

Published by
Harlequin Mills & Boon®
Level 5
15 Help Street
CHATSWOOD NSW 2067
AUSTRALIA

® and ™ are trademarks owned by Harlequin Enterprises Limited or its
corporate affiliates and used by others under licence. Trademarks marked
with an ® are registered in Australia and in other countries. Contact
admin_legal@Harlequin.ca for details.

Cover art used by arrangement with Harlequin Books S.A.. All rights
reserved.

Printed and bound in Australia by
McPherson's Printing Group

THE EARL'S
RUNAWAY BRIDE

Sarah Mallory

Author Note

The Retreat to Corunna is one of the less well-known episodes of the Napoleonic Wars. The Spanish allied armies had been overwhelmed, and Sir John Moore found himself and his British troops alone in northern Spain and facing Emperor Napoleon's victorious French army. Moore retreated to the port of Corunna and managed to keep his exhausted men together as they struggled across the mountains during the depths of winter. He fought off the French at Corunna long enough to allow the British transport ships to come into the harbour and carry the remains of the army safely back to England. Traveling that same route in January 2009, I realised just how awful that journey across the mountains must have been. Many soldiers perished from cold and hunger, stragglers were cut down by the French and the ragged, starving wretches marching back into Corunna roused the sympathy of their Spanish hosts.

The story of *The Earl's Runaway Bride* begins amongst the mayhem and confusion of that winter in Corunna. Felicity Bourne is alone and penniless in the city, and when she is rescued by a dashing British soldier she thinks him the hero of her dreams. Unfortunately, those dreams turn into a nightmare and she is separated from Nathan Carraway for five long years, until the premature Peace Celebrations of 1814 bring them together again in London. Nathan and Felicity are both scarred by their wartime experiences. They must learn to forgive the past and work together for their future happiness.

I do hope you enjoy *The Earl's Runaway Bride*. As an author I set scenes and drop my hapless characters into predicaments that I would certainly not wish to experience, but they battle through, survive and succeed, often in ways that surprise even me!

DEDICATION

For my editor, Lucy, with thanks for all your help
and support.

Chapter One

Felicity was angry, blazingly angry. All her terror and anxiety at being alone and penniless in a strange country was forgotten, superseded by rage that the portmanteau packed with her last remaining possessions had been snatched away from her. Without a second thought she gave chase, following the ragged Spaniard in his leather waistcoat away from the Plaza and into a maze of narrow alleys that crowded about the harbour at Corunna. She did not stop; even when a sudden gust of wind caught her bonnet and tore it off her head she ran on, determined to regain her property. Only when they neared the harbour and she found herself in an unfamiliar square bounded by warehouses did she realise the danger.

She saw her bag handed to a young boy who ran off with it while the thief turned to face her, an evil grin splitting his face. Felicity stopped. A quick glance over her shoulder revealed two more menacing figures blocking her escape. Felicity summoned up every ounce of authority to say haughtily, 'That is my bag. Give it back to me now and we shall say no more about this.'

The response was a rough hand on her back, pushing her forward. She stumbled and fell to her knees. Quickly she scrambled up, twisting away as one of the men reached out to grab her. There was only the one man in front of her, if she could get past him—with a guttural laugh he caught her by her hair and yanked her back, throwing her into the arms of his two accomplices. Felicity fought wildly, but it was impossible to shake off their iron grip. They held her fast as the little man with his yellow teeth and stinking breath came close, leering at her as he ripped open her pelisse.

She closed her eyes, trying to blot out their cruel laughter and ugly jests. Then she heard another voice—slow, deep and distinctly British.

'Move away from the lady, my good fellows.'

Felicity's eyes flew open. Beyond the thief stood a tall British officer, resplendent in his scarlet tunic. He looked completely at his ease, regarding the scene with a slightly detached air, but when her tormentor pulled a wicked-looking knife from his belt the officer grinned.

'I asked you politely,' he said, drawing his sword. 'But now I really must insist.'

With a roar the two men holding Felicity released her and rushed forward to join their comrade. She backed against the wall and watched the red-coated officer swiftly despatch her attackers. He moved with surprising speed and agility. A flick of his sword cut across the first man's wrist and the knife fell from his useless fingers. A second man screamed as that wicked blade slashed his arm and when the officer turned his attention to the third, the man took to his heels and fled, swiftly followed by his companions.

The officer wiped his blade and put it away. Sunlight sliced through a narrow gap between the houses and caught the soldier in a sudden shaft of light. His hair gleamed like polished mahogany in the sunshine and he was grinning down at her, amusement shining in his deep brown eyes as if the last few minutes had been some entertaining sport rather than a desperate fight. He was, she realised in a flash, the embodiment of the hero she had always dreamed of.

'Are you hurt, madam?'

His voice was deep and warm, wrapping around her like velvet. She shook her head.

'I—do not think so. Who are you?'

'Major Nathan Carraway, at your service.'

'Then I thank you for your timely assistance, Major.'

'Come along.' He held out his arm to her. 'We should get out of here in case they decide to come back with their friends.'

'But my portmanteau—'

'I think you should resign yourself to its loss, madam. Was it very valuable?'

'Priceless.' She swallowed. 'It contains everything I own in the whole world.' Suddenly she felt quite sick as she realised the enormity of her situation. 'What am I going to do now? I have nothing, no one…'

Instinctively she turned to the man at her side. Looking into his eyes she was conscious of a tug of attraction, a sudden conviction that in this man she had found a friend. Her fear and anger faded away. He gave her a slow smile.

'You have me,' he said.

'Good morning, miss. I've brought your hot chocolate.'

Felicity stirred, reluctant to leave her dream, but when the maid threw back the shutters her room was flooded with sunlight, banishing any hope of going back to sleep.

'What time is it, Betsy?'

'Eight o'clock, miss. With Master John and Master Simon gone off to school you said not to wake you too early this morning.'

Felicity sat up. She hadn't bargained for the extra hour's sleep being haunted by her dreams!

She did not linger in her bed but dressed quickly and

made her way down to the schoolroom. It was eerily quiet: after four years of looking after two energetic youngsters and watching them grow into schoolboys it was not surprising that she now missed their presence. As their governess she had grown very fond of them, and they had provided her with an excellent distraction from her constant, aching sadness.

'Fee, Fee, where are you?'

Felicity heard Lady Souden's soft calls and hurried across the room to open the door.

'Do you need me? I was just tidying up.'

Lady Souden entered the sunny schoolroom and looked around, sighing.

'It does seem so *quiet* with the boys away at school, does it not? But you are no longer the governess here, Felicity.' She rested her hands upon her stomach. 'At least not until this little one is of an age to need you.'

'And that will not be for some years yet,' observed Felicity, smiling.

'I know, but oh, Fee, is it not exciting? The boys are darlings, and I adore being their stepmama, but I cannot *wait* to have a baby of my own.' Lydia shook her head, setting her guinea-gold curls dancing. 'After five years I thought it would never happen! But that is not what I wanted to say to you. Come away now; you do not need to be toiling up here.'

Felicity scooped up another handful of books from the table.

'This isn't toiling, Lydia, I enjoy being useful. Besides, the boys will still use this room when they come home, so it is only fitting that it should be as they left it.'

'If it is to be as they left it you had best spread their toys over the floor and pull *all* the books from the shelves! Oh, Fee, do leave that now and come into the garden with me. It is such a lovely morning and I want to talk to you.'

'Oh, but another five minutes—'

'No, now. It is a command!'

As Felicity accompanied Lady Souden down the stairs she reflected that few people could have such an undemanding mistress. They had been firm friends at school, and when Felicity had come to her, penniless and desperate to find work, Lydia had cajoled her doting new husband into employing her as a governess to his two young sons—Lydia's stepchildren. Felicity knew she was very fortunate. Sir James was a considerate employer and she was thankful that her excellent education allowed her to fulfil her duties as governess to his satisfaction. So pleased had he been with her performance that when the boys finally went away to school he raised no objections to Lydia's suggestion that Felicity should stay on at Souden Hall as her companion. The arrangement worked extremely well, for Sir James was often away from home and said it was a comfort to him to know that his wife was not alone. Felicity's only complaint was that she had so little to do, but when she taxed Lydia with this, Lady Souden merely laughed and told her to enjoy herself.

Now, walking in the shrubbery arm in arm with Lydia, Felicity gave a little sigh of contentment.

'Happy?' asked Lydia.

Felicity hesitated. She was content: there was a world of difference between that and true happiness, but very few people could aspire to such a luxury. She said, 'Who could not be in such lovely surroundings? The gardens here at Souden are so beautiful in the spring. Are you still planning to lay out a knot-garden? I have been studying the pattern books in the library and would dearly like to help you draw it up.'

'Oh, yes, if you please, but I am afraid that will have to wait. James has written to say he wants me to join him in London next month. For the Peace Celebrations.'

'Oh. Oh, well, while you are away I could—'

'You are to come with me, Fee.'

Felicity stopped.

'Oh no, surely that is not necessary.'

'*Very* necessary,' said Lydia, taking her hands. 'With the boys at school there is no reason for you to hide yourself away here. Besides, you have read the news sheets, you know as well as I that any number of important personages will be in London for these celebrations: the Emperor of Russia and his sister the Grand Duchess of Oldenburg, the young Prussian princes and—oh, too many to name them all now! And James has already been informed that he will be expected to entertain them all. Just think of it, Fee, dinners, soirées and parties—dear James has also said he wants us to hold a ball! So I shall need you to help me with all the arrangements. I could not possibly cope with it all.'

'Should you be coping with any of it when you are with child?'

'Oh, Fee, I am not *ill*! I am more likely to die of boredom if I stay here with nothing to do. Besides, the baby is not due until the autumn and the celebrations will be over by then. Do not look so horrified, Fee, look upon this as a rare treat.'

'A treat! Lydia, you know I am…not good in company. I fear I should let you down.'

'Nonsense. You have very good manners, it is merely that you are out of practice—and that is because your horrid uncle dragged you away from the Academy to make you his drudge!'

'Lydia! Uncle Philip was not horrid, he was…devout.'

'He was a tyrant,' returned Lydia with uncharacteristic severity. 'He tried to beat all the joy out of you.'

Felicity hesitated.

'It is true my uncle considered all forms of pleasure a sin,' she conceded, 'but that was only because he was deeply religious.'

'Then he should have hired a *deeply religious* servant to take with him rather than dragging you off to deepest Africa!'

Felicity laughed at that.

'But he didn't! We only got as far as northern Spain! Poor

Uncle Philip, he convinced himself that the Spanish Catholics were as much in need of saving as any African tribe, but I have always suspected the truth was he could not face another sea journey.'

'Well, it was very wrong of him to take you away instead of giving you the opportunity to marry and have children—'

Felicity put up her hand in a little gesture of defence; she did not want to contemplate what might have been.

'What's done is done,' she said quietly. 'I am very happy here at Souden, and I would much rather stay here while you go to London.'

'But I shall need you!'

Lydia's plaintive tone carried Felicity back to their schooldays, when her friend had often begged her for company. Poor Lydia could never bear to be alone. Now, as then, Felicity found it impossible to resist her. Sensing her weakening, Lydia pressed her hand.

'Do say you will come, Fee—you are so *good* at organising parties.'

'But you will not expect me to *attend* any of these parties.'

'Not unless you want to, my dear.'

'You know there is nothing I would want less!'

'Then you may remain behind the scenes, invisible.'

Felicity laughed at her.

'But I cannot possibly be your paid companion if I never leave my room. Sir James will not countenance such a thing!'

'I shall tell him that you have a morbid fear of strangers,' said Lydia. 'He will understand that, for he has a cousin who is very much the same, only because he is a man, and rich, it is *quite* acceptable for him to be a recluse. And James knows how much I rely upon you, especially now that I am increasing.'

'Perhaps you should not go at all,' said Felicity, clutching at straws.

Lydia gave a little gurgle of laughter.

'But of course I should! I have never felt better, and the doctor says I must not pamper myself but carry on very much as normal. Oh, *do* say you will come with me, Felicity: you are very necessary to my comfort, you know.'

Felicity could not resist Lydia's beseeching look.

'You have been so kind to me that I cannot refuse you.'

'So you promise you will come to town with me?'

'Yes, I give you my word.'

Lydia gave a huge sigh.

'I am so relieved!' She linked arms with Felicity again and gave a little tug. 'Come along, now: we must keep moving or we shall grow too chilled. It is only April, after all.'

They walked on in amicable silence for a few more minutes.

'Is that what you wished to say to me,' asked Felicity, 'that we are to go to town?'

'Well, yes, but there is a little more than that, my dear.'

'Now, Lydia, what mischief are you planning?'

'None, I promise you, but there is something you should know.' Lady Souden gave her arm a little shake. 'Remember, Fee, you have given me your word!'

'Very well. Tell me.'

'The Earl of Rosthorne will be in town.'

Felicity's heart lurched. The Earl of Rosthorne—Nathan Carraway, her handsome hero. The man who still haunted her dreams, but had proved to be a master of seduction. She swallowed nervously, trying to remain calm.

'How do you know that?'

'James wrote to me—'

'Lydia, you haven't told him—!'

'Of course not, I promised I would not give you away. No, his letter was full of the plans for the celebrations. He said that Carraway had been ordered to London, not only because he is now Earl of Rosthorne, but because he is— or was—a military man and Prinny is quite *desperate* to impress. The royal parks are to be opened, there will be displays, and fireworks, and—oh, Felicity, it will be so exciting—are you not the *teeniest* bit curious to see it all?'

'Not if there is the teeniest risk of meeting Lord Rosthorne!'

Lydia turned her wide, blue-eyed gaze upon her.

'I know he treated you badly, my dear, but are you not curious to see him again?'

Felicity hesitated. Nathan had rescued her, given up his lodging for her, bought her new clothes. He had taught her to love him and then broken her heart.

'No. I have no desire to see him again.'

'Felicity, you are blushing. You still care for him.'

'I do not! It was five years ago, Lydia. I am over him.'

'Well, perhaps you no longer cry yourself to sleep every night, as you did when we first took you in, but at times, when you are sitting quietly, there is that faraway look in your eye—'

Felicity laughed.

'Lydia, you are too romantic! That faraway look was most likely exhaustion, having had the care of two energetic boys for the day!'

'Well, it does not matter what you say, I have the liveliest curiosity to see the man who—'

'Lydia!' Felicity stopped abruptly. 'Lydia, you promised me when I came to you that you would respect my secret.'

'And so I shall, my love, but—'

'Pray let us say no more about the odious Lord Rosthorne! If you insist upon my coming to town with you then I will do so, but pray understand that upon no account must he know I am there. It would be embarrassing to everyone.' She swallowed hard. 'I am dead to him now.'

Lydia threw her arms around her, enveloping Felicity in a warm, scented embrace. 'Oh, my dear friend, you know I would do nothing that would make you miserable!'

'No, of course you would not. Not intentionally, that is.' Felicity glanced up. 'The rain clouds are gathering. The sun will soon disappear; I think we should go indoors now.'

They did not speak of London again, or of the Earl of Rosthorne, but when Felicity retired to her room that night he was there, in her head, as close and as real as ever.

'The Earl of Rosthorne, sir.'

The butler's sonorous tones filled the small, book-lined study, investing the announcement with considerable gravitas. Nathan squared his shoulders. After twelve months he was still not comfortable with the title. The gentleman sitting behind the large mahogany desk jumped up immediately and came forward to meet him. Nathan regarded him with interest. He knew Sir James Souden only by reputation but even if he had not heard that the man was an active supporter of Lord Wellesley, he would have been disposed to like him, for there was a look of intelligence and humour in his face and an energy in that lean body. Here was a man who was used to getting things done. He was smiling now at Nathan and waving him towards a chair.

'Welcome, my lord, and thank you for coming so promptly.'

Nathan bowed.

'Your message was waiting for me when I arrived in town this morning, Sir James.'

'Ah, but knowing the object of this meeting I would not have been surprised if you had put it off.'

The twinkle in the older man's eyes drew a wry grin from Nathan.

'Always best to attack the unpalatable without delay, I find.'

'Spoken like a true military man.' Sir James gestured towards the decanters lined up on a side table. 'You'll take a glass with me, my lord? I've a very fine cognac—stolen from the French, of course, so you might appreciate it.'

'I would, thank you.'

'So,' said Sir James, when the glasses had been filled and his guest was sitting in one of the comfortable padded armchairs that faced the desk. 'So, my lord, how much have you been told?'

'Only that his Highness wants me to help with the entertaining of his royal visitors.'

'Aye. He's turning the town into a damned bear-garden for the summer,' said Sir James, shaking his head. 'But there, it's all in a good cause. Peace, don't you know, so I suppose we shouldn't complain.'

Nathan sipped at his brandy. It was smooth and aromatic and definitely not to be hurried.

'I am at a loss to know why he has summoned me here,' he said at last. 'I would have thought there were hostesses enough in London to entertain all the crowned heads of Europe. Mine is a bachelor establishment; my mother does not come to town. You may know she is an invalid and spends all her time at Rosthorne Hall—'

'Oh, his Highness ain't looking for you to give parties and all that sort of nonsense. The ladies will be falling over themselves to do that—and in fact I have asked Lady Souden to come to town for that very purpose—not that she needs any persuading to hold a party! But the Regent wants military men around him, especially to accompany Marshal Blücher: the old Prussian is so highly esteemed that even Prinny is in awe of him. There will be so many of 'em, you see: Blücher, the King of Prussia and all those princes, not to mention Tsar Alexander. And his sister, of course, the Grand Duchess… So we are all recruited to help: an army of attendants to ensure that his royal guests are not left to themselves for a moment. Your first task is to head up the Tsar's escort from Dover. I know, I know, my boy; I can see from your face that you don't like the idea.'

'You are right,' replied Nathan. 'I begin to wish I had never left the army!'

Sir James laughed and got up to refill their glasses.

'Do you miss it, my lord, the military life?'

'It was the only life I had ever known, until last year. I obtained my commission in the Guards when I was sixteen.'

'The title came as a surprise?'

Nathan nodded. 'Quite. The old Earl, my uncle, had three healthy sons, so I never expected to inherit. But the two youngest boys perished in Spain.' Nathan paused for a moment, recalling the icy winters and scorching summers: the torrential rain, cloying mud, flies and disease that took their toll of the troops. It was said more men were killed by disease and the weather than by Bonaparte's army. The scar across his left eye began to ache. Too many memories. He shook them off. 'Their loss may well have hastened the old man's end. He died at the beginning of the year '12 and his heir took a fall on the hunting field less than six months later. When the news came I thought it my duty to come home. Boney was on the run, after all.' He allowed himself a little smile. 'Since then I have been so tied up with my new duties I've had no time to miss the army.'

'And do your new duties include looking for a wife? You will need an heir.'

Nathan's reply was short. 'My cousin is my heir.'

'The ladies won't see it that way.' Sir James winked. 'You are now the biggest catch on the Marriage Mart.'

An iron claw twisted itself around Nathan's guts. 'I do not think so.'

'Oh? From all I've heard of you, my boy, you have never had trouble attracting women. Your reputation precedes you,' said Sir James, when Nathan raised his brows. 'It is said that Europe is littered with the hearts you have broken. Although to your credit, I have never heard that you seduced innocent young virgins.'

No, thought Nathan bitterly. *Only once did I break that rule, to my cost!*

His lip curled. 'With such a reputation I would expect the doting mothers to keep their chicks away from me.'

'But they won't, believe me. They will be planning their own campaigns once they know you are in town.' Nathan's hand briefly touched his temple and Sir James smiled. 'And don't think that scar will frighten them away—'tis more likely to fascinate 'em; it will add to your attractions!'

Hurriedly Nathan rose. 'If there is nothing else to discuss I must be away.' He saw his host's brows rise and tried to moderate his tone. 'I do not think there is much that can be done until the allied leaders arrive next month.'

'You are right, of course. We will meet again before then to discuss our roles.' Sir James chuckled. 'Thank God his Highness is too busy designing new uniforms for his troops and working on his plans for a grand spectacle in Hyde Park to worry about us. Goodbye, then, for the moment, my lord. If you have no other engagements, you might like to join me for dinner on Wednesday night. I am expecting Lady Souden to be here by then, but we shall not be entertaining: just a snug little dinner, if you care for it.'

Nathan bowed. 'My presence in town is not generally known yet, so I have no fixed engagements.' He bowed. 'Thank you, sir. I should be delighted to join you.'

London, thought Felicity gloomily as she gazed out of the carriage window, was crowded and noisy and so very dirty. The roads were thick with rubbish and droppings from the hundreds of horses and oxen that plodded up and down, the cobbles only visible in the wheel tracks or where a crossing sweeper cleared a temporary path for a pedestrian and earned a penny for his pains. The cries of the flower-seller mingled with those of the knife-grinder and the hot-pie man as they hawked their wares from street to street. Rows of tall houses lined the road, mile upon mile of brick and stone with barely a patch of grass to be seen.

In one corner of the carriage, Lady Souden's severe-looking dresser was snoring gently while Lydia herself was sitting bolt upright, staring out of the window, her eyes shining and a little smile of anticipation lifting her mouth. She was born to be a society hostess, thought Felicity. She delighted in parties and balls and could not understand Felicity's reluctance to come to town. After all, she reasoned, if Felicity refused to go into society, what did it matter if she was in London or at Souden?

But it did matter. Felicity knew that there was danger in London.

Nathan Carraway was in London.

Chapter Two

The carriage drew up outside Sir James's house in Berkeley Square and Felicity followed Lydia through the gleaming front door and into the study on the ground floor, where Sir James was waiting for them. Lydia ran in, cast aside her swansdown muff and threw herself into her husband's arms. He kissed her soundly before holding her away from him.

'Well, well now, puss, have you missed me?' he said, laughing. 'What will Miss Brown think of this very unfashionable display of affection?'

'Miss Brown is delighted with this display of domestic harmony,' murmured Felicity, her grey eyes twinkling.

Sir James grinned at her, keeping one arm about his wife's still tiny waist.

'I'm glad to hear it. And I am glad to see *you*, Miss Brown. I hope Lady Souden has warned you, we are to be very busy for the next two months.'

'She told me you would be entertaining a great deal, Sir James.'

'Aye, dukes, duchesses, crown princes—and never a moment to call our own. What do you say to that, Miss Brown?'

'I say Lady Souden is equal to the challenge, sir.'

'Aye, so do I,' declared Sir James, giving his wife another kiss. 'But I rely upon you to look after her when I am not here, Miss Brown. Lydia is far too careless of her health, especially now.'

Felicity met his eyes and said resolutely, 'You may depend upon me, Sir James. I would not wish any harm to come to Lady Souden or the unborn child.'

Sir James bestowed a grateful smile upon her.

'Thank you, I am sure I may. Lydia has told me of your fear of going out, Miss Brown, and I will do everything I can to lessen your own discomfiture. A carriage shall be at your disposal at all times, you have only to say the word. Now upstairs and unpack, the pair of you, for we have a guest for dinner.'

'Oh?' Lydia clapped her hands delightedly. 'Is it someone I know?'

'No, a young man I met only t'other day, but he is very agreeable, I assure you. He will set all the young ladies' hearts a-flutter this summer, I have not a doubt.'

'Oh, who?' cried Lydia. 'Do tell me, my love!'

Sir James kissed her nose.

'He is a young nobleman. Rich, handsome and most clearly in want of a wife.' He looked from Felicity to Lady Souden, his smile growing. 'It is the new Earl of Rosthorne.'

Felicity's hands tightened on her reticule. What cruel trick was fate playing upon her, to force the earl upon her notice so soon? She cast an anguished look at Lydia, who attempted a little laugh as she turned to her husband.

'R–Rosthorne? Well, bless me! How is this, my dear?'

'He is newly arrived in town,' explained Sir James. 'We met to discuss the arrangements for looking after his Highness's guests at the forthcoming Peace Celebrations and he struck me as a very pleasant young man. I thought it would please you to meet him, my love.'

'It—it does,' stammered Lydia. 'It is a little sudden, that is all. Having just arrived…'

'Well, he is not expecting any formal ceremony. Just a snug little dinner, I told him, so off you go and put on one of those pretty gowns of yours, my love. You are required to look charming tonight, nothing more.'

'Then perhaps Lady Souden should come upstairs and rest for a little while,' suggested Felicity, edging towards the door.

With another slightly hysterical laugh Lydia allowed Felicity to lead her away, leaving Sir James still chuckling to himself.

'I am sorry, Fee,' she whispered as they went up the stairs. 'I had no idea James would invite Rosthorne to the house!'

Felicity sighed. 'It was inevitable, I suppose, but I did not expect it to be *today*.'

Lydia squeezed her hand. 'You must not worry, my love, you need not see him. This house has so many rooms the earl could be *living* here and not know of your existence!'

Despite Lady Souden's assurances Felicity found herself growing ever more anxious as the hour approached for Lord Rosthorne's arrival. For five years she had done everything in her power to remain hidden from Nathan Carraway and the thought that he would shortly be in the same house terrified her. Not least because she had an overwhelming desire to see him again.

It was dangerous, but she could not resist. A few minutes after Lydia had gone down to the drawing room, Felicity slipped out of the little chamber that Lady Souden had decreed should be set aside as her own private sitting room. The entrance hall of Souden House extended up to the roof and a glazed dome provided natural light for the ornate staircase that rose from a central point to the half-landing before splitting into two flights that curved around the side walls to the first floor and the main reception rooms. From there a narrower stair curled up to the second floor where a small balcony overlooked the hall below. During past seasons Felicity had often brought her young charges on to this balcony when Sir James was entertaining and they had spent many a happy hour watching the arrival of the guests. Now she decided to use it for her own purposes.

Feeling very much like an errant schoolchild, she crept towards the edge of the balcony and sank down. Felicity knew from experience that visitors rarely raised their eyes beyond the ornately decorated first floor. Her dark-grey gown blended well with the shadows and through the balusters she had an excellent view of the front door and entrance hall as well as the first rise of the staircase. The long-case clock on the landing below chimed the hour. It was followed almost immediately by the sounds of an arrival. Felicity knew a sudden, irrational desire to laugh— trust Nathan to be so punctual, it was the soldier in him.

Then he was there. They were in the same house, the same space. She leaned forward, straining to see him. Her heart turned over as he walked into the hall, but his curly-brimmed beaver hat obscured her view of his face. She had never seen him in anything but his scarlet regimentals and thought him handsome in uniform but now, seeing his tall, athletic figure in the plain black swallowtailed coat, she almost fainted with a wild yearning to run down the stairs and throw herself into his arms. She stifled it, reminding herself of how he had betrayed her. She hated him, did she not? She had vowed she was done with him for ever. Yet here she was, hiding in the shadows, desperate to see the man who had broken her heart.

He spoke to the footman as he handed over his hat; she could not make out the words but his warm, deep voice awoke a memory and sent a tingle down her spine. She noticed that his brown hair was no longer tied back but cut short so that it just curled over his collar. He turned to ascend the stair and she was momentarily dazzled by his snowy white neckcloth and waistcoat. As he lifted his head she put her hand to her mouth, stifling a cry. A disfiguring scar cut through his left eyebrow and down across his cheek. His face was leaner and his mouth, which she remembered as almost constantly smiling, was turned down, the lines at each side more pronounced. She had expected him to look a little older, but the severity of his countenance shocked her.

Felicity had followed his career as closely as she could. She knew Nathan's regiment had been involved in several bloody battles so she should not have been surprised to see he had been wounded, but the scar made it suddenly very real.

Do not be so foolish, she told herself. *You should rejoice that he has been punished for the way he treated you!* She closed her eyes and shook her head slightly. It had been her uncle's way to call down fury and retribution upon the heads of those that had offended him. But she was not like her uncle and the thought of Nathan's suffering sliced into her heart. She stared again at the tall figure ascending the stairs.

Look up, she pleaded silently. *Look at me.*

As Nathan reached the top of the first flight of stairs he paused. Felicity's heart was thudding against her ribs: if he raised his head now he would see her! For one joyous, frightening, panic-filled moment she thought he would do just that, but then he was turning to greet his host and Sir James's bluff good-humoured voice was heard welcoming him.

'Come along up, my lord, do not hesitate out there! Here is my lady wife waiting to make your acquaintance…'

The drawing room door was closed, the voices became nothing more than a low drone. Felicity slumped down, her head bowed. She had seen him. He was alive and apart from that scar on his face he looked well. A burst of laughter reached her; he even sounded happy.

And he was not aware of her existence.

Hot tears pricked her eyelids and she berated herself for

her stupidity. It had been foolish to come to London, knowing he would be here. She should have known it would only bring pain. She dragged herself back to her room. It was senseless to think of him, laughing and talking with Lydia and Sir James in the gilded splendour of the dining room below. She would be best to put him out of her mind and go to sleep. That was the sensible thing to do.

But when the Earl of Rosthorne left the house several hours later, the silent grey figure was again watching from the upper balcony.

Having lost his first wife in childbirth, Sir James was morbidly anxious for Lydia. Felicity was aware of this and resolutely stifled her own misgivings as she offered to ac- company Lady Souden about the town. Lydia's delighted acceptance of her company was at least some comfort.

'Oh, I am so pleased! I knew how it would be, once you saw how exciting it is going to be in town this summer. I only wish we could have been here for the procession in honour of King Louis last month, but there is so much to look forward to; it will be *so* entertaining.'

'I am sure it will,' said Felicity bravely.

Lydia gave her a long look. 'And Lord Rosthorne?'

Felicity hesitated. 'I must do my best to avoid him. If I dress very plainly I shall not attract attention. It is possible that he would not even recognise me now. Perhaps, when we go out during the day, I might be veiled.'

Lydia clapped her hands. 'How exciting! But people will be so curious! We could say you are a grieving widow…'

'No, no, Lydia, that will not do at all.'

But Lady Souden was not listening.

'Smallpox,' she declared. 'You have been hideously scarred—or mayhap your head was misshapen at birth.'

In spite of her anxieties, Felicity laughed.

'Shall I pad my shoulder and give myself a hunchback as well? That is quite enough, Lydia. We will say nothing.'

'But people will think it very odd!'

'I would rather they think me eccentric than deformed!'

Glancing at her reflection in the mirror the following day, Felicity could see nothing in her appearance to cause the least comment. Lydia had informed her that they were going to drive out in Hyde Park at the fashionable hour. Felicity's russet-brown walking dress was not quite as fashionable as Lady Souden's dashing blue velvet with its military-style jacket but it looked well enough, and the double veil that covered her face was perfectly acceptable for any lady wishing to protect her complexion from the dust kicked up by the carriage horses.

The drive started well, but there was such a number of carriages in the park and so many people claiming acquaintance with the fashionable Lady Souden that it was impossible to make much progress. Lydia was enjoying herself hugely. She introduced 'my companion, Miss Brown' with just the right amount of indifference that very few bothered to spare more than a glance for the plainly dressed female with her modest bonnet and heavy veil. Felicity was beginning to relax and enjoy the sunshine when she spotted yet another carriage approaching, but this one was flanked by two riders, one of them the unmistakably upright figure of Lord Rosthorne.

She gripped Lydia's arm and directed her attention to the coach.

'Heaven and earth, Lady Charlotte Appleby! I had no idea she was in town.'

'But Rosthorne is with her,' exclaimed Felicity. 'Can we not drive past?'

'Too late,' muttered Lydia, pinning on her smile. 'They have seen us.'

She was obliged to order her driver to stop. Felicity held her breath and sat very still, praying she would not be noticed.

With the two carriages side by side, Nathan brought his horse to a stand and raised his hat to Lady Souden.

'Good day to you, ma'am. You know my aunt, of course.'

'Yes indeed.' Lydia Souden turned her wide, friendly smile towards Lady Charlotte and was rewarded with no more than a regal nod. Nathan's lips tightened. His aunt made sure no one ever forgot she was the daughter of an earl. Lady Charlotte raised her hand to indicate the second rider.

'Let me present my son to you, ma'am. Mr Gerald Appleby.'

Nathan grinned inwardly as his cousin took off his hat and greeted Lady Souden with all the charm and courtesy that his mother lacked. Young scapegrace!

'Delighted, ma'am! But we are remiss here, I think—will you not introduce your friend?'

Nathan blinked and berated himself. It was unusual for Gerald to show him the way, but he had not even noticed the rather dowdy little figure sitting beside Lady Souden, still as a statue.

'Oh, this is my companion, Miss Brown. Lady Charlotte, you are in town for the Peace Celebrations?'

'Yes. We were obliged to hire, since Rosthorne House is no longer available.'

'You know that if you had given me sufficient notice I would have had rooms prepared for you, Aunt,' replied Nathan.

'In my brother's day there were always rooms prepared and ready for me.'

'Heavens, Mama, the house has been shut up for the past year or more,' replied Gerald Appleby. 'Nathan wasn't expecting to come to town this summer, were you, Cos?'

'No. Consequently I have only opened up such rooms as I require.'

'Fortunately my man was able to secure a house in

Cavendish Square,' Lady Charlotte addressed Lydia. 'With so many visitors in town this summer there was very little to suit. So different in Bath, of course, where I have my own house…'

'My dear ma'am, there was any number of apartments that would have been ideal if you had not insisted upon having so many servants with you.' Gerald glanced at his audience, a merry twinkle in his eye. 'Only imagine the task: not only had her poor clerk to find somewhere with sufficient rooms for Mama's household, but *then* he was obliged to find stables and accommodation for her coachman and groom, too!'

'Really, Gerard, do you expect me to do without my carriage?'

'No, but you might well do without your groom. You no longer ride, ma'am.'

'Harris has been with me since I was a child. He comes with me everywhere.'

'I wonder if perhaps he might have enjoyed a holiday,' observed Gerald, but his mother was no longer listening.

'My man had instructions to find me the very best,' she announced. 'And I do not think he has managed so ill.'

Nathan's attention began to wander as the ladies discussed the forthcoming arrival of the foreign dignitaries. Gerald, he noticed, was passing the time by trying to flirt with the veiled companion. While his mother's attention was given to speculation about the Grand Duchess of Oldenburg's latest conquest, Gerald was leaning over the side of the carriage and murmuring outrageous remarks. The poor little dab looked quite uncomfortable. Nathan tried to catch Gerald's eye. Damnation, why couldn't the lad behave himself? Nathan's hand clenched on the reins. He must get out of the ridiculous habit of regarding Gerald as a boy. He was eight-and-twenty, the same age as himself, but his cousin had not served a decade in the army, an experience that Gerald declared had left Nathan hardened and cynical.

It might well be the case, but it was quite clear that the little figure in the carriage was not enjoying Gerald's attentions. He was leaning closer now, his hand reaching out towards the edge of the veil.

'Cousin, you go too far!' Nathan's voice cracked across the space between them. It was the tone he had used on new recruits and it had its effect. Gerald's hand dropped.

'I beg your pardon,' Nathan addressed the rigid little figure. 'My cousin sometimes allows his humour to go beyond what is pleasing.'

She did not reply and merely waved one small hand. He threw an admonishing glance at his cousin, who immediately looked contrite.

'Indeed, Miss Brown, Rosthorne is right; I went too far and I beg your pardon.' Gerald directed his most winning smile towards her. 'Well, will you not speak? Pray, madam, take pity on me: I vow I shall not rest until you say that you forgive me. Miss Brown, I *beg* you.'

Nathan could not but admire Gerald's tenacity. He was—

'I do forgive you, sir. Let us forget this now.'

His head jerked up. That voice, the melodic inflection—it struck a chord, a fleeting memory: surely he had heard it before. He stared at the lady, trying to pierce the thick curtain of lace that concealed her face.

'Forgive me,' he said, frowning. 'Have we—?'

'Forgive *me*, my lord,' interposed Lady Souden with her sunny smile. 'We are causing far too much congestion on this path. That will never do; we must drive on. If you will excuse us…'

There was nothing to do but to pull away and allow the carriage to pass.

'Well, well, one must admit Lady Souden to be most charming,' declared Lady Charlotte graciously. 'She intends to hold a ball later this year. I have told her I shall attend. And you must come too, Gerald.'

Mr Appleby grinned across at his cousin. 'Not really my line, Mama, but if you insist. What of you, Cos?'

Nathan shrugged. 'If I receive an invitation I must go, I suppose.' His thoughts returned to the veiled figure in the carriage. Something nagged at the back of his mind, a thought that he could not quite grasp. He said, 'Who was the female with Lady Souden? Miss Brown. Have you met her before, Aunt?'

'Lady Souden said she was her companion,' replied Lady Charlotte. 'No doubt she is some penniless relation.' She turned to address her son. 'And as such she can have no attraction for *you*, Gerald.'

'Devil a bit!' responded Gerald, grinning. 'Just trying to be friendly, Mama.'

'Better that you should remain aloof, like your cousin,' retorted Lady Charlotte.

'What, be as grim as Rosthorne?' Gerald laughed. 'Impossible! I swear his dark frown could turn the milk sour!'

Nathan allowed himself a smile at that. 'Try for something in between, then, Cousin.'

'Precisely.' Lady Charlotte nodded. 'You must remember your breeding, my son.'

As the carriage pulled away Gerald threw a rueful glance across at Nathan. 'When am I ever allowed to forget it?'

'So. It is done. I have met him.'

Felicity closed the door of her little bedchamber and leaned against it. Her legs felt very unsteady, so much so that she dare not even attempt to walk across the room to her bed. She closed her eyes. Nathan's image rose before her, so familiar, so dear. She had studied him closely while the two carriages were stopped. In profile she thought him even more handsome than when they had first met, his face leaner, his look more serious. Even when she saw again the scar across the left side of his face she was no longer horrified by it. She was thankful the dreadful disfigurement did not seem to have affected his sight; his eyes were as keen as ever and for a moment she had quailed beneath her thick veil, convinced that he would recognise her. Even worse than the fear of detection was the fierce disappointment she had known when he had addressed her; he was clearly unaware of her identity and his indifference hit her like a physical blow.

'But it is done,' she said again. 'Now I have seen him I know what to expect, I am prepared.'

However, being prepared did not prevent her from feeling slightly sick when Sir James announced cheerfully that she would be required to accompany his wife to Lady Somerton's later that night.

'I know I promised to attend, but I have fallen behind with drawing up my plans for Tsar Alexander's arrival in London—I gave my word that I would report to Carlton House tomorrow morning.'

'Then you must remain here and finish them,' replied Lydia calmly. 'But there is not the slightest need for Felicity to come with me: Lady Somerton is such an old friend...'

Felicity felt Sir James's eyes upon her and she said immediately, 'There is nothing I should like more than to go with you, Lady Souden.'

Lydia blinked. 'You would?'

'Of course,' Felicity lied valiantly. 'You will recall you showed me Lady Somerton's invitation and said she hoped that Lord Byron would be there and would read for her.'

'But I thought you disliked Byron,' objected Lydia.

'His style of living, perhaps,' Felicity persisted. 'His poetry is quite—quite impressive.'

Her friend looked at her in surprise. Felicity maintained her calm, aware that Sir James was also regarding her, but with approval, and she drew some comfort from this as she ran upstairs after dinner to change her gown. And what if Nathan should be there? Felicity knew this question would be on Lydia's lips as soon as they were alone together. She had no answer, and could only pray that the earl was not a lover of poetry.

Lady Somerton's tall, narrow town house was crowded and noisy. Felicity followed Lydia as she swept up the stairs to the main reception rooms, ostrich feathers dancing, and was immediately surrounded by her friends and acquaintances. Felicity stayed very close. In her plain grey gown she elicited barely a glance from the gentlemen vying for the beautiful Lady Souden's attention and no glance at all from the matrons who came up to claim acquaintance with one of the most fashionable personages of the *ton*.

Lady Somerton laughingly chided Lydia for arriving so late and ushered them into a large salon where the poetry reading was about to begin. Felicity followed on, but such was the crush that she was unable to secure a seat beside her friend and was obliged to find a space for herself towards the back of the room. This suited her very well, for she was able to observe the crowds from the shadowy recesses.

Any hopes that Nathan might not attend were soon dashed when she saw him stroll into the room. At first she thought it was her imagination that there was a change in the atmosphere as he entered, but there was a definite murmur of excitement rippling around the salon. A young lady to her right fluttered her fan and muttered, 'Mama! The Earl of Rosthorne is come.'

'Then stand up straight, Maria,' retorted her turbaned parent. 'You will not catch his attention if you slouch. Shoulders back, my love; he is surveying the company.'

The young lady plied her fan even faster. 'Oh, Mama, he looks so severe, I vow he frightens me!'

'Nonsense, child, it is merely the effect of that dreadful

scar. Smile now… Oh, how vexing, Lady Somerton is carrying him off. Never mind, Maria, while he is in the room there is still hope. Keep your head up. And do not squint, girl! You will need all your wits about you if you wish to become a countess.'

A cold chill settled around Felicity's heart. Was that the reason Nathan was in town, to find a wife? Why should he not? she asked herself miserably. She had done her best to disappear, doubtless he had forgotten her in the inevitable confusion of removing the army and its followers from Corunna.

The evening dragged on. Felicity heard very little of the poetry—her attention was fixed on Nathan. At one point he looked around, as if conscious of her gaze, and she was obliged to draw back into the shadows. When there was a break in the recital Felicity noticed that he was immediately surrounded by ladies, all eager for his attention. The turbaned matron lost no time in joining the throng and was soon presenting him to her daughter. Felicity longed for it to be *her* hand he was carrying to his lips, *her* words that made him smile. She forced herself to look away. It would do her no good to dwell on what could never be.

She spotted Lydia at the centre of a laughing, chattering group of ladies and seeing that she was as far from Nathan as the room would allow, Felicity made her way across to her. Lady Souden looked up as she approached, excused herself with her charming smile and stepped away from the group to take Felicity's arm.

'Well, my dear, what do you think to it?' Lydia giggled. 'I have rarely heard such execrable verse, I think.'

'Was it so very bad? I was not really listening…'

'Dreadful, my dear,' Lydia murmured, smiling across the room at their hostess. 'Rosthorne is here, have you seen him?'

Felicity almost laughed at that. She had eyes for no one else!

'Yes. By staying in the shadows he has not noticed me.'

'But you are uneasy.' Lydia patted her hands. 'Shall we make our excuses and leave? If Lord Byron had been here I might have made a push to stay and be sociable but as it is, I think I would prefer to be at home with darling James.'

Felicity nodded. She looked across the room at Nathan. She would have liked to stay and prolong the torture of watching him, but she knew that was senseless, so with a word of acquiescence she turned and followed Lydia out of the room.

They were in the entrance hall, waiting for their carriage when Lydia reached over and deftly flicked up the hood of Felicity's cloak.

'Cover yourself,' she murmured. 'Rosthorne is coming.' She gave Felicity's shoulder a reassuring pat before turning. 'My lord.'

Felicity stepped behind Lydia and out of Nathan's direct gaze.

'Going so soon, madam?'

'Why, yes, my lord.' Lydia gave him her charming smile. 'I find a little poetry goes a long way.'

The corners of his mouth lifted. 'Well said, ma'am! I expected to see Sir James with you.'

'Unfortunately his work on plans for the Tsar's entertainment would not allow him time to come with me this evening. I have no doubt that when we get back we shall find him still poring over his notes.'

'Well, ma'am, if you have no escort, you must let me accompany you to Berkeley Square—'

Lydia gave a little laugh. 'I would not dream of taking you away from Lady Somerton, my lord.'

'If your opinion of the readings this evening is the same as mine, you will know that I welcome the distraction.'

The boyish grin that accompanied the words was like a physical blow to Felicity. Nathan suddenly looked so much younger, so much more like the handsome hero of her dreams.

'But I will not hear of it,' Lydia was saying to him. 'We have our footmen and link boys, so I need not trouble you, my lord.'

'It will be no trouble at all,' replied Lord Rosthorne, walking to the door beside her. 'In fact, it suits me very well, for I need to see Sir James and it is so early that I am sure he will not object to my disturbing him. Therefore I will come with you—I beg your pardon, Miss Brown, did you say something?'

'She coughed,' said Lydia quickly. 'But really, my lord, there is no need—'

'Madam, I insist.' Nathan held out his arm and after a brief hesitation Lydia placed her fingers upon his arm and allowed him to escort her to the waiting carriage. Felicity followed closely. She was aware of an unnerving and quite illogical temptation to reach out and cling to the skirts of Nathan's black evening coat.

Nathan had been quite sincere in his assurances. He was glad of an excuse to quit Lady Somerton's soirée. He had never intended to remain there for long, and if by escorting Lady Souden to her home he could have five minutes' conversation with Sir James it would save him time in the morning.

He handed Lady Souden into the carriage then turned to her companion. The little hand in its kid glove trembled beneath his fingers but that did not surprise him; Miss Brown seemed to be a very nervous person. She did not even lift her head to thank him as he helped her into the coach.

The journey to Berkeley Square was short and Lady Souden kept up a flow of conversation to which Nathan willingly responded, although he found his attention straying to her companion, sitting quietly in the corner. Even enveloped in her cloak there was something familiar about the way she held herself. Who was she? Why did he feel that he should know her?

He thought of the women he had met during his days

with Wellington's army and a silent laugh shook him. Perhaps one of the lightskirts he had known had come to England and decided to turn respectable. They would be very likely to take an innocuous name such as Brown! He glanced again at the little figure sitting bolt upright by the window. No, that was not the answer. His instinct told him the chit was no straw damsel. From what he had seen of her, she behaved more like a nun.

Nathan realised Lady Souden was still talking to him, and he broke into her nervous chatter to say with a touch of impatience, 'I fear my presence makes you uncomfortable, ma'am.'

'No—no, not at all,' stammered Lady Souden.

'Be assured that I have no intention of stepping beyond the bounds of propriety. Besides, you have Miss Brown here to act as your chaperon.'

'Oh—no, no, you misunderstand me, my lord,' Lady Souden stammered. 'If—if I seem a little anxious, it is because—because I have a headache!'

Nathan was thankful for the dark interior of the carriage, for he was sure his scepticism was evident in his face. Something was upsetting Lady Souden, but if she wished to lie to him rather than explain, then so be it. He had long ago given up trying to understand women.

'I am sorry to hear it,' he replied quietly. 'But if that is the case, perhaps we should not talk for the remainder of the journey.'

The uncomfortable silence that ensued was mercifully short. When they arrived in Berkeley Square, Nathan lost no time in handing down Lady Souden and escorting her to the door, where she thanked him prettily enough for his trouble. As soon as she had directed a footman to take him to Sir James, she grabbed her companion's hand and hurried away.

Felicity said nothing as Lydia almost pulled her up the stairs and into her luxurious apartments. As soon as she was sure they were alone, Lydia leaned against the closed door and let out a long sigh.

'Of all the unfortunate circumstances! When Rosthorne insisted upon coming with us I did not know where to look.'

'That was quite apparent,' replied Felicity, a reluctant smile tugging at the corners of her mouth. 'I have never seen you so flustered.'

Lydia shook her head wearily. 'Oh, Fee, I cannot like this! Rosthorne is not a man I like to deceive. Will you not call an end to this charade?'

Felicity put back her hood. 'I cannot, Lydia. You know I cannot.' She turned away, her head bowed as she struggled with the strings of her cloak. Too much had happened that neither of them could forgive. She sighed. 'I am dead to him. It is better that way.'

Lydia swung her around, saying fiercely, 'No, it is not! You have not given him a chance to explain himself.'

'There is nothing to explain. He was desperately in love with another woman.' Felicity shook off her hands. 'He has forgotten me. Let it be, Lydia, it is over.'

'If you do not wish to tell him then there is an end to it. But I do not see how you can maintain this subterfuge. The earl is not a fool, he will recognise you eventually.'

Felicity sighed. 'If I am very careful he need never know I am here.' A sad little smile pulled at her mouth. 'After all, there are plenty of pretty young ladies to distract him.'

'Then you must go back to Souden. You would be safer there.'

'But then who would look after you? A poor companion I would be if I deserted you now! No, I shall do my duty, Lydia, and accompany you whenever Sir James is not available. After all, I am not likely to see Lord Rosthorne so very often: Sir James will be at your side for most of the balls and concerts you will attend this summer and I may remain safely indoors.'

Lydia did not look completely satisfied with this answer but Felicity was adamant, and at length her friend shrugged.

'Very well, if you are sure it is what you want,' she said. 'Ring the bell, Fee. We will take hot chocolate here in my room. I would like to change out of this gown and go and find Sir James, but Rosthorne may still be with him, and it would look very odd if my headache had disappeared so very quickly!'

An hour later Felicity made her way back to her own apartment. It was not yet midnight, but she felt very tired. The strain of being so close to Nathan had exhausted her, and yet as she lay in her bed thinking over the evening she realised she would not have missed seeing him for the world. It was not without pain, to be sure. He knew her only as Lady Souden's companion, Miss Brown, and his indifference cut her deeply, but there was some comfort in watching him, in being near him. More comfort than she had felt for the past five years.

As the first grey light of dawn seeped into the master bedroom of Rosthorne House, Nathan threw back the bedcovers and sat up, rubbing his temples. Why, after all this time, should he dream of little Felicity Bourne?

He went to the window and pressed his forehead against the cool glass. The view from his bedroom was a pleasant one, for it overlooked the Green Park but this morning Nathan saw nothing; he was thinking of those hectic days in Corunna five years ago. He had been sent ashore by Sir David Baird to help with the delicate negotiations with the local Spanish *junta*, trying to persuade them to allow the British troops to disembark. It was slow, frustrating work and it took all his attention—until one day he had turned a corner and seen three men attacking a young woman. Felicity.

She had looked magnificent with her dark gold hair in disarray about her shoulders and her eyes flashing with anger. He summed up the situation in one glance and when they dared to lay hands on her, he intervened. It was a brief tussle and they soon retreated, leaving Nathan to receive his reward, a grateful look from those huge grey eyes.

'So, madam, where may I escort you?'

'I do not know. That is, I have no place to stay here in Corunna.' She paused. 'I—I need to go to Madrid. I have friends there.'

Nathan hesitated. With no effective government in Spain he would not advise anyone to set out for Madrid without an escort, especially such a fragile little thing as this.

'After what has just happened perhaps it would not be wise for me to travel alone.'

Her quiet words touched a nerve deep inside him, awaking every chivalrous instinct. It was all he could do not to tell her she need never be alone again. His reaction surprised him and he took a small step away.

'On no account must you travel out of the city,' he said decisively.

She turned to him. 'But what am I to do? I am homeless, penniless—' she indicated her muddied pelisse '—and now I am not even presentable.'

'Hookham Frere, the British Envoy, will be setting out for Madrid in the next few days,' said Nathan. 'I have no doubt that he would be happy for you to travel with his party. Will you allow me to escort you to him?'

The relief in her face was evident. 'Thank you, yes, that would be very kind of you.'

Nathan gave her what he hoped was a reassuring smile. He had little experience of dealing with delicately reared young ladies and this one unsettled him. The sooner he could pass her over to the relative safety of the diplomatic party the better. He held out his arm again and hesitantly she laid her gloved hand on his sleeve. He noted idly that her head barely reached his shoulder.

'How comes it that you are separated from your friends, Miss Bourne?'

'Oh, as to that I…' Her words trailed off. He felt the weight of her on his arm.

'Miss Bourne, are you ill?'

'I beg your pardon, I—that is, I have not eaten for a few days…'

She was near to collapse. Nathan quickly revised his plans.

'If you can walk a little further, I have lodgings near here in the Canton Grande. Allow me to take you there, and when you are fed and rested we will continue.'

A slight nod was the only answer he received. He put his arm around her and led her through the narrow streets to a neat house whose wide door and shuttered window sheltered beneath a mirador, an upper-floor balcony completely enclosed by glass panels. He saw his man sitting in the doorway, smoking his pipe.

'Sam, run and fetch Señora Benitez!'

'Now that I can't do, Major,' Sam replied slowly. 'She's gone to stay with 'er daughter for a couple o' days. She told you so herself, this morning, if you remember.'

'Damnation, so she did.'

Felicity gave a little moan and collapsed against him. Swiftly he lifted her into his arms. She was surprisingly light, and fitted snugly against his heart. Something stirred within him.

'And just what have we here, sir?' asked Sam, jabbing his pipe at Felicity.

Nathan allowed himself a swift, wry smile. 'A damsel in distress, Sam. Go ahead of me and open the door, man.'

'You ain't never going to put her in your room!'

'Where the devil do you expect me to put her?'

'Well, there's always the nuns…'

'No.' Nathan's arms tightened around her. He remembered the look in her eyes when she had turned to him. It was a mixture of trust and dependence and something more, a connection that he could not explain, but neither could he ignore it. 'No,' he said again. 'I shall look after her.'

Chapter Three

'Well my love, you can be easy now,' said Lydia at breakfast a few days later. 'James and Rosthorne have gone off to Dover to meet the royal visitors and bring them back to London. The Prince is planning a royal procession through the town to St James's Palace and James has hired rooms for us overlooking the route, so we will be able to watch the procession in comfort.'

Felicity received the news with mixed feelings. She should be relieved that there was no possibility of meeting Nathan for a while, instead she was disappointed.

'Will Sir James and the earl be riding in the procession?' She tried to sound indifferent but she blushed when she looked up and found Lydia smiling at her.

'Yes they will. James tells me the Prince has insisted that Rosthorne should wear his dress uniform: he will look so dashing that I am sure all the ladies will be swooning over him.'

Felicity scowled into her coffee cup.

'Let them swoon,' she muttered. 'I am sure I do not care!'

But when the day arrived Felicity could not deny a frisson of excitement as she and Lydia sat in the window of the hired room.

'People have been gathering since dawn,' remarked Lydia. 'Everyone is eager to see the Emperor. They have even erected stands along the route, but I doubt that even they will have such a fine view as this.'

There was a sudden stir in the crowds below.

'They are coming,' declared Lydia, leaning towards the open window.

Felicity could hear the rattle of drums. A cheer went up as the cavalcade approached, a long column of bright colours and nodding plumes. Felicity watched, fascinated by the never-ending ranks of soldiers and dignitaries passing beneath her.

'There's Prinny!' cried Lydia, pointing. 'And that must be the Prussian King.'

Felicity looked down at the upright, soldierly figure in his topboots and white pantaloons. He looked very serious, but she could not help thinking that was much more regal than the portly Prince Regent. Lydia grabbed her arm.

'Look, there's James!' She waved her handkerchief wildly at a group of riders following the royal party and was rewarded when Sir James looked up and raised his hat to her. 'Oh, he is so handsome. And he looks so well on horseback, does he not?'

Felicity murmured a reply. She was searching the colourful columns, eager to catch a glimpse of Nathan. What had Sir James said about their escort duties? Nathan was to accompany the Emperor of Russia.

'I have not yet seen the Tsar,' she murmured, her eyes raking the crowds.

'Perhaps he is gone another way.' Lydia laughed. 'I would not be surprised if his sister has told him to come direct to her at the Pulteney Hotel. James says she has taken a dislike to the Prince Regent!'

Felicity was aware of a searing disappointment and

berated herself fiercely. For five long years she had resolutely tried to forget Nathan Carraway—now he was out of her sight for just a few days and she was pining for him! She stared out at the colourful cavalcade passing beneath the window and made a decision. She would speak to him. At the very next opportunity she would reveal herself to Nathan. She would watch his reaction carefully; if he wanted nothing to do with her then she would ask Lydia to send her back to Souden and she would do her best to make a life for herself without Nathan Carraway. But perhaps, just perhaps… She hugged herself, trying not to fan the tiny spark of hope that refused to be extinguished. Whatever was decided, surely it would be better than this half-life she was living at present? Beside her, Lydia gave a little tut of exasperation.

'It does not look as if the Tsar is going to appear. How tiresome! But we shall discover the truth tonight.' Lydia sighed. 'Such a lot of new faces, and James will expect me to know them all, for he will be inviting them to our ball! Well, Fee, my dependence is upon you to remember them, so that you can prompt me if I forget their names!'

'So, James, what happened? Where was the Tsar?' Lydia drew her husband into her private sitting room. 'It is no good telling me you have been ordered to dine at Carlton House; you are not leaving until you tell us everything. Is that not so, Felicity?'

'If you could spare us five minutes, Sir James, we would be grateful.'

Her calm tone belied her impatience to know why Nathan had not been in the procession. Sir James allowed himself to be pulled down on to a sofa beside his wife.

'Oh, very well So you and Miss Brown watched the pro ceedings, did you?'

Lydia shook his arm. 'You know very well we did, sir,

for you saw us there when you rode past. But what happened to the Tsar?'

'Aye, well…' Sir James shook his head. 'We made good progress coming up from Dover. There were people lining the streets and hanging out of upstairs windows, all cheering, but the crowds were so thick as we came into London that the royals grew nervous.' He tried and failed to hide his grin. 'They ain't used to the mob, you see. All the people wanted to do was to cheer their heroes, unbuckle the horses and draw the carriages through the streets themselves, but the sovereigns didn't want it. Then someone took a pot-shot at the Tsar.'

'No!'

'Yes, my love. Only the shot went wide and hit Rosthorne instead.'

'Was—was he badly hurt?' Felicity asked, her hands straying to her cheeks.

Sir James laughed. 'Not at all, but the bullet took his hat clean off! I didn't have a chance to talk to him, for he was obliged to set off after the Emperor, who was determined to join his sister.'

'At the Pulteney.' Lydia nodded sagely. 'You said he might do that.'

'Did I, by heaven?' exclaimed Sir James. He lifted her hand to his lips. 'What a clever little puss you are to remember that! Well, I hope he's comfortable there. The Lord Chamberlain, two bands and I don't know how many others had been waiting since dawn to receive him, then Rosthorne sends a message to say Tsar Alexander came into town by way of the turnpike at Hyde Park Corner and would be staying at the Pulteney. Prinny is as mad as fire, of course, but forced to put on a brave face. That is why I must go now, my love. His Highness is not in the best of moods, so it will not do for me to be late!'

'Poor James,' said Lydia, kissing his cheek. 'I think these celebrations are going to be anything but peaceful! But I must confess a desire to see this Emperor of Russia. Will he be at Lady Stinchcombe's ball tomorrow night, do you think?'

'He has certainly been invited; we must see if Rosthorne can bring him up to scratch!'

Felicity looked up to find Lydia giving her a rueful glance.

'Then I regret I must ask you to come out with me again tomorrow, Fee—I cannot wait for James to finish his interminable meetings before going to the ball.'

Felicity nodded. Inside, she was aching to see for herself that Nathan was unhurt. Tomorrow night could not come soon enough.

The carriage turned into a cobbled street off Piccadilly and pulled up outside a pretty red-brick house set back in its own grounds. Lady Stinchcombe greeted them warmly.

'There is no ceremony here tonight,' she said gaily. 'The Emperor sent Lord Rosthorne to make his apologies, but we shall do our best to enjoy ourselves without him. Wander where you will, although the garden illuminations will not be at their best until it is properly dark.'

'I suppose we should wait until the last of the daylight has gone before we look at the gardens,' said Lydia. She led the way towards the card room. 'Have a care, Fee,' she murmured, pausing in the doorway. 'Rosthorne is here.'

Grateful for the warning, Felicity stayed in Lydia's shadow as she followed her into the room. She spotted the earl almost immediately. He was playing picquet with another gentleman while a crowd of admiring ladies stood at his shoulder, vying for his attention.

'Poor man, how very distracting for him.'

Hearing Felicity's comment, a gentleman standing near them gave a laugh.

'There's no distracting Rosthorne! Even being shot at don't make him turn a hair. Some dashed fool nearly blew his head off yesterday.'

'Aye, I heard about that.' A bewigged man in a faded frockcoat nodded. 'Pretty wild shot if it missed the Tsar and hit Rosthorne. Who did it, some drunken lunatic?'

'They didn't catch him,' replied the first man. 'He got away in the crowd. Made no odds to Rosthorne, he merely followed on after the Tsar.'

'He is very brave,' murmured Lydia.

The bewigged man shrugged. 'Rosthorne's a soldier. He thought nothing of it. Ruined a perfectly good hat, though.'

Pride flickered through Felicity. Of course Nathan would think nothing of the danger. He did not know the meaning of fear. Lydia took her arm.

'Even so, we shall not add to the distraction,' she murmured. 'Let us move on to the music room.' She patted Felicity's hand. 'My dear, what is this? You are shaking.'

'I am a little shocked to hear of such violence,' whispered Felicity. 'Pray do not mind me, Lydia; let us go on.'

She was being irrational, she told herself. Nathan had been in danger any number of times when he was a soldier, so why should the news of this incident affect her so? She chewed her lip. Because it was here, in London, where one did not expect such things. She glanced back at Nathan, sitting at the card table.

And because she still cared for him.

They wandered into the next room where Miss Stinch-combe was performing upon the harp. As the final notes died away and they applauded her performance, Felicity saw Gerald Appleby approaching them.

'Lady Souden, how do you do! And Miss Brown. A de-lightful evening, is it not? Mama is sitting over there by the window, may I take you over? I know she will want to talk to you…'

He led them across the room, chatting all the time until they came up to Lady Charlotte, who greeted Lydia with a regal smile. Felicity she acknowledged with no more than a flicker of her cold eyes before engaging Lady Souden in conversation. Felicity gave an inward shrug and would have moved away, but Mr Appleby stopped her.

'How are you enjoying the music, Miss Brown?'

'Very well, sir, thank you.'

'I think the harp very over-rated and much prefer the pianoforte,' he continued, smiling at her. 'Do you play at all, Miss Brown?'

'The pianoforte, a little.'

'Ah, all young ladies say they only play a little and then they perform the most complicated pieces for us. Shall we have the pleasure of hearing you this evening, ma'am?'

'No, Mr Appleby, I do not play in public.'

'What, never? But why? This must be remedied immediately,' he cried gaily.

Felicity tried to step away but found the wall at her back. 'No, I assure you, sir—'

He took her hand and leaned toward her, smiling. 'This is no time for bashful modesty, madam. Let me take you to the piano—'

'Gerald!' Lady Charlotte's strident tones interrupted him. 'Gerald, leave the gel alone. It is beneath you to flirt with the hirelings.'

'I beg your pardon, Lady Charlotte, but Miss Brown's birth is equal to my own,' said Lydia, bristling in defence of her friend.

'So I should hope,' returned Lady Charlotte, unperturbed. 'I would expect nothing less in any companion of yours.'

Felicity observed the angry flush on Lydia's cheek and slipped away from Gerald to take her arm.

'You wished to look at the lamps in the garden, my lady '

'Insufferable woman,' muttered Lydia as they walked away. 'She is so set up in her own importance!'

'I was quite thankful for her intervention,' returned Felicity. 'Mr Appleby is far too mischievous.'

'Perhaps he is trying to fix his interest with you.'

'Oh, Lydia, surely not!'

'You may look surprised, Fee, but he is quite taken with you.'

'But I have done nothing—'

'No, nothing more than look adorably shy.' Lydia gave a soft laugh. 'There is no need to colour up, my love; you have an air of fragility that makes men want to protect you.'

Felicity put up her chin. 'But I do not want to be protected! Oh dear. I had hoped, by dressing plainly and not putting myself forward, that I would not be noticed.'

'And in general that is the case,' Lydia reassured her. 'Mr Appleby is perhaps trying to make amends for his mother's ignoring you.'

'Yes, that is very possible,' mused Felicity. She looked up, a smile lurking in her eyes. 'And it is a very lowering thought!'

Her companion laughed. 'Yes, it is! But it is quite your own fault, Fee. If you were to put on a fashionable gown and stop dressing your hair in that dowdy style I have no doubt that we would have dozens of gentlemen clamouring to make your acquaintance!'

Still chuckling, they wandered out on to the terrace where a familiar voice cut through the darkness.

'So there you are! Now what in heaven's name are you two laughing at?'

Sir James's bemused enquiry brought his lady flying to his arms.

'Oh, my dear, you are here already! How wonderful! No, no, you must not ask about our silly jokes. I did not expect to see you here for another hour yet!'

'Well, having delivered his Highness to our hostess I have left him being toad-eaten by any number of the guests! What a crush. Scarcely room to move in the ballroom!'

'I know, that is why we came out here to look at the lamps. They are very pretty, are they not?' Lydia took her husband's arm. 'Shall we take a stroll through the gardens? Come with us, Fee.'

'If you do not object, I think I might stay here for a little while.' Felicity had spotted the earl slipping out of the house on the far side of the terrace. She nodded at Lydia. 'Please, go on without me. I shall be perfectly safe here.'

As soon as Lydia and Sir James had disappeared into the gardens, Felicity ran across the terrace and down the steps in the direction that Nathan had gone. This was her opportunity to reveal herself to him. It was much darker on this side of the house, for the path led away from the main gardens, where myriad coloured lights were strung between the trees. As she hurried through the gloom her step faltered. Nathan might have an assignation—how would she feel if she came upon him with his arms around another woman? She put up her chin. If that was the case then she would rather know of it. Then she could put him out of her mind and end this growing obsession.

Away from the house there was just sufficient light for her to see the grassy path. It ran between tall bushes with the ghostly outlines of marble statues at intervals along its length. Nathan's tall figure was ahead of her, no more than a black shadow in the darkness. At the end of the avenue he hesitated before disappearing to the right. Felicity followed and found herself stepping into a rather unkempt shrubbery.

'Why are you following me?' Felicity turned to flee, but Nathan's hand shot out and grasped her wrist. 'Oh, no. You will not leave until I have an explanation!'

Felicity swallowed. It was far too dark to see clearly and she only recognised Nathan by his voice. She lowered her own to a whisper in an attempt to disguise it.

'I—I came out here to…' Felicity hesitated. Should she

reveal herself, tell him she had followed him? Her courage failed her. 'I do not like the noise and chatter.'

That much at least was true. She heard him sigh.

'Nor I.' He released her. 'In fact, I can't think why I came tonight.'

Felicity knew that she should pick up her skirts and run away, but her wayward body would not move. To be here, alone with Nathan, talking to him—it was very dangerous, but she could not resist.

'Why remain in town, sir, if you do not enjoy society?'

'I have duties to perform.' He turned his head suddenly, peering at her. 'Do I know you?'

Felicity shrank back. 'No,' she said gruffly. 'No. I do not move in your circle.'

Nathan shrugged. He had come out into the gardens to enjoy a cigarillo in peace but it was not his house, he could hardly tell this young person to go away. The strains of a minuet floated out on the night air.

'The dancing has begun. Do you not wish to join in?'

'No.'

Her laconic reply surprised him into a laugh.

'I thought all young ladies love to dance.'

'I do not dance. I have not danced since I was at school.'

He heard the wistful note in her voice and held out his hand to her. 'Would you like to try now? Here?'

The stillness settled over them. Nathan had the impression the little figure before him was holding her breath. He saw her hand come up, then it dropped again to her side.

'Thank you, but no. Companions do not dance.'

So that was her role. He felt a stir of pity.

'But out here we do not need to abide by society's rules.' He reached out and took her hand, pulling her towards him. 'Here we are no more than a man and a woman. We may dance if we wish to, or…'

His words trailed away as he drew her closer. He had not

intended to take her in his arms, but as she stepped forward it seemed natural to embrace her. She leaned against him, her head just below his chin. He breathed in the subtle fragrance of flowers and sunshine and—

'Oh, dear heaven, let me go!'

She was struggling like a frightened bird against this hold. Immediately he released her.

'Oh, I do beg your pardon,' she gasped. 'That was not meant to…I must go!'

'As you wish.' She stood before him in the darkness. He could not see her face, but he knew that she was troubled. He said gently, 'Did I frighten you?'

'No…' Her voice caught on a sob. 'No, never.'

She turned and disappeared into the night. Nathan watched her go, then with a faint shrug he reached into his pocket for his cigarillos.

Felicity flew out of the shrubbery and stopped, panting once she reached the grass path. What had she been thinking of? To talk to Nathan had been foolish enough, to allow him to take her in his arms was sheer madness. Why had she not told him who she was? She bowed her head. She could imagine his reaction. Anger and revulsion. How had she ever dared to hope that he might want her back? Yet even now she could not bring herself to walk away.

Give him the chance to decide.

Felicity crept back to the edge of the path and peeped around the corner. She could just make out Nathan's dark figure a short distance away, only his white neckcloth and waistcoat showing against the black shadows. He was moving quite slowly and as she watched he tilted his head back and exhaled a little cloud into the night air. A tangy, unusual fragrance wafted towards her. He was smoking a cigar. She had seen the officers in Corunna smoking these little cylinders of rolled tobacco and guessed that Nathan had picked up the habit during his years as a soldier. A movement in the shadows caught her eye. There was someone else in the shrubbery. Immediately she was on the alert, sensing danger. Nathan had turned away from that corner of the garden and Felicity saw a sudden flash, a glint of metal in the moonlight.

'Behind you, sir!' Felicity's shout cut through the silence.

Nathan wheeled about, fists raised. 'Who's there?'

A dark shape broke away and fled, all attempts at stealth gone as it crashed through the bushes.

Felicity stepped back into the shadows. She had succeeded in putting Nathan on his guard. Now she must remove herself. Picking up her skirts, she raced back towards the terrace, veering off along the path leading to the main gardens.

'Sir James, Sir James!'

Lydia and her husband were strolling arm in arm beneath the coloured lamps. They looked up at her call. She ran up to them.

'Sir James, there is—an—intruder,' she gasped out the words, impatient to make him understand. She pointed. 'Over there in the shrubbery.'

Sir James immediately ran to the terrace and pulled one of the torches from its holder, calling to a footman to follow him. He turned to Felicity.

'Very well, show me.'

'James, be careful!' cried Lydia, running along behind them.

They were halfway along the path when they met Nathan coming the other way. Felicity dropped back immediately into the darkness.

'Rosthorne,' Sir James called to him. 'There's a report of an intruder. Have you seen him?'

'Aye, there was someone. He took off through the garden door when I challenged him. I followed him outside, but the alley was deserted.'

Sir James turned to the footman. 'Could he have got in that way?'

The servant shook his head. 'No, sir. Her ladyship insists we keep the door locked.'

'Well, it was used tonight,' said Nathan. 'There are bolts top and bottom. I was close behind the man as he opened the door. He did not have time to draw them back. Either he had prepared his escape, or someone let him in.'

'Good heavens!' gasped Lydia, clinging to her husband's arm.

'I will talk to Stinchcombe,' said Nathan. 'He can have the servants search the house, to check if anything is missing.'

'Make sure you do not alarm the rest of the guests,' Sir James called after him. He patted Lydia's hand. 'There is nothing more to be done here, so I suggest we go back indoors. Come, Miss Brown. You may rest easy now; there is no one here.'

Sir James took the ladies back to Berkeley Square soon after, and the incident in the Stinchcombes' garden was not mentioned again, but it remained in Felicity's mind when she went to bed that night. Sir James had spoken to his hostess before they had left and she had assured him that nothing had been taken from the house, and no uninvited guests had been seen in the building. For all that Felicity was still uneasy. It would be a very bold thief who would risk entering a house full of guests. There had been something menacing about the way the figure had moved in the shadows, the way it had approached Nathan and the glint of metal she had seen. Could it have been a knife blade? She shuddered. There were so many strangers in London for the Peace Celebrations: perhaps not all of them were friendly.

'Now you are being fanciful,' she muttered, pummellling her pillow. 'It was probably some poor starving creature looking for a little food, nothing more. You were overwrought. Most likely you are making a mountain out of nothing more than a worm-cast!'

Nevertheless, the feeling persisted that by being there she had saved Nathan's life.

However, there was no talk of intruders the next morning; Lydia's thoughts were all on a forthcoming treat.

'In general James does not like masked balls and I feared that he would cry off from Lady Preston's masquerade next week,' she said, with a twinkling look at her husband. He grinned back at her.

'His Highness insists we all attend, and that we wear a costume of his own designing.'

Lydia laughed. 'How galling that I must be grateful to the Prince Regent for my husband's company!'

Felicity turned to Sir James. 'His Highness wishes you *all* to attend?'

'Aye, Miss Brown. Neither Rosthorne nor I will be escorting the royal party that night, but we are still obliged to wear the Regent's costume.'

Felicity digested this while Sir James took his leave of them and went off to his study.

'I am glad for your sake that James will escort me to Lady Preston's,' said Lydia, when they were alone again. 'It means that you are not obliged to come with me, Fee, so it works out very neatly.'

'Actually, I would like to go to the masquerade, if I may.'

Lydia turned an astonished gaze upon her. 'Fee, my dear, you cannot wish to go!'

Felicity looked down at her hands. 'It is not so long ago we thought I should be attending as your companion,' she reminded Lydia. 'You expressly requested Lady Preston to send me an invitation, did you not?'

'Yes, yes, I know that, but…oh, Fee, are you sure you want to attend? Have you considered?'

'Yes, I have. It is to be a masked ball, so I may be quite disguised. And I shall leave before the unmasking at midnight.'

'But Rosthorne will be there!'

'I know. That is why I want to go.'

With a tiny squeal Lydia sat up. 'Have you run mad?' she demanded. 'Do you know the risk you will be running to attend a masquerade?'

Felicity nodded. 'I have considered that. But I want to see him again, Lydia.' She clasped her hands tightly in her lap. 'It is the perfect opportunity for me to talk to him.'

'But as soon as you speak to him he will recognise you.'

Felicity shook her head. 'He will not be expecting to see me there.' She thought back to their time together in the shrubbery. 'I doubt he even remembers my voice.'

'This is madness,' Lydia said again. 'Think of the danger, Fee. These events can be very…wild.'

'It is no matter,' said Felicity calmly. 'All I want is to dance with Nathan. We have never danced together, you see. And I would so like to know how it feels. Just once.'

Lydia looked at her, tears starting in her blue eyes. 'Oh, my dear—'

Felicity quickly put up her hands. 'No, please, Lydia, do not pity me or I shall start to cry, too. Instead I would like to ask you to help me in another way.' She fixed her eyes upon her friend. 'I will need some dancing lessons. Apart from a few country dances at Souden I have not danced, not *properly* danced, since we were at the Academy together…'

'And you were always such a graceful dancer. I shall ask my old dancing teacher, Signor Bellini, to come here and I shall play for you,' declared Lydia. 'Oh, Fee, this is so exciting. And when Rosthorne discovers who you are…'

'You go too fast, Lydia!' Felicity frowned. 'I am not at all sure I am ready to reveal myself to him.'

Lady Souden looked as if she would say more, but after

a brief hesitation she merely smiled, and nodded. 'Very well, my love. Now, let us think of a disguise for you.'

'I thought you might have a domino that I may borrow. And a mask.'

Lydia sat back and regarded her friend. After a few moments a mischievous little smile tugged at the corner of her mouth. 'I think I can do much better than that for you, my love.' She shook her head. 'No, I will tell you nothing more now, except that you must leave everything to me!'

Lady Souden refused to say any more.

Felicity was obliged to curb her curiosity until the very day of Lady Preston's masquerade, when she accompanied Lydia on another of her shopping sprees. This included the purchase of a pair of scarlet stockings, which Lydia presented to her friend.

'What on earth would I want with these?' asked Felicity, laughing.

'They will add the finishing touch to your costume this evening.'

'What are you planning for me, Lydia? Do tell!'

But Lady Souden merely looked mysterious and bade her to wait until the evening.

'How fortunate that dear James could not dine with us tonight,' remarked Lydia as she took Felicity upstairs to her apartment. 'I can help you to dress without fear that he will want to know what we are doing.'

'I am becoming mighty anxious about this myself,' said Felicity as she followed her hostess into the white-and-rose dressing room. 'The thought of those scarlet stockings is quite alarming.'

Lydia giggled. 'Nonsense, they are just right!' She smiled at her maid, who was standing beside an open trunk. 'Well, Janet, have you put everything ready, as I instructed?'

'Aye, m'lady.' She reached into the trunk and with a rustle of tissue paper she pulled forth a gown. Felicity stared.

'Lydia,' she breathed, 'I couldn't…can you not find me a plain domino? That is all I require…'

'Nonsense, you will look wonderful in this. We are very much of a height, so it will fit you very well. I would wear it myself but…' Lydia smiled and placed her hands on her waist '…I would not look my best in it this year.'

Felicity looked again at the gown the maid was holding up for her inspection. It was a heavy brocade gown with full skirts and a narrow, boned bodice, but it was not the old style that made Felicity's eyes widen. It was the colour. The gown was a vividly patterned scarlet-and-black, trimmed with black lace.

'Begging your pardon, my lady, but I am not sure this is a suitable gown for Miss Brown,' offered Janet, eyeing the gown doubtfully.

'Pho, it is for a wager,' Lydia responded in an airy tone. 'Come now, we must help Miss Brown to dress. Quickly, Janet, for there is much to do.'

Felicity submitted meekly to their ministrations. Soon her light, flowing muslin gown had been replaced by pads and hoops and petticoats. She gasped as Janet tugged on the laces of her bodice, fitting it tightly into the curve of her waist. When Lydia sent the maid off to pack away her discarded clothes, Felicity gave a little whimper.

'I can scarce breathe.' She regarded herself in the mirror. The tight bodice emphasised her tiny waist and the creamy swell of her breasts above the low neckline. As she raised one hand to her throat the black lace ruffles fell back softly from her white arm. 'Oh dear, Janet is right: I should not be wearing this.'

'You want to dance with Rosthorne, do you not?' said Lydia, eminently practical. 'Trust me, he will not be able to resist you in this gown.' She sighed, a faraway look creeping into her eyes. 'The modiste named this gown "Temptation". I remember when I wore it: James could not take his eyes off me.' Lydia gave another sigh, but as her handmaid came back into the room she recollected herself and said in a very businesslike tone, 'Now for the headdress. Sit down here, my love, while Janet helps me.'

A heavy black wig was fitted over Felicity's soft gold-brown hair and she watched in some consternation as Janet pulled up a side table and began to set out a frightening array of powders and paints.

'Is this really necessary?' protested Felicity. 'I am sure—'

'Hush,' Lydia told her. 'You must look the part.'

'Why, 'tis no more than a little powder, miss,' said Janet. 'Thirty years ago no lady would ever leave her room without painting her face as white as snow.'

'And what is that you are putting on my eyes?'

'Nothing more than a little burnt cork, miss.'

And so it went on. Felicity stared ahead of her as Lydia and her maid worked their transformation. The daylight faded and was replaced by the soft glow of candles before the maid began to pack away the little pots and brushes.

'Can I look in the mirror now?'

'Just a few more touches,' said Lydia.

She handed Felicity a length of black ribbon embroidered with gold thread.

'To tie up your stockings, of course,' she said in answer to Felicity's questioning look. 'And finally, these.'

She produced a square leather jewel case and lifted from it a heavy ruby necklace. 'This belonged to my grandmother, but no one wears such things now. There…and the ear-drops…well—' she caught Felicity's hands and pulled her up to stand before the long glass '—what do you think of yourself?'

For a long, silent moment Felicity gazed at her reflection. A strange, exotic creature stared back at her. A dark-haired stranger with white skin and light grey eyes framed by long dark lashes.

'Well?' said Lydia again.

'Even *I* do not recognise myself.' Even as she spoke her eyes were fixed upon her mouth: plump, sensuously curving lips painted a vivid red contrasted with the whiteness of her skin.

Lydia gave a little crow of laughter. 'That is precisely what we want!' She handed Felicity a mask, a black-and-gold creation with long black ribbons to fasten around her headdress. 'Now, you are to sit down and keep still while Janet helps me into my dress. Tonight I shall be Aphrodite, the goddess of love.' She gave her friend a mischievous smile. 'Quite appropriate, do you not agree? Goodness, look at the hour! We must be quick, Janet, Sir James will be here any minute and we cannot risk him coming upstairs and finding Miss Brown dressed like this!'

The maid's head shot up. 'Sir James doesn't know that Miss Brown is attending—?'

Lydia shushed her maid and waved an impatient hand. 'I told you it is for a wager. Now not another word from you, Janet, and make haste to help me into my costume!'

Lydia was giving her golden curls a final pat when word arrived that Sir James was waiting below.

'I must go,' she said. 'I have given instructions for your coach to be at the door for you in half an hour. Janet has looked out a domino for you, so your costume will be completely concealed when you leave here.' She gave her friend a final hug. 'Do take care, Fee. I will be sure to keep James away from you tonight.'

'Are you afraid he might recognise me?'

Lydia picked up her mask. 'No,' she said, going to the door. 'I am afraid he might find you too, too attractive.'

Chapter Four

Nathan prowled restlessly around Lady Preston's magnificent ballroom. The walls were covered with swathes of midnight-blue silk that seemed to absorb the light from the huge chandeliers. The colourful costumes lost something of their brilliance as the movement of the dance took the dancers away from the centre of the room and they were eager to push back into the middle of the swirling, swaying mass. Not so Nathan, who took advantage of the shadows to hide himself away against the dark walls or in the shadowy corners of the room. He tugged at his collar: it was very warm, despite the tall windows being thrown wide. Impatiently he fiddled with the strings of his mask and heard a quiet laugh at his shoulder.

'No, no, my lord, it's not time for the unmasking yet.'

He turned to find Sir James and Lady Souden beside him.

'Fie upon you, sir, that is no way to address someone at a masquerade.' The lady was smiling at him through the scrap of lace that served as her mask.

'Well, I'm dashed if I'm going to ask Rosthorne if I know him,' retorted Sir James. 'It's perfectly plain to see who he is. But you don't look as if you're enjoying yourself, my boy.'

Nathan shrugged. 'I have been here for most of the day,

sir. His Highness got wind of the fiasco in the Stinch-combes' garden and I was despatched to check that the grounds here are secure.'

'Ah, yes. We cannot risk another assassination attempt,' replied Sir James. 'That would really put a damper on the celebrations. But having done your duty you are free to enjoy yourself now, Rosthorne.'

'To tell the truth I wish this whole evening was over,' replied Nathan, grimacing.

'Is it really so bad?' Lady Souden gave him a sympathetic smile.

'I would be more comfortable in a plain domino, but this—' Nathan indicated his costume, an over-elaborate variation of a hussar's uniform in royal blue, red, white and gold.

Sir James nodded. 'Garish, ain't it? And even the mask don't conceal one's identity. But his Highness insists. A display of solidarity for his guests, I think.'

'And they haven't even put in an appearance,' declared Nathan bitterly.

'But they will.' Sir James patted him on one heavily gilded shoulder. 'Bear up, Rosthorne. Prinny and his royals will turn up shortly and depart again even sooner, no doubt. When they have gone you can take your leave.'

'Aye, I'll go home and change.' Nathan grinned. 'I pity those poor fellows in the Prince's Own if their uniform is anything like this.'

'Well, I think you both look very dashing,' laughed Lydia as Sir James led her away to join the dancing. 'Every woman will want to dance with you.'

And that's the problem, thought Nathan as he drew back once more into the shadows. It seemed to him that all the matchmaking mothers in London had begged, borrowed or stolen an invitation to this masquerade for no better purpose than to fling their marriageable daughters at his head. Lord, what a conceited fool everyone would think him if he expressed such a view aloud, but it was true Sir James himself had called him—what were his words? The biggest catch on the Marriage Mart. Nathan's mouth twisted in distaste. When he had been a mere Major Carraway no one had cared about his marital status, but the wealthy Lord Rosthorne was the subject of constant speculation.

Nathan had not expected to become Earl of Rosthorne, but when he had inherited the title he had thought it his duty to sell out and interest himself in his estates. Now, as he dodged behind a pillar to avoid the gaze of another predatory matron, he began to wish he had remained in the army.

'Do I know you?' A soft voice at his side uttered the familiar words.

He looked down to find an exotic, black-haired creature standing beside him. Her silvery eyes glittered through the slits in her black velvet mask and as he met her gaze she looked away, bringing up a black feather fan to hide her face.

'Do I know *you*?' he countered.

Running his eyes over the delightful figure enshrined in the rich scarlet-and-black gown, he could not bring to mind any woman of his acquaintance. As if aware of his appreciative glance at her full, rounded breasts she lowered the fan a little to cover them.

'I am Temptation,' she murmured. 'Have you never known me?'

'Not recently,' he responded, entering into the spirit of the game. A footman walked by with a tray full of glasses and Nathan reached out to seize two of them. 'Will you take wine with me, madam?'

Her scarlet lips curved upwards. 'With pleasure, my lord.'

'Ah, you *do* know me!'

She looked at him over the rim of her wineglass. 'Everyone knows the rich Lord Rosthorne.'

'Then you have the advantage of me, madam, for I cannot put a name to you.'

'I am Temptation,' she repeated. 'I exist only for tonight.'

Her voice was low and slightly breathless. He found the combination very alluring. Nathan leaned closer.

'And are you Temptation for all men, or only for me?'

The eyes behind the black mask widened slightly. 'For you alone, sir, if you wish it so.'

He stared at her, intrigued. There was something vaguely familiar about the woman, in the tilt of her head, the soft cadences of her voice. Those carmined lips belonged to the mouth of a wanton, but her low, musical voice was cultured and there was no suggestion of a bold swagger in her movements, nothing to suggest she was anything but a lady. And yet...

'Tell me—' He broke off as a female dressed as a milkmaid dashed by, screeching. She was closely followed by two gentlemen in Turkish costume. For a moment he watched their progress. They were heading towards Sir James. He was standing nearby with his wife upon his arm and was obliged to pull Lady Souden out of the way of an imminent collision. Catching Nathan's eye, he shook his head at him.

'What is it that makes these affairs so dashed boisterous?' he demanded, coming up. 'Damme, but my poor Aphrodite already has wine stains upon her skirts!'

'I told you we would be safer dancing,' remarked Lady Souden, dismissing her spoiled robes with an airy wave of her hand. She pulled Sir James back into the crowd and they were soon lost to sight. Smiling faintly, Nathan looked around for the lady in the scarlet-and-black gown, but she had gone.

Lady Preston presented a dancing partner to Nathan, a young woman in a pink domino who appeared to have no conversation and even less sense. Nathan led her on to the dance floor, but soon grew tired of trying to talk when the only response to his efforts was a giggle. The music ended and he escorted his partner back to her party, where her effusive mother made every effort to keep him at her side. A flash of scarlet and black caught Nathan's eye. The dark-haired beauty was moving across the floor almost within arm's reach. His curt 'Excuse me' cut off the matron in mid-sentence but he hardly noticed her indignant gasp for he was already pushing through the crowd.

He was closing on his quarry when a large be-whiskered cavalier stepped in front of her. She tried to move around the fellow but he blocked her escape, pushing himself against her and laughing at her attempts to evade him. Nathan did not hesitate. In two strides he was beside her.

'My dance, I think.' His tone was pleasant, but the savage look he bestowed on the cavalier made the man step back, muttering something that could have been an apology. Triumphant, Nathan put his arm around the lady's tiny waist to lead her away.

'You are trembling,' he said.

'Because you are holding me.'

Her words were quiet, almost lost in the noise and chatter of the room. Almost, but not quite: a bolt of pleasure shot through him. He was unaccountably pleased by her reply. With some reluctance he released her to take her place in the set.

'I thought you were going to tempt only me this evening.'

She smiled, displaying white even teeth between those luscious scarlet lips. 'For that I need your company, my lord.' She reached out for his hand as the music began.

Nathan had never danced such a measure before. Perhaps it was the wine and the warm, heady atmosphere of the crowded room that had confused his senses. His partner fascinated him; he had to force himself to turn away from those glittering eyes when the movement of the dance demanded that he should do so. The laughter and chatter around him died away, he heard nothing, saw nothing, only her. They danced down the line and separated and he found himself impatient to have her beside him again, resenting the other men who enjoyed her smiles, however brief. The dance brought them back together and as he reached for her hand he felt her fingers tremble in his grasp. His heart leapt; so she felt it too, this attraction. The music was ending, the couples were bowing to each other, walking off the floor. Only Nathan and his partner remained, standing breast to breast, staring at one another. As if in a dream he reached out his hand to her. Slowly, the fingers in their black satin glove came up, slid into his. Pulling her hand on to his arm, he led her through the crowd. He saw Sir James ahead of him, his mask failing to conceal his curiosity as he observed Nathan's partner. Even as Nathan was wondering how he would introduce his mysterious companion, Lady Souden glanced in his direction, gave a faint smile and with a word to her husband she led him away. Nathan could not be sorry; he wanted nothing to break the spell that surrounded him.

The orchestra was striking up again as they moved to the side of the room and he took his partner to a less crowded spot near the wall. A nod at a hovering footman provided two glasses of wine; in the dim light it appeared as black as the panels of her gown.

There was a sensuous pleasure in watching her take a sip from her glass. A ripple of excitement pulsed through him when the tip of her tongue slid across her lip. She was temptation indeed. He moved closer until the skirts of her gown brushed his legs.

'So, madam, will you stay with me for the rest of the evening?'

A warm sense of satisfaction spread through Felicity. She looked up at Nathan, noting the way his dark eyes glittered through the slits of his mask. He wanted her! Or, rather, he wanted the beautiful, entrancing creature she had become.

Felicity had no illusions; people behaved differently as soon as they put on a mask. She had experienced it herself. As soon as she walked into the ballroom she had been aware of the admiring glances, and safely disguised beneath the mask and the beautiful scarlet-and-black gown, her nerves had disappeared. She was not herself, but an enchantress, powerful and alluring, capable of seducing any man in the room. It was a role she was happy to play, if it kept Nathan by her side. She smiled up at him.

'If you so wish, my lord.'

'I do wish,' he said softly. 'I wish it very much indeed.'

Slowly he lowered his head and touched his lips against hers. Felicity trembled but did not recoil. She tasted the wine on his lips, breathed in the subtle spicy fragrance that hung around him and knew a momentary desolation when he raised his head. He gave her a reassuring smile and turned to watch the dancers. She stood beside him, observing the little smile hovering around his mouth, wondering if she dare reach up and plant a kiss on his lean cheek. She desperately wanted to be close to him, to feel his arms around her. She realised with a shock that she wanted him to make love to her.

It is the wine, she told herself fiercely. *It is making you reckless. You must be careful.* A little devil in her head mocked at her caution. *This may be your only chance,* it taunted her. *Take it!*

As if aware of her scrutiny Nathan turned and looked down at her. He put down his glass and held out his hand. 'We should dance again, I think.'

Nathan was entranced: the woman had intoxicated him. He was aware of the envious glances of the other men and the glares of the ladies, but only for a moment, for he found he wanted nothing more than to look at his partner, to watch her eyes glint with laughter when he said something to amuse her, to admire the slender column of her throat, the white, smooth skin of her shoulders and the soft, rounded breasts that nestled in the lace of her bodice. A flurry of activity near the door indicated the arrival of the Prince Regent's party, but Nathan took no notice. He only had eyes for the temptress beside him.

They danced and danced again and when she declared herself too warm he led her to one of the open windows and out on to a narrow terrace.

'Here.' He took the feather fan from her hands and began to wave it gently.

'Thank you, that is much better.' She leaned back against the wall and closed her eyes, smiling slightly.

Nathan looked at her. The ruby necklace glinted in the moonlight, inviting him closer. He reached up one hand to cup her face and slowly brought his mouth down upon the side of her neck. She trembled and slipped her hands over his shoulders, her fingers driving through his hair, holding him close. A tiny, whispering breath escaped her and he lifted his head.

'What did you say?'

'I sighed, merely.'

'You called me Nathan.'

'No. You are mistaken.'

He looked at her closely. 'We *have* met before, I know it.'

She gave the tiniest shake of her head. 'In our dreams, perhaps.'

'Now I have it! You were the mysterious lady in the Stinchcombes' shrubbery. My guardian angel.'

Her grey eyes glittered and a small dimple appeared at one side of that delicious mouth.

'That is a compliment indeed, my lord.'

'I must know who you are.'

He reached out towards her mask but she caught his hand, her eyes darkening, suddenly serious.

'No. If you unmask me I shall be obliged to leave. Let us enjoy this one brief moment.'

'But—'

She put her fingers to his lips saying softly, 'I am Temptation, nothing more.'

Her hands cupped his face. Gently she drew him to her until their lips were touching. The first, gentle contact deepened almost immediately into something much more passionate and Nathan gave himself up to the desire that had been building all evening. He gripped her shoulders, his mouth coming down hard upon hers, forcing her lips apart. She responded eagerly, tangling her tongue with his. Again, he revised his opinion of her: this was no shy lady out of her depth. The passion of her response fired him. She was eager for his touch and offered herself with a fierce abandon. He slid one hand around her back while his right hand caressed her neck, his thumb moving lightly along the line of her jaw. She clung to him, her body leaning into his. The blood pounded in his veins. He felt more alive than he had for years. He tore himself away from the delights of her mouth and began to kiss her breasts, desire slamming through him when he heard her moan softly.

Cry off, before it is too late.

The warning flashed through Felicity's head. She had never intended to let it get this far tonight—one dance was all she had hoped for, but the wine and Nathan's attentions had swept her up into a dream world where nothing else mattered, except being in his arms. The warning cried again in her mind but she ignored it; her body was yearning for Nathan to make love to her as he had done during those brief heady days in Corunna. She was overwhelmed by the white-hot passion cascading through her. She clung to him, giving him back kiss for kiss. She revelled in his touch, gasping as his hand slipped beneath the black lace of her bodice and caressed her breast. A fierce elation filled Felicity—she felt alive, irresistible. Dangerous.

Nathan raised his head, gazing deep into her eyes. 'Shall we finish this?'

She rested her cheek against his coat and heard the rapid beat of his heart beneath his jacket. 'We should go back into the house,' she whispered.

He sighed. 'I am not ready for this to end.' His hands tightened around her. 'Come with me,' he whispered urgently. 'Come away with me, now. Tonight.'

It was tempting. They could run away and continue this idyll—until he discovered her identity, then the questions would begin. There would be accusations, bitterness. Sadly, Felicity shook her head. 'I cannot.'

'Why? Is there a jealous husband ready to call me out?'

'No, but I cannot leave here with you.'

Silence stretched between them. Finally, with a little nod Nathan stood back and held out his arm.

'Then shall we go back inside?'

For a moment he thought he saw a shadow of unhappiness in her eyes and she stared at him as if trying to memorise every detail of his face.

'One last kiss,' she whispered.

Nathan obeyed. The heady fragrance of flowers filled his senses. He looked down at the woman in his arms. 'This cannot end here.'

'It must, my lord. It is the nature of the masquerade.'

'But you must tell me your name.'

A smile trembled on her lips. 'I have done so, sir. You need know nothing else of me.'

He gave a little growl of frustration. 'I need to know everything about you. I shall not let you go until I know everything about you!' A nearby church clock struck the hour. Nathan raised his head, counting. 'Twelve.' He laughed. 'Midnight! It is time for the unmasking.'

She put her hands against his chest. 'You go in—I need a moment to compose myself.'

He hesitated, covering her fingers with his own as his eyes searched her face. He said at last, 'Very well, but only one moment.'

She nodded. 'I will follow you. Now go.'

Nathan could not resist stealing one final kiss before he tore himself away and slipped back into the ballroom.

The orchestra played a fanfare as the last strokes of midnight died away and amid much laughter, cries and shouts the guests abandoned their disguises. Through the crowds Nathan could see Sir James and Lady Souden embracing, their masks discarded. Now was the moment. He tore off his own mask, glad to be free of it at last. He looked around for his lady. She had not yet come in and impatiently he stepped out on to the terrace.

It was empty. He walked the length of it and back again, but there was no sign that she had ever been there, save for a black feather fan lying discarded on the floor.

Swiftly Nathan ran down the steps into the garden. He tore around the side of the house to the front drive. Just in time to see a carriage driving out through the gates.

'Damnation!'

He watched the coach vanish into the darkness. It was too late; even if he called for his own chaise his quarry would have disappeared by now, effectively hidden amongst the other carriages filling the London streets.

Exhaling slowly, Nathan sat down on a low wall and stared into the darkness, aware of an overwhelming sense of loss. Temptation. She had named herself well. She had moved him more in a few short hours than any other woman he had ever known. His head went up. All except one.

Chapter Five

Only when she was safely inside the carriage and on her way back to Berkeley Square did Felicity allow herself to consider what she had done. She had spoken to Nathan, danced with him—and so much more. For a few brief hours he had been hers alone. In vain did she tell herself it meant nothing to him, that he would view it as a mere flirtation with a stranger. She had been in his arms, experienced his passion and nothing could crush the little seed of hope growing within her. She crossed her arms, hugging herself. Her body still burned from his touch. She closed her eyes and relived the evening, going over every word he had spoken to her, every little action. When she thought of their time together her insides melted again, just as they had done when he had taken her in his arms. She had spent so long trying to forget him and it had all been for nothing. She loved him now quite as desperately as she had done five years ago.

The pain and anger she had felt at his betrayal were diminished. Perhaps she had expected too much of him. Seeing Nathan again, being in his arms, had convinced her that she would rather be a small part of his life than to be out of it completely. If he would take her back. Slowly she removed her mask. Perhaps she should have revealed herself to him; she had heard that men would promise anything when they were in the grip of passion. She had been very tempted, but something had held her back, a fear that when his passion cooled he would regret his actions, and she could not bear to think of that.

She nibbled pensively at the tip of one finger as she considered what she should do next. It was a problem that occupied her thoughts for most of the night.

With the morning light came a solution. Determined to waste no time, she dressed quickly and made her way to Lydia's bedchamber. As Felicity followed the maid into the room, Lady Souden gave a little shriek.

'Heavens, Fee, what are you doing here so early? Go away, do, until Janet has had time to make me presentable!'

Felicity regarded her friend's frothy lace bedgown and the very fetching cap tied over her golden curls.

'You look very presentable, Lydia, and you are well aware of it. Now do, pray, let me talk to you. It is important.'

'Oh, very well.' Lady Souden waved her maid away. 'I confess I am desperate to learn how you went on last night— I saw you dancing with Rosthorne and could scarce contain my curiosity. If James had not been with me I vow I should have had to come to your room last night to find out what happened! He did not recognise you?'

Felicity perched herself on the edge of the bed. 'No. I left before the unmasking.' That at least was true.

'But he danced with you, several times, and I saw him taking you outside.'

Felicity's cheeks grew warm under her friend's scrutiny. 'Yes. He…kissed me.'

'Yes?' Lydia put down her cup. 'Is that all?'

Felicity hung her head, feeling the heat spreading from her cheeks—even the tips of her ears felt warm. 'It was a very—a very *passionate* kiss,' she mumbled.

'Oh, I knew it!' Lydia clapped her hands. 'I knew he would not be able to resist you! And he looked so preoccupied when we saw him later in the evening.'

'He did?'

'Quite distracted, my love! He left soon after midnight. Ring the bell, Fee! I must get dressed and we must think what to do—'

'I have decided what I must do,' Felicity interrupted her. 'I must write to him. I shall not give him my direction; I would not have him blame you or Sir James for my deception.' She clasped her hands together tightly in her lap. 'I shall explain everything, and throw myself upon his mercy. If…if he wishes to see me again it shall be arranged. If not…' she tried to smile '…I hope you will let me go back to Souden.'

'Of course you may, but I do not think that will happen. Once Rosthorne sees you again he cannot fail to want you.'

Felicity could not share her friend's optimism—there was so much Lydia did not know. She said in a low voice, 'There is no guarantee he will want to acknowledge me. In Spain he looked after me out of pity.'

'It was not pity that kept him at your side last night,' observed Lydia drily. She reached out and clasped Felicity's hands between her own. 'Have faith in yourself, Fee. I am confident the earl will want you back.'

'We shall see. Whatever the outcome, I am truly sorry to leave you without a companion—'

'That is of little consequence compared to your happiness. Besides, there is always my widowed cousin Agnes; she would dearly love to come and bear me company. But we have talked enough. I have arranged for us to go to the silk mercers in Covent Garden this morning, but after that I shall not need you, and you will be free to write your letter!'

However, when Lydia peeped into her room just before the dinner hour, Felicity was still at her writing desk.

'But how is this? Have you not finished yet?'

Felicity indicated the scrunched-up balls of paper littering the floor. 'All my attempts so far have come to nought. It is proving far more difficult than I thought to explain everything.'

'Perhaps you should just ask him to meet you.'

Felicity grew cold at the thought. 'But I behaved like a wanton last night—what will he think of me?'

'You have hidden yourself from him for five years,' retorted Lydia. 'Do you think Rosthorne will forgive that more easily?'

'No, I suppose not.'

'I do wish I could stay and help you with your letter,' said Lydia, 'but James and I are promised to attend the Prince Regent at the theatre tonight. You must wait up for me and I will tell you all about it. James has heard that the Princess of Wales will put in an appearance!'

'Poor woman,' murmured Felicity. 'I am sure she regrets her marriage. I know she does not behave very well—both she and the Regent are shockingly indiscreet—but one cannot help but feel sorry for her.'

'Feel sorry instead for James,' Lydia urged her. 'He will have the unhappy task of soothing the Prince's ruffled sensibilities if the Princess makes an appearance, as well as explaining away any awkwardness to the Tsar and his sister!'

After a solitary dinner Felicity returned to her desk, but soon discovered that her wasted efforts had exhausted her supply of paper and ink. Rather than disturb the servants she decided to go down to the morning room and make use of Lady Souden's elegant writing cabinet.

One of the best things about living in Berkeley Square, thought Felicity, was that Sir James ordered candles to be kept burning throughout the house during the evening, in readiness for his return from the nightly round of balls and parties that he and Lady Souden were obliged to attend. There was therefore no need for Felicity to use her bedroom candle to light her way down the stairs, nor did she have to send for more lights in the morning room: she had only to move a branched candlestick to the top of the writing cabinet to provide her with ample illumination. She spent some time searching for plain paper and mending her pen, then, unable to put it off any longer, she began to write.

She had scarcely finished the first line when she heard the door open and the footman's echoing utterance.

'The Earl of Rosthorne!'

The pen dropped from her nerveless fingers. She turned in her chair and stared as Nathan strode into the room.

The candlelight, which Felicity had thought so beneficial moments ago, now seemed far too glaring. There were no concealing shadows that she could step into, even if she could have made her limbs obey her, which she couldn't—they seemed to have turned to stone.

'So. It *is* you.'

Felicity could not speak. The footman withdrew, closing the door behind him. Fear tingled down her spine as she saw the glitter in Nathan's eyes. The thought flitted through her mind that she would be safer shut in with a wild animal.

'I thought you were dead.'

'No, I—' Her mouth felt very dry. 'How did you discover me?'

He put his hat and gloves upon a side table. The candlelight glinted on the heavy signet ring he wore on his left hand.

'Your disguise last night was very clever, but there was something…familiar about you. I couldn't put my finger on it, until you had gone.'

'How…who told you I was here?'

'You did.' .

She shook her head. 'But I never—'

'The Stinchcombes' garden,' he cut in. 'You told me you were a companion. It did not take any blazing intelligence to think of the self-effacing Miss Brown, Lady Souden's drab little attendant.'

She flinched, hurt by his scathing tone as much as his words. He crossed the room and stood over her.

'What was your plan?' he demanded. 'Did you think to ensnare me? To entangle me in a web of desire before revealing yourself?'

'No! I am even now writing a letter to you—'

'More lies!'

'No, I swear—' She forced herself to stand up. It was not quite so intimidating, even though her eyes were only level with the snowy folds of his cravat. 'Nathan, listen to me, please. I had no intention of *ensnaring* you. When I left Corunna I had no thought of ever seeing you again.'

'Until I became an earl!' he bit out. 'You had no wish to be the wife of a poor army officer, but a countess—no doubt you find the title irresistible.'

'That is not true!' She stepped away, trying to ignore the sheer animal power that emanated from him. She said slowly, 'Last night should not have happened. I meant only to dance with you.' She winced at his bark of disbelief. 'I thought, later, that there might still be some...hope for us. I have been trying to compose a letter to you.'

'Do you think you can explain everything?'

She was silent. The idea of baring her soul to this hard, angry creature was unthinkable.

'I tried to find you,' he said at last, rubbing at the scar above his eye. 'I put notices in the newspapers. Did you not see them?'

'Yes,' she said unhappily, 'but—'

'I told myself there could only be two reasons why you would not respond. The first was because you were dead, the second that you did not want to be found. I had hoped it was the first.'

She closed her eyes. How many times in those first months back in England had she indeed wished to die?

'What did you do with the money?'

'I beg your pardon?'

'My prize money. Every penny I had saved. I left it with you before I marched out of Corunna.'

'I…spent it.'

'Oh? How long did it last you?'

'Six, seven months.'

She shrank from the blaze of anger in his eyes.

'By God, madam, you must have lived high to spend it all in so short a time! Well, I hope you enjoyed it, because you won't get another groat out of me!'

'I do not want your money!' she shot back at him. 'I want nothing more from you. Ever!'

'Then why did you seek me out last night?'

Felicity glared at him, her bottom lip caught between her teeth. Her hopes and dreams seemed foolish now, but even so she could not bear to have him sneer at them.

'Think what you like of me,' she said coldly, turning away. 'I do not need to explain myself to you!'

He caught her shoulders and swung her round to face him. 'By God, I think you do, madam! Last night you seduced me—'

'I did not seduce you!'

'Hah! Then what would you call it? No mere maid would know such tricks.'

'If I used any *tricks*, sir, then I learned them from you!'

'Do you expect me to believe there has been no man in your life since you left me?'

She wrenched herself from his grasp. 'I do not *expect* you to believe anything I say!'

He folded his arms. 'Then you wrong me. I am very

ready to be convinced.' He waited, and when she did not reply he said, 'Perhaps you can explain what brought you to this household?'

'Lydia—Lady Souden and I were at school together. When—when I came back to England I had nowhere else to go, so I contacted her and—and she took me in.'

'And you have been her pensioner for the past five years.'

'Not at all.' Felicity's chin went up. 'Until very recently I was governess to Sir James's two sons.'

'And you call yourself Miss Brown.'

She looked away. 'I wanted to forget the past.'

'You thought that could best be done by starting a new life, with a new name?'

She shrugged. 'I did not wish to be any trouble…'

'Trouble!' With a grunt of exasperation he turned and strode about the room. At last he stopped by the fireplace. 'Did you think you would cause no trouble if you disappeared? Heaven and earth, do you have any idea how it was in Spain that winter?' He stared down into the empty, blackened hearth. 'We marched through hell to get back to Corunna, and all the time the French were snapping at our heels! My men were starving, we had scarcely one good pair of boots between us and we knew we would have to make a stand against the French with the sea at our backs. I expected you to be there, in Corunna, waiting for me—and then to find you gone! The town was in chaos, I did not know what to think, where to look. There were more than twenty thousand soldiers to be ferried out to the waiting ships and brought home. Do you think anyone had time to help me find one woman at such a moment? I prayed you had found safe passage back to England, but I could not discover it. Five years. *Five years* and not one word from you. Then I find you living here, right under my nose!'

'I did not plan this!' she cried.

'Then why did you come to London?'

'Lady Souden is in a—a delicate condition and asked me to accompany her, to be with her when Sir James cannot be at her side.'

'No doubt you both thought it a good jest to bamboozle me.'

'Not at all! I—I did not want to come to town. I knew it might be difficult but Lydia begged me—and I owe her so much.'

'Well, consider that debt paid. It is time to consider what you owe me.' He held out his hand to her. 'Come.'

She eyed him warily. 'I do not understand you.'

He grabbed her wrist. 'I am taking you back to Rosthorne House with me.'

'No! It is far too late at night. What will everyone think?'

'I neither know nor care.'

She tugged against his iron grip. 'No, I will not go with you!'

'And I say you will.'

He pulled her towards him and lifted her easily into his arms. Felicity gasped, then began to kick and struggle, but it was useless. His hold tightened, pinning her against his chest.

'Be still, woman. You did not fight me thus last night.'

She gave a sob. 'Let me go, you monster!'

He laughed harshly. 'Monster, madam? I am your—'

'What the devil's going on here?'

Sir James Souden stood in the open doorway, Lydia behind him, her eyes wide with amazement. Felicity's cheeks flamed. She stopped struggling and glanced up at Nathan. He seemed quite unperturbed.

'I am sorry to tell you, Sir James,' he said, 'that you have been harbouring an impostor.'

'Have you been drinking, Rosthorne? Put Miss Brown down immediately.'

Nathan merely tightened his hold. 'Ah, now there we have it. This is *not* Miss Brown.' His angry gaze scorched Felicity. 'This is my wife, the Countess of Rosthorne.'

Chapter Six

Sir James's brows snapped together. 'Good God, man, now I *know* you are foxed!'

A sardonic smile stretched Nathan's mouth. Felicity wished she could free her arm, for her hand itched to slap his face.

'Not at all,' said Nathan smoothly. 'Ask Lady Souden. I believe she knows the truth.'

Lydia pulled her husband into the morning room and shut the door upon the interested gaze of the footmen standing in the hall.

'I was aware of a connection, but not…' She stared at Felicity. 'It is a little complicated…'

Sir James had been a diplomat for too long to be shocked by anything. With a sigh he gently disengaged himself from his wife's grasp and turned again towards Nathan.

'Very well, then I demand an explanation of just what is going on in my house. Rosthorne, kindly unhand the lady and tell me what this is all about.'

Sir James's calm tones had their effect. Nathan set Felicity on her feet. She stepped away from him, smoothing down her crushed skirts and glowering fiercely.

Sir James smiled. 'Well now,' he said, at his most urbane. 'Shall we send for some wine?'

Nathan waited silently while Sir James rang the bell. The speed at which its summons was answered suggested that the footman had been standing very close to the door. Probably with his ear to the panel. Lady Souden had coaxed Felicity to the sofa where she sat very stiffly, her eyes downcast. With her disordered curls tumbling about her shoulders and a delicate flush on her cheeks he thought she had never looked more tantalising. Damn her.

Nathan had been perfectly ready to carry the wench off to Rosthorne House, but as his white-hot anger cooled he realised the situation would have to be handled much more delicately if they were to avoid a scandal. His only thought in calling at Souden House had been to prove that his guess was correct, but the shock of finding Felicity had been overwhelming. She was even more beautiful than he remembered, her face a little thinner, the cheekbones more defined, but those huge grey eyes still had the power to send his thoughts crashing into disarray. And remembering her passion last night on the terrace he had become prey to such a bewildering array of emotion that he had quite lost his usual iron control. Relief, joy, pain and anger had all fought for supremacy. Anger had won the first victory.

They waited in silence until refreshments were served. As he sipped at his brandy Nathan noted that Felicity's hands were not quite steady when she took a glass of burgundy. It was some consolation to know that she was suffering too.

'Now,' said Sir James, sitting back at his ease and smiling at the company. 'Who is going to explain? Lady Rosthorne, perhaps you would like to begin.'

Lady Souden sat up, her eyes shining. 'Rosthorne rescued Felicity from a group of desperate *bandidos* in Corunna!'

'Perhaps, my dear, you would allow the lady to tell her own story.' Sir James turned to the Felicity. 'I think I should like to know what you were doing in Spain in the first place—succinctly, please. It has been a long evening and I would appreciate brevity.'

Felicity was very still for a moment, as if gathering her thoughts. 'My parents died when I was very young. I was left in the guardianship of my uncle, but he was a bachelor and could not be expected to take me in. However, my parents left sufficient funds for me to live at an excellent school.'

'The Academy,' nodded Lydia. 'Where we met. She was Felicity Bourne then, of course—'

'Thank you, my dear,' said Sir James. 'Please continue, my lady.'

'I travelled to Spain in June in the year '08 with my uncle, Philip Bourne. He is—was—a clergyman. He had planned to go to Africa, as a missionary, but our ship docked at Corunna and we came ashore. Uncle said we would remain there, that it was his calling. He hired rooms for us and talked of opening a church, to cater for English travellers, but somehow it never came about. He was never well enough. He caught a fever within weeks of arriving in Spain, you see, and never recovered fully. In October he fell ill again and this time—' Felicity bit into her lower lip but Nathan observed how her little chin trembled. 'My uncle was not the best at keeping his accounts. I did not know how little money there was until—' She sighed. 'By the time I had paid the doctor and buried Uncle there was not enough left for my lodgings.'

Nathan watched as she collected herself and settled her hands once more in her lap. Pity stirred; this was difficult for her. There was a look of great determination in her face as she continued.

'I sold everything I could, hoping the money would last until I could find some kind of employment, but I was too young.' She raised her head. 'I was nineteen. If I had remained at the Academy I would have had charge of the younger girls by then, and in Corunna I saw women of my age with families of their own, but it seems that I was not to be taken seriously, except for…'

Nathan's hands clenched into fists. He had heard this. He knew what she was about to say.

'Except for?' Sir James prompted her gently.

Felicity shuddered. 'Our landlord said I could stay on in the rooms if—if I allowed him certain…favours. So I left. I was on my way to the town centre when I was accosted, and my bag was stolen.'

'Which is when the then-Major Carraway came to your aid.'

'Yes, Sir James. We…we were married a week later.'

Sir James sipped at his wine. 'Incomprehensible,' he murmured at last.

Nathan leaned back and shut his eyes.

Incomprehensible indeed, when stated so baldly. But not then. Then it had seemed the most logical thing in the world.

He had taken Felicity to Casa Benitez, fed her and put her to bed, removing her muddied clothes, bathing the dirt from the cuts and bruises on her arms. He held her when she awoke, terrified, from a nightmare, and watched over her when she drifted back to sleep. Even now he remembered staring at her exquisite profile with its straight little nose and determined chin, and her hair fanned out over the pillow like a deep, golden storm.

He had planned to be the perfect gentleman, but when she woke up and gave him a sleepy smile, he leaned over to drop a kiss on her forehead. Her eyes widened and he recognised the spark of desire in their grey depths. Her mouth had formed a little O of surprise and Nathan could not resist. He brushed her lips with his own and when she did not recoil he slid his mouth over hers. A little tremor ran through her, then she was kissing him back. Her inexpert embrace ignited his soul. He sensed the passion within her, wild and untamed and he wanted to be the one to release it. Their first, long kiss was deep and satisfying, but her inexperience tugged at his conscience and he broke away. She lay back against the pillows, breathing heavily, her eyes the colour of a stormy sea. Reluctantly he pulled himself away from her.

'Felicity. Listen to me: I have work to do this morning, but later today I shall take you to the British Envoy and we will explain your situation. Once he takes you under his protection you will be safe.' He turned, afraid that if he looked into her huge grey eyes again he would forget his honourable intentions. 'I must go out now. I have to talk to the local council about bringing our men ashore. You must remain indoors, do you understand? You must stay here where I know you are safe.' He heard her sigh and added more gently, 'I am sorry I have to leave you here, but I have a job to do.'

'Of course,' she said quietly. 'I understand that you must do your duty, Major.'

Three hours later Nathan had returned to the Casa Benitez, grinding his teeth in frustration and consigning all bureaucrats to the devil. He ran quickly up the stairs to his apartment to find Felicity waiting for him. As he entered the room she gave him her wide smile. It was like a burst of sunshine. Suddenly the day did not seem quite so bad. He felt his tension draining away.

'Is that your old dress? It has come up very well.'

She spread her skirts and dropped him a little curtsy.

'Thank you, Major. Sam managed to get nearly all the dirt out of it, and I have reworked the lace that was torn around the neck.'

'Very ingenious. Has that taken you all morning?'

'Most of it.' She pointed to the enclosed balcony. 'Since then I have been sitting in the mirador, looking out for you.'

He grinned. 'A tedious job!'

'Not at all. The Canton Grande is very busy, so there is always something interesting to be seen.' She indicated a little tray. 'Sam brought in your sherry. He thought we should fortify ourselves before we go off to see the British Envoy.' She poured out two glasses and handed one to Nathan. 'I admit I am a little nervous.'

'There is no need—Hookham Frere will find you charming,' said Nathan.

She sighed and put down her glass. 'I have had time to reflect upon my situation, Major, and I can quite see that you might not wish to be associated with me.'

His brows snapped together. 'What the devil—?'

She put up her hand. 'You have done more than enough for me already, sir, and I know you are very busy. I have no wish to importune you further, so if you would give me Mr Hookham Frere's direction I will make my way there alone and ask for his protection. If I can find someone to lend me the money for my passage home, I can contact the family lawyer; it may be that there is something left of Uncle Philip's estate to allow me to pay my debts. And if not I can return to the Academy and earn my living as a—'

'No!'

She turned her clear grey eyes upon him. 'I beg your pardon?'

'You should not do that.'

'You are being nonsensical, Major. I must do *something*.'

'Then you should marry me.'

'You said something, Lord Rosthorne?'

Nathan opened his eyes to find Sir James and Lady Souden watching him.

'The chaplain married us,' said Nathan crisply. 'It was a drumhead wedding, but perfectly legal. I marched out of Corunna with my regiment later that day, and that was the last I saw of my wife. I could find no trace of her and was forced to assume that she was dead. Until tonight.'

'And do we know why the lady ran away from you?' Sir James asked quietly.

Nathan glanced at Felicity. There was a hunted look in her eyes. No doubt she expected him to announce to all the world that she had stolen his prize money!

'A misunderstanding,' he replied curtly.

Her grey eyes flickered over his face. 'Yes,' she whispered miserably. 'A misunderstanding.'

Sir James bent an enquiring gaze upon his wife. 'And you knew all this, my dear?'

Lydia plucked nervously at her skirts. 'Not *everything*. Felicity came to me for help, and I could not refuse her.'

'Please, you must not blame Lady Souden,' Felicity put in. 'She knew nothing of my marriage.'

'Besides,' said Lydia. 'Lord Rosthorne—or Major Carraway as he was then—had returned to the Peninsula by the time Felicity wrote to me, so—so there really was nothing else to be done.'

Nathan could not but appreciate the imploring glance she cast at her husband. It was a nice mixture of regret, apology and entreaty. He found himself wishing that Felicity would direct such a look at *him*, but she merely sat with her head bowed. A sudden irritation came over him.

'Enough of this,' he declared, rising. 'It is very late. If you will excuse me, I will take my wife home now.'

From the tail of his eye he saw Felicity's head snap up.

Sir James set down his glass.

'I appreciate how eager you are to be—er—reunited with your wife, Rosthorne, but perhaps Miss…perhaps Lady Rosthorne should remain here for a little longer.' Before Nathan could object Sir James continued in the same thoughtful tone. 'A couple of points for you to consider, my dear sir. One, Rosthorne House is a bachelor establishment, is it not? Surely you would wish to make a few changes before you install your bride there. Two— and possibly of more concern—if the *ton* wake up tomorrow morning and discover you have a wife it will make you the object of speculation for every gossip-monger in town.'

'After what has occurred here, your servants will already be speculating,' Nathan retorted.

Sir James dismissed this. 'I pay my people well for their silence, but once outside this house you will find the world is less discreet. You will not deny that you have allowed everyone to think you are unmarried.'

Nathan flushed at the gentle rebuke. 'It was unconsciously done,' he said stiffly. 'Those who knew of my marriage were fighting in the Peninsula with me. Most perished there. When I came back to England, there seemed no point in dragging up the past.'

'Quite, but now it will be—er—dragged up, discussed and pondered over in every salon and coffee house in London,' observed Sir James. 'It cannot be avoided.'

'Yes, it can.' Felicity spoke up. She was very pale and was holding tightly to Lady Souden's hand. 'I could disappear again.'

'No!' Nathan's anger flared. In heaven's name, why did this woman hold him in such aversion? Even the French prisoners he had taken in battle had shown less desire to run away from him.

'I'm afraid that is impossible, my dear,' said Sir James, gently. 'You are Rosthorne's legal wife—we cannot ignore that fact. But perhaps we can take a little of the sting out of the gossip and speculation.'

Nathan sat down again. 'Go on, sir.'

'We could spread it about that you sent your wife back to England for safety,' suggested Sir James. 'After all, the war was going badly at that time, so no one would think anything amiss there. And what more natural that she should wish to stay with her lifelong friend?'

'For *five* years?' Nathan could not keep the sceptical note out of his voice.

'The war has only been over a few months, my lord.'

'And why did she not take my name?'

Sir James allowed himself a little smile. 'A foible. Women are prone to them, I believe.'

'Oh, well done, my love!' exclaimed Lydia, clapping her hands. 'An excellent notion!'

Sir James accepted his wife's praise with a faint smile, but his eyes were fixed upon Nathan, awaiting his response.

Nathan shrugged. 'I have no objection, but will Lady Rosthorne agree to it?'

Silently Felicity nodded, so pale and unhappy one would have thought she was agreeing to her own execution. Pity gnawed at Nathan and made him uncomfortable. Impatiently he rose again to his feet.

'Good, then it is settled,' he said. 'I shall return in the morning to collect my wife—' He observed the look upon Sir James's face and said impatiently, 'Good God man, what is it now?'

'I said at the outset that your wife should remain here and I still think that. Not only would it give both of you time to come to terms with the new situation but...' Sir James gave the slightest of pauses '...one must consider his Highness.'

Nathan stared at him. 'What the d—! What in heaven's name has the Regent to do with this?'

Sir James spread his hands. 'We are in the middle of his Peace Celebrations,' he said apologetically. 'They are not going well. Only tonight the Princess of Wales appeared at the theatre and drew everyone's attention. The sensational news that the Earl of Rosthorne has a wife could have very much the same effect, and you know how Prinny hates anyone to steal his thunder.' He paused. 'The Regent would make a powerful enemy, Rosthorne.'

Nathan was about to damn the Prince to perdition when his eyes fell upon Felicity. The abject misery in her face gave him pause. He could shrug off whatever the gossips said of him—it did not matter to him if the Prince turned him into a social outcast—but it would be different for his countess. He might disdain the Regent's good opinion, but there was no doubt that his Highness could make life very difficult for his wife. If the fashionable tabbies of the *ton* decided to unsheathe their claws they could destroy any chance she had of being accepted in town. They could make her unhappy, and much as he was tempted to wring her pretty little neck he was damned if he would let anyone else hurt his wife. He rubbed his chin.

'Your duties as escort to the Emperor of Russia will leave you very little free time for the next two weeks,' Sir James reminded him. 'I understand there are visits planned to the Royal Exchange, the Tower and the Abbey as well as various engagements in the City…'

'Very well, you need not go on. I will leave her in your care until the Tsar leaves London,' agreed Nathan. He directed a hard look towards Lady Souden. 'I make you responsible for my wife, madam; I shall hold you accountable if she slips away from me again!'

'P-perhaps I should leave town,' suggested Felicity.

Nathan shook his head. 'No. I want you here, where I can see you.'

Sir James agreed. 'If you remain here, my dear, it will give you and Lord Rosthorne an opportunity to get to know one other again.'

Lydia looked up, a speculative light in her eyes. 'My lord, will you allow Felicity to continue as my companion while she is here?'

'I do not see that that is his lordship's decision,' Felicity objected.

'Well, it would need both of you to agree, of course,' replied Lydia, unabashed, 'but it would mean that you could come about with me, at least until Cousin Agnes arrives.'

She turned a hopeful face towards her husband. 'Would you agree to that, my dear?'

'Since my primary concern is your welfare, love, of course—but I think it is for Lord Rosthorne and his countess to decide.'

Nathan hesitated. He did not want Felicity to be anyone's companion save his own, but after making such a mull of this encounter he realised that it might be to his advantage.

At last he nodded. 'I will allow this charade to continue for a while longer.'

'Excellent.' Sir James rose. 'Now I think that is quite enough for one night. I think we would all benefit from a little sleep. Allow me to escort you to the door, my lord.'

Nathan turned towards the ladies, but observing the way Felicity shrank away he merely bowed to them before accompanying Sir James out of the room.

'A most interesting evening,' murmured Sir James, linking his arm through Nathan's.

'That, sir, is an understatement!'

'So you and Miss Bro—Miss *Bourne*—met and married within a week? Hardly time to get to know one another.'

Nathan thought back. He had known after one day that Felicity was different from any other woman he had ever met. That she was the only woman he wanted for his wife. Nothing had happened in the last five years to change that.

Sir James continued, 'It is to be hoped you can find some time amid your duties as royal escort to plan your campaign.'

Nathan lifted an eyebrow. 'Campaign, sir?'

The older man's smile widened and he patted him on the back. 'Why, man, to court your wife all over again!'

Chapter Seven

Felicity awoke to the usual morning sounds: birdsong, the clatter of wheels and hooves on the cobbles beneath her window, the creak of floorboards. Sounds she had heard every morning since her arrival in Berkeley Square, but this morning something was different, something that made her stir restlessly against her pillows. Then it all came back to her and she was sitting up in bed, clutching at the bedcovers. Last night had not been a nightmare, Nathan really had come to the house. He really had recognised her.

She slipped out of bed and went to the chest by the window. Reaching beneath the neatly folded chemises and petticoats in the top drawer, her fingers closed around a small leather pouch. She pulled it out and tipped it up over her hand. Two rings tumbled into her palm.

Felicity remembered with perfect clarity when Nathan had given her the diamond ring. It was the eve of their wedding. Nathan came to collect her to take her to dinner, to meet his fellow officers. They had not gone many yards along the road when he stopped.

'Almost forgot. I bought you this today.'

He reached into his pocket and pulled out a small box.

Felicity took it, a smile of anticipation hovering around her mouth, which turned into a gasp as she opened the lid to find an exquisite diamond ring winking up at her.

'Oh, it is beautiful.'

'We are to be married tomorrow, and I cannot introduce you as my fiancée if you have no ring. Take off your glove and put it on. I hope it is the right size.'

'It is perfect,' she breathed. 'Thank you, Major.'

'I have a name, you know; I think it is time we were a little less formal.'

She looked up at him, smiling shyly. 'Yes, of course. Thank you, *Nathan*.'

She smiled up at him, flushing as she observed the warm glow in his eyes. She thought that only the fact that they were on a busy thoroughfare prevented him from pulling her into his arms and kissing her. Instead he looked away and cleared his throat.

'You had best put your glove on again.'

'Must I?' She looked down at her fingers. 'I want everyone to see my ring.'

He laughed at that. 'Very well—' he tucked her hand in his arm '—but these sea winds will chap your skin.'

'It will do no harm, this once. But should I not give *you* a ring?'

'That is not necessary; I have this.' He pulled a heavy gold ring from his right hand. 'My mother gave me this when I came of age three years ago. I shall wear this on my left hand from now on.'

'And the other ring, the band on your little finger?'

'A present from my grandfather when I joined the army. He said it would buy a few nights' lodging, or a pair of boots if ever I was in need.'

'It is very unusual,' she remarked, leaning closer to study the ring by the light of the torchères burning outside one of the houses.

'Yes, it is a thorn bush, the Rosthorne family symbol—a rose thorn, you see.'

Felicity looked at the gold band with its engraving of thorns running around it. She had a fleeting thought that he might have given her the smaller ring, rather than buying her a new one, but a glance at the little diamond on her finger, flashing fire as it caught the light, quelled any dissatisfaction. The diamond ring fitted her slender finger perfectly and she would treasure it always.

'Tell me again where we are going, Major.'

'To the hotel Fontana d'Oro. I want to introduce you to Adam Elliston. He and I grew up together, we are almost like brothers.'

'Then I should be delighted to meet him,' she replied, smiling.

He hesitated. 'He will be accompanied by a…' he coughed '…by Mrs Serena Craike. She is the wife of Colonel Craike.'

'And will Colonel Craike be there, too?' Felicity asked innocently, but then she glanced up at him. 'Oh, you—you mean that she, that she and your friend are…are *lovers*?' she whispered the last word.

'Well, he is besotted with *her*, but as for *love*—' Nathan's mouth twisted in distaste.

'Perhaps she is unhappy in her marriage,' mused Felicity.

'Perhaps. Adam is not the first man to fall under her spell.'

'Oh. Is she very pretty?'

'A beauty, if your taste runs to ripe redheads.'

Felicity picked up the second ring, a plain gold band, and held it between her fingers. She could remember only disjointed images from her wedding day. Being surrounded by men in bright uniforms, a loud-voiced officer with bushy side-whiskers barking orders at the chaplain, telling him to get on with it since the Guards were already marching out of Corunna, the officer's wife pressing a small posy of wild flowers into her hands. One or two of the officers she recognised, but Nathan's best friend, Adam Elliston, could not be spared from his duties and she was sorry for it, for Nathan's sake. She had no friends there but she wanted none, for Nathan was constantly at her side, making his vows with clipped assurance, sliding the wedding ring on to her finger, brushing her lips with his own.

'Well, Mrs Carraway…' Nathan turned his head to look at her. 'How do you feel?'

'Very strange,' she said slowly. 'I feel—no different.'

'Forgive me—to be married in such haste, at the drum's head—'

She put her hand to his lips. 'It is the vows one makes that are important, Nathan, not where one makes them.'

He handed her a small purse. 'This is all I have now. There is more than enough to keep you until we are together again. I have paid for board and lodging here for the next three months, by which time I hope to be able to send for you.' He put his arm around her. 'I am sorry to be leaving you so alone…'

'No, no, you must not worry for me. You have your duties to attend to, and as for being alone, I lived very isolated with my uncle, so I am used to that. At least now I have Señora Benitez, who is very kind, and I shall soon become acquainted with the other English ladies of the town.'

Smiling, he caught her hand and pressed a kiss in the palm. Then he put his hand under her chin and tilted her face up to kiss her, very gently, on the lips.

The shock set the nerves tingling throughout her body. She closed her eyes, relishing the sensation of his mouth on hers, the scent of his skin. She wanted it to go on for ever.

He took her back to the apartment on the Canton Grande and carried her into the bedroom.

'But, Nathan, your men.' Her protest was half-hearted. 'The colonel said you have to catch up with them…'

'Let them wait,' he muttered, setting her gently on her feet. 'I will ride all night if I have to.'

He put his hands on her shoulders and she trembled at his touch. She said shyly, 'How much time do we have?'

Nathan smiled at her. It sent a warm thrill down her spine and on, right to her toes.

'As long as we need, sweetheart.'

Felicity gave herself a shake. She dropped the rings back into the pouch and buried them deep in the drawer again. It was over. She had loved him, trusted him, and it had cost her dear. She would not allow that to happen again.

'Oh, what a fool I have been!' she exclaimed.

'What was that, my love?' Lady Souden came in, closely followed by Betsy with her morning tray.

'I wish I had stayed at Souden,' said Felicity morosely.

She allowed Betsy to place the tray on the bed, but she did not drink her hot chocolate, merely stared into its muddy depths. When the maid had left the room she looked up.

'Oh, Lydia, what am I to do?' she wailed.

'Do?' Lydia helped herself to one of the dainty strips of buttered toast lying on the tray. 'Why, my love, you must learn to be a countess.'

'But Rosthorne hates me!'

'No, no, Fee. He was a little put out last night, to be sure, but that is understandable. It was quite a shock for him to find you in London.' She giggled. 'It was quite a shock for *me*, when I followed James to the morning room and found you in Rosthorne's arms. I had not considered him to be such a passionate being.'

'It was not funny,' retorted Felicity, offended. 'It was quite frightening. I have never seen Nathan so angry. Heaven knows what would have happened if you had not arrived when you did.'

Lydia gazed at her, a knowing twinkle in her eyes. 'Do

you not, love?' Felicity's cheeks flamed and with a soft laugh Lydia reached out and patted her hand. 'I beg your pardon; I will not tease you any further. I thought James handled the whole thing very well, did not you? He is always so calm and sensible. And how delightful that Rosthorne has agreed to your remaining here with me.'

'But for how long?' replied Felicity. 'I am very tempted to keep to my bed, knowing that he might call at any time.'

As if to prove her words, there was a light scratching on the door and a flustered maid peeped in to announce that Lord Rosthorne was below and wishful to see Miss Brown. Felicity grew pale and turned her frightened eyes towards her friend. Lydia merely patted her hands.

'Tell Lord Rosthorne that if he would care to wait, Miss Brown will be with him in thirty minutes,' she said to the maid. She turned back to Felicity. 'Betsy shall help you into your gown and I will send Janet to dress your hair for you. Now that the earl knows who you are there is no need for you to look quite so Quakerish!'

'My uncle would have said it was a very appropriate look.'

'Your uncle tried to beat your self-esteem out of you,' retorted Lydia. 'The Academy trained us to be fitting partners for our husbands, not meek little servants. Remember that.'

Slightly more than half an hour later, Felicity was ready to descend. 'I wish you would come with me.' She gave Lady Souden a beseeching look.

'I am not yet dressed,' exclaimed Lydia, fingering the folds of her frothy negligee. 'Besides, Rosthorne would only request that I leave the two of you alone, I am sure.' She gave Felicity a reassuring pat on her shoulder. 'Go on now, and stand up to him; he is a gentleman, after all.'

Felicity cast her a darkling look. 'I hope Lord Rosthorne remembers that!'

★ ★ ★

She found the earl waiting for her in the library. He was standing by the window, his buckskins, topboots and the tight-fitting jacket he wore combined to accentuate his athletic form. He was idly spinning the terrestrial globe on its stand and did not look up immediately.

Felicity waited. With the light behind him she could not read his expression.

He said abruptly, 'I came—that is, I wanted to apologise for my boorish behaviour last night.'

She inclined her head. 'We were all a little on edge, my lord.'

'You have dressed your hair differently.'

Flushing, she put a hand up to her head. It felt strange after so long to have curls falling about her shoulders.

'Lady Souden suggested…'

'Ah, I should have guessed. She knows how to please a man.'

Felicity's cheeks burned at the inference. She pulled herself up a little taller. 'What can I do for you, my lord?' Her tone was as frosty as she could make it, but it had no visible effect upon the earl.

'May we not sit down?'

She sank into a chair, tensing herself as he chose to sit opposite her. She tried to ignore his searching gaze.

'You do not look to have slept well,' he said at last. 'If it is any consolation, neither have I. Your appearance in town was quite a shock for me.'

'I had hoped to break the news a little more gently.'

'It should not have been necessary to break it to me at all,' he ground out. 'You entered into a legal contract when we married, madam. It seems those vows that you professed were so important meant very little to you, since you ran away from me at the first opportunity!'

'No, no…' She must try to make him understand. 'You had a…' She fought to speak calmly. 'Someone said you had a mistress.'

'A mis—!' He raised his brows. 'And you believed that? Without even asking me?'

'It is unlikely that you would have told me the truth!' she retorted. 'Besides, you had already left Corunna.'

'Then you could have written to me—but that is not the point. What did it matter if I had a whole *string* of mistresses, you were no less my wife! You had no right to leave without a word. What in heaven's name was I to think?' He paused and drew a breath. 'When I returned to England I tried everything. I set the lawyers to work, I even sought out your late uncle's man of business. You might have applied to him for funds, you know, your uncle did not die a pauper.'

'I was afraid if I went to him he would tell you of it.'

Felicity kept her head bowed, but she could feel his eyes boring into her.

'Did I frighten you so much,' he asked quietly, 'that you cut yourself off from everyone who could help you?'

'Not quite everyone…'

'No.' The sneer in his voice was unmistakable. 'You went to Lady Souden. No doubt she thought it very romantic to take you in, to hide you away—'

'She wanted me to contact you! I made her promise to tell no one, not even Sir James!'

'So not only did you disregard your own marriage vows, but you persuaded your friend to deceive her husband.'

Felicity jumped up. 'When I left Spain I was hurt and angry. I wanted only to get away from you. I was…ill for a while and by the time I had recovered your regiment had sailed again for the Peninsula. Lady Souden offered me a home, and an occupation. It seemed best to take another name, to forget that we had ever married. I never thought to see you again.'

Nathan watched her, his arms folded across his chest and a cynical curl to his lips. 'Do you take me for a fool, madam?'

It was Felicity's turn to sneer. 'Is it so hard to believe that I wanted nothing more to do with you?'

'Oh, no, I am quite ready to believe that you were happy to abandon a penniless officer. Quite a different matter when you realised your husband was the Earl of Rosthorne.'

She gave him a scorching look and turned away from him.

'Yes, that would make sense,' he said, getting up and coming to stand behind her. 'To be married to a rich lord would be much more comfortable than to be the wife of a poor soldier, would it not? A handsome jointure might even reconcile you to my—ah—diversions.'

She swung round to find him so close that she was obliged to look up to meet his hard, angry eyes.

'I have never wanted your money! If I had done so I should have declared myself as soon as you became the Earl of Rosthorne.'

'Why did you not? Why leave me to think myself a widower? Good God, I might have taken another wife. Would you make a bigamist of me?'

'Of course not!'

She went to step away, but he grabbed her arms.

'So what *would* you have done if I had chosen another bride? Come to the church, perhaps, and declared yourself on my wedding day!'

'No! I never thought of that—I merely planned to hide myself away, to live quietly, under another name…'

'And now? What are we to do now?' His fingers dug into the flesh of her arms. 'Well, madam?'

She struggled angrily against his grip. 'I could go away, live abroad.' Her head went up. 'Or there is always divorce—heaven knows your name has been linked with any number of women!'

She met his gaze squarely. There was a flash of something in his eyes. Rage, surprise, she could not tell. He released her and she quickly moved out of reach, rubbing her arms. Scowling, he walked away from her and stood for a moment, staring out of the window.

'Is that what you want?' he said at last. He waited, then said harshly, 'I presume your silence means you do.' Slowly he turned to face her. 'Well, I'm *damned* if I'm going to make it that easy for you, madam. You married me, for better or worse. I give you fair warning that I intend to claim my wife!'

'That smacks of vengeance, my lord,' she challenged him. 'Hardly the sentiments of a civilised man.'

'Very likely,' he retorted. 'But I do not feel very civilised at the moment.'

'Well, let me remind you, sir, that this is a gentleman's house, and until you can act in a civilised manner I suggest you stay away!'

With that she swept out of the room, closing the door behind her with a decided snap.

Felicity flew the stairs. Her spine tingled. She was afraid that Nathan might follow her and drag her back, but it was only when she reached the second floor that she heard his booted tread on the marble floor below. Running to the balcony, she was in time to see him leave the house.

'Felicity, my dear, what happened?' Lydia appeared on to the landing. 'I heard raised voices.'

'As well you might,' replied Felicity, her voice shaking with anger. 'The man is a boor and a bully. I cannot think how I ever thought I could like him!'

Lydia drew her into her room and closed the door. 'What did he say?'

Felicity hunted for her handkerchief and defiantly blew her nose. 'I told him I knew of his mistress and he—he did not even care! He said he might have dozens of them, but it did not give me the right to leave him!'

'Well, legally, he is correct…'

'I do not *care* about the law,' declared Felicity. Her eyes narrowed. 'He says he will not let me go.'

'Well, that is a good sign, isn't it?'

'I am not sure. I think it is just that he does not like to be thwarted.' She sighed. 'He is so hard, Lydia, so angry; nothing like the kind, gentle man I knew in Corunna. Perhaps I was naïve to expect him to be the same; perhaps I never really knew him at all.'

Lydia patted her hands. 'You have startled him, that is all. I have always found Rosthorne a most charming man, and James thinks very highly of him. I think he will make you a very considerate husband.'

'And what of his mistresses? You have heard the gossip, Lydia—Europe is littered with them. It is not to be expected that he will change.'

'But it *is* possible,' said Lydia. She added gently, 'We must face facts, my dear. Many men take a mistress, although I do not think that James has ever…but he is the exception, I fear. To have a kind, generous, considerate husband is more than most women dare hope for and I think Lord Rosthorne is all of those things. When you have had a little time to grow accustomed I feel sure you will deal very well together. But, there is nothing else to be done about it at the moment, so go and change into your walking dress. A little exercise will do you good. I shall expect you downstairs in half an hour.'

'Why, where are we going?' called Felicity as Lydia went to the door.

'To New Bond Street,' came the airy reply. 'We are going shopping!'

It was three days before Nathan managed to catch up with his wife again. In between riding out to Richmond to escort Tsar Alexander back to town and accompanying Marshal Blücher when he attended a military review, he had called at Berkeley Square, only to be told that Lady Souden and Miss Brown had gone out and were not expected back until the evening. He had called again while the Tsar and his sister were at one of the innumerable parties being held in their honour and was informed that the ladies of the house were dining out.

The following day he had dashed off a terse note, requesting an appointment and received a very civil response from Lady Rosthorne explaining that the ongoing Peace Celebrations were causing such a clash of engagements that she could not possibly say with any certainty when she would be at home. Nathan was not taken in by the apologetic tone of the note, which he ground savagely between his fingers. It was plain that Felicity was avoiding him.

When he had worked off his anger with a strenuous bout of fencing practice Nathan was able to look back upon his last meeting with Felicity, and to acknowledge that he had given her little reason to seek out his company. It seemed they could not meet without ripping up at each other. But surely he had reason to be angry. Her erroneous belief that he had been keeping a mistress in Corunna was a feeble excuse for running away from him. It was much more likely that she wanted his money—he would not be the first soldier to fall victim to a heartless adventurer. But Felicity was not heartless, he would stake his life on it, and it was quite possible that she had needed his money when she returned to England—had she not told him that she had been ill? He needed to talk to her.

With this in mind he presented himself at Lady Templeton's rout the next night. He was in no very cheerful mood as he entered the crowded ballroom. When he was given leave from his escort duties the last thing he wanted to do was to attend another party, but this promised to be one of the most glittering occasions of the season and he was confident he would run his quarry to ground there. It appeared that all London was crammed within its elegant walls. He stepped quickly into the crowd to avoid Lady Charlotte, looking magnificent in diamonds and lace, and he soon spotted his cousin Gerald flirting outrageously with the Tsar's sister, the Grand Duchess of Oldenburg.

He turned away, thankful that for tonight at least the royal party was not his concern. His height gave him the advantage as he swiftly surveyed the room and he soon spotted Lady Souden talking to their hostess and—yes, standing behind her was Felicity. He noticed immediately the subtle difference in her appearance. She wore no concealing fichu around her neck and her gown of rose-coloured muslin accentuated the creamy whiteness of her flawless skin. Her honey-coloured hair was no longer combed flat and constrained in a knot but now hung in soft curls about her head, with one glowing ringlet coaxed to hang down beside the slender column of her neck and rest upon the gentle swell of her breast. Little changes, but the effect took his breath away.

Felicity saw Nathan as soon as he entered the room and it was with some unease that she watched him pushing his way through the crowd, a determined look on his face. She touched Lydia's sleeve and was gratified when her friend reached out to give her hand a reassuring squeeze. As Nathan came up Lydia smoothly ended her conversation with Lady Templeton and turned to greet him.

'My Lord Rosthorne, how delightful.' She held out her hand and he could do nothing but take it, although his impatience was ill-concealed.

'Your servant, my lady. Miss Brown.'

Remembering their last meeting, Felicity gave him only a cool nod of recognition.

'I wonder, Miss Brown, if you would do me the honour—'

'Oh, you would like Miss Brown to dance with you!' Lydia broke in. 'Yes, yes, do go along, my dear, I do not need you for the moment.' She put her arm across Felicity's shoulders and pushed her forward. 'There you are, my lord, a charming partner for you. But be sure to bring her back to me directly the dance is ended!'

'You were not going to ask me to dance, were you?' Felicity challenged him as he led her away.

'No. I want to arrange a time to see you. Alone.'

Her spirits dipped. There was nothing of the lover in his tone. 'That may not be possible, we are very busy…'

'So I understand.' He took his place opposite her in the line, his frowning gaze never leaving her face. 'But it must be done.'

The music began. Felicity gave him her hands, stepped close, then back, all the time gazing up at her partner. He looked so stern that it was difficult to believe he was the same man she had danced with at the masquerade. Then there had been a smile on his lips and a glint in his brown eyes. But *then* he had not known who she really was.

'You sigh, Miss Brown. Do you find me so tedious as a partner?'

They were so close it was safe to reply without anyone overhearing.

'I was thinking of the last time we danced, my lord.'

'At the masquerade?' He brought his head closer. 'I have told you, madam—that was not so much a dance as a seduction.'

She flushed. 'I beg your pardon. I behaved then like a wanton.'

His grip on her hand tightened painfully, but before he could respond the dance drew them apart. Her spirits dipped even further. He had not contradicted her; perhaps such behaviour was acceptable in a mistress but not in a wife.

'So will you tell me when I may see you?' he asked, when at length they came back together. 'I could call tomorrow morning.'

'Lady Souden and I are going out—'

'Tell her you cannot go.'

'No.' Felicity recalled the scandalised faces of the servants the last time they had been alone together in Berkeley Square. She did not think her reputation would withstand another such meeting. 'I cannot meet you alone at the house.' A muscle flickered in his cheek, as if he was keeping his temper with difficulty and she added quickly, 'I—I will think of somewhere… Pray give me a little time.'

Again that iron grip squeezed her fingers. 'You have until the end of the evening, madam!'

They finished the dance in stony silence and Nathan escorted her off the floor with almost indecent haste, his countenance shuttered and cold. It seemed to Felicity that he could not wait to part company. She moved towards Lady Souden, only to find Gerald Appleby blocking her way.

'Well, well, Miss Brown I must take you to task! I was led to believe you never danced, yet I have been watching you on the dance floor with my cousin here. If you can dance with Rosthorne, then you cannot say nay to me! Come along, Miss Brown.' As he reached for her hand Nathan stepped up and grabbed his arm.

'You are too impatient, Appleby. The lady has not consented.'

Felicity blinked, startled by the icy menace in his tone.

Gerald regarded him with a mixture of laughter and surprise in his face. 'What have you done to my cousin, Miss Brown? He looks ready to call me out.'

Nathan released his grip. 'I would not have you importune the lady, that is all,' he said coolly. 'If she wishes to dance with such a fribble that is her choice.'

'A fribble, am I?' Gerald grinned and cocked an eyebrow at Felicity. 'Well, ma'am, will you dance with me?'

She hesitated. Beyond Gerald, Lady Souden was smiling at her and nodding, but Nathan bent on her a furious glare. Perhaps he was not quite so indifferent after all. Her shoulders straightened. She lifted her head. 'Why, yes, Mr Appleby, I will dance with you.'

Nathan's lips thinned and he bowed, unsmiling, to Felicity. 'Until later, Miss Brown.'

Chapter Eight

Dancing with Gerald did much to restore Felicity's spirits. She was amused by his cheerful banter but more than this, she was aware of Nathan's eyes upon her throughout the dance.

'I vow I am much encouraged by Lord Rosthorne's behaviour,' murmured Lydia as they made their way to the supper room soon after. 'To accost Mr Appleby in such a manner is most unlike him. There can be only one explanation, Fee. He is jealous!'

'Do you really think so?'

'Why, yes, I do! The whole time you were dancing he stood by and watched you, his arms across his chest and such a dark and brooding look upon his face I declare no one dared approach him.' She gave a little giggle. 'Very romantic—just like Lord Byron's *Corsair*.'

'I have not yet read that so I have no idea what you mean.' Felicity tried not to think of Nathan as dark and brooding, it made her knees grow weak. Instead she tried to think of somewhere safe to meet him on the morrow.

In the supper room a deferential footman approached and murmured quietly to Lady Souden. Following his oustretched hand Felicity observed Lady Charlotte

Appleby on the far side of the room, nodding and smiling towards them. Lydia allowed herself one swift, rueful glance at Felicity.

'We are summoned,' she murmured.

Lydia led the way across the room, greeting Lady Charlotte in her soft, well-modulated voice and sinking gracefully on to a chair.

'My dear Lady Souden, such a crush, is it not? I thought it best to bring you here—heaven knows whom you might have found at your table with you.' Lady Charlotte's strident tones carried around the room and Felicity found several pairs of eyes turning towards them. Lydia turned off her comment with a soft, laughing rejoinder, but Lady Charlotte's attention had already moved on. She called for wine, then sat back and ran an appraising eye over Lydia.

'Sir James is not with you tonight?'

'No, ma'am, he is accompanying Marshall Blücher to a dinner in the city.' Lydia glanced briefly at Felicity and gave her a smile. 'But I am not unaccompanied.'

'No, I noticed.' Lady Charlotte sat up very straight. 'I saw your companion earlier. She was dancing.'

'Why, yes. Miss Brown is a very elegant dancer.'

'That is not the point,' declared Lady Charlotte. 'I saw her dancing with *Gerald*. It will not do.' She beckoned Lydia towards her. 'You should drop a hint to her, my dear Lady Souden. My son is a very engaging young man, but she must not set her sights in that direction. Gerald is not for her.'

Her carrying whisper reached Felicity's ears and continued on to the surrounding tables.

'No,' continued Lady Charlotte with a regal disregard for the smiles and smirks around her. 'He is Rosthorne's heir, you know. Gerald is destined for Great Things.'

Lydia's eyes darkened with anger, but she returned a non-committal answer and neatly turned the subject. Felicity kept her head down and picked at the choice morsels provided by Lady Templeton for the delectation of her guests. It was depressing to realise that if Lady Charlotte thought her too lowly for her son, she would certainly not consider her a fitting consort for Lord Rosthorne.

She was relieved when at last Lady Souden rose from the table and carried her back into the ballroom, murmuring as she went, 'Poor Fee, what an evening we are having. Shall we go home?'

'When you are ready, my lady.'

'Then pray go downstairs and bespeak our wraps. I will take my leave of our hostess.'

Felicity hurried out of the room, but just as she reached the top of the stairs a drawling voice stopped her.

'Are you planning to run away without seeing me?' Nathan stepped towards her. Instinctively she put out her hand as if to ward him off. He took it in his own.

'L-Lady Souden wishes to leave.'

'But you would have sought me out, to say goodnight.'

'I—' All she could think of was his thumb gently massaging the inside of her wrist. It robbed her of any power of speech.

'So have you decided upon a meeting place for us tomorrow?'

'It—it is so difficult,' she stammered. 'I am very busy.'

'So too am I,' he growled, pulling her closer. 'Let it be early then. Shall we say six o'clock? I do not think even Lady Souden will require your services at that time in the morning.'

She swallowed. 'N-no, of course not. A-and where shall we meet?'

'Green Park—the Queen's Walk. I shall be there at six.' He lifted her hand to his lips. 'Do not fail me!'

Felicity nodded. As Nathan turned and walked away, a movement to one side caught her eye—Lady Charlotte was standing at the supper room door, her cold eyes snapping.

'Quite the little belle of the ball tonight, are you not, Miss Brown?'

Without a word Felicity hurried off down the stairs.

London was surprisingly busy at six o'clock on a summer's morning. The *haut ton* were still in their beds, but an army of servants was already hard at work scrubbing and cleaning and polishing the grand houses while in the streets a steady stream of carts and wagons rumbled by, carrying everything from fresh vegetables for the markets to paper and board for the bookbinders. Felicity slipped out of the quiet house in Berkeley Square and into this busy, bustling world. No one took any notice of a little figure in a serviceable cloak and bonnet and she moved without incident through the early morning streets until she came to the gated entrance to Green Park. The path Nathan had mentioned was easily found. It was lined by trees and to her left the tall houses of Arlington Street rose up, their rear windows overlooking the path. One of those houses, she knew, belonged to Lord Rosthorne. She would be living there now, if Nathan had his way. She pushed the thought aside.

She moved deeper into the park, where the buildings were screened by high walls or bushes and the noise of the streets was replaced by birdsong. An early morning mist clung to the trees and she pulled her cloak about her, unnerved by the stillness around her after the bustle of Piccadilly.

Felicity began to wish that she had brought a footman with her. The path was deserted, but she glanced left and right, half-expecting a menacing figure to jump out. She had reached a slight bend in the path when her straining ears heard sounds that set her heard pounding: a grunt, succeeded by several dull thuds. She should turn and run, but instead her feet carried her on past the bush that obscured her view.

* * *

Nathan arrived at the rendezvous early, admitting to himself his eagerness to see Felicity again. He was still angry with her for hiding from him for all these years, but she was his wife and he was anxious now to bring this matter to a close. He swiped at one of the bushes with his cane; Sir James had told him to court Felicity, but he was damned if he would do any such thing. Confound it—a man should not have to woo his own wife! A still, small voice in his head whispered that if he had courted her properly five years ago she might never have run away from him, but he swiftly quelled the thought.

A sudden sense of danger intruded into his thoughts. He was instantly on the alert. A slight sound behind him made him turn, just in time to see a heavy cudgel swinging towards his skull. Nathan ducked, but not quick enough and the club caught him a glancing blow to the head, sending his hat flying off. He dropped his cane and closed with his assailant, seizing his wrist in an iron grip and twisting until the club fell from his nerveless fingers. His vision clearing, Nathan drew back and delivered a well-aimed fist to the man's body. He grunted and as he bent forward, winded, Nathan sent a second blow slicing upwards to his chin. The man collapsed and Nathan stood back, pausing to drag one arm across his eyes to wipe away the blood. In that brief moment his opponent scrambled to his feet and dashed off into the bushes. Nathan was about to give chase when he heard a noise behind him and he looked round to see Felicity staring at him, white-faced.

'I beg your pardon,' he said. 'I would not have had you witness that.'

'You are bleeding.'

'It's nothing.'

'No, do not use your arm, you are wiping the blood over your face.' She came forward, pulling a handkerchief from her reticule.

Nathan reached into his pocket, saying, 'I have my own—'

'Then use it as a pad over the cut, while I clean your face.' She guided his hand to his head. 'There, you have covered it.'

Nathan held his breath; she was standing very close to him, her whole attention on the wound, but her face was only inches from his mouth. He was greatly tempted to lean forward and kiss her. As if suddenly aware of his thoughts she dropped her hand and stepped away.

'I am sorry,' he said. 'So much blood on my face—and with my scar, too, I must look monstrous.'

She smiled at that. 'Hideous,' she agreed. She moistened her own small handkerchief with her lips. 'Allow me to clean you up a little.'

He stood passively while she wiped the blood from his cheek and brow. Her hand faltered as she touched his scar.

'When did this happen?' she asked.

'Spain. We were withdrawing from a little village called Pozo Bello. I got in the way of a French cavalry sword.'

'I am so sorry.'

Nathan shrugged, uncomfortable with her sympathy. 'I was one of the fortunate ones. Elliston died there.'

Felicity's large grey eyes filled with tears. 'Adam Elliston? Oh, I did not know.'

'No, you had disappeared and I had no way of informing you.'

She recoiled at his tone and Nathan cursed himself for his clumsiness. He tried to think of something conciliatory but she forestalled him, saying in a matter-of-fact tone, 'You look a little more presentable now, sir. Has your head stopped bleeding? We should move back towards Piccadilly, I would prefer to be able to call for help should your attacker return.'

He picked up his hat and placed it gingerly upon his head, wincing a little as the brim pressed upon the fresh wound.

'He will not come back.'

'You cannot be sure of that.' She handed him his cane. 'I wish you will take care, my lord.'

'I do take care, but footpads are a hazard in London. I do not heed them, I have broad shoulders.'

'And a broad back for an assassin's blade!'

'Now what nonsense is this?' demanded Nathan.

'Three attempts upon your life, sir—'

He laughed. 'Are you thinking of the supposed intruder at the Stinchcombes' garden?'

'There *was* someone there, my lord, I know it, I saw them. And I saw something glint, like the blade of a knife. And the shot that took off your hat—'

'That was merely an accident.'

'But what if that was meant for you and not the Tsar?' she persisted.

With a smile he caught her hand and pulled it on to his arm. 'I am touched by your concern, but you must not let these events worry you. Why should anyone want to kill me?'

'I do not know, but—'

He put up his hand. 'Enough, now. I will give the matter some thought, I promise you.'

They began to walk back towards Piccadilly. Felicity tried not to cling too tightly to Nathan's arm, but her spine tingled uncomfortably as they made their way to the park entrance and she breathed a sigh of relief once they were in sight of the busy road.

'You are shaking,' observed Nathan. 'I shall escort you back to Berkeley Square.'

'There is no need, my lord.'

'There is every need.'

Felicity inclined her head. Secretly she was relieved that she did not have to make her way back to the house alone. She had been shaken to come upon Nathan fighting off an attacker and her knees were still inclined to be a little wobbly.

'You have not yet told me why you wanted to meet, sir.'

'Because I only ever see you in company. I confess I did not intend to put you in any danger; I thought the park would be safe enough at this time of day. Which puts me in mind of something,' he said suddenly. 'What in heaven's name are you doing abroad unattended? Why did you not bring a footman with you, or at the very least a maid?'

'I was trying to avoid gossip,' she retorted. 'Like you I thought it would be safe enough at this early hour.'

'Thank God that you did not arrive first in the park and fall victim to that ruffian. He was probably loitering near the gate, waiting for someone to turn into the park.'

Felicity bit her lip. She was still convinced that it was no random attack and was about to say so again when Nathan forestalled her.

'You are too careless of your own safety, Felicity. I begin to think it might be better for you to leave London after all.'

'But why should I do that?'

'Until it is known that you are my wife I cannot protect you.'

'I do not need your protection,' she retorted, nettled.

'No? Appleby is already paying you far too much attention.'

She raised her brows. 'Are you jealous of him, my lord?'

'Good God, no! I am merely concerned for you. Discretion is not one of Gerald's strong points.' He glanced down at her. 'So will you go out of town?'

Felicity hesitated. 'I am sorry, I cannot,' she said at last. 'Lady Souden needs a companion and her cousin cannot be here until the end of the month.'

'Two weeks! Surely Lady Souden can manage without a companion until then.'

Felicity shook her head. 'You know, of course, that Lady Souden is expecting a happy event in the autumn and Sir James wants someone to be with her at all times.' She paused and added with some difficulty, 'I know you cannot like the fact that she helped me to deceive you, but she has been a very good friend to me. Besides, carrying a child is an anxious time for any woman. I want to be with Lydia, to support her.'

Nathan did not reply immediately, but at last he put up his hand and briefly covered her fingers where they rested on his sleeve.

'Very well, we will keep to the original plan.' He exhaled and Felicity heard a wealth of frustration in the sound. 'But you must take care—remain in the house as much as you can.'

Her lips twitched. 'That would hardly make me a good companion, sir.'

'Lady Souden cannot be out all the time!'

'Well, during the day there are carriage drives and morning calls to be made and at night of course there are parties, routs, balls—'

Nathan swore under his breath.

'My lord?' She glanced up innocently.

'And you have to be present at all these events?'

'Oh, no, not all of them. Only those that Sir James cannot attend.'

His jaw was clenched. 'Then when you are out make sure you do not attract attention.'

'Yes, my lord,' she answered meekly.

'And at the balls you are not to dance.'

'No?'

'No,' he said forcibly. 'At least, you are to dance with no one but me!'

Chapter Nine

Felicity's return to Berkeley Square did not go unnoticed and it was not to be expected that Lady Souden would let her rest until she had given her all the details of her morning adventure. Felicity was disappointed when Lydia made light of the attack upon Nathan.

'My dear, it happens all the time. No one is safe on the streets—and that reminds me: you should not have gone out without a footman—Sir James's staff are most discreet, especially if you slip them a few extra shillings! But what is this about Rosthorne wanting you to go out of town?'

'He is anxious for my safety.'

Lydia gave her a sideways look. 'He is very possessive of you, Fee.'

'He is not jealous, if that is what you mean.'

'No? Yet you say he gave you orders to dance only with him.'

'Yes.'

With a little cry of delight Lydia clapped her hands. 'It is a Case, I know it! Oh, if only we can persuade a few more gentlemen to flirt with you under Rosthorne's nose…'

'No! I will not tease him, Lydia. When he is in a passion he is…ungovernable.'

'That is because he is desperate for you, my love,' replied Lydia sagely.

Felicity shook her head. 'It is merely that he does not like to be crossed.'

'We shall see—oh, I know what I shall do!' declared Lydia, jumping up. 'I shall dash off a note to the earl now, asking him to join us for dinner before we go to the reception at Carlton House tonight.'

'Lydia, no!'

'Felicity, *yes!*' retorted Lady Souden, adding with spurious sympathy, 'Poor man. It pains me to think of him dining alone in that enormous town house of his.'

'Lydia, *please* do not write to him,' Felicity begged as she followed her down to the morning room. 'I would as lief not see him again so soon.'

'My dear, if it would upset you so very much then I shall not invite him, but why, my dear?'

'I am in turmoil, in here.' Felicity pressed her fist against her chest. 'I need a little time to think everything over.'

'What is there to think of? He had a mistress so you packed your bags and left him. That was five years ago, my love. He was very angry that you ran away, but now you have explained it all to him, have you not?'

Felicity said nothing. There was a secret that she could never bring herself to share with anyone, especially Nathan Carraway.

When Sir James declared that he would be escorting his wife to the ridotto the next night, Felicity declined an invitation to accompany them.

'Pray do not think that I shall be bored here alone,' she explained, smiling. 'I have my books, and I think perhaps I should write to my uncle's lawyer, to advise him of my direction. If there is anything due to me from Uncle Philip's estate, it would be a comfort to know I do not go to Rosthorne penniless.'

As soon as Sir James and Lydia had left the house, Felicity made her way to the morning room. After several false starts she managed to compose a satisfactory letter and was fixing the seal when she heard the low rumble of voices in the hall. Some premonition of danger made her jump up, but before she had reached the door it opened and Lord Rosthorne entered.

'Miss Brown—please—do not run away.' Without taking his eyes from her he raised one hand and dismissed the footman. The door closed and he stood for a moment, watching her. His lips twitched. 'Poor Fee, you look as if you have been locked in a cage with a tiger.'

'S–Sir James and Lady Souden are out, my lord.'

'I know, I met them at the ridotto. That is why I am come here, to see you. Will you not sit down? I promise I mean to behave myself.' He guided her to the sofa and gently pushed her down, seating himself at the other end and turning a little so that he could look at her.

'How is your head now, sir?'

'Sore, but mending.'

Felicity bit her lip and twisted her fingers together nervously.

'You were not wont to be afraid of me, Fee.'

'You were not wont to be so severe.'

'No. Those years fighting in the Peninsula have taken their toll. I am not the same man I was five years ago.'

'I followed your progress as closely as I could,' she told him. 'Sir James has the London newspapers sent to Souden; I read all the reports.' She glanced at him. 'Such a long campaign. It must have been very difficult for you.'

'I found it more difficult when I sold out and took control of the Rosthorne estates.'

'But war is so terrible, so much violence and death—the loss of your friends, like Mr Elliston.'

He frowned and she thought for a moment he would not reply.

'Yes, that was bad,' he said at last. 'His parents live near Ros-thorne Hall. I brought back what possessions he had when I came home, but at the time, writing to tell them Adam was dead was the hardest thing I ever had to do, I think.'

He stared down at his hands, his thoughts far away. Felicity let the silence settle around them for a few minutes, then she spoke again, trying to keep her voice light and indifferent.

'Do…do you ever see any of the people who were at Corunna? Colonel and Mrs McTernon, perhaps, or Mrs Craike…'

He looked up. 'The colonel and his wife are in France now. As for Mrs Craike, her husband died on the retreat to Corunna and she came back to England. Within a year she had married Sir Alfred Ansell.'

'Married! But I thought—' Felicity broke off, flushing.

'Did you think she would marry Adam?' His lip curled. 'Adam was a diversion for her, but he was never rich enough to keep her interest. It amused her to beguile naïve young men.'

And you, Nathan, did she beguile you? The question hovered on Felicity's tongue, but she could not bring herself to voice it.

'Elliston was devastated when he heard,' Nathan contin-ued. 'I think he could have borne it better if he thought she had married for love, but Ansell was old enough to be her grandfather—it was plain she took him for his money.' His next words answered her unspoken thought. 'I don't doubt you would have seen her in town, but Sir Alfred died last winter and she is still in mourning.'

Felicity looked down at her hands, clasped tightly in her

lap. 'You seem to have followed her career quite closely,' she observed.

'One cannot avoid hearing the gossip.' He waved an impatient hand. 'Enough of this. I came here to talk about you.'

'A—about me?'

'Yes. I meant to ask you yesterday, but we were—er—distracted. I want to know all that happened to you after you left Corunna.'

'I—I bought my passage home.'

'And lived like a duchess until the money ran out.'

Felicity did not reply.

'I would not have left you with a penny if I had known how you would spend it!' growled Nathan.

Felicity's head went up.

'We had known each other but a se'ennight,' she challenged him. 'Would you have me believe you were heartbroken when you discovered I was gone?'

'Of course not. Inconvenienced, merely.'

She jumped to her feet and walked over to the window, staring out into the near-darkness. 'If I was such an...an *inconvenience*, I am surprised you want me back.'

Nathan had wondered about that himself. He believed it was because he could not resist a challenge, but there was something else. When he had danced with Felicity at the masquerade she had gazed at him as if he had been the only man in the room. It was an image that disturbed his dreams, but it would not do to own it. For now he needed to provide a logical answer. He said roughly, 'You are my *wife*, madam. We may have been married by an army chaplain but it is the vows that are important. *Your* words, Felicity, remember?'

'Yes, I remember—and I remember you promising to forsake all others.'

His brows snapped together. 'What the devil do you mean by that?'

'I too have heard gossip, my lord! You have not been monk-like these past few years.'

With a smothered oath he crossed the room in two strides and caught her by the shoulders, roughly turning her towards him. 'Dear heaven, you try my patience! By running away you gave me no *opportunity* to be faithful to you!'

'You blame me, then, for leaving you?'

'Yes, I do! I blame you very much for not waiting for me, for not giving our marriage a chance!'

Felicity stared at him, shaken by the violence of his outburst. Was it possible that she had been mistaken? Had she been wrong to leave him? If she had stayed, if she had not been weakened by that rough sea crossing...

Abruptly Nathan released her and turned away, running a hand through his hair. He did not mean to hurt her, but every time they met she roused such a passion in him!

'Perhaps,' she said haltingly, 'perhaps I should not have left Corunna. Perhaps it would have been better to wait, to talk to you.'

'Much better,' he said grimly.

She was hunting for her handkerchief. He held out his own and she took it, silently. His arms ached to hold her, but even as he reached out she stepped away from him. He said quietly, 'Let us leave the past. We can deal together better than this, Felicity. We need to get to know one another all over again.'

She blew her nose defiantly. 'I do not think we ever really knew each other.'

He risked stepping a little closer. 'Then we have that pleasure to come.'

One of her curls had worked itself loose. He reached out a hand to tuck it gently behind her ear, his fingers trailing lightly down her neck. She did not bat his hand away: that must be a good sign. He moved nearer.

'Do not be afraid of me, Fee.'

She finished wiping her eyes. 'I'm not,' she muttered, her restless fingers tugging at the handkerchief.

Another step brought him within kissing distance. He put his fingers under her chin. 'Then will you cry friends with me?'

His fingers, gentle but insistent, tilted her face up.

Felicity raised her eyes to his face and found him gazing down at her with such a tender look that it made her feel very weak. She was obliged to put her hands against his chest to steady herself.

'F-friends?'

Felicity could hardly hear his words over the pounding of her heart; it seemed suddenly to be trying to leap out of her breast.

'Yes. Very—good—friends.'

He smiled, sealing her fate. He bent his head, gently touching her lips with his own. It was the lightest kiss, as soft as a feather, and Felicity found herself stretching up on tiptoe to respond and prolong the pleasurable sensations he was arousing within her. Nathan took her in his arms, cradling not crushing, while his thorough, unhurried kiss went on and on, dispelling all the anger and the tension until there was nothing left but the warm, heady sensation of floating away—flying or drowning, she was not sure which.

After some time—but all too soon for Felicity—the kiss ended. Nathan kept his arms around her, and she still clung to his jacket, afraid that if she let go she would collapse.

'Oh, how can I *think* when you kiss me like that?'

He gave a low laugh. 'What is there to think about?'

She rested her head against his chest, listening to the steady thud of his heart.

'I need to think about what to do—how to behave properly.'

He kissed the top of her head. 'I consider you are behaving very properly.'

'No, no. I should not be alone with you,' she murmured, but she knew her words lacked conviction.

'Sir James is a diplomat; his servants are well known for their discretion, although I have no doubt it will cost me at least a half-crown when I leave here.'

He led her again to the sofa, but this time they sat together, Nathan keeping a protective arm about her. He reached for her left hand, looking down at her bare fingers.

'I do have the rings you gave me,' she told him shyly. 'They are safely hidden in my room.'

'And will you wear them again for me?'

'Of course. I will look them out tonight, my lord.' She looked at his hands. 'You were wont to wear two rings, my lord.'

'What? Oh, yes.' He lifted his right hand and stared for a moment at the little finger where he had worn the small gold band with its pattern of rose thorns. He said curtly, 'That one was lost, a long time ago.'

The faraway look in his eye and the faint sigh that accompanied his words pricked at the bubble of happiness inside Felicity, but she stifled her doubts. It was time to forget the past.

She went to rise, but he pulled her back.

'No, stay and talk to me.'

'Talk of what, sir?'

'Anything. The weather, the theatre—I do not have to be back at the ridotto for another hour.'

With a laugh she settled back against him. 'I am afraid I cannot converse to order, my lord.'

Nevertheless, she found that, once they began, the conversation flowed very easily. She was surprised and a little disappointed when the clock in the hall chimed the hour.

Nathan raised his head, listening.

'I must go,' he said. 'The Tsar and his sister are engaged to go on to Lady Collingwood's at midnight and I must be there to escort them.' He pulled Felicity to her feet. 'Soon we shall be done with all this pretence. I shall carry you off to Hampshire.' He kissed her and stood for a moment, looking down at her. The look in his eyes sent a pleasurable shiver through Felicity; even her toes curled when he said softly, 'It will be our honeymoon.'

Chapter Ten

Lady Souden's ball was the last event the royal visitors would attend before the Emperor left London at the end of his visit. Nathan was escorting the royal party to Dover and when he returned he would carry Felicity off to Rosthorne Hall. Lydia confessed herself grateful that Felicity would be there to help her through the ordeal.

'Lydia, how can you call your ball an ordeal?' laughed Felicity. 'You love entertaining, you know you do!'

'True, but I have never entertained a grand duchess before, nor had so many crowned heads of Europe in my house!'

'It will not be necessary to introduce me to them all, will it?' asked Felicity, nervously.

'No, no, not unless you wish it,' murmured Lydia, soothingly.

'I do *not* wish it, most decidedly!'

'Then you may remain in the background, but pray do not go too far away from me; James must attend to his guests so I shall feel happier knowing you are there to support me if I need you.'

Something in Lydia's tone made Felicity look closely at her.

'My love, are you unwell?'

'I am perfectly well, thank you.' Lydia laid her hands on

her stomach. 'But I *am* increasing, and James is concerned—I think he has passed some of his anxiety on to me.'

Felicity promised to look after her and went up to her room to change into her green satin gown in readiness for the evening. Lady Souden sent her own maid to dress Felicity's hair and to fix around her neck a collar of fine pearls that Sir James and Lydia had given her—'Look upon this as a wedding gift,' Lydia had said when she had presented it to her that morning. 'For soon you will begin your new life as Countess Rosthorne.'

Lydia's words came back to Felicity as she sat before her mirror while the maid's nimble fingers finished their work on her hair. She trembled a little, but with pleasure at the thought of Nathan carrying her away.

'No need to be nervous, miss,' said Janet, misinterpreting her shiver. 'You look as fine as fivepence, if you'll forgive me saying so.'

Felicity stared at her reflection. There was an alarming amount of skin exposed by the low neckline of her gown.

'Is it not a little…revealing?' she murmured when Lydia came to collect her.

'Not at all. It shows off your lovely shoulders and that beautiful, slim neck of yours. You look quite beautiful!'

'I think it would be better if I were to throw a kerchief about my shoulders…'

'No time, love.' Lydia caught her hand. 'We must go down now to welcome our guests!'

An hour later the rooms were so crowded Felicity knew the ball would be hailed a success. The arrangements had been very thorough, and Sir James's staff so well drilled that there was nothing for her to do except move from room to room, keeping a discreet watch upon Lydia. Society had grown accustomed to the sight of Lady Souden's companion, but she was aware of the surprised looks from several of the ladies, as well as admiring glances from the gentlemen. Her chin went up. Let them look and speculate on her improved appearance; in a few days everyone would know the truth. She watched the royal party arrive and was entertained by the jostling that ensued as the guests tried to make sure they were noticed by the Grand Duchess of Oldenburg or the Emperor. She was surprised and enormously gratified when she saw Nathan making his way over to her.

'I hope I can persuade you to dance with me this evening, Miss Brown,' he said, a smile glinting in his eyes.

'I think not, sir.' Laughter trembled in her voice. 'If I dance with you, my lord, how can I say nay to any other gentleman who asks me?'

The mockery in his eyes deepened. 'Easily. You inform them that you have a jealous lover.' He leaned closer. 'Or tell them you have a husband.'

She brought up her fan and fluttered it nervously. 'My lord, have a care,' she begged him, looking about her.

He laughed. 'There is no one to hear us. But I suppose I must agree with you; if you dance with me and refuse everyone else it might rouse suspicions. Very well, dance with anyone you wish.'

'If I do *that*, sir,' she responded, greatly daring, 'it will only be with you.'

His brows went up, but there was no mistaking the triumphant look in his eyes. He bowed over her hand. 'I am engaged for the first dance with the grand duchess, but after that, I shall seek you out, *Miss Brown*.'

Smiling, Felicity watched him walk away. She did not expect to dance much, and certainly not the first dance, but she hoped that Sir James might ask her to stand up with him, and perhaps one or two of the other gentlemen of her acquaintance. She saw Gerald Appleby striding purposefully towards her until his approach was halted by Lady Charlotte, who took his arm and led him away in the opposite direction. Felicity's smile grew—if only Lady Charlotte knew that she was wasting her efforts.

'So, madam, are you free to dance with me?'

Felicity turned to find Nathan at her side.

'Is that how you invited the grand duchess to stand up with you?'

'No, ma'am, she asked *me*.' He held out his arm. 'Well?'

'Despite your rag-manners, Lord Rosthorne, I will dance with you.'

With a laugh he swept her off to join the set. Once again she knew the exhilaration of dancing with Nathan, the touch of his hand, even though they were both wearing gloves, sending shockwaves through her body. His intimate smile turned her insides to water. When the dance required him to take her left hand his grip on her fingers tightened.

'You are wearing your rings!'

'I thought it was time,' she said.

'And has no one noticed?'

She met his eyes, her own twinkling with mischief.

'It is customary when dancing only to *touch* the tips of your partner's fingers, my lord. *Your* grip is far too familiar!'

He grinned. 'Baggage!' he hissed as the dance separated them once more.

When the music ended he led her off the floor and procured a glass of wine for her.

'Thank you.' She glanced around; there were laughing and chattering groups on all sides, but none close enough to overhear her. 'I received a letter today, from my uncle's lawyer.' She glanced up at him. 'It seems my uncle's legacy has grown into a very useful sum. I have you to thank for that, I think.'

'I sought out the man when I got back from Corunna. I thought you might have contacted him. Once he knew I was your husband he disclosed to me details of your uncle's estate. I advised him to invest it for you.'

'As my husband you could have taken it for your own,' she said carefully, 'to replace the money you had given me.'

'I could, of course, had I wanted to do so.'

She kept her eyes upon the wineglass, held tightly between her hands. 'You did not think, then, that I had stolen your money?'

'No, I never really thought that of you.'

She gave him a tremulous smile. 'I am very relieved to hear that, my lord,' she murmured, her spirits lifting.

Nathan was in no hurry to move away. Felicity was surprised at how easily they conversed, but eventually she felt obliged to comment.

'We are attracting attention, my lord. You should not be spending so much of your time with...' she hesitated '...Lady Souden's drab little attendant.'

A smile glinted in his eyes. 'Is that what I called you? Damned impudence!'

She laughed. 'It was no more than I deserved. But truly, you should leave me now, sir. People will talk.'

He moved closer. 'Let them talk. In a few days it will not matter.'

A shiver of anticipation ran down her spine.

'There will be waltzing later,' he said. 'Will you stand up with me?'

'Perhaps, my lord, if I am not engaged.'

His eyes narrowed. 'I believe you are laughing at me.'

'Would I dare to do that, my lord?'

'I think in this mood you would dare anything!' He kissed her hand. 'Tomorrow morning I leave with the Emperor and the grand duchess for Portsmouth. One night there and I take them on to Dover. As soon as they have sailed my duty is done and I shall come for you.' He added quietly, 'I cannot wait to have you to myself again, Fee.'

The blazing look in his eyes set her pulse racing. Such

was its intensity that for a moment she thought he might sweep her up and carry her off that very instant. It shocked her to realise how much she wanted him to do just that. He held out his arm to her.

'Would you like me to escort you back to Lady Souden now, Miss Brown?'

Felicity gave herself a mental shake. This was Lady Souden's ball, part of the Prince Regent's Peace Celebrations. Nathan had his duties to attend to, as had she. But soon…

'Ah, there you are, Cos!' Mr Appleby's cheerful voice called out behind them. 'I've been looking for you.'

Impatience flickered over Nathan's face.

'Well, Gerald, now you've found me.'

'Aye. Here's an old friend eager to meet you again,' said Gerald as they turned towards him.

Leaning on Nathan's arm, Felicity felt him tense. There, standing beside Gerald, was Serena Craike.

Chaotic thoughts reeled through Felicity's mind. What new torment was this? She had helped Lydia write the guest list and had seen all the replies; she would have known if Serena Craike—or Ansell—had been amongst the guests.

'Lady Ansell arrived in town only this morning,' Gerald continued. 'Knowing you were old friends, General Rowland brought her along with him.'

He beamed at them all. The lady gave a soft laugh, released Gerald's arm and stepped forward, holding out her hand.

'Well, Nathan, I can see that I have surprised you into silence. How gratifying.'

Nathan touched the lavender-gloved fingers and bowed over them. 'Ma'am. What brings you to town?'

Another of those soft, seductive laughs. 'Oh, boredom, and a desire to seek out old friends.' She spread her hands. 'As you can see I am still in mourning.'

The lady's gown of silver-grey silk was cut very low at

the neck and very high at the waist, making the most of her ample bosom, while the thin skirts clung to her shapely legs. Felicity thought she had rarely seen anything less suited to a widow. No wonder then that Gerald could not take his eyes off her.

'Lady Ansell,' said Gerald, 'you will not know Miss Brown. Let me present you.'

Felicity froze. The widow subjected her to no more than a cursory glance. There was no sign of recognition, but Felicity's relief was tinged with anger when she realised that she was being dismissed as being of little importance. Lady Ansell lost no time in turning her limpid gaze back to Nathan. Gerald immediately began to chatter again.

'Well, well, I am sure you would like to catch up on old times. Miss Brown, this is our dance, I think…'

He was holding out his hand to her, but Felicity did not know if she dared let go of Nathan's arm. She hesitated, but found Nathan lifting her fingers from his sleeve and handing her to his cousin, saying, 'Yes, thank you for your company, Miss Brown, but I must not monopolise you.'

Felicity allowed Gerald to lead her away and as she did so she was aware of the widow stepping up, taking her place at Nathan's side, her voice almost purring as she said, 'Well now, my lord, let us find somewhere we can be private…'

'Up to your old tricks, Serena?' asked Nathan, gently removing her hand from his sleeve.

'I have no idea what you mean.' When he made no reply she pouted and once more tucked her hand in his arm. 'What, still sulking with me because I preferred Adam Elliston to you?'

'I was never one of your admirers, Serena, you know that.'

He was aware of heads turning in their direction and his irritation grew. The knowing looks being cast towards them showed that many of the guests were drawing their own conclusions about his relationship with Serena Ansell. Thank heaven Gerald had taken Felicity away. He did not want Serena to destroy the fragile trust he was building there. The widow gave a little sigh.

'My period of mourning is almost over; I think I might risk dancing with you.'

'But first you must wait to be asked,' he replied.

She laughed gently. 'Oh, how ungallant, my lord! Well, at least escort me down to supper, Nathan.'

'I regret that is not possible. I am required to attend the grand duchess this evening.'

'That did not prevent you from dancing with the little chit who's just walked off with your cousin.'

'No, but I promised to return directly, which I am now going to do. I suggest you go back to General Rowland and let him escort you.' He disengaged himself once more, gave her a quick nod and walked away, leaving the widow staring at his retreating back.

'Do you…do you know Lady Ansell well?'

Felicity's voice sounded very odd, but Gerald did not seem to notice.

'Lord, no, never met her before tonight. Heard of her, though.'

They took their places in the set and Felicity hoped she would remember the steps. Her mind seemed to be working very sluggishly. For the first few minutes she concentrated on the dance. When she closed with Gerald she could smell the wine on his breath. That was why he was so garrulous. She thought she could use it to her advantage.

'What have you heard of her?' she asked.

'Oh, things. Not really fit for a lady's ears.'

She gave him what she hoped was an encouraging smile. 'Surely you can tell *me*.'

'Oh, very well.' He lowered his voice a little. 'She has a

bit of a past.' He mouthed the next word, *lovers*, and winked at Felicity. 'I shouldn't be surprised if Rosthorne had an interest there at one time.' A sly grin curled his mouth. 'Perhaps she's come back to rekindle an old flame. There's no doubt that she is a dashed attractive woman. That glorious hair and those green eyes—irresistible combination!'

Felicity did not reply. The light-heartedness that had been growing within her was now replaced by a lead weight. She declined a second dance with Gerald, pleading a headache, and as he led her off the floor she looked around for Nathan, but he and Serena had disappeared. An ice-cold hand clutched at her heart. Gerald obviously believed that no red-blooded male could resist the luscious beauty of Serena Ansell.

And Nathan was every inch a red-blooded male.

There was a sudden flurry of movement in the corner of the room. A lady had fainted, a common occurrence in hot and overcrowded ballrooms. As she crossed the room to see if she could help, Felicity caught a glimpse of rose-pink skirts and a tremor of alarm ran through her as she pushed her way through the crowds. Her fears were realised—it was Lydia. She was lying back in a chair, her eyelids fluttering as someone waved smelling salts beneath her nose. Felicity rushed forward.

'What happened?'

'Is that you, Fee?' Lydia put out a trembling hand. 'I am a little faint. Perhaps you could help me to my room?' As Felicity helped her to her feet, Lydia smiled at the crowd around her. 'No need for this fuss. Pray continue to enjoy yourselves; I shall be better in a little while.'

'We should find Sir James—' said a voice in the crowd.

Lydia waved her hand. 'No, he is busy with our guests. Miss Brown will look after me.'

While Janet put her mistress to bed, Felicity sent a footman running to fetch the doctor. She returned to find

Lydia lying back against her pillows. She was alarmingly pale, but gave a wan smile when she saw Felicity.

'A lot of fuss about nothing,' she murmured.

'Not at all. We have to look after you and the baby. I shall sit with you until the doctor comes.'

Felicity pulled a chair beside the bed and reached for her hand. Lydia sighed and closed her eyes. After a few moments her steady breathing indicated she had fallen asleep. As the silence settled around them, Felicity was left with nothing to do but to think back to the last time she had seen Serena.

Felicity had stood in the mirador, her hands pressed against the glass as she watched Nathan ride away to join his regiment. She was determined not to cry, but loneliness pressed in upon her, and after a restless night she knew she must find some activity to fill the long days until she heard from Nathan. She remembered the kindness of Colonel McTernon's wife at her wedding and decided to seek her out. She was about to put on her warm pelisse when the little Spanish housemaid knocked on the door and announced a visitor.

Serena Craike sailed into the room in a cloud of olive-green velvet, her hands buried in a swansdown muff.

'Ah, my dear, I thought I should come and see how you go on.'

'I was about to go out,' Felicity greeted her shyly, indicating the pelisse thrown over her arm. 'I thought I might visit Mrs McTernon…'

'Oh, it is far too early for that; she will not yet have broken her fast.' Mrs Craike laughed gently. 'I can see that you are not yet used to our ways, Miss…I mean, *Mrs* Carraway.'

Felicity turned to put her pelisse over a chair. 'Will you not sit down, Mrs Craike?'

'Thank you, but I can only stay a moment. I thought I might drop a little word of warning in your ear.'

'Warning?'

'With our menfolk gone we shall be left to entertain ourselves, and when ladies get together there is nothing they like better than gossip.'

'Oh? How does that affect me?'

Serena gave another soft laugh. 'Bless you, my dear, you must know that your marriage is quite the *on dit* of our little circle.'

Felicity shifted uncomfortably. She did not want to talk about her marriage.

After a minute or two Serena continued. 'Yes, when the handsome Major Carraway suddenly announces that he will marry, you can imagine the speculation.'

'But there is no secret about it. My circumstances—'

'Yes, that must be very hard for you, my dear.'

'Why should it be?'

Serena's smile was all sympathy. 'To know he married you out of pity. Oh, there is no need to colour up, child. I am sure Mrs McTernon and her circle think that he acted most honourably by you, but you must be prepared for a little talk.'

'Talk, madam?' Felicity shook her head. 'I cannot think why—'

'Can you not?' Serena's green eyes were fixed on her face. 'But everyone knows Nathan is desperately in love with *me*.'

Felicity was stunned. She felt as if she had been hit by one of the huge white waves she had seen rolling on to the beach. Fearing she might faint, she sat down on a chair, but not for a moment did she take her eyes from her visitor. Serena Craike regarded her with a mixture of amusement and sympathy.

'Did he not tell you? Perhaps he thought you knew of it already.'

'I do not believe you.' She remembered Nathan's words when he first told her of Serena—*Adam is not the first man to fall under her spell*. Dear heaven, did he mean himself? Trying to fight off the thoughts and images that crowded in upon her, she muttered, 'It is not true.'

'I thought you might say that.' Serena pulled a letter from her muff and held it out. 'You will recognise the writing. Nathan gave it to me yesterday.' Her smile grew. 'Did he not tell you? He came to see me, shortly after he had left you.'

With trembling fingers Felicity took the folded paper. It was a single sheet and covered with Nathan's familiar black writing. The words danced on the page and she was obliged to blink several times before she could make sense of it. My Passion. The very first words cut into her heart. She forced herself to read on. Nathan had not used the word love, but it was apparent in every line. Felicity's eyes filled with tears.

'No.' She shook her head. There must be some other explanation, although her poor brain could think of none. She turned the paper over. 'There is no name on this. It is not addressed to you.'

She raised her eyes. Serena met her challenging look with a contemptuous smile.

'He did not need to address it; he gave it to me personally.' She pulled off her glove and held out her hand. 'With this.' A black cloak of unhappiness wrapped itself around Felicity. There, on Serena's slim finger, was a thin gold band engraved with thorns.

In the ballroom, Nathan looked in vain for Felicity. If she did not appear soon it would be too late to join the dancers gathering for the waltz. He recalled hearing someone say that Lady Souden had fainted, so perhaps Felicity was looking after her. His jaw tightened. His wife should not be playing nursemaid to anyone. The sooner he restored her to her rightful place the better! He heard a heavily accented voice behind him, and turned to find the Emperor approaching with Serena Ansell on his arm.

'Ah, Lord Rosthorne, the man for whom we look.' The Emperor beamed at him. 'Lady Ansell, she wishes to dance the waltz. Myself, I would escort her, but we have already danced twice tonight and the tongues, they will wag, no?'

'Majesty, I regret…' Nathan paused, casting one more look about the room. Still no sign of Felicity. He turned back and bowed, trying to ignore the triumph in Serena's cat-like eyes. 'Majesty, it would be my pleasure to dance with Lady Ansell.'

Felicity wiped away a tear. So Serena had come back. To rekindle an old flame, Gerald had said. As the maid opened the door she could hear the orchestra striking up in the ballroom. They were playing a waltz. Nathan had asked her to dance a waltz with him. Lydia stirred.

'I am glad I have not broken up the party,' she muttered. 'You should go downstairs, Fee.'

'Yes, yes, I will, if I may. Just—just for a few moments.'

She sped out of the room and down the stairs, pausing halfway down to look across to where the double doors stood wide. Just in time to see Nathan whirling by with Serena Ansell in his arms.

She gripped the handrail, afraid that her knees might give way. Then she turned and made her way back up to Lydia's room.

'Back so soon?' Lydia murmured. 'There is no need, Fee. I shall be perfectly safe with Janet to look after me.'

'No, I shall stay with you, Lydia, until the doctor comes.' Felicity dragged up a smile that went slightly awry. 'There is nothing for me downstairs.'

Chapter Eleven

The night was giving way to a clear dawn when Felicity finally left Lydia's bedchamber. The doctor had come and gone and Felicity had stayed with Lydia, holding her hand until she had fallen asleep, by which time the orchestra had finished playing and the last guests were leaving the house.

Felicity decided against going back downstairs. She was desperately tired. The re-appearance of Serena had awakened all her old anxieties. Gerald's words echoed in her brain and her last image of Nathan waltzing with Serena did nothing to convince her that he was impervious to the widow's obvious charms. She thought that the little bubble of happiness growing within her must have been made of glass, for now that it had fractured, the sharp pain of her disappointment was unbearable.

It was a week later when Nathan returned to London and he made his way directly to Berkeley Square. There had been no opportunity to speak to Felicity before he left the Soudens' ball. Understandable, of course, with Lady Souden being carried off to her room, but he was anxious now to see her again.

'So,' said Sir James, when Nathan was shown into the study, 'your royal charge has left England.'

'Yes, Sir James. We stopped off at Portsmouth where there were sufficient cheering crowds and 21-gun salutes to please his Highness, then on the Saturday morning the Emperor and the Prussian royals breakfasted with the Duke of Clarence before leaving for Dover where, thank heaven, the weather was favourable and nothing delayed their departure.' Nathan drained his glass. 'And now I am back, and wish to see my wife.'

There was the slightest of pauses.

'Ah.'

Nathan watched Sir James get up and refill the glasses.

'Is something amiss?' He was suddenly tense. 'Is Felicity ill?'

'No, no, your wife is very well, Lord Rosthorne.' Sir James handed Nathan his glass and returned to his seat. 'You may recall that Lady Souden was taken ill on the night of the ball.'

'Of course. I trust she is now recovered?'

'Unfortunately, no.' Sir James's face was unusually solemn. 'We feared she might lose the baby, but that has not happened. However, her doctor prescribes complete bed-rest. I wanted to take her back to Souden, but she is too ill to be moved.'

'I am very sorry to hear it.'

'Thank you. Your wife has been a great support during this time—you will know that Lydia had asked her cousin to come and live with her, but unfortunately the woman broke her leg and is now tied to her own house. And even if she was available—' Sir James broke off, sombrely regarding his glass. At last he looked up, his grey eyes meeting Nathan's. 'My wife needs peace of mind, Rosthorne; Dr Scott insists that she must not be upset or disturbed in any way. You know the bond that exists between your wife and mine; I very much fear that if Lady Rosthorne was to leave now, it would distress Lydia greatly. I would therefore ask if you would spare her to us for a little longer.' He put up his hand. 'I can see by your face that you are minded to refuse, and you have every right to do so. Felicity is your legal wife. But I would ask you, as a friend, to let her stay.'

Closing his lips tightly against any unwary comment, Nathan jumped up. 'And what does Felicity say about this?'

'Lady Rosthorne is anxious not to do anything that could endanger Lydia's health.'

After a few hasty turns about the room Nathan found himself by the window and paused there, staring out. 'Another delay—how long could this last?'

'Possibly until October, when the baby is due.' Sir James came to stand beside him at the window. 'We might lose the child. If that is the case, then so be it, but my concern is Lydia. I will do everything in my power to save my wife.'

Nathan looked at the older man. He noted the sadness in his eyes, the lines of worry etched upon his face. It shocked him to realise that Sir James was so desperately concerned for his wife. This man, this great diplomat who had the ear of princes, who consorted with royalty and advised the government, was actually begging him not to take Felicity away. With a sigh Nathan turned again to look out of the window. The bright sun was still shining down, the day was as full of promise as it had been when he had arrived, but not for him.

'I would do the same, in your place,' he said quietly. Sir James placed his hand on his shoulder, his touch eloquent of relief, gratitude and a measure of sympathy. 'I would like to see my wife for a few moments, if that is possible.'

'Of course. I will send her down to you.'

Felicity entered the study. Nathan was standing at the window, staring out into the street.

'I am glad you are back safely, my lord.'

'Are you?' He turned and crossed the room to greet her. He kissed her hand and would have kissed her cheek, but she drew back with a tiny gesture of denial.

'I cannot stay long,' she said quickly. 'Lydia becomes very restless when I am away from her.'

His hand cupped her chin. 'Are you in constant attendance upon Lady Souden? Poor Fee—that would explain the dark shadows beneath your eyes.'

Forcing a little smile, she freed herself from his grasp. 'Yes, that would be it. Sir James has told you—explained…'

'Yes. I was hoping to take you into Hampshire tomorrow. I have already written to my mother—she is eager to meet you—but it seems that that meeting will have to be postponed.'

'I am very sorry.'

'So too am I. Perhaps I should stay in London. I could take you to the town house tonight—'

'No. Lydia often needs me during the night.'

His brows drew together. 'I am beginning to think you are trying to fob me off.'

'That is not so, my lord. Lady Souden is ill, she needs my attention.'

'Perhaps you should consider devoting some attention to your husband!'

She put her hands together. 'And I *will*, I give you my word, as soon as I can safely leave Lydia.' She looked down, conscious of his frowning stare.

He said quietly, 'What is it, Fee? What makes it so important that you stay here?'

'Lydia must have love and comfort and careful nursing, all the things that—that a new mother needs if she is to have a healthy baby.'

'I suppose it is no good suggesting that she could find these things elsewhere.'

'She could, of course, but…it is important to *me* to help her through this ordeal.'

'And why is that?'

'She…is my friend, and I will do everything in my power to make sure she does not suffer the agony of losing a child.'

Nathan fixed his eyes upon Felicity. She stood before him, eyes downcast and looking distinctly uncomfortable. There was something she was not telling him. She was removed, distant, no longer the delightful companion he remembered from their last meeting.

He wanted to take her arms and shake her, but that would not release the lively, loving creature he knew was inside her. It might drive her even further from him. He decided to change tactics. 'Then you had best remain here.'

Felicity did not know whether to be most relieved or disappointed at his calm acceptance.

'It seems our marriage must wait a little longer, my dear. I will go down to Rosthorne and set everything in readiness for you.' He took her hand again. 'I will let you get back to your patient. Write to me; let me know as soon as you can be spared.'

'I will, my lord.'

His hand tightened on her fingers. 'So formal? I would rather you called me by my name. Can you do that?'

'Of course…Nathan.'

Gently he drew her into his arms, placing two fingers beneath her chin to tilt her face up for a brief, gentle kiss. Her heart cried out against such restraint. She wanted him to crush her to him, to override her sensible arguments and carry her off to his town house. She thought she would happily do without sleep if she could spend a few hours each day with Nathan.

'So, madam, will you miss me?'

This was her chance—she could ask him to stay, tell him how much his presence would support her, but even as the words formed on her tongue the vision of Serena's green eyes and flaming curls intruded. She would not demean herself by admitting her need when he was besotted by another woman. So she summoned up a bright smile and stepped away from the comfort of his arms.

'Of course, my lord, but I am so very busy it is best if you are not here to distract me. But…the Peace Celebrations are to continue for some months yet—do you not wish to stay in town for that?'

He grimaced. 'I have had enough of crowds and spectacle. There is plenty of work to be done at Rosthorne.'

'And you will set out for Hampshire tomorrow?'

He nodded. 'As soon as it is light.' He paused. 'If there is nothing more to say then I shall leave you now.'

'No,' she said brightly. 'I wish you a safe journey, my lord.'

His gaze rested upon her for a long moment and it was as much as Felicity could do to maintain her cheerful countenance. Then, with a word and a nod, he was gone. Felicity ran to the window and peeped out. A groom was walking Nathan's great black horse up and down the road. As she watched, he turned quickly and brought the animal back to the door just as Nathan appeared. He mounted effortlessly into the saddle and exchanged a few brief words with his groom as he gathered up the reins. Felicity drew back quickly as Nathan cast a last, unsmiling look at the house before he turned his mount and trotted away.

'Fee? What are you doing?'

Felicity looked up. 'Oh, are you awake, Lydia? Janet and I thought you might sleep for an hour or so, yet.'

'No, dearest, I have been lying here watching you. Are you writing to Rosthorne?'

Felicity put down her pen and walked across to the huge bed, where Lydia lay propped up against a bank of snowy white pillows.

'I am, but it can wait. Shall I draw the curtains? The afternoon sun is very bright—'

'No matter, I like to see the sun shining.' Lydia patted her hand invitingly. 'Come and sit on the bed and tell me all that you are writing to him.'

'Well, he asks after your health, so I have said that Dr Scott is very pleased with you, and that you now spend a little time each day on the daybed by an open window.'

Lydia placed her hands on her swollen belly and chuckled. 'Did you also tell him that I am becoming grossly fat?'

'Of course not! I described you as being in high bloom now.'

'Did you? Then he will be demanding that you leave me.'

Felicity's smiled slipped a little. 'Not for a while yet; his letter said that he is off to Yorkshire for a few weeks, to visit his estates there.'

'No word of his coming to town?'

'No. Lydia, do not look at me in that way. It was agreed that I should stay here with you for as long as you need me.'

'And I *do* need you, love. With James obliged to spend so much time dancing attendance on the Prince Regent I should be moped to death here without you.'

Felicity smiled. 'How can you say that when every post brings you a shower of letters and we are forever taking in flowers from your friends? Even Lady Charlotte sent a bouquet.'

'Lord, yes, I was surprised to see she was still in town. Keeping an eye upon her son, I think.' Lydia chuckled. 'I hear he is very taken with the red-haired widow, Lady Ansell. Lady Charlotte will wish to squash *that* connection.'

Felicity tried to smile. She wondered if she should tell Lydia about Serena, but decided against it. Lydia stirred restlessly.

'I am most disappointed in Rosthorne,' she complained. 'I thought he was very much in love with you, but if that was so I wonder that he has stayed away from town for so long.'

'Clearly he was not so besotted as you thought,' returned Felicity, trying to keep her voice light.

'Oh, Fee, I am sorry—if I had not been ill you would have been happily settled with your earl by this time.'

Felicity shrugged, sadness squeezing at her heart. What happiness could there be for her if Nathan was still in love with Serena Ansell?

The months dragged on: the hot summer days gave way to the cooler mists and rain of autumn and still Nathan did not come to London. He wrote several times to Felicity, his letters polite, friendly even, but with no hint of the lover in their tone and Felicity resolutely buried the hopes that had burgeoned so strongly at the beginning of the summer. She would do her duty, when the time came, but before that there were nervous weeks ahead as the time drew near for Lydia's confinement.

It was the news Nathan had been waiting for. The brief note from Sir James informed him that Lady Souden had been safely delivered of a strong, healthy girl. Mother and baby were both doing well, Dr Scott was confident that there was no risk now of childbed fever and declared that they would both be well enough to travel to Souden at the end of October.

Nathan penned a short message of congratulations to Sir James and his lady, and an even shorter one to Felicity, informing her that he would be in London by the end of the week and requesting that she should be ready on the Friday morning to travel with him to Hampshire. As he fixed the seal to this second missive, he thought over all the frustrations of the past few months, when he had thrown himself into the business of his estates rather than giving in to the urge to post up to town. He was surprised how much he had missed her; it was a physical pain and now that the waiting was almost over he allowed himself to think of her again, to remember her shy smile, which would light up a room for him, and the mischievous twinkle he would sometimes surprise in her eyes. He had been very forbearing; she had said she did not want him there to distract her so he had kept away, but now, climbing into his travelling carriage on a misty October morning, he was returning to claim his wife.

Chapter Twelve

'Of all the arrogant, unfeeling—!' Felicity almost stamped her foot as she read Nathan's hasty scrawl.

'What is it, Fee?' Lydia, with a sleeping baby in her arms, did not look up.

'This note from Rosthorne. He informs me I am to leave here tomorrow morning, without so much as a by your leave!' With a little huff of frustration she twisted the paper between her hands and hurled it across the room.

Lydia merely smiled. 'He has been very patient, my dear, and I cannot keep you with me for ever, much as I would like to, for you are so good with your little god-daughter.'

Felicity's anger drained away as she regarded the mother and child. 'Baby Elizabeth is so good, it is not difficult to love her.'

'She *is* a darling, isn't she? But you have such a way with you.' Lydia twinkled up at her. 'I find it hard to believe you have no experience in the nursery.'

Felicity gazed for a long moment at the baby. She had to breathe deeply to remove the constriction in her throat.

'No,' she said at last, and with perfect truth. 'No, I have never held a baby before.'

'Well, once you are back with your husband I am sure

it will not be very long before you have a family of your own—'

.'Oh, Lydia, pray do not go on!'

'Darling Fee! What is it?'

Felicity hesitated, then with a sob she threw herself on her knees beside Lydia's chair. 'I am afraid,' she confessed, resting her head against Lydia's knee.

'Frightened of the bedroom? I am sure there is not the least need…'

Felicity blushed. 'No, it is not that. It is Nathan.' She searched for her handkerchief. 'I am not sure of him. I—I do not think I know him any more…'

Lydia, still euphoric after the worries of the past few months, merely smiled and laid a gentle hand on Felicity's head. 'This is nothing more than nerves, Fee. You love him, do you not?'

Felicity sighed. 'Yes,' she whispered. 'That is, I *did*, but he is so different now.'

'You are both different—five years older, for one thing. I have seen the earl's face when he looks at you. He desires you, Felicity.'

'But does he *love* me?' she persisted, wiping her eyes.

Lydia smiled. 'For gentlemen, love and desire are very closely linked,' she said softly. 'With James, one followed the other, and look how happy we are now.' She gave Felicity a little push. 'Go and pack your bags, my dear, and consider your good fortune: Rosthorne is a kind and honourable man. He is also very rich and exceedingly attractive, despite the scar across his brow. I vow if I was not head over heels in love with James I would set my cap at him myself!'

Nervously, Felicity tied the ribbons of her bonnet. She had seen the handsome travelling carriage pull up outside the house and had received a message that Lord Rosthorne was awaiting her below. A glance out of the window showed her that even now the servants were carrying her trunk out of the house.

Sir James was standing with the earl in the hall and both men turned as Felicity made her way down the stairs. Her new pelisse and bonnet were a present from Lydia, who had insisted that the soft sage-green colour suited her very well and would boost her confidence. Very necessary, she thought, as she met the earl's unsmiling look.

Felicity dropped a curtsy. 'My lord.'

He bowed. Sir James stepped forward.

'Well, Lady Rosthorne, we must say goodbye to you.' He reached for her hand and kissed her fingers. 'My wife has already told you how grateful we are to you?'

'Yes, sir. I have just left her bedchamber.'

'Then it only remains for me to say goodbye and to wish you and Lord Rosthorne every happiness.'

Nathan held out his arm to her. 'Shall we be on our way, ma'am?' She met his eyes and observed the glint of amusement there. He knew how much she wanted to turn and run. But his look was not unkind. He said gently, 'Come, my lady.'

Felicity gave him her hand and he led her to the waiting carriage. She had time for one final, smiling wave to Sir James before they were away, clattering out of London. She was very aware of the earl, sitting in one corner of the coach. He was watching her and his gaze made her spine tingle. She had the impression that he could see every curve of her body, despite the jaconet muslin pelisse that enveloped her. She did not know whether she was most alarmed or excited by the thought. Excited, she admitted to herself. She had certainly missed him.

'I was surprised to receive the letter from Sir James,' remarked Nathan. 'I thought perhaps you might write first, to tell me the good news.'

Felicity cleared her throat. 'I—I was waiting, to be sure…'

'Putting off the evil day?' His dry tone sent the blood rushing to her cheeks.

'Not *evil*, my lord.' She risked a quick glance at him and observed that he was smiling. She was emboldened to add, 'I confess I am a little apprehensive.'

'There is no need.'

'No? The tone of your note was very peremptory, and we left Berkeley Square so quickly this morning...'

'I am sorry to rush you away from your friends,' he replied. 'Naturally I am anxious for you to assume your role as my wife, but there is another reason I wish to be at Rosthorne in good time today. My mother is expecting us and she keeps early hours—her health is not good, you see. She injured her hip in a riding accident years ago and it has never healed properly. She tires very easily.'

'Oh, I am sorry for that,' Felicity responded with ready sympathy. 'How far is Rosthorne?'

'A little over fifty miles. It is just west of Petersfield, near the village of Hazelford. It is not the biggest of my houses—judicious marriages by my ancestors added a couple of substantial properties in the north—but it is the one I use most.'

'And Mrs Carraway lives there?'

'Yes, she has her own apartments in the east wing.'

'I am looking forward to meeting her.'

With nothing more to say, she turned her head to gaze once more out of the carriage window. She heard Nathan shift his position, felt his thigh against hers.

He said softly, 'Don't be afraid of me, Felicity.'

She did not move. His fingers were playing idly with the curls at the back of her neck, causing a sensation akin to ice trickling down her back.

'I—I am not afraid,' she stammered, fighting the desire to lean back against his hand.

'Good. I would not have you afraid.' She could feel his

breath on her cheek. 'We could deal very well together, if you would only trust me.'

She remained perfectly still, her eyes fixed on the landscape flying past them. 'I do, Nathan. I do trust you.'

His lips brushed her neck. She trembled, her breath exhaled in a tiny moan. Nathan put his hands on her shoulders and turned her towards him, his lips seeking hers. The next moment she was locked in his arms and he was kissing her, tenderly at first, but with increasing passion. Her arms crept around his neck. She was aware of his fingers unbuttoning her pelisse, exposing the soft column of her throat to his caresses.

Nathan's pulse leapt erratically when she responded to his kiss. She pressed against him, her fingers tangling gently in his hair. Her touch excited him and he felt the latent passion behind her hesitant, tentative responses. He drew back, suppressing his desire to lose himself in her soft, innocent beauty. He kept one hand on her neck, his thumb tracing the fine line of her jaw. She gazed at him, her eyes dark beneath half-closed lids and her reddened lips parted slightly, inviting him in. It was irresistible. He kissed her again, then gently put her away from him.

'You are too tempting, madam wife. I will have to move back into my corner before I forget myself.' He saw the flash in her eyes, half-surprise, half-pleasure, and he laughed. 'You do not realise just how bewitching you are, do you?'

The blush in her cheeks deepened. 'Am I, truly?'

'Yes, *truly*.' He lifted her hand, turning it to place a kiss on the exposed skin of her inner wrist, between the edge of her glove and the lace cuff of her sleeve. She did not pull away and he saw that she was watching him, a soft glow in her eyes. What he read there sent his heart soaring. He placed her hand back in her lap and released it.

'Compose yourself, madam. We shall be stopping soon for a change of horses and some refreshment. I shall not be able to leave the carriage if you continue to look at me in that way.'

Felicity flushed, laughed and looked away, inordinately pleased with the effect she was having upon her husband.

The coach rolled on, the bustling, dirty streets and the acrid smell from the coal fires were soon left behind and they were rattling through towns and villages where small children stared in open-mouthed wonder and labourers in the fields straightened their backs to watch them go past.

Felicity gazed at everything with interest, especially when they reached Hampshire and Nathan pointed out the rich pastures and thickly wooded slopes of his estate.

'When shall we see the house?' she asked him, glancing up at the sun, low on the horizon. 'Shall we be there before dark?'

'Yes, we are nearly there now. Rosthorne Hall is too well screened to be seen from the road. You must wait until we are in the park.'

Even as he spoke the carriage slowed. A sharp blast of the horn brought the lodge-keeper hurrying out to throw open the gates leading to a tree-lined drive. Nathan let down the window to exchange a few words with the man as they drove past then sat back, reaching for Felicity's hand.

'Welcome to Rosthorne, my lady.'

Even as he spoke the carriage emerged from the belt of trees and Felicity had her first glimpse of her new home. The sun, which had been fitfully breaking through the clouds all day, now made a final, blazing appearance, as if determined to present Rosthorne Hall at its best.

The house stood on a slight rise. It was built of red brick and creamy stonework with three rows of windows that gleamed in the evening sunlight. A stone pediment containing the Rosthorne coat of arms stood over a central doorway, which opened on to a set of shallow stone steps. From the neat square windows of the semi-basement to the hipped roof with its dormer windows and tall chimney stacks, the whole house had such symmetry that Felicity thought it quite perfect.

'You like it, I am glad,' said Nathan, when she had voiced her opinion. 'There have been some alterations and redecoration to the interior—for one thing the dining room is now much closer to the kitchens, so the food arrives hot at the table, but the outside is very much as it was when the house was built more than a century ago.'

As the carriage came to a halt, a crowd of servants came running out and lined up on the steps. Anxiety fluttered through Felicity and must have shown in her countenance because Nathan grinned at her.

'They wish to welcome their new mistress,' he explained as he helped her to alight. 'You need only smile at them for now, my dear—Mrs Mercer will introduce them all to you tomorrow, isn't that so, Mercer?'

The stately butler waiting at the door to receive them allowed himself a fatherly smile.

'Indeed it is, my lord. Mrs Carraway has given instructions that dinner should be put back an hour and has requested that you join her in the little drawing room, if you are not too exhausted from your journey.'

Nathan looked a question at Felicity. She nodded and they followed the butler into the hall where Nathan tossed his hat and gloves on to a console table and a wooden-faced footman waited for Felicity to divest herself of her bonnet and pelisse. She tried not to cling to Nathan's arm, but as he led her into the little drawing room her heart was beating a rapid and nervous tattoo against her ribs.

The likeness between mother and son was very marked. They shared the same keen brown eyes and both had an abundance of brown hair tinted with reddish-gold, although the lady's was also sprinkled liberally with grey. Mrs Carraway was sitting in a wing chair beside one of the room's long windows, an embroidery frame between her hands. A tall, thin woman in an iron-grey gown with hair to match was sitting opposite, reading to her in a low voice.

As they entered she stopped reading and looked up. A rather overweight spaniel emerged from behind the sofa and ran forward, barking. Mrs Carraway put down her embroidery and held out her hands to Nathan, smiling.

'So you are here, and in good time, too. Norton said you would be, but I did not look to see you before dark.'

Nathan bent to make a fuss of the spaniel gambolling around his ankles, then went forward to take her hands, kissing each one in turn and then her cheek. 'Mama! I promised we would be here in time for dinner. Mrs Norton knows I am true to my word.' He paused to acknowledge her companion. 'The roads were clear; there was nothing to delay us. And how are you, Mama? Well, I hope?'

'I am very well, now you are come.'

Felicity hung back, watching this interchange while the red-and-white spaniel snuffled around her feet.

'You see, Mama, I have at last brought my wife home.'

Felicity curtsied. 'How do you do, ma'am?'

Mrs Carraway held her hand out to her. 'You must forgive me for not getting up. I am sure Nathan has told you I have a tiresome problem with my hip. Don't mind Bella, she will soon lose interest in you once she knows you have no food for her.'

'I do not mind her at all, ma'am,' murmured Felicity, stooping to fondle the spaniel's ears.

'Well, that is fortunate,' murmured Nathan, smiling, 'because Bella has the run of the house.' He clicked his fingers and the little dog ran over to him, gazing up adoringly with her big brown eyes while he scratched her head. 'I bought her for Mama when I first joined up. Thought they would be company for each other.'

'And she has been with me ever since,' nodded Mrs Carraway. 'She is very old now, of course. She has almost no sense of smell, and her eyes are growing weaker, but she is still my constant companion. Bella rarely leaves my side.'

'Because you spoil her, Mama.' He gave the dog a final pat and straightened. 'You feed her far too many titbits.'

'Perhaps I do, but I will not quarrel with you over that today, Nathan. I want to talk to your wife. Come along, my dear; come and sit over here where I can see you.' She smiled as Felicity perched nervously on the edge of a chair. 'Norton, I would be obliged if you would order refreshments to be sent up. And then you may take Bella out for her walk while I talk to Lady Rosthorne. That is, if you are not too tired after your long journey?'

Felicity knew a craven impulse to say she was exhausted, but she suppressed it. In a very short time a jug of raspberry shrub had been provided for the ladies and Mrs Carraway ordered Nathan to go away and drink a tankard of ale with his steward, who had a mountain of notes to discuss with him.

When she and Felicity were alone, Mrs Carraway fixed her dark eyes upon her guest and said gently, 'Well, my dear, you have led my son a merry dance, have you not?'

'Indeed, I am sorry for it, ma'am. I never intended to cause so much trouble.' Felicity stared down at the cloudy liquid in her glass. 'You have every right to condemn me.'

Mrs Carraway was silent for a moment. 'Any mother will tell you,' she said at last, 'that it is very hard to forgive an injury to one's child. But I promised myself I would not judge you until I had met you. You have your chance to explain it all to me now, my dear. Nathan has, of course, told me his version of events, but only the barest details.'

'Did he tell you I stole his money?' asked Felicity bluntly.

'He was very careful *not* to say so.'

'I am no fortune hunter, ma'am, I assure you. I left him because…because he did not love me.'

'Odd, then, that he should marry you.'

'It was an act of chivalry, ma'am. He was in love with someone else. A—a married woman. When I found out, I was determined to go away. I needed the money he gave me to get to England and then…I was very ill for a while, you see, and there were doctors to be paid. I thought he would forget me.'

'I thought he had,' returned Mrs Carraway. 'His attempts to find you evoked little interest and when he was obliged to return to the Peninsula, having heard nothing from you, I was more than happy to allow the matter to rest. After all, I had no real desire to find the woman who had deserted my son.'

Felicity closed her eyes. 'I am so sorry,' she whispered.

'The matter was forgotten. By the time Nathan became earl it was as if your marriage had never happened. Nathan never mentioned you, until a few months ago, when he came to tell me that you were alive and living in town.'

'Was he…' Felicity ran her tongue over her dry lips '…was he pleased to have found me?'

'Perplexed, I think,' Mrs Carraway said at last. 'But he is determined to honour his obligations.'

'Oh.' That did not sound very encouraging. 'I never meant for him to find me again, only…'

'Only?'

The gentle understanding in the lady's countenance invited Felicity to confide. She said, 'Lady Souden took me to London with her and once I had seen Nathan, I…I could not help myself. I wanted to see him again and again. I knew it was dangerous, that I should go away, but I could not resist. It was inevitable, I suppose, that he should discover me.' She spread her hands. 'And here I am.'

'Yes, here you are,' agreed Mrs Carraway. 'You love him very much, do you not?'

Felicity gave a little sigh. 'Yes, I do. Very much indeed.' She leaned forward, saying earnestly, 'Oh, ma'am, if only he will let me, I mean to be a good wife to him. It was very foolish of me to run away, but now I really do want to make him happy.'

Mrs Carraway watched her and after a long moment

she nodded, apparently satisfied. 'Yes, my dear, I think I believe you.'

There was a soft knock on the door.

'May I come in?' Nathan hovered in the doorway. 'Collins has nothing for me that cannot wait until the morrow.'

'Then by all means join us, Nathan.' Mrs Carraway looked at the clock. 'I was about to summon Norton to take me to my room, and you two must change for dinner. I told Mercer to lay covers on the table in the small parlour,' she added. 'Much cosier for just two of you.'

'Oh, will you not be joining us, ma'am?' asked Felicity.

'Not tonight, my dear. I am a little tired, so Norton will bring my supper to my room. Besides, I think the two of you should have some time alone.'

Chapter Thirteen

The dining table in the small parlour was capable of seating only four couples in comfort but to Felicity, entering the room upon her husband's arm, there seemed a vast expanse of white linen between the two places set at each end of the table. There was also an inordinate amount of silver on display, including an oversize salt cellar and mustard pot, a pair of bell-shaped goblets, a variety of candlesticks and a very ornate wine cooler.

Nathan's lips twitched and his glance flickered over Felicity. He turned to address the butler.

'Are you trying to impress Lady Rosthorne with all this magnificence?' He murmured a few brief instructions before leading Felicity back to the drawing room.

'Is that your normal style of dining?' asked Felicity, looking up at him with eyes that were at once apprehensive and wondering. Nathan was quick to reassure her.

'When we have visitors of consequence, perhaps, but they would be entertained in the dining room, not the little parlour.' He chuckled. 'Poor Mercer. He was here in my uncle's day, and the late earl enjoyed a great deal more ceremony than I care for. I am sorry to delay your dinner, my dear, but I think you will find it much more comfortable once Mercer has carried out my orders.'

★ ★ ★

When they returned to the parlour a short while later, the table had been transformed. Most of the gleaming silver had been cleared away and the covers had been laid at one end of the table only with a place for Felicity set on Nathan's right hand. A cheerful fire crackled in the hearth and instead of the glare of dozens of candles, the room was illuminated only by those in the gilded girandoles on the walls and one carefully placed branched candlestick on the table.

'That is much better,' Nathan approved.

He led Felicity forward and held her chair for her himself before taking his place at the head of the table. After the soup she took a little of the fish and allowed Nathan to carve her a few slices of chicken. At first she was too nervous to eat more than a few mouthfuls from the array of dishes spread out on the table, but Nathan's quiet attentions and gentle manner soon put her at her ease. She refused a second glass of wine, in favour of a glass of water, but when the dishes for the second course appeared she took a small helping of the fricassee and a little of the plum pudding.

Conversation was desultory. Nathan was very aware of Mercer's silent presence behind him at the sideboard. Ostensibly the butler was polishing glasses, but Nathan knew he was listening attentively to every word that was spoken.

'We must hold a ball, my dear, to introduce you to the neighbourhood, but I would as lief wait a little while, until we are more settled.

'There must be an announcement, of course; I shall send something to the London newspapers and journals tomorrow, but I see no reason for any formal entertaining until the new year.'

'As you wish, my lord.'

'Of course, it may be impossible to keep my aunt Appleby away,' he mused. 'She lives not twenty miles from here and will insist upon driving over to hear the whole story for herself.' He laughed. 'Do not look so horrified, I shall not allow her to bully you.' He reached out and covered her hand with his own. 'I shall not allow anyone to hurt you.'

The sudden change in tone and the warm grasp of his fingers brought the blood rushing to Felicity's cheeks. She raised her eyes to his but looked away immediately, for the intense glow in his eyes made her suddenly very shy. Nathan squeezed her hand before releasing her and they sat in silence while the covers were removed to reveal the highly polished mahogany table. A number of pretty little sweet-meat dishes were placed on its gleaming surface. Nathan raised his hand and signalled to the butler.

'Leave the wines and glasses on the table, if you please. I will serve my lady. You may go now; I shall not need you again tonight.'

Perhaps it was the removal of the snow-white linen that made the room seem smaller, and a little darker, but there was a different atmosphere in the parlour once she and Nathan were alone. She was intensely aware of him sitting beside her. She need only reach out her hand and she could touch him.

She felt a sudden rush of affection for him. He was her husband, and he was exerting himself so much for her comfort. *This is my life now*, she thought. Serena Ansell and all the problems of the summer seemed as distant as the moon.

He pulled one of the little dishes closer. 'These confits are made by a French émigré in London. I have them sent down for my mother, she is especially fond of them.'

Felicity shook her head. 'I do not think…'

He reached out and picked up a small shell-shape between his long fingers. 'Try it.' He held it up to her mouth. 'It is chocolate.'

Felicity's lips parted and he slid the small, fragrant sweet meat into her mouth.

'There,' he said, smiling. 'Do you like it?'

She could only nod, her mouth still full of the rich, velvety confection.

'Good. Now let me find you a little wine to follow it. Which shall it be, the claret, port, or…?' He reached out for one of the decanters. 'Madeira, I think.'

Felicity watched him pour the wine into two glasses. 'I have never tried that,' she admitted.

'Then you shall do so now, and we shall drink a toast, to many such nights as this.' He handed her a glass and she sipped at it, enjoying the slightly nutty flavour and warmth in her throat as she swallowed. Nathan was watching her, waiting for her opinion.

'I like it, sir. Very much.'

Nathan smiled, the slow curving of his lips drawing an answering smile from Felicity.

Sitting within the golden glow of the candlelight, they began to talk. In response to Nathan's gentle questions she found herself telling him about her years with Lady Souden, describing the joys and frustrations of life as a governess, albeit a well-loved one. She was encouraged by his mellow mood to ask Nathan about his work on the estates. She sipped at her wine and listened attentively as he talked to her of his various houses and the improvements he had put in progress. His deep voice flowed over and around her, smooth as the chocolate he had given her. She watched him, observing the animation with which he spoke of his plans for new building works, better drainage and crop rotation.

'I think you love your role as Earl Rosthorne,' she ventured when he paused to refill their glasses.

'It was a little daunting at first, but I have some good people around me, like Collins, my steward here. There is much to be done, it is a lifetime's work.' He met her eyes. 'And you can help me, Fee, and you will.'

She returned his look, her spirits singing.

'There is nothing I should like more, Nathan.'

'Good. Then you must come riding with me—get to know the land and the people. That is the first step.'

She sipped at her Madeira. A warm glow was spreading through her, making her feel comfortable, and happy and...reckless. Nathan gestured towards the sweetmeats.

'Would my lady care for another?'

'No.' She put down her glass. 'It is my turn.'

She selected a sugared plum and held it out to him. Smiling, Nathan opened his mouth. Her eyes widened as his teeth closed gently on her finger. He reached up to capture her hand and with infinite care he began to press kisses on her palm. Slowly he moved his mouth to the inside of her wrist, then placed a series of butterfly-light kisses along her arm towards the hinge of her elbow.

Felicity stilled. She caught her bottom lip between her teeth and tried not to move. The touch of his mouth on her skin was sending little shocks through her. A pleasurable lightness was pooling in her belly. She fixed her eyes upon him. The candlelight reflected in the red-gold tints in his hair and enhanced the strong lines of his countenance. She marvelled at the concentration on his face as he gave his attention to the soft white skin of her arm.

'Oh, heavens,' she whispered, unable to contain herself.

Immediately he looked up. 'Do you not like that?'

'No—yes,' she confessed. 'Too much.'

To her disappointment he released her hand.

'I should go,' she said, her voice not quite steady. 'It is time for me to retire to the drawing room.'

'What, would you leave me here in solitary splendour to enjoy my brandy?'

'It is the custom, my lord.'

'In general, of course, but not tonight.'

'N-no?'

The warmth was spreading through her again, but this time it was caused not by the wine but by the look in

Nathan's eyes. He rose and held out his hand to her. Silently she gave him her own and his fingers closed around it, safe. Secure. She followed him out of the room and up the dark stairs, the only light coming from the bedroom candle that Nathan picked up from the hall table as he passed. Her heart was hammering hard against her ribs. It was five long years since she had been in Nathan's bed. Then he had been very patient with her. What would he expect of her now? She knew so little, she might as well be his bride of five days rather than five years.

In the main bedchamber they found the candles burning on the mantelshelf and Nathan's man on his knees before the fire, coaxing it into a blaze. He jumped to his feet as they entered.

'It's good to see you again, my lady,' he said with a little bow. 'Welcome to Rosthorne Hall.'

'Thank you, Sam.'

He gave her a quick smile, half-saluted Nathan and went quickly to the door.

'Sam.' Nathan's one quiet word halted him. 'Find my lady's maid and tell her she may go to bed. She will not be needed again tonight.'

With a nod he was gone, and they were alone.

'Very cavalier of you, my lord,' said Felicity, trying to conceal her nerves with a flippant remark.

He looked down at her, his eyes glinting. 'Do you think I cannot undress you? Come here.'

She walked towards him and he put his hands on her shoulders, drawing her closer. His kiss was slow and thorough and Felicity's senses took flight. She was no longer nervous but eager now for him to make love to her. The memory of their wedding night, a memory that she had suppressed for so long, flooded into her mind and she wanted to feel again the soaring, intense pleasure of his body against hers. She put her arms about him, hugging him close while his own hands loosened the thin drawstrings that fastened the little puff sleeves of her gown. Then they slid around her back to tease open the hooks. When Nathan raised his head and gently pulled away from her, Felicity felt bereft. She wanted only to be back in his arms, to be kissing him once more.

The little part of her brain that was still working registered some satisfaction at his laboured breathing and the way his hands trembled as they moved up over her arms and pushed the gown off her shoulders. It fell to the floor with a whisper. Her chemise followed swiftly and he turned her around, pressing kisses on the back of her neck while he drew the laces from the confining corset that imprisoned her. But even as the linen and whalebone stays fell away she was imprisoned again as Nathan's hands slid around to cup her breasts. With a little moan of frustration she turned within the circle of his arms, pulling his face down to hers, seeking his mouth. Impatiently she began to tear at his clothes. Jacket and waistcoat were quickly discarded, shirt and breeches followed. He swept her up and carried her to the huge tester bed.

Nathan laid her down gently on the covers, deep in shadow, and she reached for him, eager for his touch. He obliged with kisses and caresses that sent her spirits soaring. She responded with caresses of her own, revelling in his closeness, the feel of his skin against hers. She was like a flower, unfurling in the heat of his sun, opening up, offering herself with an abandon that shocked her. Their coupling was wild and urgent. They rolled together in a tangle of limbs, crying out as excitement surged through them until at length they fell back on the covers, spent and exhausted.

A warm sense of well-being had settled over Felicity. She put her hand up to Nathan's face, her fingers moving up the soft ridge of scar, following it from his cheek to his temple. He covered her fingers with his own.

He said with difficulty, 'This—disfigurement. Does it—do you find it…repellent?'

'No,' she said softly. 'It is part of you—it is what makes you who you are.' She drew his head down and placed her lips gently against the mark.

With a sigh he caught her against him, burying his face in her hair. Felicity wrapped herself about him and allowed him to possess her once more, before finally succumbing to a deep, contented sleep.

Felicity awoke to find herself alone. She sat up when she heard the soft creak of the door as her maid peeped into the room.

'Ooh, I beg your pardon, my lady, did I wake you?'

'No, Martha. Where is the earl?'

'His lordship is already gone out riding, my lady. He left orders that you was to be allowed to sleep on and he will join you for breakfast.'

Felicity threw back the bedcovers.

'Then you had best help me to get dressed.'

It was an hour later when Nathan returned. Bella heard his approach; she was sitting at Felicity's feet under the breakfast table but came out and uttered a joyful bark as Nathan appeared in the doorway. Felicity was every bit as happy to see him as the little spaniel, but she contented herself with a wide smile. He was dressed for riding in jacket, topboots and tight-fitting buckskins. She thought how well he looked as a country gentleman. He was relaxed, his complexion still glowing from his early morning exercise, and he sat down beside Felicity, eager to discuss his plans for her entertainment. After listening to him for a full five minutes she put up her hands, laughing.

'Enough, my lord,' she said. 'Much as I would enjoy visiting all your neighbours and attending the local assembly you must remember that I have very few gowns suitable for a countess.'

He poured himself a cup of coffee. 'It is not the gowns but what is underneath that is important.' He turned his head towards her, his eyes glinting. 'And what is beneath your gowns is *very* suitable for a countess, my lady.'

She flushed scarlet and was thankful they were alone in the room. She said seriously, 'I would not wish to embarrass you, my lord.'

He took her hand and kissed it. 'You could never embarrass me but you are quite right, we did not buy you a trousseau. Shall we post back to London and open up the town house? Or will you put yourself in my mother's hands? She rarely leaves Rosthorne and has local dressmakers and milliners that attend her here.'

'I would rather not return to town, sir, and would gladly talk to your mama,' replied Felicity. 'An excellent solution.'

After breakfast Nathan took Felicity along to Mrs Carraway's apartments. She was only too pleased to help.

'In general I use Jannine, in Winchester. She has a sister in town who is very useful for providing details of the latest fashions. I shall write to her immediately and explain that we need pattern books and fabrics sent here as soon as possible. I shall tell her that you need a complete wardrobe: walking dresses, morning gowns, pelisses, spencers—and we shall need a milliner, too...'

'Dear ma'am, you must not overtax yourself,' cried Felicity, alarmed. 'I had not thought to give you so much work!'

Mrs Carraway brushed aside her concerns.

'Norton and I will positively enjoy being involved in such a task. Of course, the decisions on styles and fabrics must be yours, my dear, but I do hope you will allow us to help you.'

Felicity's response was heartfelt. 'I do not know quite where I should begin, ma'am, and should be very glad of your assistance.' She added hesitantly, 'My Uncle Philip did not approve of elegant clothes. He thought they were the trappings of the devil.'

'Then he was wrong,' replied Mrs Carraway robustly. 'They are the trappings of your position as Rosthorne's countess. Nathan is lord of the manor here, and as his consort people will expect you to dress accordingly.'

Thus it was that within a few days an army of seamstresses and dressmakers descended upon Rosthorne Hall together with ells of muslin, chintz and silks in a bewildering assortment of patterns and colours. Felicity allowed herself to be pinned, prodded and measured, but her reward was to slip away every morning to ride out with Nathan. Her riding habit was serviceable rather than elegant, but the blue jacket showed her neat figure to advantage and Nathan announced that it was perfectly suitable for riding around the estate.

He introduced her to the tenants and lodge-keepers, gardeners and gamekeepers that they met during these rides, and on one particularly sunny day when they had reached the limits of the Rosthorne land he suggested riding a little further.

'That is, unless you have to get back to the house.'

'To be stitched into even more gowns?' she laughed at him. 'No, I thank you!'

'I thought you would enjoy buying new clothes.'

'I do, but not all at once! Mama Carraway has been so good as to take charge of the sewing room. I have only to choose the fabric and the pattern and she does all the rest. I am very grateful to her.'

'And I am grateful to *you*,' he responded promptly. 'You have provided my mother with a new interest and she is greatly enjoying herself.'

'I am glad. Your mama has been very kind to me.' She paused, then added haltingly, 'I thought, at first, that she might not like me—and she had every right—I behaved abominably to you.'

He reached out for her hand. 'No, she likes you, very much.'

'Thank you,' whispered Felicity. She blinked rapidly and said after a moment, 'Well, my lord? Where are we going now?'

'To West Meon, no more than a few miles away. Adam Elliston's parents live in the village—I should like to make you known to them.' Felicity did not reply immediately; the mention of Nathan's friend brought back vivid memories of Corunna. Nathan said quickly, 'Perhaps it is too much to ask of you, after all we have been riding for—'

'No, no,' she interrupted him, smiling. 'I should be very happy—honoured—to meet them, if you do not think me too shabbily dressed for the visit?'

'No. You have a little mud on your cheek, but if we remove that I think you will pass muster.'

'Mud? Where?'

Nathan brought his horse closer. 'Keep still and I will deal with it.' He pulled off his glove and took her handkerchief from her fingers. 'You did the same for me, in Green Park, do you remember?'

She shivered. 'How could I forget? Have there been any more attacks since you left town?'

'No, none. So you see, there is no grand plan to dispose of me.' He cupped her chin with one hand while he wiped the mud from her cheek. 'There, you are respectable again.' Felicity remained very still, gazing into his face. Nathan's mouth curved upwards in a tantalising smile. 'What say you we postpone our visit to the Ellistons? We could dismount here and—ah—take a stroll in the woods.'

Her heart began to race. She could not mistake his meaning, nor the warm look in his eyes. It was an outrageous suggestion, but she was not at all shocked by it, only by her own impulse to agree. She swallowed convulsively and said in a rallying tone, 'If we do that, my lord, I shall certainly not be fit to be seen!'

He laughed. 'No, you are right, we must go on to West Meon.' He released her, sighing. 'Pity…'

A chuckle escaped Felicity, but she said severely, 'Fie, my lord. Let us ride on; you must attend to your duty.'

'That is what I was planning to do.'

She choked, decided it would be unwise to try to respond and instead she spurred her horse on, hoping that she would regain her composure before they reached their destination.

'So Nathan has been introducing you to our neighbours.'

Mrs Carraway joined them for dinner, and they were seated within the candles' glow in the small parlour.

'He took me to West Meon today to meet Mr and Mrs Elliston, and their daughter,' replied Felicity. 'They send their regards to you, and Mrs Elliston promised to call very soon.'

Mrs Carraway nodded.

'A delightful couple, and their daughter Judith is a lovely girl. She has been their sole comfort since they lost Adam—such a good-natured boy. I felt for them most deeply when I learned of his death.' She added, her voice breaking, 'And I feel my own good fortune even more.'

Nathan reached across the table for her hand. 'So, too, do I, Mama. But let us not dwell on the past—tell me how you have gone on today. Have you been busy with the dressmakers all day?'

'No, for Mrs Orr, the vicar's wife, came to take tea with me. A pleasant woman, but addicted to gossip.' Mrs Carraway smiled at Felicity. 'I think her object in calling was to find out all about you, my dear. You need not be anxious, I told her only that you had been living quietly with friends in London until Nathan could bring you home. She thought it very romantical! Everyone is eagerly awaiting your appearance at church tomorrow.'

'Good heavens,' exclaimed Nathan, startled. 'Do we have to go? You will remember how they stared the first time we came here, as if I were a prize exhibit!'

'Of course you must go, my son! It is most important that you and your wife are seen abroad, and you know that they will soon grow tired of staring at you.' She reached out and lifted a chocolate shell from the sweetmeat dish in front of her. 'And Felicity will not be the only new face for the congregation to gape at. Mrs Orr tells me Godfrey Park is let.'

'I had not heard that. Godfrey Park is a neat little property about three miles north of here,' Nathan told Felicity. 'We passed it on our way here from town. So, Mama, who are our new neighbours?'

'Well, according to the agent—and he should know the facts, should he not?—it is a widow. The relict of a wealthy gentleman from Somerset. A Lady Ansell.'

Chapter Fourteen

The warmth and contentment Felicity had been feeling vanished in an instant. Her eyes flew to Nathan. He was very still, looking at Mrs Carraway.

'Ansell? Formerly married to Colonel Craike?'

'That I do not know, only that she is a wealthy widow.'

'Well, we shall find out soon enough,' Nathan responded coolly. 'Did I mention that I have given instructions for the track through the Home Wood to be cleared? It has become sadly overgrown this summer…'

Lady Ansell's name was not mentioned again, but Felicity felt her presence like a cloud over her own happiness.

As she made her way upstairs to their bedchamber that night she resolved to say something to Nathan. She was at her dressing table, brushing out her hair, when he came in. Even in the candlelight the colourful pattern on his heavy silk banyan was garishly bright.

'You are the devil of a time about your undressing,' he told her.

Felicity dismissed her maid.

'I have been looking at my new gowns; two of them are ready and I have been trying to decide which one I shall wear tomorrow. If Mama Carraway is correct we shall be under scrutiny when we go to church.'

He came up behind her and placed his hands on her shoulders, meeting her eyes in the mirror. 'It is only natural that everyone will want to see my new countess.'

She smiled a little, and looked away, idly straightening the glass pots on the table. 'They will also wish to see the new tenant of Godfrey Park.' She risked a fleeting look up. 'I wonder what brings her to Hampshire?'

'I have no idea.'

Words filled Felicity's head, but they would not be spoken—she wanted to ask Nathan is he still loved Serena, if he had invited her to be near him. If she was his mistress. She knew such arrangements were not uncommon and the questions battered at her head, even as Nathan pulled her up into his arms. *Ask him*, the voice inside her screamed. *Ask him to tell you the truth, now.* But as Nathan swept her up and carried her into the bedroom, she buried her head in his shoulder and quelled the nagging demon inside her, wretchedly acknowledging that she would not ask the questions, because she was too afraid of the answers.

The dawning of a bright and warm Sunday morning did much to restore Felicity's spirits and her confidence was greatly increased by Nathan's look of admiration when she presented herself in a new flounced gown of white muslin with an olive-green velvet spencer and matching high-poke bonnet.

'Well, my lord, will I do?' she asked shyly, fingering the green ribbons of her bonnet.

'Admirably.' He held out his arm to her. 'Shall we go?'

They found Mrs Carraway waiting for them in the carriage, the faithful Norton at her side.

'Well now, you make a very handsome couple,' she declared as Nathan handed Felicity into the carriage. 'Just one thing, if you will permit me, my dear. Norton, re tie the ribbons of Lady Rosthorne's bonnet, if you please. Yes, that's it—a large bow, just beneath her ear.'

As Mrs Carraway's companion sat back to admire her handiwork, Felicity cast an anxious glance at Nathan. He was grinning at her.

'Very dashing.'

'Oh,' she said, daunted. 'Not *too* dashing for a Sunday?'

'Not at all, my love,' declared Mrs Carraway. 'It is perfect for a young bride, as is the colour in your pretty cheek. Give the driver the word, Nathan, we do not want to be late.'

The little church in Hazelford village was crowded and Felicity was glad of Nathan's arm as he escorted her to family's box pew below the pulpit. The congregation stared at her with unashamed curiosity and she guessed that many of them had come especially to see the new Lady Rosthorne.

'Well, Mr Orr's sermon was not too long, thank heaven,' muttered Mrs Carraway as they prepared to leave the church after the service. 'Now, my son, you must take your countess outside, and face the dragons!'

Felicity accompanied Nathan out of the church, blinking in the sunlight, and was confronted by a bewildering number of strangers, all wishing to be presented to her. With Nathan beside her she smiled and said all that was proper. From the corner of her eye she saw Norton escorting Mrs Carraway to the carriage; another few moments, she thought, and they could drive away, back to the peace and privacy of Rosthorne.

'Ah, my lord—' the vicar's blustering tones shattered her hopes '—we cannot let you and your good lady leave without introducing another new member of our congregation.'

Felicity turned to find Serena standing before her, tall and beautiful in a lavender carriage dress, a single ostrich feather curling around the edge of her bonnet and framing her perfect features.

'The earl and I were in Corunna together,' Serena told the beaming vicar.

Felicity bridled at the implication of her words.

'I knew him even before he married.' She turned to Felicity with the merest hint of a curtsy. 'But you were only Mrs Carraway then, my lady.'

'Yes, of course.' Felicity was surprised that her voice did not shake. 'And you were Mrs Craike.'

'I was. Poor Craike, it was such a long time ago.' The widow sighed and turned her gaze upon Nathan. 'My congratulations, my lord. You must be very happy to have found your bride again.'

'Thank you, ma'am. I am very happy.' Nathan's attention was sought by the vicar and he turned away, leaving Felicity alone with Serena Ansell.

'So—' the widow was smiling but there was no warmth in her green eyes '—you could not resist the idea of being a countess.'

Felicity's lip curled. 'Think that, if you will.' She was determined not to be intimidated by this woman. She turned and began to walk towards the carriage. Serena followed her.

'It is what everyone will think when they know the truth.'

'Why should they? I have merely been living quietly with friends.'

'Using an assumed name.'

Felicity shrugged. 'I did not wish to draw attention to my situation.'

'And just what is your situation now, my lady?' purred Serena. 'Does Nathan know why you left him in Spain?'

'Yes.' Felicity stopped. 'What happened five years ago is no longer of interest.'

Serena's brows rose. 'Are you quite sure?'

Felicity drew herself up. 'I will acknowledge you as an acquaintance, madam, but nothing more.'

'And I will acknowledge *you* as Nathan's wife in name, but nothing more.' Serena glared at her, all pretence of friendliness gone. 'I will allow you your title, Lady Rosthorne,' she said contemptuously. 'But do you think someone as innocent, as unskilled as you can keep the man?'

'I intend to try,' retorted Felicity, thoroughly angry. 'And if you still have his ring, I think it is time it was returned.'

There was an arrested look in the widow's face.

'Well, madam,' said Felicity coldly, 'Do you still have it?'

'Why, I…it may well be in my jewel case,' came the careless reply.

Felicity's indignation swelled. If Nathan have given *her* such a token she would cherish it. Serena was watching her, a cold little smile playing around her lips.

'You never told him of our final meeting, did you?' she said softly. 'You never challenged him.' When Felicity did not reply the widow gave a soft laugh. 'No, you did not dare. And even now, you will not confront him.' She leaned closer. 'You poor fool, you were a nobody that Nathan plucked from the streets of Corunna—you know you can never be worthy of him!'

Felicity stared at her, inwardly flinching as Serena put into words her own deepest fears. Before she could summon a suitable retort, Nathan came striding up.

'I beg your pardon, my dear, I never intended you leave you alone.' He placed his hand under her elbow.

'Your wife and I have been getting better acquainted,' said Serena, smoothly. 'It is such a comfort to know I have such good friends living nearby.'

With a final smile she turned and walked away.

Silently Felicity accompanied Nathan to the carriage where Mrs Carraway was waiting for them.

'You look pale, my dear,' she observed as Nathan handed Felicity into the carriage. 'Such an ordeal for you, to meet so many new people.'

'Is that it, Fee?' asked Nathan, regarding her closely. 'I trust Lady Ansell said nothing to overset you?'

Felicity knew that even if she had wanted to tell him everything Serena had said, she could not do so here, in front of his mother. So she shook her head and disclaimed, dismally ashamed at her own cowardice.

'I admit I am intrigued by our new neighbour,' mused Mrs Carraway as the carriage rattled its way back to Rosthorne Hall. 'Very beautiful, of course. One wonders why she has decided to bury herself away here in Hampshire? Perhaps we should call—'

'No!' Felicity's involuntary gasp caught Nathan's attention.

'I pray you will not seek for too close an acquaintance with Lady Ansell, Mama,' he said.

'Oho,' cried his mama, her eyes twinkling. 'I smell some story here, Norton! Well, my son, are you going to tell us what is so very bad about the widow?'

'Certainly not,' returned Nathan, smiling faintly. 'I abhor gossip. Suffice to say that I knew the lady in Corunna, and she is not good *ton*.'

'But we cannot ignore her. Such a wealthy widow—she will be invited everywhere.'

'But not into my house. Is that what was worrying you, Fee?' He took her hand and squeezed it. 'Serena Ansell has her place, but it is not at Rosthorne Hall.'

Felicity sank back into her corner, deriving some small measure of comfort from his words.

When they arrived back at Rosthorne, Mrs Carraway went off to her apartment with her companion. As soon as Felicity had divested herself of her bonnet and spencer, Nathan escorted her to the drawing room.

'Well, that is the biggest ordeal over,' he remarked. 'To be obliged to sit in church while every man and his dog gawps open-mouthed—'

'It was not so very bad,' she said, preceding him into the room. 'I had your mama there to support me.'

He reached for her hand and pulled her down on to the

sofa. 'They were very taken with you.' He raised her fingers to his lips. 'I was told several times how lucky I am to have found such a wife.'

'Nathan.' She clung to his hand. 'You never told me what happened to your ring, the one engraved with the rose thorns that you wore on your little finger.'

'I told you it was lost during the war. There is nothing else to know.'

Felicity screwed up her courage. 'Did you…did you give it away?'

Gently he removed his fingers from her grasp. 'It was a long time ago, Fee. We will forget it, if you please.' He rose. 'Collins tells me they have now finished clearing the path through the Home Wood. I was going to ride out there later—would you care to join me?'

His face was impassive, but there was a hardness about his eyes, a look that told her not to ask more questions. She capitulated.

'Yes,' she said. 'I would very much like to ride out with you.'

Let him keep his secrets, she thought, *and I will keep mine!*

Felicity settled into her new home. She enjoyed the companionship of her mama-in-law and fell ever deeper in love with her husband. He encouraged her interest in the estate, was always kind and attentive, yet doubts continued to haunt her. She longed for the courage to talk to him, to confide her fears, but she could not bring herself to risk their new-found happiness.

Mrs Carraway's excellent dressmaker delivered another selection of gowns in time for the Hazelford Assembly and Felicity spent a pleasant afternoon choosing just what she would wear.

'You will be the first in consequence there so it is important that you are looking your best,' Mrs Carraway told her when Felicity asked for her opinion.

They were in the large sunny apartment that was designated as the countess's dressing room and Felicity was trying on her new muslin evening dress. It was a very pale cream decorated at the neck, sleeves and hem with exquisite green-and-gold embroidery.

'I am aware that every eye will be upon me when I walk in,' murmured Felicity. 'I shall be so nervous.'

'Just be yourself and everyone will love you.' Mrs Carraway turned in her chair. 'Martha, my dear, run along to my room and ask Norton to look out my gold shawl.'

'Oh, please, no, you have done so much for me already,' cried Felicity, dismayed, as her maid ran off on her errand.

'Heavens, why should I not? You are my daughter now.' She held out her hands. 'What is there in that to overset you?'

Felicity went to her and dropped down on her knees beside her chair. 'You are so generous, and since I have been at Rosthorne everyone has been so kind…I do not feel that I deserve it—I came here with so little.'

'Now enough of this foolish talk. You have won all our hearts and that is all that signifies.' She put her hand under Felicity's chin and turned her face up, smiling down into her eyes. 'Have a little more confidence in yourself, my love, and you will do very well.'

The words echoed in Felicity's head as she entered the ballroom at the Swan Inn that evening. With her hand securely on Nathan's arm, she thought it was easy to be confident. Easy to convince herself that they could be happy together. A quick glance at him made her heart swell with pride. She had seen Mr Brummell in London and knew that Nathan followed his precepts, but privately she thought her husband looked much more handsome than the arbiter of fashion himself. His tall figure and broad shoulders were ideally suited to the superbly cut evening coat and tight-fitting knee-breeches he was wearing that evening. The snowy whiteness of his intricately tied cravat accentuated his dark face, tanned by years of soldiering in Spain and France, but Felicity much preferred this to the ruddy cheeks and bushy side-whiskers of the other gentlemen present.

Nathan glanced down at the silent little figure beside him. He knew how nervous she must be to be opening the dancing in a crowded room full of near-strangers and her quiet dignity impressed him. A number of gentlemen were already heading towards the card room, but he decided he would not leave Felicity until he was sure she was more comfortable.

'I insist upon at least the first two dances with you,' he told her and was inordinately pleased at the way her face lit up. Even now, after a month together, desire stirred his bones whenever she smiled like that.

As they danced together he found he had eyes for no one else. He enjoyed watching the way she moved to the music, taking in every graceful step. He wanted to draw her aside and plant kisses on the delicate curve of her neck, but that must wait. He could not even dance with her again, at least not yet; having brought his new countess to the assembly, he could not monopolise her. Seeing his cousin as they left the dance floor, he buried his frustration and hailed him cheerfully.

'Gerald, well met, Cos! I thought you would still be in town.'

Mr Appleby came up, grinning. 'So I would be, but when Mama received your letter she insisted upon posting down here immediately.'

'Ah, I see.' Nathan looked down at Felicity. 'My dear, may I present to you my cousin, Mr Gerald Appleby?'

Gerald grinned as he took Felicity's outstretched hand.

'Well, well, Lady Rosthorne, you fooled us all very neatly! When Nathan wrote to explain that you had been living in town all this summer, under our very noses, I could scarcely believe it! Mama was for once almost speech-less when she realised that little Miss Brown was in fact Nathan's wife! Depend upon it, I told her, the whole charade was a scheme concocted by Lady Souden to keep you out of the public eye while Nathan here prepared Rosthorne for his countess. Am I right?'

'Y-yes.' Felicity cast a laughing glance up at her husband, who grinned.

'Very acute of you, Gerald.'

Mr Appleby nodded. 'There is a rumour running around town that my cousin had lost you, Lady Rosthorne. I can only say that it was incredibly careless of Nathan. I hope he means to take better care of you in future!'

Felicity blushed and murmured something incoherent.

'Forgive my cousin's attempts at humour,' retorted Nathan, smiling in spite of himself. 'Is Lady Charlotte with you tonight?'

'No, we only arrived at Appleby Manor this afternoon and she was too exhausted to come here. I, on the other hand, was eager to meet my new cousin.' He turned again to Felicity. 'If you are not engaged, madam, would you honour me with the next dance?'

Nathan was aware of Felicity's hesitation. He gave her a reassuring look and a slight nod. Immediately she smiled.

'I shall be delighted to dance with you, Mr Appleby.'

'Capital! I shall return to claim my prize,' exclaimed Gerald, adding irrepressibly, 'I charge you not to lose her before then, Cousin!'

'What a pleasant young man he is,' murmured Felicity, as Gerald lounged away. 'He was always very attentive when I was in town.'

'I am aware,' growled Nathan. 'Insolent puppy!'

She laughed at that. 'He was merely being kind to Lady Souden's impoverished companion.'

'Aye, and putting me to shame. I paid you very little attention.'

'If you had done so, I should have been obliged to retire from society rather than risk discovery.'

He stopped and turned towards her.

'And now?' he asked. 'Are you sorry that I discovered you?'

A faint blush mantled her cheeks. She did not look up, but he saw the slight shake of her head. Surrounded by the noise and chatter of the room, he had to bend his head to catch her words.

'No, I am not sorry.'

His heart swelled with pleasure. He hoped he was not strutting like some arrogant coxcomb as they continued their perambulation of the room.

Felicity was enjoying herself. Nathan's obvious approval did much to calm her nerves and she almost skipped off to dance with his cousin. After that her hand was solicited by any number of gentlemen, including Mr Elliston, who had arrived with his wife and daughter while she was dancing with Gerald.

They were talking with Nathan when Mr Appleby escorted her back after their dance.

'Ah, here is that lovely wife of yours, Rosthorne!' cried Mr Elliston, in great good humour. 'Good evening to you, Lady Rosthorne. We were just saying what a blessing it is that Rosthorne here is no longer in the army.'

'I count myself very fortunate, sir,' replied Felicity, smiling up at her husband.

'But what if Boney should get free?' put in Gerald. 'What then?'

'If he posed a threat to England then I suppose I might be called upon to join up again,' said Nathan.

Mr Elliston cocked an eyebrow. 'And what would you say to that, Lady Rosthorne?

Felicity smiled. 'If my lord considers it his duty to go and fight then naturally I should support him. And I think I might best do that by staying here and looking after his estates.'

'A truly excellent answer, my love, thank you.' Nathan

picked up her hand and kissed it. He smiled into her eyes. 'I knew you would make me a perfect wife.'

Later, when Nathan asked Miss Elliston to stand up with him, her father turned a kindly smile towards Felicity.

'I'd be honoured to tread a country measure with you, Lady Rosthorne, if your husband will allow it.'

'With pleasure, sir, if your *wife* will allow it,' responded Felicity, twinkling.

'Away with you both,' laughed Mrs Elliston. 'I shall take myself over there to enjoy a comfortable gossip with my friends!'

Two lively country dances left Felicity and her partner breathless but upon excellent terms, and Mr Elliston took her off in search of refreshment in the supper room.

'If you will forgive me for saying so, ma'am, it does my heart good to see Nathan in such spirits,' he told her as he handed her a glass of punch. 'The war took its toll of him, you see. Losing so many comrades.'

'Including your son,' she ventured, shyly.

'Aye. That shook him badly. Even now he don't like to talk of it and shies away from any mention of Adam. Feels he is somehow to blame, you see, because Adam followed him into the army. He came to see us, you know, as soon as he could get leave. Brought back Adam's effects, such as they were. They were like brothers, growing up, and Nathan is like a second son to us.' Mr Elliston shook his head. 'I don't say it didn't break our hearts to lose our boy, but it was some consolation that Nathan survived the war, albeit marked. It don't frighten you, that scar down his face?' he shot at her.

Felicity smiled. 'I do not notice it.'

The old man beamed. 'That's the spirit! Now, I suppose I had better return you to his lordship, before he thinks I have run off with you!'

★ ★ ★

Nathan observed Felicity going down to supper with Mr Elliston as he returned Judith Elliston to her mama, where she was immediately carried off by Gerald Appleby to dance again. Nathan made his way to the card room, satisfied that Felicity would not need his company for a while. However, he found he could not settle to picquet or whist and it was not long before he was heading towards the ballroom once more to look for his wife. As he crossed the deserted landing he heard his name and stopped. Lady Ansell was coming up the stairs.

'I am very late—have I missed all the dancing?'

'Not quite, the orchestra will play for another hour yet.'

'I suppose it is useless to expect you to partner me.'

He returned her speculative look with a bland one of his own. 'It is.'

'Ah well, then you can at least escort me to the ballroom.'

He made no move to offer her his arm. 'Why have you come here, Serena?'

'Why, to dance, of course.'

'I meant why have you chosen to settle in Hazelford?'

'Do you not know, Nathan?' she murmured, looking up at him from under her lashes.

'Should I?'

She laughed and waved her hand dismissively. 'I have been invited to go to Bath at Christmas,' she told him, straightening her long silk gloves. 'I have family there. But I can easily cry off, if you would like me to stay.'

'Your actions are of no interest to me, madam.'

'No?'

'Not in the least.' He held her eyes. 'You are wasting your time with me, madam.'

'Am I?' She stepped close, sliding her fingers over his chest and on to his shoulders. 'Are you not just a little bit tempted?' Her voice was warm and inviting. She was leaning into him, so close that he could smell the heady perfume of the flowers pinned to her corsage. 'I liked you well enough in Corunna,' she murmured, 'but Adam Elliston was before you and you had such *chivalrous* ideas about not stealing his lover. Besides, *then* you were only a boy. Now I would like to try the man…'

She reached up, brushing her lips against his. For a moment he did not move, but allowed her to kiss him. Her hands slid up and around his neck, but her touch awoke no answering spark in him. He placed his hands on her waist and gently but firmly detached himself.

'Enough, madam. Man or boy I never was, nor ever will be, for you.'

He saw the flash of anger in her eyes. It was gone in an instant, and she was smiling again. She shrugged.

'I suppose it is still honeymoon for you and that innocent little bride of yours. But when the novelty wears off, I shall be waiting for you.'

Without a word Nathan turned away. Her self-assurance was incomprehensible. As he walked back into the ballroom, his uppermost emotion for Serena Ansell was pity.

Chapter Fifteen

'Well, upon my soul!'

It was only the briefest moment before Mr Elliston whisked Felicity back into the ballroom, but the vision was imprinted upon her brain: Serena with her arms around Nathan's neck, *his* hands placed possessively upon her waist.

'Really, I would not have expected such behaviour from Rosthorne!' muttered Mr Elliston, distressed.

'Y-you misunderstand, sir,' replied Felicity. 'The earl has known the lady for many years. I am sure it was no more than a friendly greeting.'

The words sounded hollow, even to herself. She had gone happily with Mr Elliston when he had suggested they should look for Nathan in the card room, but as they stepped out of the ballroom there had been no avoiding the sight of the earl locked in a passionate embrace with Serena Ansell. This was no friendly greeting—she and Mr Elliston both knew that.

'By Gad, I wish we had not walked away,' declared her partner. 'I wish I had told him then just what I think of such outrageous behaviour! When I see him—'

'No!' Felicity stopped. 'I pray you, Mr Elliston, please, for my sake, say nothing of what we have just seen.'

'But it is scandalous! I had not thought it of Nathan.'

'Then pray do not think it now,' she begged him. 'Please, let us go and find Mrs Elliston, and forget the last few minutes.'

Mr Elliston puffed out his cheeks and stood, frowning down at her. Felicity looked up at him imploringly and gave his arm a little shake.

'Please, sir. For my sake.'

He let his breath go in a long, disapproving sigh. 'Very well, my dear, if that is what you wish. But it goes very much against the grain. And it has destroyed all my pleasure in this evening.'

'Yes.' Felicity nodded sadly. 'So, too, has it destroyed mine.'

Mr Elliston guided Felicity back to his wife, who was watching Judith Elliston dancing with Gerald Appleby. Felicity was content to join her, a fixed smile upon her face while inside her heart was breaking. She glimpsed Nathan through the crowd, but made no attempt to attract his attention and it was some time before he found her. As he approached, Felicity cast an anguished looked at Mr Elliston, who was visibly bristling. Reading the entreaty in her eyes, the old man harrumphed and walked off with barely a nod towards the Earl as they passed.

'So there you are. I thought I should find you wearing out your slippers on the dance floor.'

Nathan's smile roused Felicity to a speechless rage. How dare he act so unconcerned, when only moments ago he was locked in the arms of his mistress! Felicity was pleased when Mrs Elliston answered for her.

'I think it is the Countess who is worn out,' she told him, smiling. 'The poor child has been sitting here this past half-hour and spoken barely a word!'

'I am a little tired,' admitted Felicity, unable to meet Nathan's eyes.

'Then I shall take you home.' He reached out for her

hand and pulled her to her feet. 'No one will miss us if we slip away now.'

'Yes, yes, take her home and cosset her,' cried Mrs Elliston. 'Goodnight to you, my dear. I shall call in a few days to see how you go on.'

Felicity kept her head high as she accompanied Nathan out of the building. She had come in so full of hope and happiness and was leaving now enclosed by a fog of misery. She wanted very much to burst into tears, but that would not do: she was the Countess of Rosthorne and must keep her smile in place. As they left the room they passed Lady Ansell, surrounded by a group of laughing gentlemen. She looked up as they passed and her smile reminded Felicity of nothing less than a cat that had lapped a whole pot of cream.

The carriage was blessedly dark and Felicity could stop smiling. Anger still simmered inside her. Should she confront Nathan? Would he admit his involvement with Serena or would he perhaps tell her it was none of her business? She remembered his words that night in Berkeley Square, when she had first challenged him: *'What did it matter if I had a whole string of mistresses?'*

She stifled a sigh. Her knowledge of men was woefully inadequate. Apart from Sir James Souden, who was a most devoted husband, the only other man with whom she had any close acquaintance was her late uncle, Philip Bourne, and she had learned very quickly that any attempt to confront or question his authority resulted in physical punishment. She did not think that Nathan would actually harm her, but the thought of hearing from his own lips that Serena Ansell was his mistress and that she must accept the fact was worse by far than any beating.

Nathan tucked a carriage rug around her knees and climbed into the coach beside her.

'There…' he reached for her hand. 'Was it the noise and the heat that overset you?'

'I think so.' She hesitated. 'Lady Ansell came in very late. She is very popular with the gentlemen.'

'It has always been the same.'

'Mr and Mrs Elliston do not know she was…acquainted with Adam?'

'No.'

'Should—should they not be told?'

Nathan put his head back against the squabs and exhaled slowly. 'Why rake up old coals?' he said at last. 'It would only cause them distress. Besides, I do not think she means them any harm.'

Felicity bit her lip.

She could readily believe that Serena had no interest in the Ellistons—she had her sights fixed on another prey entirely.

Felicity retired as soon as they arrived at Rosthorne, but she did not sleep. Every time she closed her eyes she saw Serena Ansell clasped in Nathan's arms and the image had her fighting to wake up. She lay very still when Nathan came to bed, hardly daring to breathe when he leaned over her and dropped a gentle kiss on her neck. She heard him sigh and turn away, but did not stir until his regular breathing told her that he at least was at rest.

She used the same tactics the following morning, waiting until Nathan had left their chamber before she sent word that she was too tired to join him for their usual morning ride, and when at last she did appear in the breakfast room she looked so haggard that Mrs Carraway insisted upon sending for the doctor.

Nathan knew nothing of this until he returned from the stables to find the house in uproar and a message from his mother to attend her immediately.

'Well, Mama, what have you done to set the house by

the ears?' Nathan strode into her sitting room, his riding crop and hat still in his hand.

She smiled up at him, accepting his kiss upon her cheek. 'Doctor Farnham has called to see Felicity.'

'The devil he has!'

'No need for alarm, love.' She gestured to him to sit down. 'She was looking so worn down and tearful this morning that I asked him to look in. He thinks it is nothing more than an irritation of the nerves. He has bled her, and she is quieter now.' She studied the rings on her fingers. 'He recommends separate bedchambers.'

'What?'

'Pray, do not look so black, Nathan. You know that the old earl and his wife always maintained their own rooms.'

'Of course I know that! It was I who ordered one of them to be redecorated as the countess's dressing room.'

'Yes, well, Mercer is organising for a bed to be made up in there for Felicity. It is only a temporary measure,' she added quickly. 'Doctor Farnham thinks her recovery will be swifter if she is allowed to rest.

With a smothered oath Nathan got up and began to prowl about the room. 'Is Farnham saying it is my fault? That somehow I—'

'No, no, love. Many young brides find the transition to married life difficult, and you must admit that the circumstances of your marriage are a little…unusual.'

Nathan shook his head. He walked over to the window and looked out. The view was a particularly fine one, stretching out over the formal gardens and to the park beyond, but today Nathan saw nothing of its beauty. He thought only of his wife.

'I must see her.'

'Of course.'

Felicity lay in the great bed, her head and shoulders supported on soft white pillows. Doctor Farnham had been very kind, telling her cheerfully that her spirits were a little disordered, but it was nothing that rest would not cure. When he had suggested she should have her own room she had agreed to it, although with a little anxiety as to Nathan's reaction. But now, with the doctor gone and only her maid bustling quietly about the room, she felt too tired to be anxious about anything.

She opened her eyes when she heard the door open. Nathan came in. He was still wearing his riding jacket and topboots and when he came closer she saw the tiny furrow in his brow. He dismissed her maid and smiled at her.

'Now then, Fee, what's all this?'

The concern in his voice nearly overset her.

'I am a little out of sorts, but I shall be better directly, if I rest.'

He sat on the edge of the bed and took her hand. 'Will you tell me what is the matter?'

His gentle tone brought the tears welling up, clogging her throat. She gave the tiniest shake of her head. Muted thuds and bangs could be heard coming from the adjoining room.

'So, madam, you intend to abandon me again—' He broke off when she gave a little sob. 'Ah, love, I did not mean to make you cry, I was merely teasing you.' His brows contracted. He said quietly, 'Is that it? Have I frightened you with my love-making?'

Her cheeks flamed and she covered them with her handkerchief. 'No, no,' she said, her voice muffled. 'You have been so kind, so gentle…'

'There was nothing gentle about our first night in this bed,' he said drily. 'Nor when I threatened to carry you off by force from Souden House! But you may rest easy, love—I shall not touch you again until you command it and I will not enter your bedroom uninvited, I give you my word.' He leaned forward and kissed her forehead. 'I shall leave you to sleep now.'

He was gone as swiftly as he had come and Felicity was

left staring at the closed door. He had not countermanded the doctor's orders; she was to have her own apartment, her own bed. With a heavy heart Felicity could not help thinking that she was driving him even more surely into the arms of Serena Ansell.

It was not to be supposed that Felicity's youthful spirits could stay at low ebb for very long. The following day she left her bed, and by the end of the week she was well enough to venture out of doors, although she declined Nathan's suggestion that she should join him once again on his morning ride. She thought a little innocuous conversation over breakfast and again at the dinner table when Mrs Carraway was present was far less dangerous than being alone with Nathan. And for the rest of her day there was plenty to occupy her: the final fittings for her new wardrobe, gentle drives with Mrs Carraway as well as receiving morning callers. Mrs Elliston and her daughter were regular visitors and very welcome, unlike the appearance of Lady Charlotte Appleby.

'I vow,' said Mrs Carraway, when her sister-in-law had departed, 'she came with no other purpose than to see what changes you have put in place and to criticise them! I begin to wish that we had not invited her and Gerald to stay at Christmas, I swear we shall come to cuffs!'

Nathan laughed. 'Nonsense, Mama, you never fight with anyone. You are far too sweet-natured, just like Fee.' His eyes rested upon his wife, who was picking at her dinner. 'Were you subjected to my aunt's caustic tongue, my dear?'

She glanced up, a distracted, unhappy shadow in her eyes. He wished he knew how to banish it.

'Only a very little, my lord.' She tried to smile. 'I was very properly engaged with my embroidery when she arrived, and apart from telling me that the new curtains in the morning room are entirely the wrong colour, she was more aggrieved that you were not there to greet her.'

'But I had no idea she was coming!'

'That is no excuse, Nathan,' said Mrs Carraway, chuckling. 'My sister-in-law expects the world to wait upon her pleasure! However, I told her that since she chose to call before noon there was little chance of finding you at home, since you spend every morning on estate business, usually riding here, there and everywhere!'

'Well, I am very glad I missed her,' declared Nathan. 'But talking of riding—the weather looks set to be fine tomorrow morning. Felicity, would you like me to have your mare saddled up for you?'

'Th-thank you, that is very kind, but, no, I think not.'

Nathan bit back his disappointment. He said coolly, 'Just as you please, my dear. But if you change your mind, you only have to send a note to the stables.'

Felicity remembered his words when she awoke the next morning to find the sun streaming in through her window. When she heard the door open she looked up hopefully, but it was only her maid bringing in her morning cup of hot chocolate.

'It is very quiet next door, Martha. Is the master sleeping late?'

'No, my lady. He was on his way out o' doors when I came up to you.'

The disappointment was severe. Now the opportunity was lost, Felicity realised how much she would have liked to go out riding with Nathan. But the sunny weather was having its effect upon her spirits. Suddenly she wanted to be up and doing something. She threw back the bedcovers.

'Find my walking dress for me, if you please, Martha. I am going out!'

Despite the sunshine there was a chill in the air as Felicity set out to walk across the park, but she strode on, conscious that her mood was lifting. She stopped and looked about her. The park stretched away in every direction with avenues of sycamore and lime leading the eye beyond the palings to where the Rosthorne estate continued in the form of meadows, pastures and forests as far as the horizon.

'I am mistress of all this,' she murmured and her heart swelled with a curious mixture of wonder, apprehension and pleasure.

Nathan was fond of her, she did not doubt that. He might not love her, but he was kind and generous; other women managed with far less. She quickly buried the thought that she did not deserve his regard; she would earn it. The past was over; it was time to make amends. A few nights sleeping alone had convinced her that she no longer wanted to keep him at a distance—she missed him too much. And if she had to share him with a mistress—or even a whole string of mistresses—then so be it. She turned her head to look at the trees on the southern horizon, their autumn leaves blazing yellow, gold and brown in the sunlight. The route around the estate might change, but she knew that on his return Nathan always rode through the Home Wood. There were several footpaths through the trees, but only one track suitable for riders. She turned her footsteps in the direction of the wood. She would cut through to the bridleway and meet him.

Twenty minutes of brisk walking brought her to the edge of the wood and she plunged in, following the leaf-strewn path that meandered through the undergrowth. She did not slow her pace, for she was eager to reach the bridle-way to meet Nathan, who would be approaching from the opposite direction. The wood was dappled with shade and she picked her way through the drying leaves and felled branches that littered the path. There was no wind to stir the trees and disturb the peacefulness. A tiny doubt disturbed her—what if Nathan had already passed this way? She quickened her step; she did not want to miss him and have to walk back to Rosthorne alone. She was just beginning to wonder if perhaps she had taken the wrong path when her ears caught the soft drumming of hoofbeats somewhere ahead of her. Relieved, she quickened her pace. The steady drumming was growing nearer. He was moving fast; she recalled following Nathan through the wood, always at a canter. Suddenly horse and rider were visible through the branches, one huge dark shape surging along the track. Then the regular thudding stopped, there was a shrieking neigh from a horse, a crash, then silence.

Her heart in her mouth, Felicity raced the last few yards to the bridleway. The big black hunter was standing riderless, trembling and snorting nervously. She looked around, a giddying wave of nausea sweeping over her when she saw Nathan lying motionless on the ground.

'Nathan!' She ran forward and dropped to her knees beside him. He was very pale, but she noted with relief that a pulse throbbed steadily in his neck. Her instinct was to call for help, but the wood seemed unnaturally quiet now. Frighteningly so. She looked around. There was something lying on the path: a length of thin cord, snaking amongst the fallen leaves. Intrigued, Felicity walked across and picked up the end. The cord pulled taut across the bridleway, just level with the horse's knees. A cold chill scurried down her back. She dropped the cord and swung round, her frightened eyes searching the trees. She could see no one, but she picked up a stout stick and kept circling, ears straining for any little noise. She did not know whether to be frightened or relieved when she heard another horse approaching. An instant later the Earl's steward trotted into view.

'Collins! Thank heavens!' cried Felicity 'You must help me—my lord is hurt!'

The steward threw himself from the saddle and followed

her to where Lord Rosthorne was lying. She dropped to her knees again and dashed away a tear. She must try to think clearly.

'We must get him back to Rosthorne. Ride to the house, Collins. Fetch some men, and a carriage—'

'Wait, my lady. He's coming round.'

Even as the steward spoke, Nathan's eyelids fluttered.

'Oh, thank God!' whispered Felicity. She reached for his hand. 'Do not try to move, sir, until you are sure nothing is broken.'

'Only my pride,' he muttered, struggling to sit up. 'I shall have a few bruises tomorrow, no doubt. Heaven knows what caused Jet to stumble—'

'He didn't stumble, my lord,' growled Collins, who was examining the hunter's legs. 'He was brought down. There's some nasty gashes here.'

'There is a rope across the path,' added Felicity.

Nathan stared at her and raised one hand to his head. She said quietly, 'This time there can be no question. Someone deliberately tried to harm you.'

'We must get you home, my lord,' said Collins brusquely. 'If my lady will stay here with you, I'll ride on to the Hall and fetch a carriage.'

'You had best have some of the men search the woods and park, too,' said Nathan. 'Although I have no doubt the attacker is long gone. And send a boy to walk Jet back to the stables.' He waited until the steward had ridden away before fixing his gaze upon Felicity once more. The scar across his eye was very noticeable, enhanced by the bruise beginning to form on his cheekbone. His eyes fell upon the stick lying beside her.

'What is that? Did you mean to cudgel me to death while I lay helpless on the ground?'

'Pray do not joke, sir. I picked it up for protection.'

'Hmm.' He put a hand to his head, wincing. 'What were you doing in the wood?'

'I walked out to meet you. I regretted not riding out with you this morning.'

'Tell me what you saw.'

'Nothing, my lord. I was approaching the track when I heard your horse fall. I ran here and…found you.'

'And you saw no one?'

'No.' She pointed towards the cord, still lying across the path. 'Whoever was holding the rope was on the far side of the path. They were gone by the time I came up.' She shivered and looked around apprehensively. 'It is another attempt upon your life, Nathan. This time you cannot deny it.'

'No. I shall take care not to ride out alone again.'

'Good.'

'You must come with me, for my own protection.'

That drew a reluctant smile from her. 'I will, my lord, gladly, but my presence is not sufficient.'

He waved his hand towards the discarded cord. 'I beg to differ. Whoever is trying to kill me is very keen not to be detected.'

'I disagree, my lord. I—'

Nathan held up his hand. 'Enough.'

He struggled to his feet. Felicity jumped up, putting her arm about him as he swayed.

'You are still dizzy, you must not stand.'

'Neither can I remain on that damp earth.'

She guided him to a fallen tree and sat down beside him. She shivered.

'Are you cold, Fee?'

'No. A little frightened, perhaps. Your attacker might return.'

'I doubt it.' He took her hand and squeezed it. 'Not with you beside me.'

Their companionable silence lasted no more than five minutes before Nathan exclaimed, 'Oh to the devil with this sitting about! We will walk on and meet the carriage.'

'But, Nathan—'

'I am not an invalid,' he retorted, getting up and walking towards his horse. 'If you would kindly pick up my hat for me, it is better for us to be moving than to grow chilled to the bone sitting here. Come along.'

He held out his hand to her. Felicity took it and, with Jet hobbling along behind them, they made their way slowly out of the woods.

Word of the attack spread quickly. Nathan met with neighbouring landowners and extensive searches were made of the surrounding area. When it was known that it was not the first time someone had tried to kill the Earl, patrols were organised to keep watch on the local roads and fields. Gerald Appleby was one of those who volunteered for this duty.

'I thought you were off to London,' remarked Nathan, surprised.

Gerald merely grinned at him. 'I have no intention of returning to town when there is such excitement going on here,' he said.

Despite all the activity, Felicity remained anxious and could not relax until Nathan was safely returned to the house every evening. However, there was one piece of news that cheered her—she learned that Serena Ansell had left Hampshire and would not be returning until the spring.

Mrs Elliston conveyed these tidings when she came to visit Felicity and Mrs Carraway just days after the attack.

Mrs Carraway, who had not taken to the widow on the few occasions they had met, proposed her own theory for Lady Ansell's departure.

'You do not suppose that she was responsible, and has gone away until the dust has settled?'

Felicity was immediately upon the alert. 'What makes you say that, ma'am?'

'I have seen the way she looks at my son.'

Mrs Elliston gave a very girlish giggle. 'Do you think he spurned her advances? A woman scorned, as they say…'

Felicity hurriedly changed the subject. 'S-several of our neighbours have left Hampshire,' she observed. 'Do you plan to remain at Hazelford for the Christmas period, Mrs Elliston?'

'Yes, we always spend Christmas very quietly at home. Judith is making her annual visit to her aunt in Bedfordshire, but once she returns we shall not stir again until the new year. And you, ma'am? The neighbourhood will be expecting grand entertainments here, now that Rosthorne has a new mistress.'

Felicity was at a loss to answer and it was Mrs Carraway who replied quietly, 'Not this year. We shall keep the season very quietly. However, I hope you can be persuaded to join us for dinner one evening. Lady Charlotte and her son will be staying with us for a few days and I know they would be very happy to see you both—and your daughter, of course.'

'We shall be delighted,' replied Mrs Elliston. 'Judith and Mr Appleby were getting along famously at the assembly the other week, and I have no objection to continuing the acquaintance.' She added, with a touch of defiance, 'Though I doubt Lady Charlotte will be quite so sanguine about her son's friendship with a mere *Miss* Elliston, being herself, as she never fails to remind us, the daughter of an earl!'

Chapter Sixteen

'We will soon be back at the Hall now, my lord.'

Nathan heard a hint of relief in his steward's voice. They had ridden out to look at the plantation Nathan had established the previous year and the short December day had closed in upon them very rapidly. Collins still insisted upon accompanying the Earl whenever he rode on the estate, even though there had been no sightings of any strangers in the area and the regular patrols set up after the attack had ceased. Felicity, too, colluded with his staff to make sure Nathan was never alone.

He thought of his wife as he rode through the gates and into the park for the final part of his journey. She was so anxious for his safety, yet she still kept him at a distance. They had resumed riding together every morning and during the day she would be friendly, affectionate even, but she resisted his every attempt at intimacy, putting up an invisible barrier between them. He was careful not to allow his impatience to show, but he wondered how long he could continue before his resolve snapped and he broke his promise not to enter her bedchamber.

The icy December wind cut at his cheeks and the scar over his eye throbbed in the cold. A good thing, he thought bitterly. It took his mind off the ache in his loins.

They clattered into the stable yard, where a large, old-fashioned travelling carriage was being manoeuvred into one corner.

'Lady Charlotte has arrived, sir,' observed Collins.

'Oh lord,' he muttered ruefully, 'I had forgotten she was coming today.' He jumped down and handed the mare's reins to his groom. 'Take a look at her left hind fetlock, Pat, I fear it might be sprained.'

A shorter, thickset figure came running out of the stable, tugging at his forelock.

'Will 'ee let me take 'er, Mr Patrick? I'll look at 'er.'

Patrick handed over the reins and turned back to Nathan with a slightly apologetic smile.

'It's Harris, my lord. Lady Charlotte's man,' he explained as they watched the man lead the horse into the stable. 'He's a half-wit, but a natural healer. He seems to know just what to do with animals.'

Nathan nodded. 'Very well, if you are sure, Patrick. Report back to me later.' He turned and saw Felicity coming across the yard to meet him, a paisley shawl pulled tight about her shoulders and Bella trotting at her heels.

'I was watching out for you, my lord; you are very late.'

'I beg your pardon. My mare went lame and I didn't want to push her.' Her anxious eyes flew to his face and he shook his head, smiling a little. 'It is all perfectly innocent; with Jet's knees not fully healed I have been riding Juniper a little hard lately.' He put his hand on her elbow. 'Shall we go indoors, out of this biting wind?

'Where is my aunt?' he asked as they walked through the flagged passage leading to the hall.

'Your mama is entertaining Lady Charlotte and Mr Appleby in the drawing room.' She glanced up. 'You are cold, sir. I had Sam build up the fire in your dressing room; you will need to change.'

'Should I not make my apologies to my aunt first?'

She chuckled. 'I fear that whatever you do, you will be

in the wrong. It is her way. Go upstairs, sir. I will make your
excuses.' She began to move away, but he caught her hand.

'Shall we leave my mother to look after our guests?' he
murmured, drawing her into his arms. 'You could come
upstairs with me and help me out of my muddy clothes…'

The light in the passage was very poor, but he thought
he saw a sudden longing in her eyes. A swift flash of desire.
It was gone in an instant, replaced by the wary, anxious look
she wore so often these days. He ran his hands gently up and
down her arms. 'What is it, my dear? What is worrying you?'

'W-worrying me?' She gave a nervous little laugh. 'Why,
nothing, my lord, only the thought of entertaining Lady
Charlotte. I have already had to bring Bella away, because
she objects to dogs in the drawing room…'

Felicity looked past Nathan towards the hall, then down
at the little spaniel, anywhere rather than into Nathan's
face, for there was no mistaking his look and it made her
knees grow weak. She wanted so much to give in to him
and to her own yearning, but the spectre of Serena Ansell
haunted her and she could not rid herself of the conviction that Nathan would always compare her unfavourably
with the beautiful widow. Her thoughts returned to their
first meeting at Souden House, when he had swept her up,
intending to carry her off with him. If only he would show
the same forcefulness now. If only…

Nathan's hands fell away from her shoulders. 'Of course.
Take Bella to my mother's apartment, Norton will look
after her. Then go back to your guests and I will join you
as soon as I may.'

Felicity watched him stride away. Bella scampered after
him, but a curt word sent her back to Felicity, her ears
flattened.

Since neither Mrs Carraway nor Lady Charlotte kept late
hours, the evening came to an end before midnight.

'I hope that was not too intolerable for you,' said Nathan as he escorted Felicity to her room. 'My aunt is not the most amenable of guests. Her comments concerning the attack in Home Wood were outrageous. I hope you did not take her seriously.'

'No, indeed. Do you…?' She hesitated. 'Does she *truly* think I tried to murder you?'

'My aunt likes to make mischief, nothing more.'

'But it *is* suspicious! When Mr Collins came up I was holding that stick…'

'Hush now. You have already explained it to me.' They had reached the door of her bedchamber and he stopped, turning to look down at her. 'When I came round to find you bending over me, the look in your eyes was not that of a murderer.'

'It—it wasn't?' Felicity gazed up at him. She suddenly felt very short of breath.

'No.' He lowered his head until his lips were just touching hers. She put her fingers against his chest and grasped the lapels of his evening coat. Smiling, he captured one hand and turned it.

'Remember,' he said softly, pressing a kiss into her palm, 'I am in the next room if you want me. You only have to walk through the door.'

'I—I—'

He dropped a light, butterfly kiss on her forehead and walked away. A moment later she heard the soft click of his door closing.

Sam was laying out his master's nightgown and banyan when he entered the room. With a word Nathan dismissed his valet and stood, head bowed, straining his ears against the silence. He heard Felicity go into her room, the soft pad of feet across the boards, the murmur of voices. She was not indifferent to him, he would swear to it. He had noted her relief when he had arrived that evening, seen the shy longing in her eyes, felt her cling to him when he had kissed her goodnight. He could have taken her then, swept her into his room, into his bed and kissed her into submission. She would respond to him, he was certain of it, but he wanted more from his wife. He wanted her to come to *him*. Nathan walked across to the adjoining door and rested his shoulder against the wall, staring at the door handle, willing it to turn, willing Felicity to come in.

But the door between them remained resolutely closed.

Christmas Eve dawned grey and windy, the blustery weather reflecting Felicity's restless mood. Lady Charlotte was a difficult houseguest, but Felicity was determined not to be intimidated by her autocratic manner, nor her constant references to the way Rosthorne used to be run. Her courage dipped a little when she found only Gerald and his mother at the breakfast table, but she scarcely had time to say good morning before Mrs Carraway came in, leaning on Nathan's arm.

Gerald, pouring coffee for his mother, bade them all good morning and offered to fill their cups.

'Yes, thank you.' Mrs Carraway took her seat beside Felicity. 'I have given Norton a holiday to visit her family in Petersfield, so Nathan came to fetch me for breakfast.'

'Then do not hesitate to tell me, ma'am, if there is anything I can do for you today,' put in Felicity.

'Must we have that animal in here?' demanded Lady Charlotte, frowning at Bella who was capering around Gerald's feet, her paws pattering and skidding on the polished boards.

'I am afraid so, Aunt,' said Nathan cheerfully. 'She is used to having the run of the house in the mornings. But you need not worry; we never feed her from the table. She merely waits for any scraps that might fall.'

'And saves the servants the trouble of sweeping up.' Gerald grinned, still wielding the coffee pot.

'Exactly. No coffee for me, thank you.' Nathan picked up the ale-jug from the sideboard and filled a pewter tankard. 'This is one of the old earl's customs that I *have* continued,' he said, a smile glinting in his eyes.

Gerald looked towards the window, where the rain had started to drum against the glass.

'We must entertain ourselves indoors today,' he remarked. 'What time did you say the Ellistons were coming?'

'We expect them before dark,' said Felicity, 'unless the storm persuades them to cry off.'

Nathan shook his head. 'It is only a few miles and Elliston is not one to fight shy of a little bad weather.'

Gerald walked over to the window. 'When I saw them at the assembly, Mrs Elliston gave me permission to call at any time; I could always ride over and escort them.'

'By all means,' said Nathan, 'if you think it necessary.'

'I do not see the least need for such a thing,' stated Lady Charlotte. 'Indeed, if the weather remains inclement this afternoon, I shall want you here to entertain me.'

Felicity's lips twitched.

'We must not expect the gentlemen to wait on us the whole day, ma'am. I am sure we shall be able to entertain ourselves. We might play at battledore in the long gallery, or charades.'

Gerald chuckled. 'Mama's idea of entertainment is to have someone read to her while she sleeps on her daybed.'

'Then I shall be very happy to do that,' declared Felicity gallantly. 'In fact, Lydia—Lady Souden—has sent me a copy of *Waverley*. I was going to share it with Mama Carraway, but I can easily read it to you both!'

With Lady Charlotte's entertainment organised, Gerald went off to order his horse, and when breakfast was over Mrs Carraway took her sister-in-law away to the morning room. Nathan detained Felicity as she was about to follow them.

'It is very good of you to give up your time.'

Felicity was warmed by his compliment; suddenly the day seemed much brighter. 'Nonsense, I am only being a good hostess. I very much wish to read *Waverley*, so it will be no hardship for me.' She chuckled. 'I hope it is sufficiently diverting to keep Lady Charlotte happy throughout the day, and then perhaps she will behave herself this evening.'

In the event Felicity's hopes were realised, for Lady Charlotte was at her most gracious during dinner. She greeted Mr and Mrs Elliston with a condescension that made Mr Elliston's eyes twinkle and proceeded to dominate the conversation.

'She behaves as if she were the hostess here,' murmured Mrs Carraway as she and Felicity led the ladies to the drawing room after dinner.

'As long as she refrains from making any of her more outrageous remarks, I am very happy with that,' returned Felicity, a glimmer of a smile in her eyes.

The evening was going much better than she had expected; Mr Elliston had been a little brusque with his host at first, but he observed Felicity's anxious look and soon took the opportunity to reassure her.

'No need to make yourself uncomfortable, ma'am,' he muttered, during one of Lady Charlotte's many reminiscences of how past Earls of Rosthorne had been wont to celebrate Christmas. 'Much as I would like to take Nathan to task for his dastardly behaviour at the assembly, I gave you my word and we will say no more about it.'

Her only other concern was that Lady Charlotte might take exception to her son's attentions towards Miss Elliston, but although her cold stare rested upon the young couple several times during the evening, she made no comment, and even expressed mild disappointment that the party was such a small one.

'When I was young the events at Rosthorne Hall were on a much grander scale,' she stated, fixing Nathan with an accusing stare. 'All the principal rooms would be opened up and the house would be full of guests. Although I admit that this year the country is exceedingly thin of company. If Lady Ansell had been in residence you could have invited her.'

'No, ma'am, I could not,' retorted Felicity. She added, aware of the surprised glances of her guests, 'I am not well acquainted with the lady.'

'No more are we,' put in Mrs Elliston. 'My husband does not wish for the connection. The lady has a reputation for being rather *fast*.'

'Is that so, Rosthorne?' demanded Lady Charlotte. 'I believe you knew Lady Ansell when you were in the Peninsula.'

Felicity risked a quick glance in Nathan's direction. His face was quite impassive.

'Yes, she was in Corunna.' Nathan's tone was slightly bored. 'She was Mrs Craike then, but I believe she was quite a favourite with the officers.'

'I wonder that she should choose to live here,' mused Mrs Carraway. 'Hazelford is very quiet, and there are few enough single gentlemen to attract her interest.'

'Perhaps it is not a *single* gentleman who interests her,' muttered Felicity.

Nathan's head came up. 'Would you care to explain that remark, my dear?'

She flushed under his searching gaze and was relieved that her mother-in-law had not noticed the interruption and was continuing with her own conjectures.

'I do not like to think that any gentleman of our acquaintance would set up such a liaison.' Mrs Carraway laughed. 'Imagine respectable Dr Farnham being caught in her web, or even the vicar!'

Mr Elliston harrumphed in disapproval and stalked away.

'You may rest easy, then,' replied Gerald, smiling. 'Your speculation is very wide of the mark—Mama had a letter from Lady Ansell to say she is not returning to Godfrey Park, but means to remain in Bath.'

'Which is very inconvenient,' announced Lady Charlotte. 'There are few enough families of note in this area with whom one can dine.'

Mr Elliston, who was standing at the unshuttered window, announced that he was anxious to set off in good time for West Meon.

'This wind shows no sign of abating,' he said, 'and I fear there may be a few trees blown down before morning.'

A particularly fierce gust of wind rattled the window at that moment, giving substance to his argument, and the party broke up shortly afterwards, with Gerald escorting the ladies to their coach.

'I was tempted to saddle up and ride back with them,' he said, coming back into the drawing room. 'I would like to be sure they have a safe journey.'

'Their way lies mainly through the valley, which will afford them some shelter,' said Nathan. He raised his head as a door slammed somewhere in the house. 'I will have Mercer check all the shutters tonight.'

'Yes, please do.' Lady Charlotte beckoned to her son. 'Give me your company to my door, please, Gerald. These stormy nights are very alarming.'

'I did not think that anything could alarm Lady Charlotte,' remarked Felicity, when Mr Appleby had escorted his mother away.

Mrs Carraway chuckled. 'Nor does it. The woman has nerves of steel.' She struggled to her feet, leaning heavily upon her stick. 'I think I shall retire now.'

Felicity jumped up. 'Then let me give you my arm, ma'am,' she said. 'We will leave Nathan to make sure the house is secure.'

Walking back a short time later, Felicity was obliged to use her hand to shield the flame of her bedroom candle, for the howling wind seeped into the house and whined along the dark corridors. She was relieved when she reached her own chamber and lost no time getting into bed and blowing out her candle. She lay tense and nervous under the covers, listening to the storm battering the house. There was a crash as something smashed on the terrace below her window and a growl of thunder added its own menace to the darkness. Felicity curled herself into a ball and snuggled down beneath the bedcovers. Finally, she fell into an uneasy sleep.

Once he had make a last tour of the house, Nathan too retired, but sleep eluded him. He tossed restlessly in his bed. The storm would almost certainly do some damage. He had already heard the sounds of a pot or a tile shattering on the terrace and he hoped the young trees on his plantation would survive. He turned over. He could do nothing about it until it was daylight.

A sudden cry caught his attention. He sat up. The sound had come from Felicity's room. He heard her cry out again. Reaching for his tinder box, he fumbled to light his candle, then, pulling on his dressing gown, he went across to the connecting door. As he stepped into the room the door from the corridor opened and the maid appeared, holding aloft her candle with a shaking hand.

'Ooh, excuse me, m'lord, I heard m'lady calling out...'

They both looked towards the shadowed bed where Felicity lay restlessly muttering.

'It is all right, Martha,' said Nathan quietly. 'I will look after my lady.'

With a little curtsy the maid withdrew. A sudden gust of wind rattled the window shutters and the flame of his candle flickered wildly. Felicity muttered and gave another anguished sob. Nathan moved towards the bed.

'Felicity.'

Nathan put the candle down beside the bed. Her eyes were closed and she thrashed out, throwing off the covers.

'No, no. Leave me alone—*Déjeme!*'

She was crying out in Spanish, just as she had done five years ago when he had rescued her from the robbers in Corunna. And just as he had done five years ago, Nathan climbed on to the bed and took her in his arms. She fought against him, but he held her close, muttering soothing words. She began to cry.

'I have lost everything! There's nothing left, nothing!'

'Hush now.' He stroked her head. 'We can buy you new things.'

'No, no, I have lost him!' She was rambling wildly. 'It is God's punishment! Why must I live…?'

'It is only a dream, Felicity. Wake up.'

'It's too late. I have lost him! If only God would let me die…'

Nathan's arms tightened about her. He said sharply, '*I* won't let you die! Wake up, Felicity!' She stopped fighting and he felt her flutter, like a little bird in his arms. 'You are safe now, Fee,' he murmured the words into her hair. 'You are with me.'

'I am so sorry, so sorry.' She sobbed into his chest. 'Don't leave me!'

Nathan settled himself more comfortably on the bed and pulled her against him. 'Hush now. I will never leave you.'

She continued to cry, great, wrenching sobs that racked her body. Nathan felt powerless to do anything but hold her. He pulled the covers over her shoulders to ward off the cold night air and remained there, cradling her in his arms while the storm raged at the windows.

The candle had burned itself out before Felicity finally grew calm. She lay quietly in the darkness, her head resting against his heart. Nathan felt her stir.

'Nathan?'

'I'm here.'

She pulled the sheet up to wipe her eyes. 'I don't deserve you,' she murmured. 'You have been so forbearing with me. I wish I knew why you are so good to me.'

'You are my countess.'

'I don't deserve you,' she said again, sleepily. 'I don't know why you should want me.'

He smiled to himself.

'Because you are irreplaceable,' he murmured. 'God knows I tried! All those stories they tell of me, the women, the broken hearts that litter Europe; I was trying to forget you, to prove to myself that you did not matter to me. But you do, Fee.' He kissed her hair. 'You matter very, very much.'

She did not reply but lay against him, her breathing deep and regular.

She was asleep.

Chapter Seventeen

Felicity did not wake up until Martha came into the room to open the shutters. The storm had blown itself out and bright sunlight flooded the room. She stretched.

'Is it very late? I had such dreams!'

'The master said not to wake you early, m'lady.'

'Oh, he was here?' Felicity pulled the sheets around her. She remembered him holding her, but she had thought it part of her dream.

'Yes, m'lady. He came in last night, when you was crying in your sleep. Terrible dreams you must have had, ma'am.'

'Yes.' Strangely, the horror of the night was gone and Felicity remembered only feeling safe and secure in Nathan's arms.

Martha stood beside the bed, smiling at her. 'The master sends his compliments, madam, and says he will escort you down to breakfast in half an hour.'

'Heavens, then we must be quick!'

Felicity scrambled out of bed, bubbling with an equal measure of happiness and alarm. She was inordinately pleased that Nathan should want to attend her, but a nervousness remained about what she might have cried out during the night.

★ ★ ★

When Nathan knocked at her door some thirty minutes later, Felicity was ready for him.

'I fear I disturbed your sleep last night, my lord.'

He took her hand. 'Nigtmares,' he said. 'You were very distressed.'

'And you stayed with me. I thank you for that.' She gave him a smile.

'Do you often have such bad dreams?'

'No, not now. I think it was the storm that disturbed me.' She hesitated, then said shyly, 'I am very glad you were there, Nathan.'

He squeezed her hand. 'I shall always be there for you.'

She accompanied Nathan down the stairs.

'We are exceedingly late, sir. And it is Christmas Day— I very much fear we shall miss the morning service.'

'I am certain of it.' Nathan grinned at her. 'I do not doubt that my mother has gone on without us, but we shall not be missed; my very regal Aunt Charlotte will more than make up for our absence!' As they reached the hall Nathan paused. 'You go on, my dear; I will slip down and speak to Collins. I want to know if there was much damage last night.'

He strode off in the direction of the servants' wing and Felicity made her way into the breakfast room. Bella came dashing up and Felicity bent to make a fuss of her.

'So where have you escaped from?' she murmured, fondling the spaniel's soft ears. 'Have they all gone off to church and left you here? Never mind, I will take you for a walk later.'

Felicity straightened and went into the breakfast room with Bella capering around her. The room was empty, but even before she had taken her seat Mercer entered with a fresh pot of coffee. She had just filled her cup when Nathan came in. His warm smile made her toes curl with pleasure.

A young footman hurried in with a plate of hot toast which he placed on the table.

'Coffee, my lord?' he asked reaching for the pot.

'No, no, Toby, bring me some ale, if you please.' Nathan sat down beside Felicity. 'The crash we heard last night was one of the pots from the balcony shattering on the terrace. The shrub had grown too large and the wind caught it. Collins has already ridden over the park; we have lost a couple of trees but nothing more serious. I shall go out later, to check the damage for myself. Perhaps you would care to come with me?'

'But, our guests...'

'I think they can spare you to me for an hour.'

'Then, yes, thank you. I should very much like to come with you.'

Her eyes fell on Bella, who was scampering about the room. She opened her mouth to utter a warning, but it was too late—the footman was carrying Nathan's tankard of ale upon a tray and did not see the little dog under his feet. Servant, tray and tankard crashed to the ground and Bella, delighted with the chaos she had created, hurried to lap up the frothing ale that was spilled on the floor.

'Never mind, never mind.' Nathan waved away the lackey's anguished apologies. 'Just go and find a cloth to mop up this mess. Leave that, Bella!' He looked at Felicity and said severely, 'And I would be obliged, madam, if you would refrain from laughing at my servant's misfortune.'

Felicity was not deceived; she saw the smile tugging at the corners of his mouth and took her hands away from her own.

'I should not, I know, and I shall be sober again by the time the poor man returns, I give you my word.'

With a laugh Nathan took her face between his hands. 'I love to see you so happy. I have missed your smiles.' He kissed her, then sat back, glancing down at Bella.

'Hmm, by the time Toby returns I think that damned dog

may have licked the floor clean.' He picked up his tankard from the floor and wiped the edge of it with his napkin. 'I had best fetch my own ale while Bella is preoccupied.'

Still glowing from his kiss, Felicity began to butter a piece of toast.

'Thank goodness Lady Charlotte was not here to witness the accident,' she remarked. 'She would want poor Bella banned from the house! What a poor start to Christmas Day, I feel sure your mama will ring a peel over us when she—oh heavens—*Nathan*!'

Felicity jumped to her feet, sending her chair toppling backwards. Nathan had just finished filling his tankard. He looked around. Felicity struggled to speak.

'Look—Bella—' She turned her horrified gaze towards the little dog, who was staggering across the floor, her legs giving way beneath her.

'Nathan, what is it?' whispered Felicity.

The dog had collapsed on her side, her breathing laboured.

'I'm not sure.' He picked up the tankard and sniffed at it, frowning. 'Poison. In the ale.'

Nathan crossed the room to Bella in a couple of strides. Felicity looked down at the spaniel, who stared up at her with wide, frightened eyes. She put her hands to her mouth.

'Is there nothing we can do?'

'I have heard that coffee sometimes works.'

Felicity reached for the coffee pot on the table, then put it down again. 'This one will be better, it is cold,' she said, running to the sideboard and picking up another silver pot.

'Quickly then.' Nathan cradled the little dog, forcing open her mouth while Felicity gently poured the coffee down her throat.

Bella struggled, but Nathan held her firm.

'I hope that's a good sign,' he muttered. 'Try a little more.'

'There is no more,' she said, her voice breaking. 'Shall I fetch the other pot?'

'No, wait.' Nathan released the spaniel and moved away a little as she vomited.

The footman, returning at that moment with a mop and bucket, stopped in the doorway, staring open mouthed at the scene before him.

'Will she be all right?' asked Felicity as Bella lay on the floor, panting heavily.

'I cannot say.' Nathan lifted Bella carefully into his arms. 'I shall take her down to the stables. Patrick will know better than I how to doctor her.' He turned to the servant. 'Pick up my lady's chair, if you please, and clear up the mess on the floor, but on no account allow anything else in the room to be touched.'

Felicity started forward. 'I shall come with you.'

'No, I would prefer you to stay here and make sure no one comes into the breakfast room.'

When Nathan had gone, Felicity sat back down at the table. Her appetite had quite disappeared; in fact, she felt a little sick, but she fought against it, and when the servant had gone she remained staring fixedly out through the open door, waiting for Nathan to return.

The chimes of the long-case clock in the hall told Felicity that she had been sitting alone for only a half-hour, but it seemed a lifetime before Nathan came striding back towards her. He looked very grim, and her heart turned over.

'Well?' she said, hardly daring to breath.

Nathan shifted his eyes to her face, as if recalled to the present and his frown lifted a little.

'Patrick is hopeful she will recover. It seems we did the right thing.'

'Thank heavens.' She watched him pick up the jug of ale and pour a little into a clean water glass. He lifted it up to the light, then sniffed at it cautiously.

'What is it, my lord?'

He held the glass out to her. 'What can you smell?'

'I am not sure. Hops, perhaps...' she wrinkled her nose '...and a faint, unpleasant odour...like mice.'

'Quite.' He put the glass back on the sideboard. 'Hemlock, but the smell is so faint that anyone might quaff half a tankard before becoming aware of it. And poor old Bella, as we know, has very little sense of smell these days.'

Felicity put her hands to her mouth. 'If you had drunk it...' she whispered, growing cold at the thought. 'Who would do such a thing?'

He took her hands and sat down beside her.

'There is a bottle of hemlock tincture in the stables,' he said slowly. 'You will recall my mare sprained a fetlock; Patrick used the tincture in the poultice he applied to bring down the swelling.'

'Oh, dear heaven! Has the bottle disappeared?'

'No, but Patrick thinks some of it may have been used. However, he cannot be sure.'

'But who would want to do such a thing?' she repeated.

'Who would have the opportunity to put the hemlock into the ale?' he countered. 'I stopped at the kitchens on the way back and spoke to Mercer. He tells me he drew off some of the ale for himself this morning and he also filled the jug and carried it here. My mother and Lady Charlotte were already at breakfast when he brought it in.'

'And the other servants?'

He shook his head. 'They are all local people and have worked here since they were children. I shall have to question them, but I cannot believe that any of them would be capable of such a trick.'

'But if it is not a servant...' She left the sentence unfinished and stared at him in horror. Nathan held her gaze.

'Who was in this room when you came down this morning, Fee? Think carefully.'

She frowned.

'No one,' she said. 'Mercer followed me in with the coffee pot and placed it directly on the table, but he touched nothing on the sideboard.'

'Then it is possible that someone put the hemlock into the ale while the room was empty, knowing I had not yet broken my fast.'

She clung to his hand. 'Oh, Nathan, I do not like to think of someone here in this house, wishing you harm.'

'No more do I.' He smiled slightly. 'But despite everything, we must eat, you know. I shall call Mercer. He will have everything cleared away from here and bring us a fresh breakfast in the morning room.'

Felicity could not enjoy her food, despite Mercer's earnest assurances that he had watched every stage of its preparation. However, she admitted she felt better for having eaten something and was able to await the church party's return with tolerable equanimity. Their shock and horror when they discovered what had happened was understandable, but Felicity found the repeated questions and conjecture distressing and made her excuses to slip away. As hostess she knew she could not absent herself for very long and after a suitable period she went back to join her guests. The short December day was overcast and the house was very gloomy. In the drawing room everyone was gathered about the hearth, where the light from the blazing fire combined with the candle flames to provide a comforting glow around the little party.

Felicity entered unnoticed and she was still in the shadows when Lady Charlotte said emphatically, 'Look at the facts, Rosthorne; she had every opportunity to slip something into the ale. And it would not be the first time— was she not in the wood when you came off your horse? And I had not been in the house five minutes before I could see that you and that wife or yours are estranged.'

The little group became aware of Felicity's presence. All

eyes turned to her as she emerged from the shadows, the damning words hanging in the air around them. Felicity looked at Nathan. She prayed for him to defend her, but it was Mrs Carraway who said with a touch of asperity,

'That is utter nonsense, Charlotte. I would ask you not to repeat such foolishness! Felicity, my dear, pray you come and sit here by me. You must not take any notice; we are all a little upset. Nathan has asked Mercer to gather all the staff together in the servants' hall and he will speak to them all, but I cannot think that any of our regular people would do such a thing. They have worked here for generations and have nothing to gain from such a trick.'

'What about the stable hands?' asked Gerald, pouring a glass of wine for Felicity.

Nathan shook his head. 'I questioned them when I took Bella down to the yard.'

'I trust you did not trouble Harris with your questions,' put in Lady Charlotte. 'You know that he is very simple, and as like to tell you a lie if he thinks it is what you wish to hear.'

'No, ma'am, I did not question him. He came forward immediately to help Patrick look after Bella. He was over-wrought when he saw her; I do not see him harming anyone.'

Felicity hardly heard them. She was still staring at Nathan, wanting some sign of reassurance, but he avoided her eyes. Surely he could not think that she had tried to poison him?

'If you will excuse me,' said Nathan, rising, 'I will go and talk to the servants now.'

'And I think we would all do well to rest before dinner,' said Mrs Carraway. 'Felicity, would you give me your arm, please?'

'My sister-in-law grows ever more eccentric,' she murmured as Felicity accompanied her along the darkened corridors to her apartment. 'We do not heed her, I promise you.'

'But it is true, ma'am, that I was alone in the breakfast room for some time before Nathan joined me.'

'And he told us you warned him not to drink the ale. Nathan has had a trying day, my dear, but he would be a fool indeed if he did not know that you would never do such a thing.'

Felicity took some comfort from Mama Carraway's words, but the memory of Nathan's cool, unsmiling look would not go away.

Once she had settled Mrs Carraway in her room Felicity made her way back towards her own bedchamber. She ran up the back stairs and along the corridor that looked down on the stable yard. The short winter's day had already ended and in the corridor the feeble light of the candles in their wall brackets was enhanced by the glow from the braziers burning in the yard below. Felicity glanced out of the windows as she passed. Harris was coming out of one of the stalls and she heard someone hail him. Gerald Appleby crossed the yard and put his arm about the groom's shoulders, engaging him in earnest conversation. Felicity watched them for a long moment, a slight frown between her brows, then she turned and made her way slowly to her room.

When Felicity came downstairs nearly an hour later she found there was an unusual amount of activity in the hall. Footmen were carrying a number of corded trunks out of the door. Gerald Appleby was standing to one side, talking with Nathan, but when he saw Felicity he came across to her, a rueful smile on his lips.

'My dear Lady Rosthorne, what can I say? How can I apologise? I was just telling Nathan that Mama is rather overcome by the events here and wishes to return to Appleby Manor.' He lifted his hand. 'No, no, ma'am, I know you would protest that the Christmas dinner is almost on the table, and that it is very dark, but I am afraid Mama is adamant that she wishes to leave immediately, so we do our best to accommodate her.'

Felicity, who had not intended saying anything at all, merely nodded and walked across the hall to stand beside Nathan as Lady Charlotte came down the stairs, leaning on her dresser's arm.

'I have never been in favour of allowing animals to roam loose in the house, and look what comes of it.' Lady Charlotte's clear, uncompromising tones preceded her.

Felicity stiffened indignantly. She looked up at Nathan, but there was no reading anything from his impassive countenance.

'Well, we must hope the little dog makes a full recovery and no harm done,' put in Gerald, stepping forward. 'Come, Mama, let me escort you to your carriage.'

'My compliments to your mother, Rosthorne,' announced Lady Charlotte as she walked slowly towards the door. 'She will be sorry I am cutting short my visit.'

'I have already explained everything to Lord and Lady Rosthorne, Mama.' Gerald flashed a quick, apologetic smile towards them. 'And I have sent Harris on ahead to Appleby Manor so I hope that when we arrive everything will be in readiness for you. It is a clear sky, and the moon is already rising, so I think we shall make good time.'

Nathan and Felicity walked to the door and watched as Gerald ushered his mother into the coach. Lady Charlotte's dresser climbed in and while the two ladies made themselves comfortable Gerald ran quickly back up the steps.

'Goodbye, Nathan.' He held out his hand. 'I do hope Bella recovers; I dare say you will be glad to have us out of the way at this time.' He gripped Nathan's hand, gave a quick nod to Felicity and ran back down the steps to the coach.

Nathan watched the carriage drive away, but his thoughts were elsewhere, going over and over the events of the day.

After questioning the servants he could not bring himself to believe that any one of them had put the hemlock into the jug, but if that was so, then he had to face an even more unwelcome thought. Beside him Felicity shivered and pulled her shawl a little closer about her. Nathan put his hand under her elbow.

'There is a chill wind blowing. We should go in. There is a good fire in the drawing room, and Mama will join you soon.'

'You are not coming in?'

He looked away, not wanting her to guess at the turmoil in his mind. 'Not yet. I have some work to complete in my study.'

'Then I shall come with you, for I need to speak with you, alone.'

'As you wish.'

His heart sank. At any other time he would have welcomed her confidences, but now he needed to be alone, to think through the events of the day. He ushered her into his study and closed the door. Candles were already burning around the room and after the chill of the night air the blazing fire was a welcome sight.

'You were working here, perhaps, when you heard that Lady Charlotte and Mr Appleby were leaving?'

'I was.'

'Their departure is very sudden.'

'Yes, it was a surprise to me. I would have sent for you to bid them adieu but Gerald begged me not to disturb you.'

Nathan sat down and idly shifted the papers on the desk while Felicity paced the room.

'Nathan.' She stopped in front of his desk. 'I think your cousin knows something of this attempt to poison you.' Her words were rushed rather than considered.

'And why should that be?'

His voice was harsher than he had intended and she

hesitated before continuing. 'I saw him talking with his mother's groom.'

'When was this?'

'After I had taken Mama Carraway to her room. I was on my way to my own chamber and saw them in the stable yard. It did not look as if Mr Appleby was giving Harris any ordinary instructions,' she added quickly, 'I thought they looked more…secretive.'

'It is most likely that he was giving him his orders to quit Rosthorne.'

'I do not think so.' She shook her head. 'The groom was looking very frightened.'

'Harris is simple. You heard Lady Charlotte say so.'

'Yes, but he could have fetched the hemlock from the stable if Mr Appleby asked him.' He watched her as she considered this. 'You sent word that you would be late,' she said slowly. 'Gerald could have returned to the breakfast room when it was empty and put the poison into the ale. Nathan, he must be involved.'

'No, you are mistaken.'

'How can you be so sure?'

'Never mind that for now—'

'Never mind!' she exclaimed, an angry flush on her cheeks. 'You would prefer to think that *I* poisoned you!'

'Of course not!'

'Then tell me what you suspect.'

'At this moment I would rather not—'

'No, of course,' she said bitterly. 'It is easier to think ill of me than of your own family!'

'Now you are being foolish!'

'Am I? Would you not be pleased to have some excuse to be rid of me?'

Nathan's brows snapped together. 'Now what the devil are you talking about?'

'I know you would like to put Serena Ansell in my place.'

'What?'

Felicity dashed a hand across her eyes. 'She is the wife you really want, is she not? I saw you, at the assembly—embracing!'

'That was *not* what you saw! Felicity, listen—'

She put up her hand. 'You need not deny that you love her, she told me of it herself.'

Nathan stared at her, frowning. He forced himself to speak quietly. 'And just when did she tell you that?'

Felicity sank down on to a chair and pressed her fingers to her temples. 'In Corunna, just after you had left town. She came to tell me that you were in love with her.'

'And you believed it?'

Felicity threw up her head. 'Why not, when she had your letter and your ring to prove it?'

'Impossible.'

'How can you deny it?'

'I *do* deny it.' He sat back, arms folded. 'And this was your reason for leaving me? Upon the word of a woman with the morals of an alley cat?'

'She had *proof*!'

'Preposterous. I have never written to her.' Her look of disbelief angered him. 'Damnation, Felicity, after five years, how am I supposed to convince you?'

She turned away. 'There is no need,' she said dully. 'You said yourself the past is over.'

With a smothered oath he jumped up from his chair and reached out, grabbing her wrist.

'Well, I was wrong! There is very clearly a need to talk about the past! We must clear this up now, Fee, or every time we have a disagreement it will be there, between us.'

She glared at him, her grey eyes positively smouldering. There was no shuttered look in them now.

'Sit down, Fee. It is time we were done with any secrets.'

He gently pushed her down into a chair and took

another for himself, turning it to face her, so that when he sat down their knees were almost touching.

'Very well, Fee, let me tell you the truth now. Serena *did* kiss me at the assembly, but if you had stayed another minute you would have seen me push her away. The woman delights in making trouble. When we were in Corunna she liked to think that every man would fall at her feet. I never did, but I do not think she understood that. I can believe she told you some fairy tale to drive you away from me.' He rubbed his temple, his fingers coming to rest on the ridge of his scar. 'Perhaps I should have warned you about her, but she was Adam's mistress; foolishly I thought that was enough for her. As for writing to her—no, I never did that.'

Felicity stared down at her hands clasped tightly in her lap. Perhaps she had been foolish; she had not wanted to believe Serena, but…

'She had your ring, Nathan. The band engraved with thorns, I could not mistake it.'

She risked a glance at his face. She knew him well enough now to realise that although his eyes rested on her, his thoughts were far away.

'I gave that ring to Adam Elliston,' he said at last.

'To Adam? But why did you not tell me so, when I asked you about your ring?'

He rubbed his chin. 'I find it…very hard to talk about Adam. When he died it was like losing part of my soul. We were neither of us rich, but when we arrived in Corunna he spent all his money on Serena, every last groat. It is possible, I suppose, that he loaned her the ring. After all he was quite besotted with the woman. But he had it later, I know, for I saw it. He wanted to give it back to me, but I told him to keep it, for good luck…' He dragged himself back to the present and looked at her. 'If only you had stayed, Fee, we could have put this to rights in a few minutes.'

She did not answer. If only she had stayed.

'I understand why you wanted to get away from me,' Nathan said. 'I realise you must have been hurt and angry, but later, when you had time to think, why did you not contact me? Why hide yourself away for so long?'

He leaned forward, his eyes fixed upon her. 'Well, Fee?'

Silence stretched between them. Felicity stared at the floor, her arms wrapped across her stomach.

'When I arrived in Portsmouth I was still intent on dis-appearing, but I had been violently ill during the sea voyage and could do no more than find myself safe lodgings, calling myself Mrs Brown, the name I had used on board ship. Then, I realised my condition. I was carrying your child.' She began to rock herself on the chair. 'I wish I could explain to you that first, joyous realisation: suddenly anything seemed possible. I decided I should move closer to London, where I would be within reach of the best doctors. I reasoned you could not object to me spending your money to protect the baby.

'My landlady had a sister in Camberwell with a lodging house and she recommended me to her.' Felicity stopped rocking and glanced up at him. 'Since she knew me as Mrs Brown I did not like to confess the truth, lest she thought me not respectable enough for her house, but I thought that once the baby was born I would write to you and try to effect a reconciliation.' She shivered. 'Then the sickness returned. I gave money to my landlady to engage a good doctor. Unfortunately, not all his skill or the careful nursing of my landlady proved effective. The baby—a little boy— was born three months early and died within a few hours. I did not even hold him.'

Felicity blinked hard, and stared at the Turkey rug beneath her feet. She would finish this now.

'It was then that I regretted being introduced into such an honest household; all I wanted then was to sink into oblivion. It would have been so easy for the landlady to let me die and keep my money for herself. Instead she paid the doctor to visit me regularly and undertook to nurse me back to health. Gradually, I recovered my strength and from somewhere came the will to live again.

'I saw a notice in the London papers, announcing my friend Lydia's marriage to Sir James Souden. I decided to write to her and ask for her help.'

'Why did you not write to me?'

She gave the slightest shake of her head. 'I buried all hopes of resuming my life with you when I buried my baby. I thought it was a punishment. Y-you see, when my uncle had died, I felt no grief, no remorse, only relief that I was free of him. Then, when you rescued me in Corunna, it seemed too good to be true, such happiness could not come without a price.

'It was at this time that I read your notice, seeking information about me. Of course no one in Camberwell knew who I was, so I was able to ignore it. I saw one or two more notices, but then they stopped and I learned that the Guards had returned to the Peninsula.' She lifted her head to look at him, her eyes swimming with tears. 'I lost the baby, Nathan. *Our* baby. How could I expect you to forgive that, since I could not forgive myself?'

Nathan put a hand up to his eyes. So many thoughts battered him; he grew cold at the thought of her being so alone. Now he could understand why she had been so determined to stay with Lydia this summer.

Felicity gave a little sob. 'I beg your pardon—pray tell your mama that I, too, am overset by the events of today and I will not dine with you!'

She was at the door before Nathan could collect his scattered thoughts.

'Fee, wait!'

By the time he reached the study door she had disappeared. His mother was standing in the hall, staring into the darkness of the upper landing and without a word he dashed past her and up the stairs.

Five minutes later he came back down to find Mrs Carraway waiting for him.

'Felicity was crying,' she said. 'Have you quarrelled?'

'No, Mama, not exactly, but she is upset.'

'Then should you not go to her?'

'I tried, but she has locked her door. She does not want to talk to me.' Nathan's chin went up. 'I am not such a monster that I would force myself upon her.'

His hand was gripping the carved handrail and she covered it with her own.

'Do you want to tell me, my son?'

He rubbed his eyes. 'Later, perhaps, when I have made sense of it all myself.'

Chapter Eighteen

A prolonged bout of tears left Felicity drained and exhausted, but when she had cried herself out and could
think rationally, she found she was not sorry that she had
told Nathan about the baby. She had no secrets from Nathan
now. Her maid arrived at the door, saying that the master
had sent her up with a dish of hot soup for m'lady's supper
and Felicity's spirits rallied a little. Tomorrow, she told
herself, tomorrow we will start afresh.

She rose early the following morning and dressed with
care before going down to the breakfast room, only to have
her burgeoning hopes dashed when Mercer informed her
that the earl had already breakfasted and gone out riding.

'He is not alone?' she said anxiously.

'No, my lady, Patrick is with him.'

With this she had to be satisfied, but she had no inclination for a solitary breakfast and went in search of Mrs
Carraway.

She found her mama-in-law sitting in her sunny
morning room, writing letters.

'Do come in, my dear, these can wait.'

'Thank you.' Felicity stooped to fondle Bella's ears when

the spaniel came up to say hello to her. 'She seems fully recovered now, Mama Carraway,'

'I believe she is, and Nathan tells me he is inclined to believe he was mistaken, that there was no poison in the ale.'

'But Bella—'

'She is an old dog and may well have suffered a slight stroke. She would have recovered even without Nathan's pouring coffee down her throat.' The older woman sighed. 'We must hope that is the case, for I cannot bear to think that anyone wishes to harm my son.'

'Nor I, ma'am,' added Felicity earnestly. 'But can he really believe this was not another attempt on his life? I cannot credit it.'

'Nathan and I discussed it last night. He says it is all coincidence and conjecture. He was at pains to assure me that he does not think his life is in danger.'

'Well, ma'am, I wish he had been at pains to reassure *me*.'

'That is difficult, of course, when you lock yourself away.'

Felicity flushed at the gentle rebuke in the words. She said quietly, 'We quarrelled last night. Did he tell you?'

'No.' Mrs Carraway moved over to the sofa and beckoned Felicity to join her. 'Nathan has never worn his heart on his sleeve. He does not readily discuss the things that matter most to him.'

Felicity clasped and unclasped her hands nervously. She took a deep breath. 'Then, I think *I* should tell you. Everything, ma'am.'

Haltingly, and with a few tears, Felicity told her story. She blushed when she spoke of mistresses and hesitated before voicing her suspicions about Gerald Appleby, but Mrs Carraway was not shocked, and merely patted her hands when she had finished.

'Thank you for your honesty, my dear; I may live retired here at Rosthorne, but my friends keep me well informed about the ways of the world. I do not think you need worry about Lady Ansell. I recognised her as a schemer almost at once, and you may be sure that Nathan knows it, too.'

'But what of his cousin, Mama Carraway?' Felicity twisted her hands together. 'I believe Nathan is in danger and—'

'I have never thought Gerald anxious to inherit the title. However, I am sure Nathan would not dismiss your suspicions without good reason.' She smiled. 'I will talk to him when he comes home. For now, I think we should—' She broke off as the door opened and Mrs Norton came in carrying a letter.

'Excuse me, madam, this has just arrived for you. From the earl.'

Felicity did not need to hear the last few words, she recognised the heavy black writing immediately. With a word of thanks Mrs Carraway broke open the seal and unfolded the crackling paper.

'Oh,' she said. 'He is on his way to Bath.'

A cold, hard hand clutched at Felicity's heart. 'Was there a message for me, Mrs Norton?' she asked.

'No, my lady. Patrick brought only two notes, the other being for Lord Rosthorne's valet. Patrick is having the horses put to the earl's travelling carriage and plans to join him again tonight. It would appear his lordship intends to be away for some time.'

'Yes, it does, Norton. Thank you, that will be all.' Mrs Carraway waited until her companion had retired before turning her attention again to the letter.

'He is going to Lady Ansell,' muttered Felicity. 'You see, ma'am, I have driven him away.'

'Well, it is Nathan's usual untidy scrawl,' said Mrs Carraway, not noticeably disheartened. 'But he wrote this from Appleby Manor. So *that* is why he went out so early this morning.'

'Do you think he went to confront his cousin?' asked Felicity.

'He does not say so, merely that he is accompanying Gerald and Lady Charlotte to Bath.' Mrs Carraway looked up, a decided twinkle in her eyes. 'That does not sound to me like a man going off to seek his lover.' She folded the letter. 'It does seem odd that they should set off today. I suggest you pen a note for Patrick to take back to his master, requesting an explanation. After that, you should put it from your mind, for it is Boxing Day, and we have work to do!'

Felicity made an effort to smile as she carried out her duties as mistress of Rosthorne, distributing the Christmas boxes to the servants and taking baskets of food to the poorest villagers. Somehow she managed to get through the day, but despite her resolve not to allow herself to fall prey to useless conjecture, when she retired to her bed that night her dreams were disturbed by images of Nathan whirling around the dance floor with Serena Ansell in his arms.

'Three days and still no word from Nathan, save a short scrawl to say he has arrived safely and is staying at the York,' remarked Mrs Carraway as they sat down to breakfast. 'One would have thought he might by now have written to explain just exactly why he went to Bath.' She looked over the rim of her coffee cup at Felicity. 'Did you write to him as I suggested?'

'No, Mama Carraway, I did not. I have tried his patience too far—Lord Rosthorne is no longer interested in me.'

'Oh, my dear, that is not true!'

'No?' Felicity put up her chin. 'When he did not have the courtesy to write to tell me he was going away?' She pushed back her chair. 'If you will excuse me, I think I shall take Bella for a walk. I feel in need of a little fresh air.'

She took the little dog out into the park and while Bella spent a happy hour snuffling around the trees and bushes,

Felicity wondered how on earth she was going to survive the rest of her life. It was her own fault. Perhaps if she had not told Nathan about the baby he might have forgiven her for running away from him, but they had agreed, no secrets. She had kept to that, but now Nathan had gone to Bath without any word at all to her.

She blinked rapidly. She would not cry, that would do no good. She must make a life for herself as mistress of Rosthorne. It was not so very bad, she told herself—she had a comfortable home and could command almost any luxury. She had every reason to be happy.

Except one.

Nathan did not love her.

Felicity returned to the house quietly resolved to do her duty. She spoke to the gardener about the spring planting for the gardens then went off to see Mrs Mercer to discuss menus for the week. With such activities she was determined to keep herself busy but when the stable clock chimed the hour she realised with dismay that it was still only noon. The rest of her day stretched interminably before her, and with a feeling of despondency she sank down on the sofa in the morning room and wept.

'My dear girl, whatever is the matter?'

Mrs Carraway's concerned voice brought Felicity to her feet.

'Oh, it is n-nothing, ma'am! A mere irritation of the nerves, that is all…'

Felicity went to the window to wipe her eyes. Knowing signs of her distress would still be in her face, she kept her back to the room as she heard her mother-in-law murmuring instructions to a servant.

'Come and sit down by me, Felicity.'

Slowly she returned to the sofa. 'Oh, ma'am, you must think me so foolish,' she muttered, kneading her handkerchief between her fingers. 'Nathan should never have married me, and now—'

'Hush.' Mrs Carraway patted her hands. 'I think you and Nathan are both a pair of very silly children.' She looked up as the door opened. 'Ah, Norton. You have brought the box? Bless you, my dear. Put it here, on the sofa between us—thank you.' She waited until they were alone again, then she put her hand on the box and said quietly, 'I think it is time I shared this with you.

'Nathan brought this box home with him from the Peninsula and gave it to me for safe keeping. It contains his most precious mementos: the miniatures of myself and his father; letters from me and from his friends.' She opened the lid and sifted through the papers. 'And this.' She lifted a folded paper and handed it to Felicity. 'It is a letter he wrote to Adam Elliston the day he marched out of Corunna. I think you should read it, because it mentions you.' Felicity took it and stared at the heavy black letters of the inscription. Mrs Carraway continued, 'I know you are convinced that Nathan married you merely to protect you, but I think this tells a very different story.'

Felicity unfolded the two sheets of stiff paper. She began to read.

Adam

Forgive this hurried scrawl and God grant that you read this before you leave Corunna. My orders have arrived. We march today and I know that you will not be far behind us. It was our intention that we should drink a toast together before setting off to join up with Moore's army marching north from Portugal, but the usual confusions of providing food and billets for so large a force as this, added to the delays and frustrations of our disembarking here, have made it all but impossible to do more than snatch a few moments with you. And of course there is my dear wife now to consider, but you will not begrudge me any time I have spent with her, for you know that she has stolen my heart. Felicity— aptly named indeed, for she has become my Life,

As she came to the end of the first page Felicity gave a little sob and put a hand to her mouth.

'Oh,' she breathed. 'I never knew.'

'No,' murmured Mrs Carraway, smiling. 'And Nathan never told you. You had best read on, although the rest of the letter may not concern you quite so much.'

'Oh, but it does,' murmured Felicity, turning to the second page. 'This concerns me very much indeed!' Her heart thudding in her chest, Felicity realised she had seen this page before, but not in this context.

my Passion.

You will understand how it is, a new husband has his duties. This unforeseen marriage has made demands upon my purse as well as my time, so I am unable to leave you any coin, but to ease my conscience at abandoning you at this time I enclose my ring, an infinitesimal token of my regard. Wear it for me—or if circumstances dictate and you are in dire need, pray sell it, I know you would only do so out of the greatest necessity and I shall never reproach you for it.

Yours etc, as ever

Nathan C.

'Adam died in Spain in the year '11,' said Mrs Carraway, when Felicity had finished reading. 'Nathan told me that he was charged with returning Adam's personal effect to his parents, and this letter was amongst them.'

Felicity handed the letter back to Mrs Carraway. 'I believe Serena read this letter before Adam saw it. She used the letter and the ring to trick me!'

And Serena was now in Bath. With Nathan.

'So, my dear…' Mrs Carraway carefully folded the letter and placed it back in the box. 'He did love you, and loves you still, I think. Will you not write to him, before it is too late?'

Felicity sighed. She *could* write to Nathan, but a piece of paper seemed poor defence against the wiles of Serena Ansell.

'No,' she said slowly. 'I shall not write to him.' She turned to Mrs Carraway, a determined tilt to her chin. 'I shall go to Bath,' she announced. 'This time I am going to fight!'

As Nathan strode away from Bladud Buildings, he thought there was no more dismal place than Bath on a winter's afternoon. It was no longer raining, but there was a chilly dampness in the air that crept into one's bones. He longed to be back at Rosthorne, sitting with Felicity in front of a roaring fire. Dear Fee. He had spent most of the night writing a long letter to her and sent it off express. He hoped, once she had read it, that she would understand why he had been obliged to post off to Bath so urgently.

Gerald pounced upon him as soon as he entered the house in Laura Place.

'Well?'

Nathan shook his head. 'Doctor Thomas is not expected back until tonight.' He let out an exasperated sigh. 'Surely there is another physician we could consult.'

Gerald drew him into the morning room and shut the door. 'I would prefer to wait for Dr Thomas. He has been Mama's physician for years. She will be less suspicious if he comes to see her.'

'Very well, I will call again tomorrow morning.'

'I will come with you,' said Gerald, 'and we won't leave Bladud Buildings until we have seen him!' He put a hand on his shoulder. 'I am very grateful to you for coming with me, Cos. There was no one else I could trust with this. I have not even told the servants here the true state of affairs, only that Mama is not well.'

'Is that wise? Surely it would be better to bring in a nurse—'

'As soon as Dr Thomas has examined her and we have his opinion, then I will hire as many people as I need to look after her,' Gerald interrupted him, looking uncharacteristically grim. 'Until then I do what I can to prevent the news of her…affliction…from spreading.'

'Very well.' Nathan rubbed his chin. 'I can give you one more day, Gerald, then I must get back to Rosthorne.'

'I understand, and I appreciate all you have done for me.' Gerald raised a smile. 'Will you dine with us?'

Nathan shook his head. 'Thank you, but given my aunt's state of mind I think it would be better if I did not stay. Sir James Souden is in Bath with his wife, and they have invited me to dine with them tonight.'

'Until tomorrow then.'

Nathan gripped his hand. 'Until tomorrow. And let us hope we can get this matter settled quietly!'

It took Felicity two days to reach Bath. The earl having taken his elegant travelling carriage, she had been obliged to use the more elderly barouche and Mrs Carraway's equally elderly coachman, who refused to entertain the countess's suggestion that they should drive through the night.

As they drew up outside the York House Hotel Felicity glanced at her elegant little carriage clock. It was still early and she thought there was a good chance that the earl might not yet have left his rooms. Head high, she sailed through the hotel and up to the earl's apartment. Her spirits dipped a little when Sam opened the door to her and announced that the earl had already gone out.

'He is gone to Laura Place, I believe, m'lady,' said the

valet, eyeing the large corded trunk that was being heaved up the stairs under the watchful eye of Felicity's maid.

'Laura Place?'

'To call upon Lady Charlotte.'

Felicity realised she had been holding her breath. She gave a little sigh of relief, but another anxiety quickly crept up on her.

'Oh. And Mr Appleby will be there, I suppose. Has the earl taken Patrick with him?'

'No, ma'am. His lordship was walking, and had no need of his groom.' Sam looked at her closely, then gave a reassuring smile. 'You've no need to worry about Mr Appleby, m'lady. Sound as a gun, he is. Bit of a rattle, but 'tidn't him who means his lordship any harm, if that's what's worrying you.'

She read the understanding in the valet's eyes and allowed herself to relax a little.

'I confess, I was a little anxious,' she said with a rueful smile. 'Thank you, Sam. I shall walk to Laura Place and join the earl, if you will tell me the way.'

Sam grinned at her. 'I think I have a map here somewhere, madam…'

Arriving at Laura Place, Felicity was shown into an over-furnished room while the servant went off to fetch her mistress. Felicity wondered if she had been too impetuous, and if she would have done better to change out of her travelling dress before setting off in search of Nathan. She was sure Lady Charlotte would think so, but Felicity realised with a little kick of pleasure that she did not care what Lady Charlotte thought. A glance in the mirror told her that her hair was still tidily confined beneath her modish bonnet with its swansdown trim and her olive-green pelisse looked surprisingly fresh despite her long journey. Added to this, Nathan had said he liked her in that particular shade of green and that was all that mattered to her. The door opened and she turned with a calm smile to greet her hostess.

'Lady Charlotte. I understood my husband was here.'

'He has gone out with Gerald.' Lady Charlotte regarded her with her cold stare. 'I did not know that you were in Bath. Rosthorne did not say.'

'I arrived this morning.'

'So the earl does not know you are here?'

'No, madam. I walked here with my maid to surprise him.'

Lady Charlotte gave a flicker of a smile. Could it be a little sign of approval at last? wondered Felicity. The old lady's tone was certainly a little warmer when she next spoke.

'The gentlemen are likely to be some time. I wonder, Lady Rosthorne, if you would give me the pleasure of your company in a walk to Sydney Gardens? The sun, you see, is trying to shine, and it would be a pity to miss the best of this short winter day.'

'I should be delighted to come with you, ma'am.'

'Give me a moment, then, to put on my coat.' At the door Lady Charlotte turned. 'Your maid can go back to the hotel, Lady Rosthorne. You will not need her in the Gardens—we will be much more comfortable on our own.'

Felicity waited, smiling to herself. This was a change indeed, if even the proud and haughty Lady Charlotte was warming to her!

Ten minutes later they were at the entrance to the Sydney Gardens. Lady Charlotte had set a surprisingly swift pace, hurrying along Great Pulteney Street with her hands tucked deep inside a huge fur muff.

An icy wind was blowing and Felicity was not surprised to find the gardens almost empty.

'This must be a delightful venue in the summer,' remarked Felicity, looking around her. 'I think, though, we might have the gardens to ourselves today.'

Lady Charlotte did not answer and Felicity was faintly irritated. Why had Lady Charlotte requested her company if she was not going to talk to her?

They crossed the wide carriage-way that ran around the perimeter of the gardens and followed one of the winding paths into the centre, where the trees and bushes blocked out any sounds from the traffic on Sydney Place. Felicity was about to suggest that it was time they were turning back when Lady Charlotte stopped.

'This will do.'

Felicity looked about her. 'Do for what?' she asked, laughing a little. 'There is nothing here save bushes! Perhaps you could show me the sham castle, or the maze—' She broke off. Lady Charlotte had stepped away from her.

'No, we shall go no further, Lady Rosthorne.' She pulled one hand from the fur muff and levelled a small silver-mounted pistol at Felicity.

'I—I do not understand.'

Lady Charlotte's eyes narrowed. 'I know your little game,' she hissed. 'And you will not succeed. You tricked my nephew into marriage, then left him because he was not rich enough for you. You came back only when he became earl, and now you are determined to deny my son his inheritance.'

'Lady Charlotte, I assure you—'

'You think to secure the title with an heir, do you not? While you and your husband were estranged you did not matter, but now—! Bad enough to have my nephew in the way, but I cannot allow you to give him an heir.'

Felicity saw her raise the pistol. She said quickly, 'I have no wish to deny Gerald the title, ma'am, if you consider it his right.'

'Of course it is his right!' Lady Charlotte's eyes snapped angrily. 'Appleby died soon after Gerald was born and we returned to live with my brother, the earl. Gerald was brought up as one of his own.'

'Nathan told me the old earl was a very kind man…'

'Kindness had nothing to do with it! He wanted Gerald to inherit. Nathan was never his favourite, never!'

Felicity said gently, 'But the old earl had three sons of his own, ma'am, no one could have foreseen—'

'I did.' Lady Charlotte drew herself up. 'When the three boys died, I knew it was meant to be. It was a judgement. Nathan was a soldier; it was only a matter of time before he too perished in battle.'

Felicity fixed her eyes on the old woman's face and tried not to think about the little pistol pointed at her heart. She must keep her talking.

'But Nathan survived the war and came back to London.'

'Yes, and I knew then what I had to do.'

The cold was eating into Felicity, joining with her fear to make her shiver.

'So it was you behind the attempts to kill Nathan. But how? Did you pay someone?'

Lady Charlotte's lip curled. 'Nothing so vulgar. Harris did it for me.'

'Harris! Your groom?'

'Yes. I have to tell him everything in detail, of course, because he does not have all his wits, but he is devoted to me. Unfortunately he is a poor shot, so his first attempt failed.'

'As did the second,' put in Felicity. 'In Lady Stinch-combe's garden.'

'Yes. I thought he would manage that better. I knew Rosthorne liked to smoke that horrid tobacco so I sent Harris out to the garden. I told him to unlock the garden door to make his escape, but somehow he failed, as he did in Green Park. But you were there, my dear. You were in the park, were you not? You saw him.'

'I did not recognise him.' A faint sound caught Felicity's attention. Voices. Someone was in the gardens. If only she could buy a little more time! 'And was it Harris, too, in the Home Wood?'

'Yes, but you foiled that attempt, did you not? Harris was obliged to flee or risk being recognised. Poor Harris, he came back gibbering about the injury to Rosthorne's horse. That was when I knew I would have to take a hand to do the job myself. Harris brought me the hemlock from the stables and I poured it into the ale. It was very simple.'

'If Bella had not tripped up the footman.'

The voices were growing louder. Felicity longed to cry out, but she knew that as soon as she drew breath to scream Lady Charlotte would shoot. Her hand was so steady Felicity had no doubt she would hit her mark. She raised her voice a little.

'So where is Harris now?'

For the first time Lady Charlotte looked confused. 'Gerald sent him on an errand, before we set off for Bath. He said he would follow us...'

There was a movement in the bushes behind Lady Charlotte. Felicity was aware of several figures moving closer, but she dared not let her eyes wander, she must keep Lady Charlotte's attention fixed upon her.

'Let us return to the house, ma'am. Perhaps Harris has arrived...'

'No!' Those cold eyes narrowed, immediately suspicious. 'No, we shall finish it now. At least with you dead it will give me time to dispose of my nephew!'

She raised the pistol, taking careful aim. Felicity held her breath. Everything happened at once. Felicity saw Nathan spring from the bushes and launch himself at Lady Charlotte even as her finger closed on the trigger. A shot rang out and something whistled past Felicity's head. She jumped back, her mind whirling as the tension of the past few minutes caught up with her. Suddenly it was all too much and she felt herself falling into blackness.

'What do you think you are doing?' Lady Charlotte's outraged voice made itself heard above the confusion. 'Unhand me at once!'

'It is all right, Mama, I am here.' Gerald came running up. He gently prised the weapon from her fingers.

'Did I kill her? She was in your way, my son. I could not allow that.'

Nathan glanced towards the gentleman in the frock-coat kneeling beside Felicity.

'Doctor?' Anxiety made his voice harsh.

'The bullet missed her, my lord. She is concussed by the fall.'

'Doctor Thomas.' Lady Charlotte stopped struggling with her son and looked across. 'What are you doing here?'

'Why, I came to see you, madam,' said the doctor cheerfully, getting to his feet.

'See to your patient,' muttered Nathan, brushing past him and taking his place beside Felicity's still form. 'I will look after my wife.' He tore off his own gloves and Felicity's and chafed her cold hands. A wave of intense relief washed through him as her eyelids fluttered.

'Where am I? Uncle Philip?' She stared up at him, a slight crease in her brows. Nathan saw the shadow of alarm darken her eyes and she snatched her hand away. 'You are not my uncle. Go away! *Déjeme!*'

'Felicity.' He tried to lift her, but she fought against him wildly.

Dr Thomas hurried over. 'Hysterics,' he muttered, 'brought on by the shock of her ordeal or the blow on the head when she fell. Allow me, my lord.' He bent over and caught Felicity's hands. 'Come along, Lady Rosthorne. No need to be afraid, I am a doctor.'

Nathan watched, helpless, as the doctor raised Felicity to her feet. Her eyes were staring and she continued to ramble.

'He must not find me. I am his wife in name only…it is a judgement. We can never be happy. Forgive me, Uncle, I did not mean to be so wicked…'

She collapsed again. Nathan looked to the doctor. He was frowning.

'Go and find a cab, my lord. I will attend to Lady Rosthorne and bring her to the entrance of the gardens. Mr
Appleby, if you can look after your mother I shall call upon
her later.'

Fear gnawed at Nathan as he accompanied Dr Thomas
back to the hotel. Felicity was laid in his bed and he could
barely contain his impatience until the doctor emerged
from the bedroom.

'Is she all right? May I see her?'

'You may go in if you wish, but she is asleep now—I have
given her laudanum to help her rest. She has a lump on her
head, but I do not think it is anything to worry about.'

'But she was rambling—'

'Her thoughts are scrambled. It means nothing.' He
smiled. 'She is young and strong, my lord. She will wake in
a few hours none the worse for her ordeal, I am sure. Now
if you will excuse me, I shall go back to Laura Place.'

When the doctor had gone Nathan went back into the
bedroom. Felicity was lying motionless in the centre of the
bed. She looked very frail, her eyes closed and her dark lashes
resting against her bloodless cheeks. During all his time as a
soldier he had never known such fear as he had experienced
when he and Gerald had arrived back at Laura Place with Dr
Thomas, only to be told that Lady Charlotte had stepped out
some half-hour earlier with Felicity. He had led the way to
Sydney Gardens, not caring for the stares of passers-by as he
raced along the street and into the trees, expecting at any
moment to hear Felicity's screams splitting the silence.

He reached out and placed a gentle hand on her
forehead. There was no fever, but her unnatural immobility
unnerved him. What if she awoke and did not know him?
She had called out for her uncle—what if her mind was
trapped in the past, would she not be terrified to find
herself being cared for by a stranger?

He jumped up, unable to bear the idleness any longer. With a curt word to Felicity's maid to look to her mistress, he plunged out into the street. Darkness had fallen over the city and a cold drizzle had set in but Nathan did not heed it, nor the surprised look he received from Sir James's butler when he demanded to see Lady Souden.

'I regret my lady is not at home, my lord. Sir James and Lady Souden are dining out and then going on to the ball at the Lower Rooms.'

Nathan found himself back on the street. He glanced down at his sodden coat and muddy boots. It was not to be expected that he would be allowed into the Assembly Rooms in such a state. Jamming his hat more firmly upon his head, he turned and headed back along the street.

The heavy blackness that engulfed Felicity was lifting. She lay very still, her eyes closed. Something was not right. The bed was very comfortable, but it was not her bed. She was not at Rosthorne. She could hear the steady tick, tick of a clock in the room, and the sound of voices and the occasional rumble of a carriage outside. Perhaps she was in London, at Souden House. Slowly she opened her eyes. The candlelight was too dim for her to see in any great detail, but she was certain she had never seen this room before. She looked at the figure sitting beside the fire and some of her unease drained away.

'Martha.'

Her voice sounded a little strained, but it worked. The maid hurried over, a beaming smile on her face.

'Milady! We've been that worried about you.'

Felicity frowned and closed her eyes. Her memory was trickling back.

'Oh yes, Sydney Gardens.' Slowly she put up her hand and touched the base of her skull. 'Did someone hit me over the head?'

'No, miss, my lord says you banged your head as you fell. He and the doctor brought you back here.'

'Doctor?'

'Doctor Thomas, my lady.' Martha helped her to sit up. 'I hear he's one of the best in Bath, and Lady Charlotte's physician, too. He left you more laudanum, if you wish to take it madam…'

'No. No, thank you, Martha, just a little water.'

Felicity leaned back against her pillows and tried to think. She felt weak, but apart from a bruise on her head she could feel no other damage. She recalled staring at the black muzzle of the pistol. Lady Charlotte had fired, she was sure of it, but something had happened.

'Where is Lord Rosthorne?'

'That I don't know, m'lady.'

Felicity slid her legs over the edge of the bed. 'I shall get up.'

'Ooh, my lady, I think you should not get out of bed until his lordship returns.'

'And when will that be?' Martha hesitated. 'You do not know that either, I suppose. Well, help me into my wrap.'

Felicity was pleased to find that her legs still worked. She walked to the door and found Nathan's man tending the fire in the sitting room.

'Where is your master?'

Sam jumped to his feet. 'My lady, you surprised me! I thought you was still asleep.'

'Quite clearly I am not,' retorted Felicity, feeling stronger by the minute. 'Where is Lord Rosthorne?'

'He's gone out, ma'am.'

'Oh. Did he have an engagement?'

'No, madam, not that I know of.'

'And when did he leave?'

Sam looked at the clock. 'About a half-hour since. He said something about a ball at the Lower Rooms, changed into his evening dress, and went out.'

'A ball?' Felicity steadied herself with a hand on the back of a chair. Why would Nathan go to a ball while she was lying unconscious in his bed? Unless… 'A ball at the Lower Rooms would be quite well attended by Bath residents, would it not?'

'I would think so,' replied Sam slowly. 'I believe the entertainments in the Lower Rooms are highly regarded.'

Entertainments. Felicity's fingers dug into the back of the chair. He had left her in a laudanum-induced sleep while he attended an entertainment! Slowly she turned on her heel and went back into the bedroom, closing the door behind her with a snap.

Bath might believe itself very thin of company, but Nathan considered the three hundred or so people crowded into the Lower Rooms to be far too many. It was almost impossible to find anyone. Suddenly he spotted Sir James Souden and he cut through the crowd to intercept him.

'Well now, Rosthorne.' Sir James stopped, smiling. 'What do you mean, to be scowling so at everyone?'

'Was I scowling?' returned Nathan mildly. 'I was not aware of it.'

'Be damned to you, of course you were scowling,' retorted Sir James. 'Can't say I blame you, either, if it keeps the inquisitive at bay. I can't tell you the number of people who have asked me about this mysterious marriage of yours. It's becoming tedious, my friend!'

'Tell 'em to mind their own business.'

'I do, but it don't stop 'em speculating. Should have brought the lady with you, Nathan. That's the only way to stop the gossip.'

'As a matter of fact, she *is* here, but she is not well. Confined to her room. In fact, I wanted to talk to Lady Souden about her…'

'Here to take the waters, is she? That's precisely why we

are in Bath, so that Lydia can regain her strength after her lying in.' Sir James looked past Nathan and smiled. 'Ah, here is my wife now, and Lady Ansell, too. You know her, of course, Rosthorne—she tells me you are neighbours in Hampshire. Servant, ma'am!'

Nathan turned to find Lady Souden approaching with Serena by her side. He swallowed his frustration; he had no intention of mentioning Felicity to anyone but Lydia Souden.

'You are both looking far too serious,' said Lydia, twinkling. 'Lady Ansell suggested we should come over and put an end to that.'

Serena gave them her brilliant smile. 'Good evening, Sir James, and to you, Lord Rosthorne.' Nathan's curt nod had no visible effect. She merely smiled more broadly. 'Do you mean to intimidate me with your severe frown, sir?'

Sir James laughed. 'Just what I was telling Rosthorne, ma'am; his scowls are likely to frighten the ladies.'

'I fear the earl has been too long without company,' murmured Serena.

Nathan met those green eyes and read the blatant invitation in them. 'Thank you, madam, but I am well content.'

'How can one be content at a ball if one does not dance?' purred Serena. She stepped across to stand beside him, looking up at him under her lashes. 'Come, Nathan—will you not tread one little measure with me?'

'Thank you, but I do not dance tonight.'

'No doubt the earl is missing his wife,' remarked Lady Souden, frowning a little at this exchange. 'Why did you not bring Felicity with you?'

Before Nathan could speak, Serena was taking his arm.

'I found Lady Rosthorne to be very shy,' she murmured, flashing him a conspiratorial smile. 'We do not look to see her in Bath, do we, Nathan?'

He observed Lydia's disapproving look. She began to pull Sir James away towards the supper room. Damnation, Serena was intimating that she was his mistress! He would have to get rid of her before he could go after Lydia and ask her to visit Felicity. Serena turned towards him.

'You are very elusive, Nathan. Did you not receive my note?'

'Yes, but I came to Bath on business, madam.'

'Surely your business cannot take up all your time.' Her voice was very soft, caressing. 'If you cannot visit me, I could come to York House…' He looked down at her and she gave a low laugh. 'You are a fool to resist me, my dear, and for what? A little mouse who is no real wife to you.' Her hand in its silk glove slid over his chest. 'We could…comfort one another.'

He stared down at her, wondering why it was that those perfect features and brilliant green eyes held no allure for him. All he wanted was to have a pair of candid grey eyes smiling at him as if he was their whole delight…

'The Countess of Rosthorne!'

Chapter Nineteen

Nathan's head snapped up as the servant made his announcement. Surely he had misheard?

A hush fell over the ballroom and all eyes turned towards the door. Felicity stood in the doorway, pale and beautiful in rose silk, a shimmering gold scarf across her arms and her hair falling in soft curls around her face. His heart swelled with pride as Mr Guynette, the MC, escorted her across the room towards him.

'Not such a little mouse, madam,' murmured Nathan, detaching himself from Serena's grasp.

He realised he was grinning as Felicity came towards him, her head held high and a confident smile on her lips. Little witch—just when had she turned into such an indomitable woman?

Nathan's look of surprised delight bolstered Felicity's spirits. She was his countess, and he was proud of her—she could read it in his eyes. She was no longer shy little Felicity Bourne, afraid to speak out for fear of reprisals. She was the Countess of Rosthorne! Felicity crossed the room, trying to ignore the fact that everyone was staring at her and her knees were shaking. Mr Guynette was talking to her, but she was not listening. Her whole attention was fixed upon her husband.

'My lord, I regret I could not be here earlier.' Her eyes flickered over Serena Ansell, standing tall and beautiful beside Nathan. She breathed in, pulling herself up another inch as she held out her hand. 'But I am here now, sir, and await your pleasure.'

For a long, long moment everyone in the room seemed to hold their breath, watching the little tableau being acted out before them. It took all Felicity's courage to keep her hand extended and her eyes upon Nathan. Not by so much as the flicker of an eyelid did she reveal the fear that gnawed at her, that he might reject her. Then slowly, she saw Nathan's smile deepen. He walked forward, reaching out to take her hand in his own.

'The pleasure, ma'am, is all mine.'

His words and the look that accompanied them made her heart soar. Nathan tucked her hand into his arm and walked away with her. The ballroom, released from its spell, began to hum again with conversation, the orchestra struck up for the next dance, and everything returned to normal. Except that Felicity and Nathan found themselves almost mobbed by Rosthorne's acquaintances, demanding that he present them to his lady.

It was almost an hour before they could talk together undisturbed. Nathan escorted her to a secluded alcove.

'I thought I should never get you to myself,' he said when at last they were seated. He subjected her to a searching gaze. 'Are you sure you are well enough to be here? I left you sleeping.'

'I am well aware of that, sir, and I took it very ill that you should go out enjoying yourself without me!'

His lips twitched. 'I beg your pardon, madam. I came to find Lady Souden; you did not know me earlier, and I thought that if you were still confused when you woke again you might feel more comfortable if your friend was with you.'

'How thoughtful of you!' Felicity smiled up at him, blinking away a tear. 'You are so *very* good to me!'

A smile glimmered in his eyes. 'I look after my own, madam! But you are very pale. Tell me truthfully, you have no pains, no headache?'

'No, no, I am quite well, now. I was a little dizzy when I first woke up, but that soon passed.'

'Good. Then tell me now how you come to be in Bath.'

'Your second-best travelling carriage, my lord…'

'Yes, yes, saucy Jane, but why?'

'I came to be with you, my lord,' she said simply. 'Mama Carraway and I decided I should follow you. Of course, if I had known about Lady Charlotte I should not have followed you to Laura Place.'

'Imagine my surprise when Gerald and I arrived back there to be told you had walked out with her! I was afraid we would not find you in time—'

'I kept her talking as long as I could.' Felicity shivered. 'She told me *everything*, Nathan. The poor woman is quite deranged.'

'I know. That was why I rode over to Appleby Manor on Boxing Day, to talk to Gerald about it, but he was already making plans to bring her to Bath. He begged me to accompany him. I wrote to you yesterday, explaining everything.'

'Then your letter will be waiting for me when I get back.' She took a deep breath and looked him in the eye. 'I have stopped running, Nathan. I want to be a proper wife, if you will let me.'

'If I will let—oh, my love that is all I ever wanted!' He reached across the table for her hand. 'In fact, I want to kiss you right now.'

She squeezed his fingers, warmed by the soft look in his eyes. 'I would like that too—but not here…'

'No, of course not.'

He sat back, and she saw the light die out of his face, leaving him looking very serious.

'My dear?' Felicity watched him, a tiny frown creasing her brow. 'Nathan, what is it?'

'Talking to Sir James last night. There are rumours, hints of unrest in France. If that is so, if Bonaparte should rise again—'

She caught his hand. She said quietly, 'If you think it is your duty to rejoin your regiment then I shall not stand in your way, Nathan. But make sure you come back to me, my love.'

He raised her hand to his lips. 'You may be sure of that! Do you know,' he said, gazing deep into her eyes, 'I am suddenly very tired.' The message she read in his eyes made her blush to the roots of her hair. 'Shall we go?'

'Yes,' she whispered, her insides turning to water. 'If you please.'

He rose and held out his hand to her. 'Come along; let us take our leave.'

They walked out through the ballroom where the dancing was still in progress. Felicity saw Lady Ansell going down the dance with a fair-haired youth. The widow looked up and Felicity met her cold stare with a brief, haughty look of her own before turning away to accompany Nathan across the room to Sir James Souden, who grinned at them.

'Leaving us so early, Rosthorne?'

'It has been an eventful day,' said Nathan. 'Pray give our regards to your wife.'

'She will be sorry she missed you. She is off dancing somewhere.' He shook his head. 'She told me she wanted to come here to take the waters, but there doesn't seem to be much amiss, if she can dance all night the way she does.'

'I wish I could stay and talk to her—' Felicity broke off, aware of Nathan's hand under her elbow. 'But we must leave this instant. Give her my love, Sir James, and tell her I will speak to her tomorrow.'

She turned to accompany Nathan to the door, but they had not gone many paces before Serena Ansell stepped in front of them.

'So your little wife still hangs upon your sleeve,' she sneered. 'Quite the picture of marital harmony. How provincial.'

Felicity stiffened. It was unfortunate that the music had stopped, and Serena's words fell into the sudden quiet. She heard someone close by titter.

'Is it so unfashionable to dote upon one's wife?' returned Nathan.

'You were not always so devoted a husband.'

'Possibly not.' He smiled down at Felicity. 'That was an error and I admit it. But my lady and I have no secrets from each other now.'

Serena looked up at him under her lashes. 'What, none, my lord?'

The meaning was so transparent that Felicity's fingers curled into claws. Nathan put a restraining hand over hers.

'None, Lady Ansell. We have discussed…everything.' He gave a smile as false as her own and turned to leave.

'Then I wish you joy of her, my lord,' Serena called after him. 'Until your countess runs away from you again!'

Felicity gasped. Nathan came to a halt, then slowly he turned back towards Serena.

'Let us speak plainly, madam,' he said coldly. 'And let me correct any misapprehension that others may have. We have never been lovers. I was never susceptible to the charms you offered so freely, and the fact that you were married to my commanding officer and the mistress of my best friend only diminished any regard I might have had for you. You have tried on more than one occasion to make my wife believe that I have an affection for you; I believe you even intercepted my letter to Elliston and used it for your own purposes before passing it on to him. But your stratagems failed, madam. I am happy to state here, quite publicly, that I never was, and never will be, an admirer of yours!'

A look of shock and horror replaced Serena's smile as his voice carried across the room. Others were sniggering now, but Felicity ignored them. She was astonished at Nathan's open avowal and her heart swelled with pride as she realised how difficult it must be for her reserved husband to speak quite so openly.

'Oh, bravo, my lord,' she applauded him as they left the ballroom. 'That will give the Bath tabbies something to talk of.'

'I fear there can be no reconciliation with Lady Ansell.'

Felicity laughed. 'That is one acquaintance I am happy to forgo!' She looked back over her shoulder. 'I wish I had stayed to speak to Lydia. I fear Sir James will think you most boorish to drag me away so intemperately!'

'Souden is too much of a gentleman to think anything so impolite,' murmured Nathan, leading her out of the building. 'I think he is more likely to excuse my conduct as the actions of a man violently in love.'

Felicity stopped. 'Oh. Oh, do you mean that?'

'Mean what?'

She felt herself blushing in the darkness. There was a constriction in her throat, making it difficult to breathe.

'That…that you are in love. Violently.'

He dragged her into his arms. 'Of course I mean it. I am so very much in love with you that I am going to kiss you here. Now. In the street.'

Before she could protest Felicity found herself swept up in a crushing embrace. When at last Nathan lifted his head, her mouth felt bruised from his savage kiss. She heard a discreet cough and realised that the earl's carriage had drawn up beside them and a wooden-faced footman was holding open the door.

'In with you, baggage,' growled Nathan, 'before I forget myself again.'

Felicity sat beside Nathan for the short journey back to the hotel, her head on his shoulder and her hand clasped in his.

'Nathan?'

'Yes, love?'

'What will happen to Lady Charlotte?'

'Gerald will make provision for her to be looked after at Appleby Manor.'

'And her groom, Harris?'

'We have sent him to my estate near Newmarket.'

Felicity sat up. 'But, Nathan, he tried to kill you!'

'The man is an innocent; he is no danger to me or to anyone else if he is removed from Lady Charlotte's influence. He has a gift for healing; he can work on the stud farm and my men there will keep an eye on him. He can be useful there, Fee, and I think he will be happy.'

She eyed him doubtfully. 'If you are sure, Nathan…'

He nodded. 'I am sure.'

'Poor Lady Charlotte,' murmured Felicity. 'I wish you had explained. When you were so reserved, I thought you suspected me…'

'That was never my intention, but I could not tell anyone until I had confirmed my suspicions.' His grip on her hand became momentarily painful. 'I did not want to admit to you that my aunt, a blood relation…'

'You thought that I would think ill of you because of Lady Charlotte's illness? Oh, my dear, I could never do that!' She turned to hug him. 'Only think of my own uncle, eccentric enough to drag me to northern Spain and to spend every penny he had, trusting to God to provide!'

'Eccentric, yes, but not the same!'

'Not so very different, when you think he condemned me to the life of a missionary with no concern for my own wishes.' She caught his hands. 'It is *you* I love, Nathan, for the good, kind man that you are. I love you for your forgiving nature, and your forbearance, when I have been so foolish.'

He pulled her on to his lap. 'We have both been foolish, my love, but no more—let there be no more secrets between us.'

'No,' she whispered. 'None.'

Nathan's hold tightened as Felicity responded to his kiss. She filled his senses, he was drowning in the taste of her, the touch of her fingers on his skin fanned his desire and it was with difficulty that he resisted the temptation to tear away her silken gown and lose himself in the delectable flesh he knew lay beneath it. Reluctantly he eased away from her.

'Enough,' he muttered, breathing heavily. 'We should stop now while I am still able.'

Felicity sighed. 'I never want this to end, Nathan.'

She snuggled into him, her head against his chest and her curls tickling his chin. With admirable resolution he put her gently but firmly on to the seat beside him.

'A jolting carriage is not the place to make love to one's wife. Besides, we are already at York House.'

Felicity straightened her wrap and waited patiently while the carriage slowed to a halt outside the tall, imposing frontage of the hotel. Nathan jumped down and turned to help her out of the carriage, then with one hand possessively about her waist he swept her up the steps and into the building.

Sam was waiting at the door of his apartment.

'Bring some brandy, and wine—or perhaps ratafia for Lady Rosthorne, if you please, Sam,' said Nathan. 'Then you may leave us.'

There was a cheerful fire burning in the sitting room and Nathan helped Felicity to remove her voluminous cloak before drawing her down beside him on the sofa.

'Now,' he said, when they were alone, 'tell me what it was that made you come to Bath.'

'Your mother showed me the letter you had written to Adam before you marched out of Corunna.'

He kissed her neck. 'And what was so special about that?' he murmured.

She closed her eyes, enjoying the touch of his lips on her skin. 'You wrote that you…loved me.'

'Mmm.'

'You never said that to me.'

He raised his head. 'Did I not?'

'Never, until tonight.' She added shyly, 'I did not believe it could be so, until I read your letter.'

He pulled her on to his lap in a rustle of silk. 'How very remiss of me,' he murmured, his mouth against her ear. 'Because I *do* love you. To distraction.'

She slipped her arms about his neck. 'Oh, Nathan, that makes me so happy! I—'

He cut off her words with his mouth, kissing her ruthlessly. She melted beneath the onslaught, almost fainting with love and relief and the sheer bliss of being in his arms again.

At length he broke off, but he kept her on his lap, safely enclosed in his arms and for a while they sat in silence, listening to the crackling of the fire.

'One thing,' said Nathan. 'At the Hazelford Assembly— did anyone else see Serena kissing me?'

She nodded against his chest. 'Mr Elliston.'

'Hah! So that was why he has been so distant of late. Oh, Fee, you little idiot, why did you not challenge me at the time, or come up and slap my face for me? Come to think of it, why did Elliston not charge me with it?'

'B-because I begged him not to say anything.' Felicity dared not look up. 'Serena Ansell is so beautiful, so assured—all the gentlemen think her very desirable.'

'Not all of them, Fee.'

'I am so sorry I doubted you, Nathan,' she whispered.

His arms tightened around her. 'You are not wholly to

blame. If I had been more open with you, perhaps you might not have believed her so readily. Hell and damnation, no wonder you have been so unhappy! Did you think I had installed my mistress in the neighbourhood? What a scoundrel I should be to do that! Fee, I should ring your neck for thinking me capable of such a thing!'

'I am sorry,' she said again. 'Sometimes my temper overwhelms me, and I find it impossible to think rationally.'

He kissed the top of her head. 'I'll make sure she does not hurt you again.'

She raised her head and looked into his eyes. 'She cannot hurt me, now I know the truth. Oh, Nathan, I was a fool not to trust you.'

'Let us put all that behind us now, love.'

In one swift, fluid movement he swept her up into his arms and carried her to the door.

'What are you doing?'

'Taking you to bed.'

She gave a little, shaky laugh and buried her head in his shoulder. 'Nathan, the servants! They will see us!'

'Let them. It is a tradition in my family to carry a bride to her bed.'

'It—it is?'

He looked down at her, a wicked glint in his eyes. 'It is now.'

Felicity said no more. He carried her into the bedchamber where a fire blazed merrily in the hearth and a few candles burned around the room. There was no sign of Sam, or Martha.

'I think they knew they would not be needed tonight,' grinned Nathan, gently setting her on her feet. 'Now turn around and let me undress you.'

Amid fevered kisses they began a breathless, undignified scrabble to shed their clothing. It involved many oaths on Nathan's part and much giggling from Felicity until the last stocking had been removed and Nathan scooped her up and placed her none too gently upon the huge bed.

A sudden stillness enveloped them. Felicity lay on her back, looking up at Nathan, his shape outlined blackly above her. In the near-darkness her other senses were heightened—she breathed in the smell of his skin, a mixture of spices and musk and brandy, but at the same time she was aware of the scents from the perfumed candles burning in the room and the hint of herbs coming from the freshly laundered sheets. It was like lying in a meadow on a summer's night.

She reached up and ran the tips of her fingers down Nathan's body, from his neck to his navel. A fierce joy filled her: this was where she belonged. With Nathan, as his partner, his wife.

'By heaven, but you are beautiful,' he muttered hoarsely.

He lowered his head to kiss the valley between her breasts. She held him close, her hands moving over his back while he covered her body with delicate kisses. She stretched beneath him, throwing back her head as she gave herself up to the sensations his touch was arousing. He did not hurry, devoting himself to each area of her body, caressing and kissing her until her senses took flight and she was writhing beneath him, crying his name while her fingers dug into his shoulders. With a wild abandon she gave herself to him, aware of his own growing excitement as their bodies met in a tangle of limbs and hot passionate kisses. Her senses climbed higher and ever higher until she was no longer in control. She clung to Nathan, their two bodies moved together, harder, faster, and they shared a brief moment of exultation before they collapsed, panting, on to the covers.

Felicity lay in the darkness, worn out by the force of her passion. She sighed, trembling, and Nathan wrapped himself around her. Then, in the safe cocoon of Nathan's arms, she slept.

* * *

Nathan's first action the next morning, even before opening his eyes, was to reach for Felicity. She was not there. Quickly he looked around the room, his initial alarm fading when he saw her standing at the window.

It was quite dark, but the moonlight shining in through the window filtered through her thin nightgown, outlining every curve of her body. Desire stirred again. As if aware of his eyes she turned towards him.

'Fee? Is anything wrong?' She came across to stand beside the bed. He sat up. 'What is it, my love?'

She ignored his outstretched hand. 'We said no secrets, Nathan.'

Immediately he was on his guard. It was an effort to keep his voice neutral. 'Is there something you need to tell me?'

She nodded. 'I am going to have a baby.'

At first he thought he had misheard. Then in a bound he was out of bed and standing before her. 'Truly?' He took her hands. Even in the darkness he could tell she was smiling.

'Truly,' she said unsteadily. 'I suspected it some time ago; but now, I am sure.'

Nathan could not restrain himself. He gave a whoop of joy and caught her up in his arms, swinging her around even as he kissed her. Just as suddenly he put her down again.

'I should not have done that. You will need to lie down, to rest—'

'No, no.' Laughing, she put her hands against his chest. 'I am very well, I promise you.'

'But after the last time,' he said decisively, 'you must see a doctor.'

'And so I shall, as soon as we return to Rosthorne Hall.' Her voice softened as she realised the depth of his concern. 'Perhaps, since we are in Bath, I will take the waters. They are said to be most efficacious.'

'Perhaps.' He kissed her, wrapping his arms about her and holding her close. 'Listen.'

He lifted his head. Outside the window the church bells began to chime. 'It is the first day of the new year, my love.'

Felicity laid her head against his heart. 'The first day of our new life, Nathan.'

Epilogue

Notices: *Morning Post* and *St James's Chronicle*:
25th July 1815:

BIRTH
On Monday last, the Countess of Rosthorne, of a
son and heir, at the Earl's seat in Hampshire. Lord
Rosthorne, a hero of Waterloo, is reported to have
returned to England two weeks before the birth.
Mother and son are in a fair way.

A Supper and Fireworks held for workers and tenants of the Rosthorne Estate was hailed a great success.

★ ★ ★ ★ ★

IN-STORE 16TH SEPTEMBER

Historical™

Available Next Month

Carla Kelly

Marrying The Captain

The Surgeon's Lady

Marrying The Royal Marine

Available from Big W, Borders, Kmart, Target,
selected supermarkets, bookstores & newsagencies.
OR call 1300 659 500 (AU), 09 837 1553 (NZ)
to order for the cost of a local call.

Visit **www.millsandboon.com.au**

HIO610_1

Historical™

3 Brand New Stories
Each Month

tantalising period romances

HI0610_2

Mills & Boon™

Keep an eye out for this brand new collection of historical romances.

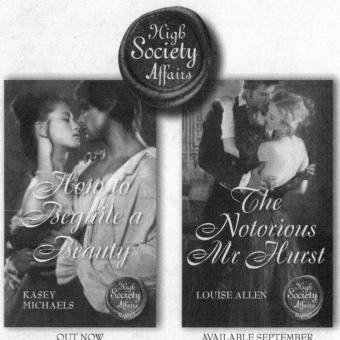

OUT NOW

AVAILABLE SEPTEMBER

Enjoy tales from chivalrous knights, roguish rakes and rugged cattlemen to impetuous heiresses, unconventional ladies and defiant bluestockings. These rich and vivid romances will capture your imagination.

1 NEW STORY EACH MONTH

www.millsandboon.com.au

HS0810A-